Also by Lolah Burford

THE VISION OF STEPHEN: AN ELEGY

VICE AVENGED: A MORAL TALE

Edward, Edward

Edward, Edward

A Part of His Story and of History

1795-1816

SET OUT IN THREE PARTS
IN THIS FORM OF

A New-Old Picaresque Romance

THAT IS ALSO

A Study in Grace

BY

Lolah Burford

Macmillan Publishing Co., Inc.
New York

Dedicated to Shelley, who liked novels, with apologies, and to the Romantic Spirit:

> *"—there are some by nature proud*
> *Who patient in all else demand but this—*
> *To love and be beloved with gentleness;*
> *And being scorned, what wonder if they die*
> *Some living death?"*
>
> *"Me—who am as a nerve o'er which do creep*
> *The else unfelt oppressions of this earth . . ."*

Julian and Maddalo, A Conversation
(1818)

Contents

PART ONE

❀❀❀❀❀❀❀❀❀❀❀❀❀❀❀❀❀❀❀❀❀

The Beginning of the Story

(1795 – 1805)

◊⧓◊⧓◊⧓◊⧓◊⧓◊⧓◊⧓◊⧓◊⧓◊⧓◊⧓◊

How It Began:
1795

I

WHEN the message was brought to him, the Earl of Tyne was at breakfast in his dressing gown, dividing his attention between the *Gazette* and his kidney-and-eggs, the late morning sun streaming in the windows behind him, bringing the scent of late roses. He looked up, displeased, the hard lines of his face at variance with the peaceful room and the pastoral view immediately through the window behind him.

"A lady to see me, at this hour?" he said, annoyed. "Send her away. It is too early, I am not interested."

"She asked me particularly," said the footman, with an apologetic cough, "to give you her card, if you would not see her. She was most persistent, my lord, and she would not take *no* at all." He coughed again, more apologetically yet, for he knew well, no one better, his employer's wishes and habits.

"If you could not suffice to throw her out," snapped the Earl acidly, "why did you not call George to assist you?" But he did take the card, with a certain idle curiosity, and saw to his surprise that it was sealed inside a sheet of paper. The name engraved on the card inside was a simple one, without title, "Mrs. George Armstrong," and so were the words written simply on the sheet of paper, as if in explanation: Lady Anne. His face did not noticeably change in expression, but the paper shook in his fingers as in a draft, and he hastily put it down. The coincidence struck him forcibly and unpleasantly, for he had just read the announcement of the sudden death of the Rev. Mr. George Armstrong in a small space in the *Gazette* when his breakfast hour had been, without precedent, interrupted. The notice was printed below that of the passing of the Grenville-Pitt Bill against Treasonable Practices and Seditious Meetings. He did not wonder now that the footman had found the lady difficult to dismiss. His lips twisted slightly in a grimace that might have been a smile, but held nothing of pleasure or delight, and he said to the footman to show the lady into his dressing room upstairs. He ignored the footman's look of astonishment that even his training could not suppress, and continued his study of the *Gazette* and his breakfast, waving the footman out with the words: "Go on, man, go on, be about your business. I will follow presently." He made no effort to hurry himself, but after some minutes he rose, shaking out the folds of his gown, and laid the *Gazette* down on the table, but the card and the sheet of paper he took with him.

He mounted the steps, wondering only slightly if he would find the lady before him, or if she would have been dismayed at his directions and taken her leave at the door. He could not imagine what she wanted of him or why she had come to his house, when he had hardly seen her to speak for seven years. He opened the door, and she was there. She stood facing the door, a slight, heavily veiled figure in black, from her shoes to her gloves to her hat. He could not see her face, but memory painted it in for him, behind the black veils. He waited a moment for her to speak, but since she did not, he walked over nearer to her, and bowed slightly, but he did not attempt to take her hand in its black glove.

"I am surprised at this honour, Lady Anne," he said. "I have only this morning read of your husband's death in the *Gazette*. I offer my condolences."

"It was sudden," she said, her voice faint behind the veil. "It was an accident, a hunting accident. He was shot, by mistake, walking in the fields behind our house."

"Did you find him?" he asked, with interest as faint as her voice.

She shook her head. "The hunters brought him to me, and he died the next day."

"I am sorry," said the Earl politely. "I hope he did not suffer great pain?"

She nodded. "He did, but he did not complain. He was a good man, and a very brave man. I did not come to speak of this, Noel," she said, dropping formality.

"I am glad to hear it, Lady Anne," he said with relief, but not matching her tone. "I have been wondering why you did come, and I suppose now I am to know." He stood waiting, his face as masked and inexpressive as hers was veiled, except for a questioning, unpleasant light that gleamed behind his eyes.

"I have come to you for help, Noel," she said simply.

"I am not a good man to come to for help," he said equally simply, "for I never give anything for nothing, and my price is very high. Why do you need help, and why should you come to me?" He paused, and then he said angrily, "For God's sake, Anne, take off that silly veil. I cannot talk to a veil." He reached forward with his long fingers and lifted the veil back himself, over her hat. Her face, revealed to him, shocked him, as it had before, in years past, and the violence of the emotion he felt shocked him, too. He shut his eyes for a moment and turned away from her, but he could not find control over himself, and he found his hands shaking again. He said, not looking at her, "Anne, I cannot answer for myself. You know what I am. Take warning and go now, at once, and ask help of your relatives, whom you should have gone to first. You should not have come here alone, like this." He had locked the door behind him as he entered, and he now gave her the key.

He heard her move, but he did not hear the door, and when she spoke her voice was some steps nearer him.

"I have no one else to go to," she said simply. "That is why I came to you. I must have your help."

"If you do not go now, Anne," he said again, his voice harsh, "in a moment I will not let you. Do not deceive yourself about me. This warning is the limit to my generosity. Believe it." When she still did not move to go, he gasped suddenly, in a kind of shuddering sigh, and grasped her in his arms, and kissed her, not a kiss such as she knew, but his lips simply open on hers, framing hers, breathing her breath into him and his into hers. He stood so, holding her to him, until she grew dizzy and her legs began to fall away from her. He picked her up in his arms, his mouth not releasing hers, and carried her into the next room, and laid her on the bed, and himself beside her, his breath still locked in hers, in a kind of ecstasy of suspended motion, which she herself broke.

"Noel, you cannot, like this, I am in weeds."

"I see you are, Anne," he said harshly, "and I agree with you. Take them off."

"You cannot mean it," she said faintly.

"I do," he said. "I warned you. You should have gone. It is too late now."

He watched her intently, but although he read shock and dismay in her face, he read nothing to repulse him. He reached forward with his practised fingers that were like whip steel and unfastened the tiny buttons down the front of her dress, and those at the back, and slipped it down to her waist.

"My God," he said, "your underthing is black. I shall keep on until the black is gone."

"It is all black," she said in a stifled voice, her face hidden.

He sat up and took off his dressing gown. "Here," he said, "have this, and do it yourself. I'll have no black here." He continued unbuttoning the small buttons in back of her shift.

"I did not come for this, Noel," she said desperately.

"Of course you did not," he said reassuringly, "you came for my help, but payment first, as Jew King says, and then we'll see. Will you do it, or shall I?"

"You would not," she said, unbelieving. "My husband is not three days buried."

"My dear, when I was at Oxford these many years ago, I read a novel, not the kind you read, it was an old one, in which a man, a soldier, I believe, kills a woman's husband, and takes the woman, very much against her will, on her husband's dying, still-warm corpse. If it suited me, I am quite capable of that myself, and this is nothing to it. It has been a week, his body is not even here. There is only you, and your tight-crossed legs are no more obstacle to me than hers to him, as you will see. I want this black off. Will you do it, or shall I?" he repeated.

"Noel," she said, her voice entreating, "Noel, I am dying, too." He only laughed, not understanding her, and she said in despair, "How do I know that you will help me after all?"

"You don't," he said, "But you haven't any choice now. Be quick. I or you?"

"You will have to," she said. "I could not."

She shut her eyes, but she did not dismay him. He proceeded as he had indicated he would, noting the ravages of time but the beauty that yet clung to her. His hands explored it with a tenderness his face did not promise. When the offending black was gone, dropped on the floor, he handed her again his dressing gown, and she took it this time and wrapped herself in it, hiding herself in its large folds.

His fingers parted the dressing gown, and his steel thighs parted her quivering ones.

"Are you so desperate, my dear, as this?" he asked, as he began his descent.

"I am so desperate, Noel," she said, her breath caught in a gasp that was half pain, half pleasure. "You are not kind."

"I am never kind," he said briefly, proving it, "unless it suits me, and it seldom suits. You will shortly tell me what you need, though, and we will see."

She did not respond to him, but he had hardly expected it. The passage over, they lay back, remembering the other time, seven years before. They did not speak of it, but it was in both their minds, sharp and fresh as if it had only happened.

He had been—God, how old had he been? Thirty? Not so much? Older? Seven years ago. He would have been thirty-one, and she had been twenty-six, on the shelf, as they put it, but still very beautiful, in his eyes, although not every man's style. He raised himself up then, on his elbow, and with his other hand he turned her face to him, and saw again the wide-spaced grey-blue eyes, frank and innocent and yet seeming to look into his uninnocent self in a way that had shocked him as with lightning on a kite string, and shocked him now. His breath caught convulsively, and he drew her down against him, hiding her eyes in his neck.

"Oh, God, Anne," he said, "how many times I have dreamed of you, like this."

"And I of you," she said simply. She raised her head, and took his hard, lined face in her hands in her turn, and gently kissed his eyelids and then laid the imprint of her lips on his. He caught her face again in his hands, and held it near his, tracing the clear arch of her brows, and following her hairline with his fingers, and the pure line of her nose, kissing her heavy black eyelashes, fringing eyes that had not laughed at him again for those years, and did not laugh now.

"You have such beautiful bones, Anne, in your face, beneath your skin," he said, tracing them with his finger lightly, along the lines of the cheekbone and the jaw. "I never saw such lovely bones in a woman's face. I never understood why no one else could see them. You were born to be a Duchess."

"I had unfashionable hair, and no fortune," she said, lightly, "and I was much too small."

"You dressed it unfashionably," he said, "then as now. Why did your mother not teach you how to do it?"

"She was too busy, I had too many other brothers and sisters, and they crowded in on her and me. And their hair curled."

His hands busied themselves, then as now, among the steel pins that held it back in severe braids, pulling them out and loosening the tight plaits, letting the pale gold strands fall across her face, burying his face in them. "Did you do this for your husband, for the good brave George?" he asked thickly into them.

"You are wicked still, Noel," she said, but she shook her head in answer to his question, destroying the force of her words.

"Did you ever think I was not?" he asked, from her hair. "I have never given you reason to think it, and I never will. Even a wicked man might love this hair, and still be damned. There is no virtue in loving your hair."

He sighed, and pulled her down close again to him. "I am thinking of how we first met," he said. "Are you?"

"I was thinking of it too," she said.

"And the maze?" he asked.

"That too," she said.

She did not know all the story, though, and she would not, for he did not mean to tell her, then or now. He would be damned, he had thought, if he would let Gore outdo him, a mere boy in age compared to his five years' seniority. They had been rivals in many things, and Gore had the lead on him, being beautiful and better born and unscrupled and uncaring in an insouciant gay way that was inimitable. But Gore had been caught out, and he did not intend to be, and he had not been. The money meant very little to him, he did not need it. They did not call him Cripplegate, but they might have, with his lame, still slightly clubbed foot. The pain he had gone through as a child, dragged from doctor to doctor, as his parents tried to mend it, had even changed his face, he thought. If it had changed his disposition, he did not know, for so far as he could know it had always been as it was now, disagreeable and prematurely old.

He had taken his time, for, the Viscount Rockfort then, he had time to spare. He had made acquaintance through an acquaintance with the Lady Anne, as she escorted her brood of brothers and sisters, more like a governess to them than a sister. He had taken Lieutenant Wrexham with him, who nursed a tendre for the daughter who had just come out, an auburn-ringletted dimpled charmer of seventeen who did not cause his heart to stir, and Lieutenant Wrexham's married sister. They had made a proper party, unexceptionably escorted, despite his reputation, for no one, knowing him, could believe he had an interest in the Lady Anne. Nor did he at first, nor did he ever show more than might be natural from the two older members of the party. He contrived to meet them in the Park, and helped the younger boys sail their boats on the Round Pond near the Long Water. He even made one from a five-pound note, with another for a sail, and then blew it into the middle of the pond, and while they scrambled after it with sticks, whooping and laughing, forbidden to wet their white socks and shoes, he had contrived to fix his interest with their older sister. Fingers at last found fingers and trembled, eyes engaged eyes, and fell, lips briefly found lips, beneath the bonnet's rim, touched and did not draw away, and then withdrew, quivering, trying to smile.

He knew he had her then. She should never have let him advance so far, so quickly, so improperly yielding and indiscreet. In his experience, he undergauged the extent of her sheltered innocence, and in this one humility, he never imagined the extent to which he himself might draw her. He looked now only for opportunity, and until then he kept his distance, contriving to meet her, but with a grave mien and no attempt at further familiarity. He escorted her and her brood with Lord Wrexham and their duenna to the Botannic Garden, without finding it, and to a picnic at Tunbridge Wells, without success, and then, having first secured the key to it, to the Maze at Hampton Court. He took her quickly to the center of the Maze, which would have suited him very well had it not been for the eye upon them of the Maze keeper, watching for signs of exhaustion among the struggling laughing maze-bound children and adults between the high thick hedges. Then, pleading shamelessly his crippled foot for excuse, he had led her out by a side entrance, and into the bluebell wood that neighboured the Maze, to which he had a different kind of key.

They had wandered more deeply in until, out of sight or hearing, they had sat on a grassy knoll beneath the trees, sheltered by flowering bushes, carpeted with the bluebells of the woods and wild violets and mosses. He had spread his white riding cloak on the ground for them to sit upon, and picked flowers for her, and persuaded her to untie her bonnet strings. He had kissed her then, first gently, laughingly, then more lingeringly. He produced wine from his pocket flask, and persuaded her, laughing, provocative, wooingly, to drink with him, and then he drank from her lips, and she from his. If he misunderstood her, it was not surprising. It was stronger than she knew, and what inhibitions passion had left her, the wine withdrew. She returned his embraces lingeringly, hungrily, her body warm and unresisting in his arms and then beneath him, as if as bent on her own ruin as he. When finally she was sensible that his intentions were not those of the gentleman she had thought him, and that incredibly they were to give her a slip on the shoulder, then and there among the bluebells, without promise or assurance, her will had left her too far, and she could not resist him and she did not try to, except in a futile, ineffectual way, weakly crying and weakly pleading. She did not try to scream, she only lay, in her lavender dress, her strength dissolved in his greater strength and in the wine, crying quietly in her betrayal. He removed with a quick ripping of his too strong, too practised fingers the material resistance, uncovered himself, and holding her tightly in his hands beneath him, and stopping her mouth with his, made his entrance. He felt her stiffen, heard her cry beneath his lips, and then he saw she had fainted. He paid her no heed but finished his work and took his pleasure, and took the torn garment from her. He was not a coward, and he did not leave her. He stayed beside her until her senses returned to her, and then he offered her again his wine, which she drank a little of.

She made no outcry, and no reproach. She looked at him with her wide, grey, innocent eyes, so long and so penetratingly, the tears falling from them, until his own dropped, and then, in perfect trust, that was misplaced, she gave herself into his arms. She pressed herself to him, desperately, searchingly, clingingly, drawing him to her, until his astonished passion returned, and met her own. He did not understand his fortune, but he did not question it, and his mind, as he took her again, was making rapid revisions of his intentions. She was inexperienced, but the fresh intensity of her released passionate love for him surprised and shocked him and left him more shaken than she. They kissed one another again and again, as if striving for something they could not find, and he picked the blue flowers, bluer but not clearer than her eyes, and covered her face with them, and kissed her through them.

He became aware of the sun, and he said abruptly, "We shall be missed, we must go back to the Maze."

"When shall I see you again?" she murmured in trusting confidence.

"I do not know," he answered truthfully, a disturbing note in his voice. She heard it, and she did not mistake it.

"You will not marry me?" she said falteringly, "it was not your intention?"

"No," he said briefly, "it was not, and is not."

She stared at him in horror and dismay, but more at herself than him.

"Do your parents know of me, that you have been seeing me?" he asked cruelly and shrewdly.

She shook her head dumbly, her shamed eyes on his.

"Does that not seem strange to you? Why did you not tell them? I will tell you, Lady Anne. You knew, my dear, whether you knew you knew or not, what kind of man I am, and that they would not approve of me or of your seeing me." She nodded dumbly. "And yet for reasons of your own, you kept on seeing me, and you, as well as I, found excuses to meet, even clandestinely, and with covering engagements. Does a lady, whom one would wish to make his wife, do that, Lady Anne, or go with a gentleman she hardly knows, alone, and out of call of her friends into an isolated woods, when they have hardly met, or let him kiss her lips beside a pond?"

She shook her head, her eyes still on his. He found their gaze disconcerting.

"But I am not a marrying man for anyone, Lady Anne, not for foolish young girls like you, or any girl. And why do you think that should be?" he asked, not expecting her to answer. Her lips formed some words soundlessly but he did not catch them. "Did you think you could entrap me where no one else could? Were you so proud? If I had lacked birth and wealth, I should have been no prize for anyone, and no one knows that so well as I. But I do have both." He looked at her soberly, and then he took her in his arms, and kissed the top of her head resting beneath his chin. He stroked her, and comforted her, and despite his harsh words, she nestled against him, and then he said, softly and gently, against her hair, "I have not married because I know my own nature. I have only one kindness, not to inflict it for very long on any other human being but myself. Do you think I exaggerate, Lady Anne? Believe me, I do not. I have perceived myself, long ago, that I have no heart, and in place of it I have a very real cruelty. I enjoy being cruel. You surely know it is true. If somehow you did not know it before, you know it now." He held her more closely to him as if to deny the effect of his words. "The odd thing is that now, for the first time, I am sorry for it, too, but I cannot change it or myself. I cannot, Lady Anne, do not deceive yourself. I cannot, and the truest measure of that, is that I do not even mean to try. If you think you love me—I cannot imagine why you should, but if you do—you do not love me, for there is nothing there to love. You love some figure of a man you have yourself invented. And I do not love you." He softened the brutality of his words by the gentleness of his hands, which gave her his handkerchief. "I do not love you. I shall leave you in a few minutes, and I shall not look back, or think of you again."

"I cannot bear it, if you do," she said simply and sincerely.

"You will have to bear it, for that is how it will be. I have done now what I set out to do, and tomorrow I am going abroad, to stay for some months, perhaps more." He looked at her narrowly. "But if you really mean it, you may come with me, and stay with me, until you tire of me."

"Or until you tire of me?" she said faintly.

"Or until I tire of you," he agreed, "but until then we shall make a good time for both of us, I think, and you may spend and do as you like. That might amuse you. You will not find me ungenerous, and in Paris you will not find yourself shamed."

"I cannot do that, Noel," she said sadly, "that is not *my* nature. And I need more than that, much, much more. But I wish I could. I wish you would just take me, make me go, but I cannot make myself."

"I don't want you enough to take that trouble, or that risk," he said brutally. He had thought she might cry, but she did not. He caught her looking at his hands appraisingly, with a strange look on her face.

"Give me your wine, Noel," she said. "Or have you anything stronger?"

"I have my Hollands," he said, puzzled, "and a little wine. What do you want them for?"

"Give them both to me," she said, holding out her hands; she took first the wine, and drank all that was left, and then she took the Hollands in her hand, holding it.

"I am going to drink this Hollands, Noel," she said, "and make myself very drunk. But before I do, there is something I am going to ask you to do for me, when I have done it." She spoke so calmly, her next words overthrew him. "I want you to kill me, to choke me with your fingers, which I have found are very strong."

"Strangle you?" he cried. "Are you mad? I may be cruel, but that is lunacy. We are going back now."

She shook her head. "You cannot watch me all the time, Noel. But I would rather have your help. You will be quicker, and you will hurt me less, than what I can contrive myself."

The mask-like expression of his face was gone, replaced by astonished horror.

"Anne, I cannot. You are serious, I think, but I cannot."

"Drink some of your Hollands, then," she said, "and fortify yourself, Noel, for you will have to. For if you do not, I shall scream, and if you make it so I cannot scream, unless you kill me, at some time I shall be able to tell someone what was done to me and by whom, and I will, and I will ruin you too."

"I am a hard man to ruin," he said, "being much ruined already," but she saw the dubious look in his eyes.

"I love you, Noel," she said brokenly, "but I believe you. So now believe me: if this is how you are, being now what you have made me, I do not want to live with it, I want to die." (Her voice caught on a sob.) "I wish I were already dead."

"Tomorrow you will feel differently."

"Perhaps," she said. "You will not be there, and my resolution may fail me, but it is now where we are, and now I have to live through, and by tomorrow I will have ruined you, too, indeed, much sooner. But I do not want to ruin you. By tomorrow, by the next few minutes, I want to be dead." She looked at him. "You owe me this. You know you do. It is all you can do for me."

She saw that he was wavering, but that she would have to help him by frightening him, if he could be frightened, and angering him beyond restraint. She took the Hollands resolutely and began to drink, gasping at the bitterness. He wrenched it from her, and drank himself, rather desperately. He hoped she had had enough. She lashed out at him now, softly at first, but gradually growing louder, inviting him to stop her.

"Are you afraid? You, Rockfort? I am frail, it will not take much. Are you afraid of explanations, of being made to stand a trial? You will find a way to explain. Your brain will work, you know how to contrive. It will be easier than explaining what you have already done to my father and my brothers. They will not duel you, but they will have you to the law, or have you killed. Never think they will not, Noel; once roused, our family does not take its honour lightly. You will not escape us."

He believed her now, and at any moment she might be heard. He took her in his hands, and felt her tremble, but she did not resist him. She put her arms behind her, letting the weight of her body and his hold them. He put his hands on her throat, and his mouth on her mouth, pressing both desperately. There was some point, he had heard, that would kill her quickly, but he did not know where to find it. She struggled, but she did not struggle much, and he pressed his weight against her until her struggles beneath him stopped. He had felt as if he were in a dream, but as she grew limp abruptly he woke from it, aghast at what he had done. He could not believe he had killed her, had killed a woman. He felt her heart, and it was beating, and the suffusion in her face, the pressure of his fingers gone, was beginning to leave. He opened her mouth, and breathed into it, as he had heard the Methody doctor John Wesley had done, until she began to moan slightly, and recover first her breath and then her senses.

"God, Anne," he said, horrified, "what you nearly had me do. You won't try again, surely you won't." He felt at once nineteen and ninety.

She shook her head wearily. He helped her to her feet, and they went back slowly to the party, who were just beginning to emerge, giggling and laughing, from the Maze. She had arranged her scarf about the marks of his fingers on her throat, and put her bonnet again on her head, and her gloves on her hands, but she could not speak. He had explained that she had suffered from the heat in the Maze, and they had walked apart in the cool shadows of the trees, but that she had taken a headache and had not much revived. Her pale face and wilting looks bore up his story, and they went home at once, not even stopping for ices. She went in with no word and hardly a glance at him. The next day he left early for the Continent, where he stayed for several months. Her notes to him were not delivered. When he returned, he learned that she had married, within that week, the youngest son of the Earl of Havermore, the Rev. George Armstrong. It had been a marriage that had met with approval of neither her overlarge family, of finer blood but present impoverishment, that had at least enjoyed her services, if no settlement, nor his, that had expected him to marry into some competence, if not of fortune, at least of advancement. They had moved to Devon, to a small living, and they met with no material success of any kind.

He touched her throat now, remembering, and kissed the places where the marks had been. He saw by her eyes she remembered, too.

"Do you forgive me?" he asked.

"For what?" she asked. "For that?" she asked, touching his fingers on her throat with her own. She smiled slightly. "I asked you to. Of course I do. Though it hurt more than I thought for. Please don't again."

"And for the rest?" he asked.

"No," she said in a faint voice, and buried her face against him. "No, I do not."

They lay together, two strange lovers, he that he loved at all, and she that she loved him, and then, as before, she caught him to her fiercely, and clasped him to her fiercely, as if she would force his skin and bones to melt into her own.

"Oh, God, oh, God, Noel," she sobbed wildly, kissing him with wild abandon, wordless, full of both love and grief, for many things. His passion, as before, rose to meet her own, and they joined in it, in a sudden breathless ecstasy that ended as quickly as it had come.

He suddenly turned to her, his mood of reminiscence gone as abruptly as it had come, his hard self again to the fore, and asked, "What do you want of me, Anne? You have told me it was not myself, and we have had that now anyway. It is your turn now. What do you want?"

"I want your help for my son," she said simply.

"Your son?" he exclaimed in complete surprise, sitting up. "Are you serious? I did not know you had a son."

"I have a son. He is six. He will be seven soon." She saw his eyes narrow. "I have shown I am serious by coming here alone."

He grew suddenly angry, in a way she could not understand. "Do not try to bargain with me, Anne. I will do nothing for you if you do. I cannot be bought and I cannot be bargained for. There is nothing I need. I admit you've given me a shock, and I must think." He got off the bed, and walked around to her side with his slight limp, and gave her his hand to assist her to rise.

"Put your clothes on," he said with unreasonable curtness, "and go downstairs to my book-room." He saw her surprise. "Do you wonder at my having a room for books? There is much you do not know about me, Anne; in fact, I would say with most obvious truth there is more you do not know than that you do." He had taken the dressing gown from her, now, noting, as he had not done before, how thin she was, standing up. He ran his fingers over her lightly, in a practised way, as he would have done a horse, a filly, or a bitch that interested him, or as a doctor might have done, without passion. She stood quietly, her eyes meeting his without shame or fear. He looked at her with shock in his eyes: "Are you ill, Anne?"

"I have told you, but you would not listen to me or believe me: I am dying, Noel," she said quietly. "I knew it even before George died. Do not be afraid," she added, misreading the dismay on his face. "I shall not infect you."

"I never thought it," he said, clasping her to him, "I care nothing for that, or think you could." He could not speak for a moment, and then he released her, and gave her chemise and her petticoat to her, and began to button the tiny buttons with patient though shaking fingers. When she was dressed, he put his hands on her shoulders, and looked hard in her face. "Have I hurt you?" he asked. She shook her head. "Go downstairs then to my book-room, as I said, and I will have my George bring you coffee, or ratafia, or brandy, or whatever you would like. I will join you when I am dressed, Anne. You will not go away?" he added anxiously, suddenly and incongruously.

She almost laughed. "Do not think it, Noel," she said, and left his room.

II

When she was gone, he sat down for a long time with his head in his hands, before he called his valet to him. It was longer than an hour before he finally joined her.

"Was I long?" he asked, when he came into the room.

"You were very long," she said, lifting her veil again. "Were you thinking of ways in which you could refuse me, and reasons why you should?"

"I do not need to do that," he said shortly. "I have only not to say yes. You know that. Let us not waste any more of your time. You have a son. Have you other children?"

"No," she said, "just the boy."

"And he is six, nearly seven. The significance does not escape me, Anne. Is he my son?"

"I do not know, Noel," she said simply.

"Do you know he is not? Do you know he is George's?"

"Noel, I have told you. I do not know. I was married within the week, fully married. I do not know whose son he is. He could be yours, he could be George's."

"Did George, this Armstrong, did he know this? Did you tell him?"

"He knew," she said, "I told him."

"My God!" said Tyne, and sat down in the chair, at the small round table, across from her.

"He had known me, and wanted me to marry him, and I would not. I did not love him, my family did not wish the marriage, his family did not wish it. But when you left me—as you did, Noel—I went to George, and told him what had happened to me, all except your name." She met his shocked looks without embarrassment. "I had no one else in whom I dared at all confide. I knew him for a just man, and a kind man, and a brave man, fully courageous, and one who loved me—"

"All that I was not," he interposed with unwarranted bitterness.

"All that you were not," she agreed. "He would have married me, I think, without my saying anything. I do not know. But when I told him, he had no hesitation, and we married very quickly, without our families' knowing."

"Being in the trade, he could do it quickly, I suppose," Tyne said, again bitterly.

"A friend of his performed it," she said, "for us. You might have done it yourself, Noel, had you wished."

"I did not wish," he said bluntly, "not then, not now. Is that what you have come for? If you are wanting me to marry you now, you are wasting your breath and your time, and mine."

"I wish you would, Noel, but I did not think you would," she said. "I did not come to ask you for that, or for your name."

"What do you want, then?" he asked her curiously.

"I want you to be the guardian for my child," she asked.

"My God!" he exclaimed, standing up, in disbelief. "Is that all!"

"That is all," she said simply and sincerely. "Will you do it?"

"No!" he exploded, "and no! I will *not* do it!"

She did not expostulate, or reproach him, but she put her head in her hands, and he saw by the shaking of her shoulders that she was weeping silently. He could not bear it. He put his hands awkwardly on her shoulders, and then he took his seat again.

"Who does the boy look like?" he asked.

"He looks like me, now," she said.

"That is in his favour," he said simply. "What is his name?"

"His name is Edward," she said, and her eyes widened in surprise at his start.

"Did you do that on purpose?" he asked.

"Do what?" she asked, bewildered.

"Did you name the boy that on purpose?" he asked.

"It is a family name, in George's family. George named him. I don't know what you mean."

"We have an old song up here, about a boy named Edward who killed his father, by the counsels of his mother, when he was a young man. He has lost one of his fathers already. Did he kill him?"

"Not directly," she said faintly, "it was an accident. He was in the field with George's gun, and the hunters were shooting, and George ran to get him, and he was shot, instead of Edward."

"My God!" exclaimed Tyne. "You mean, the boy himself shot George your husband."

"George did not say so, he said it was the hunters."

"He would say so, being the man you say he was. Were you there?" She shook her head.

"What did the hunters say? Did they see?"

She shook her head again.

"And the boy?"

"He is too distressed, Noel. I have not questioned him. I had, I have, no reason to question him. George told me enough. He was naughty to take his father's gun, but it was an accident—even the way you think it, it would have been an accident."

"Is your husband truthful, or would he change the story, would he do that?" He did not notice he used the present.

"I don't know," she said. "Anyone might."

"God!" he said again. "And you want me to take this viper to my bosom and rear him up to sting me!" He looked at her savagely. "Is this your means of revenge on me? It will not work, Lady Anne, I will not take the lure."

She did not answer at first, but only looked at him quietly, and then she said in a low voice, "You cannot think that, Noel. You know that is not my intention or my wish."

He sat down again, more quietly. "Well, I wish he had another name. So we have this boy who takes other people's guns without permission, and looks like an angel, if he looks like you, and is in the field when his father is killed with someone's gun. Can Edward shoot well?"

"I do not think so. I do not know. His father was not one to teach him, but he might have learned from someone else."

"Well, I hope he cannot. But I shall find out—" he saw her look of surprised hope—"if I take him. I have not said I would. I would have whipped him for taking the gun the first time, for I am sure this was not the first."

"Did you never take your father's gun without permission?" she asked, worried at his sternness.

"Never," he said briefly, "and it was *guns*. I might have liked to but I knew I would be skinned for it, despite my foot, and so I did not ever. If you are afraid of my strictness, we may end this discussion now. There are other things with me far worse than strictness that you would do well to be afraid to trust your son to me for, but not strictness for stealing or lying. If you think me a liar or a thief, you mistake me." He paused suddenly. "Is that why you suddenly after seven years think I am his father? You do not flatter me, madam."

"I love my son Edward," she said with dignity, "and you are making up these bitter fancies out of whole cloth. I wish only the best for him, and now that his father is dead, and I may die without great warning, I wish only to do the best for him I know. He has no fault in him, unless he is your son, and that would have been put there through no fault of his own."

He winced at the blow she aimed at him, which hit him squarely, though why it should have wounded him he did not know, since he enjoyed his life. It was her intention, he supposed.

"I wish you were less truthful, Anne," he said wryly. "I like my life and my ways; and my viciousness and my depraved habits, are, I believe, acquired, not inherited. My parents would say so. And your strain, and his upbringing by the clergy, is surely enough to blot mine out."

"I wish you were an easier man to deal with," she said wearily. "I am glad now you did not marry me."

"I can*not* be dealt with, at all, by anyone," he said stringently. "I wish you would learn *that*, Anne. Where is the boy, Anne, now?"

"He is at an Inn in town."

"Here?" he asked, shocked more than he thought he could be.

"Where else should he be?" she said, smiling slightly. "I could not leave him at home, so young, with his father newly dead. We have been too poor, Noel, he has not had a nurse. We live in Devon, and you are here in Northumberland."

"Yes, I have acquitted myself recently too well in London, and I thought it well to cool my heels and my reputation for a time here at my ancestral home." He did not offer to explain. "Were you so sure I would take him?"

"I was not sure at all. I am still not sure. If I were you, I would— but I am not you," she said with a faint smile. "I did think you might like to see him."

"I *would* like to see him," he said sincerely, "even if I persuade you to take him elsewhere." He saw the faintness of her cheeks, and he would have ordered some restorative for her, but she waved aside his offer. He took her hand in his and put his other over it, and held it so, looking at her almost pleadingly.

"Why will you not take him to your husband's family, who will love him for his father's sake, and bring him up in a proper way suitable for a young boy, with friends, and relatives and a more usual life, Anne? Why do you want for him the strange life he will lead with me?"

"There are so many reasons why I cannot, Noel, and why even if I could, I do not wish to, I hardly know where to begin."

"Try," he said, encouragingly. "I am listening carefully. I really want to know, I am really trying to understand." He smiled faintly. "It may prove important to me, too, in the end."

"Edward looks like me," she said, "I told you that he does, or more like me at six, being a young child, than anyone else, and his family did not like me at all or George's marrying me, at all in any way, or particularly in the way he did, so quickly and with no warning. They never forgave me for it, and they will not, especially now, and I do not think they will love Edward at all, because he looks like me. They never came to see me once, Noel, not once, nor to see their grandchild, nor their son. Perhaps he saw them and did not tell me, but I know I never did. I find that hard myself to forgive, Noel, and Edward is at least half my son. I do not want him in their hands. Can you understand that?"

"Yes, Anne," he said, "I can. I can very well, and I honour you for it, but none of your choices seem very good ones to me. Will he not have some advancement, some inheritance through them?"

She shook her head. "I do not think they even loved George, somehow, very much. His own mother, you see, is dead, she died when he was very young, and he has a stepmother with children of her own, as well as older brothers and sisters. They are not so wealthy, I think, as they would like to seem, and he will have no title there."

He smiled, not pleasantly. "You think he will with me? A bastard, at best, at worst another man's child?"

"If you are his guardian, you will be fair, at least, I think. And if you wished, if you found you thought he was your own son, or if you grew to like him, you could adopt him, or make him your heir."

"I could," he said thoughtfully, "yes, I think I could, but I would have to check the law, what under entail I could do. This question is not one I have given any thought on. But I would not count on it, Anne, I really wouldn't, if that is why you bring him to me. I feel no disposition towards it, I find none in me at all, no hint of it. I have a feeling for you, that is true, but my feelings are not as strong for anything as you might imagine, and we do not know each other well, we cannot, we have hardly been together. What you ask, though, is for a long, long time, and a close association with your boy."

"Ah," she said, "but you have not seen Edward yet."

"What of your own parents, Anne? Could they not take your boy?" he asked, disregarding her remark.

"I would laugh," she said, "except I have a little pain here in my chest and it would hurt me. They could not even raise *me,* and they have not been to see me since I married either, and they have let me know I was not welcome to come there. And you think they'd want to raise my child for me?"

"Why do you not raise him yourself, Anne? If you are so desperate, I will give you an income. I can afford to do it, and I would like to, and you could stay as you are, where you are, with your friends, and I would come to see you from time to time to see how you did and what your requirements were. Would that not be best? Come, Anne, think!"

"I am thinking," she said. "I think you are misjudged, by yourself, and by your friends. I think you are both generous and kind."

"I am neither, Anne. I wish to spare myself trouble, which means a great deal to me, and I do not mind sparing money, which once meant a little something to me, but now means nothing at all. I have enough to do it, and not miss it, that is all. I owe you something, I would feel I had in some measure repaid it. Will you accept it?"

"With gratitude and pleasure and affection, from you, Noel, but it would not be for very long, and then Edward still will have no guardian. You did not believe me and you still do not, but you must act as if you did."

"That is nonsense, Anne," he said, "nonsense, utter, arrant nonsense you must put from your mind. If you are ill, you must come here, and I will see that you are nursed, and then you will put this morbid nonsense from your mind."

She smiled at him, her sweetest smile. "But that is just what I wish to do," she said, "I do wish to come here."

He fell into a slight panic. "I did not say I would marry you, Anne. I do not need or want a wife."

"I did not ask you to," she said again, smiling. "You made me once another offer, it is that one I would accept now, if you made it again."

"I find this hard to believe," he said slowly, "your husband just dead, and you with a young child to care for. What do you want in exchange?"

"Nothing," she said, "only what you wish to give me."

"I accept then, your acceptance," he said slowly, his hand tightening on hers. "What shall I give you?"

She drew her breath in, hesitantly. "Will you hear me out? I will come, even if you say you cannot give it." He nodded, watching her. "I want you to call your lawyer here now—oh please, Noel, do not frown so, hear me out—and have him draw up the papers of guardianship for Edward, you to be his guardian, under any terms you like, Noel. And you may keep the paper. I will not tell Edward or anyone about it. But when I die" —at his face, she amended—"but should I die, if I died suddenly and there was not time to draw them up even if then you wished to, you would have the papers and you could use them to protect him, if you chose to."

"That is not very much to ask," he said thoughtfully. "I will do that for you. Will it relieve your mind? And we will have lunch while we wait for him." He rang for his footman, and while he came, he wrote a note to his lawyer, summoning him on immediate business of some urgency.

"It will relieve my mind very much," she said shakily. "You are good to me, Noel."

"If you keep saying that," he said, "I might believe you, and then where should we be? A villain believing himself a good fellow. That would never do, Anne, never. Shall we have Edward here for lunch, or go to him?"

"I would rather finish with the lawyer, first," she said, "then we can go."

"You are persistent, Anne," he said with a slight frown.

"Only desperate, Noel, as you said yourself."

He looked at her queerly, as the footman entered, and gave him instructions: "Take this at once to my lawyer's house, George, and if he is not at the first address, try the second, and the third, until you have found him. If he has not lunched, he can lunch here. When you have done that stop by the Inn, the 4 Trees Inn," he said looking at Anne. She nodded. "You will find a little boy there, whose name will be Edward Armstrong. Is that his full name?"

"Edward Clare."

"Edward Clare Armstrong," the Earl repeated thoughtfully. "You will see that he makes a good lunch, George, and that he makes no mischief, but that he enjoys himself. What is he doing now, Lady Anne?"

"I think he is reading," she said with a faint smile.

He looked amazed. "Does he do that already?"

She nodded.

"Well," he said, "George, you will stay with him until we come."

"I understands your lordship," the footman said, bowing.

"And as you leave," Tyne added, "have our lunch brought to us here."

They waited to speak until the footman had gone, the Earl observing his visitor closely.

"You are tired, Anne," he said without preamble. "You have had much strain, and a long journey with a little boy, and you have what you want now, at least a part of it. Lie down on my bed, until lunch comes." He smiled at her look of dismay. "By yourself, of course. Or on the chaise longue here, if you prefer."

"I think I would prefer it," she said. "You are kind, and I am tired. Will you sit by me?" They rearranged themselves.

"You think Edward is my son, I think," he said to her, without warning. "Why?" As she opened her mouth, he put his fingers on her lips. "I know you do not know. You told me that. I want to know why you think it. I am not a fool; of course, Anne, that is why you brought the child. You would not otherwise have so presumed upon our so brief connection. And you think I will see it too. I wonder what mark it is I am to look for, what stamp?"

"You are right, Noel, as you always are. I do think it. That is why I came. But I do not know. There is no mark. I wish there were."

"Like the mark of Cain?" he said bitterly. "Let us spare him that in our wishes, since another has. Why do you think it then?" he added gently.

"Because he is unusual, Noel. He is not an ordinary child. George was extraordinarily kind and extraordinarily good, but he was not an unusual person, as Edward is. Nor am I. But you are, Noel." (She ignored his flush of embarrassed displeasure.) "That is why I think it. You will have to learn to know him and then decide for yourself."

"That seems small grounds to me."

"Perhaps." She seemed too exhausted to speak further.

"I am going to do as you ask, Anne, because you ask it, under the conditions you propose, which seem fair to me, and do not commit myself now, but do you understand what you are doing? I wonder. I know nothing at all of young children, or children at all. I think I must have been born old myself. And I remember no love shown me by my parents. I remember only strange nurses and strange doctors and strange rooms and strange governesses and then strange tutors. I cannot imagine showing love to a child, or feeling any, or wanting to show or feel it. I feel only bitterness, as if in revenge for the poor unhappy child I was myself, lonely and unwanted and in pain. I have never spoken of this to anyone, or even thought of it, but fairness makes me speak of it now to you. I would not want such a man as I a guardian to my child," he added, unaware of the irony there might be in what he said.

She was aware, but she did not refer to it. She only said, "If your intention is good, and I hope it is, you have money, as you say, and you can hire a loving nurse and a loving governess. They do exist, Noel. They can be found if one looks."

"True," he said, "I had not thought of that. What you say is true. But I might not recognise the right kind myself. You will help me, Anne."

"I will try," she said.

"But that is by no means the worst obstacle or hazard. The worst is myself, the kind of man I am, Anne. You do not know me. I am a man of violent passions and angers and strange appetites. I have never tried to control them, and they largely control me. Do you consider I may very well hate your child, Anne, and then God help him, if he is left with me."

"Would you, Noel?" she said soberly. "Do you think you would?"

"It might very well be that I would. Loving you—I do, you know, Anne"—he bent and gently kissed her lips—"loving you, I would love your child, you think, but that is with a different man than I am. I might very well hate him, quite as easily and more likely—seeing you in him, and you not with me, for if I should have to be his guardian, you would not be with me, even if you had only left me—and wondering whose act with you produced him—seeing his father that reared him in him too, and hating that, for he cannot help being most like the man he knew his first six years, I think."

"Edward is himself," she said, "he is no one else. I have rarely known anyone so much himself. I do not think anyone, even you, Noel, could hate him, unless they first hated me and wished to hate him."

"Perhaps I do hate you too, Anne, as well as love you. Perhaps it would please me to raise your child in depravity. Give it thought while you can."

"I have, Noel. I do not think you will, I trust you will not, but if you choose to, it is your choosing."

"You are a strange woman, yourself, Anne. You are always surprising me. I do not understand you at all, and perhaps that is why I love you. But it is not enough," he said, "for raising a child I don't want."

Lunch was announced then. Lady Anne ate very little, but she revived somewhat, and the colour came back briefly to her lips, though not to her cheeks. The lawyer came before they had finished. She pushed aside her cup, as if to have no more of it, in her impatience. He started to comment, but at the look of her face, he thought better of it.

He talked quietly and at length and to a degree frankly to the lawyer, Anne listening carefully, and answering carefully the questions put her. In the end, the affair did not prove a difficult matter, and she signed the release to him, and Tyne also signed, and witnesses were called in from the downstairs hall. As he finally escorted the lawyer to the door, and turned back, he saw she had fallen from her chair onto the table, her hand at her throat. He called the lawyer back, and gave him two hurried instructions, a sudden fear gripping him, and rang for his footman, and as he had rung, walked to her as fast as he could, with his gait, and lifted her up, unbuttoning again her dress and her bodices to give her air.

He did not know what to do for her, and his distress in its way equalled hers. He felt for the first time since he was a child as if he would faint. He carried her upstairs to his bed and pulled the coverlet about her, and he only knew to hold her hand tightly, as she was holding his, murmuring endearments and assurances. The footman came and went, on hurried errands. The doctor came next, and proceeded to work as best he might, to lessen her pain and ease her breathing. He asked if his patient had had such attacks before. The Earl could only say he thought so. The clergyman came then, expecting to administer the last comforts, and was surprised to be asked to marry the Earl to the ill woman. She looked at him then, barely conscious, but understanding, and pressed his hand in grateful assent. While the doctor worked on, the ceremony was read.

"Anne," he said urgently, before he made his final answer, or she hers, "I do this under duress of your extreme illness, only in case it should be necessary later to protect the interests of your boy. Can you hear me? Do you understand me? If you can, signify your assent to these gentlemen to an arrangement of present secrecy that may seem strange to them." He dropped to one knee by the bed, to be on a level with her, and took her hand. "Recover yourself, Anne, only recover yourself, and we will make no secret of it."

She caught her breath faintly, and fixed her gaze first on the doctor and then on the clergyman, and said, "Whatever this lord urges on you in the interests of my son, as his guardian, I also urge you do. I do entreat you to it, gentlemen. Please reassure him that we may finish."

They reluctantly, at the mutual entreaty of the two most concerned, agreed to leave the fact of the ceremony a present secret, and the marriage was completed.

"I think I may be dying," she said to the clergyman, "I feel so very ill, but you can give no other comfort than you have. I have no fears except to leave this life and my son, and you cannot help me stay, if I must leave it. I want to speak to this lord, before my son comes. Will you leave us, please?"

The clergyman reluctantly withdrew, but Tyne would not let the doctor leave, for he was frightened, a state he rarely found himself in.

"Did I do this to you?" he asked contritely.

She put her arms about his neck and guided him near her, for she had no strength to draw him. "You have made me very happy," she said, "in ways I had not thought to be. Remember only that. This would have happened, if not today, tomorrow, or next week, or next month. Any time. The London doctor warned me when George took me up to see him. It frightened George. I am glad I did not frighten you. But I had hoped, seeing you again, for much more time."

"Oh, God, Anne," he cried, "am I to lose you? Not now, not now." He fixed his desperate eyes on her. "I have sinned, and I see I am damned in this life, too." He began suddenly to sob.

The doctor was shocked at his lack of control, and came forward and touched his shoulder, not very gently. "My lord," he said in a horrified whisper, "this violence will not do when your lady is so ill. If you cannot contain your personal grief, you must go away from this room until you can!"

"Do not send him away," said the Lady Anne in a stronger voice. "He can do me no harm." She took his hand and pressed it to her lips. "Come, Noel, you cannot say I have been so important to you. You will recover. You are disappointed, and I own I am, too, that is all. But we must not shock this good man."

"I did not know how unhappy I had been," he said simply, "and then you came, and I saw you, and then I knew. I began to hope"—he smiled wryly—"even I, for ordinary happiness, and to hope that you might even know how to teach me to be good. I have never wanted to before. One must be happy, I think, to be good."

"We must be good just for ourselves, Noel. You taught me that." She kissed his fingers, softening the effect of her words.

"I?" he said, disbelieving. "How I?"

"You were necessity, and necessity teaches us that lesson."

III

He was aware suddenly, as he knelt beside her, on his bed, her arms again about his neck, of the fixed gaze upon him. He turned his head, and saw a small boy, of indeterminate age to him, a child, not a baby, staring at him, with a fixed, and somehow, it seemed to him, disapproving gaze. He flushed, disliking the embarrassment the child produced in him, and the child for producing it, and rose awkwardly to his feet, and withdrew a little. The child did not speak to him, or question him, or look at him again, but went straight to his mother, to the place he had himself left. The tears were brimming from his eyes, that the Earl saw were his mother's eyes, and as large, they seemed, but he did not sob, and his voice was curiously steady for a little child's.

"Are you ill, Mama?" he asked. "Some gentleman came for me, and said you needed me, and I must come at once."

"I am a little ill, Edward," his mother said gently, trying to smile at him. "I have hurt myself, but I am trying to be better. But I could not come to you, and so I asked you to come to me."

"Like Papa?" he said doubtfully, the distress growing on his face. Like his mother he was dressed in shabby black.

"No, not like Papa, little mouse," she said. "I shall be better soon."

"Whose house is this we are in?" he asked, in a whisper. "And who are all these gentlemen?"

"They are footmen," she whispered back, putting her arms about him, "and the doctor, and the tall man who was by the bed is a friend of mine and of yours, Edward, who will take care of us, now that your papa is gone."

He accepted this, without comment or further question, without enthusiasm and without dismay. The doctor wished his patient to rest, and sent them all for a time from the room. The Earl, going towards the stairs, found the little boy had followed him. He wished to be alone, and he was displeased, but he found it hard in the circumstances to rebuff him. They were in the gallery, below the long line of forbidding picture faces. He found the little boy's eyes also upon him questioningly.

"I am your Uncle James," he said severely to the little figure. He winced under Anne's eyes fixed upon him.

"I did not know I had an uncle," the little boy said, "but I suppose it is a good thing to have."

"I am going to take care of you," the Earl announced, rather desperately.

"I do not need anyone to take care of me," Edward said. "I have my mother, and I do not need anyone else. Or do you mean while she is sick?" He looked at his new uncle in sudden comprehension and dismay. "I hope she does not want to go to be with Papa," he said simply. "I could not bear it if she did."

The boy's words fell unpleasantly on Tyne's ears, expressing too bluntly his fears, and curiously and irrationally awakening his jealousy. "I hope not," he said discouragingly. "I do not think I could myself," he added, with sudden springing sympathy, "but if she does, then we must learn to bear it, that is all, Edward."

"Do you love my mother?" the child asked without warning. Tyne found himself, at his age, blushing, having no idea of what was behind the child's clear eyes, and hating the child for his disconcerting questions, when his nerves were so frayed.

"I suppose I do," he said slowly, not looking at the child.

"Then I shall love you, too, Uncle James," the child said simply, and slipped his hand into the Earl's long-fingered white one. "What is the matter with your foot?" he asked abruptly, in his quick way of changing from subject to subject. The Earl dropped his hand. "Have you hurt your foot? Why do you walk the way I saw you walking, like this?" he said, demonstrating.

The Earl's face grew white with anger that he was dismayed at feeling at a child, particularly this child. He had no guide to measure the child by, though he dimly felt such a guide would help him to take less seriously the child's questions, if he had one. "I was born with it, Edward, I have a club foot, and I don't want you to ask me about it ever again. But if you want me to, I will take off my boot, which is specially made, and show you now, once and for all."

"That will not be necessary," the little boy said, his head high, the Earl's tone having penetrated even his understanding, suddenly in his pride so like the Earl himself that the Earl found himself shocked and aghast at this image of himself. "I am sorry I asked. I did not mean to hurt you."

"*Hurt* me?" exclaimed the Earl, unconsciously talking to the child as to another adult.

"My father says that people are never angry with us unless we have hurt them in some way."

"Your father is mistaken," the Earl snapped. "You have not hurt me."

The boy's eyes upon him never wavered in their clear gaze, and his own fell.

"I forgot," the child said, in sudden despair. "My father is dead."

The Earl was conscious of a desire to pick the child up, and soothe or joke or in some way banish the old look from his face and the stiffness from his small back and shoulders, but in the face of his tiny pride, he did not dare, and he would not have known how to begin. "Shall I take you to the stables?" he asked hesitantly. "Would you like to see my horses, Edward?"

"I would rather stay with my mother," the little boy answered.

"Your mother is resting," the Earl said, "and she cannot see either of us."

"But I am near her here. I would rather stay here," he said simply.

The Earl sighed. "Come down, and have your tea, and let George my footman take you for a little walk in my gardens, or on the lawn, if you do not want to see my horses." He smiled a little at the little boy with his serious grave face. "A footman, Edward, is just a kind of servant, it is the usual name. Perhaps I shall get you a pony, Edward. Would you like that?"

"Must I stay here?" the little boy said directly.

"Don't you want to, Edward?" the Earl asked, indifferent and yet irrationally hurt.

"I want to go home," the little boy said, his composure shattered. "I want to go home, with my mother, and I want to go home now."

"Well, you can't, Edward, your mother is sick," the Earl said, driven to brutal frankness. "You will have to stay here, at least for a little while. You can't go home now."

The little boy measured him with his eyes, and then he sighed. "Well, if I cannot go home, I suppose I will go as you say and have my tea with your—with your footman? Where must I go? Or will you take me? But when I have had my tea, may I come back here and see my mother then?"

The emotions the child produced in him in his state of anxiety for the child's mother exhausted and bewildered the Earl, unaccustomed to children as he completely was. The child's gravity and sudden acceptance of thwarting fate moved him unbearably, and he took the child's hand, saying only, "I will take you," and led the way down the broad stairs. Even a day ago the idea of himself, Viscount Rockfort, Earl of Tyne, scandal and bane of London, helpless in the merciless hands of a child, would have amused him, but the reality did not amuse him at all.

He left Edward and went back to his room. The doctor was on the point of leaving.

"I am going to my supper," the doctor said, "and I have two more cases I must look in on, but I will send a nurse up for the night from the village, and I will be back before long. I am leaving the names of the houses I must go to, if you cannot wait for me. But your lady seems now to be resting easy. She is uncomfortable in these clothes, but she says she has no clothes with her."

"I will find a nightgown for her," the Earl said. "What other instructions do you have?"

"None, except to let her rest, and not let her distress herself for the child or any worry." He packed his bag, and made a last visit to his patient's bed. He found her with her eyes closed, breathing easily, and he did not disturb her. The Earl walked with him to the door of the room, and then he shut it, and locked it, and walked over to the bed. He found she had not been asleep after all, for her eyes were open, and on him.

"I am such a trouble," she murmured faintly.

"And you are going to be more," he said, "for I am going to put you in a nightgown on the doctor's orders." He walked to his clothes stand, his limp more pronounced than usual, and returned with a white ruffled gown of his own.

"How pretty," she said, "I did not know you wore things like that."

"You know now," he said smiling.

"It will be much too large for me."

"It is not meant to fit," he said, again smiling. "It does not usually take a valet to put on, but I will valet you tonight," his fingers once more at her buttons.

"Is it night already?" she asked. "The room seems light."

"It is not six yet," he said, "and Edward is having his tea, with my George."

"Do you like Edward?" she asked. "Have you talked to him?"

He did not know what to answer, but he decided on a version of the truth. "I do not know what to make of Edward. He disconcerts me."

She laughed a little. "He sometimes disconcerts me, too. As you do. I think you do not like him, but I hope you will." She winced a little as his hands, very gentle, lifted her clothes from her. He winced too, at the sight of her flesh, and then he slipped the nightgown over her.

"Did the doctor leave me water to drink?" she asked.

"It is here," he said, handing her the glass, and helping her to drink, his arm behind her.

She looked at him, her eyes near his eyes, speaking, over the glass, and she saw the water shaking, in his hands, not hers. Her eyes pled, and his refused, and hers pled insistently.

He reached to put the glass down, for her arms were clasped about him, and though they had no strength, he let them hold him.

"The pain is coming back, a little," she gasped. "Do I repulse you, like this?"

"Not at all, Anne," he said, "you do not at all."

"Take me one more time, Noel," she begged softly, "let me be in your arms, which are my only home."

"That is madness, Anne," he said, "even I know it. The doctor would not forgive me."

"The doctor is not here," she said, "and the pain is. Nor is it his affair. Help me, Noel. You are all I want, all I ever wanted, and this pain is taking me away from you. Hold me now, while I am here, hold me, Noel, before the pain takes me away, or other people come, and I have to die with them here."

She held out her arms to him, pleading, and unable to resist her desire meeting with his own, he loosened himself, and took her to him, as gently as he could, murmuring endearments to her all the time. As the pain within her grew larger and fiercer, threatening to blacken the world from her, she clasped him to her the more fiercely, kissing him desperately, until with a rending cry, she fell back limp in his arms. He thought she had fainted, but he discovered to his horror and his grief that she was dead. He tried breathing again into her mouth, but the breath was simply gone. He held her, still warm, unbelieving, for a long time in his arms, until sense returned to his mind, and he realised Edward, and the doctor, would be wanting to come in. He was at first too shaken to move, but then he summoned his years of hardness to his aid and made himself rise. He took his handkerchief, and moistened it in the glass of water, and gently wiped the traces of their folly, if such it was, from her legs, and then he closed her eyes, and covered her, but not her face. He adjusted his clothes, put on his coat and his boots, unlocked the door, and went down to have the doctor called.

Edward, incredibly, was still at his tea. It was, incredibly, not yet seven o'clock. The long light fell upon the rose gardens and the box hedges, and on the little candles of the yew. He took the boy by the hand, without a word, and walked with him out into the garden. The air was warm, Autumn not yet approaching, a few roses yet bloomed, their petals full blown and ready to fall. He did not know what to say, but he found he did not have to say anything. His exhausted face, with its drawn lines, told the child, too experienced in the signs of grief, what he could not find words to tell.

"My mother is gone," he said, half questioningly, half wonderingly. "My mother is dead, she has gone away too, and left me too. Is that what you want to tell me?"

He nodded his head, still unable to speak.

"Why would she leave me?" the child cried in accusing grief. "Wasn't it enough for my father to leave me? Oh, mother," he cried suddenly, to the air about him, "you have left me, oh, why did you go? I have no one at all now." He did not cry, but his face was white with grief and repeated tragedy.

"You have me," the Earl said slowly. "Your mother left you to me. I will take care of you."

"I have you," the child repeated, with faint fright and disgust in his voice, repelling the Earl, who released him. The child, uncanny, the Earl thought, in his sensing of others' emotions, he himself being so blind to them, suddenly threw his arms about the Earl's waist, as high as he could reach, burying his face in the Earl. "I did not mean it. I do not know you. Forgive me, Uncle James, I did not mean it."

The child began to cry now, and the Earl knelt down so that the little boy could put his arms around his neck. He picked him up, a light sobbing weight, and carried him to a bench in an arbour, still thick with leaves, and sat down with him, holding him. He felt suddenly that Anne was very near him, and he tightened his arms about the little boy convulsively, but the child did not cry out if his arms hurt him, but only held to him more tightly himself. The Earl felt tears in his own eyes, and his throat tight and painful and constricted with emotion he held in it.

The little boy sobbed on and on, until gradually he wore himself out, and his sobs changed to hiccoughs, and then to silence. Finally, he lifted his head, and said, "I want to see my mother. May I see her? Will it frighten me?"

The Earl shook his head. "Come," he said, "I will take you to her."

He stood beside the boy, not watching him, ravaged by his own emotions, at last, finally and completely and too late, prey to them, not they to him. But he saw the child stretch a timid hand out, as though to touch his mother, and then draw it back, as if afraid. The Earl took the child's hand in his, and placed it on his mother's hand, and her cheek, which were not cold, only cool, as a sleeping person's might be, a faint warmth left. He thought she did seem to be sleeping, and as if to show the child, he bent down and kissed her farewell lightly on her lips.

"You may kiss her cheek, Edward, if you wish to."

"She is not there," the boy said.

"It is a kind of farewell," the Earl said, "all the same we sometimes make."

He took the child's hand, and laid it on her heart, to show him there was no pulse, and on her face, to show it did not stir and had no breath.

"I know what death is," the child said with dignity. "You forget, Uncle James, my father is just dead, too."

"If you know that," the Earl said, "you know what most of the world does not. What is death, Edward?" he asked curiously.

"It is the parting of the spirit that we love from the body that we love. The body will decay, and worms will eat it in the ground, and we cannot have it or touch it or kiss it again"—as he spoke he leaned forward, and kissed quietly and sombrely his mother's forehead, her cheeks, her lips, and her hands, his tears falling on the places he had kissed, but his voice did not cry, as he continued, after a moment—"but the spirit we love will not decay, for it is not here any longer, it has gone to God who is our home and our rest and our peace and our release from pain, and from there it can look down upon us and watch us and love us and see what we do, if we remember and call upon it; and someday we shall see it again, someday I will be with my mother again." Here he did begin to cry. "But I may not care, at least not so much, then. I just want her now."

"Shall I take you out now, Edward?" the Earl said tenderly, picking the little boy up.

"Yes, Uncle James, please," he said, "I would rather remember my mother not so still and not so white."

He nestled his head under his uncle's arm like a little bird, very tired, very forlorn.

"Who taught you these things, Edward? Your father?"

The little boy nodded, in a muffled way, and said, from the shelter of his arm, "And my mother, too. Do you believe it, Uncle James?"

"Not entirely, Edward. I wish I did. But my believing or my not believing does not make it any the less true, for you or for itself."

"I know that," the child said. "I just wondered if you did. Do you go to church, Uncle James?"

"No," the Earl said, "not often, unless I am here, when it is expected of me. But you may go."

"I mean, what about my mother?"

"Do not worry for that, Edward, she will be well taken care of, as you and as your father would wish."

The child sighed. "I shall never go to sleep."

"Of course you will, Edward. Shall I make a sleeping potion for you? I may make one for myself."

"No, thank you, Uncle James. Tomorrow my mother will be even farther away. I am not sure I want to sleep tonight, I do not want today to end. I can still say, 'This morning we breakfasted together, this morning she helped me dress . . .'"

The Earl could not bear it any longer. "That is enough, Edward," he said more sharply than he meant, torn by his own different memories of the day.

The child looked at him in hurt surprise. "But tomorrow I can't say that. It will not be true any longer. Is it not right to *grieve*, Uncle James, for the person we loved best in all the world?"

"It is right, Edward," he said heavily, "but it has only begun to hurt, our loss, Edward, and I cannot bear to think about it anymore tonight." He changed the subject abruptly. "Was your father Church of England? He was, I suppose."

"No," said the child, "he was of Mr. Wesley's persuasion."

"My God!" exclaimed the Earl, "a Methody!"

"His family did not like it, you see," the child said, "for they were Church of England, like my mother's. They did not mind his being a clergyman, since he was a younger son, but they minded the kind he was."

"You are too wise, Edward," the Earl said, "too wise too young. I must get you a pony. Would you like a Welsh pony or a Shetland pony, or one from Skye?"

"I do not care," the child said. "Choose for me what you want for me."

"Was your mother Methody too?" he asked, incredulously.

"She was what my father wanted, that was all," Edward said.

"Well," the Earl said heavily, "we will do the best we can by her up here. What shall we put on you, Edward? I suppose your nightshirt is at the Inn?" The child nodded. "That is too far to go. My nightshirts are too big for you, but one of my shirts should just about be right. Now my George will bring your bath up, and help you into bed."

"Can you not help me, Uncle James? My mother always did."

The Earl shook his head. "I have things to see to, Edward. George will help you, and I will look in on you again and say goodnight." He had taken the little boy into the only other bedroom that was at all made up, not far from his own, and he left him sitting disconsolately on the windowseat, staring out into the darkening garden, and the deepening sky where the stars were just beginning to show. He had his eyes fixed on the evening star.

"Venus," the Earl thought, and wondered what was in the child's mind.

He saw the doctor, who had arrived, and made arrangements for another room, and for the laying out in it. He bore the doctor's shock, and the unexpressed reproach of his eyes, and made preparations to have the funeral the next morning with the clergyman whom he summoned, despite the haste, because of estrangement between Anne and her two families. He was not certain it was well-done of him, but he did not care. She had come to him, because they would have none of her, or had made her feel so, and here she would stay, and he would deal as he liked. He composed a brief notice for the *Gazette* and sent it off to be posted by a footman.

He was very tired now himself, though sleep seemed far from his mind. He heard a sound of bitter sobbing, wrenching tearing sounds, from Edward's room, but despite his promise he did not go in. His moral nature was cowardly, as he well knew, and he had put more upon it already that day than it could well bear. He felt stretched, through it, to a point of breaking, and past thought. He had a bath brought up, and bathed himself, at last, sadly and regretfully, and got into his bed that had born such different weights and emotions that day. But once there, sleep evaded him. He wished for laudanum, but the boy's bravery had shamed him. He lay, his eyes open, watching the light from the rising moon creep in a square across the floor. When it reached the door, it caught a white figure in its path. He gasped, and then he said, sternly, "Edward, is that you?"

"You said you would look in on me, Uncle James, but you didn't," Edward said, his voice worn out from lonely weeping.

"I am sorry, Edward." He did not know what to say. Somehow he found himself disliking to tell even white lies to the child, but he did not like the position.

"Why didn't you come? Don't you keep your promises?"

"I heard you crying, Edward, and it put me off," the Earl said roughly.

"That was not very brave," Edward said, his voice stifled.

"Then you be brave for us both, and go back to your bed, Edward," the Earl said, dismissing him.

"I am not very brave either, at least not just now," said Edward, and his nose seemed to be stopped up a little. "I am only six, and you are much older, quite old, you are supposed to be brave."

"That may be, Edward," said the Earl. "But I am not, and it is late and you need a handkerchief and to go to bed. Goodnight."

He turned over, away from Edward, resolutely, and shut his eyes. After a moment, he heard the door close softly. He sighed, but sleep continued to evade him. After an hour, he gave in to himself, and got out of bed to find the bottle of laudanum. He wished he had put it ready by his bed. He had stumbled over the little huddled heap by the door, in the shadow, before he saw it. It was Edward, of course, he should have known it, by the door. He stared at the sleeping child with a mixture of exasperation and pity and other emotions he did not try to define for himself. He bent and picked the boy up, and carried him to his bed, and laid him down, not on the particular side his mother had lain on, for she had been on both, but where he had last seen her. He was too tired to carry him again, down the hall, with his foot, and he supposed persistence deserved some reward. He found the laudanum and mixed it and drank it, welcoming its bitter promise of relief, and put himself back in bed. The night was still warm, although a slight wind promised a cooler day. He stared at the sleeping boy, whose pale features in the moonlight might have been Anne's. It seemed to him, dizzy with sleeplessness and fatigue and the first effects of the opium, that it was Anne herself, and he started back in dismay, gasping, and then, his conscious brain attempting to stop him, but his will and his need overriding it, he bent down and kissed the child's pale face, lingeringly and hungrily, his fair hair, his eyelids, his pale brow and cheeks, and his lips that lay in sleep like Anne's only a very little smaller, and the child's fair neck, and then his lips again. The child stirred, and returned the caress, and put his arms about the Earl trustingly. "I am lost," the Earl thought, "totally lost," but it seemed to him that he held Anne in his arms, passionately and lovingly though chastely. "Oh my God," he thought, "is he depraved too, already, so young, is it in the blood—or is this Christian love?" He fell asleep, the child's arms clasped innocently about his neck, his warm soft limbs nestled against his own.

IV

Though he slept late, the next morning, the child was still asleep when he woke. The Earl would have liked to have carried him, still sleeping, back to his room, but he was afraid to wake him. He went into his dressing room, shutting the door quietly between the two rooms, and called his valet to dress him. He had set the enterrement for ten that morning, and he had no time to spare, not even for breakfast, nor appetite for it, had he time. He was not certain of his duty to Edward, but he was certain he did not care. He did not know whether the child had been taken to his father's funeral or not. He hated funerals himself, and he was so uncertain of being able to get through this particular one that he wanted no eyes upon him, least of all her child's, and he had no reserve of strength to cope with the child's shock and grief during the harrowing ordeal. He wished he need not go himself. He could have set the hour for a time when the child would have been awake, but he had set this hour intentionally for an unfrequented, unusual one, to be alone. If the child minded, he thought, it would just have to mind.

He absented himself from both his mind and from his body, a trick of relief he had learned during the painful and humiliating operations and manipulations upon him as a child, and as a stranger with remote eyes, spoke civilly to the Vicar, who had so recently married him to this woman now to be put in earth, oblivious to his kind, mildly curious eyes, and to his sympathetic words of comfort. He felt no longer any need for comfort, his moment of open vulnerableness had passed. He had the flowers he had brought placed on the mound of earth, refusing to consider or imagine what lay there underneath. He had chosen a remote corner of the churchyard, but one that by chance, he discovered, overlooked from a distance, being higher, his own land. It seemed appropriate, and he supposed angrily Anne must have arranged it. "It is too late, now," he addressed the grave angrily, "you have left him and given him to me, and I did not want him. Go your way now, and do not trouble me." And then, he thought, "Oh, God, I am mad. There is nothing here. It does not matter what I can see from this place."

He arranged for the stone, with the name of Armstrong to be written on it, not his own. He realised also, suddenly, that he had not put her in his family's vault. Well, it was quiet, out here on this hill, and more private. If he decided to claim her, and honour publicly their private ceremony, he could have her moved, he supposed. But he thought now he would rather be placed here by her himself, in the clear free air, and perhaps he would make arrangement for it. He had some explaining, he knew, to do with the Vicar, and much as he disliked explanations, he bent himself to it. He talked with the Vicar for a long time, and though he did not convince him of the wisdom of his plans and intentions, he persuaded him that he had no intention of claiming the child for his own, at this time, if ever. The Vicar, hoping the Earl might be persuaded of his own will to it, agreed to continue to not speak of the marriage, to the child or to anyone, understanding it would advance no one's interests and had not been the dead woman's wish. The Earl persuaded the Vicar more easily to allow the little boy to come to him daily for a fee to be taught Latin and English grammar.

"He reads fluently and well already in his own language. I shall engage to find a nurse for him, but he can wait, I think, for a tutor living in for some years. He will not need divinity," the Earl added. "He is

already well instructed in it, and thoroughly advanced. But you will probably enjoy discussing it with him, as I do not. His father, as he will tell
you, was a clergyman, but of the Methody persuasion." He enjoyed the
Vicar's look of shock, that was immediately replaced by a speculative
interest as he considered future delights of conversation and possible
conversion. "But he will sooner convert you, than you him, Vicar. Stand
warned."

The lightness of their conversation, and the subject, though necessary
in part and convenient for the rest, suddenly wearied him, and he rose to
take his leave. "If you know of a good woman who can be a nurse to
Edward, will you let me know? I know nothing of the needs of small
boys, and I don't wish to learn."

The Vicar smiled indulgently, for he knew the Earl could not completely avoid learning a great deal about small boys, but he promised to
give the problem his attention. Mrs. Pigot he thought might be available,
when she returned from her sick sister's. The Earl sighed at the disruption
of his routine and of his calm, and returned to his house into a storm such
as he had never experienced.

Edward, waking, had learned from George the footman where the
Earl had gone, and what he had gone to do. It was too late for Edward
to follow, even had he known where to go and even had the footman
allowed it, but the footman, considerably larger and stronger than Edward, though not in himself large, had managed to contain the child in
the house. He met his Uncle now at the door, where he had been waiting,
on his return.

"I shall never forgive you for this," Edward cried, "never. You had no
right. She was my mother." He struck at him with his fists, beating him on
the chest, with both hands, with both fists and flat palms, sobbing
tumultuously all the time in an ecstasy of grief and wronged fury. The
Earl, tried beyond his small endurance, gave him a sharp slap on the
cheek that happened to overbalance him, and sent him tumbling to the
floor. He sat up, holding his face, nursing it, shock and pain written on
his face, hatred glaring from his eyes, but he did not speak, and he caught
back his sobbing breath and held it checked. The Earl could not have
been more surprised if one of the stable kittens he had just passed when
he left his horse should have reared on its legs in the size and fury of a
tiger. For a moment two pairs of eyes, both blazing with hatred and
anger, held each other in a glare more suited to the field of battle than
the front hall of a country estate. The ghosts of the dead kings of
Northumbria seemed to have risen and walked the fields on which the

house now stood. The Earl came to himself first, realising the justice of the boy's anger and its provocation of grief and his own peremptory dealing and the ridiculousness of the extent of his own anger, but he did not know what to do to mend the situation.

He held out his hand to the child, to help him rise, but the child refused to take it.

"You struck me, you hit me," the child cried in a voice of strained emotion, "and no one ever has before."

"Well, you hit me too, Edward, and you hit me first," the Earl said reasonably, "and nobody has ever done that to me either. I thought you had run mad. Will you forgive me?"

"No," the child said simply.

"You are too like your mother," the Earl said less reasonably, his anger rising again, "I will not ask you again. But she did forgive me, and with more cause not to." He did not at the moment care whether the child understood him, or not, or what he made of his words. "Have you had breakfast, Edward?"

"No," Edward said. "I will not eat in your house."

The Earl sighed, exasperation in readier supply than patience. "You have nowhere else to go right now, Edward. Your mother wanted you to stay here, and she would want you to eat."

"I see I have to stay here," Edward said bitterly, "your footman George made me see that, but you cannot make me eat, and my mother would not want me to eat the food of a man who struck me in the face, after stealing my mother from me."

"Did you go to your father's funeral, Edward?" the Earl asked more gently than his friends who knew him might have expected.

The child looked at him blankly.

"Did you see him buried? Did you see him put into a box and the dirt and earth piled upon the box in a hole, until there was nothing to see?"

The child shook his head slowly, horror in his eyes.

"That is what it is like, you know. That is all there is to see."

The child shook his head, unconvinced, the tears spilling over from his eyes. "But it was my mother, my only mother, and not yours. You could have waited for me, Uncle James, you did not have to hurry so to put her away like that. And I was her only son. I should have been there. You should have let me come, you should have told me." His voice was dry and tight with held-back sobs. "Can I go there at least now? Will you take me now?"

The child's request was reasonable, but the Earl, exhausted, wishing no more scenes of any sort and knowing the rawness of the new grave, shook his head. The child's anger flared out again.

"You are *too* cruel, Uncle James. How *could* my mother leave me with you?"

The Earl felt an apology in order, and he made it, slowly, and carefully: "I have made a mistake, Edward. I am sorry for it. But you will just have to decide for yourself whether you can forgive me and whether you can eat my food. I am tired, and I am going to have my own breakfast. If you don't want to eat with me, why don't you go to your own room, the room you have just now, and think it over. Perhaps you can even find a way to talk to your mother about it. I couldn't, but perhaps you can."

"Am I a prisoner here? Cannot I go outside?"

"If you mean to run away, yes, Edward, I suppose you are, though I wouldn't myself have put it quite like that. And you can go outside after you have your breakfast."

He walked wearily out of the hall, away from the child, into his breakfast room, and sat down. He called George to him and asked him to take a message to the Vicar, asking him to come and talk to the child, as soon as he might, and when he had delivered it, he asked him to take Edward his breakfast up to his room and leave it with him, or stay with him, as he thought best.

"If he eats anything at all, George, take him down to the stables and let him stay among the horses and the kittens for a while with you, or Ross." He had a thought. "Better, George, on your way back from the Vicar, put a kitten in your pocket, just one, and take it up to him. But I wouldn't say it was my idea to him, if I were you."

He dismissed George from the room, and Edward and Anne from his mind. He could not believe that only twenty-four hours had passed since he last sat, unprovisioning, at his breakfast. The tumultuous passions, hopes, shocks, griefs, of the intervening twenty-four hours exceeded his wish or his capacity to dwell on them. His figure, as he sat eating, to anyone uninformed of his actions, would have seemed heartless, and to Edward, creeping in heartbreak past the room up the stairs, he did appear heartless.

He lost his way several times, his eyes filled with tears, and stumbled over the different varying levels of the floor. Once, half faint, he clung to the rail of the balustrade, in the upper gallery, and looked down, with more bewilderment than hatred, at the figure of his Uncle, quietly sitting in the sunny room. Even the day with its quiet sunniness seemed to taunt his despair. He had no words for it, and not even any more tears. He was sitting in his room, a sad disconsolate little figure, erect in a chair, when George knocked and put his face around the corner of the door.

"You *are* here," he said with a sympathetic smile. "May I come in?"

"Do you have to ask? It is my Uncle's house and my Uncle's room, and I suppose I belong to him, too," Edward said bitterly.

"I always ask," George said, unruffled, and not understanding all Edward's words, or shrewdly pretending not to. "It makes good manners." He withdrew briefly, and pushed the door wider, and entered with a large tray. "I have brought breakfast and lunch, the hour is so odd. I will leave it with you, and you can choose what you want, or would you like some company, like myself, here with you while you eat it?"

"Did my Uncle send you with this?" Edward asked, his eyes flashing fire.

"Of course he did," said George, clearing a place for the tray on a table and drawing up a chair. "Who else would be having the authority to have trays sent up in this house but himself?"

"I don't want it," Edward said truthfully, for he was so hungry he did not feel hungry any more. "I wish you would go away, and take it all with you."

"I can't do that altogether," George said, his sun-browned face smiling sweetly and kindly at Edward. "I can go, but I have to leave the tray here."

"Do you always do as you are told?" asked Edward wonderingly.

"Well, that depends upon who does the telling," replied George. "If it is the Earl, I would say *yes*. You see, he is not *my* guardian, he is just my employer, and he could send me away any time if I did not." The novel light of this situation did not fail to strike Edward. He looked less hostilely at the tray. The look did not escape George, and he pressed his small advantage. He had been reared in the middle of many brothers and sisters, both older and younger, and he had not reached twenty-four without knowing much about their ways in most situations, including the loss of their parents. He now said coaxingly, "You were not so strange with me at the 4 Trees Inn yesternoon. We had a good time together then, we did that. Have you forgotten?"

The mentioning of that lunch, before the second tragedy wholly changed Edward's life, was unfortunate in that it brought back reflections that brought tears to Edward's eyes, but their softer emotions worked upon his rage.

"Here," said George suddenly. "Feel my pocket." It was moving in a strange way, and he had seen Edward's eye upon it.

"There's something in it, that's alive," Edward cried.

"Ay, and what do you think it might be?" said George with a twinkle in his round brown eyes. Edward was given permission to unbutton the flap, and a yellow kitten poked its head out at once, like Jack-in-the-Box.

"Oh," cried Edward, "did you bring him for me?"

George nodded, equivocating.

"Will my Uncle let me have him in my room?"

"He will that." George fished the kitten out, and dropped it into Edward's jacket, so that its head stuck out the top. It seemed to like its new home better than its old, and after a few surveys with the tiny pinpricks of its claws, it settled itself down comfortably.

"Oh!" cried Edward, his attention diverted. "Oh!" George, taking immediate advantage, put the glass of milk in Edward's hands and told him to save some for the kitten, for he could have more. Edward, not thinking to protest under this kind of request, drank the milk, and then, discovering he was hungry, proceeded to finish his breakfast-lunch with no more fuss. He then went down to the stables, his hand tucked in George's, the kitten still buttoned inside his jacket. The hard weight of anger and hatred within his chest, behind the kitten, began gradually to loosen and seem less imminent to choke him.

When the Vicar, coming to the house, found them walking back from the stables, he found a more malleable little boy. He would not have imagined the storm that had raged within him, shaking both himself and his Uncle, had the Earl not told him.

"Will you walk with me, Edward?" the Vicar asked. "Do you know who I am?"

Edward shook his head. "No, but I have seen you before. I saw you come out of the room where my mother was last night. And I know what you do by your clothes."

"What is that?" the Vicar asked gently, interested.

"You are God's minister. I thought you knew," Edward said.

"Then you surely will not mind walking with me," the Vicar said, half smiling, half grave. He held out his hand, but Edward did not take it.

"I will like to," he said, "but I have this kitten in my jacket, and I must take it back to the stable and its mother then. Little creatures do not like to be away from their mothers for very long, when they are so young as this kitten is." He ran back, but he was not gone very long, and when he came back, he put his hand trustingly into the Vicar's.

"Can your kitten drink milk yet?" the Vicar asked thoughtfully.

"Yes," said Edward. "I gave him some of my milk at lunch in my saucer."

"Then I think you could perhaps keep it with you for company, for if it can be fed by you, instead of its mother, then it does not need her the way it did."

"Well," said Edward, "I will do that then, I would like to, if George will give me a box for its mess, and my Uncle does not mind, but still I think it would sometimes like to go back to visit its mother and its brothers and sisters in the place it knows, and be with them again for a little. Don't you? And a bouncy walk is not what I should think a kitten would like very much."

"It is old enough, though, to live with other people besides its mother, if it has to. It is old enough to survive your taking it from her or her leaving it."

"You are trying to tell me something," said Edward directly. "What is it?"

"Don't you know, Edward?"

"Yes," the little boy said, his eyes lowered. "Yes. I do. I hope it is true for both of us. I am not so sure right now as you are."

The Vicar sighed. They walked on in silence for a little while, and then the Vicar said, "You are very aware of what your kitten needs, are you so aware of the needs of all the creatures about you, Edward?"

The child lifted his eyes in surprise. "I don't know. I was just thinking about the kitten."

"You were paying attention," the Vicar observed. "That is a gift of God, Edward, to be able to pay attention to another creature or to another person. That is how we love them, and how we love God. It is how we pray. It is even how we read books. Your Uncle tells me you already know how to read."

Edward nodded. "My father taught me," he said, but he did not say anything more.

"I am to teach you now, Edward, and I think you will be an apt scholar."

Edward squeezed his hand to show his approval but he only said, "I would like that."

"I am glad you would, Edward. I shall like it too." He smiled at the little boy and returned the pressure of his hand, and then he continued thoughtfully. "You are fortunate to have that gift, Edward. It may cause you pain sometimes, but it will cause you less pain than it will give you joy, and it will give joy to those around you, especially those who do not themselves have it. Did your mother or your father have it?"

"My father was a clergyman, and paid attention to God. My mother loved my father and she loved me. I suppose they did then."

The Vicar smiled again encouragingly, a little sadly. "You seem to have enough for more than one little boy, Edward, and I am glad, for you are going to live now with a man who in my experience of him has very little of this quality, this ability I spoke of, of paying close attention to another's needs."

"You mean my Uncle? He sent me lunch even though I was naughty, and held me when I cried last night, and I think he had George bring the kitten to me, though George did not say so. Don't you like my Uncle?"

The Vicar noted with surprise and relief that the Earl seemed to have been more kindly and more thoughtful than he had pictured himself to the Vicar, and that the little boy seemed already more attached to the Earl than the Earl gave him credit for. It might simply be his loneliness and his need, but the Earl was a strange substitute to pick, and the little boy seemed unusually quick to rise to his defence at the Vicar's criticism, if the Earl was merely a strange substitute that had lain to hand.

"I do, Edward, and I am glad you do too. But I have been acquainted with him a long while, and he is sometimes a difficult man to know or to understand. I only wanted to say"—he bent his kind, mild but sharp eyes on Edward's clear ones—"that sometimes you may have to pay close attention enough, that is, to be understanding enough and to be loving enough, for two. Do you understand me?" he added, a little worried.

"I think I do. I have seen my father do that. You mean really that I should not have shouted at him. He told you about that, didn't he?"

The Vicar nodded, almost non-plussed.

"He asked you to come to see me and to talk to me, didn't he?"

"Yes," the Vicar said, "but I would have come later myself anyway."

"That was very kind of my Uncle," Edward said thoughtfully. "I am sorry for the things I said. I should not have said them to him. I will tell him so." He looked at the Vicar with candid eyes. "I think my Uncle grieves for my mother, too, though not the way I do, and I do not know why he should. That is probably why he was cross. It is why I was. And he has much to do, and I have caused him trouble with my coming."

The Vicar only patted his hand reassuringly.

"How much I am going to enjoy seeing you every day, Edward," he said. "I will teach you and you will teach me, too, I think." He was surprised by the fierce hug the little boy suddenly flung about his neck, and he hugged him quickly back, and lifted him up into his arms, and swung him high, laughing. Edward laughed back, and then scrambled down. He ran ahead of the Vicar, exploring, more like a little boy, and after a few minutes, he came back with his hands filled with prints summer had left on the moors.

"I have never been here before," he confided to the Vicar. "I don't know this country at all, and it seems strange to me. I have never been anywhere but Devon. Tell me the names of these flowers I have found and what bird this feather comes from." They paused, and the Vicar, who was also interested in such things, told him the names and histories as best he could of what Edward held carefully in his fingers.

"Edward," he said, when he had finished, "would you like to go with me now, to see where your mother is?"

The little boy looked so startled that the Vicar quickly changed his words, though he found the true words hard to say. "Would you like to see the place where she is buried?"

"Is the stone there yet?" Edward asked surprisingly.

"The stone? No. Not yet. It must first be carved."

"Is there grass or is there just dirt? Does the box show?"

"There is no grass, but it does not show."

Edward shivered. "I hope there are trees." He looked about him. "No, there wouldn't be any here, would there? We could plant one, but the wind would just kill it too. I can tell it must be windy here, for it blows even now a little." He walked along beside the Vicar, and the Vicar, looking down, saw he was crying, but without a sound, the tears running down his face. He handed Edward his handkerchief, but he did not say anything. "I wish my Uncle had taken my mother back to Devon, near my father, and our house, and my friends, where there are trees, and flowers I know. I wish he had," the little boy said in a choked voice.

"I wish he had, too, Edward, but he did not."

"Couldn't you ask him to wait, and ask me what I thought my mother would have liked, and what I would have liked?"

"I could have, Edward, but for reasons of my own, as well as your Uncle's reasons, I did not. And he would have paid rather little heed. I think I could not have changed his mind, or stopped him."

"Couldn't you?" Edward asked, a little incredulous.

"No, Edward. Your Uncle some day may tell you all his reasons. And you are here, Edward, and you will be here for many years, you know." At his words Edward began to cry harder. "Don't you wish her to be where you are?"

Edward did not answer directly, but he cried hard for several minutes. The Vicar finally sat down on the heath and took him in his arms, but then Edward shook his head resolutely, shaking the tears out of his eyes, and began to walk back towards the Earl's house that they had come some distance from.

"If you are going to be my teacher, I mustn't cry with you," he said, catching his breath. "I do so want to go home, but my mother wanted me to stay here, and I see I must. I shall try very hard to be brave, and I shall even try to enjoy myself. My father told me it is not enough just to endure, we must feel joy if we can, or we make the world a misery about us, for ourselves and everyone around us."

"I agree with your father," the Vicar said.

"But it is hard." He had a certain thought. "What will happen to my house, and to my things? Will I see them again?"

"Your Uncle will have your things brought here, I imagine, Edward."

"Will he sell my house?" Edward whispered.

"I do not know, Edward. Did your father own your house? Clergymen often don't."

"I hadn't thought of that," Edward whispered. He hunted at his feet, and found a little stone, and threw it as hard as he could, and then another.

"You didn't answer me, Edward. Would you like me to take you?"

"To see my mother's grave? No," Edward said, "my Uncle does not want me to, and since I live with him now, I would rather not until he says I may." He looked at the Vicar's troubled face, and he said as if to reassure him: "He must have his reasons for that, too, though I do not know them. It does not matter as much as I thought. My mother is as much here, with me here, as there. I see that now." They had come to the house. "Did you want to see my Uncle, too?" he asked.

The Vicar shook his head slowly, "I have seen him already today. I came only to see you, Edward."

"Thank you very much," Edward said politely. He looked at him with his clear gaze. "You have helped me see my way. I know that's what you came for, but I think I would have found it anyway, but not so soon. Do you mind now, if I leave you? I would like to go on by myself."

The Vicar nodded, and shook the hand offered him, with equal politeness. "I do not mind, Edward. I will see you again soon." He watched Edward's figure walk quickly towards the house, noticing that he did not go to fetch his kitten. His head was held erect, and his thin shoulders squared back, and he looked as if he were going towards a disagreeable task he had set himself to do, as the Vicar supposed he was.

V

His Uncle, however, was not to be seen. He had called his agent, and they were shut inside the Earl's study together until Edward's supper, when the agent left, and the Earl left too. Edward ate his supper quietly with George, and then he let George again bathe and undress him into the Earl's shirt, for his own had not yet been fetched from the Inn. He had nothing of his own about him, and he felt very lonely and sad and uncomforted.

"George," he said, "I want my things."

"Your things, Master Edward?"

"My clothes and my book, and my mother's things. They are still at the 4 Trees Inn. Will you get them for me?"

"I can't tonight, Master Edward, but if the Earl says I may, I'll go tomorrow and take you with me. Can you thole it until then?"

"Would you, George? I should like that very much." After a moment's silence, he looked at George and asked, "What does *thole* mean?"

"I never thought. It is just a word we use here when there is something unpleasant we have to go through we don't like to."

"Oh," Edward said, without comment. Then he asked, "Why do you call me *Master Edward* when I call you *George*, and I have just come here?"

"You are the Earl's ward, Master Edward, it is proper."

"I don't like it very much, George, won't you just call me Edward?"

"I can't do that, Master Edward, the Earl wouldn't like it."

"Oh," Edward said, again. "Well, then, I must just thole that too. Could you do it sometimes just when we're alone? Would the Earl mind that?"

"I might, Master Edward, but it might just confuse me. I do not notice it, myself."

"I suppose by this *Earl* you do mean my Uncle?" he asked rather hopelessly. The footman nodded, his face oddly sympathetic. "I know what Earls are, I have read about them. My Uncle will be a very powerful man then." He sighed softly. "He will be able to do what he wishes."

"He is that," the footman agreed. "Let me tuck you in your bed now. Shall I leave a light burning?"

"Yes, please, George. Did you know my father's name was George, too?"

"No, Master Edward, I didn't. I have always fancied the name myself. You weren't named then for your father?"

Edward shook his head. "Is one usually? My names are family names. Isn't it strange," he said yawning, "that I should call you George, when I hardly know you, and yet I never did my father. Everything I know, everything I knew, seems upside down now, nothing seems the same. Go away, George, I may cry, and I don't want you to see me."

"Wouldn't you like me to stay?" asked George in a friendly, concerned voice.

Edward shook his head. "No. It wouldn't help much. You haven't had your supper either, have you, George?"

"No, Master Edward."

"Will you bring me a drink of water when you finish? I shall be all right." He gave George a brief smile and turned his face away to the wall. But he was not all right. After George left, having brought his filled glass right away, he lay awake, unhappily, his mind thrashing wildly in his head, thoughtless but disturbed, and he could hear the wind crying in the eaves outside his bedroom window.

"I hate it here," he thought. "I shall never get used to it. The wind is crying where they put my mother too." He cried for a long time, with nothing to hold to or to steady him, but he did not cry himself to sleep. He cried his mind empty, and he lay quietly, his eyes wide open and staring, until he heard his Uncle's step in the hall. His heart leapt into his throat, it seemed to him, for apprehension and yearning seemed to choke him, but the halting footsteps did not pause, and passed him by and went down the hall. Agitation seized him again. He began to tremble, from head to foot, and after a few minutes of it, he climbed down from his bed and made his way on his bare feet down the long shadowed hall to the Earl's room. The door was tightly shut. He stood shivering, wondering what to do, but he could not go away again. The crack of light under the door went out and he was completely in the dark. He put his hand up to the knob of the door handle, and it turned easily, being well-oiled, and without any sound. He pushed the door open a little way, and slipped inside and closed it behind him. He stood by the door a long time, it seemed to him. The moonlight fell whitely on the objects of the room, and it was lighter inside than it had been in the hall. He walked softly to his Uncle's bed and stood hesitantly near it. A glass stood on a table by it. He supposed it was his Uncle's sleeping draft, and he thought he would like to try it and escape from himself into sleep. He raised the glass to his lips, and had taken a sip, drawing in his breath at the burning bitterness of the taste, when his Uncle's voice startled him. It seemed to come from a long way away, although his Uncle lay beside him close enough to touch.

"Don't drink any more, Edward," his Uncle's strange removed voice said, "it is too strong for you."

He replaced the glass, and found a second glass of water near it. His Uncle's hand lay uncovered, and he touched it with his own.

"I will do anything you like, Uncle James, only take me tomorrow to see where you have buried her. Please, Uncle James. I do not hate you, Uncle James, I only hated what you did. Perhaps you did right. I don't know. Will you forgive me?" He climbed into the bed, and put his arms lovingly around his Uncle.

His Uncle lay as if he had not heard him. He took his Uncle's face in his two hands, and his lips slightly parted, gently kissed his Uncle's, his child's breath sweet and warm. The Earl gave a long shuddering sigh, and turned, and placed the child beneath him.

When he woke, the sunlight streaming through the uncovered windows, whose curtains he had not drawn the night before, the child lay still asleep beside him, breathing lightly. He explored the child's face with his own delicate fingers, tracing the lines along his brow, like the wing tips of a bird flying in, the Earl thought, and along his cheek, to the small shell of his ear. The child stirred, and turned in towards him. The Earl took him in his arms and held him closely, his body warm and limply heavy and compliant against him, his soft hair beneath his chin, his face nuzzling into the hollows of the Earl's throat, his arms about his neck.

"I am going to go away," the Earl whispered to the child, "today, and I would like to take you with me. Would you like to go on a holiday with me, Edward, and leave this house for a little?"

"Yes, Uncle James, I would," Edward said.

"Then we must dress ourselves, and make ready to go," the Earl said, and he gently unclasped the child's arms from his neck.

The Earl did not understand the child he took away with him late that morning. He looked at him sometimes, in the days that followed, and wondered. He knew Edward grieved for his mother, and he had some notion of how much, but though the child was willing to speak of her, he rarely did, and he did not cry for her again. He was often pensive, but the expression of it, cast on the delicate beauty of the bones of his face, and in his clear eyes, the Earl did not find distasteful or oppressive. His lips were ready to smile, even to laugh, and his eyes to fill with merriment or high glee, when occasion caught his or the Earl's fancy, and he included the Earl always in his own frank joys and delights without hesitation or imagining that he might not wish it; the Earl found himself enjoying himself as he had not since he could remember. At night he lay in the Earl's arms without shame, with a wild innocence and a tender abandon the Earl had not imagined to exist and which startled and enchained him. In the day Edward seemed to remember nothing of it, or to consider the night so natural as to need no remarking. The melancholy that held him the first days lifted, and his active fancy that the Earl had not yet experienced reasserted itself. After some hard, wearying days of travel, down the moors, by night across the channel, and across the North center of France, they passed the low French mountains towards Italy, towards the Apennine hills.

"Look, Uncle James, the mountains look as if the sunlight on them was a coverlet, and one could lie down in the folds and pull the sunlight right over one. Perhaps giants do. I am such a giant," he said, his imagination running off with him, "and my name is Ellen. That is a word," he explained for his Uncle's benefit, "that means strength. In the morning, I shall wake up, and throw off my coverlet of sunlight, and stride over the tops of the hills that are my bed, and my table, and my playground. You can see me standing in the limbs of the beeches, motionless among the trunks of two, and I like one; or my fingers in the clusters of the pine. I shall find you sleeping, Uncle James, and make you fight me, and pierce you to the heart."

"Why so?" the Earl asked, startled.

"For no reason, it is just the story." He yawned, and leaned back into the circle of his Uncle's arms sleepily, in the jolting chaise, and then without self-consciousness, he twisted his body, so that his arms were about his Uncle's neck, and his head on his Uncle's breast.

The Earl stroked his hair with gentle fingertips, his long fingers playing among the fair elflocks. "You are rather small to have such a big name," he said teasingly. Then he realised that Edward had fallen asleep, quietly and unpretentiously and without any warning. He held him protectively against the jolts of the road, for the chaise he had hired was not so well-hung as his own, but one particularly severe shock tossed them both, and Edward waked. He did not go back to sleep then, but lay in his Uncle's arms, watching the line of the long undulating hills, black now, the blue-grey sky of evening transparent behind them and one large star shining, as it had in his new home on the moors.

"We should reach an Inn soon," the Earl said, to reassure him, but Edward did not need to be reassured. He enjoyed the movement of the coach with the security of the Earl's body behind him.

"Do you see that star?" he asked.

"I do," said the Earl, "it is the Evening Star. I have seen it many times."

"I have too," Edward said, "but now I like to think my mother can look at me through it and watch me."

"God forbid," the Earl thought to himself, but aloud, he only said, "And your father? Does he watch over you too?"

"I do not think about him now," Edward said, "at least not so much. He has my mother now, to keep him company, and that should be enough for him," he added almost angrily.

It was ten o'clock before they reached a small Inn, poorly furnished, but it did not seem dangerous or filthy, and the Earl felt they must stop. He carried Edward in, and undressed him into his nightshirt, and put him in the single bed he had been able to obtain without a bath for either of them. He could hardly find the strength to undress himself. He thought Edward asleep, but the child turned to him, and pressed his cheek against him. They slept so, their lips just touching, Edward nestled in the hollows of the Earl's body, assuaging his loneliness in his new Uncle's nearness.

The next morning at breakfast the Earl watched him make what appeared to him as the most unusual motions, not being himself familiar with a six-year-old boy's ideas of necessity. Edward was rolling his eyes, it seemed heavenward, his popover held up high in his hands, before the orbs of his eyes, gently being rotated in his fingers with total seriousness and concentration. He looked like a small angelic John the Baptist. The Earl could stand it no longer.

"Edward," he snapped, "what are you doing? Where are your manners?"

Edward gave him a happy, involved, slightly sticky smile of welcome. "I am coating the inside of my popover with honey," he explained, "all the way around. Have some. It's very good this way." The Earl accepted the offering in the spirit in which it was made, and pronounced it as good as Edward promised, but please, he asked, would Edward not do it anymore, for the motion made him dizzy, and the other people in the Inn were staring.

"Do you like the sun, Edward?" he asked.

"I love the sun," said Edward simply.

"Good," his Uncle said, "for we are going into the country of the sun. I am going to take you all the way into the boot to Naples and Baiae where you shall find all the sun you could want."

Edward basked in the sunlight like a chameleon and plunged into the clear shallows like a fish though he could not swim. It could not be too hot for him, despite his fair skin, and he would have browned, had they not spent so many hours inside the coach. A restless spirit drove the Earl on, and he did not stay long in any place, but his companion did not complain. He had hardly reached the South, than his restlessness impelled him North again, and they drove again towards Switzerland, avoiding the great cities of Italy as they had those of France and England, breaking their journey by the Lake of Como.

"Some day, Edward," the Earl said, as they were sitting by the lake, the dark furry wooded hills rising up smooth and sheer about them, "when you are older, I will take you to Florence and I will show you four great figures like your giant. They are so beautiful, they do pierce me to the heart."

"Like my giant? What are they?" asked Edward, who had already forgotten his story. "Describe them to me, tell me what they are like."

"They are four figures of the four great changes of light that you love, carved by Michael the Angel himself." His musing voice for a moment seemed to forget the child's presence. "One may stand there, and look upon them, as they are: the painful beauty of Dawn, the tired rest of Twilight, Night with worn dugs, Day with muscles, and back turned."

"Like you," said Edward thoughtfully, and the Earl found himself blushing.

"No," he said firmly, "not like me. Very large, very beautiful."

"Like you," Edward's eyes said, but he accepted the rebuke and said nothing for a full minute. "I wish you would take me now," he said then.

"No, not now. When you are older." He saw a look of distress cross the child's face, and he looked as though he were about to cry.

"What is it, Edward?" the Earl cried in alarm, and some distress himself. "Do you hurt? What can I do?"

"Yes," the child said, "I do, but you cannot help me, or you will not.

It was the thought of so much time I must spend—" He did not finish the phrase, and the Earl was glad to let the matter drop.

That night, in the middle of the night, Edward woke with a cry that woke his Uncle. He stared straight ahead of him, and he hardly seemed awake. His Uncle shook him gently.

"Edward, you are having a bad dream," he said, "Wake up and then go back to sleep." He tightened his arm sleepily about the child, and pulled him to him, reassuringly. In the morning Edward told the Earl his dream, although the Earl had little interest in dreams, his own or those of anyone else.

"I was by a lake, Uncle James, that angels used to bathe in." His Uncle cast a surprised incredulous eye towards him. "It was like this lake, only even more beautiful. I could see the angels coming down to it, in their formations, like great shining white birds. One by one, taking turns, they would leave the air and dive into the lake. The water was so clear, Uncle James, I could see their wings beneath the water, and I could see the drops splashing from them as they kicked themselves out and flew up into the air again. Their wings had purple and blue and green feathers that glistened on them and shone in the water and in the sunlight, and they all had short gold hair that shone too, and they wore short white tunics and their skin shone through them. Can you imagine such a thing, Uncle James?"

"I never have," he said a little dryly, "but I do now. Why should they frighten you, even in a dream?"

"Oh, Uncle James, one stayed behind, drying its wings on a stone, and then it stood up, to dive once more, I suppose, into the water, and it slipped and hit its head on a stone. And then I saw an old man come up with a horrible black net, and throw it over the angel, and then he carried it back to his cabin that was nearby in the forest, like these forests, and on a wooden table he cut off the angel's wings with his axe, leaving only the poor stumps of them, and threw them back into the lake. But he made the angel put on clothes like his, and be his servant, and it could never fly away again, back to its real home. It just had to stay there, forever and ever."

The significance of Edward's dream was not lost on the Earl, and it pricked his hard conscience, as if Anne herself had spoken.

"Did you see what the dreadful man looked like?" he asked, with apparent disinterest.

"I don't remember," Edward said, his eyes shuttered. He showed little interest in his breakfast, and after a little, he crept over by his Uncle's side on the bench, and sat against his arm, tired and sad. The Earl put his arm about the little boy and drew him close inside it against him.

"Was I the man, Edward?" he asked.

"I don't remember," he said again.

"Well, Edward, dreams are just dreams, and they all fade. This one will, too. But sometimes they point a warning. I think we have travelled enough. You are growing tired, and I am too. It is time to go home, and for you to have your schooling with the Vicar, and for me to go about my affairs again."

"You will stay there with me, Uncle James, won't you?" Edward asked, his dream forgotten in this new apprehension.

"Sometimes, Edward, but mainly I live in London."

"May I live there too, Uncle James?"

The Earl smiled, regretful himself. "No, I am afraid not, Edward. You need country air and country food. The milk is dirty and is carried in a big can with a ladle through the streets, and might make you sick."

"I am too big, I don't need milk any more," Edward said, his breath caught.

"I have no way to keep a little boy there," the Earl said gently, but firmly.

Edward thought he might, if he wished to, but he did not argue. He only wedged himself even tighter against his Uncle.

"Here, Edward," his Uncle said, forcing cheer, "our trip is not done, and I shall come to see you. You will hardly miss me, with George, and the Vicar, and your pony, and your nurse."

"I don't want a nurse. I am too old." He did not say, "I just want you," but the Earl heard the words as clearly as though he had spoken them, and Edward heard the Earl's reply, "But you can't have me, any longer," in his silence, as clearly as if he had answered aloud.

But if he must leave this association, as he saw he must, or be damned even in his own eyes, the Earl did not intend to yet, while it was yet so dear to both of them, not until they had reached home. The return took them several more days, and until the last, as they began the journey north across England, their conversation at Como might not have happened. But on the last day, Edward's spirits drooped so, as the hated moors enclosed him, the Earl reverted to his former self and finally lost patience and at length brought his carriage, left at Dover, home and turned Edward over to George with feelings of relief. He spent the remainder of the afternoon with the Vicar about Edward's education and the hiring of Edward's nurse, and his agent about the estate. He gave scant time to either, made a visit into the village to inspect Mrs. Pigot, whom he agreed to engage, introduced her to Edward, ignoring his shattered face and quivering mouth, and to the household, and with a perfunctory goodbye to the child, he left for London before night. His swift departure shocked no one except Edward who despite the efforts of George and Pigot, did not recover from the third sharp severing of the summer outwardly for several days, or inwardly at all.

◊﹥◊﹥◊﹥◊﹥◊﹥◊﹥◊﹥◊﹥◊﹥◊﹥◊﹥

CHAPTER II

Edward, Child & Youth: 1795–1805

I

THE Earl, true to his promise, had a Welsh pony sent to the stables for Edward, within the week. Boxes arrived at Christmas time, a new game children played in London, a book of voyages, a crate of fruits and sweetmeats from Spain and France, and Christmas crackers, but the Earl himself did not come. He remembered the date of Edward's seventh birthday, which he did not attend, in late February, and sent a box of wooden soldiers and a book of famous battles, in which Edward began to learn the history of the countries he had visited, and places he had been near. He conceived an interest from it in Hannibal and a passionate dislike of the Romans which the Vicar found hard to understand, despite his growing fluency in their language and his love for their land.

"You do not know anything at all about the people they destroyed," he exclaimed passionately at the Vicar. "They were very clever, those Romans. They destroyed the records of the people they conquered, and all their men, and so there is no one left to speak for them."

"Except you," said the Vicar, with a slight smile.

"Except me. Look what your Caesar did to the Nervii and their beautiful city of Bourges. And even the Romans say Hannibal was a just and merciful man, as well as a very clever general, though they took his records too. Why, they were afraid of him even after they defeated him, for they knew he was the better man. I would rather have known Hannibal than Caesar, who never kept his word unless it suited him, and had brave enemies strangled in his dungeons. I hate Romans, and I would rather be destroyed and forgotten than a destroyer."

"I cannot gainsay what you say, Edward," the Vicar said, and began to reread his history more critically.

Edward wrote his Uncle polite formal notes of thanks and acceptance, but he otherwise did not write to him, for he felt, and with reason, that had his Uncle cared to hear what he might have to say, he would have come to see him. He knew his Uncle wrote from time to time to the Vicar, who sent accounts of Edward's progress, and to his agent, and that sometimes George or Pigot wrote the Earl, but that was all. Edward had himself no communication with him or from him, and he gradually steeled himself to live without him, and consciously did not often think of him. The Earl's activities were varied and beyond Edward's comprehension. He visited his other estates, he took his seat occasionally in Parliament when the impulse or the Season moved him, he turned down invitations to innumerable houseparties which he found dull, accepted an occasional few, such as to Coke's Clippings, or Sheep Shearings, at Holkham, or to the Lansdownes' at Bowood where the conversation was good, saw that his annual fetes for the neighbourhood gentry and the neighbouring poor were given but did not attend them or permit Edward to, kept his Northern estate closed to visitors but allowed his Anglian holdings, rented out, to be open, kept a careful check on his tenants, both their needs and their produce, through his agent's accounts and through infrequent personal visits, paid scant attention to the activities of the new little Corsican General acting for the French Directory, and generally spent the rest of his time out of the country entirely, untroubled by the attacks against Italy and Venice.

Edward did not see the Earl again until the summer of his seventh year when he hurt his foot. He had run a thorn into it that broke off and that infected it. George had had a younger brother who died of blood poisoning, and his cousin had contracted lockjaw two years before. He did not wait for the red streaks to appear in Edward's foot, but wrote at once urgently to the Earl in London, and sent the letter by a groom. Both the Earl and a London surgeon arrived the next night. George was much relieved, for he had not expected the Earl to act so quickly or to come himself.

"Edward will be relieved," he said.

"Where is he?" asked the Earl, not staying to remove his driving coat.

"He is in his room," George answered, to the Earl's back. The surgeon removed his own coat, and gloves and hat, giving them to George, ordered water to be set to boil and a garlic root he had brought with him to be mashed and brought to him, and followed the Earl, overtaking him on the stairs.

Edward was propped uncomfortably against two pillows in his bed, his foot bandaged and out of the bedclothes, his face flushed. His eyes lit at the unexpected sight of his Uncle, despite the presence of the surgeon and his bag.

"This is Dr. Knighton," the Earl said to Edward in his gentlest voice. "He comes from Devonshire, too, and he cannot go back to his own home either."

"Oh," said Edward, forgetting his throbbing foot and his apprehensions. "Why not?"

"It is a long story," the young doctor said, smiling. "But my father made his father angry, and his father told him to go away and never to come back or bring his family back either to the home that otherwise would some day have been his."

"Oh," said Edward, amazed. "Do fathers do that to their sons?"

"Sometimes," Knighton said. "His did. When it is an eldest son, they call it 'disinheritance.'"

"Oh," said Edward. "Didn't he mind? Don't you mind? Not seeing his father any more, I mean? Or his home?"

The surgeon smiled. "If that was the way it was, there was no use minding, was there? Some things can be even more important than an inheritance. Myself, I do not think about it, Edward, anymore."

"My father is dead," the little boy said, "and my mother is dead too. I was his eldest, and his only son. But he was not an eldest son. I would have been his heir, but he did not have anything to leave me except to remember him. But I think that is inheritance enough. And one can never be—disinherited of that."

"No, Edward, not of that."

The surgeon unwrapped the bandages, and put them on a paper to throw away, and examined the tender swollen foot as gently as he could.

"I shall have to lance this, Edward, and it will hurt," he said. "I have brought a clean knife, and I am going to try to find the thorn or the splinter that may be still inside. You must be a brave boy." He turned to the Earl. "I shall give him a dose of laudanum now, I think, to help him bear it. Call your footman to hold him still for me."

"If Uncle James will sit beside me, and talk to me, while you do it, I will be still and I won't move," Edward said. "I don't need to be held." He drank the laudanum, recognising its bitter burning taste. The surgeon smiled at the face he made.

"Would you think that poppies could be so bitter?"

"Is this made from poppies?" Edward asked, astonished.

"Have you not ever heard that poppies make you sleepy, Edward, and to be careful not to stay too long in a full field of them? The next time you are near some, pick several, and smell how heavy their scent is. If you put them in a glass in a room, the whole room will take their scent, and the air will be too cloyed for you to be quite comfortable in." As he spoke, he had been preparing himself and his instruments, and now he addressed himself to Edward's painful foot. Edward held tightly to the hand his Uncle, sitting beside him, gave him to hold. He fixed his eyes on his Uncle, and set his teeth, and tried to listen to his Uncle's talk, and he did not move, or cry out, as he had promised, though his face grew white and beads of sweat pricked out on his forehead.

"You are a fine boy, Edward," the surgeon said. "I have finished now, and I have the tip of the thorn. It was not deep, the infection was pushing it out. You managed very well not to cry, and I have never had a patient stay so still." As he spoke, he poured a stinging liquid over the wound that made Edward jump.

"I pretended you were Caesar," Edward said, "and I would never let Caesar see me cry. And Uncle James was here to help me."

"Now," the surgeon said, as George came with what he had ordered. "Edward, when you do not have your foot in this hot water I want it propped up, instead of you, as high as it will go on as many pillows as you have, and no bandages on it, except hot salt rags. But I want you to stay almost all day with it in this salt hot water. Your George, I think, will see you have it every hour, and stay with it until it cools." He took the garlic from George. "I want you to swallow this, now, Edward, with this glass of water." He turned to the Earl. "It should help drive out the infection."

"Good Lord," said the Earl, smelling the pungent scent, "that's garlic! I thought that was an old wives' tale."

"It is, but it often works," the surgeon said bluntly, "and some of us are not ashamed to use it. I would like a poultice of it on his foot this evening when he goes to sleep. I will leave a saline solution here for you to give him, to drink, if he becomes feverish, and let him have all the honey and lemonade he will drink. I have brought lemons with me, thinking you might not have them. I shall spend the night at the Inn, and look in on you in the morning, young man." He rose to go.

"You will stay here, I hope, after coming this way, Knighton," the Earl said, and turned to go with him. He paused by the child's bed a moment.

"I think you were very brave too, Edward," he whispered, and kissed the small hand that had left marks on his own with its hard grasp. "I will look in on you tomorrow morning, and you shall tell me all about this Caesar."

Unfortunately that next morning they spoke of other things than Caesar, and they parted on less happy terms. After his Uncle had inspected his hurt and seen him seated at his hot foot bath, Edward had asked: "Uncle James, what has happened to my things in my house?"

"They were sold, Edward, some months ago."

Edward's face whitened, but for a minute he did not say anything at all. Then he said, "I thought they were mine, Uncle James, mine and my mother's and my father's."

"I am your guardian, Edward. Your father had debts. The property he had did not cover them."

"Could you have paid them?"

"I could, I did not choose to, Edward," the Earl said briefly.

"And all my things are gone?"

"Yes, Edward, I suppose they are. I did not go. My agent attended to it for me. I will ask him about it." He picked up a book by Edward's bed and began looking at it, and paid no more attention to Edward, or to the emotions that raced across his upturned face, of shock and grief and disappointment and bewilderment and fury, both separate and mixed together. But the child did not say anything, and after a few minutes, he brought his emotions and his face under control, and lowered his eyes. He gave a little cough in his throat, as though swallowing something hard.

"It does not matter, Uncle James," he said. "They were just things, and not very important. May I go back to bed now?"

His Uncle nodded. Edward dried his foot and limped quietly back to his bed under his Uncle's eyes and sat staring at the book his Uncle returned to him without comment, the *Commentarii de Bello Gallico.*

"You had my things taken away from the Inn, too, while we were gone. Did you have them destroyed?"

"I don't remember," the Earl said, truthfully.

"Why must you destroy my records?" Edward asked, his voice quiet, his eyes accusing. "How can they hurt you? I have no pictures now, not even the miniature of my mother, nothing at all, except what I can remember. Why was it necessary to take it all away? Why did you have to take it all?"

"I will ask my agent about the miniature," the Earl said, evading Edward's direct questions, and asking one of his own. "Are you thinking I am like this Caesar?"

"Are you?" Edward asked, his eyes hurt and bewildered. "I don't know. Are you?"

The Earl found no answer. Their conversation flagged, and after a moment more of silence, the Earl excused himself. Edward limped, "like my Uncle," he thought, to the window, and sat, looking out for a long time. He saw his Uncle ride out with his agent, and he wished he could ride with them, but since he could not, he returned to bed as the surgeon had instructed him.

Edward's foot responding to the surgeon's care and the household's subsequent efforts, the Earl and the surgeon both left late that afternoon. After they had gone, Edward cried as he had not under the surgeon's knife, but he put away in his mind the surgeon's parting words: "Remember, Edward, it is the simplest measures, making no show and costing little, but requiring our attention and our trouble, that often produce the best effects in the end."

"Uncle James is not fair to me. He does things that are not just to me and he asks things he has no right to," Edward said bitterly to George that night. "He leaves me by myself, and yet he will not let me be myself."

"Hush, Master Edward," George said. "I cannot listen to these remarks."

"Why not? Are you afraid of him, too?"

"Yes, Master Edward," George said.

Edward was silent, thinking. After a while he said, in a dispassionate voice, "My Uncle James cannot bear to be crossed, in anything."

"If you know that," George said, "then why do you do it, Master Edward?"

Edward shook his head slowly. "I am afraid I am going to cross him many times," he said, in a voice much too old. "I wonder what will happen to me, for it." He was silent again for a moment. "And yet my Uncle is so kind. He came all this way just to see about my foot. I wish he had not left." He sighed, and let George blow out his light.

Edward did not see his Uncle all his eighth year. He did not even know where he was. The Vicar heard from him occasionally, but at no length. He sent his letters to the Earl's London address, and they were not returned, but the Earl gave no indication in his own letters that he had read them. Adequate moneys were sent regularly to the house on the Earl's estate from the Earl's bank. Life settled down to a routine without him.

As it so happened, the Earl had left London and had taken himself to the Continent where he proceeded to live, in his own fashion, after his own manner for all the winter of Edward's eighth year, while Napoleon took Corfu, kept Venice, and dreamed privately of breaking the British blockade and invading England. That year the Earl instructed the bank to send money for his agent to buy Edward's Christmas and birthday presents, and he so completely forgot Edward's existence that his adventures, which were numerous, have little to do with Edward's story. He was thirty-nine, and despite his reputation, which occasionally made him leave London for some weeks to allow it to forget his excesses, his birth and his wealth kept him in demand by the ton, more than he cared to exercise. He had a particular taste for music and for art, more perceptive and more discriminating than the greater number of his friends. He set up his current mistress in Paris partly for herself, and though she did not know it, more for her ability to hold his salon for him where he gathered certain of the literary figures, but more of the musicians of that year. He spent considerable time travelling to look at the art treasures in France and Italy, which he had not done when Edward was with him, and he spent the Spring in Vienna where he might hear the old Haydn at sixty-five, the young Beethoven at twenty-seven, Salieri conduct, and the music of Mozart, who had died at thirty-five six years before. Undeterred by the devastated countryside, he went to Genoa particularly to hear the infant prodigy of the violin, Paganini, fifteen then, whom he had heard of in Vienna.

Edward continued his lessons with the Vicar, and went to church with Pigot, whom he tolerated, unlike George, whom he loved, and listened to the old organ in the church and yearned after it. He knew his Bible well, from his days with his father, surprisingly well, the Vicar thought. Nevertheless, he set him passages to con by heart, and questions to look up, on Sunday afternoons, and when he had finished, he could only read, besides the Bible Testaments, in Fox's *Actes and Monuments of These Latter and Perilous Days,* better known to him as the *Book of Martyrs,* which he hated, and the *Pilgrim's Progress,* which he liked, with its small black and white woodcuts. *Paradise Lost* and *The Divine Comedy* the Vicar considered unsuitable for his youth or the day in their detailing of Wickedness, and in the last, of Papacy. He learned to tolerate the wind and the otherwise chill silence of the moors, though not to like it. He learned to ride well, and he went frequently with one of the younger grooms on rides over the moors, and sometimes with George on long rides into the Cheviot Hills where they would stay overnight.

He followed everyone around who would let him, learning the secrets of their different trades and skills or mysteries. He baked cakes and scones and custards with the cooks and scullery maids, and learned to clean fowl and to roast meat. His curiosity was endless. He learned the names of all the garden plants, both vegetable and flower, and all the herbs, their scents and properties, and appointed himself chief assistant to the gardener, and with the underboys weeded and raked and planted so industriously that the gardener suggested he take a part of the kitchen garden for his own. He inspected the dairy, and talked to the cows, and learned to make butter, though he declined to learn to milk. He learned how a stable was put together and managed, and listened for hours to tales of the road, and polished harness, and learned to care for his own pony, and its saddle and its stall, although he stayed as quiet as possible around the dour unbending Scot who held the stables in his charge, for he was a little frightened of him. Sometimes George took him to see his own large family nearer town, and sometimes he brought the children nearest Edward's age to play with him. Edward kept himself very busy, and apparently thrived on his life, and no one, not even George, guessed the extent to which he missed the Earl.

At Christmas, Edward's third in the house, when again only money arrived from the Earl, the Vicar, having observed Edward's interest, suggested a small spinet be purchased for a surprise for Edward. It was a particularly happy thought, although the outcome was not happy, and gave Edward such pleasure he almost forgot the absence of the Earl from the festivities. The Vicar promised he should have lessons from the organist, and they all went down then into the great kitchen to greet the Mummers who had come.

Edward had never seen them until he came North, and he did not know which he liked best or most wanted to be. They marched in, ceremoniously singing, and took their places in a semi-circle. First they introduced themselves, speaking particularly to the little boy who watched them so wide-eyed: the Three Kings, not the Wise Men but familiar English Kings, the Queen who was a boy dressed out with long hair, Little Jack with his family tied to his back, and Giant Blunderbore; the Merry Andrew, with his foolstick and his bells, and the Hobby Horse galloping about, impeding the progress of the play, the silver-scaled Dragon with his snapping jaws, and long claws, and St. George with his silver cross and his sword longest and brightest of all the swords. The Morris-Men danced, their bells jingling in a raucous music, their sticks clashing, while the drum and the recorder kept time for them. Edward loved their stiff rhythmical dance and their high leaps, so precise and exact, and he hesitated between wanting to be a Morris dancer or St. George. The Dragon roared, and menaced St. George, St. George drew his sword, and all the performers drew their pipes, sticks, clubs, swords, and laid about them, while Edward laughed, put his hands over his ears, and screeched with the flute, and the drum sounded, until they all fell upon the floor in heaps of shining ribbons and velvet rags.

This part never failed to frighten Edward, and each time he wondered if this time they would really rise again. Old Dr. Ball limped out with a stick from the back of the ring, with his magic potions and pills and his long speech that Edward could never completely understand, but he enjoyed the sounds of the nonsense, as he had that of the other mummers. He watched, his eyes round as the Doctor's huge pills, as the Doctor went from one to the other, pouring his magic water or poking in a giant pill, exhorting each to rise. And each time Edward could not believe that the silly Mummers would no sooner be resurrected back into life than they would start to fighting again. He felt like shouting into the noise, "Stop! Stop!" but instead he waited breathlessly for Father Christmas himself to appear with his silver beard and his wreath of Holly, and he sang under his breath with him as he gently admonished the roustering kings and knights, "Hold, men, hold, put up your sticks," until finally peace reigned and they broke their swords, and marched about the room holding out their hands for money and singing.

Edward threw his gold and silver coins at them with joyful abandon, and sometimes they would throw the gold ones back to him with a wink. He plied them with hot ale and Christmas cakes, and they picked him up in their arms and set him on the cavorting hobby horse and gave him a sword, miraculously restored, to wave. The Dragon chased him, and St. George rescued him, and the Dragon, tamed, laid its head against his knees to be stroked, and the Morris-Men lifted him up on their shoulders and danced with him. And then suddenly, with a rush, they flung the door open, and were gone singing into the night, and it was over until next Christmas. He stood waving, as long as he could see them, or hear them, the snow crisp and white and even, and their footsteps crackling through it, the stars bright and frosty above them. He hardly heard the Vicar beside him, talking to himself, musing that "Georgius" might be only a mistake, a corrupting long ago of the Latin of St. Gregory's name, who had sent the first Christian mission into England when it was still the savage isle of Britain. He could not have less cared. The Carolers had come the night before, on Christmas Eve, but they would come again on Little Christmas. But the Mummers were gone. It was hard to believe they were all men he had met in the village when he had gone there with George. He walked slowly back inside, his eyes glowing with the marvel of it, and sat down quietly by George, wishing for his Uncle to enjoy it with him.

II

When Edward was nine, the Earl put in a surprise visit unannounced at his Northern estate. Walking into his study, that was both study and gunroom, he found Edward with one of his duelling pistols in his hand, his back half to him. He was shocked, and horrified, and frightened, all at once, because as best he could see, the child had cocked it, and he thought it might be loaded.

"Edward," he exclaimed, and in as cool a voice as he could muster, he said, "will you put my pistol on my table, please."

He had underestimated the effect of his sudden presence, unforewarned, on the child. Edward gasped, and spun around, and the pistol fell from his fingers to the floor, exploding as it touched. The Earl felt the shot pass by him, and bury itself in the door. He strode over to Edward, with his halting gait that made his stride the more purposeful and the more menacing, his face a grooved mask of anger, and holding the little boy by one hand, with the other he thrashed him as mercilessly as he would have a delinquent adult, with the riding whip he still held in his hand that he had not put down. It was only when he realised he had made tatters of the child's clothes with the sharp crop that he came to himself and threw both it and the child from him. The child himself had made no sound. He turned his back on Edward, panting from his fright and his exertion, and walked over to the windowseat, and stood by it, looking out of the window, attempting to compose himself.

"You may go, Edward," he said harshly, not turning around. "I will speak to you later." He did not hear the door close, but he was not listening for it, and he was shocked to feel a small hand put itself into his. He shook it off roughly, but he turned and looked down at the child, who had picked himself up and come over to stand beside him.

"What did you do that for, Uncle?" the child asked him, wonderingly, the trust in his face bewildered but not gone.

"You are not supposed to be in my study, or to touch my guns," the Earl said, still harshly, "and you know that very well, Edward."

"I did not know that, Uncle James," the child said. "I won't do it again."

"You might have killed me," the Earl said, unrelenting. "What did you want in my room?"

"I did not know you were back, Uncle James," the child gasped.

"I see that. What did you want?"

"I wanted a book to read, and I saw your pistol and I was curious."

"My pistol was not out," the Earl remarked.

"It was out. It was in the glass case there, and the door was not locked. I should not have opened or taken it out. I am sorry." The tears were hard behind his eyes now.

"Don't let me see you cry, Edward," the Earl said with distaste. "You should have thought. You might have killed yourself, as easily. I do not want you ever again to come in this room, unless I am here, in it, and I ask you to. Do you understand me?"

"Yes, Uncle James. But may I not use the books? You are not here very much, and I do like to read them. I did not know it was wrong."

"I will have a book-room made," the Earl said, "straightway, as soon as shelves can be made, and all the books I put there you may use when you like, whether I am here or not. But I do not want you in my study." His face softened just a little. "I keep papers here, all kinds of important things here. It is *my* room, Edward, as much as my room upstairs, per-haps more. I would not come in your room."

"Wouldn't you? Everyone seems to."

"No," the Earl said shortly.

"You may if you like," Edward said. "You can come in whenever you like, and stay as long as you like, and do anything you like, in my room. Why were you so afraid, Uncle James?"

His Uncle did not answer, but the child's grave eyes perceiving what lay in his face, widened in horror.

"I heard a noise like that once before, when I was smaller, and my father was hurt. I had forgotten that until now, but you hadn't. You were afraid of that, Uncle James." He looked at his Uncle in the eyes, straightly. "Did I shoot my father, Uncle James?"

The Earl found he could not bear the look in the child's eyes. His own fell. "I do not think so," he said, his face a little aside. "Your father did not say so. He said it was an accident, from some hunters."

"I saw them," Edward said, "but I had a gun, too, of my father's. I was naughty then, too. I remember the noise. It could have been me." He pulled at his Uncle's coat. "Please don't be afraid of me, Uncle. Is that why you never come here anymore? If I did, I did not mean to."

The Earl looked straight into the child's eyes. "Your father said you did not, Edward, and he was a clergyman, and he would have spoken the truth." The Earl found himself lying without any hesitation. "And I am not afraid of you. But any man is afraid of a loaded pistol in the hands of a child, he would be a fool not to be, of a loaded pistol in any man's hands."

The child put his arms about his waist in a rush of gratitude, and the Earl felt the old emotion surge within him, drawing him towards the child. He sat down on the windowseat, and drew the child into his lap, and hugged him tightly to him, and held him so for long minutes, until he realised his hands and his coat were stained from the cuts on the child's back. The child himself had not winced.

"Go to George," he said abruptly, putting him down with a last small hug, "and tell him I have whipped you for meddling with my guns, and have him fix you up and change your clothes. Throw these away," he added with distaste.

The little boy slid down from his knees, but he did not immediately go away. He stood in front of his Uncle, his legs slightly apart, his hands clasped behind him, the look on his face pensive.

"If I were my father, even though I generally told the truth, and my son shot me by accident, I would not say so either, especially if he was a very little boy and there was something else I could say," Edward said reflectively, but with a slight question behind his voice.

"No," the Earl agreed, "I would not either, but on the other hand it could be the truth, that you didn't, just as easily as that you did. If it was an accident, what does it matter, either way?"

"It matters to me," said Edward sombrely, "but I suppose I'll never know, unless I can remember better how it was. My mind doesn't seem to want to."

"I wouldn't think about it anymore," the Earl said, half-kindly. "Now go to George. When you come down I have something for you on the floor of my coach."

"You have?" asked Edward in surprise, his lips parting and his eyes shining. "Did you remember after all it was my birthday yesterday? I thought you had forgotten."

The Earl had, but he masked his embarrassment, and put on a face that let Edward think what he wanted, and it was clear what he wanted to think. His face grew pale with joy, and he threw his arms again about his Uncle's waist.

"Here," said his Uncle sharply, "that is enough of that!" He gently disengaged the little boy, but his hands lingered on his arms and his own eyes grew dark and bright. He gave him a sharp pat of dismissal and sent him from the room.

While Edward was following the Earl's orders, the Earl had his agent called, and made quick plans with him about the conversion of a small parlour downstairs into a book-room with maps. He went to his shelves, and going quickly through them, pulled down several stacks of books, amounting to some hundred volumes, which he instructed the agent to transfer to the new room. He arranged for the Vicar to order direct from his bookseller any books he thought desirable for Edward, and he suggested that he himself might send several boxes on his return to London. He also arranged with the agent to have the ammunition for his guns removed from the house to the agent's, and to have cabinets with solid doors and new locks built to house his guns.

By the time he had finished, he could see Edward outside, with George, and his nurse. He could tell by the nurse's compressed lips that she was angry, and he was angry in his turn, and considered dismissing her at the end of the quarter. Edward, he thought, was old enough now not to need a nurse. But since he had resolved to leave again immediately, without staying the night, as he had first planned to do, he left that matter for further thought.

"You may go inside, Nurse Pigot," he said coldly, "and you may go too, George," as he walked out to them. He smiled suddenly, disarming their disapproval of his discipline. "You will know all too soon all about the surprise I have brought Edward, but let us give Edward the pleasure of re-surprising you after I have left."

Edward tugged at his hand, his joy in his present eclipsed. "You are not going, Uncle James? You have only just come. Why must you go? We have all missed you so. I have missed you very much." He looked up beseechingly in his face, but the melting look of his eyes only firmed his Uncle's resolve.

"You must see your present, Edward." He smiled. "It demands to be seen at once. I have been in Skye, with a party of friends, for a kind of winter joke, and when I saw what I have brought you, I decided to stop on my way down to bring it here without delay, but I have business in London, and I cannot stay." He ignored the bewildered hurt in the little boy's eyes, and pulled a basket out from under the driving seat of the chaise. The wicker lid was fastened, but as soon as Edward's light eager fingers pulled out the stick that held it, the bright eyes and ragged head of a Skye terrier poked its head out and licked Edward's hands and face.

"Oh," cried Edward, "oh, Uncle James!" He could find nothing else to say, but his face said what his voice did not. But when he saw his Uncle call his coachman and step into the chaise, the happiness left his face, and his lips quivered, and he held the puppy, wriggling as puppies do, for comfort, as he watched his Uncle drive away.

The spring of Edward's ninth year, George took him to see the gypsies that had camped near the village. They had spread out their brown tents on the land once the Commons, now the enclosed property of an absent land-owner. They had caravans now, knowing they were subject to removal, and there was an even more enticing air about them than about the small fair they had set up. They reminded Edward of the Mummers and his eyes shone. They had even a trained bear that was kept on the end of a chain. Edward wanted to go into the camp itself; but George would not let him.

"They take boys, sometimes, Edward, especially small pretty boys like you. Though I do not think they would dare, because they know who your Uncle is. They don't want money, you see, they just like sometimes to take children."

"Why do they take them?" Edward asked.

"I don't know, Master Edward. I think myself they just like an extra pair of hands about, or perhaps they hate those who are not like them and like to abuse the children of them, if they can do it without fear of being found. They would not take you. My mother thought they sold them to the Sweeps. My sister says the gypsies kill them, being heathens, and use them to make the potions they have to sell that they claim has special powers, but I don't believe that myself, though they do have some strange customs. I'm going to take these pans now to be mended—they have a very good tinker—and you stay here, Edward, well away, until I come back."

Edward stayed by the edge of the field, watching with interest and a little fear, but not very much, for he did not believe either that gypsies boiled little children. One of the men walked by him, and put a hand out, and touched his fair hair with interest, and smiled at him, with white teeth, and Edward smiled back, and several children came near him and stared at him with as much interest as he at them. The man passed by him again, and stopped to speak to him.

"Are you with that man?" the gypsy asked, his voice light and strangely lilting.

Edward nodded.

"Is he good to you?"

Edward nodded again, but the gypsy, wise in a way peculiar to the gypsies, recognised the unhappiness in Edward that escaped those around him, and perceived a kinship between them. He squatted down beside Edward, and with a quick practised movement, flipped up his shirt and uncovered briefly the scars on Edward's back that had not completely gone away.

"We are not good to our children in this way," he said briefly, his black curls near Edward. "Is he your father?"

"No," said Edward.

"Your brother, your Uncle?"

"No," said Edward again. "He is my Uncle's footman."

"And who beat you like that? This footman or your Uncle?"

"My Uncle," Edward said with a catch in his breath.

"I would not stay with such a man myself," the gypsy said to the air about him.

"I have to stay. He is my guardian," Edward said.

"Is he here now?"

"No," said Edward, "he doesn't often come here."

"He is a foolish man," the gypsy said. "Have you been to the fair? Have you seen the bear?"

Edward nodded.

"Would you like to see more?" Edward nodded. "If you will come here, by yourself, tonight, I will show you things you have not seen at our fair."

"You might steal me away," Edward said.

"What an idea," cried the gypsy in innocent amazement.

"Besides, George will not let me come by myself, and he is taking his own brothers that are older than I am to the fair tonight. I am too young, he says, to go after dark."

"Is he," said the gypsy with interest. "Where do you live?"

"Not very near here. You can see the chimneys of my house from here, but it is a long walk," Edward said a little wearily, "especially when there is no shade."

"Didn't you ride?" asked the gypsy with interest.

Edward flushed a little. "George says it is not safe to bring horses here."

The gypsy smiled again at Edward, and Edward smiled politely back, and then, seeing George reapproach, the gypsy touched his hand to his head in salute, and moved off, gracefully and with a casual and indifferent insolence. George looked after him with disapproval.

"Has that Egyptian been talking to you, Edward?" he asked.

"Yes," said Edward, "He asked me about my Uncle."

"Oh, that is all right then," said George with relief. "I was thinking I should not have brought you."

He saw Edward safely tucked into bed, and then he and several of the other servants went off to the fair. Nurse Pigot retired to the kitchen for her supper and a cup of tea. Edward, just dozing off, heard his puppy his Uncle had brought him whining, he thought, outside his window. George must have let him out by mistake, he thought, when he left. He got up and put on his robe and his night shoes, and slipped quietly down the stairs and out onto the lawn near the shrubbery about the house. He called, but the puppy did not come, and suddenly a large strong hand was clapped over his mouth and nose. His frightened eyes recognised the face of the gypsy he had spoken to that afternoon, and young as he was, he realised he had been a fool to talk as freely as he had. The gypsy took out a long sharp knife, and Edward thought he was to be butchered, then and there, on the spot at once, and he hoped the gypsy had not also killed his dog.

"Lie still, little master," the gypsy hissed, "and I shall not prick you." He held the point suggestively beneath Edward's ear, so close it broke through the skin. Edward ceased thrashing about, and the gypsy stuffed rags in his mouth and bound a rag about it, and then, throwing him over his shoulder, he picked up his sack in which, though Edward fortunately did not know it, his puppy lay, butchered in truth, with two of his Uncle's birds. "I am going to take you away from your cruel Uncle, and you will never have to see him again," he said without consoling Edward. "I do not like your Uncle myself. He ran me off his land on our last visit where we were camped and were doing no harm to him." He slung Edward before him on his horse, and set off at a gallop for the gypsy camp.

Edward was not missed until late the next morning, and by that time the gypsies had decamped. They had eaten the dog and the birds, and had transformed Edward, except for his blue-grey eyes, into a gypsy like themselves. They had dyed his skin with a tannic juice, and his hair, even his eyebrows, and burned his clothes, and put their own on him. He sat now, miserably enough, behind a curtain of one of their caravans with two older gypsy boys who regarded him with amusement. Every moment, he knew, he was going farther away, and his Uncle did not even know he was gone. He did not know where he was to be taken, but he remembered from his books that gypsies migrated swiftly and quickly all over the world, from country to country, and had their own kings and one queen and their own laws, and recognised the authority of no one, and he despaired of rescue. He was tired from his long walk in the afternoon and his visit to the fair, and from his struggle with the gypsy on the lawn, and from the lowness of his spirit. He did not want these amused boys to find amusement in the sight of him crying, though he felt like nothing else more, so he compressed his lips and winked back the drops that filled his eyes, and after a bit, he made his way to the darkest corner of the lurching caravan and curled up on a heap of dirty rags and tried to go to sleep, but he found he could not after all. He was very worried about his little dog, but he had not had the courage to ask about it, for he knew now it was either at home, quite safe, as he was not, or else that it was no use at all asking. He was cold, in the Spring night air, and uncomfortable on the rags, being thrown about by the jolting of the wagon. His Uncle's face kept rising in his mind. He hoped his Uncle would not think he had gone willingly with the gypsies just because he had whipped him. If he did, he might not even look for him, when finally someone found where he was to tell him one small boy was gone. Even if he did look, Edward could not see how he would find him, for he no longer even looked like himself. He finally fell asleep despite his worries.

In the morning, the caravan did not stop, and he supposed they were making particular haste because of having taken him. He could see that they were travelling by back country lanes, and despite his grief at being taken, he found himself interested. He was not afraid for himself, for no one seemed to show any disposition to harm him, except in having taken him at all. He heard a disturbance ahead, at one of the caravans, that grew louder, and then approached his own wagon, and to his amazement he thought he recognised the voice of George. He hoped desperately George would find him, and he was going to cry out, when the gypsy by him thrust a rag in his mouth and held his arm, and whispered fiercely to him to sit quietly or his friend would be hurt. He looked piteously away from George, in his dark corner, afraid now he would see him, and George of course did.

"I want to see that little boy there, in that corner, sitting on that rag heap, by the older boy," he heard George demand in a fierce voice he had not heard George use before, and that came strangely from George.

"He is just my little brother, you can see that," the gypsy said in a placating whining voice, but as George bent forward, Edward, powerless to help, saw the gypsy quickly lift a bottle and bring it down with a hard crack on George's head. No one cared about Edward now, and he pulled the horrible rag out of his mouth, and stumbled over the clutter of the caravan to the front where George had been pushed in. The gypsies bound his hands and feet, and left him, with the older boys and Edward, as before.

"Well, Master Edward," said George, groaning, as he recovered his senses, "we are in a pickle now, the two of us, but especially me. What for would you run off with these Egyptians, Master Edward, what come over you?"

"I didn't, George," Edward cried in a voice of grief at the accusation. "They just took me. They had a knife, and poked me with it here, and they stuffed my mouth with dreadfully dirty rags, as they did just now so I couldn't warn you. Oh, George, they have hurt your head," he cried, exploring with his fingers, "there is a dreadful bump there."

"I do know it indeed, Master Edward," George said feelingly. "I do hope you will not catch some wicked disease from these Egyptians, and I hope your Uncle James will catch up with us before they think to cut my throat. They'll not harm you, Edward, not intentionally, but I doubt they have much use for me."

"Oh, George," Edward cried, "then why did you come?"

"Why, I could not let them make away with you, Master Edward, particularly seeing as how it was through my carelessness they caught sight of you at all. But I doubt not your Uncle has my message now, and

I have left signs behind me at the inns and crossroads, like a regular Hansel and Gretel I was. And I do hope he finds them," he added more feelingly than before.

The gypsies chose to rest their horses in a wood during the heat of the afternoon, and to leave the lane they had travelled, in case George had been followed by friends. Despite the haste of their travel, they did not seem worried. They lay about at ease, and one had a violin he played softly, its wailing notes rising and falling, drawing Edward, for he had never heard the sounds before. He crept to the front of the caravan, and then drawn despite himself, and George's helpless voice calling him, he climbed down, and walked hesitantly forward until he found the source of the sound, the instrument and the maker of it, the gypsy who had taken him. The gypsy did not seem to notice him, and Edward sat down a little way from him, and shut his eyes and forgot his fears and his concerns, and let the music carry him away on its river-like flow of sound. The tempo abruptly changed, and he opened his eyes, and found the gypsy looking at him.

"A little tzigane at heart, as I thought," the gypsy said. He handed the instrument to Edward, who shrank from it, yet longing to touch it.

"Take it, take it," the gypsy said impatiently. "Try it!"

"I cannot," Edward said, in a whisper, "I don't know how."

"Take it," the gypsy said, continuing to hold it out, his black eyes snapping bright, and his mouth smiling.

"I would break it," Edward whispered, hesitant and longing.

"You break it, I fix it," the gypsy said, his eyes encouraging. "Try it, try it! Don't be so afraid, little tzigane." He put it out towards Edward again into his timid hands which rose to receive it, and showed him how to hold it, and how to pluck it, and to draw the bow, tremulously and discordantly across the strings. The discords broke the spell holding Edward, and he remembered George, and what had been done to George and to himself. He thrust the violin back into its owner's hands, and gave a quick disturbed glance at the amused, sympathetic eyes watching him shrewdly. He started to run back to the caravan, but the gypsy pounced upon him like a cat, lithe, lean, and muscular. For a moment he could smell the grease on the gypsy's hair, close to him, and the smell of his sweat, which he did not mind, and found oddly reassuring in its humanness.

"You stay, I teach you to play," the gypsy said, his voice enticing and humanly warm. "You be like my son, and my violin's son. No?"

"No," Edward said, his breath a sobbing gasp. "No! I don't belong to you at all." He wrenched himself away, hearing the low amused laughter of the gypsy behind him, and ran back unhindered to the caravan and the unhappy George, sobbing and shivering. He crept very close to George, away from the gypsy boys, as the wagon began to move again.

"What for did you go out, Master Edward?" George asked, worried and reproachful. "Natural matters?"

"No," Edward whispered, "it was the music I heard, it was the sound of the music, I had to find out what it was."

"Heathen fiddle!" said George sharply. "Here, Master Edward, has that Egyptian hurt you? If he has, I'll—I'll—I don't know what I can do. Has he hurt you?" he asked in genuine concern.

"No," Edward said, choking back his sobs, "No, he didn't hurt me at all. But oh, George, I want my Uncle James, I want to go home."

George did not know whether to worry more that the gypsies would keep them, or weary of them or take fright, and leave them, but he had not long to worry, for by noon of the next day the Earl had found them. They heard the galloping hooves of a horse furiously ridden, behind them, and then the Earl swept in upon them, like a hero from a panto-mime, his cape flying in the wind of his speed, and his pistols shooting fire. Knowing gypsies and their love of the flamboyant, he did it purely for effect. Edward ran to the curtains at the end of the wagon, eluding the hands of the boys, and would have cried out to him, but the boys caught him and pulled him back. Nevertheless, his Uncle must have seen him, for he came straight to the wagon, and ripped the curtains down with his dress sword. Edward thought he looked magnificent. He was in full dress, beneath his riding cape, and his boots shone like black glass. He leaned down with his sword, and cut the rags that bound George, and without a word indicated they should come out. He handed George a small loaded pistol, from his pocket, and then he asked Edward in cold fury to point out to him the gypsy that had taken him. Edward had no need to look. The gypsy had walked forward, knife poised in hand, towards the Earl.

"Cover me, from anyone's interfering," the Earl said to George, and sent the knife flying out of the gypsy's hand with the point of his whip. Without dismounting, holding in his horse, he sent his long driving whip snaking again about the gypsy, marking his face and raking his back, and he did not stop until the gypsy rolled onto the ground to evade him. Then he reached over, and lifted Edward up with his arm, and set him in front of him on his horse, and called George to mount behind him. The gypsies screamed at them, and pelted them with sticks and rubble, and some had drawn knives, but George fired the pistol he held, and the Earl laid a path open for himself with his whip and the flying hooves of his horse, and vanished with what he sought, almost as quickly as he had come.

That the Earl was in a rage as towering as the cumuli above them, they discovered, as they rode, with them as well. Besides a curt direction to hang on to him, he had no word to say. It was not until he reached the main road, and his curricle, and George had reharnessed his horse with the other three, that his mood began at all to abate.

"What did you *say* to that gypsy, Edward?" he snapped. "Don't you *know* you must never speak to them? George, didn't you warn him of that? They are like the *good people*, Edward, they will never take you unless you call them first. This kind of business with them is most unusual, but they can be dangerous in a corner."

"I did *not* call them," Edward cried, his eyes flashing, stamping his foot, angry like his Uncle out of relief after his scare. "I was merely polite." His lip began to quiver. "I have had a horrible time, Uncle James, and I was never so glad ever to see anyone, as you. And I doubt George was, too. You might be a little more glad to see us."

"Little silly," said his Uncle, his voice softening, "why then do you think I have disrupted all the boroughs of England and all the ports, and scoured the countryside on horse myself for a day and a night? And here you are not fifty miles from my doorstep, looking a perfect fright, both of you. But I have George, I think, to thank for having found you so soon, and for that I am not going to dismiss him completely." His sense of humour began to return at the combined sight of his frightened and half-cowed disreputable-looking retainer and ward. He grinned suddenly, a wide boyish grin Edward had never seen before. "I think you cannot imagine how you look. What *have* they done to you, Edward? When I think of you in that foul wagon, black as a gypsy, looking out at me with your blue eyes—" He stopped laughing suddenly, and caught the little boy to him tightly against his gold coat and his lace, now spattered with mud and unmentionable refuse. "I would have been well served, to have lost you, for leaving you in the hands of an incompetent like George who lets a gypsy catch sight of you."

"You look rather awful yourself, Uncle James," said Edward, beginning to recover.

"Then let us get home quickly," his Uncle said. "I would not venture in our conditions to stop at an Inn."

After they returned home, however, there was no pleasing the Earl at all, and his temper was a force to be reckoned with. He dismissed Nurse Pigot, and sent George away on a two-week probation, with grim threats about not rehiring him. Edward he put under the particular charge of Ross, and the housekeeper's assistant. He was in and out of his house unpredictably at all hours, for several days, unusually demanding and critical and capricious, but he did not stay in it. He had been spending some time at a country house of certain London friends some twenty miles distant from his own, but his household soon wished he would spend his nights in and his days out.

Edward did not mind Nurse Pigot being gone. He did not care what happened to his buttons and his rents, and he hardly noticed the condition of his shirts at any time; to him, they appeared as naturally as the rain and the sun from heaven, and he gave them less thought. But he did miss George, and he resented his dismissal, and the substitution of Ross whom he could not now avoid, put in power over him. The effects of his kidnapping, and the sudden loss of his familiar rocks of steadiness and comfort combined to shatter his disposition. The Earl's own moods he did not understand, but he felt them, and he felt the strained uneasiness of the house. He refused to help himself or to tidy his room, as he usually did, and he made such a nuisance of himself as if purposely to an already distraught and overburdened household that he soon received a sharp set-down from the Earl, and promise of worse. He then sulked, and brooded, and the dye on his hair and skin refusing to fade away or be scrubbed away, he made an odd figure in the house. The climax to his misdeeds and the Earl's mishumour came over his spinet three days after his return.

He had gone to it, as he often had since its arrival at Christmas, for solace, and he was sitting at it, not attempting to play, although he was beginning to learn, but softly and idly pressing one tone at a time, thinking of nothing at all, and then imagining what nothing must be. It would not be grey and formless, he thought, but a kind of sparkling shimmer, made up of all the colours and everything in the world, ground all together into a million, no, trillions of coloured bits of atomies, like the motes in the dusty rays of sunlight, or like the light filtered through his eyelashes into peacock rainbows. He was startled from his reveries by a sharp box on the ear that knocked him from the fragile bench to the floor, overturning the bench as he fell. He looked up, bewildered, to see his Uncle staring down at him, his face cold as a stranger's, white, masked with incomprehensible and frightening hatred that the child felt pierce him.

He could not imagine, having no reason to, the Earl's shock at hearing the soft sounds as he entered his house unannounced. He had followed them, until they stopped, to the little unused room where the spinet had been placed, and there, like an image and an echo of himself at that age, he saw the thin back and dark hair of a child, his fingers arrested on the keys, his eyes brooding into space on nothing. He himself had not known until much later why his own father had struck him, finding him so. It was much later, when he was grown, that he had pieced together the story of how his mother had run away from his father to Vienna, with a musician, and how his father had pursued her and killed her lover with a pistol shot and brought her back and forced himself immediately upon her, and how the child born within the year that was himself had been born deformed. He had not connected the memory or the history later learned, and until this moment when his eyes saw again, as through his father's, the scene, he had forgotten it. He stood there, in blind horror, not seeing Edward anymore, remembering how his mother had cried, and his father had raged, and how his father had had the pianoforte, his mother's, burned then.

Edward, knowing nothing of the Earl's mind, felt only the injustice of the blow, and in sudden unreasoning fury, flew at his persecutor, screaming in a culmination of the three days' strain and bewilderment, hitting out at his unresisting Uncle, and then as his Uncle, waking to himself again and the present moment, caught his wrists and held them in his own steel hands, he bit, and scratched, wherever he could. His Uncle, losing all patience, transferred his two hands to one of his own, and with the other systematically slapped his cheeks in turn, until his screaming voice quieted to sobs, and all fight left him. Then his Uncle took his hand, without a word, and led him to his room, and still without a word, but a chilling look of distaste and disdain on his face, he shut the door on him. Edward took himself to his bed, and lay down, and cried himself to sleep. His quick anger had left him, and he was only bewildered and hurt. He hoped his Uncle would come back, but he did not. The Earl directed Ross to have the spinet removed and sold, not asking how it had come there, and left, not meaning to return soon, if at all.

But he did return, and sooner than he imagined. A weary, listless, lonely week passed for Edward, made bearable only by his lessons, and then both Nurse Pigot and George and the Earl were all three returned to him by reason of an illness that came on him. He had at some time been infected with measles, most probably in the gypsy caravan, and his resistance being at all points low, he took them badly. Informed of it by Ross by letter, the Earl wrote both to George and to Nurse Pigot, asking them to return. He was himself not at first alarmed, counting it only a necessary childhood disease with a silly name, but when it appeared that Edward was very ill, fetched by Ross himself on horseback, he returned, again with a London doctor, as fast as horses could bring him. He found Edward delirious, in a high fever, not knowing him or anyone. He was as sick as a little boy could be. The surgeon, with calm efficiency, proceeded to bring him out of the fever safely and to settle the frightened household, but it was many days after that before he felt much better, and it would be weeks before he would feel as he had before the gypsies took him. In some ways, he never did again. Another part of his childhood had left him, and though it did not show in his face, a part of his trust.

III

The Earl, exhibiting a novel patience and concern, shared the watches over Edward. The London doctor had left, once the crisis had passed, leaving medicine and warning them to protect his eyes and his nerves from light and exertion, and only the village doctor paid his calls. Edward minded the Earl better than anyone about taking his medicines and drinking scraped beef teas and lemonades and the cold saline solution when he wanted nothing at all. He had dreamed one night during his high fever that George had been ground up and made into sausage his Uncle had required him to eat, and the nauseous taste of it was still always in his mouth, impeding him whenever he tried to eat or drink. As he grew better, he spoke sometimes hesitatingly to George or his nurse, but he did not speak at all to the Earl. He only shook his head for yes or for no when the Earl spoke to him, but he seemed to rest most easily when the Earl kept his hand in his own larger one. Sometimes he opened his tired, weak eyes, and fixed them briefly on the Earl's face or figure, and then closed them, and the slow tears of an invalid would fall silently from under his lashes down his cheeks.

The Earl did not know what to make of him. George thought, thinking of one of his sisters, even not knowing what had passed while he was gone, that Edward had a broken heart, but the idea seemed impossible to him, and he did not consider mentioning it to the Earl. The Earl, however, sensing that something was very wrong with Edward, besides the weakness of his illness, bent every effort of his considerable powers towards cheering him up. He read to him for hours on end, in his darkened room. He had sent up several of the late Mr. Newberry's books for children from his London Bookstore, and Mr. Goldsmith's reputed *History of Little Goody Two-Shoes,* but to his relief Edward found them as dead and insipid as he did himself. But they served a purpose, for Edward suddenly laughed, with an amused chuckle, and spoke for the first time.

"Oh, Uncle James," he said, "I am long past books like these, don't you know that? I love to have you read to me, I wish you would never stop, but isn't there something else you could choose?"

So the Earl read to him *The Life and Adventures of Peter Wilkins,* shipwrecked among the glums and the gawries, a race of winged creatures whose eyes could stand light no better than Edward's could, which Edward loved, and also *The Life and Strange Surprizing Adventures of Robinson Crusoe,* and M. Perrault's *Histories or Tales of Past Times, Told by Mother Goose, with Morals,* about Riding Hood, Bluebeard, Sleeping Beauty, Cinderilla, Little Thumb, the Master Cat, and Riquet with the Tuft. He then read to him, for there were few books written for children, parts of Gibbon's *Decline and Fall of the Roman Empire,* which Edward was interested in from the point of view of his bias against Romans, and North's translation of Plutarch's *Parallel Lives,* which Edward preferred.

"I hope you are not still thinking I am like that Caesar," the Earl remarked, his eyes once again gentle and kind on Edward.

Edward did not answer, but he turned his head away into the pillow. "I am sure people who knew him loved Caesar too," he said to the pillow.

The Earl found the answer less than satisfactory. "I have been reading reports in the paper this morning," he said, "of the works of a man in my opinion much like your Caesar in real truth. He has seized Malta and Egypt with some shows of mercy, and God knows where our government had then put Nelson, but he has massacred in Jaffa—which did resist him—three thousand prisoners he took, as well as all the people of all ages of that town, and then, when he was forced into retreat from Syria, he ordered his own soldiers who were ill with plague in hospital to be put to sleep with laudanum. Am I like that to you, Edward? Do I appear so to you? I hope I do not."

"I don't know," Edward said drearily to his pillow. "You do not have the power to do that. And *massacre* means to butcher, I know that, the Vicar told me in my Latin, and you are not a butcher. But you do what you can. I don't want to talk about Caesar, Uncle James. Read me something else."

"Shall I read you *Julius Caesar* then?" the Earl asked wickedly.

"Read me what you like," Edward said, with a slight smile, but tiredly and without enthusiasm. His Uncle, penitent, took his hand, and they sat in silence, until Edward fell asleep for his nap, and the Earl did not bring up the subject again or the play.

But of all the books Edward liked best for his Uncle to read to him Shakespeare's comedies, which the Earl read with verve, taking the various parts, and enlivening the darkened room with moving scenes and clashing characters. Edward, unable to see anything else, saw them all, before his closed eyelids, in the vividness of life. The words and passages he did not understand he ignored. He liked *A Midsummer Night's Dream* exceedingly, he tolerated *As You Like It*, and he liked the unravelling of *All's Well That Ends Well*, but his particular favourite was *Measure for Measure*. The golden Duke and particularly the seducing and self-knowing Angelo, dark and light, caught his fancy. It seemed to him even more a fairy tale than the play in which Oberon and Titania held court, and he loved the final resolving and pardoning, in which mercy exceeded justice, and the seeming dead lived, and seeming hatred became love.

> " 'Mercy and Truth are met together;
> Righteousness and Peace have kissed each other,' "

he said softly.

"What is that?" asked the Earl sharply, a little embarrassed by the plot which he understood very well. He had tried to change to a different play, but Edward had begged him to finish.

"My father taught me that," Edward said. "Go on, please, Uncle James. Is it over?"

"It is quite over. We shall read *The Tempest* next," he said, "and you will find a character very like yourself, my former Ariel who has now turned gypsy, and a wicked Duke, and a banished Duke who can make magic and holds all the creatures of his island in his thrall, and a savage deformed beast who yet loves music."

When Edward was tired of being read to, the Earl told him the more tellable of his adventures, but of things he had seen and done, not of himself. He saw that the kitchen exerted every effort to tempt Edward's flagged appetite, and as he grew better, the Earl took him for drives, a scarf wound about his eyes. He was too weak to wish lessons or visits from the Vicar, but he enjoyed telling off his exercises and his declensions and his verbs to the Earl by rote, who held his book. Gradually, with the Earl's new patience and tact and forbearance, they slipped back into some of their old friendship.

The Earl had the gardener plant an arbour, with flowering vines and trees bought ready grown and blooming from the South, and he had a reclining chair made for Edward to lie on, and a long cushioned swing. He would often sit there himself, his long legs up, leaning back, the little boy in his arms, watching the clouds pass in great armadas and finding changing shapes in them, of animals and gnomes and trolls, wise men on camels, and angelic winged creatures blowing trumpets. On impulse he told Edward the story of the angelic child-musician Mozart fainting with ecstasy when he first heard the sound of the French horn, but he was startled by the raptness of Edward's attention, and before Edward could speak he quickly found another image above them to point out. He taught Edward how to tell the weather from their different shapes. Edward would sleep, and wake, and sleep again, each time finding his Uncle's quiet steady breathing behind him. But he was older now, and though he took present comfort and recuperation in his Uncle's steady quiet presence beside him, he knew now it was only for a time with limits. He did not want again the intenser relationship he had known, he wanted only this, and he wanted it whole and continuing. With his child's heart, he felt it a bitter thing that he could not have it. Even as he felt his Uncle's chest by him rising and falling with his breath, his bones and skin firm and reassuring beneath the cloth of his coat, he felt the time approaching when he would not feel it. He began, finally, to talk to his Uncle again, but he did not ask where his spinet had gone or if he might have it again or speak of it at all, and he did not encourage his Uncle to explain his sudden violences to him, or his sudden fears about him. He already knew as much as his brain could understand or bear to know.

His Uncle did ask him, when they were sitting quietly and companionably together, "Shall I get you another little dog, Edward?"

"No," Edward said, "please don't."

"Perhaps later then."

"No," Edward said, with finality in his voice. "Something would happen to it. Everything I love goes away from me."

His Uncle could not deny what he said, but he held the little boy tightly to him.

"My father told me once Mr. Wesley said even animals could go to heaven," Edward said, with a slight question in his voice. "Do you think my puppy is there? I am not sure. There was so little of him. He was here such a little while, there was not much of him," he added, for his Uncle. "But I hope so, all the same."

He had begun, after the whipping his Uncle had given him just after his ninth birthday, to daydream in earnest and to make up stories for himself. His Uncle, discovering this, encouraged him to tell them aloud to amuse them both on the long light summer evenings before Edward fell asleep. Edward smiled, but he did not tell them all.

"I imagine," he said once, "that I am riding down a road, an ordinary road," he said, "like any one I know, and suddenly I see a great round hedged garden before me. A squared thick hedge. Sometimes it is there, blocking the lane, and sometimes it is not there at all, and sometimes I meet it on another street. Sometimes there is no way in, and other times, a section of the green hedge slides into itself, and one can pass in as through a door, and then it slides to again, and the place seems to have no crack in it, no opening at all. Sometimes through it I see a woman who wears a pink dress. I am riding a white horse, a large one, and I have courage, and I ride through the opening, the next time it slides into view, and then the hedge closes behind me, like a dance, and I cannot leave even if I wanted to. But I don't wish to. There are rooms built into the sides of all the hedge." His voice fell off, and he did not go on with that story, even at the Earl's prompting, though he clearly knew more of it in his mind.

"Then tell me another," the Earl asked, but Edward yawned and said he was too sleepy. The next night he told the Earl part of another.

"There are seven Russian Princesses whose skin is as clear as diamonds, and the fifth is the most beautiful of all, but they are very hard to see. They have been cursed since they were born that they will be carried off by a white cloud, and they are never allowed outside. I am a Prince, but I take the post of a footman in order to see them. The King has a great party, and the footmen brought in specially from the village have to stand, one on a step on each side of the red velvet stairs all night. They can see the crystal chandeliers winking, and hear the music, and the perfumed air is very heavy and hot, but the Princesses do not faint.

Some of the footmen faint, and are replaced, and I am one that does. I am to be taken out and thrown into the snow, being of no use, except the fifth Princess stops them and has me taken into a room. I become then a tutor to the Princesses, for I am a learned Prince." The Earl smiled a little, but not much, for he found himself interested.

"There have been other tutors before me, who have lost four of the seven Princesses, and now there are only three left. The cloud has somehow gotten them, and then the King has gotten the tutors. But I am resourceful, and I think I will not fail. We are in an enclosed garden, with white flowering pear trees and pink apricot trees, and snapdragons and roses and white larkspur. We should not be there, but the fifth Princess has begged so pitifully that I have let them go into it, being too proud of my abilities. It is summer, and suddenly a cloud of white ice, full of cries like white swans in it, falls upon us, and I cannot see anything. It is very cold, I can hardly breathe, or move my arms or legs, and then the cloud is gone, and the sun shines again and warms me, and then I see the three remaining Princesses are gone. The King is very angry with me, and he has my hands bound behind me and throws me into a cell in his castle, that has only straw in it, and is not even private, but has other people in it. I stay in my corner and wait, and I am very uncomfortable, and after a long time, the King comes to see me. He is very angry and very stern, as he certainly might be, but I promise that if he will let me out, I will find where the ice cloud has taken the Princesses, not just mine but all the seven, and why, and I will bring them back." Again his voice died away.

"You always stop at the most interesting place, Edward," his Uncle complained. "I wish you would finish."

"Then it would be your daydream, not mine," said Edward, "and it would be of no more use to me. I have said enough, you can finish it for yourself.

"Do you have others?" asked the Earl.

"Oh, many others," said Edward. "They are like books in the shelf of my mind. When I cannot sleep, or am very lonely, or sad about something, I take one down and I reread it or I add to it or I make up a new one, but I can't just do that, an idea has to come to me, and then I go on with it. I'm tired of talking about my daydreams, Uncle James, tell me about yours."

"I haven't any," the Earl said, "I haven't any at all."

In the Autumn, his Uncle left again, with one quiet kiss on Edward's brown forehead and a friendly assurance to his little gypsy, and this time, he was gone for longer than two years, without making explanation or a reappearance. Shortly after he had left, Napoleon, having slipped through the British Blockade during August, arrived in Paris and manoeuvred himself to become First Consul of the Republic in name and Dictator in effect. This news reaching England was hailed by the Whigs, but not by the Earl or his party. Despite these events in the world at large, for the first year, the Earl's letters were regular, and his gifts appeared at the proper seasons, while Edward's hair grew out fair again and his skin faded to white, but the second year, both, as before, began to fall off, as Edward's existence again receded from the Earl's mind. Edward took his meaning: that he must learn to live his life without the Earl's presence, except in emergency, and as before, he did it as well and as uncomplainingly as he could. But as the months passed, he found the rigid limits of his life more confining, and more and more he widened them within his mind.

In his eleventh year, as in his tenth, Edward attended to his studies. He read Tacitus' *Germania* and Livy's history of Rome, *Ab Urbe Condita*, with the Vicar. He was interested in Tacitus' castigation of the Romans and his account of the purity of the Germans, and he was fascinated by Livy's account of the disappearance of Romulus in a miraculous dense thunderstorm.

"That is Romans for you," he said triumphantly to the Vicar. "Their king lies bleeding and murdered in front of everyone, if they will only look; and what happens. One of the fathers who tore him into pieces lifts a finger and points it up at an eagle that happens to be flying up (or more likely a vulture and looking into the sun that has come suddenly out, they can't tell the difference), and he cries: 'Look! It is Romulus who has been turned into a God!' And all the people—they are Romans, too, you see—like silly sheep look up into the sun and shout *Io!*, instead of looking down for the poor butchered body underneath their feet. It disgusts me. What a mockery of religion and sense."

"Your imagination is running away with you, Edward, that is not in the text. There is no bird."

"I see it, all the same," Edward said, brushing aside the objection. "And it is all one. The end is the same, and the means are the same."

"But Livy was a Roman, too," the Vicar murmured, "and he did not believe the story."

"True," said Edward thoughtfully. "That is true."

He read Horace, but found little in his sedate Mean or his gentle playfulness to appeal to his passionate spirit. He did not read Catullus,

in whose poems *"Da mi basia mille"* and *"Odi et amo"* he would have
found a kindred spirit, because the Vicar did not approve. He read the
Aeneid, and he thought it interesting, though in imagination somewhat
tame, he said, and he enjoyed the verse and its challenge to his wits, but
he was anxious for the Vicar to teach him Greek so that he might read
the *Iliad* and the *Odyssey* for himself. He applied himself so diligently
that he kept himself out of trouble, and after his ninth year, which had
fallen on the household like the Ninth Wave and left them trembling
in trepidation for what might come next, the household accepted in
grateful relief two years of apparent peace.

Edward seemed content, to a casual and even a fond eye, but he was
not. He seemed to have learned to accept the North as the place he must
live: and on moonlit nights when he stole away from his room, called by
the night from his window, unseen and undiscovered, and walked abroad
on the moors, smelling the rank scent of an unseen fox that raised small
prickles of fear at the nearness of something wild, and watched the tilted
three-quarters greenish-white moon above the far-off low hills, pressing
their shapes down, sharpening their smooth outlines, or the bright stars
on moonless nights throwing their red and blue sparkles into the darkness as sharply as lances; and when he saw the snows as Autumn changed
to Winter that first capped the high distant mountains gradually descend
them and take the moors in their unsteady elastic grip, he even loved
them. He knew all their seasons now, heat, snow, rain, sleet, white mist,
and early Spring and Autumn days with air as clear and fresh as his
Uncle's white wines over the springing green Northern grass (that twelve
men with scythes were continuously occupied in shaving to keep the
lawns near his Uncle's house). But for him it was a house without center,
and the sharp yearning pain within him grew sharper, not less, as the
years passed. It was as sharp as the point of the gypsy's knife that had
brought the blood beneath his ear, and he walked always with the little
unseen point at the edge of his heart, for he knew what it was he had
not, having had it once. In memory, he found himself thinking of the
gypsy who had perceived his unhappiness, and whatever his reasons, had
acted upon it to take him from it. He had not wanted to go then, and
he had been frightened by the violence of his taking, but in memory, as
the Earl continued to stay away, he found himself curiously grateful to
the gypsy and had it not been for his little dog, he would have been sorry
now for his whipping.

IV

When Edward was twelve, he began to run away. He chose his twelfth birthday, at the end of February, for his first attempt, with what significance or reason for him he did not explain. Nothing in particular seemed to have happened to provoke it. The Earl was not at home, and he had not remembered the boy's birthday. That afternoon Edward simply went out on his pony, and did not return. George and the footmen, finally alarmed and alerted, scattered out on their horses over the park. George, on an instinct, went towards the frosty foothills of the Cheviot, and saw him, higher up, ahead of him. On his stronger horse, he eventually came upon him. Edward looked at first as though he might try to run from the footman, but in the end, he did not.

"That was too long a ride, Edward," was all the footman said. "I think the Earl would rather, next time, that you did not go so far alone." Edward did not reply or make any explanation, his teeth chattering, and his fingers and lips blue with cold. But there was no next time in which to use the footman's advice. The Earl, informed by the groom, directed the pony to be sold, and for the groom to whip Edward for it. The letter arrived some ten days after the event, but the groom Ross, a rough Scot who believed in stern upbringing of the young, particularly young boys, did not feel any loathing for his assignment and carried it out strictly. Edward did not cry very much, though his eyes were shocked, and he did not complain to George, who tried to make him comfortable afterwards, but the next day, when George came to find out why he did not appear for breakfast, he found Edward's room empty. The footman wasted no time in misplaced confidence. This time, Edward being unmounted and on foot, they found him rather quickly, at the edge of the park. He had had breakfast, cheerfully and leisurely, at the gate lodge with the caretaker, and had started naively down the road. George galloped up beside him and swung him with one arm up into his saddle, and gave his ears a quick perfunctory box.

"It is into trouble you will be getting us all," the footman scolded him with a worried look on his face. "What mischief has come into you, Edward? What is the matter with you these days?"

"The Earl does not want me," Edward said with a dry sob, "and I do not want him. I am going to my father's people where I belong, if I can find them."

"Then I am going to lock you in your room, Master Edward," said the footman regretfully, "until the Earl can arrive here and take charge of you himself, for he has put you in my charge particularly in his absence"—he looked at Edward's set face thoughtfully—"unless you will just tell me yourself you will not go running off again."

"Will you have to tell the Earl about it?" Edward asked, his voice uncertain.

"Ay, Edward, I will that, I'm afraid. He made particular mention of it to me, and if I did not, then someone else would anyway."

"Need they know you hadn't?" asked Edward rather desperately.

"When I can, I go my own way on matters, Edward, but if I broke my orders, I should lose my place here, Edward, and I value it. It would not help you, much, in the end, either, and I should have just lost my place. Besides, it would be a kind of lying, and I don't lie easily, Edward, or lightly. Do you?" he asked, knowing what Edward's answer would be.

Edward shook his head. "Then you had better lock me in my room, George," he said rather wearily with a sigh.

He was there at lunchtime, finishing *The History of Rasselas, Prince of Abyssinia,* and his adventure or his apprehensions did not seem either one to weigh heavily on him, for he left nothing on his tray. He was also there for his tea, and for his supper, after having spent a long afternoon in his room working out his Greek exercises, a language he was beginning, in addition to his Latin, with his tutor the Vicar, and reading a book of Mythology, throughout the long afternoon hours on his bed. But when George came, after his own supper, to see that he was making ready for bed, he found the room empty and the window open. The distance to the ground was a long drop, even with his two sheets that he had knotted together inside the window to a heavy chair. He thought Edward must have swung out on them until he could reach the lone tree that grew a little way from the sheltered southern window. He pursed his lips in admiration at Edward's daring, and felt a faint sweat at the risk the boy had taken. The light was fading, but he roused the house, nevertheless, and set out with the groom and the stable hands and the second footman, on horse, to look for him. When dark fell, they returned without success, to find the remaining horse, with its saddle, was gone from his stall.

"Ay, the canny lad," said Ross, with a respectful gleam, "he has waited right here until we ourselves be gone, and the stable quiet, and he has taken the master's horse and gone off with it. There will be a skinning for that he will be having, that will make the first one look like nothing at all."

"That may well be," said George, "and it probably will be, if we get him back, but it is black night now, the moon is down, and where has he gone?"

"He will come back when his belly be empty," said Ross.

"He will not that, I'm thinking," said George, "for he left nothing at all on three trays. I should have known it then. And he gave me a fair warning with it, and I was that blind."

The next day they searched the immediate countryside, in the villages and farms, and among the colliers in the mountains to the southwest, but they found no trace of any boy like the one they looked for, or any unaccounted for juvenile at all.

"He has gone to ground," said Ross, "until he thinks he has shaken us off his tracks and made us lose the scent. I am at a loss to know what to do now. With me he has won out."

"It will be another matter when the Earl comes home," said George. "I hope it may be soon."

He had now written the Earl twice, but the second letter the Earl had not received, for he had left London immediately on receipt of the first. He arrived in great haste, to deal with a culprit who had not waited to receive him. He was astonished, even thunderstruck, by the news, and after a conversation with his footman George, very thoughtful. He wasted no time in recovering his ward, who had already been gone three days. He employed runners whom he sent to all the posthouses on all possible roads that led south, and to all villages and towns on them or near them, offering a reward of fifty pounds for the recovery of a runaway schoolboy ward, and ten pounds for information alone, twenty-five for information that led to his recovery. He described his horse, and offered to rebuy it. He then sat down to wait, and to think, and to have long conversations with his ward's nurse and with his tutor. He did not have long to wait. Within four days, he had word by a messenger on horse that a boy answering Edward's description, obviously of schoolboy age and unconnected, obviously a runaway, had been found. The Earl himself, surveying the virtuous face of his informant, thought privately that had word of the reward reached his informant earlier, he would have had word of Edward earlier, but he made no remark or comment, except to pay his informant the first promised ten pounds, and to ask about his horse.

"Us has no horse, but us knows where horse be," his informant said.

"Will he stay where he is?" the Earl asked. "The boy, I mean. Have I time to take my coach by the roads?"

"He will stay," his informant said, grinning slightly. The Earl's frown quenched his grin, and he left the room, at the Earl's curt command, to wait below in the kitchen, where he refreshed the ears of the kitchen staff with accounts of Edward whom he described as a game spirit, full of pluck, and requiring both himself and his brother and his cousin to subdue, when he sensed from their looks they had learned who he was, and from their actions that they did not mean to let him leave. He described the scene with a gusto that George moderated when he told the Earl of it later, on being summoned to his room. The Earl, with his valet, was dressing for the journey, for he gathered Edward was some hundred miles away.

"He was on a farm, working for his supper, when this man came back from the public room at the Inn," George said, "and recognised that he might be the boy the runner was describing."

The Earl only said "Well" repressively, and ordered George to call his coachman to have his fast curricle, rather than his chaise, brought round, which he meant to drive himself. He took his London groom with him, to ride the horse back. He exchanged horses twice, leaving the stableboy at the first exchange house handsomely provided to care for his horses until his return, and drove on, as quickly as the road would let him. Having started late, he was forced to spend a night on the road, and he did not arrive at the particular Midland village until well in the day. He was not particularly concerned about the time, despite his pressing as fast as he could. He thought it would do Edward no harm to wait on him.

His informant led him so far into the country, off the main road, that for a time he wondered if his purpose was to rob him, and he wished for his footmen, as well as his groom, but the generosity of the reward made that seem unlikely, if Edward really was to be delivered to him, and in any event he had his pistols and his sword which, despite the new fashion to leave it off, he had brought, and was prepared and able to use them. They arrived finally, in a deep-rutted road, sunk between hedges and tall fields, at a low-thatched stone farmhouse. The Earl had to bend his head to enter the doorway, under the thick beam that formed the lintel. The whitewash was peeling away with damp, and it looked as if they could use the help of anyone's reward, or any money. The sunlight barely penetrated the small windows, and it took his eyes a few minutes to adjust to the gloom and to discover Edward, sitting on the floor by the embers of the morning's fire, his knees drawn up, and his hands clasped around them, a piece of dirty string knotted tightly around his wrists. He had raised his head at the opening of the door, and kept his eyes fixed upon his Uncle's figure, but he did not otherwise move, or attempt to say a word. The room was crowded with the tenants of the farmhouse, and several curious visitors, staring avidly at the Earl and at Edward and grinning, but the commanding presence of the Earl, despite his limp, silenced their remarks.

The Earl did not go over to Edward on his first entrance. He nodded to his informant, and said curtly, "That is the boy. I will pay you, if you will clear this room." He waited until it had been done, except for the tenants of the farm.

"What school did he run away from?" asked the older man of the farm.

"Sion House," the Earl said briefly, naming his own. He paid the money quickly, and walked over to Edward. He found himself pitying the boy, as he saw the frightened, miserable look in his eyes that did not flinch from his own angry ones.

"So you have learned, so young, what betrayal feels like," he said softly, bending to cut the string that held Edward's ankles with his knife. "Well, you will not have to learn it so completely again, you will be prepared for it. It is a bitter knowledge, is it not—especially when it is for money." He helped Edward to his feet, but he did not cut the string on his wrists. He put his hand under his elbow, and led him out of the room and helped him up into the curricle, and then he had a word with his informant about leading him to his horse, and sparing an extra horse briefly for his groom, since there was only room for two persons in the curricle.

Then he climbed into the curricle beside his ward, and prepared to take the reins, as soon as his groom was mounted.

"How much did you pay that man?" Edward asked with tight lips.

"Enough," the Earl said briefly. "Console yourself you come expensive, though less might have served."

"Please, Uncle," he said, holding out his hands. "I cannot bear it any more."

"You will have to," the Earl said tersely, "until I have recovered my horse. I don't want to have to pay too much for him because I am worried about your running off across the fields."

"Is it far?" asked Edward whitely.

"I have no idea," said the Earl curtly. "You would know better than I would." He looked to see the effect of his words on the boy, but none was visible. "It may do you good to suffer a little," he added savagely, and was glad to see the boy wince at his tone. Edward was silent then, but the Earl saw in the sunlight that the string was stained, and his wrists were rubbed raw, and he guessed his struggles to escape during the night. He wondered a little at the intensity the mute string bore witness to, for Edward did not seem afraid of him now, or excessively disturbed to see him.

They proceeded in silence down the rutted road, the Earl guiding the wheels of the curricle as skilfully as the road allowed between the worst of them, until they reached another farmhouse, where he discovered and rebought his horse. He saw tears glistening in Edward's eyes when he returned, but he ignored them. He kept his groom by him, a little behind, as escort in this remote countryside, as they made their way back to the highway. When they finally reached it, he sent his groom and his horse on ahead, with a message, given privately, that he might not at once come home, and to see that his own horses were brought home. He then cut the string tied about his ward's wrists, who had wedged himself into a corner of the curricle to brace himself against the joltings on the bad road. He saw, to both his annoyance and dismay, that the tears were falling from Edward's eyes, though he was trying not to cry.

"Do you have a handkerchief?" he asked. Edward shook his head, sniffing. The Earl pulled out his own and handed it to him. "For heaven's sake, blow your nose, and stop that revolting noise, Edward," he said, crumpling his ward's dignity. "What are you crying for *now?* You are safe now, or are you afraid of me? I suppose you should be."

"I never was not safe, until you bought those men," Edward said defiantly, but his defiance like his dignity crumpled suddenly beneath his Uncle's cold stare. "I'm sorry, Uncle James. That is a lie. Sometimes I didn't feel very safe at all. I'm crying"—he hiccoughed slightly—"because I've made you pay so very much money, and I took your horse, and—and—my wrists sting so—and I can't seem to stop myself." He looked fair to dissolving himself, and his Uncle stopped him on the verge by a quick unsympathetic and repressive glance.

"If you are sorry at all, Edward," he said coldly, and more repressively yet, "then please try not to snivel. I have had a wearing day myself. And as for the money, I dislike wasting it of course, but I could easily afford to buy ten naughty boys twice as expensively as you, and think nothing of it, so please will you not give it another thought, either. I do not intend to myself." They had come to a crossroads, and the Earl turned his horses onto one of them. Edward looked at him in surprise.

"You are going in the wrong direction, aren't you, Uncle James? This is not North."

"I have no fancy to go home just yet," said the Earl, "do you? Shall we let your escapade blow over there and be forgotten? Nothing, Edward, is more than a nine days' wonder. You will learn that." He put his hand for a moment on the boy's head. "You have had no holiday this year or last—when did you last have a holiday, Edward? I think I have been the one to take them all. The Vicar tells me you have been working very hard, even excessively, at your studies, and I think a holiday for you is in order now."

Edward's face filled like any boy's with joy at the prospect, but then the joy faded. He shook his head.

"I have been very naughty, and I have intended to be. You should not reward me for it, Uncle James, that would be so bad for me."

"Do you now venture to tell me what to do, Edward, and how to conduct my affairs?" the Earl said, smiling slightly. "That is coming it a little too strong, even for a young moralist like you."

"I did not mean that," Edward said, flushing.

"Well, what else did you mean?" the Earl asked. "While you are my ward, you are my affair; and I will conduct my affairs in my own manner, not yours. But if it bothers you," he added, less severely, " you may think that it is I who need the holiday, which especially after this escapade will be quite true, and you, being with me, will just have to go along. That can be your penance."

The little boy sighed, half in relief, half in weariness. His eyes closed, and suddenly he was asleep, and he did not wake until the Earl turned into an Inn and stopped the horses. He roused himself sleepily then, at the noise the ostlers made. His Uncle lifted him down, and took him into the Inn room. It happened that night, being on the main London road, to be noisy and crowded. The Earl could only manage to obtain one room for the night, but he did manage to find a small private parlour for their supper, for they were both weary.

They did not either have anything to say, while they waited for the food to be brought to them, but after they had eaten the most part of it, and the air between them had become easy, the Earl looked at his ward and said abruptly, though gently, "You see, I shall find you, Edward, and the next time you run away, if there is a next time, I shall whip you myself, Edward, and much harder than Ross. But I hope there will not have to be a next time. Why must you run away, Edward? What do you lack at my house that you do not have?"

Edward looked at the Earl sombrely, but he did not answer the Earl's last question. Instead, he said, "I will not run away again then. I do not want you to whip me." He smiled suddenly, wryly and frankly, at his

Uncle, his eyes much older. "I do not think I would do it again anyway. It was not much fun. Not being found was almost as bad as being found." But he did not offer to tell his week's adventures.

"It hurts me, Edward," the Earl said then, "that you would tell a footman more than you will tell me."

"I don't know what that means," Edward said, evasively.

"Of course you do, Edward. How do you think I found you so easily? It was by knowing in which direction to concentrate my looking."

"I know the footman better," Edward said, answering the Earl's earlier statement, almost sulkily, again like a little boy. "I have not seen you for months and months and months, and you even forgot my birthday. And anyway, I knew he would tell you anyway," he added illogically, with his sudden frankness.

"Your father's people do not want you," the Earl said bluntly. "Nor do your mother's. Perhaps they might now, but they did not then. I would have been glad to let them have you otherwise, believe me, Edward."

"Am I never to see them?" asked the little boy.

"Of course you shall see them," the Earl snapped, "but I am not certain this is the time for it. Do you want to leave me?"

"Yes," the little boy whispered, his eyes downcast as though afraid to look at his Uncle's face.

"Well, you can't, Edward," his Uncle said simply, not asking Edward why, or explaining himself either, "for I won't let you, at least, not right now. So you will just have to make the best of it. Later, we will see. They could have seen you any time at all, for the six years you were with your mother and your father, and they did not choose to see you then, not even once. Do you know that?"

"Not even once?" Edward whispered.

"Not once, not one of them," his Uncle repeated harshly. "Think about it. I may not be what you want, but I have seen you more than they. Tomorrow we are going to the seashore, Edward, to a small beach that is not too crowded with fashionable people, and now we should go to bed. But Lord," he said, inspecting it, "it is not much of a bed. But it will have to do. I had your clothes packed for you, Edward. Do you want a bath?"

Edward nodded. "I have not had a bath all week."

"Then, for God's sake, have one at once, by all means, now." He rang for assistance.

It was the bath that was his undoing, and the small bed. He left, for a smoke and a walk, while Edward had his bath, but when he re-

turned, and had bathed himself, and had the baths removed, and undressed, and climbed into bed, the moon rising shone through the window
on Edward's damp hair, curling slightly about his face, and on his fair
girlish skin, and his features relaxed, though unsmiling, in sleep. The
ruffles of his nightshirt hid the chafing on his wrists.

I should have continued to stay away, he thought, I should have sent
George, I should not have allowed this to happen. Though why I should
mind, I don't know. His rational thoughts left him, and unable to help
himself, he bent gently and kissed the boy's lips.

Edward stirred, and his lips murmured in his sleep beneath the Earl's,
and then he put his arms about the Earl, as he once had, and returned his
kiss. All conscience, if he had any, swept away, the Earl gently removed
the nightgown from the little boy, though not his own, and ran his
fingers along the smooth skin of his back and the small of his back and
clasped him to him. The child did not seem to wake, but he responded,
and covered the Earl's face and lips and hands with his own caresses,
finally lying quiet in the Earl's arms, on his breast. They fell asleep in
that manner.

The boy this time awoke first, and had dressed himself in the fresh
clothes his Uncle had brought him, and was sitting in the windowseat
of the room, his knees drawn up and his hands clasping them, as he had
been sitting when his Uncle found him, regarding his Uncle thoughtfully
with his clear gaze. His Uncle, waking, looked back at him steadily with
his older, world-worn eyes, but he did not speak, and the child did not,
until his Uncle said, "Go downstairs, Edward, and play outside in the
Inn yard while I dress."

"You are not afraid I will run away again?" Edward asked.

"Should I be? I thought you said you would not, and I always believe
your promises, Edward. Will you?"

"No," Edward said, and he turned and went out the door, closing it
behind him.

At breakfast, however, he unnerved his Uncle by asking straightly,
"It is a sin, what we did last night?"

His Uncle did not choke, but he lowered his eyes on his plate, like
a schoolboy myself, he thought, and he said, after a moment, "I suppose
so."

"I do not see why it should be," Edward observed.

"Then why do you ask?" his Uncle said.

"Because you seem ashamed. If it is a sin, I suppose I must not do
it anymore."

He did not refer to the incident again, during breakfast, or on the drive to the seashore, to Margate. He ran along the shore, laughing wildly with delight, like the child he was, throwing pebbles into the waves, and looking for polished coloured ones, and chasing sea birds. It was late afternoon when they had arrived, avoiding London, and the dusk fell, and they went in for supper at the Inn where they had put up. This beach, being one of the wilder ones, was less used, and in the early Spring, hardly used at all. After supper, Edward went out to watch the moon rise over the sea, still now and waveless, except for the gentle ones of the tide withdrawing, returning and then withdrawing further, slipping in again and ebbing out, tumbling the pebbles in its wake in a rough music. The moon laid a trail of white fire before it, "like fire folk dancing," Edward cried. He walked out on one of the long piers, and watched for phosphorescent sea creatures caught in the nets by the side of the posts. At last he yawned, and took the Earl's hand, and went in for his bath. They had two rooms at this Inn, but after his bath Edward climbed into the Earl's bed.

"I thought you had decided to sleep with me was a sin," the Earl said, questioningly.

"It may be. I don't know. It does not feel like one. But if it is, I cannot help myself," the child said, his eyes shut. "Do you not want me to now?"

"I had rather you had not spoken about it," the Earl said frankly. He went downstairs, and walked along the shore in the moonlight for an hour, or longer. He knew he should take the child's room for the night, if only because he did not know whose son the child was, but he seemed no one's, only Anne's and his own self in his own person, and in the end, slowly, drawn despite himself, he went into his own room and undressed and lay beside the child.

He thought the child was awake, but he did not open his eyes or speak. The Earl took his hand, and lay still holding it like a little bird in his own, unresisting, pulsating with its own life.

"When you are older," he said quietly, "you will read in your Greek about a man named Socrates, who was named a corrupter of the youth, though not particularly for this reason, though perhaps that too."

"I do not know what *corrupt* means, but if it means what I think it means, I do not mind, you may corrupt me, if it pleases you," Edward said, in his own quiet voice.

"But it is not you I love, Edward," his Uncle said, "it is your mother who shines in you in this half light. One day you will grow up, and I will not see her so plainly in you, but as you are right now, Edward, it is very dangerous for us both, but I cannot seem to help myself. You must grow up more quickly."

If the child understood the enormity behind his Uncle's words, he gave no sign of it. He sighed.

"Why do you sigh, Edward?" the Earl asked. "Are you angry?"

The child sighed again, in a manner too old for him. "No, Uncle," he said. He began, surprisingly, to cry.

"Edward," exclaimed the Earl, taking him as he would have taken Anne into his arms, "don't cry!"

"Ah," the child said, "but you see, I love you for yourself."

"Then there is no help for that," the Earl said, and took the child to him as he had before. The child did not initiate joyously as before, but he was pliable and acquiescent. He was like a small angel freshly expelled from innocence, and his shame, so newly acquired and in its way mature, perversely intensified the Earl's desire, which might otherwise have quickly wearied, especially since despite his shame, he shrank from nothing in the Earl's nature.

The next morning the Earl drove on to Dover, and left his curricle, and the tide going out and the wind setting fair, they took ship for France. It was Spring of 1801. Pitt had just resigned, protesting George III's failure to keep his promises on Catholic Emancipation, after the Irish rebellions and the consequent Union, and Addington, to be Lord Sidmouth, was new Prime Minister. The Peace of Amiens would not be signed for a year, but the packets were still going back and forth and the decree of the First Consul making all English of military age, regardless of degree, prisoners of war, and ending forever the civilized conventions of preceding wars, was yet two years off. The Earl foresaw no great inconvenience.

Edward had never been awake on a ship before, but he proved to be an excellent natural sailor, with a sound stomach. He was in ecstasy, and could hardly watch the departing white cliffs for watching the sea swelling ahead of him. He explored the ship thoroughly, in all its parts and all its working, and declared himself for the life of a Ship's Captain. The Earl only smiled, and promised to find a ship for him at the seashore, and left him to his own devices. He avoided Paris, as he had London, hiring a chaise and horses and driver at Calais. Apart from not wishing to be recognised with his companion, he had ceased to enjoy Paris, so many of his friends dead there or away from it or outwardly altered to fit the new times. They travelled at a moderate but steady pace to the South of France, the Earl taking the opportunity to instruct his ward in the rudiments of the French language which the staid Vicar had neglected. Edward made a good travelling companion, the Earl discovered, because he had few wants, or needs, and his mind was interested in everything, and his eyes seemed to see everything. He was excited by every evidence of a way of life different from his own, and by the Spring that flowered about them the further South they went.

The Earl, despite his club foot, was an excellent swimmer, for it in no way impeded him in the water, and the next day he taught Edward how to swim. They also rented a boat to sail before the wind in, though they did not go far from shore. They spent a week in this manner, the weather holding, their days and nights divided in a way they did not speak of or refer to again.

The day before the Earl had decided they must leave, they sat together by the waves. Edward had been feeding the gulls, but now they sat together on towels, idly tossing pebbles at the waves. Edward, at twelve, was growing taller, and gave promise of being as tall finally as his Uncle. He seemed to have grown, even in the last fortnight since his Uncle had found him, and he was certainly browner.

"George may not know you," the Earl said idly, "and Ross might find you harder to whip than he did a month ago. I don't think I shall ask him to again. You are too big for that now, Edward, unless you make it necessary I have to myself. You are not a little boy, really, anymore."

"No," Edward said, with a little sigh. "When are we going home, Uncle James?"

"Tomorrow," his Uncle said. "We can find time for a last swim, and then we really should start. I do have business to attend to, and you have yours too, in your studies."

The next morning, despite the coldness of the early sea, Edward was in before his Uncle, who followed him soon out. After a few minutes, he called to Edward to turn back, but he realised, treading the cold waves, that if Edward heard him, he was not obeying. He was striking out further, as swiftly as he could swim, straight towards the outer sea. The Earl shouted once more, and then he did not waste his breath shouting anymore, or his energy imagining Edward's reasons. He began to swim strongly towards him, gaining slowly on him, justifying his claim to have swum the Hellespont on his Grand Tour at twenty. He saw the boy go under, and doubled his efforts, reaching him as he reappeared. The child looked at him in terror, and lashed out at him wildly, and threw himself away from him under the water. The Earl could not believe what his senses informed him of, but in the cold waves washing them, he found no choice. He grasped Edward's arm and pulled him, flailing, near him, and with his other hand, hit him on the chin as hard as he could, impeded by the water. The child went limp, with shock or the blow, and holding his head above water as best he could, the Earl began to swim back towards the shore.

He thought twice, in his exhaustion, he would not be able to make the land, but he himself had a tenacious will to live. He stumbled onto the sharp stones, carrying Edward, and fell exhausted on the towels, cold and shivering. They could not stay here, he thought, and he could not carry the boy, with his foot, over the rocky beach. He cursed his foot and Edward equally. In the end, having shaken the water out of Edward and satisfied himself of his breathing, he laid himself and Edward together for warmth on the towel, and drew the second over them, and waited for him to wake. He was not warm and he was surprisingly uncomfortable, but he could think of nothing else to do. He had no doubt now, reflecting, that the boy had meant to drown himself, rather than go back to his life, as it was, and as it would be, and he had some idea of his reasons, but he saw no immediate help for any of it that he cared to give. He should perhaps send the boy away to school, but he had a good tutor, and for several reasons, principally his wish to keep the child out of the public eye, he did not intend to. He felt Edward stir beside him. He could not imagine his past madness for this half-drowned, wet, lean brown water rat beside him, in whom no magic lay now, for him.

"What folly possessed you, Edward," he exclaimed angrily. "You might have drowned us both."

The child did not answer, but rubbed his hurt jaw in silence.

"You are too like your mother in this," the Earl said, more gently. "You promised me you wouldn't run away again, Edward."

"I haven't run away," Edward said in surprise.

"Don't you call this running away?" the Earl asked penetratingly. "I do—of the worst kind."

"I suppose it is," the boy said dully. "All right, then, I won't do it again. I don't want to, anyway. It hurts." He turned his face away. "It is silly to try to hurt oneself. Other people will do it enough."

"You sound as if there were nothing left for you, Edward, and you are only twelve. If I have brought you to this, I do indeed reproach myself, for the first time, but I do not so flatter myself." His glance fell before Edward's bleak one. "Well, Edward, there is always anger. Call on that. You have tried many things, but you have not tried killing me." He regretted the words, as soon as he had spoken them, but he could not call them back, either from his mind or Edward's hearing.

"Yes," the boy said slowly, as if consideringly, "there is always that." He looked up and saw the horror on his Uncle's face. "Lord! Uncle James," he said, using the word for the first time in this way, "I wouldn't try to do that. Don't you know that?"

"If you can walk now," his Uncle said stiffly, "I think we should go back now, and make ready to leave." He looked at Edward, consideringly in his turn. "I am not a good person to love, Edward, even when I happen, as it rarely but sometimes does happen, myself to love. I told your mother that, and in the end, she believed me. And I tell you that. Don't waste your energies, or your very real talents, in any such way on me. Do you understand me, Edward?"

"I understand you," the boy said whitely, "I will remember what you say. I have forgotten already I ever did."

The Earl looked at him pityingly, but inflexibly. "At some time in our lives all of us, perhaps even myself, have wished only to live for and because of another person. But it is a delusion, Edward, and it does not last. You must be yourself, for yourself, Edward, not for me or for anyone else."

"I will remember what you say," Edward said, and walked ahead of him, not looking back, up the beach.

They returned to Calais and recrossed the Channel in a very different mood than before. They drove back to the moors of Northumberland and their grey skies, of earliest unadvanced Spring, spending two nights on the road, in their separate rooms, and two full days of driving, saying very little to one another. The boy's shamed face was proud and withdrawn and averted. The Earl's heart, to his surprise, ached for his pain, but he had no wish to relieve it, and his rational self believed what he did was for Edward's best good. He let him down at the door of his house, not dismounting himself, and watched him walk in, and turned and drove himself back to London.

During the brief while they had removed themselves from it, and during their brief accord, the world had not stood still. Tsar Paul, unfriendly to the English, had been assassinated, with the knowledge of his son Alexander and with the probable help of the English; and the Danish fleet outside Copenhagen had been destroyed by a high-handed and controversial English attack without declaration of war, cutting the Northern confederation and blockade Napoleon had formed against England. During the hot battle, Horatio Nelson, one of the two Admirals, had put his telescope to his blind eye and conveniently missed the elder Admiral Parker's signals to discontinue action. Accord anywhere, in anything, was brief and not lasting.

V

The Earl, once returned to London, briefly considered the question of sending Edward to Public School, and without consulting Edward's wishes or the Vicar's opinions, rejected it. He did not probe his reasons deeply. He cherished, without formulating to himself his feeling, Edward's frank innocence and his unworldly quality and he remembered very well the too early worldliness and easy sophistication of himself and his friends at Eton, their childish entrance into an ordinary viciousness. He perceived a quality in Edward's nature that he did not wish exposed to the brutal standards of conformity that would push him into either eccentricity, which the Earl deplored, or a surface disguising of a different self, as he had himself done. Edward seemed to him to have a nature that ignored the need to dominate or to conform, in so far as he troubled to analyse it, and he was uncertain how that nature would survive the rough organised society of the Schools. He had other reasons even stronger. He did not wish to send him merely to Manchester, into the closed unhealthy life of the city, among commoners, although he knew himself the excellence of the school, and yet he in no way wished to publicize the boy's existence among his own class at Eton or to confront the problems of Edward's parentage or his relations or his own guardianship. He was wholly unwilling to make any move that would compromise his independence about the child's future, or to accept any responsibility for him beyond what he had promised Edward's mother.

Whether or not Edward might have enjoyed going away to school, he did not consider, for his reasons concerned only himself and his own motivations. The sensation of virtually owning the child gave him a pleasure he did not probe, but he was unwilling to relinquish him yet into any other organised discipline than his own, or to widen his experience sufficiently for him to question his Uncle's behaviours or dispositions. He had removed himself from the immediate neighbourhood of the child, largely because he had suffered a revulsion, partly because he had grown bored, but partly out of some small feeling of conscience; but the memories of the child's face and his young sweet smooth skin, and what he himself had found to be his essentially yielding nature, made him particularly reluctant, both apprehensive and even slightly jealous, to leave the child unsupervised among a group of adolescent boys and unmarried schoolmasters. And so he did not send him. But he contacted Oxford tutors trained in the skills of both Manchester and Eton and engaged them to live in the town where he furnished lodgings, and so Edward was educated by both the North and the South.

The course the Earl decided to continue, although going out of practise, was not yet unusual for those able to afford it. The Earl had been sent to school because he was not wanted at home, not because it was common for his class. Eton had been the only choice for his family. He had hated but had survived it, and he had learned part of his cruelty and his indifference there. Had he read them he would have agreed with those writers like Cowper who denounced the Schools for the bad habits they nursed, their tyranny, their vice, their immorality. He had been there before 1780, before any life of the intellect had come out again. He knew the Long Chamber at Eton, although he himself had been an Oppidan, not a Colleger, where the boys lived crowded together with no adult eye from eight at night until morning. He had been a fag, and had ultimately had one, and he did not wish it for Edward. The world had had little to teach him in either dissipation or depravity afterwards.

If Edward missed the companionship of a society of boys his own age, he did not know he missed it, having never known it. He continued his classical work with the Vicar and his Eton tutor, and from his Manchester tutor he was given a knowledge of his own literature unusual at that time. The Earl, who had spent two years at Manchester Grammar School, had known the unique emphasis the school placed on this native store, and had drawn on it knowingly, as also upon its self-reliant simplicity. From his Eton tutor, Edward kept his accent as pure as when he had come from the South to live with his Uncle, for his Uncle did not wish him ridiculed as countrified when he did finally take him to London, if he did. And so Edward, for all his heartaches, was spared certain more common griefs and disappointments, and his regime remained much as he had known it, and essentially healthy, with long walks, and rides, and rest, alternating with his concentrated studies, adequate food, and time both to assimilate and to eliminate it. He escaped continued exposure to Horace, and Alcaics, the syndrome of endless composition of Latin verse for competition of which the Vicar disapproved and which occupied the education of his contemporaries, and from this his imagination benefitted. He was also left particularly vulnerable to shock and to unexpected emotion or experience.

On his thirteenth birthday, the Earl sent Edward a horse for his own to replace the pony he had sold. Before that, at Christmas, he had sent him Motteaux' translation of *Don Quixote de la Mancha* and two small illustrated volumes of poems, *Songs of Innocence* and *Songs of Experience*. Reading them, Edward wondered if his Uncle could have possibly read them, or if he had sent them only for the titles. As it happened, the Earl had read them, and both the poems and the illustrations had reminded him of Edward, which judgement showed how little he understood the child in his care. Other than those gifts no word from the Earl came.

Edward rode his horse, with what thoughts only he might have known and he kept them unformulated even from himself. He walked the moors and the hills widely, and he pursued his studies. He had at last left the Romans for the Greeks, and with the Oxford tutor the Earl had sent began to read the *Iliad* and the *Odyssey*. He also read *Prometheus Bound* by Aeschylus, and it made a lasting impression upon his mind, of the gentle god subdued by Force and Strength, rivets driven through his flesh, for Greek gods had flesh and suffered, chained upon the face of the crag which in his mind he pictured like the Mont Blanc, enduring. The Vicar intended him to read the *Eclogues* and the *Georgics* with him, but his passive resistance was such that the Vicar smiled and yielded and taught him instead the rudiments of Hebrew. With the Vicar, he also read the New Testament in Greek, despite his tutor's warning it would confuse his classical forms. "I know the English already," he said, with a smile at his tutor, "in a fashion. It will not be hard."

He also learned to shoot that year. His Uncle, despite a latent fear of his ward that he had never been able completely to dismiss, with a memory of Edward's sixth and ninth years, and his angers, and the real cause he had given Edward in his twelfth year, decided he would rather be shot by intention than by accident, and sent a marksman to teach him. But both guilt and disinclination kept him away, and he rationalised his behaviour as being safest for both himself and the child. He sent money regularly, but he sent no more gifts, and he did not write.

Edward's fourteenth year passed in much the same manner as his thirteenth. He received a gold watch for his own from the Earl, but no other word or sign that his existence was known. He read Euripides and Sophocles with his tutors, and continued his studies in Homer. He rediscovered the book of plays his Uncle had read to him when he was sick, and he reread those, and read *Macbeth* which interested him only because of the nearness of that country, and his own name, the Vicar having told him his line came from the Siward who had defeated Macbeth. He read *King Lear,* which particularly horrified him and which he did not like, and *Hamlet, Prince of Denmark,* which he did, and read many times. With *Measure for Measure,* it became and remained his favourite play. When the Vicar asked him why, he answered, "Because they think, this Angelo and this Hamlet, they may do wrong, but they know they do when they do. Their eyes are open to themselves and to their natures, and they are not deluded by them. That is important, I think." He began in the next Autumn to read certain of the *Dialogues* of Plato with his tutor, and privately by himself the *Symposium,* which spoke too clearly to him. He often thought of his Uncle but he did not know where he was. He knew indirectly that his Uncle could not be in France, for war had been redeclared between England and France and a new concept of economic and commercial blockade was in effect, but the world outside of his home did not touch him. He rode, he shot with Ross, he slept restlessly at night, and he grew taller.

In his fifteenth year, which passed much as his fourteenth had, Edward did not have any word at all from the Earl, nor did the Vicar. The bank again sent money, with no instructions or communications to follow it. The Estate was left to its agent and to its own devices, and all those on it. Edward did not forget the Earl, but he thought of him less pressingly and gave his mind to his work which had become more demanding. For Edward it was a quiet year, spent in mental discovery and reflection, but for the world it was not. That Spring, Napoleon became Emperor of France. In accomplishing this, in March he had had the young Duc d'Enghien, hardly thirty-two, last Bourbon prince of the house of Condé and much beloved, kidnapped in foreign territory in Baden, brought to Vincennes and summarily shot in the night on dubious charges a few hours after his arrival and immediate brief court-martial. Less spectacularly, he had had the generals who opposed him imprisoned, and one strangled there in his dungeon cell. Pitt was recalled in May to the prime ministry, under the country's fears of imminent invasion. Napoleon continued to encourage the United Irishmen visiting him in Paris with talk and promises, despite the abortions of the three earlier French attempts to land in Ireland before Napoleon's accession, feeding these fears. He had already had his medal of victory struck to commemorate his taking of London, but Edward knew little or nothing of these things, or of Napoleon's encampment on the coast at Boulogne.

In his sixteenth year his fate came upon him in the form of an itinerant evangelist and preacher, ordained like the Vicar but now gone into the particular persuasion of Wesley, whom he had known and who had also known Edward's father. He had come to spread his particular word in the North, continuing Wesley's work there, in the Societies Wesley had begun, but he had not expected to find the son of his friend, with the face of an angel and a mind as mature in learning and in theology as his own, despite his childishness. Edward had met him, as the minister went about his work, on one of his long walks, and discovered that this man spoke much as his father had. Recollections, that time had finally pushed back and somewhat dimmed, poured in upon him. The text was "Ho, everyone that thirsteth, come ye to the water!" He went up, after the evangelist had ceased speaking to the small handful of people about him, and addressed him, so pertinently and with such sympathy the minister asked his name particularly.

"You are Edward Clare Armstrong," he repeated wonderingly, and yet not with amazement, for it seemed to him suddenly only right and natural he should be. "I knew your father. You are George Armstrong's son."

Edward, moved by a force he did not understand, dropped to his knees, and bowed his head, and kissed the circuit rider's hand.

"I want to go with you, when you go," he said. "How long will you be near my house, in this town?"

The minister shook his head. "I do not know. It is as God calls me to do."

"I hope then He will call you to stay until I can receive a reply from my Uncle, for I cannot go without his permission."

"A man shall leave his mother and his father, and shall cleave only to me," the minister said, as to the field at large.

"I know that," Edward said, "but nevertheless I have pledged to my Uncle I will not run away, and even though this is a running to, not a running from, I cannot go from him to come with you until I hear from him."

"And what if he says you *no?*" the minister asked, finding himself drawn strongly to the earnest young boy.

"I shall come anyway," Edward said, "for I am determined to leave. I had not seen my way clearly before, but now I do. But I must tell him." It did not occur to him his Uncle might prevent his going in any way except by his displeasure, and if his displeasure was strong, by a cutting off of his funds. But he could not imagine his Uncle minding, since it would soon be four years since his Uncle had seen him, or since he had come North, and he was only his Uncle, though on which side Edward realised suddenly he did not know, and his Uncle had himself told Edward he was his guardian most reluctantly.

He wrote a long letter to his Uncle that evening, attempting to explain the revelation and the grace that had fallen upon him so suddenly and yet, as he saw, so foreseen and so inevitable. His plans and his wishes were more definite, and he expressed them clearly and, he thought, reasonably. He prevailed upon George to take the letter the next morning to London and to deliver it into his Uncle's hands, or if he were absent, into a means of reaching his Uncle as quickly as possible.

While he waited, he continued to visit the circuit rider, and to converse with him, and in that time, the minister, perceiving the extent of his find, grew more anxious to have him. In his eyes, the boy had no further need of University training, being well trained to read and to speak, knowledgeable and conversant in many subjects, widely read in general and thoroughly grounded in Scripture. When he discovered Edward could sing, and to some degree play, he taught him certain other of the hymns of Charles Wesley, and urged the boy to firmness of resolve, for from what he had heard of the Earl, he privately did not believe the Earl would lend his blessing to the enterprise.

"The Methodists do not want you: but you want them," he said to him in Wesley's words: "You want the life, the spirit, the power which they have: not of themselves; but by the free grace of God. You want that deep communion with the Father and the Son, whereby you are enabled to give him your whole heart; to love every man as your own soul, and to walk as Christ also walked."

"I want it indeed," Edward said, even as he knew he wanted "the recovery of a single eye and a clean heart" that the minister had preached on, and he knew it was true in both senses, that he desired it and that he lacked it.

"You are a child of God, Edward," the minister said, "and rightly dissatisfied with your life here. 'The soul of an immortal Spirit can be satisfied with nothing but seeing God.' There is nothing under the sun that can long satisfy a spirit that is so made for God."

Edward lifted his face, struck by the truth he felt in those words, a question in his eyes.

"Those are Wesley's words," the minister said. "I have never forgotten them. They are much like Augustine's: 'We are everywhere restless, until at last we come to rest in thee.'"

The minister seemed to have perceived something of Edward's unspoken and unacknowledged reservations, for he chose his words as if to strike directly on them: "Thou shalt worship the Lord thy God, and him only shalt thou serve," he said. And another time he looked at the boy almost severely, and said, again in Wesley's words: "'Unto him that hath,' and uses what he hath, 'shall be given; and he shall have more abundantly; but from him that hath not,' uses it not, 'shall be taken away even that he hath.'"

"It is that I am trying to do," the boy said simply, "and nothing else. Teach me how." Edward settled himself at the minister's feet, prepared to listen, ignoring the warnings his divided heart and his judgement persisted in sending out to him.

Edward's own doubts of his Uncle's approval, not expressed to himself, showed in the fact he had not spoken to his old friend the Vicar about his new friend, of his wish and his decision, or in fact to anyone. While the minister waited, he continued to speak to small crowds in the fields, one sermon particularly apt to Edward on the text: "O that thou hadst known, at least in this thy day, the things that make for thy peace!" He practised the new equivalent of the laying on of hands, now that the Methodists had separated from the Church of England conclusively, and privately spoke to Edward of his father and of his own experiences. He himself was not ignorant, being able to read both Hebrew and Greek.

"I was seventeen," he said, "when I first began to ride circuit. I never had travelled alone before, so I had a long lonesome trip across some dreary country. I had no one to encourage me to go, but there was not wanting those to advise me not to go, as I was sufficiently educated to meet the demands of life. I joined the Methodists when I was thirteen, in a schoolhouse. It was Saturday night, at the close of the services, my brother and cousin were shouting when the Spirit of the Lord came upon them. I was seated on a high seat at a writing desk when the power came upon me. I sprang from the seat on the floor and gave God the glory with no uncertain sound. But soon after, the Devil led me into doubts and finally to sin, so I turned back to the weak and beggarly elements of the world. Although the Devil had gained a victory over me, as I see he has never over you, Edward, my dear son in God, it wasn't final. I began to pray God for such a victory over the world, flesh, and the Devil, that I might never doubt again. I thank God that He gave me just such a blessing as I needed. It was a glorious experience, as our Wesley said, 'strangely warming.' All doubt and fear were removed and I had a full sense of the pardoning grace of God. I shouted nearly all night. While in this blessed experience I was called to preach the Gospel. My call was as sensible to me as any experience I have ever had. I knew the moment and time and the place. From childhood, like you, Edward, I felt empressed to preach. Now, at eighteen, I was licensed to exhort. My first text that same month was from Revelations 6:17: 'For the great day of his wrath is to come and who shall be able to stand?' Three months later, I was licensed to preach. With God's blessing, Edward, and I hope with your Uncle's, so shall you be too, for I have never met a young man unlicensed and uninstructed so full and so apt of what is needful. I think in truth I must have been called here for this meeting."

They were seated on the ground, as they talked, in the foothills where the circuit rider had ridden out to see the colliers, whom he had so moved with his words that the tears falling from their eyes had made white channels down their blackened cheeks, and evening overtook them. It was an evening Edward never forgot, as they rode back; it remained printed entirely against his memory, like the black trees of the hill against the bright lavender sky, and glowing like the barren hill across the vale that had taken the soft bright colour of the afterglow to itself, and shone gold even after the sun itself had gone; and like the young man Wesley had spoken to, "he wished it was all real."

The Earl did not answer Edward's letter. He returned with George himself, and from his face, Edward realised he should have foreseen he would. His heart sank within him at the sternness he read there. His Uncle's face seemed harsher and older than he remembered it, and his plan which had seemed so clear and reasonable to him did not seem so easy now to put into effect under his guardian's expressionless eyes. His Uncle raked him with those cold eyes and passed him by, addressing himself to his groom about his horses. His limp was unusually pronounced, but he seemed in his long caped driving coat and his high hat as tall to Edward as he ever had, despite his own growth.

He waved Edward aside, both his eagerness and his problems, with a rebuff of his hand. "I am tired, Edward," he said in a voice without warmth. "I have ridden a long way and I have other affairs more pressing. I will see you this afternoon, and you may talk to me then, if you still wish to."

Edward haunted the upper gallery in a fever of impatience. His Uncle had a light lunch brought to him in his study, and talked with his agent, and with other members of his household and a gentleman unknown to

Edward. Finally, near three, George brought a message to him his Uncle would see him.

The sight of his Uncle, so familiar and so strange, seated again behind his desk as though he had not been absent from it for four years, left Edward suddenly tongue-tied. For the first time in his life he found himself speechless with shyness. The Earl was reading a paper, which he with reluctance put aside. He seemed to wait for Edward to speak, and did not help him even by asking him to sit down. When he saw Edward was not going to speak, he said in an unpromising voice, "I received your letter, Edward."

"Did you read it, Uncle James? Did you read it carefully?" Edward asked, impatience overmastering his shyness.

"I read it with extreme care, despite its length and the immoderate haste with which it was written and the incredible sentiments it contained. I trust by now, on reflection, you have thought better of it, Edward, and wished you had not sent it."

Edward flushed, but he ignored his Uncle's opening. "I am sorry my letter displeased you, Uncle James. You must not have understood me. Didn't I make myself clear?"

"You made yourself very clear, Edward, and now I shall make myself clear." He tapped a long finger gently against the lid of his snuff box. "What you propose, Edward, is preposterously out of the question, now or at any time while you remain under my guardianship. I should have thought you would have seen that yourself. It is also impossible, for I have already arranged for you to enter University College at Oxford in the Michaelmas term." The Earl did not see fit to mention that, on receipt of Edward's letter, he had persuaded the Head of the College, whom he had known, to take Edward at an earlier age than was customary, and a year earlier even than he had himself intended, although he had always wished Edward to take his degree before he left his guardianship. "I came back not to talk to you about your letter, whose absurdity a term at Oxford will show you, I hope, but to see that you are properly tailored and equipped, and to take you down myself and install you in your rooms. I have persuaded Weston himself to come here to measure you, and we will pick the suits up in London."

At his Uncle's sign, the gentleman Edward had briefly seen rose from a chair where Edward had not observed him and where he had been studiously ignoring their conversation, and took out his measures. Edward's breeding forced him into embarrassed silence, and with a reproachful look at his Uncle, he submitted himself to the tailor's skilful hands, and the anticlimax of the discussion of materials and colours in which he refused to take more than polite interest. The business seemed interminable to him, before Weston left. His Uncle seemed to expect him to leave too, and turned back to his letter, and looked up with some annoyance to see Edward still stood by his desk.

"Well," he said testily, "you may go, Edward. I have nothing more to say."

"But I have, Uncle James," Edward said desperately. "I don't want these suits, though thank you very much, and I don't want to go to Oxford, even though Wesley himself went there. I have studied things for years here, ask the Vicar, ask my tutors."

"I have. I know you have," the Earl said almost gently, "but you have not learned everything. I want you to proceed with your studies. I think you should."

"I don't want to anymore. I am tired of being of no use. I want to be about my father's work," he said, unconscious of the several ironies of his familiar words.

The Earl looked up then, and put aside his letter and held out his hand.

"You had something in your hand when you came in, Edward. Was it something you wanted to show me?"

Edward took out of his pocket several small pamphlets and gave them across the desk to the Earl, who lifted his glass and fingered through them delicately.

"These are sermons by George Armstrong," he said in surprise, "by your father. How did you come by them?"

"I have been trying to tell you, Uncle James. Mr. Davenby had them and he gave them to me."

"Mr. Davenby? Who is he?" asked the Earl.

"I don't think you read my letter at all, Uncle James. He is the minister who knew my father."

"Oh," said the Earl, "the Methody," dismissing him with light contempt. "Well, I will keep them for you, Edward." He laid them down on his desk, and took up his letter again. At his ward's passionate expression of outrage, he pushed Edward's hand back, and said, "I don't wish to hear any more about it, Edward. The matter is settled."

"But it *cannot* be," Edward cried. "Don't say that, Uncle James. Why, you won't even listen to me, you haven't heard a word I've tried to say, and you haven't let me even say very many."

"I have been listening," the Earl said with weary patience, "believe me, I have been." He looked at his ward and sighed faintly. "Very well, Edward, if I must, I must. I am listening now. What is it then you feel you have to say to me?"

Under his tired, cold stare, Edward's ardent impetuous words withered and died. "I have said it all already after all," he said dully. "It will make no difference, anyway, will it, what I say?" His Uncle shook his head. "Oh, Uncle James," he cried, suddenly pleading, "I am no use here to anyone at all, not even to myself. Let me go and be of some use to someone."

"Does this mean so much to you, Edward?" his Uncle asked slowly, with both interest and distaste, but his voice again surprisingly gentle.

Edward nodded, unable to speak.

"Then you will have to postpone it, that is all, Edward, and see if it will stand the test of time, until you can do as you like. Until then, I do urge you to moderate your raptures, for both our sakes, for I am unaccustomed to them; please to moderate this enthusiasm I find so alarming in you."

"But Mr. Davenby will be gone," cried Edward desperately, ignoring his Uncle's hand put up suddenly, as though to shield his eyes. "He has stayed longer than he intended, waiting to see you."

"To see me?" asked the Earl in astonishment. "Whatever for? I don't wish to see him."

"About my going with him, of course, Uncle James. He has to leave, he is on circuit."

"Well, there will be others," the Earl said indifferently. "You will have—" he counted quickly—"five years to find another like him. It will not be hard." He lifted his tired, weary eyes. "I have considerable reason to mislike and mistrust evangelicals," the Earl said, looking directly at Edward, and for once speaking directly to him, with no mockery and no condescension in his voice. "Sit down, Edward," he added with a sigh. "I am going to try to talk to you, though God knows what use it will be," he added with a second sigh. He waited while his ward found a chair, and brought it nearer his desk.

"I am much older than you, Edward, as I daresay you have noticed, and I have seen enough and heard enough to give me cause for this mislike and this mistrust. I am not alone in it, it is not unique with me, and it is not an idle whim based on imagination or mere speculations. If your ministerial father and his Wesley were cheerful, logical, contained men they were the exceptions, and that very Wesley for all his intentions and his efforts, if what they say is true that he did try, could not prevent the separation or the inner factions and excesses. My God, Edward, I should take you to hear Jeremiah Garrett preach, except I think I could not bear to go within earshot again by intention. Nothing, not even the opening of your eyes, could drag me to it." He stopped and looked at the boy, and any levity left his voice.

"Edward," he said, his voice holding a note of pleading, hardly audible, yet there, "it is not the religion of our class—not yours, not your mother's, and it should not have been your father's" (the Earl ignored the quick angry loyal look that came in Edward's face) "and it is certainly not mine—and you cannot escape that knowledge and that fact for long, I think you really cannot. It is my fault for leaving you so long in isolation except for servants. I would have brought you *Humphry Clinker* to read, had I thought in time, to open your eyes just a little. Its crudities would be too much for you, you do not know what you think you want." He glanced at the boy's closed face, and his voice paused, but after a moment he continued as if he had not stopped.

"But it is not only that I so deplore. The madhouses are full of evangelicals of this and all these divisions who could not bear the strain imposed upon them. I know. I have seen them, and I have heard them. It is ridiculous and absurd to me for anyone to teach and to praise this constant listening for unseen voices and unseen guidances—it induces a dangerous self-accusatory vein and a resultant melancholia in too many. The general nature cannot bear it well, and certain natures not at all. George Crabbe has seen this, as a doctor and a curate, in his parish, and he deplored the trend. Have you read his accounts with your Manchester tutor, Edward?" (Edward shook his head mutely and unhappily.) "I must find a copy of 'The Village' for you then. And here is Wilberforce, standing alone now, fighting in Parliament with Pitt and his oldest friends. He was reared in Methodism," the Earl said, looking at Edward narrowly now, and with an uncertain and assessing quality in his glance, "and though he left it, as a young man, it is a taint that one does not easily elude, and it seems in such men to recur in some form like a fever or a disease. He had some new conversion, some years back, and nothing but his conscience sways him now." He spoke with some bitterness. "God knows, though, that may become ambition's quickest route. I believe Knox, that is one of your former Methodees and one of Castlereagh's Irish secretaries, once, exaggerates your force in government, on its side or against it. I pray he does. These men will leave nothing alone, they are worse than Whigs (and I say that who esteem Fox personally, as all must). But Wilberforce is not Fox. This old man Newton has Wilberforce entirely in his hand. You know of John Newton? No? Who ran slave ships and now is reformed and converted, and preaches people mad at Olney? He has preached poor Cowper mad, but he did not begin it, those fools at Huntingdon Chapel did. Did I not send you 'John Gilpin' one Christmas? The little ballad about his ride?" (Edward nodded.)

"Cowper was a lawyer, before he was a poet, and a man of much sweetness and much intelligence and much charm, but he lost his law appointment and was bedevilled with Methody visions and melancholia and he tried many times to put himself out of his misery in the world before that end finally came to him. I should not tell you that history. He came of a clergy family," he said, eyeing Edward. "I really cannot abide this turn of religion. Whatever and wherever it touches, men cannot get their proper work done." He observed Edward's face and sighed. "You have not understood anything of what I have said to you, have you, Edward?"

"Not very much, Uncle James," Edward said, having tried to listen patiently, "and it does not seem to me very much to the point. It is now and I am myself, and it is my life I have to lead, and it is this way I want to lead it." He was earnest rather than tactless, and for once, intent upon another subject, unobservant. He did not notice the angry flush that appeared faintly beneath the cheekbones of the Earl's otherwise unchanged white face, and the withdrawal of his eyes. "I don't want to wait. I don't want to find another, I want to go with him."

"I do not see the difference between them," the Earl remarked coldly.

"But he knew my father," Edward said, his eyes pleading.

"I have had enough, Edward," the Earl snapped with sudden sharpness, "of this talk. Let us make an end to it now. I have listened to you, as you asked, and I cannot see any reason to continue this discussion, which I find both boring and distasteful. Although I appreciate your keeping the name of our Saviour out of it, as you Methodees generally do not."

Edward stood quietly, looking at his Uncle, his frank face suddenly unreadable, gauging his Uncle's words.

His Uncle looked up. "Well?" he said impatiently.

"I am going to go, I think, Uncle James," Edward said slowly.

"You cannot," his Uncle said simply.

"I am not asking anymore for your money or your help. I am sorry to go without your permission and under your displeasure, and I suppose it means I cannot ever see you again."

"You need not suppose that yet," his Uncle rejoined curtly, "for you are not going anywhere now, or later, except to Oxford, as I said."

Edward shook his head. "No, Uncle James. You are surely mistaken.

Even if you do not want me to, I cannot see how you can stop me. I am not a little boy any longer, and I am not helpless."

"Do you not?" said the Earl. "You are under age, and I will have this man, this preacher fellow, accused of seduction and kidnapping and arraigned."

"You would not!" cried Edward, shocked and momentarily shaken. "It would not be true."

"I will think it is,' said the Earl, "and I will do it. Try and see if I do not."

Edward paused uncertainly: "What am I to do then?" and the Earl pressed his advantage.

"I would have you go to your room, and stay in it, Edward, until this—this Methody is gone. That is all now." He turned away from Edward, and began to read the paper at his desk.

"And what if I say I will not go to my room, Uncle, and that I will go with this man? I am not afraid of you, and I doubt he is. Do you think you own me? I know my mother could not have meant that. I am not just a horse to be fed and watered and stabled and trained, I need so much more, Uncle."

"There is no point in our continuing this conversation, Edward. I will have Ross put you in your room if you do not go," the Earl said, not looking up to see the shock on Edward's face, "and he can do it, I think. Which way is it to be?"

"I will go," Edward whispered, his face white. He looked at his Uncle with a strange expression, and he said slowly, "I should have known better than to ask you. 'It is folly to seek grace at a graceless face.' "

"To do *what?*" asked the Earl in surprise rather than anger, lifting his head.

"That is what another Armstrong said to another James, when the James would not release him."

"I daresay he was thrashed for it too, for his impudent tongue."

"No," Edward said, "no, he wasn't, Uncle James; he was killed. He was hung on a tree, and all his men, on live trees, when he came in innocence to see him. It was King James of Scotland who had it done. He was unjust too." He turned on his heel and left before anything more could be said.

He went to his room, and stood there. He looked about it, at his books, his things he had gathered or been given, then he took the pistol he had been using for practise, and returned to his Uncle's study, his face set.

His Uncle, looking up as the door shut, saw Edward before him, the pistol in his hand pointed at the Earl's chest. His own face whitened, but he gave no other sign that he was alarmed.

"I thought better of you than this, Edward," he said quietly.

"Did you?" asked Edward, his voice pointed, as pointed as the pistol's barrel.

The Earl ignored the implication. "Give the pistol to me, Edward," he said calmly. "It is not yours, I think."

"I mean to go, Uncle," Edward said, "and if you will not tell me I may go, and that you will not come after me, I am going to shoot you dead, now, with this pistol, so that I *can* go away. For if you won't let me go, I know you will somehow bring me back."

"You are gone purely mad, Edward Clare," his Uncle exclaimed, and his voice seemed unworried for himself. "How can you imagine you can be a minister of God, or even go walking with one, if you have killed another human being, even such a useless one as me, to do it. Think again!" But his eyes watched Edward closely, and his mouth was drawn.

"I have thought," Edward said, "and I know that I cannot, but if you will not let me go, I cannot either, so either way I have lost. But I shall at least kill you for it, which is what you have always thought I would do," he added savagely.

His Uncle did not deny it. "Sometimes I have, and I see I should have today. But you have the pistol at all because of me. I wish you would put it down."

"No," Edward said. He took the watch his uncle had given him, that he had been holding in his left hand, and walked nearer the desk and put it down on it. "I need the pistol, but I don't want this anymore," he said. "I don't want anything you have given me, just my own, and I don't want you anymore either, ever anymore."

The Earl was at a loss what to do. The distraught look on Edward's face, and the wild, yet dead look to his eyes, made him believe Edward would shoot at him, if he moved, and probably even if he did not, but he did not know how accurate a shot Edward might have become. If Edward was inaccurate, or his aim thrown off by his emotions, to move or duck could be as deadly as to stay still, which also looked to be unsafe. He wasted none of his attention berating his overconfidence in his power over Edward, it being wholly concentrated on the black ring before him. His own pistol lay in the drawer near his hand, but he did not dare move his hand by so much as a finger toward it.

He spoke directly to Edward's left and a little behind him: "Ross! I am glad to see you!" As Edward, startled and taken off guard, turned his head, the Earl's hand leapt to the drawer and his own pistol, and he had fired at the gun in Edward's hand, sending it spinning.

"If you move towards it, or move at all," he said to Edward, taking out his second pistol, and standing up, "I will not kill you, but I will blow off the fingers of your right hand." He walked towards the gun on the floor, his gait very pronounced, and picked it up, as a knock came at the door. He limped to the door, his pistol still held on Edward, and sent George away with the curt explanation that he had discharged a pistol in cleaning it. He walked back to his desk, his eyes hard.

"To be caught by such an old trick shows how much you need my care," he said. He deliberately then turned his back on Edward, on his shocked, passionate, angry, yet beseeching face, and put the three pistols in the drawer of his desk where he had put the pamphlets he had taken from Edward.

"Please give me back my things, Uncle James," Edward said, his voice unsteady.

"No, Edward," the Earl said, "I will not."

"Why not?" asked Edward passionately. "They at least belong to me."

"I do not like their influence upon you, Edward," the Earl said, only briefly turning his head. "I will keep them for you until you are older."

"You will throw them away!" Edward accused him, almost crying, "I know you will."

"Perhaps," the Earl said provocatively. "We shall see." He shut the drawer with a snap, and locked it, the key in his hand, his back again to Edward, invitingly.

On that ill-advised moment, he chose to put what trust irrationally yet lingered in him. He felt the boy spring at his back, his hands reaching for the key, as the Earl had thought he might. His own hands, not much surprised and not unprepared, easily threw Edward off, and with a ruthless experience he proceeded to mill the troubling boy down without mercy, cutting his resistance quickly, but not leaving off until he had rendered him wholly senseless, his furious pitiless face the last thing Edward, his rebellion routed into terror, saw bearing down upon him, his hands raised futilely to protect himself.

The Earl was very strong, despite his lamed foot, and well-conditioned, for it was a fashion for gentlemen of leisure to keep themselves so, beneath the seeming feminine delicacy and elegance of their dress. He picked Edward up fairly easily, and adjusted his weight over one shoulder. Unlocking a door in one wall of his study, he went through an unused hallway and then down a series of narrow steps into a part of the house level with the kitchen, but also unused. He stopped in front of a small door, set closely into the wainscotting of the wall, not easily perceived, inserted a key into the lock, opened the door, and carried Edward inside and let him fall to the floor of what had been a priest's hole and mass-room when the house was built. He then relocked the door and left, without a backward glance. He proceeded to send his servants away on an unexpected two-day holiday, to their families or wherever they wished to go, had the house closed, and left himself. When Edward's friend in God came the next day to the door to find why Edward had not returned to see him, he found all the house shut. He rightly assumed Edward's guardian had received Edward's proposal with disfavour, and thinking they must have removed to London, he rather sadly went on with his circuit. The Earl visited friends and stayed away that first night, and the next day, and a second night, giving little thought to Edward's misery.

VI

After a night alone with his aching face and body, Edward was reduced quickly to complete submission, but no one came to receive it. He did not know where he was, and after the second night, in darkness and in filth, without food or water, his trust that his Uncle would return for him in his own time began to be shaken. On the second morning, the Earl returned, and removed a tile that covered a square opening in the ceiling of the room that was also the floor of a small alcove in the passageway above it.

"Is it you, Uncle?" Edward's voice asked, from the dark, in a corner of the room. His voice was spiritless, and unhappy, and without much expression, but he spoke readily still to his Uncle, without sullenness, and with his customary fearless frankness.

The Earl stood for a few minutes by the stone without answering, and then he said, rather heavily, "Yes, Edward, it is I."

"I thought it might be," Edward said. A sigh escaped him from the darkness. "I could not believe you would leave me here like this and not come back for me, but when you were gone so long, I did begin to wonder, just a little, and to think you might, and yet what I did and what I asked did not seem to me so terrible, to have deserved this. What did you do it for, Uncle James? May I come out now?"

"No, Edward," the Earl answered. He moved as if to go.

"Wait, Uncle!" Edward cried desperately. "Please don't go, please don't leave me here like this alone anymore. I cannot bear it. What do you want?" As his Uncle still did not speak, the pleading desperation in his voice changed to despair, and he said in a tone his Uncle had not heard before, wholly flat, dull, expressionless, "I will do anything you want me to do. Anything at all. Only let me come out."

"I am going to get you something to eat and to drink," the Earl said. "I think you will want that." He heard a sound from the dark, but he could not tell whether it was a laugh or a sob, as he closed the stone.

When he returned and let down a basket on a string with water and a piece of buttered bread and cold meat in it and a fruit, he heard again the same sound. Edward made no move to receive the basket or take its contents.

"God, Uncle," he cried bitterly, "what do you think I am? A beast to feed me this way? Is there no door? Nothing else to this hole? Please at least come in and talk to me. I am not a wild animal, I will not spring on you."

"You did once," the Earl said implacably, "I have not forgiven you for it."

He heard again the curious sound that was neither a laugh nor a sob.

"You have just informed me, without my asking, that you would do anything I asked. Very well, Edward, I am asking you quietly to eat this food I have brought you. I will come back after you have had time to finish."

"Then may I come out?" Edward asked, with quiet desperation.

"Not yet," his Uncle said, "but it will be a start."

He returned a quarter of an hour later, but he was greeted only by silence from his pit. He pulled on the basket, and he found it empty when he had drawn it up.

"I did not think you were like this, Uncle, to play such games with me, it is as childish and as cruel as it is dreadful." He heard with amazement Edward's stern young voice chastise him.

"My nature is all three things," the Earl said. "You do not seem yet to be afraid of me, Edward, but you should learn to be before I give you true cause."

He heard the dry sob again in Edward's voice. "Is that what you want of me, for me to be afraid of you? After all these years, Uncle James?"

"Particularly after all these years," the Earl said. "Yes, I do, Edward.

And do not call me Uncle James anymore. That was all a pretense. I am not your uncle at all."

"What are you then?" Edward's voice came after a slight pause, but with no other comment.

"I am your guardian, Edward, until you are twenty-one. As you know, your guardian in law by your mother's request."

"Why did she choose you," the boy asked, with a new incredulity in his voice, "if you are not my uncle as you told me?"

"You may make your own guesses," the Earl said with some bitterness, "they will be as good as mine."

He heard Edward draw in his breath, where he had moved directly beneath the opening.

"That is five years away. You cannot mean to keep me here five years. You cannot, it would kill me. Have you gone mad?" His voice was wild with sudden foreboding.

The Earl laughed, though not very pleasantly. "No, and no. You do not think so, Edward, or you would not trouble the air to ask me."

"What do you want then of me? Do you want me in your bed?" the boy asked challengingly.

"Whyever should I want you there?" the Earl said, disowning without qualm all past such episodes. "God forbid."

"What, then?" Edward said, his boy's voice still strong and clear, ringing up out of the dark. "Tell me and I will do it."

"What I want is very simple, Edward. I want no more such scenes enacted me as that of two days ago, in these next five years. When you are twenty-one, if you still wish, you may then call me out to account for all your wrongs."

"I shall not wish to," Edward said simply. He paused. "What shall I call you if I am not to call you *Uncle James* anymore. I do not feel like calling you James. Are you my cousin?"

"No, Edward, I am not, nor do I feel like being called James. Must you call me anything? Yes, I suppose so. Do you know my name?"

"No," Edward's voice said simply, "except the one you disallow."

"My name," the Earl said, "is James Noel Holland. I am the Fourth Viscount Rockfort, and the Sixth Earl of Tyne." A breath sharply drawn in told that the names had not passed unnoticed. "Your mother called me Noel. My friends call me Rockfort or Tyne. Suppose you call me Holland, Edward, since you fall somewhere between the two. I do not use the name now—it should suffice."

"Holland," the boy repeated questioningly and without enthusiasm. There was a silence. Then Edward's voice came again. "I promise what you have just asked, Holland, and I will keep it. What then? Is that all?"

" '*Il dit me, il tien me,*' " the Earl said slowly. "Those are the words for a king's promise, and I believe you, Edward. No, that is not all," he added, his voice still inflexible.

"What else?" Edward's voice asked, not so steadily as before.

"You will stay here quietly for a week," the Earl said, "as evidence that you mean what you have said."

"Oh, God," Edward said, his voice breaking. The Earl heard him move, to sit down on the floor. He made little sound, but the Earl heard him sobbing, and the sounds came from further away.

"Quietly, I think I said," the Earl said inflexibly. He heard the boy catch his breath and take a drink of water, and then he was quiet, waiting.

"In two weeks," the Earl said, "the new term begins at Oxford. I want you to be there and to begin it, and put your mind to your work there as I order and direct it. I want an end to this ridiculous nonsense of your being a clergyman of any sort, and certainly of the sort you propose—and I do not want you to speak of any part of your life here while you are there, or of me."

"I promise you that," Edward's voice came in surprised relief. "That is not hard to promise, and I will keep it."

"I trust you will, Edward, for I trust the promises you make, and also, I shall quickly know if you do not in any respect. Scandals about me travel fast, and someone always tells me."

"I do not believe you are so scandalous," Edward's voice came clearly through the dark, "as you would have the world and have me to believe. Why should you wish to be thought ill of, even by those who think well of you?"

The Earl was amazed at the boy's fortitude, in his situation, but he only said acidly, "I do not like to be moralised at, by you, Edward, or by anyone, and I do not have to tolerate it."

"Then why lay yourself open to it, as if you did?" Edward asked.

"You will keep your thoughts, please, to yourself, Edward, unless I ask for them," the Earl said, less helplessly than he felt, at his unquenchable ward.

"Yes, Holland," Edward said, after a moment's reflexion, submissively. "I see I must do as you say."

"Take care, Edward," the Earl said with sudden viciousness that reached the boy, "I am not as harmless as I still seem to look to you. My fangs have not been drawn, and I will make you feel them."

He heard terror then in Edward's hitherto brave voice: "Only do not leave me here again for so long, Uncle," falling into the old address.

"I will come to see you once a day, Edward, until the time for you to prepare yourself to leave. You will also spend your holidays here, although I will give you light then, if you have work to do, as earnest of your promise." He heard the boy gasp, but he paid no attention. "I am tired of you, Edward," he said harshly, and viciously, "of your voice and your face and your impertinence and your threats against me, and I do not want to see you. But this is my home, and I will come here when I choose, without interference or interruption or fear of anyone. Do you understand me?"

"I understand you," the boy said with another dry sob, "I wish you would just let me go. I would never trouble to ask you again for anything."

"But I will not," the Earl said, "not until you are twenty-one."

"It is unnatural to treat me so, to treat anyone so," Edward whispered.

"My nature is unnatural, as unnatural as my foot. This is the reality of me. I have never said or shown in any real way it was not, I think. It is with this reality you will now have to deal, Edward, anything else was just play."

"Oh, God," said Edward softly, in a whisper, "I see I must. I cannot help myself." His voice broke again.

"I think you cannot," the Earl agreed, "and you are wise to see it." His voice suddenly rose. "Do you know where I have been, these last two years?"

"No," said Edward's voice. "No, I don't know."

"I have been in St. Petersburgh, and do you know why? I was sent there because my presence in London had become an embarrassment to those with power to appoint me to that honour, and I had perforce to go. I, with my foot, shooting the black cock and the capercailzie in the black dawn in the black forests and the cold marshes of the frozen lake of St. Petersburgh to humour a court of savages, which they are, despite the civilisation of their language. My exile is finally allowed to end, I am allowed to withdraw from my position of honour which will fall on some other disfavourite or indiscreet, and I come home, to London, and before I have well recovered myself, to my own home, summoned here, to the scene you know. But I am, after all, at least master here, in these wilds. And what I have done to you is very little compared to what I saw done there, to their fallen favourites."

"I am sorry I have distressed you," Edward said sincerely, "I wish I could undo it."

"But you cannot," the Earl said stiffly. "It is done. You have revealed yourself in your true nature to me now, and I to you. It is too late." Refusing to be drawn into speaking longer, he pushed the stone back, and left.

Edward was hardly aware of the pressures on the Continent pushing in upon the Earl and his world. All August, while Edward sat quietly on the hillside talking theology, England had sat waiting in the South again for invasion, which instead, at the last moment, inexplicably, had spearheaded in the opposite direction towards Prussia. The Blockades had intensified, on both sides, and the Earl had seen on his return all his haunts taken from him by it, and his activities limited to his native and uncongenial island. The Armies of Austria and Prussia were at that actual moment joined with the French at Ulm, a battle which within the weeks that Edward entered Oxford they would have lost, leaving nothing to protect the city of Vienna from Napoleon. This news would be lightened somewhat by Nelson's victory at Trafalgar, just before the beginning of term, securing the British control of the high seas but with the loss of Nelson himself. But by December, the Battle of Austerlitz, under a sun as bright as Napoleon's fortunes, would have in effect given the Continent to Napoleon and have dissolved the power of the Third Coalition, and the Anglo-Russian Alliance the Earl had helped secure in April. "Roll up the map of Europe," Pitt would say, learning of the defeat at Austerlitz: "it will not be wanted these ten years." In January, Pitt himself would be dead. These events already cast ahead their disturbing shadows, acerbating a disposition already embittered. But these things Edward did not know.

That afternoon, late, although he was no longer clearly aware of time, he heard the tile removed again, but it was not the Earl returning, as he hoped, but Ross, who brought him two blankets, and his supper, and arranged with him how he should keep himself clean.

"Tell my Uncle for me I think he is a coward," Edward said, "and if he will not come to me himself, then will he please send George, instead of you."

"I would cut your tongue to size, if I were your Uncle," Ross said, but he delivered Edward's message to the Earl.

Edward was awakened the next morning by the sound of a door being drawn back near him, whose existence he had not discovered. It opened, letting a little more light in, by which he saw his Uncle, who entered and closed the door partly to behind him. He rose to his feet, and stood waiting.

"I am not a coward, Edward, at least, I think I am not. I simply have other affairs besides yourself. But I thought I would relieve you of your delusion."

"Is Ross outside?" asked Edward.

The Earl shook his head. "I am by myself. And I am unarmed. That takes no courage, Edward. You gave me a promise, and I remember it."

"If you trust me, here, alone, where you have abused me"—the Earl's eyebrows raised, faintly visible in the dim light—"why must I stay here, why can't you trust me in my room?"

"It pleases me to keep you here, Edward," the Earl said simply. "And so I do. That is all."

Edward sighed, helplessly and hopelessly. "Do you dislike me so much, Uncle?"

"I have asked you not to call me 'Uncle.'" The vicious displeasure of the Earl's tone eluded and passed over the boy.

"Holland, then. The name does not fit my tongue very well, or suit you. I did not think you did, despite leaving me so much alone."

The Earl walked over to Edward, and took his face in his two hands, and held it, looking at his features in the half-light, and then briefly, almost questioningly, he kissed his lips with his own. Edward, against his inclination, did not respond, or put his arms about the Earl in his old familiar way, but he began to tremble under the Earl's hands.

"You show an admirable restraint, Edward," the Earl said, "and I commend you for it, but you are stirred, as I am, I think." As the Earl kissed him again, more lingeringly, his lips suddenly hard and demanding, Edward's own parted, and let the Earl enter them, and his arms found themselves about the Earl. The Earl abruptly wrenched himself away.

"I am afraid for you, as well as of you," he said briefly, and left.

That evening it was George who brought his supper.

"Oh, George," Edward said with relief, "I am glad to see you."

"I am glad, too, Master Edward," George said simply, "I thought you might not be."

"Why not?" asked Edward. "Because my Uncle thinks I am a wild beast and treats me like one? I am still me, and you are still you, and my

Uncle—the Earl is still himself. None of us are changed. But I am just here, and I must make the best of it. We must all just get used to it. I have angered my Uncle, you know; he thinks I will shoot him, as he thinks I shot my father." He laughed a little. "He is mistaken, of course, but I cannot convince him of it, and I must admit, I went about it in the worst way. He thinks I am like Lucifer, with a pleasing exterior and a corrupt heart, but he judges me too much by himself. I cannot imagine why he should imagine I would be like him, in my nature, or worse. I am not at all like him."

"You must not say these things to me, Master Edward," George said, "and I must not listen to you, or I will not stay for you to eat your supper. But I do wish I had never sent your message for you. It was a bad day for you when I did that."

"What have I said you don't know?" asked Edward. "We must both do as my Uncle says, you because you are paid well to do it, and I—because I must. Oh, don't go, George, please. I have displeased you, too. I think I shall go mad here in the dark, you see, with nothing to do and no one to see or to talk to, just my thoughts. I won't say another word. I will eat my supper, and do just as you say. Only, please stay and talk to me. Tell me anything. Tell me what it is like in the world. I must be still somewhere in my Uncle's house, if you are here, and Ross is here, too, I think, though I cannot imagine where. No! I am quiet, see. Talk to me, please."

He was quiet, as he promised, and listened eagerly to George's quiet, shocked voice telling him of the way of things, although he did not once speak of the Earl. He ate slowly, to keep the footman who had also been his friend with him, but too quickly to suit him, for in a short while the footman regretfully had gone, and he was left alone again.

The next night Ross came again with his supper.

"Where is George?" Edward asked.

"He is not here," Ross said.

"Not here?" Edward repeated, dismayed.

"He has gone to London with your Uncle. Your Uncle took him to his house in London to be his footman there."

Edward stared upward at the faint square of light from which Ross's voice came down. To know that the Earl had removed himself completely away from him, that he was nowhere near, and that he had also removed George's friendly presence and left him to Ross's untender uncompromising mercies came near to undoing him as nothing had. After Ross had gone, he sat looking into the darkness which pressed flatly and vacantly back upon him, unable to think, unable to feel, until hours later in exhaustion he laid himself down on the blanket against the floor and covered himself with the other, shivering, sleep flying from his eyes as soon as he shut them, but too weary and too weakened to do anything but lie. He had a strange experience then that he had never had before. He had fallen off into a sleep of a sort at last when he started awake and saw with his eyes open the figure of a giant harrow bearing down upon him out of the darkness. He screamed in complete terror, like a rabbit caught beneath the teeth of the harrow that he had heard once in the field, but the image did not disappear, but hovered in the air, still threatening to drive over him. He put his hands out and shrank away, screaming still without knowing he did, and then leaped from his blankets and stood against the wall, pressing himself away, screaming then for help, for the Earl to bring him out, for George, for Ross, for any help at all, and for light, but no one heard him, and no light came. Gradually the image receded, and left him, and he came completely back to himself, wet with sweat, trembling.

He knew then he had not been awake, as he was now, and yet he had not been asleep either. His eyes had been open, and yet he knew now, his senses returned and rational, that however real the instrument had seemed, he could not have seen it in his darkness, even had it been there. He had never had such an experience before, and he did not know what to make of it, but he was afraid to go to sleep again, fearing it would reappear. He pulled the blanket around him and leaned back against the wall, as at bay, panting, sick and miserable and not wholly certain still there was nothing waiting to pierce him with its great teeth when his guard relaxed. When Ross appeared to bring him his supper, he did not speak, knowing he would break down and beg for relief and to be taken out, and knowing that Ross would never do it, even though he begged. He had begged Ross once to end a whipping, and he had not. He was both famished and nauseated, and he could not eat the dry food dropped down to him. He left it untouched in the basket, except for the water, and Ross took it away without comment.

The same experience recurred that night. As soon as sleep wrested his consciousness from him, he was jolted awake, as he thought, the image of the harrow again floating before him, and approaching him. He screamed again involuntarily, and ran from it again, pressing against the unyielding wall, but this second time his will and his rational self returned sooner. He stopped screaming, and stood, as at bay, facing the thing, watching it, until it began to retreat, shimmering, luminous, and to fade. He was broad waking, and he knew it, and yet the image stayed with him, and he watched it, knowing he was awake, knowing it was immaterial and not there, yet none the less visible before his eyes and able to terrify. "Why a harrow?" he thought, whispering the words aloud to himself, when he was alone. "Why that?" He wondered if this was the kind of waking vision Mr. Blake had had, and if it was, he hoped his had been more pleasant, less terrifying, and yet he had to acknowledge its particular beauty, even as it gripped and horrified, floating immaterially against the dark air. He wondered if it came direct from the Devil, with such a power to paralyse the will and to frighten. His senses believed it was there, and his will, while it lasted.

He was too upset to feel hunger, and his mind seemed unusually clear. He set it consciously searching, and his memory rolled back, and he remembered something he had forgotten. He had been three, perhaps younger even, able to climb, able to invent. He had wandered off to a neighbouring estate, and climbed into the hayloft, and had fallen out onto the harrow the fieldmen had been repairing for use on the ground, its teeth pointing up. But he had not been impaled, he had slipped between the great teeth, and stuck fast, badly scratched. His wails had brought the men running from their lunch, and they had discovered him, and gently prised him free. He heard the tender voice of one as clearly as if he spoke now: "Lookit the wee tyne bairn quwha' greetit caught amang the tynes." It was a Scotch voice, like Ross's, but he had not known that. "Do na greet, bairn, do na greet, the woruld's ful o grief n'tyne, and greeting wilna help it. Tha's na hurt, tha's wh'only scrapit, tha'll live to know more pain and tyne than this sharp rake. Tha Da'll birch thee, that'll be a start."

The voice laughed and scolded and comforted him altogether, and when he had been recognised and identified, had carried him home. When the Vicar had read him *The Harrowing of Hell,* his memory had stirred, but not revived. *Tyne:* he had thought only of the river flowing near, and its great flood in '71, but his memory had recalled the tines of the harrow, the sharp bitter raking points. He shivered and tried to dismiss the connection his memory made.

All that day hunger and thirst tortured and ravened him. That night he would have eaten anything resembling or promising to be food, but Ross had sent a crock of soup filled with meat and vegetables and barley, and a spoon and a fork, and he stayed with a lantern by the opening, letting the rays shine in. It was a two-tined fork, and Edward held it, gleaming, arrested, remembering his visions, and words came into his mind, their source forgotten: "to try whether they be sent of God or of the Devil." He would have drunk only half his water, thinking for the long hours ahead, had not Ross offered to refill his flask, and he put aside his bread and apple in his shirt to keep for breakfast. He was grateful, and he broke silence and thanked Ross.

He thought he would sleep easier, but his rest was again broken by visions. This time he lay quietly, and watched it unfold before him, the harrow moving across the field of air to a clump of wheat, the bearded tares half choked by the weed the farmers hated, strangle-tare, that climbed the corn and tangled it and choked it. Tyne-weed, his father had told him, when they had passed an unweeded unkempt field. "The wheat will die, unless the weed is removed from it, or unless the next harvest is sown in another uninfected field." He fell asleep, and the images of his vision repeated itself more coherently and realistically in his dream, and he answered his father in his own voice, "I cannot leave this field, it is where I must be," and he thought his father looked at him reproachfully and sadly. He had not thought of his father now for years. His distress in his sleep woke him, and he sat up, trying to shake it off, unable to completely. He put his hands about his knees, loosely clasping them, and laid his head against them, frightened and saddened by the warnings his unconscious mind persisted in sending him that he did not want to take.

Images began to fall into his mind, conscious images and memories, of a ride he had taken in the hills with George when he was thirteen, on the horse his Uncle, as he had thought him to be, had sent him. The hills were rimed with a thin sawtoothed hoarfrost, every twig, every fallen stick and leaf coated with it. It had taken away their scent, and they saw before them, they motionless and it motionless, a hill deer, a stag, with immense branching horns in the velvet, and a younger stag with hardly two points.

"The five-tined stag," George had said in awe, "look, Edward! He is showing himself to you. He is too wise to make an accident, he wants you to see him. All of us know he is here in the hills, but the gillies never come across him any more." The two deer had touched nostrils slightly, questioningly, and then side by side, without haste, had disappeared together into the farther shadows of the trees.

Edward shut his eyes, and lifted his head, the picture sharp before the eyes of his mind. His breath came fast, he did not know why, and for the first time, he began to weep, the tears running down his cheeks. "James Noel Holland," he thought. "Noel—oh God, that's Christmas"— and he pushed the name from him. Rockfort, Tyne. What harsh names.

Rock like these rocky higher hills to the Northwest, to crumble and abrade, a rock like Peter, on which to build. Or rock like the *peine forte et dure* of the Press-yard, to press the rebellious out of existence with its crushing weight. He had seen a picture in a two-penny history, of Major Strangeways, the highwayman, stretched out, the weights piled upon him, the onlookers adding the rocks in the courtyard to hasten his death and release his agony. He shivered and was cold. Strangeways had endured it, eight minutes, and died, to preserve his inheritance. Others had tried, but when they were laid down, they had cried for mercy instead, unable to bear an agony they had elected, and pled guilty, to die another way. He had found the picture in his Uncle's library, before the library was barred to him, the book inscribed: "Rockfort from Selwyn, deprived of his sport, 1772." His Uncle had explained the picture to him, when he asked, his lips curled, saying only, "This is no longer done," and then the history had disappeared. But Edward had admired Strangeways, and remembered him. The thing was to know what one's inheritance was, and to hold to that. But he had left his, he had given up his hope of it, he had thrown it aside. The pain of his Uncle's displeasure had been too much for him, he had been unable to bear its weight, and had cried to have it removed, and to die another way. He had not the stuff of martyrs in him.

He remembered suddenly the English martyr, strangled and burned at the stake for religious single-mindedness and his translation of the Testaments. Tyndale. His family had gone to Wales under the name of Huychins, but he was from the North. Had his family come from here, from the dale of the Tyne once? Were all these men here so harshly obdurate and persistent in their wills, directed towards or against Heaven? It was a formidable thought to a person like himself with so little will of his own. Well, he thought, with a brief show of spirit, I am an Armstrong, that counts for something surely, and a Clare. I could play games with those names too.

He began to laugh at himself, the tears still streaming down his cheeks, playing games with names and words that meant nothing. The reality of his Uncle suddenly presented itself to him, he saw his figure as clearly as if he stood before him, all games and names forgotten, and grief for his loss pierced him until he thought his heart would crack. He did not want to remember or to think anymore, and he buried his head in his arms, and slept as he had not for days, visionless, dreamless, timeless.

He would willingly have stayed in that condition until the time came for him to be let out, but Ross woke him to feed him, and his mind, once awake again, would not allow it. During the day it persisted in throwing like a magic lantern disconnected images against the dark of things that had happened in the immediate or the far-off past, until he wished for sleep to choke them off, but when he slept, he had terrible dreams. The least image set his mind off. Finally, he decided he must try to bring the chaos of his mind back into some order, and he pushed it back as far as it would consciously go, discovering to his surprise it had stuck fast, except for a few separate disjointed memories, at his arrival at his Uncle's house, and then slowly brought it forward. He pushed it unsparingly through the pleasant and the painful. He refused to answer Ross the night his memory travelled his twelfth year, and Ross had refused in return to leave his supper, saying only, "Eat crow, then, Edward, eat crow!" Hungry already, and brought to his senses, Edward would have eaten crow at once, but Ross had gone and closed the tile. Hunger, he thought, was a good breaker of rebellion. It was the last of his.

Unable to help himself, knowing now what fasting did to his brain, he braced himself, waiting the onslaught. It was not long coming. The homely phrase for humbling oneself that Ross had used brought back a memory he had forgotten, of the summer of his twelfth year, after his Uncle had left him. He had been angry almost all that summer, angry at himself, angry at what his Uncle had taught him to feel and then left him helpless to cope with, angry at his Uncle for leaving him and at himself for wanting his Uncle still. Shooting with the marksman and with Ross had been a relief, and he had thrown himself in it. Practise at the targets was not enough, and he had wanted to kill something, he had thought it would make him feel better to make something else suffer and for a change to inflict pain himself. He had shot a crow. It gave a terrible cry of pain, almost human in its surprised and agonized shriek, that had brought his heart into his mouth. He did not feel better at all for it. He had thrown the gun down, and run across the stubble of the field, panting, while the other crows had sat on the hayricks and the cross-fences, watching him. He was not a good shot, and he had not killed the bird. It lay, unusually large, its eye looking up at him, its beak open, and its blood dribbling from a corner onto the yellow stubble. When he approached, it looked at him helplessly and malevolently, attempted to beat at him with its beak and its maimed wings, and even as he watched, its bright eye began to film with pain and slow-approaching death. Ross came up, then, looked at him, trembling and horror-struck, and at the bird, trembling and dying and unable to die, in disgust at them both, and picked the bird up and wrung its neck. Edward had run blindly from them both, and been sick behind a haycock. Ross and the marksman came to him then and chided him gently, and told him he would become used to it, and also become a better shot, but he would not listen to them. He did become a better shot, but he never shot anything again, except the targets. In memory, looking back, it seemed incredible to him he could have ever wanted to kill the crow, but he had. He had wanted to enough to do it, but he had not imagined the afterwards and how he would feel then. He smiled faintly. He was hungry enough to have eaten a real crow now, that particular crow, any crow.

He began to remember lines from the strange little poems his Uncle had sent to him that Christmas. How had his Uncle been able to send them to him, untouched as he was? He could not understand it, that ability to do, to witness, to read, and yet to remain untouched. He said the lines over softly to himself, in the dark:

> *"For Mercy has a human heart,*
> *Pity a human face,*
> *And Love, the human form divine,*
> *And Peace, the human dress."*

He found neither Mercy nor Pity nor Love nor Peace in the man who held him. "Then what have I to do with thee?" he thought angrily and helplessly, knowing too well the answer to need to give it. He remembered parts of the little poem about the Clod and the Pebble. The piece of dirt beneath the foot sang of Love: it "seeketh not itself to please . . .

> *But for another gives it ease,*
> *And builds a Heaven in Hell's despair."*

The rock answered:

> *"Love seeketh only Self to please,*
> *To bind another to its delight,*
> *Joys in another's loss of ease,*
> *And builds a Hell in Heaven's despite."*

What did that mean? Nothing for him. He would willingly have been so bound, willingly have given away his ease, and to his shame he knew it, but his Uncle did not even wish that. He wanted nothing of him at all, he wanted him only to be nothing to him, the one thing he found it impossible to be. His Uncle did not think in such extravagant terms, nor did he himself, really; and he was after all not his Uncle. He was in fact nothing to him at all, nothing except his keeper. They were silly poems.

Holland did not *joy* in his loss of ease. He simply did not think of him at all. He, Edward, knew that now in all its terrible simplicity, and his emotions began to appear to him as tiresome as they did to his Uncle.

That night, when despite his hunger and his attempts to stay awake he did finally fall asleep, he had a frightening dream, as he had feared he would. The crow set it off. He was twelve years old again, and he was in such a stubble field, in the middle of a congress of crows such as he had seen once on his rides with George. A large crow like the one he had shot sat in the middle of a wide ring of hundreds of crows, and he stood beside the crow, but he was not aware of any advantage of size. He knew what it was about, George had explained to him how they had their leader, their wiseman, their judge, their laws, and their trials and executions. This time he was the offender, and they tried him, sitting gravely, occasionally one hopping into the air off the steel springs of his feet. They looked like a group of clergymen, he thought, and suddenly he saw that the big black priest-like crow beside him had the two white flaps of collar hanging down at his throat, like a Methodist clergyman, and instead of a bird's head, the face and head of his father. And all the crows in the circle had heads, like old forgotten faces in his father's congregation, and they were all looking at him, severely, gravely, reprimandingly, with grief, but unrelenting in their expressions, even his father's face. Then, his trial and sentencing over, the human faces faded again into nodding beaked birds.

They picked him up then, helpless among their numbers, and flew with him to a crag that was cold like ice, and bound him with briars and riveted him there with their beaks through the flesh of his hands and feet, clustering on his face, their unnaturally long beaks in his nostrils, his ears, his mouth, in all the natural orifices and clefts of his body, his body arching rigid against them, the black feathers of their black winged bodies on his face smothering and suffocating him. He could see others rise into the air and fall upon him, pulling out pieces of his flesh in their beaks, rising and falling, and all the time chanting a weird child-like rhythmic song:

>*Oh will you dine*
>*With the Earl of Tyne*
>
>*At 9 or 10*
>*If he is in*
>
>*Oh yes I will*
>*If he will call*

For me at 8,
I'll not be late.

Oh he will eat
You for his meat

And he will drink
You for his drink

Oh pray be slow,
Oh, do not go

You will be wine
For the Earl of Tyne

For he will dine
On you at Tyne.

He felt himself dissolving under their onslaught, falling through the stone crag, the birds still upon him, when all at once there was a deafening impact, that exploded about his ears, and the birds disappeared and disintegrated in little puffs of black feathers, and he saw a figure with a smoking enormous bell-like fowling piece that had his Uncle's face. And then he did not know whose face was there. The crag disappeared, and the briars, and his torn flesh was cool and free and whole and his own again, and he was again where he really was, sobbing in relief. He thought he was awake, and yet he knew he could not be, for there was a presence in the room that he sensed, though he could not see it.

"Ross," he said, sitting up, catching his breath, "did you come after all, with my supper?"

"No," he thought he heard someone say, "not Ross."

He was surrounded and encompassed suddenly by a feeling of complete peace and complete understanding and undemanding love, that filled him, until he forgot his hunger, and he understood, incredulously, without needing any longer to be told who was with him in the room. He cried out, without knowing he did, and dropped to his knees.

"O Lord," he cried, his breath catching, "is it you? Can it be you?" He shut his eyes and bowed his head. "O Lord," he whispered, "I am unworthy, leave me, I am not fit."

"It is indeed I," he thought he heard the gentle words. He heard his name called, he thought, and he opened his eyes, and he thought he saw a hand extended to him, stretched out for him to take. "Let me judge your unworthiness," he thought he heard the words, like a breath of wind over water.

But he shook his head, and refused to take the hand, and said wildly, to the dark air, "It is too late, O why did you not come sooner, why did you not help me, I have chosen now, I can't go back."

"I was always there," the words formed themselves in his mind, "but you would not look. Choose me, and I will help you."

"O do not ask me now," he gasped, "I cannot now. I cannot." The hand continued to be outstretched towards him, and he cried, more wildly yet, hardly knowing what he said, "I don't want you now, I want only Holland." He saw the extended hand withdraw. He hid his face in his own hands then, until he knew the room was again empty, and the sick pains of hunger struck him more forcibly than before. The face he had seen merged with his father's face, in his mind, and then eluded his memory, and he began to sob in hunger and in grief and loss.

He did not faint, and he did not die, and in time the time passed, and Ross came again and brought his supper to a polite, subdued boy who took it gratefully and without question, that evening and all other remaining evenings.

PART TWO

The Middle
(1 8 0 5 – 1 8 1 0)

⊙⋉⊙⋉⊙⋉⊙⋉⊙⋉⊙⋉⊙⋉⊙⋉⊙⋉⊙⋉⊙⋉

CHAPTER III

Oxford:
1805–1808

I

A T the end of the week Ross brought Edward out. He was not like himself at all. He came out quietly, but he had nothing to say. His eyes, grown used to the dark, blinked at the sudden bright light of the day, and he walked as if he were sleep-walking or in a dream. There was no visible trace left of the storms that had ravaged him, although he was thinner and whiter. He did not ask again, about his Uncle, as he continued from habit to think of him, or about George. He did what Ross asked him to do, tractably, but he did not ask to do anything himself. His face was not set in any emotion, and he did not seem to be particularly afraid, it simply had no emotion at all, and he kept his eyes lowered or withdrawn and did not look at Ross, or anyone. He answered if he were spoken to directly, in an unused sort of way, but otherwise he did not speak at all. Ross found himself feeling sorry for his charge, but he did not show it.

They made the journey down to London in virtual complete silence, but the air and the sights about him, of the countryside and the little towns, the motion and the colours, began to revive him somewhat into his more familiar self. His face began to resume its natural colour and mobility, and his eyes began to look about him with interest, at the reapers with their scythes and sickles, and the hayers with their forks, the packmen and their horses, and the fairs being set up, particularly when the landscape about them began to change into the tall trees of the South Midlands. Ross drove until late in the night, and broke the journey for several hours' sleep, and then roused his charge out of bed before dawn had fully broken. The traffic of all kinds of coaches and vehicles, open and closed, grew heavier and the waits at the toll-gates without the use of the Earl's crested coach to facilitate them grew longer, frequently blocked by moving flocks of animals being driven into London to be butchered at the Smithfield Market, Ross told him. He looked at the herds of cattle and sheep and felt sympathy with them, but he did not reply. As they approached London, constraint fell upon him again, and not even the sight of the city, new to him and beautiful in its distant shapes at any other time, could lift his spirits.

He was not allowed to go to his Uncle's house, which he had never seen, but was taken direct to Weston's where his Uncle met them. He greeted Edward with the perfunctory politeness of a stranger. His eyes veiled, the Earl inquired about the journey, whether he had lunched well, reintroduced him to Weston and checked the tailoring with a careful eye, but making no suggestions to offend the great man who in his way was as powerful as the King himself. Edward watched his Uncle's tall figure, graceful despite the deformity of his foot, negligently sauntering about the shop, surveying with his glass alternately materials, cuts of style, and his ward but with the close attention the Vicar might have given a disputed reading. His Uncle's cold and impenetrable civility withered and unnerved him, he felt neither he nor his history existed within it, and the shock of the public remeeting, when nothing could be said, penetrated his defences and shattered his small remaining pride. He thought he could not bear it, and that he might even cry, under the surprised eyes of Weston and his assistants, but because he must, somehow he did. He fixed his attention on the shine of his Uncle's gleaming high black Hessian boots, and wondered how it was produced, and if he was to have boots, but since he did not care, he found these thoughts not enough to help. He wished desperately he could hate the man who was not his Uncle, instead of feeling submerged under his helpless admiration and bewildered hurt.

As if he read his ward's thoughts in his shaken face, the Earl paused in his perusing march near Edward, and put his hand on his shoulder, and said in a low voice near his ear, for him only to hear: "You should hate me, Edward. Have you no pride? Get hold of yourself, can't you, and don't disgrace both of us in this way. You are at Weston's."

The unexpectedly intimate words, showing the Earl did indeed perceive Edward's emotions and that he was indifferent to them, and even scorned them, had an opposite effect than the Earl intended. The nakedness of Edward's face shocked even the Earl. He let his fingers linger for a moment longer as if appraising the shoulder of the coat, then he stepped back, dropped his glass, and said, "That one will do. Let's see the next," and strolled to the window, looking out while the change was accomplished.

When he once more glanced in Edward's direction, he saw that Edward had recovered himself somewhat. He gave the coat a quick inspection and passed it, with a compliment.

"My ward will be up this next term, Weston, I think I told you," he said, for diversion.

"Will he be in your own College, my lord?" Weston asked, his attention divided, primarily focussed on the piles of clothes.

The Earl nodded. "He is enrolled there. But he will find it different," he said, "than I did. It is harder now to take a degree than it was when I was there. I read, because I liked to, but I did not have to. The questions were not hard, two or three in private by an examiner who was not interested." He smiled a little, remembering. "I think I was asked who founded the University, and I gave the expected answer, about Alfred, although I did not think it was true. Edward will be there thirteen terms, at least, and then he will face a board of six examiners, although they may not all be there, and an audience of his peers and anyone else who happens to be interested. He will not just get his degree. He will have first a written examination to pass, but that is only the start. His oral could last for three hours, or even longer. And if he likes, he can elect now to try for Honours, not just a Pass. We had no such special thing."

"Do you think you will, sir?" Weston asked, addressing Edward directly, as his Uncle had not.

"I don't know," Edward said, "I hadn't thought. I don't know that I could."

"You should try, sir," Weston said. "Your uncle speaks well of you." He addressed the Earl. "I should have thought you would have entered Christ Church yourself, my lord."

"They had the better Organ," the Earl said, "but University had Chambers, then, and William Scott for Ancient History, who is Lord Stowell now, the judge, you know. I also knew Lord Eldon well, Scott's brother. He was very poor, then. He had lost his Fellowship because he had married and had to go into the town and train for the Bar as best he could, and give deputy law lectures and coaching for Chambers." His voice, soft and reminiscing about men Edward did not know, had this time the effect he intended, in relaxing Edward back into the world of the more commonplace. "They were also all Newcastle men from Tyne, and my father wished me to go there. It is in the High Street, but Edward does not know that, opposite Queens. I was there, Edward," he said, turning to the boy, "when the fire broke out, at four in the morning, two hours before Chapel, and burned down Queens. We did not all study then, I was asleep, but some did, and were awake, and saw it, and we all carried buckets of water. I was young, I enjoyed the excitement, but it was a bad fire. We carried out the Master's children, from their nursery in his wing." He continued to look at Edward, his thoughts unpenetrable. "Dr. Johnson was a friend of Chambers and the Scotts, he was often in our Common Room. You have read *Rasselas,* I believe the Vicar has told me?"

"Yes," Edward said.

"Did you talk with the Doctor, my lord?" asked Weston, interested.

"I listened," the Earl said with an amused reminiscent smile, "as most did, when Dr. Johnson spoke. It sharpened my tongue, I think. I was entered by my father as a Gentleman Commoner, which was more the practise then than now, and so I could sit at the High Table, if I liked, and go into the Common Room, when John Scott, as he was then, asked me." He smiled suddenly at Edward. "You will be spared one annoyance, Edward, of keeping a wig combed and powdered for dinner, and waiting on the Barber. Perhaps that's why we got so little done. Very tedious. You cannot imagine. But in appearance it will be much the same. The city gates had just come down, when I went up." He began to laugh suddenly, and with a familiar, mischievous look at Edward, he said, "I must tell you a story about Dr. Johnson and Robert Chambers. They were walking together, by a garden, into which Dr. Johnson observed Chambers made a practise of throwing snails over the wall, and Dr. Johnson rebuked—yes, it was that strong, as was his custom, he did indeed rebuke—Chambers himself for doing it. 'Sir,' said Sir Robert, 'my neighbour is a Dissenter.' 'Oh!' said the Doctor, 'if so, Chambers, toss away, toss away, as hard as you can.' It is true. John Scott told me the story."

Weston was too polite to look puzzled, as he was, not knowing Edward's father had been popularly thought of as a Dissenting minister, but Edward flushed with pleasure in his Uncle's warm tenderly teasing smile, forgetting in the comfort of the moment the bitterness and estrangement that he did not fully understand that lay between them, and that his Uncle had made clear he did not wish to forget; and forgetting also how easily his Uncle could put forward and as easily withdraw the charm of his manner, as quickly as the snails of his story their horns, when each chose.

The awkward moment in Weston's passed, and smoothed away, the Earl withdrew again into his frigid and aloof courtesy as soon as they had left that shop. His warmth might not have been. He took Edward to have boots fitted, at Walter's, quickly despatched that matter and arranged to have them sent when made to Edward at his College.

"Above all things, besides his coat," he said briefly to Edward, "a gentleman must look to the fit of his boots and their condition. I will see that my valet gives you a supply of his polish for your servant."

"But I am not a gentleman," Edward remarked to his Uncle's masked face. "I am not even an undergraduate yet."

His Uncle looked at him somewhat queerly. "Nevertheless I would have you behave as one, and you should have a good pair of boots. You will be known there as some connection to me."

"If you are embarrassed, why have you put me at your College?" asked Edward bitterly.

"If I were not embarrassed," the Earl said savagely and cryptically, "I would have put you at Christ Church, where I should have been myself, had my father not also been embarrassed. Be quiet, now, Edward," he said with unexpected viciousness, "and let us get through this as best we may." He was as angry with himself for allowing his emotion to betray itself, as with Edward.

But I do not care about being at Christ Church, whatever that may be, Edward thought to himself, I would rather be at the College where you were, and I am glad I am going to be, but he did not say the words aloud. They left immediately then. His Uncle had brought his full travelling equipage in style, crest, footmen, postillion, to Weston's. He had Edward's portmanteau exchanged to it, and his trunk of new clothes, and sent a groom he had brought to do it to fetch the older open carriage they had travelled down in to his London home. Edward had to ride inside the travelling coach with Ross while the Earl rode the principal distance of the way outside. He could have laughed at the absurdity of it, had he not felt so sad.

"Why are you in here? I don't want you," he said to Ross crossly, breaking their long silence.

"I am to fetch you back at Christmas, when your College is shut, and your Uncle wants me to know where you are," Ross answered with more patience than he might have.

Edward eyed him with hostility. "I don't want you to. I don't like you. Can't my Uncle or can't George?" Edward spoke with a rudeness unusual to him, and unconsciously used the older title.

"It is mine to fetch and yours to be fetched, Edward, and your Uncle may have chosen me because he knew we would neither of us find any pleasure in it."

"You are too familiar, Ross. I wanted George to call me Edward, and he would not. Why do you?"

"I am a Scot, that would perhaps be why. I own few masters, and you are not one."

"I wish you would ride outside. My Uncle is here now. I wish my Uncle would ride inside instead. I wish I had my horse, to ride outside, too."

"I would not think you would be wanting your Uncle inside with you at all."

"It is your trouble, Ross, that you don't think enough, for all your big head."

Ross compressed his lips. "That may be, but I am not all words like some. I don't threaten those I do not hate, and when I threaten I carry through."

"I shall take care with you, Ross, since I know it now." Edward looked at him angrily and then suddenly he laughed and held out his hand to Ross.

"I am sorry, Ross. I am out of sorts today. I think I must be frightened about this place I'm going to. I have lived so long in one house on one empty moor with so few people. Will you be friends with me? I don't like you very much, and I know you don't like me, but if we are going to have to make this ride together, and keep seeing one another, I would rather make peace with you than war."

"You are a strange boy, Edward," Ross said, not taking Edward's hand, "and I maybe like you better than I did, or than you think I do. I've always liked your spirit, I thought you were a plucky little boy, to stand up to your Uncle as you did. But I won't take your hand. I won't do that with anyone I may have to mistreat."

Edward continued to hold his out. "I don't mind, Ross. I know you can't help yourself."

"No, Edward," Ross said, shaking his head, "I am not your friend—

with me that word means something—and I don't want you or anyone thinking I am."

"Very well, Ross," Edward said with a faint smile. "Good enemies it is then." He turned away from him and looked steadfastly out of the window of the chaise, and did not try to speak to him again. However, just before they reached the town, Ross seemed to remember himself of something, and felt in his pocket.

"Your Uncle told me to give you this," Ross said, taking out Edward's watch, "he said you left it."

Edward's hand faltered and started to withdraw, and then, his eyes stinging, he put out his hand blindly and took the watch. He did not know what to make of the return and made in this way. He supposed his Uncle just thought he would need a watch.

It was late October, days when the sunlight already was falling in shafts instead of sheets, and the dusk came early, so that Edward did not see his first sight of Oxford as he entered. He smelled the dampness of a river, as they passed, he heard the rough stones of a town street underneath them, saw a doorway open, a figure weighing out something on scales on a table, a candle behind, and then he was at an Inn on a side of the town where he was to spend a night with Ross. His Uncle, he learned, had gone on ahead to stay the night at a Master's house, an old friend.

Edward did not sleep well, and he was dressed and had breakfasted long before his Uncle came at eleven. He had seen the swans wake up on the river, himself sitting on the lawn under the great trees behind the Inn, quietly, before even Ross was up. He had watched the grey steal into the black of the sky, and the stars go out, and he felt the dew even with his cloak and a sudden intense chill, as if night were making its last protest before the sun rose. I wonder why it should be coldest just before the dawn, he thought to himself. I wonder if I will find that out here. The night was warm compared to this moment. As he saw the rays streak upwards across the sky, hitting the clouds, the swans woke up out of their white floating balls. What a racket they make, he thought with amusement, and how conceited. "Swans are up!" they say. "Everybody wake! Swans are up!" Are we all like that? He felt better, more peaceful, more like himself, than he had for a fortnight, even longer. Even his relationship with his Uncle seemed to have faded briefly from his consciousness, and a kind of healing soothed his raw, hurt nerves. He yawned, and stood up, and despite the swans' opinions, decided to go back to sleep. He could see over the tips of the trees two tall pale towers, just showing, some little distance away, gleaming in the highest rays of the sun, though he was in shadow. Another mystery, he thought, that perhaps I will uncover. This is a beautiful place my Uncle has brought me to. One could be happy here, one should be happy here. I wonder if I will manage to be.

He slept until nine, and then he breakfasted on ham and bread and butter and ale, and porridge, and walked about, while Ross sat and smoked, until his Uncle appeared, and inspected his dress. He did not approve, and valeted him himself, and then they set out together, walking, peaceably in the quiet late morning, past the pale patches of trampled grass which his Uncle pointed out to him that were all that remained to show where the booths and tents had stood for St. Giles' Fair, to Broad Street, which they found jammed with too many carriages and horses, phaetons, gigs, of all descriptions and sizes. The Earl gave Ross instructions how to follow when he could, and turned with Edward off into the High Street. Unknown to Edward, he had already entered him in his College. He took him first to be capped and gowned and given his white tie, and then to matriculate in Divinity School beneath its carved ceiling, and then, introducing him to acquaintances as they passed, took him to meet the Master of his College, and to his rooms on his staircase.

Edward looked about his rooms with interest and pleasure. They were a pair, a bedroom and a sitting room, and although there were other suites with more and larger rooms, they were to be his own. One set of windows overlooked the quadrangle, which Edward found beautiful. He looked at his guardian with surprised gratitude, but the Earl did not seem to expect any, and had turned his back and was surveying the arrangement of the rooms and their furnishings. An older man, with one eye, whom Edward later learned was a Scout, appeared suddenly, like a Jack-in-the-Box, and asked without preface, "Shall I sport?"

"By all means," said the Earl dryly, raising his glass and surveying him through it as though he expected him to begin to dance or to handspring, but the Scout only pulled the massive outer oak door to. The Earl, surprised, promptly opened it again, and stepped out a little way into the hall.

"I had forgotten that phrase," he said, " 'to sport one's oak.' "

"What does it mean?" asked Edward, his lips suddenly dry, pounded by many emotions.

"It means that when the big outer oak door is pulled to, one is not available for company, being studying or sleeping or—occupied. We won't sport yours." He paused. "I am going now, Edward. You don't need me anymore. If you do, write me, or better, write my lawyer, Wotton. I have written his name and his address for you, here." He took out a piece of paper, carefully inscribed.

I have never seen my Uncle's handwriting, Edward thought in surprise. How much I do not know about him, how little I do. The older title still came naturally and unconsciously in his mind.

"Holland," he said desperately, pleading, holding out his hand, as he saw his Uncle turn to go, "Holland, I cannot bear for you to be angry with me, like this." He saw his Uncle's face freeze into lines of displeasure, and his voice faltered. "Must you be? Is there nothing I can do?"

"You can please not talk about it," the Earl said stiffly.

"What did I do? Did you really believe I would really hurt you?"

His Uncle gave a short bark of laughter, without amusement. "I did. I do. And must I remind you again who I am? I will not tolerate to be threatened or to be struck, by you, by anyone. If I informed them, the courts would punish you more harshly, more severely than I do for it. You have presumed always too much that way, but when you were a child, I could find to forgive you. I do not now. And I will not tolerate a Methody or your unsettling doctrines loose in my house or on my estates or among my servants. It is enough, Edward. I do not wish to speak of it anymore. It was a mistake for me to take you, I should not have done it under any persuasion. I will educate you, as I promised, but nothing can come of our speaking further." His voice, beneath the biting words, continued viciously and impatiently polite.

"And all the past . . ." Edward faltered, his voice dying, beneath his Uncle's stare.

"I do not live in the past." His eyes briefly glanced away. "Do not you."

"I am not to see you again?" Edward asked, his eyes stark.

"Not if I can help it," the Earl said, "and I can."

"I think I shall die, Holland, if you leave me, like this," Edward said simply, without pride.

"Do not be absurd, Edward," the Earl said. "Do not be absurd." He looked at him curiously, as at a strange animal, but his eyes did not soften. "This is Michaelmas term, Edward. At the end of it, Ross will come for you—as we have agreed." Without wishing Edward well, or any further speech or instruction, the Earl bowed slightly to him, and left him, there in the middle of the floor, in his new rooms, his own last words and all they conveyed of an unforgiving and relentless spirit, underneath his outer casual agreeableness of manner, hovering in the air of them.

That first term Edward spent quietly. He became acquainted with his tutor, he attended lectures faithfully, without questioning whether or not he should do so. He explored no other of the colleges, although he took walks among the drifting, scuffling leaves of the elms, the Chinese willows, the horse chestnuts, dropping their conkers, and by the rivers. The gardeners with their besoms were already at work, sweeping the lawns of the fluttering leaves that piled up again even as they swept, the cascades yet to come. He did not go far afield. He attended Chapel, he observed the hours of curfew without rebellion, he had breakfast and lunch in his rooms, and much later, supper, brought by the staircase servant from the Buttery and the Kitchen. He took dinner at five each day in the Hall, and made no attempt to speak to anyone at all, and was unaware of any distinction among the different faces. When he was not doing these things, he read, all variety and manner of books, he studied, he translated, he made notes, and listened to the college clocks strike. He followed the gentle suggestions of his tutor, whom the Earl had chosen, through his influence, and had chosen well, and he followed the suggestions of his own mind. He made no friends, and did not then wish to. Having never had any, except for people connected with him by duty or position, he would not have known how to begin, and he did not feel the lack of what he did not know. He listened to the noisy sounds of evening revelry, of breakfast parties in rooms, and luncheon parties, of the crash down the unlighted stairs of a late unwary elastic body, or the sound of flying hooves of a forbidden horse in the quadrangle, of student songs, and arguments, in two's and three's and ten's, with an unenvious but interested ear, as in beings of another planet, and watched with a quiet, interested but undesiring eye. He was himself remarked, but he did not remark it himself.

Despite the stimulation of a new and so beautiful place, and his pleasure in being a part of it, even though he had not wished to be, he was at first as unhappy in his transplanting as a boy of sixteen, almost seventeen, could be, which is an age known for its capacity for unhappiness. Although he was now free to go and do as he pleased, like a creature grown used to its pasture, he had few desires to go or do anything beyond his immediate work. He had almost no ready money available to him, but he did not miss it, and although the Earl had arranged for accounts for him at all shops, inns, coffee houses, taverns, and for all his bills there and his University *battels* to be sent direct to his agent, he made little use of this liberality. To add to his unhappiness, besides his surprising homesickness, he was aware of an uncontrollable desire, despite his Uncle's treatment of him and his expressed dislike of him, and sometimes he thought with perceptive dismay even because of it, to be again in his Uncle's arms, and to feel his lips on his. He had thought himself past it, but the brief contact with his Uncle had reawakened it. It was a desire that he knew could have no relief, and that he did not even wish to have relief for, that nevertheless haunted him and was controllable only by his inability to help himself. His misery was increased by his horror at what it revealed to him in himself, but gradually the intensity of his desire and finally even his misery left him. The gathering mists drew a curtain over Oxford and over his own towering feelings, veiling and softening both. What he did not know was that they served as a shield and an armour against lesser attachments, and in that as well as a weakness, they were a strength he did not realise to himself.

At the end of Michaelmas term, after the gathering of the mists, hiding all sharpness and extremity in the town and in himself, after the riot of the Michaelmas daisies and the wildness of Guy Fawkes, and the beauty of the choir boys in chapel and the Advent carolers in the first powdering of snow, Ross appeared at his door, shaking the sprinkling of snow from his wild tawny locks. Edward, inconceivably to himself now, had forgotten his forced bargain with his Uncle, and he could not believe he must endure, after this gracious spaciousness of air and light and bells and the merry organ, what he knew he must now endure. His face whitened, as if beholding a great lion of death ready to spring upon him. Without a word, he picked up several of his books, taking off his cap and gown, but taking none of his clothes, except his travelling coat and his hat, and walked out with Ross, shutting the door behind him.

They journeyed back, not stopping for the night, or for anything but quick meals and quicker changes of horses, in an old large enclosed coach, into deeper snow and deepening winter, and worse roads, heavily rutted, the horses' breath white and frosty in the night. It was dark the next day when they finally arrived after an upset on the road, and dark when Ross with no more word took him down to the dark priest-hole and locked him in. He did not understand why he must be there, and he did not try to. He was tireder than he knew he could be, as well as sadder, and he lay down on a bed that had been placed there, and went to sleep. He knew too well that the Earl was at home, but he did not know that he looked in on him, through the opening of the tile, with a lit candle, for a long time, with interest, before he closed the tile, and went away to spend Christmas in all its festivity at the estate of a friend in the South.

After a week of darkness, in which he slept a great deal, being tireder from his first term than he knew, he heard a crashing noise and discovered that the room did have a window that he had not known of, boarded up with nailed shutters that Ross had now removed from the outside. After that, he had light enough to read for several hours each day, although despite the glass the room was colder, and for the rest, in the dark, he thought about what he had read, developing the muscles of his memory, which had always been unusually strong and clear, quick to grasp and retain, and testing his powers of comparison and analysis. He wasted no time, although he had time enough, and no energy continuing to berate or question his Uncle or his fate. He was beginning to realise he might have led a strange life, and this seemed only a part of it, which he could change no more than he could his father's or his mother's deaths, or his remove to the harsh North, or his Uncle's nature. He sometimes allowed himself for pleasure to pass memories he had enjoyed before his mind, particularly any of warmth and sun, in Devon, or in Italy or France, and then he did weep, and so he did not let these memories invade him often. He meditated and considered, but he seldom consciously prayed. His inward unexpressed bitterness was too intense for prayer, and that part of his life seemed to him over.

Christmas passed with no marking of it, and no word or sign from the Earl or anyone. For the first time in his life Edward did not even know when the day had come and gone. Some time after, after Epiphany had passed unmarked and January had dragged its way to its third week, the door was unlocked, as before, this time to let him out, and he found Ross waiting for him. Enclosed inside the house, vented in ways he could not discover, the priest-hole had been cold, but he had been given a small brazier, of coals, and he was surprised by the icy, iron bitterness of the cold of the outside weather. Even Oxford was cold, when he returned silently with Ross. He could see skaters on the Isis and the Cherwell, and the swans and the ducks had gone inland. One wag tried to imitate the old feat of driving a coach and four down the river across Worcester Lake, but it was not that cold. When he reached his rooms and Ross had left him, and he had undone his books, he discovered a poem he had written, that he had named "To ——, On the Eve of All-Hallows," had gone. He supposed he must have dropped it, in his pit, or in his Uncle's house, perhaps even in his coach. He wondered briefly if it would be found, or read, and then he put it out of his mind, in his studies.

Ross did find it, and without reading it, being unable to, put it on the Earl's desk where the Earl found it on his next visit:

> *Here in this Autumn night, Quiet lives.*
> *We do not hear him stir, but brooding days*
> *Have shown his coming. Gilded Autumn gives*
> *What summer stored. Along the trodden ways,*
> *Under the leaves, find him. We perceive*
> *Excess to excess clings, and will not leave;*
> *But here is only quiet. The spirits hum*
> *In the wind. The moon is wrapt in a cloud. Here come*
> *No fears, but vision such as the quiet conceive.*

The Earl read it through once, and then without comment put it away in his drawer with the pamphlets of sermons by George Armstrong. Pitt had died suddenly, and his personal friend but political anathema Fox was forming with Lords Grenville and Sidmouth, recently Addington, the brief administration to be known jocularly as All the Talents. There was excess enough there; his attention was not on Edward.

Lent term passed in ice and snow, and thick grey mists, damp and bone-chilling, which the sea-coal fires alleviated but did not dispel. By 3:30 each day it was dark. Otherwise it was much the same as Michaelmas, except that in it, without public observance, Edward became seventeen. One was never really warm, but Edward's blood ran young and strong, and he did not mind. He was lonelier in this term than in the other, being more inclined to keep to his rooms and read, though sometimes he took long walks in the snow with only the crows for colour and for company. His sense of displacement continued to be strong. He would imagine sometimes that the porter at the Lodge would call him, and that he would fly down the steps, to find his Uncle had come to see how he did, or when he heard the footsteps pass by his door, that one pair would stop, and knock, but none did. Lent began in aconites with Hellebore and Heliotrope blooming in the Physic garden, progressed to snowdrops and crocus, and ended in celandine and meadow frittillaries and in Ross.

This second vacation, in which for Edward there was no public notice of the great holiday, only his private penance, was not outwardly different from the first at Christmas, except that this time, intentionally, he left an imaginary sonnet for his Uncle to find, if he wished. Half-serious, half-not, he felt a necessity to try somehow to pierce the Earl's silence, to provoke the Earl into some recognition of any sort of his continued existence:

O, I should be as true to you as books,
Which, read abroad, are yet best found at home;
For where you are is my heart's ease, and from
That stay I should not leave, when in your looks
Content. Yet be you true to me; love brooks
No inequality, nor cannot come
To credit broken faith; though shown in some,
Believe that we are fast bound with love's hooks.
Yet should you change, myself by your love's death
Would die, but my love be not killed, and that
Would haunt you. Winds would seem to you my breath,
And you would fear to sit where I had sat,
And when you looked in mirrors, it would be
Not yours, but my face there that you would see.

The Earl, finding it, saw in it a veiled threat Edward in his innocence had not intended, but he did not destroy it. His face marked briefly by distrust and displeasure, he put it away with the other in his desk drawer. Above all things, he disliked the feeling of being pressed upon, by any person, any emotion, any claim, and whenever so pressed, he defended himself from any acknowledgement of any justice in the claim by obliviating his brain of it entirely. England at that time watched the triumphant Progress of Napoleon and his armies through Europe. In March news came that he had taken Naples and put his older brother Joseph on its throne as King, although the British held Sicily and in a brief successful foray onto the mainland took and held for a few days tiny Maida with prophetic tactics Wellington would re-employ himself with lasting success at Waterloo. Two hundred British marksmen simply held their ground backed against the sea against sixteen hundred Frenchmen in two columns which broke before their fire and fled. But after the winter Treaty of Pressburg extending the Blockade to the Adriatic the Earl saw Vienna made wholly inaccessible to him with a growing concern and irritability that excluded schoolboys, in any case, effectually from his consciousness.

II

Edward, oblivious to Napoleon, returned to Oxford, and two hundred miles suddenly further South, to full Spring. The warmth, the sun, relaxed him. He availed himself of his Uncle's generosity in accounts to procure a small boat, in which he did much of his reading beneath the Pollard elms. He looked at the river, at the water flowing between the rushes and the sun sparkling on it and them, and he thought to himself, in a moment of sudden joy and delighted discovery: Look! the river is combing its silver locks of those tangled reeds.

He watched the ecstasy of the courtship and the mating of the swans, spectacular and splendid to him, their long necks inclining and entwining, the final covering half-submerged, and their rearing of their young in careless fragile floating nests. When he was not reading, he frequented the Music Hall of the University at Holywell, and the Physic Garden near Magdalen, where he held long, friendly, informative conversations with the Gardener, as he had with the Gardener on the Earl's Northern Estate. He learned that the custom of pollarding elms was very old, several centuries old, brought in from Holland as a means of preserving the banks of the rivers during the Spring freshets, because the cutting of the tops, though it spoiled their fine grace, made their roots go wider and deeper and stronger than normally they would, and that the garnering of extra fuel was only incidental. Easter and Act terms merged, for all practical purposes. The College did not close down for the brief time, and he was not taken home, although some of those students who lived close by did go, or went to London. He saw the approach of the Long Vacation with apprehension. He did not see how he could bear to be taken from the green, glowing world of summer and again immured, this time for so many weeks. But even had he seriously considered breaking his strange agreement with the Earl, and he did not consider it, he had nowhere to go, and no wherewithal to go with, for he had no way of paying for a coach or any lodging or food outside of Oxford. He looked at the pollard elms, on his last day of term, and found tears drowning the vision of his eyes. He winked them back angrily with a return of his old childish wry humour and philosophy.

I am very silly to complain of what I cannot help, he thought. I shall just have to be like one of these *pollardi*. Here they stand, and they cannot help themselves when men and events come to them and shear their tops off, and all the leaves and sprouts they have worked so hard to produce, and they are just deformed, withdrawn knots again. I must be like them, and make what is underground in me strong and wide too, and reach and grasp with my mind, which is the root of my being, even underground, even in the dark. I think I am not really a religious person after all, as my Uncle thinks. It is my mind that is everything to me. If I could hate my uncle, it would be easier to endure, but perhaps it is best not to have what is easy. What a strange time we live in, to produce men without hearts to touch, although otherwise they seem whole, and integral, and so fair. Well, he thought, as he had thought many times before, I must make my own life and live my own life. I cannot hate him, but I will not let him deform me, like himself or these poor tree tops.

Sitting, half-lying in his boat, he found lines going through his head, quietly, fashioning themselves without his conscious will:

> *Loosening from the Winter's silences . . .*
> *A seeming death to our discerning . . .*
> *Evoking buds and leaves from immanences . . .*
> *From like loveliness recalling . . .*
> *Pleasure, half-remembered . . .*

He selected and packed his books, while his Scout selected and packed his clothes. He was downstairs waiting, before the porter called him, and greeted Ross with a return of his older courtesy, that made Ross privately think to himself that the Earl would be surprised at the young gentleman Edward was growing into.

It had rained briefly, hard in the afternoon. The sun, in a clouded gold luminous sky, was setting, as they set out once again together. Edward watched it shining in the pools of water, and through and on and in the hearts of trees, gilding with its unbelievable gold the undersides of the pointed green shapes of the topmost leaves, with the quiet eye of one looking at what he loves and knows he must leave. In the East, the grey-blue clouds were yet massed, and against them, in the reflecting western gold light, the towers were sharply outlined, their gold stones soft and luminous. It was the same hour when they neared his home, if it was a home that would receive him so. Here the bare rounded hills had taken a new beauty to themselves from the gold light that turned their browning sides to rose-gold. A pool of water by the road reflected back the heavenly light, and children splashed in it, their legs spraying the water drops behind them as ducks do when they land. He looked at the billowing luminously white, gold- and rose-hearted clouds rising over the hills, and at Ross whose tawny face and hair reflected the light. It faded, as they came nearer the house, and he saw out of the corner of his eye a flash of sharp bright light, and then heard the crack of thunder, followed by a low rumbling. They had stopped at the back door, that faced the hills. He paused at the door, watching it, and he thought he could not go in.

"Let me stay," he said to Ross, pleadingly, "just until it grows dark."

"I dare not, Edward," Ross said, "the Earl is here with guests, and though his horses are out now he may return at any time, especially with these clouds." He took Edward by the arm, and guided him almost gently down.

The sudden knowledge destroyed Edward's brief peace. He was filled with a rage, a bitterness, a jealousy, he had not known himself capable of, and which he knew no way to express. He paced his narrow room, back and forth, back and forth, feeling as if his hurt and angry emotions would burst through his skin, they crowded and swelled within him like the huge clouds, rounding, inwardly turmoiling, that he had watched. The angry tears scalded his eyes, his lips were tight and yet quivering, his throat dry. To be ignored was a terrible cruelty. He took his coat off, and with his hands, consciously tore it to pieces, trying to let some of his passion escape.

He waited, torn between hope and fear, for hours and days, cursing his guardian uselessly, hoping he would appear, imagining him still there, imagining him gone.

I cannot live like this, he thought suddenly and finally, and I have to live. He sat down on his bed, his head in his hands. I have expected too much too quickly, I am not going to win this battle, I see that now, at least not right away, in one stroke. I am always going to lose it, when I least expect it and when I am overconfident. Someone or something is going to have to help me, for I can do nothing by myself. I see that now. I have been vain and overconfident, to think I could, for there is something here too strong for me, that I do not understand. I think I have somehow forgotten all my father taught me, only I have not really forgotten it.

He lay down on his bed, his eyes open, not thinking, and then he turned over and let himself begin to cry, not angrily, not in grief, quietly and gently like the rain which after a time, when his first sobs abated, he could hear falling in a passionless steady way somewhere outside. There was no one to hear him, or to pay attention, and he cried for a long time, the tears continuing to fall after his sobs ceased. When finally he had finished, his mind was exhausted but washed clean, and somehow freshened like the earth. He turned back onto his back, and he began to pray then, quietly, as he had wept quietly, not asking for anything to help him except understanding. He had not prayed, being alone, outside of church, consciously, except superficially or unconsciously, since he had committed himself knowingly to his Uncle when he was twelve, but he found he had not forgotten how. His months with Mr. Davenby, he saw now, had been an outward thing, a visible and audible satisfaction, and not this dumb mouthless, eyeless, earless flowing, as in a great dark sweeping current on which he could be carried, if he sought and yielded to it, as he did now. The Early Christians had needed no assurance of happiness or prosperity in fulfilment of their desires. The understanding that they need not ever wholly die had been enough. He had that understanding already, and no one was calling upon him to use it. It was another understanding, what he did not know, that he needed now, and asking wordlessly, not demanding, waited upon, without impatience. He did not find it then, completely, but he found again a certain acceptance and in it a certain peace. He did not know of the words carved in the porch of the temple at Delphi where Apollo's Oracle had been: "To commit oneself is to court misfortune," but had he known he would not have been able to help himself, the act had long ago been done, and now there was only the living with it.

When he was given light again, he wrote down a poem in a rhyme new to him, the *terza rima*, that he had found in *The Divine Comedy*, recalling the lines he had felt fall into his mind his last day on the Isis, and remembering the Spring he had seen progressing, unfolding, as he travelled down from Northumberland to Oxford. All his poems were a kind of dialogue between himself and his Uncle, and he entitled it only:

To——

Envision how sweet Spring to earth returning
Loosens from the Winter's silences
Late Autumn's seeming death to our discerning,

Evoking buds and leaves from immanences;
No other Spring has being now, yet from
Like loveliness recalling to our senses

Old pleasures half-remembered, pleasures come.
Look where love flowers, from a seasoned root
Arising, which in Winter cold and numb,

Hidden from sight, waited, waking but mute,
March winds to sound the reveille salute!

It was a different flowering of love, though, that he envisioned, than what
his Uncle, if he read his poem, might imagine. Nevertheless, he left it
as it stood, not his any longer, although he smiled at the idea of an un-
mute bulb, and at a poet too much subject to his rhymes.

After the Earl left, to go to Brighton to attend a levee at the Regent-
to-be's Pavilion, Ross took it upon himself to lessen the rigours of Edward's imprisonment during the long Summer. The memory of that young
figure, not quite a man, no longer quite a boy, glowing in the soft gold
evening sunlight, giving even himself on his errand the warmth of his
smile, had remained with him, and when he walked in the air and the
sunlight, and then briefly tended Edward's necessities in his darkness
and perpetual shadows, the two ideas so pictured before him moved him
to a mild revolt. Every morning, after breakfast, he brought Edward out,
without explanation, and went riding with him until before noon, when
the heat began to bake the moors. His first sight of Edward's tired, white
face, older seeming, confirmed him in his judgement. In the evening,
when a cool freshness succeeded the lowering of the sun, he again
brought Edward out, to walk as he chose, Ross accompanying him again
without any word or explanation, until the late evening finally ended
and the dark came. It did not occur to Edward to ask by whose grace
the new liberty came, for he supposed without question it was by his
Uncle's permission. Had he asked, and had he been told it was not, his
young sternness would not have allowed him to use or accept it. By
chance he did learn it, on the occasion of the Earl's stopping on his way
into Scotland, in depression of spirits at the death of his friend Charles
Fox. After his Uncle left, he thanked Ross but he did not resume his
rides or walks, and Ross in conscience could not insist. But by this time,
Fall was again approaching, and in two more weeks, he was again on
his way to Oxford with Ross for his second Michaelmas term.

That term, with its late Michaelmas Summer, and that Christmas
Vacation he spent much as he had spent the first. Christmas went un-
observed openly, but not inwardly. But as he remembered, that Christmas
Day, that it had now been some months longer than a year since he had

seen the Earl, he felt a brief resurgence of bitterness which he left a brief expression of, his Christmas gift for the Earl:

Dec. 25, 1806

> *What is more useless than old friends forgot,*
> *Dreary as birds that sing on winter boughs*
>   *Before they freeze?*
>
> *How to forget, and leave an old disease,*
> *Forcing it forth, nor suffering it to drowse,*
> *Dreaming sweet hopes where it hath used to sit?*
> *My love for you, you not desiring it,*
>   *I want it not.*

He heard the freezing rain pattering against the walls of the house, and the bare icy branches of the shrubbery where the gypsy had waited for him scraping against the brick, and he wished for his freedom and for Spring. His spirit ached with longing.

He returned to Lent term, and a particularly cold frost for Oxford, with the swans again driven inland, so that if inclined, one could walk as easily on the Cherwell and the Isis as on Christ Church meadows. Starved for exercise, and inured to cold, in the afternoons he walked far and wide, coming back only when the red opaque sun went down into the grey rising mists behind the stark black boughs of the trees, and sometimes he walked at night on the crackling ice, the black sky above him and the stars very bright and very sharp, like the frost itself, in the rare clear air.

It was at this time that Edward made the acquaintance of Marion Alleyn, in a quiet interlude of his brief ill-starred career which would lead him finally to an honour his College was unaware of since it occurred when he no longer used his own name. The eldest son of Lord Alleyn, or Admiral Alleyn as he was addressed, he was at that time a fourth-year student, in his fifth year, overdue to take his degree, having been sent down several times, rusticated, as the practise was known. He continued nevertheless to engage in various political and social revolutionary activities frowned on not only by his family but by his College, and the University at large, which had involved him already in several disasters. The more common pranks and debaucheries would have caused less stir and less concern. The latest of his misdemeanours had been the showering of his pamphlets on the state of Ireland on all unwary enough to receive them from his hand. He had even dropped them into the hoods of ladies' cloaks passing him in the street, and had prominently displayed his latest, prudently unsigned, in an Oxford bookseller's window until it was forcibly removed. That France was interested in Ireland, and that England was at war with France, gave him no concern. He regarded the use of a present war for excuse for delaying present reform as no excuse at all. Much under the influence of the writings of Rousseau and William Godwin, and exceeding both in his passion for their principles and his practical application of them, to the left even of the Radical Left of the Whigs, he was a thorn in the flesh to anyone in authority about him, particularly his Conservative Tory College.

Edward had noticed him, as a matter of course, when he was present at the College. A Gentleman Commoner, he might eat at the High Table, although he rarely chose to, having many friends, and seeming much beloved, despite his annoyance to authority. He was a tall young man, fully grown at twenty-two, with a head of black Irish locks, blue eyes, full of the devil's laughter, heavily fringed in long black eyelashes curling up like a girl's, well-shaped black brows, a wide mouth quick to smile, and bones beneath his fair skin as beautiful as Edward's in their particular own moulding of jaw and cheek. He wore his cap and his gown, like his life, with a careless ease, and gave no sign on his face of what went on beneath them. The meeting, when it occurred, was unexpected. It happened in this manner.

Edward was sitting in the study of his rooms, reading, his curtains half-drawn, the winter world outside dark and black and cold, his feet propped on the fender of his fire. It was early in the evening, he had just returned from Chapel, but he had already pulled his oak to, for quiet, not privacy, and when he heard a hesitant yet demanding knock at the door, he rose instantly, and opened both his doors. He was surprised to see two friends there of the Marion Alleyn just described, for he knew of them, but he did not know them. They were older than he was, and already walked in spheres of influence and position he did not himself aspire to. When he asked them in, they complied readily, and explained themselves charmingly and plausibly.

It was a part of Alleyn's nature that he had and held friends whose opinions and characters differed sometimes widely from his own. He dealt with them on their own grounds, according to their own interests, adapting himself, unlike Edward who was steadfastly the same. He moved among them, unfixed, in his orbit; although in another sense, he attracted them into his own, for he dealt with them with apparent frankness and considerable charm. Like Parliament, his friends were divided, although loyal to one person, into the majority and the opposition, the Conservatives and the Liberals. The two at the door belonged to the Conservative faction who had been among his friends at Eton.

"We are in a mess," they said, smiling ruefully, and the expression of their faces denied any authoritative seriousness, "and we have come to you as the only person who can help us out."

"You see," they said, alternating voices, like Tweedledum and Twee-dledee, Edward thought, "we know who you are. We know the Arm-strongs, you see, and that you are George Armstrong's son, despite this connection you have with Lord Tyne—"

"And so we thought you could be relied on."

"Discretion, you see, and fairness, and non-faction, and charity—"

"All the Christian virtues, in fact—"

"And also that you would probably be alone, and not going out after hours or having anyone in your rooms."

Edward thought now he did see the reasons for being chosen to be the repository of their confidence, and he was not flattered, and asked directly and not encouragingly, "All right, I understand you. What is it you want me to do for you?"

"Well," they said, "it's rather hard to explain it right off, bang like a firecracker, just like this—"

"We have kidnapped someone—"

"Oh, in the best of intentions, the best of motives, all the way—"

"But he doesn't know that it is us, you see, who did it—"

"And we want you to guard him for us, stay with him tonight, you see."

"Because he doesn't know you or your voice."

"And because we think we can rely on you and that you will help us."

"Why?" asked Edward.

They stopped, drawn up short by the severity of his voice, and looked at him in consternation.

"Why do you think that?" he repeated, not smiling now. "I am not very flattered. Who have you kidnapped? The Master? The Proctor? Your Scout? I don't know you, you know. I think you had better go now, and not explain anything any further."

"Well," said the taller of the two, more seriously, "it is like this, Armstrong. We have kidnapped a friend of ours. We have kidnapped Marion Alleyn. Don't go stiff on us, until we have told you why. We have done it for his good."

"I have heard those words before," Edward said. "I've never liked them. I don't like them now."

"Oh, damn and teeth," the smaller young man said to the taller, "I thought we shouldn't come here. I don't think much of your idea of it now, either."

"It's very simple," the taller said, looking thoughtfully and quietly at Edward, meeting him on his own terms. "Allister—that is, Marion—is determined to go out tonight to a meeting, after nine, and he has been gated. I am certain the Head will send someone to check on him, to see he has stayed in his room, and not gone out as someone else, or out his window and over the wall. He has lost all patience with Marion, and I hardly blame him, but we are his friends, you see, and the Head, who does not really know him except as a disturber of the peace, is not. If Marion is sent down again, we do not know what his father will do, who is out of patience with him, too. He might not let him come back. And so when we learned Marion was bent on going to this meeting, we resolved to save him in spite of himself."

"That is perhaps laudable," Edward said quietly. "I wouldn't know. It seems to me we are only saved in our own hearts and wills and intentions, and that being kidnapped would firm one, at least it would me, in another direction than my kidnappers'. Won't you get expelled yourselves? I don't wish to be at all, myself. If I do this for you, and I'm still not quite sure what it is you want me actually to do, or that I will, why do you think your friend will not just go out tomorrow night, or the next, as he planned tonight? What good will it do in the end?"

"Well," said the younger frankly, "I think we may have been a little drunk, now that I think about it, and Marion may have been too; for we were showing Petersen how to get around a sconcing, but we are quite sober now."

"We think if he has time to think it over, he may get some sense back, and anyway, at least after tonight, he won't be gated, and if he comes back by twelve, nothing will happen to him, if a brawl in town is not started at the meeting, as it likely will be. But that's another matter."

"What is this meeting about?" asked Edward curiously.

"It is the Remnant," said the taller, with no enthusiasm in his voice.

"But not of the Jews, it is the Remnant of the United Irishmen." At Edward's face, he said, in surprise, "I don't think you know what that is, or what I'm talking about."

"I don't," said Edward, "but I am listening."

"Where have you been," they asked in amazement, "how could you help not knowing?"

"Never mind," said Edward, "just tell me now, if you want to, and I see you do."

"Well, you have to know that Marion's mother is partly Irish, and in some distant way she is a relation of Curran's, Curran the artist. The Irish are all mad, and Marion is maddest of them all. Three years ago Allister left College and went to France to aid the Remnant in their new uprising. He was in Dublin, and he saw Robert Emmet hanged, and heard his ladder speech. Emmet was only twenty-five, you know, if that, and even I thought Castlereagh would have done better not to have let quite so attractive a young man to make a martyr for those patriots. It was a wild unlikely business from the start, the Dwyer had the sense to keep back with his men in the hills and not come out for it. They blew their own arsenal by mistake, and panicked."

"Was it so unlikely? They did hold Dublin for three hours, even so," the younger murmured. "The same time Colonel Despard was trying the same scheme here, blow up things, the same things, disrupt things, start a London brawl. It could have been a pretty mess. I thought they might as well have quartered the Colonel, but Nelson spoke for him, and they remitted that part."

"Emmet," the older said, as though he had not been interrupted, "was engaged to some girl in the Curran family, that is a relation to Curran the lawyer, and he could have escaped but he went back to see her, and he was caught that way. Much too romantically pleasing. McNally defended him, but McNally's men someway always lose their cases."

" 'The sacrifices to public justice restored the appearance of tranquillity,' " murmured the younger. "Do you enjoy hangings? There is one tomorrow, in Holywell, if they interest you. You can see the cockfight first in the Pit, and then the pushing off to finish. I shall probably go to both myself."

"Neither are to my taste," the taller said, "and I admit that one would not have been a pretty sight, but I think Marion is sometimes not sane on this subject, the Irish, I mean. But then, when I enter Parliament, I shall be a Tory, and I am not interested in the Irish myself except for revenue, they are dirty and illiterate, but for God's sake, don't tell Marion I said that."

"It wouldn't matter," said the younger, "he would just answer you made them so, and proceed to illuminate you."

"This meeting is about an Association he purposes to set up. I hope the Head does not get wind of it or all the Heads will meet in Golgotha about it. To miss Chapel and make derisive remarks is one thing and already enough, but an Irish Association is a thing too much."

"Well, I don't know about any of this," Edward said, "but if I spend the night with your friend, I suppose in the morning I will know. I suppose it could be said to be in the interests of education."

"That depends," said the younger, "on whether you remove the gag. Myself, I wouldn't."

"Myself, I will," said Edward, shocked. He remembered too well the sensation of one, from his stay with the gypsies. "You have really kidnapped him then. I thought you were joking."

"You do not joke this way, with Marion, you do it thoroughly or not at all," the taller said, "and we care urgently that he not find out we did it."

"Why should it matter so?" Edward asked. "Would he not be your friend?"

They both laughed. "Oh, no, Marion will love us as before, but he will make a reckoning, or his cutthroat humanitarian friends will do it for him, and it is that friendly retaliation we wish to avoid. But you will be quite safe. All the same, though, I wouldn't speak much, or let him see you, we being you. We have been careful not to speak."

"We wore masks," the younger said with a certain relish, "there are three of us. We hid in his room after Chapel, and jumped him from behind when he came in, while he was dressing, at an awkward moment." He laughed, remembering. "Lord! what a fight it was, and we had the advantage. His Scout will want to kill us."

"We have left him blindfold," the taller said. He looked at Edward. "Something we said has changed your mind, I think. Will you do it?"

"Yes," said Edward, "I'm not sure why, it seems foolish to me and futile and dangerous, but yes, I will. What do you want me to do?"

"Do you know where his rooms are?"

"No," said Edward.

"They are not far from yours. I will explain how to find them. Come down and knock in ten minutes, and I will let you in. We will arrange Allister to look as if he is reading, at his desk. If the Head knocks, you will have to unblindfold him, but you can stay behind him. You can speak, you see, he won't recognise your voice. You haven't anything else you have to do. You can bring your book and read. If his friends knock, later, don't answer."

"But for the Lord's sake," said the shorter, "if you do ungag Marion, he has the Irish honey tongue, when he wants to use it. He can talk the moon out of its course, though not the Head out of his. Don't let him persuade you for anything to unloose him. He is like Proteus, he will evade you, if you do."

"All right," said Edward, "I won't do that. Go on, I'll follow you."

When they had gone, he thought he must have run as mad as their Marion to say he would help them, and he wondered a little why he had, now their persuasive voices and merry faces had left him, yet knowing the answer. After a few minutes, he took his book and followed their instructions to Alleyn's suite of rooms. He knocked, and was admitted.

III

The air of the room seemed to crackle with the anger contained in it; it met him tangibly as he entered. The room, a shambles, books, tables, clothes overturned, was dark, the double curtains completely drawn, except for a candle on a desk, and one by a chair that the taller emissary was then lighting. He put his finger to his lips, as a reminder to Edward, and then on silent feet, he, the younger man, and a third Edward had not seen, slipped out of the door, and closed the two doors, leaving Edward alone with the angry air and a silent figure at a desk, its back to Edward, and cloaked with an academic gown, as if against the chill. Every line of his body, his back, the back of his neck and head was expressive of intense indignation and outrage, and also of attention.

For the first half hour he was there, Edward walked about the room, setting it to rights, replacing books, straightening chairs and tables, broken dishes, the clothes his prisoner had intended to wear, his cap. He had not been asked to be a servitor, but he did not wish to spend the night in its chaotic disorder, and he imagined if the Head opened the door, that it might seem odd. There was no sound in the room except for those he made. After he finished, disregarding in part the instructions given him, instead of sitting in his chair and attempting to ignore that angry back, he walked over, and put his hands on the shoulders of the momentarily tamed rebel. He felt the air of attention grow stronger, and he realised to his amazement that Marion had recognised him as new in the room. He wondered if he also knew there was now only the one of him.

"You cannot read, as you are," Edward said. "I myself have much to prepare, and you do too, I imagine." He would have slipped the blindfold off but it was fixed tightly, and so he spent some time undoing the knot. He stayed out of range of the angry blue eyes, darker than his own, which twisted surprisingly quickly to discover him.

"When I was a child," Edward said, "some gypsies carried me off one night, with rags stuffed in my mouth so I could not cry out. I hated it so, I would rather you had none in yours. It does not seem necessary. They are there now, you know it. I don't have to remove them, but I would like to." He paused, and then he said, almost indifferently: "I have several times, when brought to a place where I could not help myself, promised what, with any help for it, I would otherwise not have promised at all. But once I gave it, even though unfairly taken, I did keep my promise. I wonder if you would?"

There was no sign from the figure sitting helplessly that he was listening to Edward's words, except for the silent air of attention still about him. After a time, Edward said again, still indifferently: "I have promised I would keep you, and I am going to. If I didn't someone else would, you know. I don't know who may come to the door, I can't have you saying things to them, but if you say you won't, I will believe you. But if you want to be uncomfortable, of course, you can be. Shall I take out the gag?" He saw the dark head nod almost imperceptibly, as if humiliated. "You will not ask anyone for help, if anyone should come?" The dark head shook again, almost imperceptibly. "It is a promise?" The dark locks nodded again, inclining slightly. A faint warning doubt rippled Edward's mind. He is acting, he thought to himself, like the Mummers. I am certain he is. But the anger is not acting, I can almost smell that. And is he lying, too?

He decided to chance that his charge, in his eyes too beautiful and too high-spirited, like an unbroken horse, for anyone's safety, least his own, could nevertheless be honest. But he was not certain. He had come, he suddenly acknowledged to himself, not only to be merciful but because he wished the excitement of the brief acquaintance with a comet, and he foresaw he would have it, and he hoped he would not be burned.

He had paused, thinking, hesitating yet. He removed then, detecting an impatience beneath his fingers, the outer cloth, when he heard an authoritative knock at the oak. He put the handkerchief in his pocket, and took his book again, seating himself by the fire and calling, "Come in." The Master's figure and head appeared briefly in the doorwell. His visit was unusual, for he had little to do with the students, except to receive their bows and salutations and the reports of their tutors and of the proctor. He was surprised, and rather pleased, to see Edward there, as Marion's friends had thought he might be, Edward having shown himself quiet and untroublesome. He looked benignly on the two heads, golden and black, the black bent over his open book, and overlooked Marion's lack of proper greeting.

I do not know how loose that rag is, Edward thought, rising courteously. He can ruin me now, if he can spit it out and does. What will my Uncle have done to me if I am expelled or sent down—but he looked at the Master with a steady eye, and hoped, if enlightened, the Master would not take amiss the enforcement of his own ruling.

"Well, Mr. Armstrong," he said, "I am glad to see you begin to run to company. Even reading can be carried to excess." He coughed, and looked benignly towards Alleyn, who turned his head about and smiled courteously at the Master, letting his gaze fall full and intentionally on Edward as it passed him.

"Gating is not wholly unpleasant, eh, Lord Alleyn," he said, "and tonight it is the last one, for a time, we hope. You get some reading done, at last, hey, and no more nonsense, eh?"

"I shall try, sir," Edward heard Marion say pleasantly.

"What do you read?" the Master said with a ponderous and disinterested benevolence.

"Herodotus, sir," Marion answered. "Armstrong's Greek history is the better, and he has come to strengthen me in mine." His voice lingered with brief soft emphasis on Edward's name.

"Excellent, excellent," said the Master, moving away, and passing his hands one over the other, passed out of the door, without closing it. Edward left his chair, and closed both. Behind him, he heard Marion's voice:

"Liar and hypocrite! You knew about my meeting and you came to see if I was here; I wonder if you were disappointed to find I was." He cursed him softly and fluently in several languages. Edward walked over to him, and picked the damp handkerchief, slightly spotted with blood, out of his lap where Alleyn had spat it out.

"Who sent you here?" Alleyn asked, his eyes snapping but his mouth pleasant.

"I am not going to tell you."

"Never mind then. I will find out myself. They are fools, whoever they are, and half-drunk. Don't they know one can make considerable sound through a gag like that, though old Rowley-Powley might have taken it for mere impudence. I think he is a little deaf. I would have, too, had you not done what you did. Ineffective for what they meant, but damned uncomfortable. Were you worried? I wouldn't have delivered you into the hands of that old bag of farts. You are a merciful gaoler, there are few such, and I worship the goddess Mercy. She is all I do worship, I think. May I have some water?"

When Edward returned with a glass, and held it for him to drink, he said, urgently, "You have preserved me, will I nill I, from breaking the Head's rule, and I am glad now for it. You saw, I played your game. Untie the rest now, and let me make my meeting. I still can. I will be grateful then, and not angry. I promise you my gratitude and my anger are both worth something."

Edward shook his head, and sat down again in the chair and took out his book.

"Answer me, damn you, in plain language. Will you let me go?"

"No," Edward said, "I will not. It is no use to ask me. You waste your breath to do it."

He was interrupted by a string of Irish curses, whose like and fluency he had not encountered. Among them he heard details of his genealogy he had not imagined: "Reiver!" Marion spat out between his teeth. "Freebooter! Descendant of Armistranges—what can one expect! Rapers of England, Ireland, and Scotland!"

"Or to curse me," he finished.

There was a brief pause, like that before the electricity springs from cloud to cloud, and in which Edward could almost hear the working of the other's mind.

"Why should you do this?" Marion asked curiously, this time not intemperately. "I don't know you. Why should you interfere?"

"I suppose I was persuaded to," Edward said. "I find to my surprise too that on occasion I can be persuaded to interfere. My Uncle tells me I am a moralist, and he may be right."

"A moralist?" said Marion bitterly. "A moralist?" he repeated more bitterly. "And you would keep me here, tonight, of all nights? I damn your moralisms. I suppose you subscribe to the Thirty-nine?"

"In part," Edward said, his eyes on his book.

"In part! And to a merciful God, I daresay you do, and a kind, well-ordered world in which all is for the best, 'in this best of all possible worlds.' Or have you not read *Candide?*"

Edward shook his head.

"Read it, then. Or read Blake. And come with me tonight."

"I could not do it. This meeting—I am told—is for an instigation to riot."

"Riot? How innocently the word sits on your lips. Let me tell you, you insufferable and pious little prig, that riot is the voice of, in the words of 'Jockey' Norfolk and Fox, 'our sovereign's health—the majesty of the people.' It cannot be heard in a gentle whisper, such as you might prefer, it must have its royal roar." His voice grew dulcet. "Are you afraid of the people, wee child?"

"I don't know. In mass, I am, armed or in riot or revolution I am."

"Let me tell you, there is no riot, being the people's voice, that sooner or later did not win its point. France has won hers, America has won hers, even the Christian rabble won theirs against Rome, Ireland will in time win hers. It may be sooner rather than later. I mean to help it be sooner."

"But has France won hers? Has she not a new tyrant in place of the old?"

"Perhaps. It was what Emmet feared himself." He smiled ruefully. "Poor Emmet! The disadvantage to riot is that when the reforms do come, the original rioters are often dead or past caring. They will come all the sooner for a little blood, but I sometimes wonder if the first rioters realise that they will not see their fruits, or seldom. I mean to help them see some." His brilliant eyes flashed. "And so you could not go to a meeting for reform? You would rather sit quiet in your comfort and watch our vampire peers in Ireland suck out its heart's blood, to consume in England? See its veins, which are its people and its soil, bled dry of their own rightful prosperity to support profligate riotous princes here?

"I could tell you things I saw with my own eyes, in 1803, but you are a little boy and I will spare you that, and not make you weep. Ireland is the Devil's Walk, and you are too young for it. But look about you. In the streets of London and of Manchester, and at the looms, and at the brick factory here, and at Newgate in London, or the prison here, the Castle, without windows or light because there is a tax on glazier glass, and children with no place to go, and nothing to eat, and no life but to steal and be hung because they steal. Unless the kind parish sends them from their families to the factories and to the workhouse, to a living death." His soft persuasive voice paused, and then as Edward did not speak, continued. "Go look in the taverns at the cottagers who drink beer there because they can no longer afford to make their own and can only afford bad tea at home, and stay there because there is no reason to go home: no place to raise food or graze animals, no place to cut fuel, now the commons are enclosed, and trees prescribed for hedges, for ships, for anything except to keep them warm or cook their food. A man gets seven shillings a week here, Armstrong, that's a man with a family, and my father has sixty thousand pounds in pensions alone. That's less than the price of a loaf of bread if he can't find fuel to bake one. Did you know that, little Armstrong? And did you know that the dole is given equally to the man who does very little at all, and forced on the man who could have earned, had the law let him work? Did you know that between the tithes and the rents and the fixed rates it is more profitable for the poor to raise bastards than families? The parish will pay to support bastards after its own fashion but it deprives a man of any way to support his own. And that is here in England. In Ireland they all starve equally.

"And because I would try to do something about it, would you stop me? I am hard to stop, and I will go on until I am stopped. Or are you already like one of those who 'pity the plumage but not the dying bird'? Who jail their critics in double irons so that they have to soil themselves like the children their concern is for? Who cloak any enormity they do in concealed legal Latin words—who call desperate, hungry, robbed patriots 'the disaffected'? Are you? Are you to be a man only for assemblies? Have you not seen it, the bleeding body of the poor bird? How can you walk the streets of London and not weep? I cannot. Have you not seen it? Your God does not see, but you can. How can you keep me here? How can you spout your moralities at me?"

"No," Edward said quietly, not explaining himself, "I have not seen what you say."

"Then open your eyes and look. Even just go walk in parts of Oxford here. Go see the child who is to be hung this week for smothering her bastard baby, the bedmaker's daughter in a nameless College here seduced by a nameless Lord. Open your eyes. Walk about and look."

"I will," said Edward. "I had not thought to do it before. But I think myself it is possible to make a sufficient hell for oneself regardless of how one is fed or clothed or politically represented, and so it does not interest me very much. Sometimes even I think it is a happier life to be so obsessed by the requirements of staying alive that one has not time or energy to spend on too much refinement of one's thoughts and emotions."

"You are a strange boy," Marion said thoughtfully, "stranger than I thought for. Are you by any chance lending yourself to this because it gives you pleasure to mishandle me?"

"I don't think I know what you mean," Edward said flatly, "and for *accuracy*, I have not touched you, and I have certainly not mishandled you."

"I find your face and your form particularly pleasing," Marion said quietly. "Loose me, and I will show you what I mean."

"Then I certainly will not," Edward said, smiling without embarrassment, "if I take your meaning, as I think I do. You shall certainly stay right as you are."

Marion began to laugh in genuine amusement. "I mistook you, little Strongarm, your face deceived me, but I see you are not a woman after all. If I could, I would give you my hand in apology. I am desperate enough to leave this room to have tried any means. So you stand warned."

"I did not need to be warned," Edward said. "I know how you must feel, and I am beginning to be sorry for my part in it. After all, if you are determined to destroy yourself, why should it be my concern?"

"And is it?"

"I seem to have made it mine tonight," Edward said thoughtfully, "and I will go through with it. Be quiet now, my lord Alleyn, I have these books to read before I meet my tutor at ten tomorrow. And you do yourself."

"Is that Paley? God, how can you read him?"

"I read these books to take my degree, and please my Uncle, but I do not have to talk about them to you, or to anyone, except my tutor, and later on my examiners."

"I thought you were a religious?"

"I may be, but if I am, it does not come from Paley."

"Oh? From what then?" Marion mocked him. "Your own wellsprings?"

"Perhaps," Edward said, "but wellsprings have other sources in the end, that is the nature of them, but they are invisible and quiet to the casual observer. Be quiet, my lord Alleyn, or I shall make you be," and he pulled out his handkerchief.

"You would not," his unwilling host gasped.

"I would and I will," Edward said, and opened his book, directing only a brief glance Alleyn's way.

"Most merciful and all puissant saviour," Marion said with mock humility, "I am at your command, but instruct me how I shall turn the pages to my book."

Edward in answer left his chair and took a smaller one nearer to Marion's, and saying only, "Tell me when you want me to turn," continued his reading. His concentration and seeming indifference piqued the older boy who, not to be outdone, for some minutes also applied his mind to the pages before him. For a time, the silence was broken only by the word "turn," then a soft knock came at the door, that Edward had bolted. Edward's eyes quickly met Alleyn's, that had also turned to his, questioning, and then, not waiting for an answer, as those eyes avoided his and as the handle turned without effect, he pushed his chair back quickly but noiselessly, and stood up behind Marion, his hand without warning hard over his mouth, pressing his head backwards and against him, his other arm braced hard against his neck. The boy beneath his hands after a brief futile tensing relaxed, but Edward did not. The knock came again, and the appearance of footsteps leaving, but Edward stood tensely. He had thought to check the locks on the windows in the three rooms when he had straightened the rooms, and he had found them already secured by the three kidnappers, behind their curtains. He heard a whistle below one now, soft and urgent, repeated several times, at intervals, below different windows. Quiet finally surrounded the besieged rooms again, but Edward still held his hand over his prisoner's mouth, and when he felt teeth attempt to bite his hand, increased the pressure with his arm against the more helpless neck. They stayed this way a long time, fifteen minutes more, perhaps, until Edward, listening, heard finally what he waited for, an almost unheard footstep joining and then two retreating from the door. He sighed, and relaxed his hold, partly.

"Will you be quiet?" he whispered close to Marion's ear, and loosened his fingers a little.

"Yes, by God," said Marion, between them. "I said I would, damn you."

"I thought it too much to ask, just then," Edward replied. He sat down, somewhat shaken, in his first chair, his book in his lap, but he did not read.

"You fool—!" Edward felt the whispered words rather than heard them. He did not look up. "You should be at school still," the young man in the chair, some five years his senior, said savagely, "if you want to engage in pranks like this. Why aren't you in school?"

"I did not initiate it," Edward said quietly, and with some pity, ignoring the last question.

"Why aren't you in school? How old are you actually?"

"I shall be eighteen in a week," Edward said.

"Eighteen in a *week?* Then you are seventeen now, and you have been here over a year, you have been here five terms already. My God, how did they let you in? At seventeen I was not even ready for Montem, I was still construing verbs in class and hell outside at Eton and being flogged at the block for both."

"It did not seem to have the effect intended."

"I will thank you not to preach at me."

"I did not mean to, I was just thinking. I have never been to school, you see, I don't know what you are talking about."

"How *are* you here?" He looked at Edward curiously. "I thought only titles were educated still at home, and you do not have a title—or do you?" Edward shook his head. "This night is going to be more interesting than I thought. What is your name?"

"Armstrong."

"I know that, Reiver. I meant all your name."

"Edward Clare."

"Edward Clare Armstrong," Alleyn said thoughtfully. "Well, Edward Clare, how *are* you here? I keep asking you that and you keep not telling me. Your father must have some enormous influence. Or have you unusual talents?"

"My father is dead. I did not know it was so extraordinary."

"It may not be a rule but it is a custom. I have seen no one else here so young, in my four years here, in residence, that is. I should not think you would enjoy it much. Though Fox was fifteen, and Gibbon too, and Bentham was only twelve, but that was years and years ago and that was Fox. And Gibbon was expelled."

"I did not come to enjoy myself, but I do."

"Lord!" Marion said simply. "Are you precocious, or an incumbrance?" He observed Edward narrowly. "Which is it? Or both? I see I have hit home, but I cannot see where I drew blood."

Edward did not reply.

"So you have never been to school? Never fagged, never written Alcaics? I am still wondering why, but you have not missed much."

"Did you not like it?"

Marion would have shrugged, but he could not. "Parts I liked very much, parts not so well. I liked making theatres, and I liked boating, and picnics on the river with hardboiled eggs and radishes and bottles of warm tea stuffed in our greatcoat pockets to eat in the gaps of hedges that we called arbours, when the farmers did not find us. I liked going to the galas the Queen gave at Frogmore, and watching the dances in the pavilion and the decorations, and I even liked George III, though you may not believe that, Edward Clare, when I would meet him in the garden paths at Windsor. I liked his silly Merino sheep, and his old Queen Anne periwig, with all the silly little white curls, and I liked the way he would say to us, 'Have you had a rebellion lately, eh, eh?' I met him in a bookstore once, very early, when no one was around. He was sitting on the counter, reading Tom Paine with a kind of absent interest. Can you imagine that? No, you can't, don't tell me, you 'don't know who Tom Paine is.' He is just the man who pulled the Colonies and his peri-wig down about George's ears. What a fright it gave the bookseller, when he came down into his shop. Before he left, the old German lion looked at me rather sadly, he did not recognise me, I think, but he did my clothes, and he said, 'You are at Eton, are you not? Which form are you?' 'Sixth,' I said, it was my last year. He shook his head, with all those curls, and smiled a little, and said, 'A much greater man than I can ever make you.' I held my tongue, it was after all the King, and he was an old man, and I did not say what I thought, that I did not want him or his party to make me anything, but he must have seen something of it in my face for he frowned a little then and shook a finger at me. But his warning, you see, had no effect. I take none, ever, from tyrants, then or now, in any place." He smiled a little, reminiscently. "I was even then known as Alleyn the Atheist in the Forms. That is not your Church term, you would not know, that was just the school name, and high praise too, for anyone who knew how successfully to defy any form of self-deifying authority, and I did." He paused, and despite his discomfort, his face grew peaceful, as his mind travelled back. "I remember the first time I met the King. I was exploring Windsor Gardens with Lord Westport, whose father has spent four months in gaol for bribing some sailors in wartime to bring back some Greek marbles on a Navy ship for his house in Sligo." He looked at Edward to see what effect that fact produced, but found none. "We were tossing pebbles and coins, and Lord Westport suddenly stopped his coin on his wrist, and began to read its inscription in a voice of meaning: 'Grace of God,' 'France and Ireland,' 'Defender of the Faith,' and there was King George and his party on a crosswalk, just on the other side of the hedge, where our paths must cross."

He laughed with amused mockery at Edward's face. "Do I surprise you, Edward Clare? I am such a good hater, like all the Irish are, I can hate, and still remember with affection, as I will you, if you keep on as you are."

"Tell me some more about Eton," Edward said, passing over the remark.

"No," he said brusquely, "it is enough. I am tired of remembering."

"When did you go?" asked Edward.

"I was twelve."

"Twelve," repeated Edward slowly, remembering. "Didn't you miss your home?"

"No. I liked being away from my father, for he flogged harder than Goodall, if he was home, and oftener. Perhaps it was those ships. I don't know. I would hardly be out of the coach at vacation before I would be called in to him, sometimes I hardly knew for what. I remember once, when I was fifteen, at Easter, I left the coach in the avenue before it reached the house, and went down to the orchard by the river banks, where my brothers and sisters found me, with a message I was to go straight up to the house and meet him in his study, and then and there he had me strip and flogged me until I could hardly stand, I forget now for what, a bad mark perhaps, I think because I had not come to see him. That was his greeting. He did not even ask me how I was, or how the journey was. I could hardly walk, but I went back down to the river bank, and the cherry trees and the peach were all in bloom, and my brothers and sisters and my cousin were swinging from them, and I tried to climb and I fell. I shall never forget that, my shirt beneath my jacket sticking to my back, and my trousers sticking too, and my brothers and sisters crowding round me, puzzled but concerned, and my cousin, whom I thought I loved then, who was also there—and you think I should care to please my father?"

"I did not say that."

"You show it, by what you are doing. I vowed then I should never try to please my father again, ever, except to take what I could get from him. Have you ever been whipped, Edward Clare?"

"Twice," Edward said, remembering too clearly.

"You have experienced nothing, and I shall make it up to you, for you are still whipping age, not shooting. If you keep me here tonight, I will see to it that you are thoroughly flogged."

"I hope you will not do that," Edward said, but not withered by the other's angry eyes. "I do not like to be whipped at all, and I suppose you could do it. I don't know. But I shall just have to risk it, and hope you have a change of heart, for I am going to keep you, as I said I would."

"God!" said Marion. "Where are you from, Edward Clare?"

"From Devon, but I have been living in Northumberland."

"From Devon? There is a Lord Armstrong in Devonshire, my family knows them, but not well. But you said you were a commoner."

"Not exactly. I said I had no title. My father had none that I know of."

"Is that your family?"

"I don't know," Edward said. "I really don't. My father and my mother died when I was six. If I belong to it, they have no interest in claiming me. I live at my guardian's house." He picked up his book and moved as though to turn away.

"Do you like your guardian? Why has he sent you up early?"

"Yes, I do," Edward said, slightly baited. "I told you, I did not know I *was* up early. He may have sent me earlier than he intended. We had a disagreement."

"A disagreement? Blood again," said Alleyn, with interest. "What about?"

"I am not going to tell you."

"Why not? Is it so bad? Nothing shocks me, you know—nothing except public cruelty. Now I am going to shock you," he added, his eyes challenging and provocative. "I need to relieve myself, and I am hungry. What are you going to do about it?"

"I will contrive," said Edward. "A prisoner must be fed, and watered, and kept clean," he said with unexplained bitterness. "Not much embarrasses me. My Scout should have left my supper on the fender. I hope so. I am hungry, too. I have some bread and cheese from lunch, at least, I think. I will go see. As for the first"—he rose and walked the few steps over and took off the gown draped about his prisoner, and a look of both dismay and amusement crossed his face—"that should not be hard. I am glad the Head did not observe how carelessly dressed you were to receive him. He would not have asked only where your waistcoat was, as he did Simmons in Hall."

"At least he could not have fined me for wearing trousers. I was dressing," Marion snapped, "when those damned impudent fools sprang me. What are you going to do?"

"The obvious," said Edward. "I am going to loose your feet, like this, and the rest of you from this chair, except your hands, and let you walk into your bedroom by yourself, and then I'm going to valet you." He set to work at the knots. "I would cut them, but I haven't any other rope." He looked up, shocked. "These ropes are much too tight, I can do nothing with them."

"I know that," said Marion briefly.

"They did not need to be tied this way. You have been cruelly used. You should have told me."

"I have not complained of *that*," Marion said. "They were drunk, that's all. If you want to cut them, you can use the sashes to my dressing gown afterwards, I have two."

"I will," said Edward. "I think I can make you more comfortable. Do you have a knife? In your desk? You must be cramped." He cut the ropes, all except those about his wrists, and let his prisoner stand up and stretch his legs.

"Don't be solicitous," Marion said curtly. "Do what you think you have to do, and please don't talk about it, and when you have finished, tomorrow it will be my turn, and I shall take it. You had better read the statutes of the University, little Edward Clare, you cannot roll a hoop outside in the High, or shoot marbles on the Bodley steps. The laws are still on the books, though I thought them outdated until tonight. Look to it, Edward Clare, or you will be fined for the pastimes more proper to your age." He walked, or stalked, with as much dignity as was possible to his dishabille state into his bedroom.

When his dress was completed, with Edward's help, Edward directed him to a different chair, with arms, away from the desk, and fastened his ankles with part of the rope that had been wound around him to secure him to the straight desk chair. He used the sash to hold his shoulders to the back of the chair, temporarily, and reapplied the gag, while he left the room. He returned in some triumph with his own sash, and a dish of oysters that his Scout had left for him on his fender, a bottle of wine, some candied fruits and nuts, and the bread and cheese. He removed the gag again from his spluttering, angry charge.

"I don't think you trust me," Marion accused him, outraged. "And it is an Alleyn's word."

"Why should I? You are in a state of war, you have as much as said so, and it is your business to deceive me. Besides, I dislike myself being trusted to work harm to myself. I would really rather just have it done to me, openly, than be a partner to it. But if you can be trusted, then don't fight me in what I am about to do next. I am truly sorry you have been left so long this way. It was not necessary at all, I think." He reached behind him, and inserted the knife carefully between his wrists and sliced the rope free, and drew one of his hands and arms out, his left one. He need not have been concerned, for the hands, having lost all feeling, were useless. He laid it gently on the arm of Alleyn's chair, and loosely yet efficiently wrapped his sash about it. The right hand he brought out and left free. He brought over a small table, and served his charge and himself, and they made their late supper together in a momentary truce of hostilities, for even Marion found it impossible to retain his anger while eating someone else's oysters and bread and cheese and wine in comparative comfort before a fire on a snowy winter night, with a rising wind blowing.

Edward estimated it must be past one, and less than five hours before they must begin to dress for Chapel. He felt excessively sleepy. He bound Marion's right hand to the arm of the chair, as he had his left, using his own sash this time, and brought a cushion for his head, and left his book of Herodotus open before him, but he shut Paley, resigning himself to a bad hour's session with his tutor in the morning, and tried to go to sleep in his chair.

"Are you tired?" he asked. Marion shook his head. "I would think you would be. I am. I am supposed to keep you sitting up so that you will be too tired tomorrow to think of anything else to do. So if you want to foil their aims, you should go to sleep. Do you want me to put you in your bed?"

"I want you to be quiet, and to keep your hands off me. I will do as I am." His crossness betrayed his sleepiness.

Edward yawned, uncomfortably, in the chair, and then, used to hardness, curled up on the rug nearest the fire and fell fast and hard asleep. Marion attempted to wake him, but hedgehog fashion, he was protected from invasion even of a voice.

"Your Scout will find your bed made, and unslept in."

"I thought of that," murmured Edward. "I rumpled it."

"What was your disagreement with your Uncle about?"

"It doesn't matter. I will tell you sometime about it," he murmured, almost unintelligible.

Marion could get nothing more out of him. He looked at his infant gaoler, curled up like a real infant, his hands curled and hidden under him whose unexpected capability and strength he had himself experienced, his inventive unembarrassed mind, so surprisingly informed and so surprisingly ignorant, sheathed in sleep. I could use him in my wars, he thought, if he would come. I must try to illuminate him further, and yawned, and fell asleep himself.

Edward was waked by the sound of the hammer beaten on the staircase by the Scout, announcing Chapel was only half an hour away. When he woke, he could at first not imagine where he was or why he was on the floor, and for a moment, until his eyes properly opened, he thought himself again in the priest-hole when he first woke up there. The coal fire had gone out, and the room was cold. He sat up unhappily, wanting to go back to sleep, and put his hands around his knees, as he did in moments of perplexity or distress, and looked about, and saw Marion looking down on him sardonically, as though he had been awake for hours. It was still dark outside, without a glimmer of dawn. He heard a cock faintly crowing. The adventure of the night, and any reason he might have had for doing it, seemed as dead as the burnt-out coals of the fire. His face expressionless, he undid the sashes that bound Alleyn, leaving the rope on his feet for him to do himself, and picked up the oyster dish and his sash and his book, and walked out and back to his own rooms. He did not know that the whistler, on watch and seeing him go, went in and held brief audience while Marion, not waiting for his servant, shaved himself. Had he known, he would not have much cared. His own Scout had not come, and his rooms were colder than Alleyn's.

He found Alleyn waiting for him outside the doors of Chapel, moving to block his passage, the sardonic gleam in his eyes even more pronounced.

"As the trick was planned, I was not supposed to know who you were, was I? Surely not—you have too kind a heart. I haven't any for my enemies. You should have taken care."

Edward looked at him quickly, in turn, wondering why he troubled to say it, if it was true, and sent him a small, twisted smile, fleetingly, and raised his hand in half-salute, and passed into Chapel. He was hard put not to yawn openly in Chapel, and his mind paid no attention to the words. He watched the Van Linge windows in the beautiful Hall, to avoid seeing the black head a row ahead of him, of painted, not stained, glass, done in the early seventeenth century, when he knew the present buildings had been begun, although the College itself dated back to 1280 for its founding. He seldom looked at them, for they had the Mediterranean for a background, and that sea reminded him always of his Uncle. All the subjects were violent: Jonah and the Whale, the Expulsion from Eden, Elijah's garments floating like fallen leaves, and Elisha retrieving them. He caught the Proctor's disapproving eye directed toward him. He wrenched his eyes away, and his mind, and tried to put both on the present service.

He found his Scout in his rooms when he returned, his fire laid and beginning to burn, his bed made, his breakfast set out. He had as unpleasant hour as he had foreseen with his tutor, attended his lectures with half an ear, and returning to his rooms, fell still dressed into bed and a deep sleep. He did not trouble to lock his doors. He could not believe that in so civilized a place he would be subject to much, if any, revenge, and he did not see how he could stop it from taking place, if he was to be. He supposed for a young student to interfere in the affairs of an older one was an impertinence that might be slapped down, but he had had so little notice taken of him for a year and a half, he did not really expect any now, particularly since Marion, whom he somehow believed ultimately to be fair, despite his threats, knew he had not himself planned the attack. He slept until he was awakened by his Scout bringing lunch. He would happily have omitted lunch, and slept all afternoon, but he remembered that a concert he particularly had wanted to hear was to be given at two by the organist of Christ Church for St. Scholastica's Day.

IV

His thoughts were drowsy and preoccupied, and he did not notice other figures walking, or the converging of several near him on a quiet, deserted corner, until he was actually set upon and knocked face downwards into the snow. The attack, and its audacity in daylight and a semi-public place, stunned him, and he did not fight at all for the seconds in which his hands were twisted behind him and bound. He struggled then, his face ground into the snow, until he felt the authority of one pair of hands rested quietly on his bound ones, the whistler's though he did not know it, and in response to their quality, he grew inexplicably quiet, like a tamed or mesmerized bird.

It was done in less than a minute's time. He was picked up like a child and as lightly by the pair of hands, his face pressed into a coat front so that he could hardly breathe, and taken a short way into an alcove, where a black woollen scarf was wound about his eyes and knotted, his ankles bound, and a handkerchief pushed in his mouth, though not secured there. A cloak was thrown about over him, covering his head, and his face was once more pressed inward. No one questioned them, or even met them, as they walked across what seemed by their unevenness to be open fields, in what seemed an endless walk. When he stirred, he was pressed closer, suffocatingly close, and soothed by the pair of hands; when he lay quiet, he was again allowed a breath of air. He was taken finally into some kind of room or building, cold, with two zones, one colder, one hotter, so that somewhere he supposed in it there must be a fire. The steps of the boots of the man who carried him echoed hollowly on the floor, and in the empty-sounding corner of the room where, though he could not see, he heard voices that did not seem to be University voices now. He was truly frightened now, as he had not been, for he did not know at all into what kind of hands he had fallen.

His restraints were removed, all except the black scarf around his eyes; what followed then he tried thereafter to forget. He was stripped of his clothes, without preliminary or formality, and forced, naked and shivering, to crouch kneeling in the center of what seemed to be a pitiless, rough, jeering ring. In a mock court, with mock solemnity and form, in both Latin and English, he was read out first his personal crimes against a senior member of his College, not named and not present, and then his crimes as a loyal English citizen and incipient Tory, being from the Tory stronghold of Northumberland and having behaved like one. The Irishman who had been smuggled in to address the meeting of the night before had gone, he was informed, his errand incomplete, but one of his disciples proceeded in a lilting yet rough sing-song to enlighten Edward of the history and the nature of his crimes as an unprotesting Englishman against the subject Irish nation in graphic terms. As he listed each, he paused to have each illustrated concretely, although not ultimately completed, against Edward's shrinking person.

"So shrank Eire," the voice intoned, "so helpless was she and her sons, and so pitiless were you and your representatives." The room turned suddenly into a hell. He was threatened explicitly with emasculation, and felt the cold edge of the knife hard against him until his nerves broke and he cried out for mercy.

"You have shown no mercy," he was told relentlessly, and the pressure increased, until he sobbed incoherently that he did not know.

"The prisoner did not know," the voice mocked, but the pressure was removed. "The prisoner requests illumination."

He was held over the fire by his hands and feet and roasted while tales of Catholic burnings were told him until he screamed and fainted, with fright more than actual burning. He was revived by snow rubbed in his face and ice water thrown over his stomach, and then initiated into the term half-hanging, much in use by Cornwallis' English troops in putting down uprisings, both to terrorize and to avoid prisoners, jounced on the back of one of the taller men present, his hands clutching futilely and frantically at the noose about his neck while he heard voices chanting, "So yours have done to ours." Unable to help himself, he erected and wet himself.

Abruptly he was set down again on his knees and heels in the center of the ring, and read a history of the massacres, starting with Elizabeth and the Penal Laws, then Cromwell at Drogheda and Wexford, the Scotch settlement and the Armstrongs' part at Londonderry, the recent French Invasions and reprisals, until the room seemed filled with robbery and rapine, blood and torture and death, ashes and strangled breath and cries. The rope had not been taken from about his neck where it lay loose like a collar, and occasionally to punctuate the story, a boot pressed against the small of his back, and he felt the rope pulled tight, his hands desperately reaching inside it to loosen it again. He was told of destroyed Abbeys whose floors lay feet deep in piles of unburied bones and skulls, and read the Laws on rents, on disenfranchisement, against assemblies; prisons and slums of Dublin were described to him; the Hearts of Oak, Hearts of Steel; the United Irishmen's attempts that failed, and the formal Union with the English Parliament that followed, a union like devouring and digestion; the Heroes and the Martyrs of the rebellions and their deaths.

"Remember young William Orr," they told him, " 'basely murdered by the law': even your countrymen knew that, Fox, Norfolk, Oxford, Erskine, Burdett, Tooke, but what did they do? They toasted him at Fox's birthday dinner while he died on the public scaffold. Remember the brothers Sheares executed the both of them on the word of one man, and that man an Armstrong. Remember Edward Fitzgerald and Wolfe Tone and Oliver Bond, dead in prison of the wounds given them in their taking, and William Jackson taking the poison his wife brought him at breakfast on the day of his condemnation, to save his estate from attainder. Remember Miles Byrne in exile and Michael Dwyer transported, and James Weldon and McCann and Garrett and Thomas Russell, executed indecently without amnesty or mercy. Remember Robert Emmet whom no one will forget now. Remember those who suffered and died and whose names are not remembered, any more than yours will be."

In the end, his brain and his ears ran so with retold gore, his shock disappeared and he did not care for their agonies, only his own, except to wonder how, with it all, the Irish could also suffer from overpopulation. Later, when he could once again think, he supposed it must be some law inherent in nature for men trying to survive, increased destruction and increased birth conjointly.

He tried not to sob, but he found it hard not to, helpless and blindfold and degraded among unseen tormentors. When he did, his distress was greeted with derision and mockery. Flogging with a cat was described in explicit detail to him. He was asked roughly who had employed him, and for how much, but he could not answer anything that satisfied them; when he answered truthfully that he did not know their names, he was not believed. His hands were caught then and held, and a hard authentic leather gag given him to bite on, and one of them took a whip, not a cat, and carefully laid a pattern on his back. Between each striping he was asked again if he would reveal the names of his superior employers, but he only bit the leather in anguish, for he did not even know their names, nor would he have given them up to this. His hands finally were let go, after some word or sign in charcoal was written on him, and his breeches were returned to him. His hands were shaking so, blindfold, he could not put them on, and he had finally to be helped, to rude laughter.

Kneeling again in their midst, he was forced to learn certain Irish patriot songs, to repeat the words, and then to sing the songs, one in the Gaelic itself, but here his tormentors overshot their aim, for his voice, being unusually pure, surprised them, and in its misery, particularly suited to these songs. Unable here to mock, they were for that brief time moved in spite of themselves, and pronounced his crimes expiated.

They closed their court then, with an admonishment that afterwards he abjure interference in the activities of those his elders and his betters, but his anguish was not over, for to his horror he felt again a noose drawn about his neck, and he was lifted on a chair. He could not believe it, that having suffered so much he was to be murdered, and he had to hold to the back of the chair for support. He was then in solemn language, in a voice he half recognised, instructed to swear that he would reveal to no one whatsoever what had happened to him in that room, or to expect immediate extinguishing and execution, with no more preparation than the Irish Rebels were given. Shock took his breath away. When he hesitated, the chair, unbelievably, was kicked from beneath him, and he hung for a half-second in gasping, wretched agony, incontinent like a baby, his hands held, until he felt the chair again beneath his feet, and a hand loosened the noose.

"Courts end in hangings. The next time will be for eternity," he was told. "Swear quickly, by your hope of Heaven."

"I do," he cried, "I will never tell, not now, not ever, not anyone, by God or hope of Heaven or anything you wish. I would have sworn before, you did not give me time," he added bitterly, in pain.

He felt a hand smash across his cheek, "for impudence, in questioning the judgement of the tribunal," he was told. He was also told, in graphic language, that if he broke his oath so sworn, one of them would certainly find a way into his room at night, and leave him hanging there in earnest.

"If it is told," he said, "it will not be by me." A second blow smashed his other cheek, "for casting aspersion on the Court. Answer the Court its questions simply yes or no."

"No, I will never tell," said Edward, not adding that he did not wish to, and that nothing short of hanging could bring him ever to tell his humiliations at their hands.

He was then required to kiss the hands, the feet, or whatever part of their anatomy they chose to present him, of each member of his tribunal, and to thank each separately for their undeserved mercy to him. He was struck sharply by each in absolution. He had not known men could behave so, to one another, and he felt himself already in unending hell, but it did end in time, and he was aware finally the room was almost empty. His hands and feet were rebound, his mouth regagged, and he was lifted up again into the paradoxically gentle arms and gentling hands that had carried him there. They walked for what seemed again a long time, and then he heard the Porter's voice, and an answering one explaining he was drunk and passed out, which in his College was a plausible excuse, at any time of day. He felt himself carried up narrow steps, and into a room and still muffled, dumped without ceremony onto some surface that felt like a windowseat, and left, blessedly, alone. He stayed alone, the blessed relief changing to the torment of cramped limbs and scarce air, for several hours, not knowing where he was.

He heard finally the door open, and light quick steps enter, and cross the room. They stood still, near the center of the room, and then returned the way they had come, and he heard the oak closed and then the inner door, and the footsteps return to stand near him.

"And what package is this that I have not ordered?" he heard the now familiar voice of Alleyn say, beside him, half-drawling. He felt a hand draw the cloak off his head, then he felt fingers at the knots of the scarves over his eyes and mouth, and the hands turn him over, quickly and not gently, so that he flopped, gasping, like a fish hooked on land, he thought, onto his sore back. He could not bring himself to open his eyes. Ostrich-like, he felt if he did not somehow he would not be seen and would be somewhere else.

"It is Edward Clare," the voice pursued, faintly surprised, faintly mocking, "without his waistcoat, and with his eyes shut for once, and his moral mouth too. The tables, it would seem, have been turned, and I am to have mine, or has it been had for me?" He turned Edward half over, with a hand, and pulled the cloak down, and let him fall back, this time more gently. "I see it has." The mocking note left his voice, and he sat down at Edward's feet on the windowseat to untie the knots that held his ankles.

"Open your eyes, Edward Clare, I'm not going to hurt you. I did not intend this, or wish it. Whatever I said last night I said in anger, I have forgotten it. Whoever thought to please me in this way, sadly miscast. Who was it, Edward Clare?"

"Ask yourself," Edward said with dry, uncomfortable lips.

"I don't think I need to. Did they frighten you? I see they have. I will speak to them. But what am I going to do with you, now that I have you?"

"You might untie my hands, for a start," Edward said, feeling rather sick with hunger and reaction, "and let me go back to my rooms."

"I can't do that, not immediately right now. It would look ungrateful, for all their efforts. But what shall I do with you? I don't need a fag, I have all the servants I want, and I don't want one. I've been through that, both ways, and to me it is a bore. What will you do, Edward Clare, if I untie these strings on your hands? Fly at me?"

"I will sit up, and be more comfortable, and listen to you. And I will ask to excuse myself briefly, and return."

"Fair enough," said Alleyn. "How long have you been here? All afternoon? All evening?"

"I don't know," Edward said, "I think so. Your friends ran across me, just after lunch. I don't know what time it is."

"Good Lord!" said Marion, but he did not ask what had transpired. "You have missed Chapel, then, and dinner today, and an evening lecture. That seems hardly fair to you. I will send word in to the Proctor you have been sick and to prick you *aeger,* so that he will not frown." He had cut the knots. "You had better take one of my shirts—the second drawer—any shirt."

When Edward reappeared, he found Marion instructing the Scout he had called to bring supper for two.

"You are going to have to stay here for two or three days, Edward Clare," he said. "Will you mind? That should satisfy my friends that honour has been satisfied and justice done. Then they won't annoy you any more. They can suppose what they like. I have four rooms, and you can bring some clothes and books into one, or my servant will. And meet your tutor, and all that. Do you have a private servant?"

Edward shook his head, and sat down, hoping he would not faint.

"You live the simple life? I cannot make you out, Edward Clare."

"Nor I you," Edward said. "I cannot imagine having friends before whom I had to pretend anything, certainly not something like this."

"You are such a damned moralist, Edward Clare, you quite put my back up. I wonder if I can support your presence so long ungagged. I don't wonder any longer that your guardian has sent you off. I would myself." As he spoke, his lazy-seeming eyes were observing Edward closely. "Ah, a hit, and I see I've drawn blood again. Come here, and let me see what they have done to you. No? Who is this guardian of yours anyway who gets tired of your tongue?"

Edward did not answer, but he got up and walked to the window and stood looking out, into the quadrangle, and watched the night which lay so gently on the planes of earth. He could see the moon, round as a globe, through the open window, bathing all the black air with a white suffusion. The single shapes of house and tree were dimmed, pressed to a flat opaqueness underneath the grave weight of that still silent light.

I could write a poem, about this, he thought, wearily yet with a quickening interest.

"Do you mind so much?" he heard Alleyn's voice say behind him. "Staying here?"

He turned around, suddenly, putting the poem out of his head, his true smile lighting his face. "I shall not mind at all."

"Good, then," said Alleyn, surprised. "We shall have supper on it, which I hear arriving with the Arimaspian, and I will not tease you any more, at least not very much." He looked at him sharply. "Are you going to faint? Please don't!" He rose quickly and crossed to Edward and made him lie down on the windowseat. "You gave me a scare for a moment," he said, pouring out a glass of wine and bringing it to him to drink. "Ralph here can vouch to the Proctor that you are sick. He will do it—won't you?" he said, addressing the Scout. "A touch of ague and fever, not serious," he said. "I shall keep him here. Bring his things round tomorrow," he added.

Edward found he could eat very little supper after all. "If you really mean to have me here, and have a bed, I should like to go in it now if I may. I do feel rather ill." He found himself incapable of thinking any thoughts at all, and the room moved unpleasantly about him. Marion looked at him worriedly, and rolled out a trundle bed which he kept beside his own.

"One should never tell a direct lie," Marion said. "I have always found with me that almost at once it becomes the truth. I do hope you are not going to be really ill."

"I think I am. Send me home to my rooms."

"I certainly shall not, least of all now. You will sleep here by me, and I will hear you, if you need anything in the night."

Edward slept restlessly, crying out piteously and incoherently in the night, and holding with all his strength in his nightmares to the hand Marion held out to him, unable to wake from them. In the morning he was very ill, though not delirious, from exposure and shock. Marion neglected his requirements, which he never needed encouragement to do, and nursed him as tenderly as a woman, but he could see no improvement and his concern grew.

"You must have a doctor, and your guardian should be notified. I would like to call in Knighton."

"No," Edward said with an effort, "please no. I could not bear my guardian to know, or a doctor to see the marks on me. Knighton knows me. He would know what they are, and tell my Uncle. I will be better soon."

Marion was not reassured. "I don't want that either, but what's to do, Edward? You must be seen by someone. I could get a surgeon who is used to duels and staying quiet, perhaps." His face was troubled. "I will fetch Dr. Lind," he said with a sudden thought. "Windsor is not far, if you don't mind staying by yourself with my servant? Will you be all right? He is eccentric, but he is an excellent doctor, I think. And he hates George III, he was his physician once. He is the man for us. I knew him well at Eton. He tended me once when I was very ill and out of my head and my father wanted me put in a madhouse, and he would not let him do it. He will come for me, I think."

He returned in the afternoon with the Doctor, an elderly man with sharp piercing eyes that were yet kind. Edward's fever had gone so high, he was hardly aware of the presence of either. The Doctor reassured the Master of the College that the illness was neither infectious nor critical, and enlisted the aid of the Scout and Alleyn's valet and servant.

"He was hazed, as my father would say, by some students," Marion said, "and the hazing got out of hand."

"It would seem so," Dr. Lind said sharply. "I have seen marks not unlike this before. I thought you were beyond that, here. I hope none in this College."

"I hope not," Marion said, questioningly.

"It is not my business," the old Doctor said, severely, answering his question. "But these bruises which are quite severe complicate the illness of a common ague, and are not unlike the bruises of scurvy when it is not yet advanced, of which my father made a study, as you know, Marion, with Cook. I can bleed him, if you wish, and cut the fever quicker."

"He is weakened enough already, I would rather you did not, if you can manage."

"Oh, I can manage," the old Doctor said, with the ghost of a chuckle. "I remember you, when your father had it done; you thought you were being put to a slow death. With such an opinion, I would say, on the whole, you were very brave about it."

"I was younger then," Marion said briefly, "I know better now. I have more pleasant memories of you than that, and you know I do. When Edward is better, perhaps we may come to visit you, and you will show him the treasures of your house from your voyages. But we won't curse the King together or raise spirits. Edward is not wild, like me."

"Let us then attend to the first thing," the Doctor said, "to bring him out of this fever." He gave careful instructions to the Scout on certain fresh vegetable and fruit juices and scraped broths to be prepared, and after two days of careful tending by the combined ministrations of the four, Dr. Lind pronounced him to be mending, and asked to be returned home. He left medicines to be taken, and thorough instructions behind him, which Marion promised to see fulfilled.

When he returned, he found Edward awake, his eyes open, watching for him.

"Who was that old man with so beautiful a face?" he asked. "Has he gone?"

"It was Dr. Lind," Marion said, "of Windsor."

"I thought it had been an apostle," Edward said, smiling wearily, "to fetch me. How good you were, to bring him here. He seems very skilled. Has he gone?" Marion nodded. Edward sighed wearily and closed his eyes. Marion sat beside him, and bathed his forehead with a cloth, as he had been told to do, and smoothed back Edward's hair from his brow with a mother's tenderness.

"I am too much trouble," Edward said wearily. "I am ashamed for it."

"You are not," said Marion. "And it is I who am ashamed." He studied Edward's face carefully, and the eyes which did not meet his so frankly, and were withdrawn, when they were open. "You are not only hurt, Edward, you are troubled, and I think I know why. Do not be. Forget it, if you can. You would be surprised how many have." He smoothed Edward's brow with his fingers almost absently, and addressed the wall quietly.

"You know now what a Public School, at its worst, can be like, Edward Clare: oligarchy, made into a kind of mob rule, the tyranny of capable and unlimited power." Edward made no response, but Alleyn thought he was listening. "I have certain friends, otherwise estimable, who stayed too long in the Long Chamber. I was never there myself, or only briefly; I lived in town, in a Dame's house. But imagine a roomful of boys, Edward Clare, twelve years or younger up through all years to at least eighteen, crowded, fifty of them, perhaps, locked in by themselves all night, and every night, from eight to six. They grew immune there, these friends of mine, to the feelings of gentleness or pity through first too long a subjection to brutality themselves, to over-much servility, and then to too long a corresponding power to dominate and to retaliate in kind on others younger than they now were. I was sent many times out myself, even living where I did, when I was twelve in weather when my hands froze and the water froze, to fetch drinks, or through the secret ways of the sewers. There was no help for it, I went. I was whipped for my slowness in the first, by my peers, and in the morning, for lack of sleep, being slow in class, I was whipped for that by my masters. I was not used to such treatment then, it made me very ill, I had finally to be sent home for some weeks, but I never told my father why. I resolved, when I had power, not to do the same, and when I became one of the older boys, I did not. I remember one day, when I could still weep, when I fled from my tormentors, and flung myself down on the grass, it was Spring then, and promised myself that when I would grow up, I would break the Tyranny of the Strong over the weak, if I could.

"But it is not so strange a system for our world as you think. Did you have Bewick's *Fables* when you were a child, his picture that made me shiver of the little boy coolly hanging his dog? I could not bear it then, but why should children not practise hanging their dogs and cats and birds—it is only a preparation in hardness for what they will live with and have done for them when they grow up. It is all about them, even as children; it is no wonder they are curious, and ape and imitate what their elders do around them, and have no feelings for their victims. Lord Howick is the exception, to care. He is General Grey's son, Edward, and he understands too about the Irish. He is the Whig's first Lord of the Admiralty, and one of the rare good ones."

His quiet voice, grown bitter, stopped, and then grew impersonal again and picked up his earlier thought. "You must not blame them too much: it is a system admirably suited to train overseers. You had only the one night of it, but you will be living among men who have had years. You will learn to recognise the stamp of it in their faces, and in their behaviour, and to know where they lived, and under who, and how. Ill-usage can make one know who one is, and more often, it can make one forget; it can make one a humanitarian—or a revolutionary— or a Tory. It has happened, Edward, whatever it was. It is happening to someone, all the time, and the world still goes on. Be angry if you like but don't be ashamed or humiliated for it. It is not worth it."

"How odd you should say that," said Edward, "someone else—my Uncle—once told me to be angry, too, if I liked, but I do not like to be angry."

"I can see you don't," Marion said thoughtfully, "and yet you invite a kind of violence. I am sorry you have been ill-used," he added gently. With a tact unusual to him, he avoided all mention of Ireland, or the little Irish harp marked on Edward's back, or any further mention of politics of any kind.

The next day Edward insisted on meeting his tutors and resuming his usual responsibilities, but he agreed without much pressure put, when Marion insisted, to a continuance of his stay in Alleyn's rooms. He napped in his own rooms, but they met again in the evening, for supper, in Alleyn's.

"I think no one teases you, Edward Clare," Marion said over the last glass of wine, comfortably and companionably, "you are not as serious as I thought, but you have a serious air. You don't seem as young as I thought, either. I shall undertake to tease you. Don't your friends?"

He was startled at the look on Edward's face. "Haven't you any friends? Well, we do tend to leave people rather alone here. I think I shall extend my tyranny, and require you to come home with me. I think my father will be away in London at the Admiralty, but if he is not, he will not bother you. He might think you a steadying influence. Now don't shake your head at me, Edward Clare, for you can't help yourself. You have been delivered into the hands of the enemy. Why, whatever are you crying for? Good Lord, stop at once, or I will tell the Head and have you sent home! You are much too young after all."

"I would like to come," Edward said, putting himself under control. "I cannot think of anything I would like better, but I think my guardian will not allow it."

Marion was silent, looking at him thoughtfully.

"Who is this strict guardian of yours?" he then asked.

"It is the Earl of Tyne." He was puzzled by the intensity of the look of shock on Alleyn's face, not knowing that his "Uncle"'s name was a byword in London, in its own way as famous as those of the "Monks of Medmenham Abbey," or having believed his Uncle's own avowals of his reputation.

"Are you related to the Earl of Tyne?" asked Alleyn curiously, again with the odd look. "I cannot believe it."

"I used to call him my Uncle, but he is not," Edward said briefly. "I have lived at his house in the North since I was six, but he is oftenest at London, I have not seen him much."

"My mother, I think, knows him, there is a cousinage there, somewhere in her family, or some connection. I will have her ask him if you can come."

"She can ask," Edward said, "she can do that. I will be interested to hear his answer."

"My mother is a very influential woman. She persuaded my father to let me come here to learn to be a politician (who of course must know Latin verse) instead of going into the Royal Navy. But the kind of politician I become will surprise him. But you may have done me a better turn than I thought, Edward Clare, for if I do not take my degree this year, he has promised to put me in the Navy, will I nill I. I have been wasting my time this term, I am afraid. I have put my nose everywhere except in my books and my tutor's office."

"I do not think Latin is ever wasted for any use," Edward said seriously, picking out the one phrase that most interested him.

"And why not, little saint? Instruct me."

Edward ignored the mockery of the epithet, and said, again seriously, "It is a study that requires patience and discipline, which are two qualities of which one can never get enough. It exercises the faculties of memory and observance and logic—it encourages attention both to detail and to the governing principle. One is forced to consider and retain something besides oneself and one's own immediate interests for some time, and to concentrate on it with disinterest and to bring every faculty to play upon it. What more could Parliament require? If one can do this for one thing, being Latin, one can do it for another, being Parliament, as easily." He smiled a little. "Being tedious, it teaches courtesy in boredom, as well as patience, and being difficult, endurance. Lacking the honeyed mellifluousness and the seduction of the Greek, it is a thing in itself, teaching the lesson of an act done for no reward, and lacking in essential civilisation, it teaches in reverse by their absence the virtues proper to a true statesman."

"Why, Edward Clare, how severe you are."

"I dislike the Romans: their civilisation, their art, their buildings, their language, their virtues, their sins, their aspirations, their heroes, their laws, their literature, and particularly their wars. I know them very well. But our language and our laws are built on theirs, and we should know them, to understand our own, and to avoid their failures, if possible."

"Why, Edward Clare, I do believe you have the makings in you of a revolutionary after all." He was startled by the flash of fury in Edward's eyes like sudden lightning from a clear sky.

"I do not. Never use that word to me again. I hate your revolutions and you revolutionaries. You do all the harm and all the cruelty you inveigh against, and what does that make you? I believe in means, not ends. Ends are in the hand of God, means only in ours. I would never use the means that you employ, my lord Alleyn, never, not for any reason, not for any wrong, not for any end. It is not death that in the end is so much to be afraid of, as such as you and your friends in the pursuit of your beautiful ends."

"Well," said Marion. "Now I know what you think. Do you hate me?"

"No," said Edward, suddenly tired, "you know I do not. Go to your meeting, I know you have one. Go throw your great words about, and then do abominations, like those you criticise, and would chastise, if you could. I know why your rooms are on the first floor. I will be here when you return, but I am going to sleep." He left his chair, and walked quickly into the bedroom in which his bed now was, and stumbling with exhaustion, put himself in bed.

He did not hear Marion when he came through his windows at three, or wake as he undressed in the next room, or at the light of the candle in his own as Marion looked in upon him. The light fell on his peaceful sleeping face, and his hair, its locks slightly separated in sleep, as were his lips. He did not wake when Marion blew out the candle, or when the owner of the bed pulled back the eiderdown and slipped himself beneath it, beside Edward. When Marion, half-reclining, bent to kiss his lips, his own parted in sleep, and half-returned the pressure of the caress, and then relaxed again in sleep, but as though the touch awakened memories too painful, tears began to slip from his closed eyelids, and he turned away, still asleep. He did not resist Alleyn's explorations of his body, but he did not respond, until locked to him, he gave a cry and tightened his own arms briefly and convulsively, and as suddenly fell back, limp, never seemingly awake. Alleyn remained with him until he felt himself falling asleep, and then he roused himself enough to take himself into his own bed in the larger bedroom.

The older boy omitted the duty of Chapel the next morning, and as they did not sit together in Hall, they did not meet to speak until later that night. Edward greeted him without self-consciousness when they passed, but when he returned from the Sheldonian Theatre at nine, he saw with a shock that only one bed had been made up, and only one was in evidence, on one side of which Marion was lying. The dream-like happening of the night that he had hardly been conscious of and not remembered suddenly rushed fully into his mind, and he knew it had been no dream-image of his Uncle. He was furious and embarrassed at a meaning he did not pretend to misunderstand.

"I cannot imagine," he said stiffly, but all too aware now of the answer, "where you have taken such erroneous notions about me, or what I have said or done to mislead you. I cannot stay in your rooms like this."

"Of course you can stay. You will have to stay," Marion said lazily. "I was not kidnapped one night into the Long Chamber at school for nothing, and I know just how to deal with you. And anyway, why pretend, if you are Tyne's nephew or guardee, or whatever."

"I don't know what you mean," Edward said furiously, "but you will apologise to me and to him in me now and you will never use language like that to me again."

He hit out with his fists and struck Alleyn roundly in the face, which blow brought him off the bed where he had been lying negligently, with a leap and his fists flying. He knocked Edward with his first blow to the floor, and threw himself on top of him, aspraddle, and proceeded with his hand on Edward's jaw, to make himself master with his lips of Edward's, but this time to no avail, for like a demented girl whose virtue was threatened, Edward bit and spat and clawed, and scratched, and twisted his head as best he could under the pressure of the hard fingers holding his jaw.

Alleyn was surprised at the reality of his resistance, and after a few such moments, seeing Edward was indeed in earnest, he let him go, and retired in insulted pride.

"I thought you liked me. I misunderstood you," he said briefly. "I apologise." He did not offer any more explanation.

"I do like you," Edward said, nursing his jaw. "I still do. But that's all. I am going to take my things now, and go."

He looked at Marion, as though to speak, as he left, having gathered his books and his few clothes in his arms, but he saw only a turned back, fierce in its wounded Irish pride. He sighed, and closed the door.

V

He supposed he had seen the last of Marion, and the last of the plans of his invitation, about which he had held few hopes anyway from his guardian, but three days later, he heard an impetuous knock on his door, and Marion had entered almost before his words.

"I have heard from my mother. She is surprised and enchanted. Will you come?"

"Do you want me still?" Edward asked, amazed and feeling astonished delight, not daring even so to hope.

Marion held out his hand, and when Edward took it, pulled him from his chair, not letting go, and placed three chaste salutes, on his forehead and both cheeks, saying: "Chastity, my dear Edward Clare, chastity and morality it shall be, reluctantly, but assuredly. I abjure your sweet Greek lips, which I thought to adjure. An Alleyn's word." He smiled engagingly. "The Irish kiss before they duel, but let us not. Don't be angry. You should be flattered. It is not my natural bent, to which I shall return, like our Latin Ovid. You will be quite safe. Do come."

"I am not ever angry with you, Marion," Edward said simply, "I thought you were angry with me. I do hope I may come."

They saw a great deal of one another after that—by themselves, for Edward shrank from meeting again any of his friends at all—as much as lectures and tutorials would permit, or Alleyn's activities, and Edward did less reading. He had never known the delights of simple companionship and company. They met on many evenings, after dinner, if there were no lectures or no meetings they felt impelled to, or later, over supper, talking by the fire of sea-coals, in Alleyn's rooms, or more often in Edward's. They toasted St. Cuthbert, University's particular saint and a Northumbrian by residence like Edward, on his particular day. They took long walks into the still wintry country around Oxford, into Iffley wood, shooting Marion's pistols at knots on the oaks and papers he nailed up, and Bagley wood and up Shotover Hill, as far as Woodstock and Wantage Downs.

One late afternoon Alleyn took Edward to a strange, hidden, hedged garden he had discovered near Oxford, on one of his walks, suddenly there in the midst of the bare fields, triangular, about an acre of ground, filled with fruit trees that were then almost ready to come into flower. They approached by the bed of a narrow canal, overhung with shrubs, and made their way in quietly, into a small grove of tall trees just beginning to leaf, around a small Greek temple in its center, and heads of Greek gods, like Pan, on columns in a semi-circle about it, some fallen over in the leaves of last year's Autumn mixed with the green shoots of this Spring's bulbs. Curious, and beautiful, it stood, in its pattern of fresh flower and antiquity, sweeping away from them up the long lawn they did not venture on, away from pond and stream, towards a hidden house, and patterned parterres.

"What a beautiful place. How did you know to come here?"

"I found it by chance," Alleyn said briefly. "We should not be here, it belongs to someone, but they are never here, and I sometimes come."

"And what do you do here? Do you come here to talk treason? Is it a good place for that?"

"No, Edward Clare, I do not, and for me it is not, it is rather a place to make one forget that there is any need to talk treason. I would rather not talk at all, about anything, for a little. Does that surprise you?"

"Yes," Edward said, and smiled at him with his heart in his eyes. In the silence they heard, not far from them, a bird begin to sing, so melodiously he thought it must be a Nightingale, though he had never heard or seen one. He turned his head, and found that Alleyn with the same accord had turned to him. Their eyes met, and briefly held. They sat on the arbour wall, quietly, until the song ended, and then, without speaking, they made their way out and home.

The days slipped by. They talked of everything except their personal families or politics. On those they touched rarely.

"You cannot escape the state of the world by pretending it is not there, Edward Clare," Alleyn said once, touching on a subject on which Edward was still touchy.

"I do not try to pretend it is not there," said Edward defensively.

"Then because somehow you have managed to escape knowing it is there. Its problems will not go away because you are frightened and will not look at them."

"I am not frightened," Edward said. "I have less hopes for the world than you. To me it will always have its misery as its nature. Heaven is as real to me as the world, I don't believe in the perfectibility of men, or the glories of science, or the buried goodness in the hearts of man. I do not even believe very much in education as a cure for anything. I do believe in sin."

"Nevertheless you had better look around you. I will tell you how I see our age, Edward, or the age we have just left, when we were children, that our fathers knew and still try to see. I see it as a peaceful green island, rather like Swift's Laputa, lit by the sun of reason, but balanced on a thin stem over a boiling black gulf that preceded, and surrounded above and around it by tornadic swirling, boiling black storm clouds of passion and unreason, and all the forces of hunger and envy kept under by force and restraint and religious lies. Those clouds are growing bigger all the time and they will fall down and engulf and entirely change that idyllic timeless stationary air and island in time. It is the law of mutability, all things change, for better or for worse or for nothing at all. The great houses of Ireland are turning to slums, now the Parliament has left and been brought here. Nothing stays. Perhaps I have loved it myself, that island in time, but one cannot forever keep hanging children because they steal bread or a spoon. In the end it does not even work, it is no worse to hang than to starve."

"Is that done?" asked Edward in horror.

"It is indeed done. Shall I take you the next time I hear of it? It is a product of the Age of Reason, that lovely green island. Your Paley upholds the practise, you know."

"He is not '*my* Paley,' and Wesley nor my father would not have upheld it."

"I am glad to hear it," Marion said. "I could be hanged myself, hurdled, hanged, stripped, drawn and quartered, but I hope you don't know what that absurdity involves, or imprisoned, for things that I have said, and done, if an unkind ear heard me. Did you know that?"

Edward nodded. "I thought it might be possible."

"So I take some care what ears do hear me. I am not a coward, Edward Clare, I am a realist—in some things. I know our legislature, and I know that in the recent debate over the treason laws for women, they were not an iota changed. A woman would be, by the law, still burned, Edward Clare, with a few attendant mercies perhaps, but it is the law: can you imagine that?" (Edward shook his head slowly.) "There are not many lady traitors. It is a true deterrent, or something, to someone." He looked at Edward quickly, and looked away. "I am not a realist about my father. When we go to my house you may meet my father, the Jehovah of the Ships, and you can tell me what you think. I cannot see him straight, myself. Too much lies between us. He has ordered countless sailors hung himself, you know, and seen it done. I will not let him tell me much. I am a coward there—we are all cowards for something—

I cannot bear to know too much about the life at sea. I know more than I would like. To think of those mutinies in the Thames itself, ten years ago, for so little—even though Earl Spencer (he is the Whig Home Secretary now, Edward, thank God) was First Lord of the Admiralty then. Cook would have never let his men on his ships suffer so. He cared for his crew, and he almost never lost a man. He had been an able-seaman below decks himself and he knew what hells they were. I should not have minded sailing with Cook, into the uncharted parts of the Pacific, to disprove myths and to 'go as far as it was possible for man to go,' for no reason but to find out what could be known. He was a humane man, Edward Clare, and a just man, I could have followed such a man, and he used care and common sense in the face of misery to rid it and avoid it. But he is dead and it is wartime and there are few like him, none that I know. Do you know who Cook was, Edward Clare?"

"Yes, I know. He was a Yorkshire man. He went to sea first near Whitby. My Uncle, my guardian, gave me Hawkesworth's *Voyages* on my birthday, once."

Marion once tried to give Edward a copy of *The Adventures of Caleb Williams*, that used Howard's experiences visiting prisons, but even before Edward saw the name Godwin, he had declined it, saying his Uncle preferred him not to read novels, unless he gave them to him himself.

Marion was astonished. "You would obey him, even in a thing like that?"

"Especially in a thing like that," Edward said smiling, "it seems a request immanently suitable and sensible to me, whoever from. If you want me to read Howard's parliamentary speeches, I have already done that. Isn't that enough? It is the meat, without the fat."

"Who would know?" persisted Marion, curious and incredulous.

"I would know. And anyway, I do not care." They were by a pond formed by a disused quarry below Shotover, and as if the name suggested it, Edward bent down and picked up several pieces of shale which he put his entire attention on forming into suitable shapes for skipping across the water, and he could not be persuaded to discuss Godwin or his Uncle further by any means, or even "Monk" Lewis.

Edward waited impatiently, though without much hope, for some reply to Lady Alleyn's invitation to come to him through Marion, but the days passed with no word, and he began to think his Uncle, usually punctilious in such matters he knew by hearsay, was not going even to reply. The next day's mail brought him a franked letter in his Uncle's hand. He opened it with fingers that shook the paper and read:

London
March 8, 1807

My dear Edward,

I have received word, through Lord Alleyn's wife, that you have
been ill. I would have expected to have rather had such news from
you yourself or from Mr. Rowley. However, I suppose that is your
concern. I trust you are now better. If you wish to finish your recuperation at Alleyn's country house, as I take it you do, you have
my permission, but for one week, at most, as I am invited there myself
the end of the month, the Lady Marian and I being old friends of
long standing. Expect Ross then at that time. Since the visit is for
your health, I suppose I need not say that I will expect you to remain
quietly in the country & not gallivant to London, etc.

With due respects and regards,
I have the honour to remain,
Yr. aff. guardian,

James Noel Holland

The letter stung him, as he somehow thought it was meant to do, and
it seemed to have an elusively bitter tone that he was at a loss to explain,
but he put such thoughts aside in his simple delight that he might go.
He did not show the letter itself to Alleyn, but he kept it as his first and
only letter from his Uncle. He wrote at once to Lady Alleyn, accepting
her invitation, but he did not know how to reply to the letter of a man
who did not wish to see him and yet supported him. He tried several
times to write, discarding each letter as rude, insincere, fulsome, inaccurate, and finally admitted to himself that cowardly or not, he could not
write what was an impossible letter. Yet he did not want to leave the
letter unanswered. He resolved his difficulties in a compromise. Since he
did not know his Uncle's address, he would in any case have had to send
the letter through Wotton. He wrote to Wotton acknowledging his
Uncle's letter and sending his thanks both for the permission which it
contained, whose qualifications he would observe, and the concern for his
health, which was improved. It had been an aftermath of his hazing,
which he recognised as having occurred but which he did not try to
explain to himself, that his desire for his Uncle had abated. The other
effect had been a complete loss of interest—an interest that had never
been strong—in all questions of a political nature.

When the term ended, Easter that year being celebrated in term, he
set out with Marion in the English Mail. He had never ridden a public

coach before, and he was entranced, by the speed, with such size, by the blasts on the horn in the night and the rushing out at the toll-gate, the fast changing of horses, less than ninety seconds, by the Royal Crest imprinted on the door. Marion, having ridden it many times, endured the journey, although he took some interest in Edward's pleasure, and amusement in a package of eggs that fell and poached themselves on the road, winking at them as they sped on. He himself was merely glad to see his own coach come to meet them in the village. It was a week that passed too swiftly. Marion would have liked to take him up to London and to have attended theatres but he acceded to Edward's unexplained preference for the quiet life of his home. He had never been on a large, Southern, well-managed estate. He found it beautiful beyond imagining, in the ease and grace of the household management of the immense Georgian pile, the comfort of his room, the beauty of the park and gardens, the rose garden and the deer park, the long avenue and its prospects, the lakes and the wide lawns. He met Marion's father only once, a large impressive man, much older than the Earl, and than his wife, with a high forehead, beaked nose, but lips as curiously sensitive as Marion's own, though not so generous in the size or so easy in disposition. Otherwise, he did not look like Marion at all, but he did not seem to Edward the tyrant he had been portrayed as, despite his forbiddingly braided uniform.

Edward entering with Marion met him on the stairs.

"I am just leaving," he said to his son, "as I suppose you knew when you chose to come."

Marion flushed and looked some years younger. "I knew, of course, but I could not come sooner, sir. The term has just ended. You know that, sir."

"Your mother informs you well, better than she does me." He turned to Edward, and subjected him to an intense, piercing gaze from beneath his white bushy brows which Edward found no difficulty in receiving or meeting. He felt an instant liking he had not expected for this tall, stately old gentleman who seemed somehow so sad and so ill at ease in his own home, and with his own son.

"So you are Tyne's son," he said, looking at Edward still with his thoughtful interest, and it seemed to Edward he heard also the word "too" below the Admiral's breath.

"No, sir, your informant does not have his facts about me," Edward said with a smile to soften his words, "I am only in his care. He is my guardian. I am George Armstrong's son, of Devon."

"Well, perhaps so," the Admiral said, "but I thought I had been told that. You will excuse an old man and his memory. You do not resemble him after all, either, although for a moment I thought somehow you did, or someone I knew. I forget now who. Of Devon, eh? The Devonshire Armstrongs? I know them, too. Have my wife invite them while you're here. I shall see you the week next, perhaps, perhaps not, Marion. I am glad to have met your friend, whoever he is." He bowed to both boys, and passed on down the stairs and out of the house to his chaise that they could see drawn up waiting.

"Is not my father strange?" said Marion. "You must not take him amiss, or be offended by what he says. He has a kind of fixation these days on parentage, because he has his doubts about me. He calls me a changeling, but he cannot change the entail. He does that way with many people now. But do not be misled by him. He is kinder to everyone than to me. If he is my father. If I am his son. My father went fishing for trout in other men's streams—and other men in his. He knows too well how it can be from his own catches. There was a time, when he was younger, before he took an Admiralty post in London, when he was not often home. He suspects I am no true breeding, I think, and it preys on him. But he is what I have—and what I have to deal with."

"You shouldn't speak this way to me," Edward said, "but I think you do resemble your father, the resemblance is clear to me, though it is not obvious. You should not feed his doubts."

Marion looked at him queerly. "You should tell the old boy that. No one else does. It might make life easier for me when he is home."

"Tell him yourself," Edward said, with a slight smile. "I think I hardly could."

"I will take you to meet my mother now," Marion said. Lady Alleyn, in her boudoir sitting room, received them, looking like a feminine picture of her son. Her beauty and her friendly charm of manner, in early middle-age, was such that Edward, although inexperienced in such matters, was not surprised that her frequently absent older husband should experience jealousy, particularly since like Marion she did not appear given to the habit of reassurance, or wholly truthful. Perhaps, he thought, listening to her, it would be more accurate to say that she read the truth by her own changing lights. However, she made a charming hostess, with every care for his comfort, and a seeming delight in his friendship with her son; but for himself, he rather wished the Admiral had not left.

His hostess wished to take him almost at once to the nearby Armstrong estate, when she learned he had not met them or ever been there, but she reluctantly laid aside her designs when he pled weakness still from his illness, and his Uncle's wishes that he see no company. He held to those wishes even the one night she thought to foil them by having company in, by excusing himself politely but firmly upstairs to his room. The week passed too quickly in walks and rides, alone and with the siblings, of whom Marion as their older brother was unusually fond and careful, and they of him, and in reading and quiet talk. Admiral Alleyn had a particularly fine library, equalling and in some ways surpassing the Earl's, of Spanish and French authors, from his travels and voyages, as well as the English, the classical, and sections of philosophy, and science and law. Edward expressed his enjoyment of it all that was almost envy to Marion in terms that surprised him for something he had taken for granted: his parents, his brothers and sisters, as well as his beautiful house and fertile grounds. He had never experienced life in this manner, and when the day drew near for Ross to arrive, and he did arrive, Edward felt a physical pain tearing him, as he left the kind if erratic Lady Alleyn and his friend and his new experiences, exchanging once again the rediscovered South he loved for the colder North, knowing too his Uncle, and perhaps the Admiral were to come. His host and his hostess' surprised protests and continued urging for him to stay underlined his pain. He could not imagine why his Uncle should be so ashamed of him, or so afraid, and then, suddenly, he could.

Although then he did not believe it, even the thought was too much for him and overwhelmed him. With such thoughts he felt he could not under any circumstances return to his guardian's house. Without warning, to Ross's horrified and brief stupefaction, he jumped suddenly from the moving open carriage and began to run, his eyes blind, his feet stumbling, across the fields. Ross without thinking stopped the horses, and recovering from his surprise, leaped down and began to run in great loping strides after Edward. He overtook him quickly, without much difficulty, and threw himself upon him, knocking him to the ground and the breath out of him. As Edward choked and gasped and struggled for air, he took a rag of a handkerchief he carried in his pocket, and tied Edward's hands behind him with it. He brought him to his feet, as soon as he could stand, and marched him back indignantly to the carriage. He pulled Edward's travelling cloak about his shoulders with a reproachful stare, and without a word, drove on. Edward said nothing either. He welcomed the pain on his wrists as an antidote to the pain raging in his mind. The open, honest humiliation of his position contrasted in sharp welcome comfort to the secret humiliation and disgrace threatening to engulf him entirely, upsetting all his life and his beliefs about himself.

After a time, however, his common sense reasserted itself, and what had been a comfort became an unnecessary absurdity.

"Undo my hands, Ross," he said quietly after a bit. "I don't know what came over me, I won't again."

Ross looked at him sharply, but he held the reins in one hand and took his knife out and cut through the material. Edward brought his hands in front and rubbed their wrists, examining them absently. Whose hands were they? Whose hands, licensed or too free, had held his mother, at the moment of his conceiving? He shut his eyes, and leaned back, unable to bears his thoughts or the sight of the world or the lovely countryside, and so he did not see Marion when he first rode galloping up beside them on his black horse, its narrow delicate hooves, reined in, clip-clopping demurely beside them, his pistols drawn on Ross.

"My God, Edward Clare, *asleep!*" exclaimed a familiar voice beside him, breaking in unwelcome. "I thought you needed me, and I have come to rescue you. What was the hanky-panky I saw in the field back there?"

"I don't know what you may have seen," Edward said, his eyes clouded, "or thought you saw, but I don't need you, as you see. I am quite all right. Put your pistols up, my lord Alleyn, and go home now." As Marion hesitated, undecided, he managed to smile. "Truly I am. Ross and I are old acquaintances, we know each other well, better than I know you. Go home now, Marion, we have just seen each other, we haven't anything to say; I am tired, I want to sleep. Ross, don't mind this gentleman, he won't shoot you, please just drive on."

They left Marion, staring, undecided, in the road.

"Bloody blooming young highwayman," Ross said. "I don't understand you, but I am grateful to you, Edward."

Edward did not answer. He lay back, his eyes shut again, wondering if he would ever be able to smile easily again. Marion, on his horse, watched the carriage, puzzled by Edward's change in mood, and dissatisfied. Bored, he had happened to take his father's naval glasses to follow his friend down the road. They were an old pair, and the lenses cloudy, but not so cloudy as that. He could have sworn to what he thought he had seen. He rode slowly back a little way towards his house, and then on impulse, having nothing else to do, he turned his horse, and followed once again, but this time discreetly down the road behind them.

When he discovered that the carriage before him was not going to stop, but push on with only changes of horse, he did the same with the fixed, if frequently unwise determination of spirit that characterised him, once a purpose was taken. He did not know the location of Tyne's Northern Estate, and he was afraid to lose the track until he had managed to find it out. When finally he did, being in its neighbourhood, he himself stopped at an Inn, to sleep and rest himself and wait for his horse. The next day he presented himself at the Earl's house, to be told by the footman that Edward was not there. He had learned at the Inn that Tyne himself was temporarily in residence. Only briefly non-plussed, he now demanded so peremptorily and with so authoritative an air to be admitted to the Earl that eventually he was. The Earl was seated in his study at his desk; he did not rise.

"I would like to see Edward Clare," he stated at once, simply and directly, not troubling to smile or moderate the language of the request.

The Earl said nothing. He raised his quizzing glass, and raked the young man with it from top to toe, but his ruthless and determined young Irish inquisitor did not falter or flush under the examination, but repeated his request more impatiently, though with still a surface veneer of courtesy.

"He isn't here," the Earl said flatly, putting his glass down, "as you have already been told, and so you can't see him."

"Preposterous!" exclaimed Marion rudely. "I know he is. Where else would he be?"

"He isn't here to you," the Earl said, modifying his statement, his attention directed away. "It is the same thing."

Marion gaped at the audacity of what he now saw clearly to be his adversary, but he collected himself.

"It is not the same thing. I am his friend. I know Edward would like to see me," he stated.

"Do you?" enquired the Earl. "I do not think so, but perhaps you shall see him, in good time."

"Why in good time? If he is here now, please announce me. If he is out, I will wait."

"You are an impatient and impertinent young cock," said the Earl, smiling slightly, amused. "I believe I do not know your name."

"Of course you know my name, I have often seen you, and you have often seen me." He ignored the Earl's suddenly raised glass and his now polite disinterested stare. "I am Marion Alleyn, Lord Alleyn's son. My family sometimes calls me Allister. You are coming to my mother's house next week," he added, as the Earl's face registered no change, "as you know, and Edward has just returned from my house, as you also know, where he has been with me for a week."

"Then why tell me?" murmured the Earl. He yawned, behind a raised hand, and put his glass down. "I would think then you would have seen enough of Edward for a time," the Earl said as though dismissing both Marion and the matter. "I should have. You will see him in Oxford shortly. That is surely enough." He looked at Marion suddenly with a disconcertingly direct gaze, measuringly and assessingly, that brought the colour to the young man's cheeks. "So you are Edward's friend," he said musingly and meaningly, his eyes watching Marion's face steadily, "and you have ridden all this way to see someone who has just left you. Why?" He did not invite his unwanted guest to sit down.

"I saw something odd happen on the road," Alleyn said pointedly. "I came to reassure myself about it."

"A long ride for reassurance," murmured the Earl, ignoring most of Alleyn's remark. "Does Edward speak of me to you?" He had not really changed the subject and Alleyn knew that he had not.

"No," said Marion, "hardly at all, and with love and respect when he does, too much, I sometimes think." He looked at the Earl in a friendly way, with all his charm of manner, to which he saw the Earl was not insusceptible. "I think something is wrong here," he said, his manner at variance with his words, "and I have come here to find out what it is."

"Sit down, Marion," the Earl said quietly and pleasantly, in his turn, "I take it I may address you so, in view of your age, and mine. What makes you think so, and why do you think, if you should be correct, that it is safe for you to come here and speak to me so?" His eyes, amused again, belied his words. "What secrets do I harbour that you have uncovered? What vile deeds, which I am supposed to have done? Am I the villain of your piece, or is another? Were you not afraid, thinking such thoughts, to put yourself alone in my house, in my power and at my discretion? You are a beautiful boy, Alleyn, as I daresay you know, and I am supposed by some to eat beautiful boys before breakfast, as well as young girls. Come here," he said. "Come here," he repeated more emphatically. "You have put yourself here, do now as I say."

As the boy stood before him, his young lips quivering with audacious amusement, the Earl traced his features with his fingers, with the delicate touch of the blind. " 'They say, they say,' " he said almost angrily. "It is a matter of indifference to me what 'they say.' But what 'they say' is not always so—although almost always it is. You are an impudent boy," he said, pushing him away with a light gesture of his outstretched fingers, "but I rather like you. I imagine you are good for my serious Edward. So you have been brave, and penetrated the garden of the Beast. What then shall I do for you?"

"I have already told you, Lord Tyne," Marion said, his face and eyes warm with sudden unwished for liking. "I want to see Edward. That is all."

"Very well then, you shall see him," the Earl said with an odd expression, "but I must ask you not to speak." He rose, and took a set of keys, and unlocked the white and gold panelled door near his desk, taking a candle with him that he had lit. Marion followed him in amazed silence, until they came to the passage, and the tile, which the Earl removed. Assuring himself that Edward was asleep, he passed the candle to Alleyn and directed him where to look, at Edward below them lying asleep like a tired child on his pallet bed, his white face exhausted and desolate, his fair hair tousled and bright in the light. The Earl replaced the tile in silence. They returned in silence to the Earl's study, where the Earl again seated himself, and again invited Alleyn to sit.

The Earl said nothing, nor did Alleyn until finally, he said, "I do not know what to say."

"A wise remark," the Earl said, "and an unexpected one. I thought you might think you did."

"No," said Marion, "I do not understand. Why should you treat a gentle boy like Edward so, or why he should submit to it, as he clearly does submit. I am baffled by you both. But I see my visit was unnecessary. I will go now."

"You should stay and have lunch with me—dinner if you like, for it is late," the Earl said. "I must insist, I think, upon it, before you ride home."

"You need not insist hard," Marion said, "for I have not yet lunched at all."

During the ambiguous meal both the Earl and Alleyn exerted themselves to use their both considerable charm, the one upon the other, in counterpoint with the presence of the servants and their courses. Over the first courses, the Earl spoke politely of Alleyn's family and past visits there, of London and of Oxford, and then abruptly he said: "Of course I recognised you, you know. You look like your mother. I had forgotten you did, though, until I saw you. Does she know you are here?"

Marion shook his head and smiled. "I came away in a hurry, and I came farther than I intended. I should have sent word."

"I would not tell her if I were you." The Earl sighed slightly. "It makes me feel young, to look at you. You must forgive me if I stare. It is my youth I look at, remembering your mother's youth, seeing it in you."

Marion smiled again, his face enigmatic, his eyes, unwavering, meeting the Earl's gaze.

"You are older than Edward, are you not? By how much? Several years, I should think."

"Five, by some months."

"And you have known him long?"

"Not long. A month, perhaps, to speak."

"A month is not long."

"It is long enough. He has my heart."

"And do you give it easily?"

"Not my heart."

"I think it may be he has mine, too, but I do not mean to let him know it. And it will be of no use to him, as hearts seldom are. Have you ever seen Edward angry?" asked the Earl.

"Not really. Slightly, perhaps."

"He can be, you know, and he is dangerous when he is. He has attacked me. Has he told you?"

Marion shook his head. "He said you had a disagreement."

"A mild word," the Earl said. "He tried to kill me. Twice. I restrain him here for my safety and his good, to protect us both against his rages which it may be I may provoke." He looked at Alleyn's face, Edward's confessed friend, but he could not read any expression, doubt or conviction or disbelief. "Do you intend to speak of what you have seen? I can deliver Edward to the law, perhaps I should inform you, and let it keep him for me, in prison or in camisole in an asylum."

"A living death, and shortly not even that," Alleyn commented, his face suddenly tired.

"Precisely so."

"You have power," Marion said, in the same weary quiet tone. "Would you do that?"

The Earl nodded. "For my safety, yes, if it became necessary. And if you embarrass me, yes, to justify my actions and my name."

"Then I will say nothing. It is after all your affair and Edward Clare's. He keeps much to himself. I thought it was his temperament. Is it your orders?"

"Perhaps."

Marion smiled suddenly. "Yet you release your monster on an unsuspecting Oxford. You know, Lord Tyne, I do not entirely believe you."

"Nevertheless," said the Earl, "part of what I say is true. You would do well to remember it. He has attacked me, and as his guardian his disposition is still mine."

Alleyn lifted his hands in a graceful gesture of submission, without arguing further.

"You were with Edward, I believe, during his illness?"

"I was. He stayed in my rooms."

"Ah," said the Earl. "And what was the nature of this illness? He seems recovered now."

"He was hazed," Marion said briefly. "As my father the Admiral would say," he added.

"You entirely surprise me," said the Earl, after a startled pause, recovering his composure. "How did he provoke it? Badly 'hazed'? I think I guess correctly what your word means? It is also a Yorkshire word, but I did not know it was a University practise."

"Quite badly," Marion said. "You can ask him about it yourself, if you like, but if I were you, I would not." His eyes flickered on the Earl's. "You do wrong to treat him as you do here. His nature is much sweeter than either yours or mine."

The Earl put his long fingers over his eyes as if to shield them, in a graceful schooled gesture.

"Spare me, I pray," he said, "these reproachful looks and glances. Is it as Napoleon or as Talleyrand that I figure in your eyes?"

"Neither, Lord Tyne. In my eyes you figure always as yourself." He met the quick look the Earl threw towards him without flinching. His lips curved in a quick appreciative smile and his eyes kindled, but he only shook his head and repeated his earlier words, "Than either yours or mine."

After dinner, Alleyn asked what had been on his mind throughout. They were again in the study, with brandy before the fire. The Earl, looking thoughtfully out of the windows, before ringing to have the curtains drawn, approached his view of the subject indirectly.

"It is too late for you to begin your journey home, don't you think? You would only have to put up almost at once at an Inn."

Marion nodded, his tone careful. "I think you are right, the air is very cold still once the sun is down, and I would like to see Edward and talk to him." His fine eyes rested directly on the Earl's.

"He will not want to see you," said the Earl thoughtfully, his eyes returning Marion's look intently, "I can promise you that."

"I do not believe you," Marion said.

"Nevertheless, you will find it true, but I am prepared to let you do as you wish if you—" He paused.

"If I let you do as you wish? It is a matter of indifference to me. I have no morals."

"Good," said the Earl, "I have none myself, we should deal admirably. Let us go at once and have the interview over with and done."

He led the way this time to the door and opened it, the light shining on his face, not on Marion's who was behind him in shadow. Edward, seeing his Uncle after so long a time rose, uncertain, his heart as always in his face and in his eyes, but the hesitant words rising tentatively to his lips died as he saw Alleyn behind his Uncle. The uncertain joy in his voice changed to certain rage. He cried in a choked voice, "How *could* you? O, how could even *you*—I could kill you—" and flung himself on the Earl futilely. The Earl, catching his hands, threw him backwards against the wall, smiling slightly. He pulled out his pistol and signalling Alleyn to go in, he lounged negligently against the door, waiting.

Edward had pulled himself up, and mastered his shock, and now stood as far away as he could go, his face turned against the wall. Rage and humiliation still ravaged him, that the one place where he had thought himself to be secure to be himself, not his Pit but his College, had been connected now with his other life. He thought it wholly vile, in so far as he could think, of his Uncle to have let him be so betrayed, and yet he had to hold himself against the wall to keep himself from turning to that indifferent figure and taking that hand near him again in both his own. To Alleyn's gentle reassurances and concern he refused to answer, except to ask Alleyn bitterly to go away.

The Earl, as if determined to prove his worst in Edward's eyes, stepped forward and put his hand familiarly on Alleyn's shoulder, and said softly, "Come, Marion, it is of no use, as I told you it would not be."

Edward turned his head, startled by the intimacy in the Earl's voice, and saw the fingers on his hand caressingly near Alleyn's neck, as the Earl intended him to see. He gasped, understanding what he was meant to understand, his eyes fixed on his friend in horror. Marion shrugged slightly, raised his hand in farewell, and turned to go. He paused at the door to say, "I will see you at College, Edward."

"Do not," Edward said with dry lips. "I never want to see you again." He waited, his back tense and stiff, his face averted, until he heard the door close and lock, and the footsteps move away, not returning, and fade irrevocably. He waited, listening, even after he knew there was nothing to hear. Then he flung himself down in abandon on his pallet, racked by dry sobs of shock that tore at him and that he could not stop.

VI

"You were mistaken, you see, Alleyn," the Earl remarked upstairs again in his study, "you did not know Edward so well as you thought you did—nor he you. He is capable of far more than you know."

"Perhaps. That was cruel, what you did," Alleyn said to the Earl, "and it was intentional."

"It was indeed both," said the Earl, "but I had my reasons."

"You wished to turn me against Edward, and that failing, Edward against me. Why?"

The Earl in his turn shrugged. "Yes, I did. And I think I have. You are too corrupt for such as Edward. I took your measure from the start, you see, but to prove it will not be disagreeable to me."

"Nor to me," said Alleyn courteously. "But I think you are mistaken in your Edward, not I. I think you do not know him so well as you think. And you will not have destroyed our friendship, as you will see."

"If it is strong enough to survive this evening, I should not wish to try to," the Earl replied courteously. "Let us not talk any more now of Edward. I am tired with the subject of Edward. I feel an affection now for two things that have come out of Ireland. Will you come with me, my dear and very beautiful young lord Alleyn?"

Sobs, dry and painful, continued to tear at Edward long after the subjects of them were at rest, having taken their delights in the airy upper rooms of the house, waking him from his own fitful sleeps. Abruptly, he was sick to his stomach. He tried desperately not to be, knowing no one would come near until morning, if then, but he could not help himself, and once started, he could not stop. He retched and sobbed, and sobbed and retched, at the destruction of a last illusion, until he fell asleep, or fainted, for a few hours in his filth. He awoke, unable to help himself, and waited for a long time, miserable, until he heard the tile drawn back.

"Ross, is it you?" he whispered. "Help me, Ross. I have been sick. I am in a terrible way."

"Poor bairn," said Ross. "I believe you." He went to get his separate key, and after a bit he reappeared at the door, from the kitchen side of the passageway. "What's to do?" he said in dismay.

"Don't let my Uncle know," whispered Edward. "Please, Ross, don't let him."

"He is not down yet," Ross said.

"Is my friend gone yet?"

"Your friend?"

"Is the black horse still in the stables?"

"Ay, it is."

"Oh, God," whispered Edward, and he was sick again.

"Here, Edward," said Ross, in rough concern, "—I must get you out of here. It will be the stench that sets you on. But what's to do, if your Uncle's no to know? Come you into the scullery, quiet-like, and get scrubbed, and while you do it, I'll scrub this floor. You'll no leave, will you, or be doing it again?"

"I don't know, Ross," Edward said helplessly and frantically, "I can't seem to help myself." A wave of strangling nausea seized him again.

"You're no trying," said Ross sternly. He guided him out and helped him down the passage and into the scullery, where he set out a tub and water that had been boiling in kettles in the kitchen for breakfasts and baths. He stripped Edward's reeking clothing from him, and scrubbed him, seeing that Edward seemed unable to move or help himself, and wrapped him in a blanket.

"What's to do?" he said again. "I cannot take you to my rooms," he said doubtfully, "the Earl will not have it, while he is here."

"No," whispered Edward. "Not the stables."

While Edward was there, a bell rang peremptorily in the kitchen, audible even in the scullery. Edward's white face went ashen.

"Is it that then?" said Ross quietly. "Put your head down," he said roughly, "being sick over it will not help. You will be quiet now, and I will be taking you down to my wife then, and if the Earl finds you gone, I will be telling him why in no uncertain terms."

"No," whispered Edward.

"Hist," said Ross. He picked him up as easily as a flour sack, and would have carried him in his arms, but Edward struggled out of his arms onto the floor. He was immediately picked up again, but Edward looked at him so pitifully, his eyes so wild, saying, "Oh, Ross, he will find out, and I cannot bear him to know," that Ross, who was privately afraid of the same thing, put him down.

"I do not know what to do with you, Edward, and that's a fact," he said, puzzled.

"Can't you leave me here?" whispered Edward.

"No, I cannot, I have my orders."

"Oh, God," said Edward, "Ross, I won't do anything to them. I don't even have the strength."

"You might be pretending."

Edward laughed shakily at that, and said, half crying, "Oh, God, Ross."

In the end, he took Edward with him in his arms like a child, and left him in the passage while he scrubbed his floor, and took his blankets away to be washed, and sprinkled dried aromatic herbs, lavender and rosemary.

Edward put his head in his arms. "I am so unhappy, Ross," he whispered pitifully, "I think this time I shall die of it."

"Would it help to talk about it?" asked Ross.

"No," whispered Edward.

"Well," he said, "you won't die of it. You may think you will, but you won't. It is other things one dies of. But I am sorry for you. I have been unhappy myself."

"*You* have, Ross?" he asked in astonishment, lifting his head.

"Ay, Edward. It is a common disease. You are not the first or the last to suffer from it. But you won't die of it."

"I remember when you whipped me, Ross," Edward whispered weakly.

"I do myself."

"Would you do it again?"

"I would if I were asked to by the Earl."

"You are being kind to me, and you don't love me, you don't even like me much."

"It is sometimes easier to be kind to those we don't love, or don't like much. You will find that out, Edward. You are a child still, for all your talk. Be still now. I don't want you going sick on me. I am just doing what needs to be."

When he had finished, he brought Edward back in his arms, because he was too weak to walk, but on the threshold, as Ross returned him, Edward shrank in his arms and whispered piteously, "Ross, I shall be sick again. I cannot be in the house here with the two of them about me."

"You will have to, Edward, there is nothing I can do. I am going now to get fresh blankets," he said, "and if you mess again, I will whip you and give you a true cause and just leave you in it."

"You wouldn't, Ross?" said Edward weakly.

1 would. You must take hold of yourself now. You are not sick, and you aren't going to make yourself sick, not with me."

Much later that morning, after a night which Edward had tried vainly to erase from the pictures of his mind, Marion took his horse and rode away, but not to his house, but to Holyhead: erect and easy, his joyous black head of hair and his black horse both shining with silver lights in the sun that had broken through, his eyes glancing about him with lively interest and appreciation of the landscape of the estate. A day later, the Earl left to make his journey by fast curricle to Admiral Alleyn's country home to renew a long acquaintanceship with Marion's mother, having neither looked in on Edward or asked about him.

Ross brought Edward out then, and put him in the care of his wife who eased his tortured stomach with hot broths and teas. When he felt better, he said to Ross, his face whiter than the unbleached muslin of the pillow against which he lay in one of Ross's own coarse nightgowns, in the bed of himself and his wife: "Would you have let me die there, just because my Uncle was here?"

"It was not in any danger of that you were."

"What did you think I would *do?*"

"That's not saying, Edward. I have my strict orders on it, that's all."

Edward laughed, helplessly and angrily, and turned his face away.

When Edward had recovered himself, Ross sternly walked him back through the walled kitchen gardens to the place he was expected to be, as dour as ever, the truce in their hostilities ended.

Edward kept his oak closed after his return to Oxford. He did not answer Marion's characteristic impetuous knocks upon it, some three days later, or any knocks at all. He came back after a lecture one day, however, to find Marion seated in his chair, reading while he waited for him, as naturally as if he grew there.

Edward stopped short by the door, and his lips grew white. "I wish you would leave the room, Alleyn. I have not asked you here."

"I'd rather not. I like it here," Marion said, smiling engagingly.

For answer, Edward held the door open without a word. Marion rose, but he did not leave. He closed the door, pushed Edward down into a chair, and stood over him.

"You are being very silly, little Edward Clare. Grow up. So I know the games your Uncle or your guardian or whatever plays with you. So I do. It did not matter before, why should it now? I have had games played with me, just less spectacularly—and by my own father. Your guardian attempted to convince me, in a rather stupid way for so clever a man, that you were insane, in part, or only about him—a kind of maniac criminal, and that he acted for your good. I did not, of course, believe him, but he did convince me I would be wise, for your sake, to let matters rest as they stood.

"But you are not really angry with me for that: for my knowing how he treats you, how you spend your time at home, and why you are unusual—a little but not really. You are angry for another reason and we both know what it is." He sighed. "Unfortunately, it is not *for* me you are jealous, but *of* me. I should have known it. *Ça ne vaut rien*, Edward. It meant nothing to me, or to your Uncle. He was briefly drawn to me, and I to him. I wished to see you, I bargained with him. Does that make you feel better?"

"No," said Edward miserably, "it makes me feel worse."

"You do not understand people like your Uncle and myself, Edward. Such things mean everything to you, but they mean nothing to us. Why, your Uncle went straight to my mother after he left me. Don't gasp like a fish. Of course I knew it. I did not need to be told. I could not have stopped it, had I tried, and it would do me no good to mind. In fact, I don't mind, not anymore. I hardly think of it. I even asked my mother once if I was Lord Tyne's son—don't look so shocked, Edward, it did just occur to me—but she said it was not possible, he was in Vienna that entire year. So you see, I have not behaved so badly as I might have." He noted the aghast horror in Edward's face, but he thought it directed against himself, and exaggerated. "Come, Edward, friends? I have to go to my Divinity Exam. Is it friends?" He held out his hand. "We love you, you know, Edward. I do. I think your Uncle does."

Edward, after a moment's hesitation, took it, and said quietly, not looking at him, "Friends." He did not expect to see Alleyn again until late that evening, or the next day, and he was startled little more than an hour later to hear footsteps stop outside. There was a quick knock at the door, and it opened before him, and Marion came in. He attempted a smile, but his hands, Edward saw, were shaking, and his fair skin was startlingly white, completely drained, and the pupils of his eyes enormously black.

"Edward Clare," he said, his voice light but shaking like his hands, "you will never guess! I have been expelled."

"How could you be?" Edward said faintly, his wits in a maze. "You just left me. What could have happened?"

"It was the Divinity Examination I had to go for. I knew they only wanted cause. I never should have given it them. Oh, God," he said, sitting down, "Edward Clare, I have ruined myself, myself with my own hands." He smiled ruefully, but he leaned his head against his hand in a real despair. Feeling his cap, he took it off and sent it spinning into a corner.

"It is bad, but why ruined?' Edward asked slowly. "Will your father be that angry, to disown you for it?"

"Lord, no," Marion said, surprised out of his humour, "he would not, I even think he could not. I don't care if he's angry, he is always that with me, I could snap my fingers for his anger. It's what he'll do. I know it, and I don't know how to stop him. He'll commission me into the Navy, he said he would when I was last sent down, and I don't see how I can stop him from it, or myself from going, once he has done it."

"Won't he listen to you?"

Marion shook his head, too upset to answer the obvious.

"Can't you refuse the commission?"

"With my father an Admiral, and the Fleet ready to war with Napoleon! Once he signs my name there, and he can do it, I would be a deserter from the Royal Navy, and Edward, you are a child but you surely know what that would mean. He won't let me resign it properly. I can even imagine him having me impressed aboard if I will not go. He is a tyrant, Edward Clare, he always has been, on his ships, with me at home. Why can't he let me be?" He paused, but Edward said nothing. "I know, don't say it to me, it is my fault, I had my chance here, for five years. God, Edward Clare, I would rather go to jail than go to sea, even as an officer. I shall die of it, one way or another, I cannot bear even to see the way the ships are run."

"Could you not mutiny?"

Marion gave a brief indignant gasp of a laugh. "Have you no sense? I don't *wish* to die of it, certainly not that way. And it would serve no point. Have you any brandy, Edward Clare? Well, no matter. Oh, God, I am a fool."

He lay back and closed his eyes.

"I wish you would tell me what happened," Edward said.

"It is so complicated. It happened before today. It is my fault. I was going to make the proper answers, swear my allegiance to the Thirty-nine, all that. I could, you know, it would not bother me, I have no martyr's blood in me. It would mean nothing to me, just as it means nothing to the sixty-odd who will swear to it, and then go back and do whatever foul act they just left. It was when I saw they meant to have me, one way or another, that—fool me—I decided I would at least say what I thought and give them cause. I could not even do that. There wasn't time. They had my papers of expulsion already signed and sealed and ready for me. I had hardly said the word 'no' to the First Article when they served me with them like a warrant and sent me out."

"I do not understand it," Edward said. "I have not found them unjust men, and that is unjust, Marion."

"It is my fault, I said. After I left you, and your weird way of living with your Uncle, I went again to Dublin, to see O'Connor, and attended a meeting and made a speech that caused some stir, because the meeting was broken up by legal law, 'one cannot assemble to petition the authority of church or law,' that sort of rot. It reached the papers, though. I was arrested, but released, being English and who I was, as an eccentric—me! they little know me!—with a warning. But some papers I sent home were examined by the customs at Holyhead, a dangerous Radical, you see, and potential Revolutionary, and my father heard of it. He is a friend of Lord Spencer who is Home Secretary, or was until this month, who used to be First Lord of the Admiralty during Spithead and Nore and all that, Edward, I told you that. My mother knows his wife Lavinia. But Portland has Lord Camdon now, another Jeffreys, in his cabinet, who was the Lord Lieutenant during the '98 rebellion in Ireland. I should have known. I should have been more careful, now that the Tories are back in. Portland is all right himself, but he is an old man and he is not well." He gave a shaky laugh. "Well—enough of that. It no longer concerns me. My father was wrathful to say the least, and has shut off my allowance so I can't travel, and warned the Jews against me, and I suppose they heard of it here too. They could hardly expel me for that, but they could for this, and they knew my opinion on it, if I could be baited to some lure. And I rose! Oh, fool; fool—"

He got up, and smiled again shakily. "Well, I must go now. I only came to say goodbye. How quickly the *Vale* has followed the *Ave*, I did not expect to so soon. I don't want to contaminate your rooms, Edward Clare, with heresy or anything else. I must see my things are packed. I am to go at once, being dangerous."

"I will come with you," Edward said.

"I would rather you did not. I would rather say goodbye now, and here. I hate long, drawn-out things. I am leaving you my Swift, Edward Clare. Read it, especially *A Modest Proposal Concerning the Irish*. It is out of date, but not by much." He looked at Edward soberly. "I may not see you again. I rather think I won't." He bent quickly, and lightly and quickly brushed Edward's lips with his own. "Farewell, little Edward Clare. I mean that. I hope you do fare well."

He smiled again, briefly, and with a certain dignity, retrieved his cap and went out.

The rest of term seemed very flat with the College's bright comet whirled out of its orbit, for many besides Edward, but particularly for Edward. He had found Alleyn's older spirit, in its several complexities, warming and irresistible in its passion for life and its friendliness, and its presence would have helped divert his mind in its present upheaval. As it was, he was again completely unhappy.

How many times, he thought wearily, I have thought I have come to some understanding of myself and my situation, only to find I have none at all, and it is almost all to do over again. He considered killing himself, but he did not know how to begin, and after a moment's reflection, he realised with some sober amusement at himself and his foolish idea, that it was life itself he wanted, and more, not less of it, and to do away with the existence of his troublesome self would disturb no one very much except himself, and perhaps even relieve some. He had at this moment no wish to benefit anyone else, only himself. He attended his lectures, read for his tutorials, went nowhere, discouraged all overtures of friendship, and let his misery feed on itself and distend itself.

One brief overture refused to be discouraged. He was sitting by the quarry near Shotover Hill, where he and Alleyn had "shot" ducks-and-drakes on the water, the first walk he had taken of any length since his return, when he was aware of the presence of another person standing near him, a little away from him. Despite his despair, he found he was a little afraid, in the loneliness of the place and the depth of the quarry water, but he made himself look around, and he saw the large boy he had seen several times with Marion standing quietly by the great thorn tree, watching him, a package in his hand, though students did not carry parcels. He seemed like the Thorn himself. He was immensely tall, taller than the Earl, and heavier, and his face was immobile, with a particular peaceful quality in repose now strongly evident. When he saw he was observed, he lifted his head and raised his eyebrows slightly as if asking permission to intrude and come nearer.

"What do you want?" Edward asked wearily, not because he wanted to know but because the circumstances seemed to require him to.

"I have something for you, Allister left it with me and told me to give it to you."

"Leave it there then. I will find it." He turned his head away. "Please go away, I came here to be alone, to be quiet." He did not know which faction of Alleyn's friends the young man was and he did not care.

He did not hear the steps on the spongy moss, and he was startled to feel a pair of hands rest suddenly on his shoulders. He recognised their touch at once as the large gentle hands that had bound him and carried him to be tortured; he did not need to hear the low whistling call that the owner of the hands gave, as if to prove further the identity he purposely revealed.

"Don't," he cried, the memory bringing him real pain, wincing and trying to twist away, "don't!" but the hands held him firmly, and heavily, in their easy grasp of his shoulders. "Don't," he cried again, but there was no immediate answer.

"Have you come to hurt me again?" he asked, too hopeless now to feel afraid. "Why? I have done nothing to you. I never told, I never did, no one, not to any one. Why should you want to? Please don't, I cannot bear it again."

"No," the slow voice said, "I have not. Don't think it. I came to give you these books." He put them in Edward's lap, taking one hand away. "And I came to see how you were. Marion asked me to look in on you, he seemed to think you needed taking care of. Do you?"

"Not as you understand the word," Edward said bitterly. He felt his shoulders entirely released, and he got up at once, and moved away and began to walk off, back towards the meadow, away from the hill with more assurance than he felt. He had gone only a few steps when he heard feet running lightly beside him, and he was swept entirely from his own feet with a great swoop and back into the great arms that he had been in before. As before their touch gentled him. He shut his eyes and lay in them quietly, though his hands were not bound this time, his will to resist this particular person again lost. He was carried up the hill, onto the comparatively steep precipitous rocks over the edge of the disused quarry, and set down on a ledge. He opened his eyes briefly, and was dizzy, looking down, and was content to sit back against his captor. He was unable to think, aware only of the calm that emanates from great strength when its use is not malevolent. This did not appear to be, despite its peremptory seizure and possession of his person. He did not wonder that his restless comet friend had been drawn to this particular man, this rock as silent and solid and restful as the blocks of rock on which they sat.

"Don't go to sleep," the voice of the person holding him said, amused, "I do want to talk to you. I wasn't sure you knew me, I thought it only fair you did. I am sorry I frightened you, you don't seem frightened now. Are you angry? You don't seem to be."

Edward shook his head. "No, none of those things. Not anymore.

Only peaceful here." He was reminded forcibly of his childhood dream of strength. "But how absurd. What is your name?"

"I am the Douglas," the voice said. Edward turned his head sharply. "So Allister said. He said I was a throwback to the Black Douglas. I am not really. I am just Gavin Douglas, like the poet. My cousin is a botanist —he likes plants and trees. All very peaceful in our branch, though I am related to old Queensberry, and to the General. But not closely enough to matter. They have cornered all the titles and left none for me. I am a middle son of a middle son. But I don't mind. We have your lands, you know, now, Armstrong, your old border lands of Liddesdale. We have absorbed you there. We always wanted them. Do you want to try to push me over and even the old score?"

Edward smiled at the impossible suggestion and shook his head, listening to the quiet slow casual voice, and some of the bitter heavy pain weighting down his heart slipped away. The body against him was as undemanding and impersonal as a tree, only supporting in its nearness. He leaned back against it, and let it support him, since it seemed not to mind and to wish it.

"I am hardly an Armstrong, it is only an accident. I do not know the family at all myself."

"No?" said the quiet voice. "Alleyn said you lived with Lord Tyne, he did not explain why. A Tyneman," he added with a suspicion of a chuckle.

"Why should you find it funny?" Edward asked. "I don't myself at all."

"One of the Douglas was called the Tyneman—it meant 'the loser.'" He felt Edward stiffen. "What is it? Are you a loser? It is not so bad to be one—it is the way you lose, not the fact of losing. Though of course we all think we would rather win. But when we do, sometimes we find the roles reversed, and that we have not won after all, or not so much as we thought. You seem unhappy, Armstrong. Have I been the cause, what I had done? I have first loyalties, you know, Marion happens to be one, and the Douglas have quick honours. But the Irish are impressionable and quick to lose restraint. I thought myself it went a little far."

Edward made no comment. He was still unable to think or speak of that afternoon, and certainly not to the instigator of it, who had been willing to stand by and witness it. Except for the touch of those hands he could not have related the two, the quiet young man with him as part of it. He was not sure whether or not an apology was being made. He rather thought not.

"Well," he said, "that is what I came for. I will let you go now." He stood up, and Edward did also, and they made their way downhill. "If I can help you for anything, call on me. I will if I can. I am a Balliol man myself. A Douglas was once connected with John de Baliol, we go there when we can. An ancient rivalry. Why don't you come to my rooms tomorrow for lunch?" Edward shook his head. "Tea then?" Edward shook his head. "The wind is in that quarter? I see. Well, I hardly blame you." He smiled at Edward with his eyes and all his face. "We are all rather sad now, we are not making revolutions anymore. And I am busy myself, I go up for responsions the end of term, it is my last year. Shall I come see you this summer at your home?" Edward shook his head, his eyes shadowed. "No? Does Tyne eat Douglases still as well as Armstrongs? Our plaids are similar, the new ones, only yours has the red stripe of blood. Morton of Douglas is dead and the sieges are lifted. Come see me at Tantallon. These old things should come to an end. You have taught me that yourself. There, think that over."

He turned and walked away. Edward would not see him again that decade, but when he did, the friendship, its seeds planted then, ripened, bore fruit that was passionless, and maintained them both throughout their lives, but it is not a part of this story. Edward took the volume of Swift, without opening it, he did not need to open the parcel to know what it held, and after a while, returned to the College himself.

His unhappiness, only briefly alleviated, still held him, and he remained in that condition for several months. When taken North, he moped. Ross worried about him during the summer, and on one of the Earl's infrequent visits, secured permission to require Edward to take exercise, although he was unable to enlist the Earl's concern. He forced Edward to walk, and to ride, which he did then, spiritlessly and listlessly, in complete gloom and subjugation of spirits, to little benefit to himself. In the end, ultimately, his native buoyancy and inner stability reasserted itself and he righted himself, spiritually. His common sense, prevailing over his emotions, forced him to see he had suffered a setback, but no new tragedy, nothing insurmountable, and to resolve to stop enacting tragedies about it.

The change, as such changes do, occurred overnight. Such natures, touching the bottom of their particular despair—for no despair, supplemented with food and exercise, to a rational mind is ever bottomless for long—begin to reascend. He rode his horse into a sweat, his eyes again full of life, staying out-of-doors as long as Ross permitted, speaking to him freely, though receiving little encouragement or answer. He took pleasure gratefully in the small things immediately about him, as one does after a long serious illness from which one finally recovers. When the Earl made visits to the estate, he accepted his putting away and complete confinement as something natural and acceptable, his newfound peace still too delicately balanced to endure any probing. As when he had been a small boy of six, he knew he was unhappy, but he was resolved now as then to give as little trouble in it and to take as much enjoyment despite it as he could. Once again, he came to an acceptance of his love for the Earl, and the Earl's inability to receive it—it had changed in its outward nature several times, but its essence was constant —though he wondered why it must always be so sad, to love another person.

It seemed to him then that it must be in this way that such people as himself were drawn to the love of God, being unable to find the love and the acceptance they craved like food anywhere in anyone in the world. One must never need another person too much, he thought, they will always fail one if one does. There is in the end no help, no one finally one can go to always for this loneliness, in any other person. And so finally we are forced back upon ourselves, where we do not find much either, and then to God—who succours us, and sends us out again into the world. It is like the story of the warrior in combat who in defeat falls back upon his mother the Earth and receives strength each time from her, and rises again to fight. He took comfort in such thoughts and such things and continued to live.

The outside world in its way also continued to live, in the mud of warfare and the politer rooms of treaty. Early July saw the Russian forces defeated the fortnight before at Friedland, and at the Treaty of Tilsit passionate self-willed Emperor Napoleon for the time tenuously aligned with the rational and obstinate Emperor Alexander, a man of charm and self-control. July also saw the Danish fleet again destroyed and Copenhagen bombarded, on Canning's learning that Denmark planned secretly to join Napoleon's Continental System of economic blockade. This landing of armed troops not only destroyed the fleet and the city, but destroyed the future efficacy of the System, already weakened by smuggling, and confirmed again British control of the seas. That Denmark declared war was a little thing, in these vaster plays.

VII

Edward's third term passed without incident, much as his first had. He studied his books diligently and was looked upon as exceedingly promising. At Christmas, after almost a year's silence, he wrote some lines into a poem, which he left, like a weather flag, behind him, for his Uncle:

SONG

Wind, blow away my grief,
For I have lost belief,
In my own sorrow.
When belief fail,
Shall not relief prevail,
And say, love, tomorrow?
No, sorrow clings,
And new words sings,
To an old song,
Deceiving those
Who would suppose
Three years long.

The meaning of the poem and its tone eluded the Earl, but he did not puzzle over it. He went his way, and Edward went his.

In later years Edward would find it hard to believe that he could have so quickly let Alleyn slip from his mind, but then the attachment and the estrangement had been so quick, and the disillusionment so strong, that the brief remeeting and its recovery of some measure of friendship could not wholly outweigh in memory the scene at the Earl's house that he did want kept out of his mind—particularly since he could not reach Alleyn and Alleyn did not try to reach him. He did write once to Lady Alleyn but he received only the briefest reply from her that her son had been commissioned in the Royal Navy in the summer and was now at sea. She did not tell him on what ship or under what officer or how commissioned, for the public storms and rages of the summer before it was finally accomplished, and the private war in which she opposed the Admiral and lost, had not left her ears, or her son's despairing face her eyes, and in fact, she did not know. When letters continued not to arrive, he accepted and endured that loss too, and it too began to fade. His experience was too limited to allow him properly to conceive, even had he been told, the rigid unending misery of the man-of-war life into which his friend had been dictatorially plunged against his will. As an officer, even though an unimportant one, Alleyn's own discomforts would have been modified, but as a humanitarian, the sights daily before his eyes would have made letters back to those on the comfortable, unseeing land impossible for him, since in war all letters went through the Captain's hands.

Edward left a final poem that he constructed while he waited for the term after Easter, which he again spent in solitude, to begin, remembering an incident of winter. "The Winter Flower," he called it:

> *One day I found across the way lay blown*
> *A pine not dead, not living; and from it I broke three branches,*
> *On a vein of which there clung a hard green cone.*
>
> *Now, while all without is grey and cold,*
> *The rolled fastness with the stir of life advances,*
> *And its woody petals slow unfold.*
>
> *I could wish that I, who lay encased*
> *In greenness like this cone through hasty Summer's heat,*
> *Might after my first frost, find life encreased,*
>
> *And though blown down, be uplift from this hour.*
> *My rhymes are rough and stiff, emerging from retreat,*
> *Yet may they blossom like that Winter flower.*

His thoughts turned outward then. Imperceptibly he found he had made friends, and he was less lonely. He did not want intimacy or a single close friend, because he did not want any more close discovery or any more loss, but he found many did not either. He was invited to breakfast parties, and to lunch in rooms, and he went. The students whom he did not wish to meet had taken their degrees and gone. On his walks he had companions. His gravity and his slight air always of apartness no longer debarred him, and that last term of his third year he learned to play and to laugh like an ordinary boy. He did not seek out, but he was sought, and he did not withdraw.

The news that Spring was about Napoleon's brilliant but unfair coup of Spain, which Talleyrand likened to the unforgivable social sin of cheating at cards, at Bayonne. It gave brother Joseph another throne, and left the three young princes of Spain captive guests at the Château of their unwilling but sympathetic host Talleyrand, at Valençay. The oldest was his own age, already briefly a king himself through his own *coup d'état* against his father. Edward's first springing sympathy for any young prisoner dwindled as reports of their entertainment came through. He thought them better lodged and maintained at their enemies' hands than himself at his guardian's.

He spent the summer much as he had the previous three, outwardly obedient, inwardly rebellious, but with no tears, no agonies, no griefs. He was nineteen now, he would be twenty in the coming winter; he had much to think about.

Two weeks after his fourth year began, he was sent down, to rusticate, for a supposed involvement in a prank he did not correct, until the term after Christmas began. He borrowed a horse, and like John Wesley, he thought, with a book, and money loaned by the same indebted friend, pursued his way leisurely towards the North, by the green lanes and the drove roads, avoiding the toll-gates. He considered taking his freedom and not going home at all, but not seriously. His nature, like any religious and unpolitical nature, was essentially trusting and trustworthy, unprotesting of wrong, and obedient. It was not the fact that the College would eventually inform the Earl but his own nature that took him back. He neither hurried nor lingered, and it so happened that, irresistibly drawn to see if his Uncle was at home, he rode past the open French windows of the Earl's study at a moment of crisis. What he saw through the windows, unseen to either figure inside, caused him quickly to dismount from his horse: the Earl seated at his desk, facing a figure, whose back was to the windows through which clearly he had entered, who menaced the Earl with an outstretched pistol.

Edward, taking no time for thought, at this repeated image of himself three years before, moved quickly through the windows into the room, but not so quickly that he did not see the horrified surprise, and to his grief, the alarm, that seized the Earl's face at the unexpected sight of him. The young man, younger even than Edward, started at the Earl's change of expression, but Edward had seized him, one arm about his neck, the other his waist, before he could properly move in his surprise. Without a word, Edward relieved him of his gun, and holding him to him roughly in a bear's grip of his arms, with his hands unloaded it, putting the shot into his pocket, and then, with surprising gentleness, released the boy and returned the empty pistol to him.

"Here," he said roughly, but his eyes amused and his lips close to laughing. "You are much too foolish and too little for so adult a game. Go home now, and hurry, before anyone else besides me comes."

The boy raised large eyes, frightened, humiliated, and angry to his, but Edward only smiled.

"Go home now, fierce little chicken," he said again, pushing him. "I'm sorry I had to hurt you. But if anyone shoots this man, it is going to be me." He took his hand and aimed a sharp, well-directed spank to the boy's retreating rear, closed the windows after him and locked them.

The Earl had watched all the interchange of action and word with no movement or word of his own, his shadowed eyes fixed intently on Edward's face and his every move. The momentary open fear and shock had left his face, and only this careful, uneasy attention remained. Edward walked with a quick easy grace over to the desk, and pulled the bullets from his pocket and dropped them on the desk.

"I will go to my quarters now," Edward said without expression. His eyes did not meet his Uncle's. "I came without warning you. I am sorry to intrude upon you." He turned, without saying anything else, to go.

The Earl had no idea what Edward would find to say to him, but he had not expected words like these. Surprise held Tyne speechless and motionless for the few seconds it took Edward to reach the door. He had opened it, turning the key that the Earl's assailant had locked and left in it, when the Earl found his voice.

"Edward," he said quietly, "there is no need for this."

"No?" said Edward, his voice and his eyes veiled. "There is as much need now as there ever was." He closed the door behind him, and took his borrowed horse to the stables. "You won't have to fetch me this time, Ross," he said, "I have been sent down, and so I just came, instead of writing."

"Whose horse is this, Edward?" asked Ross. "Where did you get it?"

"I did not steal it, Ross," Edward said with faint contempt in his voice. "A friend loaned it to me," he said, with slight emphasis on the noun. "Please take care of it. It is a good horse, and it has come a long way." He took the saddle bags that held his books, and put them over his shoulder.

"Your Uncle is here," Ross said. He looked at Edward oddly.

"I know that," Edward answered. The Earl's equipage was clear to view. "You had better take me quickly to my hole, Ross, for even though I came back all this way myself, there is no telling what dreadful act I might do if I laid eyes on him. We could not have that, could we? Don't put your damned hand on my arm," he added. "You have fallen down in your job, Ross. The unforeseen has happened, and here I am, and you do not even know how long I have been here. I may have walked through the windows of my Uncle's study and shot him, while you were polishing his harness. You had not thought of that, had you, Ross? Put me in my hole and lock the door, and then you'd better go see if I did. Don't hit me, Ross, I'll hit you back."

They had reached the house and the back hall, but at the entrance to the priest-hole, Ross paused, the door open.

"Why did you come back, Edward? None of us knew. You could have gone to the friend who loaned you the horse. None of us would have known until I came for you."

Edward laughed slightly, as he bent his head to enter. "I thought of it, Ross. He asked me. But I gave my word to my Uncle, and I keep my word. That's all. Be sure to lock the door."

Ross could not see him, but he heard his voice clearly. He shook his head slowly, and locked the door, and then he went to the Earl's study, a part of the house unfamiliar to him. He walked by the now closed windows, and through them he could see the Earl sitting, apparently safely, at his desk. He went around the house to the front door, and was admitted, and knocked on the door of Tyne's study.

"Come in," the Earl's voice said sharply. Ross opened the door, and walked across the wide room rather awkwardly, and stood before the Earl at his desk. The Earl was leaning back in his chair in an exhausted manner, and his face was whiter than Ross had seen it, his dark brows standing out sharply against it in relief, the sharpness of his features particularly in evidence, but otherwise he seemed himself.

"Edward is back," Ross said without preamble.

"I know," the Earl said, "I have seen him."

"I wondered if you might have," Ross said, not noticing or intending the familiarity of his words in his concern. "He is talking very wildly. He has been sent down."

"Sent down?" said the Earl in surprise, looking less pale. "He has been, has he? That does surprise me. Where is Edward now?"

It was Ross now who looked surprised. "Where you have had me always take him. Where else should he be?"

"Good God!" exclaimed the Earl, and then noticing the amazement on his servitor's face, he added, in his ordinary voice, "You have done very well, Ross. I appreciate your having told me. I suppose he came to you himself, and asked you to take him? Did he?"

"Well, yes, he did," Ross admitted.

"Edward would," the Earl said, his lips compressed. "How did he get here? Did he walk?"

"No, he had a horse he said a friend loaned him. He brought the horse to me, to care for."

"And he was talking wildly?" said the Earl thoughtfully. "But he didn't act wild, did he?" he stated.

"I don't know," Ross said frankly, "I could not tell his words and his actions apart."

"It is important to be able to do that, of all things, Ross," the Earl said severely. "Give me the key. I have had enough of this." He dismissed Ross.

He had been sitting quietly, after Edward left, making no attempt to follow him, willing to let events take their course for once, but it seemed, after all, he must act. The violence of the preceding scene had exhausted him, more than he had thought, and he had been unnerved by Edward's sudden appearance. He had hardly seen him in three years, and never in daylight. He had been more frightened, he thought, by Edward than by his assailant. He had recognised him at once, being himself, but Edward was so much taller, and his face so much older, with so steady a look in his eyes, he almost might have been a stranger, and he had shown less recognition in his eyes than a stranger might. The Earl rose finally, and with the key in his hand, went down to the door of the priest-hole and unlocked it.

"Edward, you did not have to come here. I told you that," he said. "Come out now."

"I prefer to stay here," Edward's voice said from the dark. "I have grown accustomed to it, and I would not know what to do with myself anywhere else in your house." The tone of his voice eluded the Earl. He could not believe now, that he had treated this cool, steady young man as he had, or quite how he had been allowed to.

"Edward, please, come out," he said. "I want to talk to you."

"I am listening," Edward said. "Go ahead."

"I cannot talk to you this way." He heard Edward give a faint laugh.

"Why not? You could before."

"Edward, will you stop this nonsense, and come out?"

"Do you ask me to, Uncle?"

"Yes, Edward, I ask you to."

"Then I will stay here." His voice became suddenly angry. "God! Uncle," he said, "you make it impossible for me to hold my head up among your servants, you allow them to treat me as you would not let them treat a horse, even though you bought me too, once, and to speak to me with a familiarity that has no friendship in it, and you ask me to come out. No, I thank you. And why should you now? I am no different now than I have always been. You have just as much cause to be afraid of me now as you have ever had, you know just as little what I will do as you ever did. Had you asked me even a month ago, I would have come, and I could have loved you for it, and respected you still. But you did not. I am no different now.`I would have done what I did upstairs in your study for a stranger, I would have done it for Ross. And I even did it for you, as you saw. There is no merit in it, no reason for you to change your opinion of me because of it. I could shoot you more easily right now than I ever could. And if you bring me out, I might." His angry young voice finally hushed, leaving his last words hanging in the air between them.

"I'll risk it," the Earl said briefly. He had heard the boy out in silence. "I am glad you can at least be angry at me still. But you still talk too much, Edward. Come out now." His voice was no longer soft, and his familiar steely note was back in it.

"Do you order me?"

"I do."

"Then I will come," Edward said. The Earl heard him move the bags that held his books.

"Leave them," he said curtly. "Ross will bring them for you to your room." Edward obediently dropped them, and bowed his head and came out. He stood by his Uncle, his eyes averted, his face without expression, his hands relaxed at his side, waiting.

If this was submission, the Earl thought suddenly, a man was a fool to want it. He was not certain that he did any longer. He led the way upstairs, knowing Edward followed behind him, and into his study. He sat down in a chair by the fireplace, and invited Edward to sit in the chair opposite him.

"Are you asking me?" Edward said, his eyes briefly flickering on his Uncle.

"Yes, Edward."

"I would rather stand," Edward said, turning his face and his eyes towards the fire.

"Edward, sit down," the Earl said, his patience wearing thin.

"Do you order me?"

"I do," said the Earl.

"Then I will sit," Edward said, taking the chair. The Earl rang for a footman, and had a bottle of wine to be brought, and two glasses. The footman poured them, and the Earl handed one to Edward, who put it on a small table beside him and ignored it.

"Have you had lunch?" the Earl asked.

"I don't know," Edward said.

"Well, I know that I haven't." He turned to the footman, and ordered sandwiches to be cut and brought to them, and he also ordered the dinner hour to be set up ahead.

"I am not going to eat them," Edward said, "if you are ordering them for me, too."

The Earl looked at him curiously. "I have heard words like that before from you," he said, "but you were six then, and they were more excusable in you then. Your manners have not improved since I saw you last, they have grown worse."

Edward flushed, and the Earl was glad to see he still could.

"A beast has no manners," Edward said, looking at him with his full gaze.

"Indeed they do, Edward," the Earl said, undisconcerted, "watch any one of them in their natural state. But you mean a beast in captivity, I think." He paused. "Do you wish me to apologise? I can, you know, and if it is called for, I don't mind. I have insulted you, I have abused you, and I have misjudged you. I am sorry for all three, and I shall try to do none of them again. When you are twenty-one, you may avenge yourself properly on me if you wish, but until then I shall ask you to just accept my apology. I have been foolishly in error, and I am sorry for it. Now, will you drink your wine? Or are you an abstainer? I will not be so presumptuous as to ask you to have friendly feelings towards me now, but I do ask for some sort of truce of hostilities so that we may manage to conduct our business."

For answer, Edward took the small stemmed glass of wine and drank from it. After a moment's silence, he asked, "What made you change your mind? Being rescued?"

"I was never in much danger," the Earl said, half-smiling.

Edward looked a little surprised. "It looked to me as if you were."

"But I was not," the Earl said. "Are you going to ask me who it was that wanted to kill me, and why?"

"I do not much care," Edward said, looking at his glass.

"I had shot the young person's father in a duel recently, I believe," the Earl said somewhat absently.

"You killed her father?" Edward asked, shocked.

"So you realised that, too, Edward. You are sharper than I took you for."

"I held her," Edward said briefly. "It was not hard, holding her, to discover it. Did you kill her father?"

"It was a duel, Edward, and I do not miss. I was simply the better shot."

"He must have had considerable cause, then, if that is your reputation, or been very drunk," Edward said slowly. "Perhaps I should have let her kill you."

"I do not remember," the Earl said, "which duel it was or for what cause. I never thought she would, except by mistake, but with females one never knows for certain what they will do, by accident or by intention, or with young children. That was the only real danger, but there was some." He took his pistol from his pocket, and handed it to Edward. "You see, I had this all the time. But you may use it on me, for her, if you like."

"I should not be surprised if you had another one on you," Edward said, looking at it with distaste.

"No, Edward, I do not. I am now quite helpless. It is loaded, and you are too far away from me to make my hands of any use to me. But I won't ever give you this chance again. Take it now, if you are going to." He leaned back, and shut his eyes. He heard the small sound of the pistol being replaced on the table beside him.

"I don't think you ever thought there was much risk, when you offered that to me," Edward's voice said.

"No," he agreed, "but I did not know. You have as much cause as she did, perhaps more."

"What is her name?" Edward asked.

"I don't know," the Earl said, indifferently. "I did not recognise her, and she did not tell me. I told you, I have been in several duels of late." His face did not encourage further questions.

"When then did you change your mind about me?" asked Edward, reverting.

"The sight of you," said the Earl simply. "I had not seen you, you know, for three years, standing, in sunlight, as you were."

There was a knock at the door, and the footman entered with a tray with a plate of meat and cress sandwiches and a syllabub in glasses, and a dish of fruit.

"Where is George?" Edward asked, in his turn changing the subject.

"He is in London," the Earl answered. "Would you like to see him?"

"Yes, I would," said Edward. "But how can I?"

"I thought you might like to go down to London, until you can go back to Oxford."

"You know about that? Ross told you?" The Earl nodded. "With you, to your house?" The Earl again nodded. "Yes, I would like to go. I have never been, to London really, or to your house there. How am I to go?" He rose unexpectedly, and walked across to the Earl, and bent his head quickly, and kissed his lips: "Like this?" His face masked, he returned to his chair. "Do not say I shock you, for I don't. I just want to know why you have asked me."

"No, Edward," the Earl said simply, "not like that. That is best forgotten. You are nearly grown now, in fact, you look completely a young man, and you will soon be twenty-one. Is it next year?"

"I shall never forget," Edward said, his eyes meeting and holding his Uncle's.

The Earl sighed. "Have you been doing that at Oxford? Some do, I know."

"No, Uncle," Edward said simply, "I have not the taste."

"You relieve my mind," the Earl said. "Why me then?"

"Because it has been yours with me," Edward answered with complete simplicity.

There was a silence between them, of questions and possibilities and contradictions the Earl did not wish to explore. The Earl took a sandwich and began to eat it, knowing the commonplace and the prosaic had always the power to put the strange and the emotional in its place. Edward, perceiving his reason and being quite hungry, his dulled appetite sharpened by the wine, followed his example.

"Why have you been sent down and for how long?" the Earl asked. "You surprise me. You have surely not been expelled?"

Edward shook his head, and a smile of reminiscence lit his face. "It was a mistake, Uncle."

"You do not seem distressed," said his Uncle.

"Well, I am not, very. I have brought my books, and I think I shall not suffer for it, if I work. I may go back after Christmas, if you will write me a letter that I will behave myself, and not ride horses in the dining room, when others are eating, and even when they are not." His smile had broadened.

"I didn't think you had a horse at Oxford, Edward. I think you had better explain yourself, if you want me to write this letter, and take a properly subdued and penitent air about it. I do not see that it is a light matter."

"I know it is not, Uncle, that is why I let them fasten it on me, without making any protest, because you see, the boy who did it is in trouble all the time, and he would have been expelled for it, and not have been allowed to take his degree."

"That seems only proper to me," said the Earl. "I may write the powers at Oxford about it."

"Oh, please do not, Uncle," said Edward. "If I had thought you would, I never would have told you. He is a particular friend of mine, and he means well, but he seems always to be getting into scrapes of one kind or another and being found out. And he could not afford any more, but he can't resist a bet."

"What was this bet?"

"That he could jump his horse over all the tables in the High Hall, and not upset anything on them or touch anyone seated at them." Edward's eyes danced at the pictures in his mind the recollection brought.

"A mad bet, and rather dangerous. Did he win?" asked the Earl.

"He won, but he has hair like mine. He went so fast, no one had time to see him closely."

"Well, if you were there to see him, weren't you seen, too?"

"I was, but Averill who was there beside me, had the idea of substituting me, since I was virtuous. He is a madcap too, you know, but even he was very dismayed, and he persuaded me to slip under the table until the hall was cleared, and then when they let my name slip out, and the authorities summoned me, I didn't have to say a thing. They said it all."

"I daresay they did," said the Earl grimly.

"Uncle, come," said Edward, "did you never get into any scrapes yourself?" His guardian smiled a little, but he did not answer. "Even the heads thought I was too sober. Imagine, more than three years and nothing at all against me on their books. They hadn't any hold on me, and they were rather glad to have one. I think they would have kept me on, if they'd dared, but they couldn't, of course, for they had been sure at first, like everyone, it was—this other student, and said what they would do. They told me"—his eyes danced again—"'a little yeast was necessary to leaven the loaf,' but not to do it again. Now you won't disappoint them, surely, Uncle? Here I have a new reputation, and I am much envied, and I didn't have to exert myself at all to gain it. But I won't let it take me into any more scrapes, I promise you. You see, we all do really want our degrees." He looked pleadingly at his Uncle, whose face softened a little.

"Have you been so sober as that, Edward?" the Earl asked, somewhat incredulously.

"I have been too unhappy to be anything but sober," Edward said, his eyes darkening a little, not taking his eyes from his guardian.

"Have you been so unhappy?" asked his Uncle. "I thought Oxford was a place people enjoyed themselves."

"You know I have, Uncle. How could I not be?"

"Why so, in particular, Edward? Only because of my brutality? Could you not forget that at Oxford? It was only a small part."

Edward shook his head, but he did not answer.

"Then you have a poorer spirit than I thought for, Edward. I do not think I have managed to hurt you. You look very well to me. Your spirit is not broken, it seems tougher than ever to me, and you are not pale, and you enjoy silly jokes about horses jumping over salt cellars."

"Just one horse, Uncle," said Edward.

"Is it because you do not like the studies I set up for you at Oxford, or the fact of my setting them up?"

"I have liked them," Edward said.

"Because of my scandalous misbehaviour with your unsuitable friend?"

Edward shook his head. "Finally I understood even that, but please, let's not speak of it."

"Well, what then in God's name? Are you still harping in your mind on this God-forsaken idea of your being a clergyman, a Methody?"

Edward laughed, a little, at his Uncle's language, but his eyes did not laugh. "No, Uncle, you have succeeded there. I have no wish for that life any more."

"What life then? A poet?" the Earl said, without enthusiasm.

"Oh, you did read those then? No. I have only a most ordinary talent there, and no temperament for the life. Things do not seem so simple to me as they did, in myself or in other people," he added, "and I do not any longer really know my own wishes."

"Things? What things?" asked the Earl.

Edward shrugged, and did not reply.

"What do you wish then?" the Earl asked.

"I don't know," Edward said, his voice low. "I wish I did. Except I would like to go away somewhere, by myself, for a long time."

"To any place in particular?" the Earl asked.

Edward shook his head. "I would just like to go away."

"You have no money, Edward, and you said yourself you want your degree."

"I know. And I have promised you to stay, and you will not let me go."

"No, Edward, I won't, but you will be twenty-one in only a little more than a year, not even a year and a half, and then except with money, I cannot stop you from doing as you like. If you have put up with me for thirteen years, surely you can for not quite two more."

Edward lifted his bent head and looked at him queerly.

"This talk of my being twenty-one. Do you really think that I do not know?"

"Know what, Edward?" the Earl said, his heart beating fast at the intentness of Edward's eyes. He disliked scenes, but he had never lacked the particular courage required to face them.

"All of it. I am not stupid. I may be many things, but I am not that, and I have had time to think, more than it needed, down in that pit you cast me into."

"A pit in Dothan?"

"That was not exactly what came to my mind," Edward said.

"What do you know, Edward?" the Earl asked again.

Edward looked at him straightly. "I know that I am on trial here. I know that when I am twenty-one, you are going to decide how well I have turned out, and whether you like the way that happens to be, and how far you intend to claim me, and how much of your property you intend to settle on me, and whether you intend to see any more of me. But you have never thought, I think, that I might have my wishes too."

"You are unjust in that, Edward. It is true that I have not made up my mind yet about certain important questions I must shortly settle in it, and it is true that I do not know what intentions I have about my property, and if you said I should know by now, I would agree with you, although as it happens, I simply do not yet know my mind, but it is not true that I do not realise you may have wishes of your own. I do, very much. It is my property, and a very substantial one, and I have made no promises ever to your mother about the disposition of it, when I agreed to take you and pay for your care and education while you grew up. You cannot blame me, I think, for being hesitant about the final dispositions of much vaster sums and properties, and my land. You have surely not expected them, and I am a little surprised you venture to discuss now with me what to me is a somewhat delicate subject. I am very much alive, and I do not need to make any definite decisions even though you come of age, although I had once perhaps planned to. But I do realise that when I do make up my slow mind, you may not wish to accept what I may propose. I have always realised that."

Edward brushed the Earl's long, careful speech away with a gesture of his hand, and a few quick words. "And when I am twenty-one, you will perhaps spring a scene on me, that has been building up all these long years in your mind when you would not come near me, and I wanted you so, as any boy would, but as I particularly did, and you knew I did. And you will think then that a few words will shock me so that you can forget whatever hate you have had for me, and I can forget any you have tried to make me feel for you. I say *perhaps* because in the end you may decide not to say them. But I know them. I have known them for years."

"Known what, Edward?" the Earl asked gently, with foreboding.

"I know I am your son," he said in his young voice, hard because expressionless, ignoring the expression on the Earl's face, "and I know you are not certain you believe I am."

The words out, from which there could be no turning back, Edward rose from his chair in sudden shame at what he had said, and walked a few steps away, his back turned. The Earl rose, too, and walked with his hesitant gait to the boy, and took his hand without a word, and led him unresisting back to his seat.

VIII

"Please sit down, Edward," he said with gentle courtesy. "If you have opened this subject, we must discuss it, I think, and now, and I cannot speak well standing. That is a curse you have in any case escaped. How long have you known—what you say you know? And how do you come to know what I cannot?"

"I have known since I was at Oxford," Edward said, with a certain impatience. "I learned to understand many things there I had not before, and I had time to think, as I told you, in the hole you wanted me kept in. I could not understand it, it seemed out of all proportion, until I read a play at Oxford, and then, with other things I remembered and pieced together, it all fit."

"But is that knowing," the Earl asked, "or is it guessing? You may have guessed my mind, but do you know? What is this play?"

"It is a play by a Spanish writer named Calderón—"

"I have heard of him," the Earl said, smiling slightly, "though I do not recall reading him."

"It is called *Life Is a Dream*. A friend of mine was translating it, and I read it with him. He never knew, I never told him, how well I understood that play."

"Do not speak in riddles to me, Edward," the Earl said, "if you have something to say to me, please say it clearly."

"I am trying to. It is no easier for me than for you. This play is about a prince who has a bad horoscope, which more modernly we might call a bad ancestry, a curse from our parents rather than from the stars, as you call your foot."

"I follow you. We have this prince, who is cursed at his birth," the Earl said impatiently. "What then?"

"What then?" asked Edward. "Why, that tells it all. He will have no chance, he will be prejudged by everyone, his slightest most innocent action or must usual error will be subject to the most sinister mis-interpretations by those who know what he does not. He has been tried and condemned, with no trial, without knowing his crime, or that he has even committed one."

"Is all that in the play?" asked the Earl.

"No, but that is what it is about."

"'Jeddart justice,' as for Armstrongs," observed the Earl. "What is his particular horoscope?"

"According to the stars, he will destroy his father."

"So what happens to this prince?" the Earl said, with hardly a pause.

"The king, who is his father, his own father, has him taken a long way away from the court as a baby, to a savage place with a caretaker, where he is kept chained like a beast in skins to a stake. And he is just kept there. The wonder is that he grows up at all, but he does. It is just a play, you see, it is not real. And then when he comes of age, the king, needing an heir, is persuaded by his counsellors to have him put to sleep and brought into the midst of the court where he suddenly wakes. He is, again without knowing it, a second time on trial. Imagine. From his rocky solitude and nothing but an old man and the stones and the stars, to the world of the court, its lights, its people, its profusion of scents and colours and jewels and laughter and flirting girls and conversation he cannot follow. He does not pass the test. Suddenly given power, and space and opportunity to use it in, he is filled with savage and angry emotions, terrifying to everyone about him and probably to himself as well. He behaves like the savage beast he has been reared like, which is not surprising, and they subdue him. He is made to lose consciousness again, and when he wakes again, he is again chained in his rocky fast-ness with only the old man, and these startling images in his brain. That, you see, is what the title means. Which of his lives is the dream, and is all our life a dream, and so forth, 'Uncle.' It is a long play, full of as much talk as I am."

"How does it end?" asked the Earl curiously.

"Oh," said Edward indifferently, "in the end this Segismund learns better, and does in time become the King."

"And do you think you will?" the Earl asked pointedly.

"It is just a play, 'Uncle,' it is its world, not mine."

"Then why tell it to me? It is a good story, and it did interest me, but what was it you learned?"

"I learned why you were afraid of me, which I could never understand, before, for I cannot find much in me for anyone to be afraid of. But I did not know that you thought I might have your blood in me, as well as my mother's, instead of a clergyman's blood. And then I saw that was what you were always looking for in me, the curse of your blood, as you thought, and waiting to appear. It was foolish of you, 'Uncle,' and unjust, to yourself as well as to me. And I knew then that even if I was not your son, that you had to have known my mother at some time in a way you were ashamed of, and somehow you managed to fasten blame for that on me, too."

"You know a great deal, Edward. I cannot deny what you say, and I won't waste breath trying to. Why have you never spoken of this to me before?"

Edward laughed angrily, the anger like distant rumbling of thunder behind his voice. "When have I seen you to speak?"

The Earl acknowledged the hit with his hand up like a fencer's, and it seemed curiously also a mute cry for mercy. He seemed much the less strong of the two.

"And I should have been embarrassed," Edward added, more in the voice of his young age. "I am embarrassed now."

"I am myself, Edward," the Earl murmured. "I did not quite see the scene you imagined me planning being quite like this."

"I should not have spoken before you did," Edward said with some contrition, "but you made me so angry. You have treated me so cruelly, always a little, but so badly these last years, and mistrusted me so completely with so little cause, and then you could not even hold to your own convictions. And then for nothing but a chance coincidence, that had no relationship to anything at all, to release me, when I had prayed night after night that you would return and come, to let me out, just for myself."

"You are mistaken, Edward. Coincidences always are related, we just sometimes do not see how and why they fall into place. I saw a young man, not a child, not a boy, who did not look at all like me, and not as much as he did like his mother, who came back without being made to, at inconvenience and trouble to himself, to the most dismal and unjust of punishments, imposed for nothing except the wish to follow in

234 Edward, Edward

his father's footsteps, and for no other reason than to keep a promise exacted from him by force. No one compelled him to it. It was his own nature, no outside force, no stars. And this is what brought him at the moment when he could have seen his perscutor, so he thought, destroyed by someone beside himself, no one else even knowing he saw. These are all facts, Edward, and I saw them finally."

"Any such fact is open to more than one interpretation. If I thought you had not left me any property, I might have wanted to save you to do that," Edward said, smiling faintly.

"I think not," the Earl said.

"No," Edward agreed. "Oh, 'Uncle,'" he said impatiently, "I understand the workings of your mind so clearly. You saw all that you have described to me, and in your mind you could not see the actions coming from anyone related to yourself, and you decided then I *must* be George Armstrong's son, not yours. And then, there being no further danger to you, from me, as you thought, you had no further fear of me, and you let me out, and let me come around you. But you were rash, Holland," he said menacingly, suddenly using the name he had not, "for if I am my father's son, an Armstrong, and if you dishonoured my mother and my father's wife, why should I not kill you now, there being no tie between us, of blood or affection, with my hands, like this."

Before the startled Earl realised what he was about, Edward had taken a quick stride across the small space that separated them, knocked the Earl back in his chair, his fingers locked about his throat. The Earl, feeling the strength in his fingers, helplessly pinned against the arm of the chair, his hands futilely on Edward's wrists, unable to push him away, thought, It is fitting, I did this to his mother. It seemed now inevitable he should meet his death, as he had feared, at the hands of this boy, but he had not visualised it in this ugly way, or at this unguarded moment. He ceased to struggle against the hands and relaxed into the pain. Abruptly he felt the fingers leave his throat, and Edward sat down again, after taking the Earl's pistol and flinging it across the room.

"You were not safe after all, you see, Holland," he said coolly, again using the name. "And I have as much violence in my nature as in yours, but like you, I know too when to stop."

The Earl sat up, catching his breath, still feeling the relentless young fingers about his throat. "I did that to your mother once," he said, when he could speak at all. "She said it hurt, and she was right." At the look of shocked horror on Edward's face, he said, "I should not have said that. I am not myself. I was thinking aloud. It is too complicated to

explain. She asked me to," he added to Edward's complete incomprehension. He shut his eyes, and concentrated on recovering himself.

"I asked for that, I think," he said after a bit, when he could breathe
more easily. "Please don't do it again, though. I hope you don't mean
to," he said, somewhat worried by Edward's angry face.

Edward shook his head. "I just wanted you to know that I could,
if I wanted to. I didn't want you to think that because I did not, I could
not. There is a difference, you know, Holland, but sometimes I don't
think you see it."

"I will try to, at least when I am around you, Edward," the Earl
said wearily. "About your mother—" His words failed him at the white
look of hostility on Edward's face, but he continued resolutely, after a
moment's pause, "I did not dishonour her when she was married. Your
father was not involved."

Edward looked at him so peculiarly, the Earl felt himself flushing.
"Dishonoured, too, I mean. God, Edward, you make me feel like a schoolboy. I don't like it."

"I don't like it either," Edward said, with a set face. "But I shouldn't
be angry with you now, I have known about it for some time, and it was
a long time ago, and you have been good to me many times, and my
mother brought me to you herself. She clearly did not hate you, I think.
But if you thought I could be bought off, if I found out, or when you
told me, you were mistaken, Holland. I don't understand how people
can behave the way they do, when they grow up. Someday perhaps I
will, but I don't really want to. And someday you can tell me about
my mother, but not now. I don't like to hear you speak about her."

The Earl thought that an understatement, but he refrained from
saying so. "I had rather not myself," he said simply. "I treated her badly,
but no one knows better than you that I did love her, and in the end, I
thought perhaps through you, I might make some amends, but I never
thought to buy you off. Believe that, Edward, that never occurred to
me." He laughed uneasily. "I never thought I should have to, but children do grow up, and when they come of age, they are not children any
more. I did not think of that, I did not take it sufficiently into account,
I think. How strange. I thought, if I found out you were my son, all I
should have to do was tell you, and you would be happy to hear it. My
God, what a fool I was. I forgot what that meant about your mother.
How could I forget—and I forgot—"

"I know what you forgot. Please do not say it. I have lived with that
too, this past year and a half in my mind, and I have gotten a little used
to it, but not entirely. I have looked it up, you see, and I know how

little it means to be your son in the way I am. I do not intend to make any claims on you, Holland, and when you let me go, I mean to go."

"Even if I should wish you not to?"

"Even if you should wish me not to."

"Well, Edward," the Earl said heavily, "I see my faults. I have deserved your words. Nevertheless, I have not heard you. Make your decision when you know what I offer you, or when you come of age. I should not have asked what I did. I have forgotten I did." He found that tears had sprung to his eyes, and rather than let Edward see them, not knowing he had, he rose with difficulty and walked to the window and leaned against it, looking out. He was amazed to see the sunlight still on the trees, after the dark oppressive air of the room, its violent thoughts and emotions and actions.

"I believe you are very angry with me," he said with a novel effort at understanding the emotions of another person, which his wealth had before made it unnecessary for him to try to do. "I think you have been angry since you first came through that window, and even when you were talking about the horse. And you are angry now."

"Yes, Holland," Edward said simply, "but I have been angry for so long, for three years. You have just not been around me to know it. And you are right, I am angry still. But I can play a game, too, like you. I have learned how. Perhaps you taught me."

"Well," said the Earl. He had never felt so old. He continued to look out of the window. "I had decided this afternoon you could not be my son, as you say you knew I did. I still do not think so. But I should be proud if you were. I like your anger. You should be angry. I like your pride and your violence, for you are right to feel both against me, I think. I like your restraint where it matters." He heard Edward come up behind him, and to his surprise, he felt him slip his arms about his waist from behind, clasping him lightly. He put his own hands over Edward's clasped ones, and their shared memories were in both their minds. "I like the way you have grown up, and I claim no credit for it. I like the quickness of your intelligence, and your understanding. I like the look of your face. I even like to hear you talk. Your father would be proud of you." Edward remained as he was, not moving, and after a moment the Earl asked, "Why do you think you are my son?"

"I do not think. I know. Come upstairs and I will show you." He gently disengaged his arms. The Earl followed him up the stairs into the gallery, where Edward had first stationed himself the afternoon of his mother's death, and stopped beside the large full-length portrait of a sad-faced woman. What he should think being so pointedly assigned, he looked at the portrait with new eyes, and at Edward, and at the portrait again, and he saw what Edward had seen.

"It is very like," he said. "I should have seen this before."

"You were looking always at me, and at yourself, and at your memories of my mother," Edward said simply, "but they were none of them the place to look."

"And you saw this," the Earl said with wonder, "and I did not."

"I do not suppose," Edward said, this time without bitterness, "that you would easily have connected your memories of my mother with your memories of your mother. And you have so seldom been home to pass this way, since I came here, and you thought about who I was. You did not know my mother well, did you? To be acquainted with, I mean, as one is when one lives from day to day with someone. I know you did not know her at this age, for I did. And the eyes are not the same at all, or the colour of her hair. It is the way the bones lie beneath the cheek, I think, as my mother's did, and as mine do, and as yours do, Holland, too. Did no one ever tell you? I saw it at once, but I did not think of its significance then. Our features are not the same, and our dispositions are not. And the line of the jaw, as it sits against the ear, Holland, which you do not have, yours being like your father's in that portrait next. Her hands are mine too, Holland, and they are also yours, they are just smaller yet. You remember them when they were even smaller and even more fleshed, but you see, they are different now." The Earl glanced at them, and glanced away, remembering their brief cruelty, hands that could both caress and hurt, like his own. "Had you looked at them, since I grew up, you might have seen it, too." He placed his hand against the hand in the picture, in a similar position. "You see? Mine is not so long yet as yours, or so tightly drawn, the skin from the bones. I have been a student, sheltered, both here and there, and my hands are still smooth and more like a woman's hands. But the straightness of the bone, and the lack of tapering until the hand is here, in all our fingers. My mother's hands were not so straight, or so long, although they were somewhat the same. I thought them in their way as beautiful. She had to use them harder, too, Holland, than I have, or your mother did. And look at the width of the brow, which is not like yours, but is like mine, and like my mother's. When she drew her hair back like that, her hair sprung from her forehead just the same way, and just as mine would, if I pulled my hair back, instead of letting it fall forward as I do." He showed the Earl, gathering it back with his hand. He spoke as dispassionately as though he were proving a theorem he had developed to his tutor. "I do not wonder you never saw it, when I so resembled my mother, especially when I was softer and smaller. But perhaps something of it that you perceived, not knowing you did, drew you to my mother."

"It may have been," the Earl said heavily. "It may well have been. I have been blind, Edward."

"You never knew my father, as I thought him then, did you, Holland?" He shook his head. "You never saw him, did you?"

"Not really," the Earl said. "Not really at all. Although I have studied your father's relations and your mother's carefully, and found as little to connect you with them as I found to connect you with me."

"He did not look the least bit like me, or I like him. My mother sometimes was annoyed when her friends said how much I looked like her, and not like him. He was large-boned—not like myself, or you, or your mother or mine, Holland, and much taller than we are, though we are tall. He had bushy eyebrows, not like any of ours, and an eagle gaze with pure grey eyes; I never saw anyone else with eyes completely grey. His nose was bent, slightly at the bridge. Yours is straight, and I have a little turn-up nose, like my mother. His hands were short and square and blunt, Holland, and he was fully-fleshed, not sparse, as we are. I loved him, Holland. He was a big giant of a man, and he loved me and my mother, and he protected us. I cannot see how a little bullet could have killed so big a man. I have remembered, you see. It could not have been me. I was leaning on my gun, pretending it was a shooting stick, and had he had time, he would have been so cross with me—though he would not have whipped me for it," he interposed, with a quick glance at the Earl—"for I had buried the barrel in the soft mud and grass of the field. It had recently rained, and it went right in. I had fired it once, just to see what it would be like, and hurt my cheek, and then I rammed it down, I was so mad. It was after that my father came, and he was a long way from me when he fell. I wondered what game he was playing, but I stopped to clean the worst of the mud from the barrel of the gun, before I ran to him, because I did not want him to see. And by the time I reached him, the hunters were coming up, from the direction nearer where he had come from. And—and I don't want to remember the rest. But you see, Holland, how much you worried for so little. Couldn't you just look at me, and see I was no monster, at least after you had come to know me just a little?"

"My perceptions are not so keen, Edward, as yours," the Earl said shakily, "or so sure. Perhaps they once might have been, but I do not remember noticing other things, or other people as you do."

"I was raised by my father and by my mother, Holland, until I was six. Do you know what the Jesuits say?"

"Not in particular. Tell me, Edward."

"Give us a child until he is six, and you may then have him for the rest of his life, for he will not then depart from our ways. Something like that. I heard my father say it once, admiring it. My father had me, you see, Holland, and my mother too. Their natures were not like yours, and mine was formed by them. Of course you see my father's in me. How could you help not seeing it? But my nature is also like yours. I know. I feel things that perhaps I do not show, that you do show—as perhaps you feel things that you cannot show or do not choose to. My mother thought I was your son, didn't she, Holland? That is why she brought me, isn't it?"

"Yes, Edward," the Earl said heavily. "But she did not know, and she never saw my mother or this portrait. I do not think she did, that day. She had much on her mind, and she was not well, and it is not directly in view. When did you discover this?"

"The first night I came," Edward said. "I was so unhappy, and I walked here, and I saw the picture of this lady, and it seemed to me, though the eyes were not my mother's, or the lips, nevertheless that it was somehow my mother. I did not question why. I let it comfort me. I often came to sit here, when you were gone, and I asked George once when I was older who it really was, and he told me. But it was not until these last years, when you treated me so strangely, and I began to think, that it became one of the pieces that slipped into place in my mind. I don't remember now when exactly that happened. Last year? The year before? It was one piece, that was all. Some time ago now."

The Earl turned away from the picture. "You have surprised me, Edward," he said. He put his hands hesitantly on Edward's shoulders, but he encountered no withdrawal. He stood looking at him steadily, his eyes searching and finding what they looked for. He leaned forward, and kissed him gently, once on each cheek, the act both a valediction and a welcoming.

"I shall surprise you, too, Edward," he said, leading the way again downstairs into his study. He said nothing else, but went directly to his desk, and opened a small concealed compartment and took from it a folded piece of paper which he handed to Edward. He saw the boy's defences visibly crumble.

"In the end, you see, Edward, I did marry your mother."

"Did you?" the boy said pitifully. "Why did you not tell me?"

"Note the date, Edward. It comes too late to help you. If you wish to claim me, and own yourself my son, you are still my bastard, and there is no way that knowledge can be concealed from the world, Edward."

"I know that," the boy said pitifully. "Do not say the word. It is worse for my mother than for me."

"No, Edward," the Earl said relentlessly. "It is not. She is dead. It is worse for you. I will own you, if you wish me to, but that fact alone gives you no advantage at all, in itself, and it takes from you several advantages you do have. You bear better blood, if less highly placed, in the eyes of the world, and in mine too, as you stand now, and you have respectability, which is no mean thing, and you will value it even more later. You will not necessarily gain any material advantage you would not have anyway. I am promising nothing there. I do not even know what I could promise, or what I would want to."

"If I am your son, although a natural one, that is what I am. I wish only to be known for what I am—no more, and no less."

"So be it," the Earl said with a sigh. "I will see to it. But let me think. You have shocked me, Edward, in too many ways, and I cannot see my way clear. I am unprepared for it."

"Will you want to adopt me?" Edward asked.

"I do not know," the Earl answered truthfully. "I must think."

"I would rather you did not," Edward said, surprising the Earl. "At least not now." He surprised the Earl once again by saying, "Why can't we do as you originally thought, Holland, and wait to do or say anything at all until I am twenty-one? I must get my degree, and I am too unsettled now, as things are. I don't think I could take being any more unsettled than I am just now." He looked at the Earl squarely. "And if I still feel, as I do now, that I must leave you, then I would rather put that off, thinking of that, too, since you have said you will not let me now. I suppose you still will not?" The Earl shook his head, and Edward handed him back the certificate of marriage.

The Earl, for once wise, did not question what Edward had said. He replaced the certificate in its place, and sprung the hidden catch.

"Why did you marry my mother, Holland?" Edward asked. "To please her?"

"No," the Earl said. "My nature is not so nice."

"Why, then?"

"To give myself an easier power to do what might prove in the end necessary for the handling of her affairs or of yours, although I did not foresee it as very likely."

"What was that, Holland?"

"The closing of her house and properties, but it was not needed there. The keeping of my guardianship, should it require it and I wish it." He looked away from Edward. "Particularly, your possible adoption."

"Oh," Edward said. "I see, I suppose. But you have not needed it. Holland, you have never let me see my mother's grave. Is that why? Whose name is on the stone?"

"Your father's as you knew him; her first husband."

"Were you ashamed of having given her your name?"

"No. The other seemed more her own. I wanted no talk."

"Will you take me there tomorrow? Where is she?"

"Not far from where you had your lessons, Edward. I will take you tomorrow, before we leave for London. Or will you still go with me?"

"I will go. But I want to go now, tonight, before dinner, to see my mother's grave. You do not need to go with me. I will ask the Vicar, or find it myself. I could have looked before, but you told me not to, and I was never alone. I did not know it was so near." He looked at the Earl. "It was cruelly done, or thoughtlessly, Holland. You caused me much pain there that was needless."

"It was my thoughtlessness, Edward, rather than my intention."

"Will you tell Ross I may ride where I please now?" Edward asked, the humiliation staining his cheeks. "How shall I act at dinner?"

"Act yourself," the Earl said simply. "That will be enough."

"I am going now, then," Edward said. "Do not concern yourself for me if I seem later than you think I should be. What time shall I return for dinner?"

The Earl told him.

"I shall be home then in time to dress." He looked at the Earl hesitantly. "I would rather not speak of any of this again, at least, for a while. Would you mind?"

"I would not mind at all," the Earl said with feeling. He summoned his footman to summon Ross, and later, he watched Edward's figure cantering across the moors towards the vicarage and the churchyard beyond.

That evening they sat after dinner by the fire in the Earl's study, quietly, the Earl with brandy and Edward with coffee for which he had acquired a taste at Oxford, studying late, the early dusk fallen, but the curtains not drawn, conversing easily, like the old acquaintances they were, of many things, past, present, and yet in the future, but intermittently, with long silences that had nothing of discomfort in them.

They had touched briefly on the news of the Summer, the kidnapping by
Napoleon of the Pope, Pius VII, and the sufferings and discomfort of the
old man's hasty and summary journeys, as the Emperor transported him
across the passes to Avignon and back to Savona, at which even the
Anglicans could not feel joy; and the entering of England into the
Peninsular War in Spain, about which the two parties and their members
and the voting public were divided in opinion. Major General Sir Arthur
Wellesley, thirty-nine, the appointed Irish Secretary among other posts
in 1807, had led the British expedition succesfully against Vimeiro at the
end of August and effected the Convention of Cintra in which Lisbon
was surrendered as well to him. Wellesley, the Earl told Edward with
a glint in his eye, had spelled his name Wesley until the turn of the
century, but Edward did not rise to the bait.

Their estrangement for the moment was in abeyance, and might not
have been, for Edward had always been gifted with a lack of embarrassment, and the Earl had never known it. Edward sat quietly, resting, feeling as he had felt after he had been so very ill when he was nine, and
had finally returned to comfort, his body at last rested and easy again
and untroublesome, the Earl beside him, drained yet peaceful. The Earl
now rose and walked with no limp that Edward could see to the wide
windows through which Edward had come, that overlooked the darkened garden, and drew the curtains across them.

"Why *hooks?*" he asked, sitting down again.

Edward looked puzzled, and the Earl added, "It seemed a strange
choice of word. I wondered about it." Edward's brow cleared.

"In my poem, you mean? I had been reading Isidore of Seville.
Amicus, 'friend,' he said came from another Latin word meaning a little
hook, because, he said, 'they hold.' That interested me, Holland, because
I had been rereading *Hamlet* again and it seemed to me that Isidore's
etymology lay behind a line in that play where my tutor said the text
was ambiguous. The word seemed to be *hooks,* but one scholar said that
was impossible in sense and substituted *hoops,* and another said it referred to the grappling irons of pirate ships with which they hooked
alien ships to them, but myself, I think it is just Isidore. 'Those friends
thou hast, Grapple them unto thy soul with hooks of steel,'" he quoted
softly, his gaze on the Earl. "I liked it, and I used it myself."

"And did you tell your tutor this? Have you set them all straight?"
asked the Earl, smiling.

Edward shook his head, smiling a little himself. "I am not really a
fighter, even over a disputed meaning."

"Oh?" asked the Earl, and his hand went to his throat. Edward said nothing. He only smiled a little again, and shook his head again.

"We must cure that then," the Earl said thoughtfully. "When we reach London, I will ask Jackson to enroll you in his Boxing Saloon. He knows me well, I think he will take you on himself."

"As you wish, Holland," Edward said, but without noticeable enthusiasm.

"Can you fence, Edward?"

"I do not own a sword."

"Then we will see to that too." He looked amused at Edward's dismay. "You thought again your education was nearly finished, and again you see it has just begun. But if you like, these things can wait until Summer, after you have your degree."

"I would rather wait, Holland, until I do."

"Very well, Edward, finish your career as a scholar, and then I will see that you are educated to be a gentleman. You will find it all useful to you, I think, both kinds. You will want to make your mind wide enough to hold the world." He paused. "I particularly liked your last poem, Edward," he said, "although myself I should cut off the last two lines, I think." He paused again, looking at the young man opposite him. "My hair was fair once too, Edward," he remarked, "but that was a long time ago, it darkened before I was six. I do not think yours will, now."

Later, the Earl walked with Edward upstairs. He did not notice the eagerness held back in Edward's face, as they approached his old room, and he did not notice the sudden whitening of his face and his lips, and a look in his eyes as if he had been struck, as they entered. Edward looked about him and did not say anything immediately. It had been entirely stripped of all that had ever belonged to him. There was no trace left visible that he had ever been in it, and nothing he recognised except the frame of the window. Even the view out from it was hidden by the night. The walls were repapered, the furniture changed, the curtains, the bed hangings, the rug, all other materials and other colours. The bed might perhaps be his, but he could not tell, hidden in its new clothes. His disappointment was intense, but after a moment, he put it in proportion and collected himself. The cold fact of his banishment, however, its seriousness and its extent, its totality, had never been made so real or so definite to him as here, in his old place, his no longer, now that it was over, and he was returned.

"I am too dirty for this room," Edward said, with a wistful smile, looking about him, "but I am too tired to bathe tonight. It will have to wait for morning. You did not ever expect me back, did you, Holland?"

"No, Edward," the Earl said simply, "I suppose I did not. Why do you ask that now?"

"It was never quite so clear to me. If you had, you would have kept my room for me, and not made it new for guests."

The Earl had the grace to flush and look abashed. "I was premature, and I am glad to be able to say it, but I am sorry now to have hurt you again. But as you say, I did not expect you back, and it is my house. I have never liked dead memories, of anything. I do not even like Churches. To remember the past is only endurable to me if it is continuing pleasurably in the present."

"Did you throw my things away again?"

"I don't know, Edward, I really don't know. I will ask my housekeeper tomorrow, or the steward."

"Never mind, Holland," Edward said, as he had said years ago to his Uncle James when he was seven, and with the same little cough in his throat, "they were silly things, I do not need them now. I have long outgrown them, and the room is much prettier as it is now. I was just surprised, that's all. I had not somehow expected it would be changed, but I should have, if I had thought. It does not matter at all."

His gesture was not lost on his father the Earl, who looked at him appreciatively and half extended his hand towards him, and then let it fall, and bowed slightly instead, and after seeing his needs were attended to, told him goodnight. It was his bed, though, after all, Edward discovered, pleased. It did not look the same, but nevertheless he knew it was. One did not mistake the feel of what one had slept on for ten years. He lay there, too tired to think or imagine any more, in a drowsy euphoria that overtook him, that changed imperceptibly to sleep, but the words of St. Paul running loosely of their own accord through his mind: "When I was a child, I thought as a child, I spoke as a child, I knew as a child. But now that I have become a man, I have put away childish things." Well, he thought, in a brief flash of consciousness, they had been put away now for him, though he had not done it himself. He wondered still a little, as he had before, if it was necessary, but it had happened, outwardly at least, and the outward was the least part, if the inward was also true. He was not sure that it was. But nothing could disturb his happiness, that found its expression in the simple wondering words of joy that opened a Wesley hymn: "And are we yet alive, And see each other's face?"

◊)◊)◊)◊)◊)◊)◊)◊)◊)◊)◊)◊)◊)

CHAPTER IV

November, December, January:
An Interlude:
1808–1809

I

THE Earl was as good as his word. He took Edward with him immediately the next morning in his curricle to London, and on the way he gave Edward the reins.

"I will not generally let anyone but myself drive this set of horses, for they have exceedingly delicate mouths and a harsh hand could easily ruin them. You are inexperienced, but I see you will have light hands. With horses like these you should learn quickly."

He was patience itself on the drive, which they took slowly. He instructed Edward carefully in the names and parts of all that surrounded him, wood, leather, paint, metal, flesh, bone, hair, and made him repeat what he had been taught, and then and then only proceeded. He discovered at once, to his surprise, what Edward's tutor had already learned with surprise, that Edward's memory was broad, quick, expansive, and wholly tenacious, both of what he learned now and what he had already learned with Ross. He was amazed and commented on it.

"Part I have always had," Edward said, with his quick smile, flashing a glance sideways at his father and then returning it quickly to the road, "and part I owe to you."

"My memory is good, but not so good as this, or ever was."

"You gave me opportunity to develop mine," he said, not turning his head. "I used it, that's all."

"Are you reproaching me, Edward, or thanking me? I am not certain which. Your leader needs attention there. A good memory is worth much. On the other hand, I will not tolerate your reproaching me, even obliquely. It is a fault of mine you must bear with. I can adequately reproach myself, when susceptible."

"Neither, Holland. It is a fact. I had nothing else to do except to use my memory for considerable stretches. That should not disturb you now, for you knew it then."

"I am afraid I did not think of it at all, or of you, Edward. Another fault. The picture does disturb me now. Can we forget it?"

Edward shook his head, and smiled. "I have this memory now. But it is past, and the sadness is past with it." He gave a joyous laugh, as when he had been a child. "Oh, Holland, I am so glad to be with you here on this road, holding your horses with your reins, and you beside me all the way to London. I hope we never arrive."

"Control it, or you will have us in the ditch and we will *not* arrive. To drive horses well, even one, certainly four, requires attention and control. You may appear not to be attending but you must actually be. Stop here, and I will take the driver's seat for a change and show you what I mean by demonstration. Observe me."

It was a happy command to Edward, and easy to follow, to watch the flexible wrists and long pliable fingers flex and ply the long whip with such gentle ease it seemed impossible he had just tangled it himself so badly, and almost lost it in a low tree.

"I think you could brush a fly off the leader's ear, and not hurt him," he said admiringly.

"I think I could too," the Earl said, "if there were one there." After a time he gave the reins and the driving seat again back to Edward, and was pleased with his progress.

"We will go driving every day," he said, "while we are in London. You will soon do very well. When you take your degree, I will give these matched greys to you for your own, or a new set, if you prefer."

"Oh, Holland," said Edward, his eyes shining. "Do you mean to spoil me?"

The Earl shook his head, not answering, smiling himself at Edward's pleasure. Because of the driving lessons, they had to break their journey.

At the close of dinner in the Inn, the Earl looked at Edward thoughtfully and said, "Will you share a room with me, Edward?"

"If you like," the boy said, his eyes suddenly shuttered and his voice shuttered, too.

"I do not mean what I see you think I mean. I shall never mean that again, Edward, it is no longer possible, even should you or should I wish it, as I trust we neither do not. When we are in London, because of my reputation, to protect you, I must be particularly careful of you, until your relationship to me is clearly known, and even then. You are young, and I am old, or older, and we each have, or you will have, our ways and means of satisfying our needs. But it would give me simple pleasure to be near you, and I thought it might you, with the excuse of this Inn."

"It would, Holland," Edward said.

When they had washed off the dust of the road and dressed for bed, the Earl, sitting back against the pillows, opened his arms and Edward came into them, and lay back against him, his father's arms loosely about him. They talked briefly of this and that, of the morrow's plans.

I will not always be this happy, he thought to himself. It is not possible. We are too different, too distinct, too much has passed, and must yet happen, but aloud he said his true thought, "I have never been so happy."

"Nor I, Edward," said the Earl. "I have always wanted a son, I see now, and since I have known you, that son to be you. I have never had a child, that I knew of. I wish we might always be so peaceful as this, as we are now, but you being you and I being I, I foresee we will not always be," he added echoing Edward's thought. "It is very tiring, teaching a complete novice to drive. I am going to sleep." He unclasped his arms, and turned over and away on his side of the bed. Edward lay quietly, looking into the dark, thinking, listening to his father's even breathing, turning his eyes ever so often to look at the hump of his sleeping figure, to reassure himself he was still there, and really with him, after so many years when he had not been, refusing to be.

To wake in the grey light of early morning, with the joyous shrill yells of the birds out of his window, and find himself in a strange bed in a strange place, that he only vaguely recollected any memory of, and his father still sleeping beside him—that was a joy too sweet for him to have ever let himself imagine. He drew his knees up and clasped his arms around them, and looked down at his father's face, memorising its harsh, endeared features as they lay relaxed. The Earl opened his eyes, not moving, and saw Edward in his old position. He reached out a hand and drew Edward down to him, past his rough stubble.

"Flesh of my flesh," he said tenderly. "I am sorry, Edward, but you do not seem in the least my son." But he did not kiss him with his old passion but simply laid his cheek beside Edward's.

"Nevertheless, I am, and I know it and I feel like it, even if you don't."

"Well, I shall grow used to it, in time, I hope. Why are you laughing?"

"Your chin prickles."

"You always did say the wrong thing, Edward, Edward. You are young, and being fair, you may never know the annoyances of stubble." He saw the sudden pain in Edward's face. "What is the matter?"

"I don't want to say the wrong things to you. How can I learn not to?"

"Pay me no mind. It was a bad joke, and not really true. I shall shave it off, and we will have breakfast, and make for London, with another lesson on the whip. You shall order breakfast, and I will see how you do, and then you shall pay the account." He looked at Edward critically when he was dressed.

"Your coat is a disgrace. It is too small, and not in fashion, and it is not properly pressed. Where are your other clothes?"

"It is all I brought, Holland. I rode in it."

"All you brought?" exclaimed the Earl in horror.

"I never bring clothes to your house on vacation," Edward said. "It would just spoil them, for no use. I did not expect this to be any different. But my other coats are outgrown too."

"Didn't I leave accounts open for you?"

"You did, this coat I had made last Fall, a year ago. It isn't still Weston's, I did really outgrow those."

"I wish it were. The cut is abominable, it alarms me almost to be seen walking with such a cut—coat," he amended hastily at Edward's face, "but it must be supported, at least until we can reach Weston's." His voice became more serious. "I have neglected you, Edward."

"It does not matter, Holland; truly it does not."

"I have. Don't argue with me—" His smile removed the severity of his words. "But I shall make up for it now. I have let you run to seed, and you are much too young for that, you are hardly in flower even. I shall have your hair cut, and new boots made, and several coats, one immediately, made for you at Weston's. You shall choose the way you want them, and the colour, and Weston and I will see if you will do. And you must have a valet."

"Oh, Holland!"

"Absolutely without question, Edward. I shall look around."

"But not at Oxford."

"At Oxford particularly, or you will let yourself run to seed again reading for your Orals. I know young men, and you."

"If I must, I must," said Edward with a small sigh.

"You may find it hard, to be my son, Edward. I am a proud man, as you may know. You will find me even more demanding than I have been."

Edward flashed his most special smile at his father. "Demand, then, sir, and I will do it. But may I have George then?"

"George? He is no valet. But he has good taste." He smiled at Edward. "He has had a good example set him by admiring my valet. Yes, I think you might, if that is what you wish. But in your relations with him you will want to remember you are almost a grown man now, not a child. I hope you understand me."

Edward approached London the second time, some three years later, with far different emotions and anticipations than had possessed him on his first visit when he first went up to Oxford.

My father's city, my city, now, he thought. City, I shall be here for weeks, several at least. I shall learn to know you, and you perhaps may learn to know me.

"I do not particularly love London myself," the Earl said, as if reading Edward's thought. "Myself, I prefer Vienna first. Once I might have said Paris, but not now. But it is a place I know very well. Sometimes it is a heaven, sometimes a hell, as all our own places are—that may be why we like to visit cities not our own. I shall introduce you to the better parts of it."

I shall see at last where my father really lives, he thought, his heart beating fast, his eyes shining with eagerness. The words of a hymn rose to his mind but he did not say them aloud:

> *There would I find a settled rest,*
> *While others go and come;*
> *No more a stranger or a guest,*
> *But like a child at home.*

He was not disappointed. A large town house, its size only suggested by its narrow red brick front, it faced a quiet square, and a small park, flanked and embraced by other similar houses. No sound disturbed the peace of the grey day. Rain was imminent, the trees stood bare and black against the smoky grey sky, a leaf or two still hanging, most down, already raked away and burned, a small wind gusting the few piles left in the gutters of the brick street. He jumped down from the curricle, and stood poised, his eyes shining, his lips parted, waiting for his father to bring him in. The Earl looked at him briefly but he made no comment on the subject of rapture, modified or transported.

And there he saw George again. The Earl with uncommon tact went at once into his study to examine his mail and left them to it, without the ice of his presence to impede.

"Master Edward!" George exclaimed, with surprise and with joy. "It is you. I am glad to see you."

"Yes, George, it's me." He took George's hand in his and held it.

"And you have growed up, Master Edward," George exclaimed.

"Yes, I have, George," he said, smiling. "I couldn't help it. I hope you approve."

"It's not for me to approve or disapprove. But I am astonished. You're that good-looking, I would not have known you—not, I mean, that you was not as a little boy—but it's not been four years since I saw you—" His voice died away.

"I remember it too, George, but I don't think of it now. It was a bad time then, but 'sorrows past, their grief is with them gone,' " he said softly. "My guardian and I—we are friends again, of a sort, you see."

"I am glad, Master Edward. It is good to see you again. And edicated too. And growed into such a gentleman!"

"George," he said, "my guardian says I am to have a valet. In fact, he says I must have one. I think he thinks I've grown too countryfied, despite the lovely coats he bought me—which anyway I have outgrown. Will you do it for me?"

"I'm not a valet, Master Edward, I am just a footman."

"If my coats look like yours, George, I know the Earl will be satisfied. And he says you may, if you will. Will you, George? Foxham can show you things, if you really need it."

"You don't need to ask me, Master Edward. There is nothing I would not do for you, that I can, or that I would like better."

"Good. It is settled then. But the Earl says I am not to be familiar with you. He has expressly warned me. At least not in public. You are my oldest friend, George, and I think almost my dearest. I have missed you so very much. I must go see the Earl now, and find out what he wants me to do now." He pressed George's hand, and said quickly, "I thought I would die without you, when you went away, you know. But I didn't. One doesn't. It's a good thing to learn. But I am going to behave myself this time, so he will not think he needs to send you away again. Did you mind?"

"I minded like all Hell, Master Edward, but there was nothing I could do, but say some wicked words to myself. I have not been able to have any news at all of you, and I have been that worried. But I think I worried now for no good reason."

"No, George, that is not true. I needed your concern."

"I will tell you something, Master Edward, my Lord don't know, and you must not tell him." He looked quickly around him, disregarding Edward's suddenly disapproving face. "I have gone Chapel, I did it soon after that, and I have said prayers for you, ever since."

"Have you, George? Did you?" asked Edward, genuinely moved. "I am grateful to you for it."

"I could not think of any other thing to do."

"That was a great deal. But I hope you did it also for yourself."

"Well, Master Edward, it was like this, I heard the Methodees in Moorfields and got the Falling Sickness as the Earl laughs at. It was just like as they say, it come upon me. Do you be minding the gardener that was at Tyne when you was a little boy, that one as the Earl made send away? Him that was always shouting and thanking God and the sweet Jesus he was saved?"

"Yes, George, I do. Don't be too justified or too happy in your faith about the Earl, or he might send you away too." Edward spoke lightly, but his eyes were a little sad. "He doesn't want anyone around him that is like that, he won't have it at all." He pressed George's hand. "Now let us not ever speak of this again, George; it would be disloyal and unbecoming in me, in my guardian's new kindness, to keep what is past before our eyes. I don't, you know. I shall see you again." He disengaged his hands, and walked with his light step into his father's study.

The month of November raced itself away faster than Novembers commonly do. The first weeks in London were uncommonly busy: Edward was fitted, dressed, accoutred, and sent back to school. He did indeed find the Earl as demanding as he had promised. He was as groomed and mannered as an expensive horse before the Earl judged him fit to make his first public appearance with him. He had the coats, properly cut and buttoned and tailed, and beautifully fitted silk pantaloons that he could not help himself admiring, and court-style breeches. His silk shirts were discreetly tailored and ruffled, and immaculately kept for him, regardless of what use he put them to. His neckcloths the Earl did himself, with his own particular twist of folding them, effortless-seeming until Edward tried it himself, and spoiled all his fresh ones. He learned to dance from a dancing master imported into the house. The art of fencing he was allowed to postpone until the summer, for his father anticipated no immediate need for it. He spent some time each day driving on the streets with his father, and riding in Hyde Park's Rotten Row. He was casually introduced to the Earl's acquaintances, by his first name only, as they met on the streets or in the evenings at the opera or the theatre, which the Earl seldom attended, considering it generally insipid. Edward attracted considerable notice, because of his companion and the striking contrast in their colouring, but also on his own by his manner of bearing himself, and his quiet gravity and friendly though reserved charm that set off his face. Despite his schooling and his public life, he managed all the same, by rising earlier than the Earl, to spend several hours each day in reading.

"I shall tell you my plan of action," the Earl said, "how I think, now at least, best to accomplish our ends most smoothly. We shall accustom the polite world, this *ton*, to seeing your face, and with me, naturally; but we will not explain the mystery. With a different person than yourself, Edward, my campaign would not succeed, but your looks will make our little mystery interesting. There is no place at all so prone to gossip as this society in London which eventually you will move in and have a part in. We will give them no particular occasion for gossip, and no explanation. I myself shall continue in much my usual life, and that will leave you some time for your reading, as you have requested. I do not want at all to take you to dinners or assemblies or the routs, even if it were not the off-season, or put you up for entry in the clubs. All that can wait for Fall. You are not ready for it yet and you have not really the time, or the energy of health. I shall be asked, of course, why I do not, which is all to the good, for it will make your presence more desirable. I shall tell them you are finishing your last year at Oxford, despite this brief rustication, which strictly speaking by the word should not be in the heart of London," he added with a smile. "I shall of course be asked who you are, and I shall smile gently to some and say nothing, and to others, with an inflection and a slight dubious air, I will tell in brief your Armstrong history, to some I shall mention who your mother was, to a very few I shall say you are my ward and to a few of that few, my ward whom I intend to adopt, and to one or two only in time I will drop the word you are my son."

"It may be you will find many already think this last."

"Why do you say so?"

"Lord Alleyn, the Admiral, thinks it," Edward said, flushing, his eyes lowered.

"That signifies very little or nothing at all." He took Edward's face in his hand and forced his eyes to meet his. "You cannot change me, Edward, how I have lived, what I have done, how I am thought of. You can yet elect publicly to be a relative of Lord Armstrong."

"I do not wish to," Edward said. The Earl sighed, and released him.

"You are wondering why I am so roundabout, and if I am still playing games with you, and with our world, just because it amuses me to be torturous. And why I do not just outright say who and what you are, next Fall, in the new season, or even now."

"A little," Edward said quietly. He lifted his eyes questioningly, but with trust in them.

"It is foreign to your nature, but not to London's, Edward. London loves games. A mystery will make you interesting on your own. I want you to make your reputation on your own, which given any chance at all, I know you can do. I do not want you disadvantaged immediately by your connection with me. And you will find that although I can have you entered anywhere on the strength of my name, and invited anywhere, even to Carlton House where next year I will take you, that personally any connection with me will work to your extreme disadvantage. I am afraid I can promise you that, as I promised and warned your mother it would, and you must never forget it, though others may seem to, for they will not. Think on it, Edward. Do you understand me, Edward?"

Edward smiled slightly. "Your words are unusually obscure, but I think I do. You will stand behind me, but I am eventually to advance on my own, if I can, for unnamed reasons you suggest tactical. More clearly, you think your name will harm me."

"And do you believe me?"

"I don't know," he said frankly. "Society is out of my experience entirely. Are there not other natural sons about?"

"Many, but the husbands and the wives are all present and all married, and the children have been raised openly in the eyes of the world. The *ton* may joke about the Harleian Miscellaney, but they do not absolutely know for a certainty, and those games are carried on in more or less acceptable lines. But you see, Edward, I have never been married at all, except most briefly, as you know but no one here knows, and that at the wrong time. The acceptable course would be for you to continue as you are, as Armstrong's son and later adopted as my heir. Anything else lays you open to public scandal, which is the only thing that is not tolerated here. I find my frankness fails me."

"I love you, Holland. If you accept me still . . ."

"I do, Edward, I have told you that, the once stands now and always."

"If you do, since you do, I cannot bear to be less than I am, whatever it brings me. I should not mind not going into society at all, you know. It is not the pleasure to me you may think. The pleasure for me is your company."

"So be it," the Earl said, a second time. "But I wish I could believe you knew what you were doing. Where is Lord Alleyn's son?" he asked.

"I do not know," Edward answered, between tight lips, aware his father was baiting him to test him. "I cannot find out. He is in the Royal Navy."

"That boy? That is not the place for him."

"I know that. He knows it himself. He was sent down, and his father made him go. He is very radical in his politics, you know."

"No, I did not know that at all. I am the more glad you no longer have the association."

"Can you find out where he is, and how he is?"

"I do not know. I could try. Your friend said I underestimated you, and I see I did. I am not on good terms with Admiral Alleyn . . ."

"I know that," Edward said.

The Earl looked at him sharply, but he continued as though uninterrupted: ". . . but I will try what I can. I hold out no hopes of success, for as even you surely know, we are at war again."

"Even?" Edward said, flushing.

"We are both ready to give provocation, Edward. Let us not fight. Let us go in to dinner instead. I have invited a friend of mine to join us, whom you will like to know. Let George finish your dressing and come down."

The Earl turned away and seated himself at his dressing table. After a moment, instead of going to the door, Edward went over to him on light quick feet, and knelt beside him and bent his head over the Earl's hand that he took. The Earl's forearm, usually covered by his coat or his shirt, whose shape and strength Edward had loved for many years, was bare to the elbow. He did not speak, nor did the Earl, who disarranged his locks with roughly loving fingers that grew more gentle as they touched.

"Do not give me too much, Edward," he said softly, and warningly.

"I am too difficult a man for it." He lifted Edward's head. "Keep a distance from me."

"It is there already," Edward said, his voice suddenly and surprisingly matching the Earl's in tone. "It is there. Can you not see it? I wish only to bridge it where we can." He rose and took his father's hand and held it briefly in his own. "I will leave you to dress," he said formally, and turned away and left the room.

That evening, after their guest had left, the Earl asked, "Have you any objection of conscience, Edward, to going to church with me tomorrow?"

"To church with *you?*" asked Edward with comical astonishment. He had somehow not associated the Earl with religion at all.

"But of course. Why not? Did you think I did not go?"

"I never thought about it at all, but you do not seem to me a religious man in any way."

"I thank you for that kind opinion, Edward. The Church, however, has fewer scruples about my qualifications to attend than you. I go to see and to be seen, that is all, and all required of me since I am not ungenerous. Will you go with me?"

"Of course I will, Holland."

"You surely do not still hanker after your Methodees?"

"I am an external Anglican after three years at Oxford. How could I help being?"

"But at heart?"

"Why must you ask, Holland?"

"I would like to know. It might help our dealings. Will you tell me?"

"You cannot order out the secrets of the heart."

"I know that, Edward. I am asking you."

"I would spare you pain, Holland, and annoyance, that is all. At heart I am what I was raised to be. My heart is still 'strangely warmed,' more now than before. You do not believe yourself in private prayer, Holland," Edward stated rather than asked.

"No, I do not."

"And yet it is you who have taught me to learn again how privately to pray."

"Well," the Earl said. He enquired no further. "I had not meant to make a Methody Saint. Whatever I intended, it was not that. Nevertheless, you will attend with me?"

"It is my pleasure, Holland. You have refined too much upon what

I said. Please don't. I have not the aspirations you feared. You wished to tame me, that I believe was your intention, to your whole will, and you have done that. 'In your will is my Peace,'" he added with conscious blasphemy, whose source the Earl missed, but not its meaning.

"Do not mock me, Edward, I will not bear that willingly."

"I am not mocking you, Holland. I wish it were not so true." He stood in silence waiting for his father to dismiss him, or to speak, but the Earl had nothing to say. They stood thinking their thoughts, and after a bit Edward came to the chair where the Earl sat, and put his hands from behind on the Earl's shoulders.

"Pax?" he asked questioningly, in the old formula.

The Earl did not turn, but he reached up one hand and laid it over Edward's right that rested on his shoulder. "Pax," he said.

"I should not have answered," Edward said penitently. "I knew I would cause you pain. I so do not wish to, Holland."

"I should not have asked," the Earl said heavily. "I am a tyrant, Edward. I wish only to hear what I wish to hear. But your chief charm for me, or one of them, and also your chief irritation, is that you speak as you think. Do not let me change you. I should not ask if I am ready to hear only my own answer. So I have taught you to pray?"

"Yes, Holland. I had to learn."

"Someday I may ask you to teach *me*. Goodnight, Edward. I will see you in the morning."

II

The Earl and Edward came closest to falling out in the first week of Advent, when the Earl was gone almost all of one day. Edward was particularly restless, imagining the Michaelmas term drawing to a close without him in the next fortnight. He had not been forbidden to go out alone without his father, but it happened he had not done so. Now he decided to go to the public Reading Room at the Library. He had asked Holland and been rebuffed about the girl he had found in the Earl's study, but he could not forget her: her angry, sweet, indignant face, the feel of her in his arms, something he had never felt before, and her story whose mystery the Earl refused to unravel.

He did not expect the Earl to be pleased with his expedition, but it was important enough to him that he did it anyway. He had only to uncover the list of deaths of the past year, which he found surprisingly difficult to do, but by trying various approaches, in the end he did. By chance he came upon a pamphlet urging an end to duelling that listed the needless deaths, according to the author, of the past several years, and the parties involved, where they were known. He noted down all the possibilities, but when he came to one name, he knew with sudden certainty he had found the answer, both to the identity of the girl and the reason for his father's reticence. It had been, not his uncle, but the man he once might have believed to be his uncle, the now late William Armstrong, an elder brother to the man he had once thought was his father. He was survived by a son and a daughter, Anne. Edward sat for a long time thinking, and then he put his thoughts aside as immaterial at the moment, beyond his reach, and now perhaps impossibly complicated, it seemed. He had found, to his satisfaction, the answer to his question, but he saw no way to pursue it further.

When he returned, however, he found the Earl had returned before him, and met him in an unpromising mood.

"Where have you been, Edward?"

"Must I tell you?"

"Yes."

"I have been to the Reading Room of the Library."

"Is that the only place?"

"Yes, Holland," Edward said controlling himself with difficulty. "Do you want to know what books I used?"

"No," the Earl said, "that will be sufficient." He indicated silently they should go into his study.

"Edward," he said, after he had closed the door, "I do not want you to go about London at all at this particular time unless I am with you."

Edward gasped, but he controlled his voice and said nothing.

"I do not wish you to go anywhere, even to the Reading Room, alone. I particularly want you to have nothing to do with the Chapels or to be seen there."

"I had not yet intended to," Edward said.

"I am glad to hear it."

Edward could not wholly contain himself. "Must you ask this? Nothing does well on too short a tether, Holland."

"That may be, but nevertheless you will do as I say in this."

"Or you will send me back to the pit?" Edward said with a half-choked laugh.

"I did not say that, Edward. You did."

"Nevertheless you thought it."

"Perhaps. But haven't we gone beyond that?"

Edward found to his dismay that angry tears had sprung in his eyes, and he wiped them openly and angrily away, helpless as always before the Earl's superior armour of urbanity.

"If you are angry for so little, then I will give you cause to be angry. I will tell you where I went and what I went for."

"Ah," said the Earl. "Now we have it. But it has taken some doing to get it."

"I went to the Reading Room, as I told you, to find out who it was you killed in a duel—"

"*Which*, I think you mean," the Earl interposed, his smile surprisingly amused.

"—who was the father of the young girl. You would not tell me, and I wanted to know."

"Ah," said the Earl again, looking at him hard, but still half-smiling. "And did you find it out?"

"Yes, I think so," said Edward, "and why you would not tell me."

"Then you know more than I. I have no idea at all who the young person was, we had not gotten that far to particulars in our conversation. Tell me, and I will know too."

Edward stared at his father, who was calmly examining his nails, as if nothing else mattered to him, in amazement. "You amaze me, sir," was all he truthfully could find to say.

"Keep your secrets, Edward, if that is all they are. It is a matter of indifference to me, except I am sorry I put you to this trouble. But you see, I do not keep a list in my head, and so even had you reapplied to me, I could have been of little help."

"I do not believe you."

"Take care, Edward."

"I do not believe you capable of such callousness or of such a scale of illegal slaughter, either one."

"Well, then, perhaps I have my suspicions, which I preferred not to tell you, but it is true that I do not know. Pray do not enlighten me now. Let me rest in the words of the immortal Mr. Pope, please, Edward."

"Why, you are not angry at all."

"No, Edward. Flattered a little, sorry a little. Angry, no. My friends with sons have regaled my ears too frequently with their extreme trials with their sons for me to regard this piece of scholarship as one."

"But your prohibition still stands."

"Yes, Edward, if you will humour me so far."

"And if I do not?"

"Why do you ask? Practically or theoretically?"

Edward was forced to smile himself a little at his father's—for the moment—impenetrable good humour.

"Theoretically."

"Please, then, let us leave so serious a matter of express disobedience still untouched in the realms of theory. You may take it that it would not pass unnoticed."

"What is it, Holland, you thought I might have done, or think I might yet do?"

His father opened his snuff box, not offering it to Edward, and said carefully, after a few moments, "London is like a jungle, Edward, which you are incapable of negotiating safely yet. You have had too small an experience, as you say, your tether has been too short. I have not had time to prepare you for it, and you have, as you say, your studies on which now you wish to apply yourself. You seem to have passed unscathed, even untouched through what Oxford has to offer in its extracurriculars, with negligible exceptions." Watching Edward's shuttered face, he decided against pressing that matter. "Let us have no gaming debts, no duels, no applications to the quicksilver god's cure this Christmas or this term."

"Is that what you are afraid of? That when I have no money, I would risk yours in debt, even if anyone were so foolish as to let me? Or to take a whore? Or push a quarrel, knowing no one?"

"You would be surprised how easy any one. Particularly the last, if you are as fond of me as you say. A chance remark, and there you would be."

"Again, I do not believe you, Holland. What are you afraid of about me? Tell me: I will live by your wish, but perhaps I can reassure you."

The Earl hesitated. "I have been looking into this matter of Alleyn, as I promised." He held up his hand, to stop Edward from speaking. "I cannot find out where he is, or even where he is not. But I have also looked into what you call his radical politics, and I find you guilty of understatement. I am more glad than I can say that your association with such a firebrand was so brief, and so publicly unnoticed. I would like it kept so if possible." His voice was very quiet, and particularly expressionless. "I do not know whether you know how harsh the present laws are about this kind of thing, but I have lived through the hysteria of three revolutions and the laws that hysteria bred, and I am quite afraid of these laws myself. I know how determined the present government is to suppress any signs of one here at home. Any gathering, or loose inflaming talk, reaching the wrong ears and construed as showing hatred of the King or criticism of his policies, and you could find yourself defending yourself against a charge of high treason. A definite plot or action is no longer required to be proved. It is death now for even *inciting* the people to hate the King, the constitution, or the government, if the court chooses to convict. And Addington, that is Lord Sidmouth now, is Home Secretary. Our friend Alleyn may be adept in skirting these shoals safely but I doubt you are. I would not have you suspect yourself."

"How would my going out affect it, or anything?" Edward exclaimed helplessly and unhappily.

"You could be approached, for one thing," the Earl said, "and you are too innocent of our world to withstand importunity, I am afraid. Your Wesley was a man who went among the poor, and in the gaols, even in Oxford, but he lived before the particular laws I speak of were passed. This city, beautiful here, is built on scabs and festering sores, as I know now you must know, if you have known Alleyn even for a week."

" 'He beheld the city and wept over it,' " Edward said softly.

The Earl looked at him sharply but chose to make no overt comment. "There has always been misery for those who wished to see it but it is particularly evident now with too much produced for the economy and the Blockade halting a part of our trade. Your creed that you own you cherish in your heart demands a cognisance of these sores, and action on them. Did you know that?"

Edward shook his head.

"This time it is I who say, 'I do not believe you,' those inflammatory words, you see, Edward."

"Wesley did not approve the revolting of the American Colonies, Holland, he considered it done without just cause."

"Did he not, now? That does interest me, Edward. I did not know that. An eminently more sensible man then, than I took him for. Why did he not?"

"I cannot tell you all the reasons now. He picked no quarrel with the state or the monarchy, only the laziness of the individual soul, and he abhorred any action of any reforming mob. He had experienced it, he knew that action too well to have any illusions about it. I am too tired, and I am changing your subject. You can read them, he put his arguments in a pamphlet. He considered they had adequate civil and religious liberties, and that they owed taxes. I heard my father—my first father—talking about it with my mother once, and I saw the little book. He did not approve of the Methodists who wished to separate from the Church, either, Wesley, I mean, as I think you know." He flushed as he remembered when he had heard the Earl speak on the subject to him.

"Then I like the man more and more," the Earl said, seeming to ignore Edward's flush, "but nevertheless that happened, and times have changed. It is 1808 now and Wesley is dead, and the social enthusiasts of his sect hold the reins. I want you away from such men. I am in a brief calm of my life, Edward, and I do not want it troubled by firebrands or reformers, or you associated with me associated with such. Social justice does not interest me. I do not want your young and too impressionable sympathies worked upon."

"How strange," Edward said. "Alleyn reproached me for my disinterest, and you fear an interest I do not possess. Between the two of you, you may in the end create a conscience in me where now there is none."

"He is mad," the Earl said, "it is a dead cause. His mother is mad, too. All the Irish are. My sympathies are with the worthy Admiral."

Edward stared at him. "I do not understand you," he said in a low voice, amazed.

"Alleyn talks entirely too freely," the Earl said angrily, understanding what was in his mind. "It is his charm and will be his bane. And now you are shocked. Why? Because sometimes I say what I think? The Passion of Love does not go by perception of reason or sanity or because of it, Edward, never think it does. Rather the reverse. The Irish may be mad, but they are eminently lovable. But it is not of Alleyn I wish to speak, but of you. You have not answered me straightly."

"I have been too preoccupied with myself to care," Edward said unhappily. "I do not care now. I was christened Methodist, but I have been raised by you away from that heritage, and I have signed no covenant with them. I have been given by you a taste of a life that precludes it now for me." He laughed helplessly, and his voice grew desperately unhappy. "I am not fish nor fowl now, Holland, I lack both scales and feathers. I cannot swim with you and I cannot fly with them, both demesnes are closed to me. The furry beast and the naked helpless man, that is all I am, unable myself now to minister, needing rather to be ministered unto and unwilling to be. Please, let us not talk any more, Holland. The smoke depresses me, and makes my head ache. I find the fogs dismal. If you want me to stay in, I will."

"To be naked, that is to be a man, that is his particular condition. Even the beast is not. It is God's special dispensation and special curse," the Earl said slowly, his eyes on Edward, in a way Edward remembered and could not mistake.

Edward ran his fingers through his hair, awkward, embarrassed, half-turning his face away from those eyes.

"Will you, Edward?" he said, his eyes not leaving Edward's shamed face.

"I don't want to, Holland," Edward whispered. "I am nearly grown now, it is not the same. And you are my father."

"You knew, though I did not, that you were my son, when you offered to come with me, and not long ago. Please, will you now?"

"Oh, God," Edward said, "must I, Holland? I don't feel that way now any more."

"Don't you?"

"Not as you mean." He flushed. "I was angry then, I did not care. You did not, then. Why have you changed your mind?" He forced his eyes to meet the intense gaze of the Earl's that seemed to bore into him and impale him.

"You know why, Edward," the Earl said. "We have been too much together. You surely feel it too." He paused. "Will you, Edward?" His voice was tentative, but tenderly compelling in its very hesitancy.

Edward nodded his head slightly, unable to hurt. "All right," he whispered, "I will, then. What shall I do?"

"Go up into my room, and do not let yourself be seen. I will join you there."

He found Edward standing in the middle of the floor, his lips blanched and stiff, his eyes haunted, watching him as he closed and locked the door.

"Will you lock me in here, too, Holland?" His eyes had widened, and his voice was strained and apprehensive, but he did not move.

The Earl shook his head slowly, sorry at his distress, but undismayed. "No. I lock the world out. Leave whenever you like." He took the key in his outstretched hand and offered it to the tense upset boy, whose fingers dropped it, as if nerveless, or as if burned, to the ground; but he took no pity on him in his intense desire. He took the boy in his arms there and kissed him until he felt his limbs relax and slacken, and then he instructed him to undress, which Edward, as if helpless, and with the Earl's help did. He lay down on the Earl's bed, his eyes closed, ashamed, the tears welling beneath his eyelids and falling slowly.

"I thought I had gone beyond this at last. Oh, Holland, how could you to me, now. Why leave me at all, if to revive this?"

"I thought I could help myself, Edward, but I cannot. You must leave me entirely, or for a while live with me this way."

"I cannot leave you," Edward said, "you know that, and anyway you will not let me yet."

"No," the Earl agreed, "but I am quickly satisfied, it will not last long, and then I shall behave myself." He had undressed, and put his dressing gown about him, and lay down now beside Edward.

"But I am not," Edward whispered. He stiffened as the Earl's fingers touched him intimately as he had not when Edward was a child, shrinking within the iron unyielding circle of the Earl's arms.

"I don't want this, Holland," he protested desperately. "Why do you want me like this when I don't want you?"

"I don't know. Perhaps because you do not. It is my nature, Edward, that I should not mind hurting those I love. Your reluctance increases my desire more than your own desire would—or has. But you will soon find out you do not mind."

"That is what I'm afraid of. I want to mind. I am afraid of not minding most of all. Oh, God, I have wished for this, and now I have it," he said feverishly. "One should be more careful what one wishes for, or one may get it. Oh, God, Holland," he cried frantically, "do not hurt me, I was a child last. I never knew you really." He shut his eyes and tried to relax in the Earl's handling, but he found himself crying like a girl, with fear and apprehension, as he felt the Earl smear something cold on him. The Earl stopped, and took him more gently in his arms, and kissed him again.

"You did not do this with Alleyn?"

"No, I told you," Edward said, frightened and tense. The Earl stroked his hair, and kissed him gently, and then demandingly, until he felt the boy lay again limp and responsive.

"Do you love me, Edward?" he whispered between his lips touching Edward's.

"Yes, Holland, you know I do," Edward whispered back.

"And still now?" His fingers again touched the boy and again probed intimately and exploringly against his shrinking flesh, but although insistent, very gently this time.

"Yes, Holland."

"And still?"

"Yes," the boy gasped, "oh, yes." He shut his eyes again, trying to forget what was happening to him. The world seemed to fade about him into one fixed point, than which there was nothing else, but the Earl's voice brought him back.

"Then do now to me as I direct you. In love there is no shame."

When he had given the Earl his peace, he lay back, exhausted and in his eyes damned, and yet bound now to the Earl as he had never been, ineluctably, his guard penetrated, his brief defences assaulted, yet somewhere within him some last stronghold, a last reserve holding out and not consenting. Anne, he thought, Anne, do not let me damn myself. Let me somehow find you before I wholly do.

As if he read Edward's mind, the Earl said, "I will tell you now why I duelled with Lord Armstrong, as he led me to believe he was, using his older brother's name. He claimed I used you in this way, and he wished to recover you. He did not, of course, imagine you were not his brother's son."

"But it was true. Did you kill him for something that was true?"

"It was not at that particular time true. And a duel is not an instrument of Heaven, Edward, whatever popular belief has it, it is an instrument of man. My public honour was at stake."

He felt Edward shiver, and give a shuddering sigh, but not withdraw from him.

"Now you know. You might have been there now, had I been more generous, to let another have what I did not want, and more courageous."

"When was this?" Edward asked, his voice shaken and faint.

"Last Spring. I do remember, as you said, you see, although I did not know his girl, as I said. He came to find you at the College, but you were at Tyne for Easter. And so he found me instead. Are you sorry?"

"I am sorry for him. It was a brave gesture, but useless and too late. By then I knew. I would not have gone with him."

"Do you hate me now?"

For answer Edward kissed the Earl passionately, in his long ago, almost forgotten way. "The gesture came some thirteen years too late, nineteen even, not just one, Holland. Did nothing come of it? For you, I mean?"

"The duel was near Tyne, not in London, Edward. I did not even leave the country."

"How can I love you, Holland, I as I am, you as you are. I don't know." He turned to the Earl convulsively, his breath caught, and embraced him with all his strength for a quick moment, and then fell back again beside him as before.

They lay together, breathing quietly, motionless except when moved sometimes by an excess of tenderness.

"Can you bear me, Edward? It will not be for long. This Summer I will see it does not ever happen again."

"Oh, Holland, is it you begging me?"

"Yes, Edward. You are the stronger here. I want you, and I need you, but you must consent."

Edward in answer said under his breath, softly but distinctly, " '. . . All I am, and all I can do . . . this I do deliberately, sincerely, freely, and for ever' . . . 'without calculation of cost.' "

"What is that, Edward?" the Earl asked, recognising they were not Edward's own words.

"Blasphemy," Edward said, "but for me my truth. I have no religion but you, Holland, when you are near. It has always been so. You are the god of my idolatry, and my flesh is your altar."

"That sounds suspiciously like enthusiasm, Edward, and suspect to me. I am another generation, please spare my unused ears. No raptures! But I feel them, myself. Only please, Edward, talk less," he said turning to him again. "Where is this sacrificial blaspheming table I must have?"

He placed his fingers in the small of Edward's back, lifting him to him, and Edward, his shame lessened, put his hands and his fingers behind him loosely on the Earl's forearms that he particularly loved, pressing them against him. He could himself have been content merely with the presence and the simple embrace of that too much loved person but he submitted with less fright and less fastidious disgust again to the acts that most pleased the Earl and let the Earl educate his mature body as he pleased. With the telling of the Earl's story the girl Anne, as his cousin or not as his cousin, either way seemed hopelessly removed from his publicly as well as privately soiled and corrupt self and connection. He put her at that moment from his mind and gave himself entirely to the man who held him.

"How shall I meet you, or meet George, or anyone, after this?" Edward whispered, when the Earl released him. "Will they know?"

"Why, as always, Edward. As you did before."

"I was younger. I did not have to see anyone I knew."

"Except me."

"Except you. And it was not like this. Oh, Holland, I am so ashamed."

He buried his face beside the Earl's shoulder. The Earl turned to him, and took him in his arms, and drew a cover over them.

"They will not know," he said gently, "unless you show them in your face. All men have their secrets. Have you no secrets of your own?"

"Hardly any. You know them practically all."

"I think not. What of your illness at the College? You have not told me anything of that."

"There is nothing to tell."

"I think there is. You were 'hazed.'"

"Who told you that? Alleyn? I was not hazed. I was tortured, by Alleyn's friends."

"How? Like this?"

"No. I told you that before—I do not want to talk about it, Holland. I cannot."

"Was it so bad as that?"

"Yes. Do not ask me any more."

The Earl tightened his arm about Edward and held him closely and protectively to him, as though to shut all the world and all harm, except his own, from him, as at that moment he did wish he could. (So held, to Edward then the world and his soul seemed well lost, and then almost he did not regret.) "So you do have secrets. Then keep ours."

"When I was little you told me you wanted me because you saw my mother in me. I did not understand then as I do now what you meant. Is it that way with you now?"

"No, Edward. The years pass, finally."

"Why then? Why me, now? Is it for myself?"

"No. Another would do as well. If I love you, it is despite what I do."

"Oh, God, Holland."

"You should not talk so much, Edward. I have told you that before. You are here, and you still attract me. You always have. I am not sure how. Is it not pleasant for you simply to be here with me?"

"Yes, Holland," he said, sighing.

"Then cannot you enjoy it simply for what the moment is?"

"As Alleyn could?"

"You will not let me forget that, will you?" the Earl said. "You are much more interesting to me than Alleyn, Edward. Is it jealousy that speaks?"

"No. I was, I have been, but not for some time. I had to learn not to be. I hope I have learned. It does not matter any more. I want too much," the boy said sadly. "I cannot have it here."

"It is that, I think, that both attracts me to you and repels me, Edward. So long as you resist me, I seem determined to destroy you, Edward, even what I most love in you. It is my demon."

"And when I do not . . ."

"And when you do not, you will no longer interest me in this way. This strength you have attracts me now, and I think I am determined to make you no stronger than myself."

"Why do you tell me this?"

"As your father, to put you on your guard against myself, and show you a way out."

"I wish you would simply be my father," the boy said bitterly. "I love you so much, Holland, but I do not love this."

"Then why did you woo me?" the Earl said angrily. "I have never approached entirely uninvited."

"I did not know I did," the boy said startled. "Did I?"

"Yes, Edward, you did, and you surely knew you did, and you knew what I was. Don't be moral with me now."

There was a silence, and then Edward said in a low voice, "Yes, I did. I see it now. And I suppose I knew. But I did not know what it would mean, though once I thought I did. And as you say, the years pass, finally. I do not want to be your lover any more."

Even as he spoke, his words were cut off by the Earl's mouth. He struggled briefly, but as always, in the end he yielded to its insistent pressure, and this time he responded.

"Do they pass?" the Earl said, withdrawing, his eyes gleaming with the victory they recognised.

"No," Edward said, his voice half a sob. "No, they do not." His lips fastened of their own accord on the Earl's, passionately, and he pressed himself against him, as if to penetrate the barriers and flesh and enter him entirely.

"And you do not want to be my lover any more?" the Earl said softly.

"Yes, Holland, yes, I do," he said, his resistance swept away in the dark sweet flood of passion engulfing him and destroying him. "I want what you want, whatever it may be." He submitted to the complete violation that quickly overtook him as he had not before, passion answering passion, gasping, his eyes shut, in the ecstasy of pain and pleasure. From some seeming distance, and yet near his ear, he heard the Earl say, "Then be very patient with me now." His back arched into the Earl, away from his probing hands, and he tasted salt blood on his lips where he had bitten them, not to cry out, as the Earl entered him with his full self.

"Oh, Holland," he cried then, his breath shuddering, and all his body trembling convulsively even as it welcomed. "Oh, Holland," he cried again, "Holland," in agony and love, unable and unwilling to break from the Earl.

"You are doing very well, Edward, to be so new at this game of games. Only a moment more. Can you bear it?"

"Yes," Edward said, gasping, his heart beating so, he thought it would break, or choke him.

"Do you love me still?" the Earl whispered, near him.

"Yes," the boy whispered.

"And still now?"

"Yes, Holland."

"And now?"

"Oh," he cried suddenly, "oh, Holland," his cry matching the Earl's, "Holland, Holland." They lay still, and after a time, brought just their lips together, turning, to touch, their hands resting on each other's face.

"After all my precautions and my good intentions," the Earl said softly and ruefully.

"Will they know?" Edward whispered.

"Perhaps," the Earl whispered back. "Not through me." His hands moved to encircle the boy loosely, and his fingers slipped lingeringly and caressingly on his flesh.

"I am around people who know me and know you. It is harder, but I will try. Holland, I want to get dressed now." He kissed his father quickly, to lessen his words.

"I am going out tonight to dine, with friends, without you, Edward. It was arranged before. Will you mind?"

"No, Holland. I am glad not to go."

"It will be late when I return. I may come to you?"

"If you like, Holland," the boy said, averting his face, dressing. He lay passive in sleep when the Earl came in at three and lay beside him.

"It is snowing," the Earl said softly, "like wool, Edward. The sky is full of it." He took the sleeping boy in his arms and roused him with difficulty. In the end, he merely kissed him and let him sleep.

It snowed all the next day, making more beautiful what was already beautiful, and softening what was misshapen or ugly, hiding the dirt of the city in its fresh fall. Edward sat at breakfast, his eyes lowered but open, for the Earl did not like to be watched or stared at, intensely aware of the man across from him whose face was not in the range of his limited eyelash-veiled vision, but in the little circle he could see his shirt front and his coat across from him, and his hands, those hands Edward loved that had held him not as a person, but as an object, and done unspeakable, unrememberable things to him without loving him or caring for him, now precisely cutting their food with knife and fork, the long fingers poised against the blade and the tines, holding them too. He had known those hands for years, and thought he knew them, and now he knew he had not. Their actions against his flesh as a child were seen now for what they had been, only child's play, tempered to his age. He would willingly have continued a child. He shivered, with awareness, and fear, and longing, not for what he knew he would have from them, for something else, in an intensity of love, knowing now what they could do, and what they would probably shortly do again, helpless to refuse or resist them and their insistent, to him bewildering and ugly demands. They moved there now before him in an impersonal natural grace, so long schooled as now to be unstudied, directing kidney-and-egg as though there were no other thing in the world but kidney-and-egg, then turning the pages of the *Gazette,* seemingly oblivious to Edward. He finished, smiled at the boy, and rose and excused himself into his study. But after lunch, the Earl touched Edward on the shoulder, inviting him with his eyes, and Edward followed him without protest. He undressed, as before, shielded by the white walls of white snow outside the window panes, keeping his eyes there during this strange new necessity that had overcome him. He no longer argued or protested, and to the Earl's relief, he did not speak at all. His shame, though still intense, was less, and he could bear it.

That evening, the Earl took Edward to dine in St. James' Square, cautioning him to be modest, to talk little, and to not put himself forward. The evening after, he himself gave a small dinner for twelve, with music afterwards. In the delight of these gatherings and their conversations, in which Edward, as cautioned mixed little but listened much, so gaining a reputation of good company, he found the damp reeky cold air more endurable. He had been used to mist and fog at Oxford but not to filth and grime. Part of the Earl's large staff were continually employed in dusting, shining, and scouring the film away, and outside, the surface of the snow was blackened. Inside, however, the candles and the oil lamps gleamed, wood and silver and crystal shone, and the elegance of conversation was matched by that of deportment and dress, although ladies were conspicuous by their absence. But unaccustomed to such a life of perpetual company and talk, after a while Edward grew tired, but he kept his feelings to himself, and kept company with his books quietly when he could, when his father needed him neither publicly nor privately.

He sat the next day, quietly, near the Earl in his study, waiting his father's pleasure, whatever it might be. There was fog as usual outside the window, whose thick suffocating brightness showed the sun was up, that was all. Edward sat remembering winter mornings at Tyne when the late rising sun struck the flat bare tops of the low mountains slantway, putting the high meadows in full sunlight, the folds and one side left in shadow; or days there of morning mist when the night's humours rose off the mountains in vapourous clouds and lay like thick curdled cream among the trees at the base between the valleys. The Earl was going through his correspondence, and after a little, he raised his head.

"Sometimes one must choose between clean snow and clean wit, Edward, but at this season, we do not. Much of London is leaving it for the holidays. I, and you also, are invited to several houses in the country"— he tossed the pile of invitations to Edward for him to look over—"or we may simply excuse ourselves and stay here or we may go quietly home to Tyne. What shall we do, which life would you prefer?"

"Whichever you would like."

"No, I am *asking* you. Which would you prefer? I would really like to know."

"I would like to go to Northumberland, and have Christmas there with you there."

"Good," said the Earl, "so would I. These perpetual black fogs do not agree with me, and I winter in London as seldom as possible. We will leave tomorrow. I think I shall have an indisposition and omit Brookes' tonight, and the theatre, and stay home with you, Edward. We will have a light supper downstairs and then go up." He smiled at Edward. "I do not yet wish to take you to Brookes', and the theatre is a bore this season. Covent Garden burned this past September, before you were sent down, and the new Drury Lane is too large even for Mrs. Siddons' voice. But I will take you there all the same, Edward, another time. It was built by a Holland, an architect, but we do not claim each other. The Prince of Wales will lay the cornerstone after Christmas for the new Covent Garden theatre. Perhaps we should stay for that, or return? Would it amuse you?"

"No, Holland, unless it would you. I would just rather go to Tyne."

"It is settled then," the Earl said, and took Edward's hand.

III

That evening, and the journey up by coach, with elaborate precautions against the cold, in easy stages because of the state of the roads and of their affections, several nights on the road, in good inns, ended Edward's shame. The white peaks of the far-off high mountains, crested with pure snow, flushed rosy pink each evening just before the dark fell, and again as the first invisible light struck them just before the morning sun rose, but Edward's cheeks did not. Edward, noting the pure colour with an appreciative eye, was unaware when his shame had passed but he no longer felt it. In its place came a silent if perverse grace. He guarded his own emotions against further hurt, but he put himself at his father's disposal with a lightness, a naturalness, and an ease, that delighted the Earl, and an absence of question or demand. When the Earl wished him, he responded. When he did not, he was content. In the end it was this compliance that woke the Earl again to his responsibilities. They had arrived the week before Christmas, with George and Foxham and an expanded staff following in a second coach.

The Earl was not one with the custom then of lavish entertainment at Christmas, and knowing Edward's need for quiet to read, he omitted entirely a house party that year. Nevertheless, there was an air of suppressed excitement about him that made him seem younger, for he intended to give Edward a particular gift that had involved some arranging, and he believed it would please him, as it did. The Vicar and George and Ross were all necessarily in on the secret, for the Vicar kept it at his house. When Edward saw the small pianoforte, larger and with a purer tone than the spinet that had been taken from him, he stood transfixed, looking wonderingly and unbelievingly at his father.

"Go on," the Earl said. "It is for you. Have you forgotten all you knew?"

Edward shook his head, the tears blinding his vision.

"Play the Carols for us then, and bring the Christmas in."

Edward walked to his father, and took his hand, and bent forward and kissed his cheek.

"Pax?" said the Earl, touched at the success of his gesture. "Complete peace?"

"It is the season," Edward said. He gave his lovely smile to the Vicar, and asked him to name what he should first play. ("Play 'God Rest You

Merry, Gentlemen,'" the Vicar said.) But they were interrupted almost at once by a noise outside and the arrival of the Mummers.

"Oh, Holland," cried Edward. "I have all my wishes tonight. I have so wanted you to see them, and with me. Will you come?"

But in the midst of his happiness, as he stood beside his father, he found himself remembering the final song in an old morality play he had helped put on at Oxford the Winter before, *Nice Wanton* it had been called, unusual for them to have used an English play, even an old one that Devonshire and Hazlitt were interested in. He had been because of his face to play the daughter Dalila, who like the son Ismael had gone off with yellow-cloaked Iniquity ("My daughter Dalila is dead of the pox, my son Ismael hanged up in chains.") He remembered the gambling scene with dice with Iniquity, in which the son had thrown and lost, and the final scene, darkened, the red-gold hair of the brown-smocked good son Barnabas gleaming like an aureole as he knelt alone and invoked a prayer on all, King and Commonwealth alike, and the final chorus of all the actors, that had touched off his memory:

> *"It is good to be merry,*
> *But who can be merry?*
> *He that hath a pure conscience,*
> *He may well be merry."*

He turned and looked up at his father's profile by him, and his father, sensing his regard, turned briefly to him and smiled and briefly touched his hand with his fingertips. He did not feel merry, but he could not remember ever being so happy, and he shrugged the little verse away in his mind.

They all walked then in the crisp clean snow to church with the Vicar. As they walked back, the Northern lights shooting overhead like angels, no sound about them except the Christmas bells and then only the crunching of their feet in the crust of the snow, the breaths blowing frostily, they all sang, Edward and the Earl ahead, George and Ross and the other servants following, loudly and lustily:

> "'Now to the Lord sing praises,*
> *All you within this place,*
> *And with true love and brotherhood*
> *Each other now embrace*
> *This holy tide of Christmas*
> *All others doth deface:*
> *O tidings of comfort and joy . . .'"

The Earl in his happiness found no impediment to his limp, his eyes on the boy with him. They sat in the kitchen and boiled their feet in hot baths, all together, and had hot cups of ale with steaming crab apples bobbing in them, and drank wassail to one another and had a late supper. Edward grew sleepier and sleepier, in the warmth, as if he were still a child, until finally he fell asleep, his head against the Earl's shoulder. The Earl signalled Ross to carry him upstairs, past the still burning Yule log, and for George to put him to bed. Later, he came himself into the boy's bed and took him in his arms.

"Holland?" he murmured sleepily. "Is it you? Do you want me?"

"No," the Earl whispered, "It is the Holy Night. Go back to sleep. I have come to bear you company, that is all, in this our first Christmas together." Edward put his arms about him contentedly, and went back at once to sleep, but the Earl lay awake for a long time, holding him, thinking, before he went back to his own room.

Christmas Day dawned clear and cold, like Christmas Eve. They fasted, on the strength of their late supper, and went to church again, and took Communion. It seemed to Edward that everyone he knew, and many he did not know were all present at the great lunch the Earl held in open house: the Vicar and his family, the neighbouring Squire and his, the local gentry, and several families from further away, were all there. To his surprise Edward discovered he was after all a sociable creature. He enjoyed himself immensely. His eyes shone, and his laugh and smile in the happiness of being in his own place displaced the grave courtesy more usual to him and were in evidence everywhere. The Earl's care already bore fruit in a new poise. His popularity was immediate, and he revelled in its novelty. The Earl watched him with the traditional pride of the mother duck watching the duckling prove it could swim, and made plans.

"You will take the Season, this Fall, Edward," he said to him, in a lull before the great dinner whose preparations had the lower regions in a stir. "You will hold it in your hand with no effort." He smiled. "I am the caricature of the proud parent, Edward, *me*." He looked so mellowed and so content he hardly seemed himself.

"Holland," Edward said, seating himself on a stool near the Earl's chair, and looking up at him, "I have no present for *you*."

"I did not expect one."

"But I wanted to give you one, but I have nothing, and I haven't any money. I could not buy you anything. I could not even make you anything."

"You shall make something for me, tomorrow, Edward," the Earl said, "something I want very much."

"What is that, Holland?" Edward asked, a slight fear creeping into his eyes, but he did not lower them.

"Music, Edward," the Earl said, resting his hand on Edward's head. "I love it above all things. Did you know?"

"No," Edward said, shaking his head and looking at him in wonder.

"I will tell you sometime about my father. My real father, as I think, who was a musician, and gave me that inheritance that is my only real joy in spirit, not my father who raised me and gave me the inheritance where we sit now."

"Is there anything that I can give you today that I have to give?" Edward asked. He did not pursue the subject the Earl had raised and withdrawn.

"Do you wish to?" the Earl asked, looking at him, his eyes questioning and very tender.

"No," Edward said quietly, "but the best gifts are always those we do not wish to give away, that we cannot easily spare, that we would rather keep. I have only myself, but I thought I would give you that, if you wished it."

"I thought I had that already."

"No," Edward said. "You took it—I have not given it."

"But you would rather not?"

"I would rather keep it," Edward said, flashing a quick smile, "that makes it more precious as the gift."

The Earl took his face in his hands, and bent his own head, and drew Edward's lips to his, breathing in their breath as though it was life itself to him. He held him so, for a long time, it seemed, the boy not moving, and then he released him.

"I have taken your gift now, Edward," he said, "perhaps not the one you quite meant, but still yourself. It is indeed precious, and now I am going to give it back to you, as a Christmas gift of mine I had not yet told you of. The parting with it is a grievous loss to me, I would, like you, more willingly keep this gift." He bent once more and kissed Edward more gently, and with less length.

"Go in peace, my son," he said softly. "Take back yourself and go in peace. Here is an end now of this passage between us. Will you mind?"

"No, Holland. I shall be glad." He looked at his father straightly. "Are you tired of me?"

"I am indeed not, Edward."

"Why, then? Have I complained?"

The Earl shook his head. "I have some sense again, at last. I will not ruin you. You have not the taste yet, I hope?"

"No, Holland."

"I am glad. I was too foolish. London makes men mad, sometimes. One sees more clearly here, on these plains."

"You are sad, Holland."

"A little. I shall recover quickly. I have yet the main part. Let us be more cheerful now, Edward. The Squire is giving a small assembly, tonight. There will be no waltzing here, but there will be country dances."

"I don't know them."

"Of course you do—it is just the name here for the *contre danse*."

"But you do not like to go to dances."

"No, but tonight I shall, for I shall see the results of that most expensive Master. You may practise here for Windsor and Carlton House, where you will dance next Fall."

The next morning, or rather, the next noon, Edward sat at late breakfast with the Earl, which they combined with lunch.

"If you must yawn, learn to swallow it, Edward, or at least cover it. What I may find charming in a child, society will not."

"Yes, Holland," Edward said obediently, making a mighty effort to obey. His eyes danced. "As bigge crabbes goon, so go the crabbes smalle."

The Earl acknowledged the hit, with a fencer's hand, and tossed a sheaf of invitations to Edward.

"You are a *succès fou* already," he said. "Don't let it turn your head. It takes only one error to lose it. No," he said, removing the coffee pot. "No rot-gut for you. You must learn to take your dissipations straight. Use this for sociability but not necessity."

"Holland," Edward said, goaded, "I like you better immoral, I think. I feel you're going to race me, and I don't like the feeling."

"I am. That is precisely what I am about to do." He got up, his limp pronounced after the late night. "But not immediately. You are not sufficiently trained, and you have other work on."

"Holland," Edward said quickly, "don't go. What am I to do with these? I am doing no reading here, and how can I, if we accept these invitations?"

"Refuse them, then; these people do not matter."

"You shock me, Holland, just a little."

"Who is to care?"

"Holland, what *am* I to do? You are included, too, in half."

"Do just as you like."

"You are so cross this morning, Holland. Help me. I need your advice. I do not want to be rude."

The Earl limped over, and took the pile, and expertly sorted it. "Throw these away, I do not know these people. These, refuse; your guardian—yes, had you forgotten that?—because of your recent and unfortunate rustication requires you to absent yourself from the social scene to apply yourself penitently at home. These, if you like any of them, accept, they go only to the Little Christmas, which you can afford. You have until the twenty-fourth, do you not? Count two days at least for the trip down, or 'up,' that still leaves you three weeks undisturbed, here, or if you need more books, we can return early. If you don't like them, refuse, under a prior engagement. You are engaged at all times to me, but I excuse you if you wish to attend."

"Holland, what is it? What have I done?"

"Done?"

"You are almost nasty to me this morning. You bite your words at me and throw them down, as if I were a dog. What have I said or done to displease you?"

"Nothing. Nothing at all. The day after Christmas always finds me cross." He suddenly exploded. "And you sit there looking like a fair angel, and I know what you are capable of, and I cannot have you. God!"

"I thought it was that."

"You did,—did you?"

"Holland, if you want me, take me."

"No, damn it, I will not. No—don't touch me, Edward." He laughed shakily. "It is ridiculous, is it not? I, at such an impasse, and you are willing. It must be fought out, Edward, now as well as any time. I love you and I am in love with you. I thought you contemptible when you felt so yourself. I am well repaid."

Edward rose, and went to him. "Do you think I respect you for this? I do not. I cannot bear to see you unhappy, Holland, I am not worth it. What you want means so little to me now. Take it. How can you hurt my reputation or my character, if they are not already hurt, more than they are? See. It is I now asking you. Will you, Holland? I cannot bear your unhappiness. You will tire of me, when you have me, and then it will not be so hard."

"Finish your invitations," the Earl said harshly.

"I shall refuse them all."

"No. Keep this, it is a winter picnic, near the old Wall and the Roman fort with Lord and Lady Eddington, who are down from Scotland; and keep this Assembly; and this dinner. For the rest, do as you like. I should also keep the Masquerade set for Epiphany Eve, that is unusual here, and done just for you, I imagine. The Vicar's wife has set a *mischianza,* a small one, with her children in the afternoon tomorrow. That may bore you, but it would be a kindness all the same to go. Do you mean it, Edward?"

"I do mean it."

"Where then shall I meet you?"

"I should like for you to take me in my pit."

"You are joking." The Earl spoke with shock.

"I am not joking. I wished for you so often there, it would give me great pleasure to have you there. And being there, you will know better what I am."

"If we were in a novel, Edward, you would kill me there, or lock me up and leave me there to die."

"You have not let me read novels, so I do not know. But we are not, Holland, and I would not. Do not ever be afraid of me. I would never hurt you willingly. Take me there. I do not know the way."

"I shall come here just this once," the Earl said, moving towards the door, strangely moved at the prospect.

"The once is enough." He followed the Earl through the study door, and down the passage, and into the small room that at that time of morning was shadowed but not entirely dark. He waited, while the Earl pulled the door to, having first locked the outer door leading into the kitchen passageway. The place cast a terrible pall on the Earl's spirits.

"Is this to make me have a distaste for myself and for you?" he asked.

"No, only to make me believe I shall never have to come here again, or stay here, and then perhaps my bad dreams of it will stop. Here," he said, standing near the door, "you kissed me, and left me here. I wish you would kiss me here again."

"Don't," the Earl said. "I am ashamed."

"I lay here," the boy said, sitting down on the bed, "day after day, wanting you, unable to hate you, hating only myself, until finally someone, you, or Ross, gave me some light. Try it, Holland, see how hard it is, feel it, and for a while I had not even this, and for two days, not even a blanket. I did not die, and I did not go mad, but you must realise,

Holland, that I am tough as wire inside. I am not the womanly thing you think me, because I love you, and because I obey you. I am not past hurting. I think we never are. But I am past easy hurting."

"Don't, Edward," the Earl said again. "I thought you were mad, but I see now it was I myself who was." He sat down beside Edward and put his head in his hands.

"I was sick here, like a drunk in your slums or a Freshman in College, when you seduced my friend. I lay in it all night, the filth and the stink. Did Ross tell you?" The Earl shook his head. "He was kinder to me than you, and he did not love me, he did not even like me. He said to me, 'It is sometimes easier to be kind to those we do not love at all.' I have remembered that."

"You are not kind now, Edward."

"No, I am not. Do I surprise you?"

"Yes."

"I want you to know why I cannot forget."

"Or forgive?"

"I forgave you long ago, but it does not change what happened. Shall I lie down now? Will you take me?"

The Earl laughed in rough bitterness. "Do not be preposterous, Edward. Of course I cannot. Come out, now. I have had enough of this charade. We shall both go mad."

He opened the door, and went out.

"Come out, Edward, now, I am ordering you. It is finished. Be angry, forgive, forget, as you choose, but come out now and let us go up in the light." With no noise of footsteps, Edward appeared beside him.

"What is this room, Holland? Why do you have such a place in your house?"

"It is a priest-hole, Edward. A place where mass was celebrated, when to be a Catholic was forbidden and to be a priest was to be an outlaw. It was built for no sound to be heard outside it, and secret, for priests to hide in as well as to celebrate mass."

"In its way then, it is a holy place," Edward said. "And in the end I found it so." He saluted it, with his hand, and left it with the Earl.

"Whose room shall we go to? Yours or mine?"

"Neither," the Earl snapped. "I am out of the humour. Finish your invitations—use mine for models," he said, throwing them down, "and come into the music room with me."

When Edward joined him, he found the Earl had unlocked a cabinet, and taken out a very beautifully fashioned violin, and a sheaf of music.

"You cannot know how to play well," he said, "you have been denied opportunity, and by me, of all persons. The wonder is that you play as well as you do." He smiled. "You now know my secret vice that the *ton*, for all its scandals, does not dream of. I am not a polite performer, Edward, it is a passion with me, and I shall demand perfection of you as my student. I gave up gaming long ago, to have more time for this, and though half the stories told about me are quite true, half are mere fabrications to account for what I possibly did with my time."

"Why must you be secret?"

The Earl shrugged. "Here, and in London, I wish to. It suits me, I would not disappoint my contemporaries. In other cities, it is no secret. I have studied with Paganini himself, and with Beethoven, my father's name was known, and gave me access, and when I was gone abroad, before this cursed war, I played in chamber groups in homes and in salons. I did not use a name I would be known by. I cannot bear ridicule, Edward. I will not risk it. Anything is preferable to me but that. Let me show you now, with this concerto, what we do."

He played first the part for piano, for several pages, and then the part for violin. Had he wished for any reward, he would have found it in the look of worship Edward directed upon him.

"I thought it time we found another bond between us and something else to do. The greatest cure for misplaced passion, Edward, is simply something else to do. Remember that. Now, take only the top line first, and we will play together. Later, I will work the bass and treble out with you."

Haltingly, but gradually with more confidence, Edward began. He had known he had a talent here, why and how he did not know, and he had pursued it when he could, but he had not ever expected such happiness to come to him in it from the Earl. They worked for several hours, forgetting lunch, absorbed, each with the same capacity for sustained hard work and for detail. They lunched, Edward read, they dined alone, not in to any callers, and afterwards they played again, and then Edward read until he fell asleep.

He was awakened by the Earl's appearance in the small hours of the night. The Earl did not speak, nor did Edward, but as he bent hesitating, questioningly over the boy, seated beside him on the bed, Edward, only half awake, put his arms about him as he had when a child and drew him to him. His lips were as guileless and sweet-breathed and innocently eager as a child's. The Earl sighed, and with gentle hands removed his nightdress from him, and himself slipped beneath the covers and took him wholly in his arms. The boy stirred drowsily and turned towards him and fell asleep again, his mouth still touching the Earl's. The Earl did not disturb him further at that time.

The next morning, awakening early, Edward was surprised to find the Earl beside him.

"Holland!" he cried, "I did not know you were here."

"Didn't you?" the Earl said drowsily. "I had thought you did."

"I thought I was dreaming," Edward said. "What shall I do about George?"

"Don't ring," the Earl said sleepily. "Hush now."

"But I am awake," Edward said. He sat up and discovered he had no clothes.

"Holland," he said, "you have taken advantage of me."

"Um," said the Earl. Edward felt beneath the clothes of the bed.

"And you have kept yours. I shall catch cold and you will not."

"I wish you would find a book and occupy yourself," the Earl said sleepily.

"Why only me? Let me take yours then if you take mine."

"No," the Earl said, shocked. "Read your Bible. Authority is on my side: 'Thou shalt not look upon thy father's nakedness.' Besides, I am not beautiful."

"To me you are."

"I am raising you to impudence—I think I shall regret it. I am much older, and more liable to cold. Hush now." He reached out a hand, and pulled Edward down into his arms, holding his face against his chest until Edward lost his breath and began to struggle. "Warm now?" he enquired, releasing his head but holding him tightly in his very strong arms. Edward did not move, very quiet against him, lost in his emotions and surrendered to them. He stayed so, until the Earl's arms loosened in sleep, and then he rose and dressed himself thoughtfully, and went down to breakfast. When he returned to his room, the Earl had gone.

IV

It was the day of the winter picnic, and Edward, having never been on one, was excited, too excited to be disturbed by George's sad disapproving eyes, as he dressed him. His high spirits ran through the house and filled it. The younger members of the party were to use the Earl's troika, a great novelty, which he had brought back from Russia some four years before with him. They were so wrapped in furs and woollen coverings and mufflings, that they found each other's looks new sources of merriment. The older members of the party would come in coaches, well-padded and warmed with hot bricks, but they had all brought skates, for they were going to the Mere that had frozen stiff, not far from the ruins of the fort. The coachmen looked too cold, Edward thought, and the horses were not happy and looked as if they would rather be in their warm stables, but he did not spare much thought for them, for he was driving and *he* did not mind.

The Eddingtons had a visitor, the eldest daughter informed him, settling herself into the robes of the sledge, "but she has a cold, an influenza, or so she says, and she is not coming with us." As if he felt eyes upon him, Edward looked up, and saw a pair of dark eyes fixed upon him piercingly from an upstairs window, almost hidden by the curtaining. He returned their gaze with interest, feeling a strange thrill to be so observed, or was it himself, after all, or another person, that the eyes sought out. On impulse, he moved nearer, and the eyes vanished. His manners returned to him, and he attended to the other parties in his sleigh, but his thoughts were drawn from them, and as he lifted the whip, he turned once more quickly and saw again the bright dark eyes upon him, and saw them vanish as he turned. He wondered how he could find out the name of the Eddingtons' shy or otherwise indisposed visitor, but he wasted his time wondering, for he was quickly told by his voluble companions. She had arrived yesterday, having spent Christmas in Edinburgh with relatives, and now she was going to spend the Little Christmas with her grandmother. Lord Eddington was taking her, having business in London. Her name was Anne Armstrong.

The eldest Eddington looked at Edward with a new remembrance. "Isn't that your name, too? I keep thinking yours is Holland."

"Yes," Edward said, with his quick smile. "Yes, it is."

"Why, you might be relations, and not know it. You probably are. How too bad she should suddenly be sick."

"We might be," Edward agreed, his inward smile wider than his outward. He thought it likely the girl Anne's sudden indisposition sprang directly from the discovery that he or his father, he wondered which, perhaps both, were to be members of the expedition. He was sorry if his presence was to make her miss the outing. Did she not want to meet him again so much? He was oddly gratified to be so noticed, remembering clearly how she had felt in his arms, though it did not promise well for a meeting.

"Will she be here long?" he asked.

"No, she leaves tomorrow morning with my father, if she can recover herself enough."

"I imagine she will," he said, amused. "A day of rest, in from the cold, should work wonderfully well for an indisposition. Give her my regrets to miss the introduction. Is she out yet? You are, I think."

"No, she is not, and so she could not come to the Assembly, even if she were staying. But she will come out this Fall."

"Ah," said Edward, interested, and then they spoke more generally. The snow was hard, the air dry and crisp, the sun shining and turning the hoarfrosted trees into ice palaces. Edward loved to skate, and he had not since the winter he was sixteen. He loved these friendly people, strangers to him, who accepted him so easily; he wondered if they accepted everyone so easily, and he imagined somehow they did not. He could feel rules that he did not know or understand hedging him about, but now in their hedging they included him inside. He gave himself up entirely to the delights of the day. When they returned, exercised and rosy, he found the Earl cold and impatient. The Eddingtons themselves had skated, but the Earl of course could not. Edward had forgotten, and he was filled with penitence and left his companions and came at once to the Earl.

The Earl smiled, a little grimly. "I shall like it better when the coachman gets his apparatus working properly to heat our soup. I think my presence has surprised my host. The horses like it no better than I, we are all tasting life's bitterness and our teeth are on edge. See how they blow." He pointed to a small grove where several cold grooms were walking the horses, dressed in coats, up and down.

"I shall find you something hot, I shall stir them up," Edward said, his heart singing despite his concern. When he returned, the Earl took the tea with thanks.

"I remember," he said, "in 1788, when I was thirty, some age like that, a good deal younger than I am now, the Thames itself froze over. I say I remember, I was not there after all, I believe, but I heard about it, so I have felt I was there. It was frozen for seven weeks, from the end of November into January. The city had a Frost Fair on it, orange sellers, puppet shows, booths, a regular Bartholmews Fair. You would have loved it." He looked a little startled, and he said, "No, of course I was not there. I was on the Continent, in Vienna where it was also very cold, in parts. That was the year you were born, Edward, 1789, the end of February, when it had begun to thaw." He seemed shaken by his memories, and he waved Edward back to the other circle.

They returned at sunset when the sky and the snow were both pink, their breaths hissing and steaming, and if eyes again watched them, it was too dark for Edward to see. He was drawn to this girl of his family that he had once thought his, as to no one except the Earl himself. He would have liked to have stormed the door and battered it and demanded entrance to see her and check his conclusions of her identity and further, he knew not what. But he of course did not. Breeding forbade it, and common sense, and a reluctance for a rebuff. In his preoccupation, he found he had driven the sledge himself around to the stables. For a moment, not wanting to see Ross, he thought to drive back to the house, but he was as likely to meet Ross there, and he could not always avoid him. He doubted that the Earl, oblivious in the main to others' thoughts or feelings except where he particularly chose, could imagine the complications of his feelings towards the big Scot. He would willingly have never seen him again, but he could not ask it. He dismounted and called a younger groom he saw, and walked slowly along the panelled boxes with their polished wooden screens, remembering many things, thinking since he did not see Ross to greet his horse. In the end he had run upon him, almost into him, before he was aware. He started back, frightened, for the big man's eyes, tawny like his hair, were blazing with anger, and at him, and he could not imagine why.

"Is it here you are," he said, his *r*'s growling like the great rough lion he looked, "in my clean stables, you man's whore." He took his hand and brought the flat of it against Edward's cheek, twice, once to each side. The force of it threw Edward back against the wooden door of the stall, and he heard his horse calling out behind him in alarm and slapping its hooves against the floor. Tears of pain and anger and shame flew to his eyes, but with it, he thought in bewilderment, He cannot know, he is guessing, why would he think it?

He pulled himself up, looking at Ross straightly, his face dead white except for the red marks across it. "I could have you whipped for this," he said, "or dismissed," wondering as he said it how Ross had dared.

"Perhaps," Ross said, looking back at him straightly. "Will you?"

"You are not my groom," Edward said, "you are Lord Tyne's. If I have given you cause to do this, and I don't want to know your reasons, address yourself to him and have me punished for it by him, but do not ever dare again to strike me, Ross. I will not suffer it again." He controlled his hands, and kept them away from his stinging face, and turned to go. He did not know what to say or do, and he did not know that he had shown a dignity in the face of indignity that had unwillingly impressed Ross.

"I wish the master had left you bide where you were," Ross said sincerely, "you were better there, I think. You, sprung from the sept of Armstrong, to disgrace now the seed of Kinmont and Kilnockie!"

"I forget what you mean. I am not under your orders now," Edward said, "and if these are your stables and not Lord Tyne's, I will not come here again."

He left quickly. When he was out of sight of the stables and not in sight of the house, he picked up a handful of snow and pressed it against his cheeks, wanting to cry, but it was too cold for crying. He found George in his room, laying out his clothes that he had pressed for dinner. He was both furious and dismayed to be so surrounded and so caught out.

"I did not call you," he said to George, his voice not steady.

"His lordship did, Master Edward. Foxham has gotten him a hot bath and a hot wine, and he thought you might like the same."

"That was kind of him and of you, but I would rather be by myself, George. I am very tired."

"You are hurt, Master Edward. How did you come by that?"

"It's nothing, George. How long have I until I have to dress for dinner?"

"An hour, Master Edward."

"Is anyone coming tonight?"

"I do not think so."

"Just let me be, then, for a little. Call me in half an hour." He gave his coat and gloves and furs to George, and without removing his boots, lay down on the bed. He felt George attempt to take them, and he sat up and let him pull them off.

"Go away, now, George, please," he said, his hand across his eyes.

"No, Master Edward, you will have a chill. You are to have your hot bath now, his lordship has instructed me to it."

"God, George, whose valet are you, mine or his? Why must I have a hot bath because someone else wants one? I don't want one at all." He sighed, as his valet obstinately persisted in his preparations. "All right, George, if you must, you must."

By the time he had finished, however, he no longer felt like crying, and his cheeks stung less and the marks were less broad. The hot wine he had sipped while he bathed recovered him further. He lay down in his dressing gown and pulled his eiderdown over him and shut his eyes, not caring any more whether George stayed or went. He did not think of himself in terms such as Ross had used to him, but he supposed he was and that they were true, and they had pierced him. He wondered if he could get used to them, and if he could not, what he was to do. He was very quiet at dinner, his high spirits of the day and of the night before completely evaporated. He was not a good companion, and when the Earl remarked upon it, he answered lamely. He sat pensively by the fire afterwards in the Earl's study, listening to the Earl but speaking very little himself. When the Earl touched him upon the shoulder, he could not meet his eyes, but after a hesitation that was not missed by the Earl, he followed him. He went to his room, where the curtains had been drawn, and undressed, keeping only his dressing gown, and waited for the Earl, who came after a short while. His Christmas renunciation had, under Edward's words, been of short life, but his passion was more restrained and more considerate.

"Who has hurt you?" he asked at once, for he had noticed the marks under the light covering of powder Edward had had George apply.

"I hurt myself," Edward said, turning his face away.

"How?" asked the Earl.

"It is no matter," Edward said.

"Tell me. I do wish to know," said the Earl sternly.

"Very well," Edward said, almost pettishly. "I was clumsy, and I caught in the harness of the sledge and I fell against the supports." He turned his face away, almost crying, hating to lie and unable to do anything else. The tremulous quivering of his lips distracted the Earl from his inquisition, and he took them with his own, feeling with deliberate enjoyment the sensation of their spontaneous motion within his. His hands found the boy's body beneath his gown, caressed it, his flanks, and then slipped the gown from his shoulders, not heeding his passivity. But when he felt Edward's reluctance, his kindness and discretion left him, and determined to provoke the boy's passion, as he knew now he could, he soon did. When he had finished with him, heedless of any mood of Edward's, he was astonished to discover the boy was sobbing, but Edward would not tell him why, for any threats or cajolences, attempting unsuccessfully to choke off his sobs.

"Have I hurt you?" the Earl demanded. Edward shook his head. "Do you want me to leave you?" Again Edward shook his head. "Then what the devil is suddenly wrong with you? Are you blue-devilled? You will shortly make me so. I cannot abide tears. It is those cold picnics, I have never liked them." He would have risen and left, but Edward, shaking his mood and his passivity and his grief, put his arms about him and drew him down close to him, and held him closely to him, kissing him with a complete wild abandon. Its significance and its surrender escaped the Earl, although its intensity both gratified and alarmed him.

The Earl continued to teach Edward music, and to play together with him, but after the festivities of Epiphany, he was gone more during the days, in frequent company with his agent, and sometimes the evenings.

"Money may be inherited," he said to Edward, "but it can be easily lost, and it is not maintained by ease or lack of effort, especially in these days of high prices but higher taxation. Oak is in great demand and requisition for the Royal Navy, that has lost so many ships, but its cutting requires a judicious eye, and I do not really like it done. The Border oak is now entirely gone. Nor do rents increase by themselves."

Edward said nothing, for as yet the estates were hardly more his concern than George's.

"Next year, I will perhaps discuss such matters with you in more detail, Edward. You have your studies now, you have not time in any case. But I want you to know when I must leave you so alone why I am gone." Edward smiled faintly at his concern. With the Christmas invitations finished, and the Earl's embargo on others in effect, he had asked and received permission to let George go visit his family who lived twenty-five miles away before travelling with him to Oxford as the Earl still insisted he do. He did not explain his reasons, or mention George's open hesitation at leaving him.

"You have nothing to worry about. I shall do very well. Now go have yourself a good time and kiss all your family for me, and attend to their needs, and tell them I remember them." He sent the children tips, having requested money from the Earl ahead. If it galled him that he continued to be kept so short, he did not complain of it.

"But I do worry about you, Master Edward. I cannot help worrying," George said, his eyes troubled as always these days. "I am that fond of you I cannot help it. I do not like leaving you alone here."

So George knows too, Edward thought. I might have known. Servants are like God, especially a valet. Well, he thought, we must all live with it. As if he could do anything.

Aloud, he said, "There is no reason for you to worry. I shall take no harm for being without you, and I shall like thinking of you enjoying yourself. I shall not read too hard."

After George left, at the Earl's request, he moved at night each night into the Earl's room and remained with him until he himself woke in the morning, and then unless the Earl restrained him, he slipped away. Chastely or unchastely, the Earl liked to have Edward near him, and in this wish as in others Edward complied. He loved the Earl too much to be able to deny him anything. He was saved from complete corruption in habit at this time only by his complete detachment, a separation of his mind and his spirit from his body and what was done to that and what it was made to feel. Sometimes he wondered a little desperately if after this divorce, he could ever bring his disparate self together again, but his mind he put almost entirely on his books, and on his music. To have the Earl was almost as difficult as not to have him, he had discovered, but of the two, he preferred the pain of having him.

At the end of this week, the two coaches again progressed to London. The Earl left his staff, went with Edward by Weston's, and to the Scot Charles Sanders where he had earlier without telling Edward arranged to have a miniature of Edward painted. Knowing what would lie ahead of him, as Edward did not, he wanted it painted before he completely grew up or lost his look of the child.

"It is a present for me," he said. "I would like it done. Will you sit for Sanders for me? He may soon stop doing miniatures altogether, and I would like one."

"Ask something harder," Edward said smiling with his eyes. "Of course I will. I wish you would have one made of yourself for me."

The Earl kept Edward almost continuously by him those last few days in London. He seemed, for himself uniquely, curiously aware of the passage of time. He seemed almost visually aware of the seconds and minutes falling away. He took Edward to the theatre, despite his dislike of the building, to see Mrs. Siddons, well aware of the glasses directed towards their box, acknowledging no stares and answering no requests for introduction; and to two concerts, one at a private house in Grosvenor Square. For the rest, they dined in, then sat quietly together and read, Edward on a stool, his head resting against the Earl's knee, the Earl's fingers laced in his hair, and seldom talked. The last afternoon, their errands done, the sittings finished, the Earl called Edward into his room, and valeted him, looking at him soberly on all points, and then himself undressing him. His seriousness made Edward laugh, and he was sharply called down for it.

"But you have seen me before, Holland, every inch of me and then some. I have not changed."

"Hush," the Earl said. "Be still, impudent boy, be still now, and this time, don't talk."

Edward was moved to protest. "I am not impudent, not really, not in either sense, and I almost never talk any more."

"Hush now," the Earl said, "and undress me."

"Oh, Holland," Edward said, blushing, "I thought I was not to," but he did as the Earl asked, quickly, kissing the Earl lightly as he removed each article. The Earl then took him in his embrace, taking his breath away entirely, with his own, and then led him to the bed, his face heavy and sad.

"It is for the last time. Is that it, Holland, and why you are so sad?"

"Perhaps. I don't know. I don't know if I can bear it to be yet. If not now, almost now. Hush, Edward."

Their passion, beginning quietly, gathered intensity for both in the afternoon, but Edward was sated before the Earl, and longed for release the Earl would not allow him. He seemed bent on conquering wholly and finally the elusiveness of the boy he held, and finding him entirely, but he could not reach him, for the more he tried, the more the person Edward unconsciously retreated from him.

Finally, exhausted and in some pain, as if understanding him, Edward twisted about and said almost angrily, "You won't find me that way, Holland, it is no use trying. I am not there. Stop now. You are in the wrong place to find me, I am here, outside, and here, and here, and in the outer evidences of my speech, the rest is chaos. I cannot live in chaos. You wrong us both to think it."

He softened his words a few minutes later by burying his head in the Earl's arms. They washed themselves in water the Earl had had Foxham leave, and dressed themselves and each other, and then Edward spread the tossed bed, and lay back on it, half reclining, and held his arms out to the Earl, who came and lay in them.

"We look now what we are," the Earl said, "too old, too young, a middle-aged roué and a stripling. How ludicrous our passions make us."

"No, Holland," Edward said tenderly, "not ever ludicrous."

"Well, I hope not," he said. He lay quietly in Edward's tender, clasping arms.

"So tomorrow I am going," Edward said, quietly. "You must find another person for this, then, if you must have it. Must you, Holland?"

"Yes. In some form. One way or another. After you, though, Edward, I think I shall return to my patient mistress. Will you mind?"

"No, Holland. I want you to have what you want and what you need. Me, someone else, that is all the same."

"God's love, Edward," the Earl said, "you exceed even me in casualness, I think."

"No," the boy said quietly. "No, Holland. I am not a casual person, excepting only my birth. I am not casual about you at all, but sometimes one has to laugh, but never at you, and sometimes one has to look at what is real about another person with a clear eye."

"And are you doing that now?"

"I am trying to."

"Will you not miss me?"

"God, Holland, can you ask that? But I am not losing you, at least I hope not. You are in my thoughts always, your face is on the front of every book I read and before me wherever I walk, your name is under and above each author's name, and carved in every stone. I lie down with you at night and wake with you in the morning. There is not a moment of the day you are not with me. It has been that way with me since I saw you first, and you took me in your arms and told me my mother was dead and held me. It has been that way for thirteen years now, why should it change, when I know that you do not just seem to be in my blood, that you actually are there, in my nature and in my blood as being my actual sire. I shall miss your lips and your hands and your most dear breath and presence—as for the rest, not really, Holland. That is not the way with me. I love you better now, as we lie quietly here and do little, than when you torment me, and make me feel things against my will I would rather not feel towards you."

"Is that true, Edward?"

"Yes, Holland."

"Then why have you not told me? Why have you let me?"

"I have told you," the boy said, almost laughing but with great tenderness, "and I have told you why I let you."

"Ah, yes," the Earl said, "the endless talk."

"I feel it too," Edward said, his lips against the Earl's hair, "this need, like a compulsion within, 'to love that well which we must leave ere long . . .'"

"Whose lines are those, Edward? Not yours?"

"Oh no—not mine. Read them, Holland, read Will's sonnets again, they will strike you now, as perhaps not before. The time is too short now, to waste. Lie still now, Holland, and let *me* love *you*."

He removed himself from underneath the Earl, where he had been half sitting, and sat beside him, his eyes luminous with his feeling, and took the Earl's head most gently between his fingers, and with his lips kissed tenderly as if in valediction each separate feature, each vein, each landmark, of that familiar countenance.

> *"Rumoresque senum seueriorum*
> *omnes unius aestimemus assis!"*

he said softly. "That just means, I do not care what people think, Holland."

"I know what it means," the Earl said, "and I do care."

"I care too, but not as I once did. Hush now," he said in the Earl's words, "'for Godssake hold your tongue and let me love!' Don't you remember what comes next? *'Da mi basia mille,'*" he said, his lips smiling a little: "*'Nox est perpetua una dormienda.'* I don't believe that, of course, do you, Holland? I do not think at all we just go to sleep, endlessly, but for the purpose of kissing, we might just as well. I have counted the world well lost for these lips, knowing I should not feel this way about them, but I would like to have the world as well, and these too." He bent his head, and touched the Earl's lips with his, once, and many times. "*'Da basia mille,'*" he murmured again, "*'deinde centum, dein mille altera,'*" reluctant to leave them or part from them, and took his farewell with his lips of the Earl's neck, and his hands. "'A thousand years unto each part,'" he murmured, "'and the last age shall show your heart.' O, Holland," he said, "do you have a heart, do you, is there anything beneath your coat, or is it all here?" placing his hand on that part, and having his answer quickly. "No," he said, "I should not ask. Whatever you feel, however you do, it is what you are, and that is what I love." He looked at the Earl with a tenderness of love that flattened all expression from his face:

"Your features are grown dear to me
Through your self's use and habit in its own—
Loving, I could praise them for their selves alone,
But it would be your doubting thought,
Glancing from a narrowed eye at me;
The irritation in your foot, beating against the floor;
The pride your back, erect and thin, showed through the shirts you wore . . .
What will your lips and hands, your nose and ears to me be then
When you have left and gone to God . . .
What value may be laid on stillness when
Tension and quiet alike are unstrung under sod . . ."

He spoke quietly, half remembering.

"How shall I distinguish your proper light
Now shining, now repressed, in eyes and lips, where all is light?
O let us love, while there is limitation
Left to us in space to our control,
And the eternity of love within time's definition,
And body made desirable by soul.

But you do not believe in souls, do you, Holland?" He gave the Earl his peace, his eyes grave, quickly but tenderly, as he had learned how.

"I have found them of little use, if they are there," the Earl said, shaking his head, lying quiet beneath Edward's hands. "I am not worth this. Those lines are yours."

Edward nodded. "A long time ago," he whispered.

"I never thought of myself as thin," the Earl observed.

"You are not fat. You have some grey hairs, Holland," he said, touching with his delicate fingers the slightly pocked skin and tiny hollows in the prominent bones of the Earl's heart-shaped jaw and at the base of his neck, like the scars in his back that were now covered.

"I cannot help it," the Earl said, "they will come. If I still powdered, they would not show."

"I am glad you don't powder," Edward said. "I would not know you, I have never seen you any other way." He kissed him then, that particular part that had given him such joy and such pain and become a part of him, as he had not before at any time, and covered him, and then placed himself, clothed, so that his outline matched the Earl's, his lips once again on his. The Earl's arm tightened about him, and they lay so while the light faded and the room grew dark.

"We must have supper," the Earl said, suddenly starting, as he realised the light had left. "You have bewitched me, Edward, mesmerized me, until I have forgotten time and night and day."

He sat up and leaned forward and again their lips touched, and their hands sought one another's faces, beyond passion, in great tenderness. After supper, the Earl left Edward, but he came shortly to Edward's room, and they spent the night like two children, in one another's arms.

The next morning, George returned, on the borrowed horse. Edward's books and clothes were packed up, and they drove to Oxford, George riding on top of the coach with the coachman. The Earl asked Edward if he would like his horse, or another horse, and a groom sent down when the weather warmed a little.

"Oh, no, Holland, please, thank you very much, but my feet will take me everywhere I want to go, and I do not want to be conspicuous."

"You will be conspicuous, thank God, in the coats you have now, or conspicuously inconspicuous, or however you like to put it. This beautiful place," he said, drawing in his breath, "so dirty, so ramshackle, at its edges, at its heart so beautiful. I always forget and then when I see it, I wonder how I could forget and why I come so seldom here."

"A London Rake, callous and indifferent . . ." Edward murmured demurely. He felt a light stinging box on his ear from the man beside him, and he laughed. Looking at him quickly, dressed, on show, he wondered he could know him so intimately and take such familiarities, and that the man permitted it. In his turn, he drew in his breath slightly. This was his father, and he would claim him. He had said so. Someday, not so far away. A year, perhaps.

They installed George in his room, and then returned to Edward's rooms, after greeting the Master, and speaking with him, discussing Edward's readmittance, his penitence for his share in the prank, and at some length with Edward's tutor, about his reading.

"He is grooming you for a first, I think. We are all grooming you. I hope you do not tire, and bolt."

Edward shook his head, wondering if the moment of parting had come. Despite his light words and his more serious beliefs, he found the moment of unbearable pain. He lifted his eyes, drowning in it, and saw the same pain in the Earl's eyes, dark and drowned with it also.

"Shall I sport, Edward?" he asked, his voice hesitant and husky.

"Please, do," Edward answered, his eyes held and holding, unable to move, remembering the same scene three years and some months before when he had first come up, and he had wished then for what he saw now he was to have. He had not expected it, and his breath and his heart seemed mixed together and suffocating him. He watched the Earl close the two doors, and then the curtains in his bedroom. He knew, as the Earl surely knew, that this was the last time, unchangeably, and that they had finally reached it, after the attempts and the slidings back of the weeks since Christmas. Had he been tortured for it, he could not have told what transpired. Did they simply lie together, or did they act, one of them, or both? He could remember nothing but love and grief and the pain of parting which after a long time eventually took place at the door, which the Earl again opened.

"You will do well," he heard the Earl say, giving him his hand. "If you need me, write me. You will find 'blunt' packed in your suitcase.

Write Wotton for any more you need. I trust you, Edward. Have what you want. Ask him, he will send it. Or I will, if you do not. I shall not see you again until the Vacation, that will be best I think for us both. You celebrate Easter here, I think this year, it falls early. Goodbye, Edward—" He raised his hand, as he had before, in a half gesture of farewell.

"Goodbye, Holland," Edward said, trying not to cry. He heard the Earl's hesitant footsteps descending the stair. He imagined him speaking again to the Master perhaps, and getting into his coach, and not turning his head. He could not bear it. He ran down the stairs, after his father, overtaking him at the coach, and holding out his hand for a last clasp. The Earl held it warmly, though his figure and face seemed all at once removed and aloof.

"Why, Edward," he said, "I think you do care." The boy nodded mutely. "Don't," he said. "I am not going to.' He broke the harshness of his words by his grasp on Edward's hand. "You know then, too?" Edward nodded. "Why care, when there is no help—?" He released Edward's hand. "Go now, Edward, don't let the Master see a wicked unprincipled Earl cry, that is just for children like you. Shut the door now, we'll not make the footman dismount again." But he held the door himself with his hand. "Write me sometimes, Edward, will you? Tell me how you do. I would like very much to hear from you. I cannot, myself, but will you? Filially?" The Earl signalled to the coachman.

"Yes. I will," Edward said. Against his will, he closed the door of the coach, and watched the coach drive away.

Nothing of term had begun that day. If he went to his rooms, he was afraid he would cry. It was cold, he did not want to walk. No book had power at that moment to divert his thoughts. He decided to walk to Christ Church and see if the organist whom he had come to know was in. He did, he was, he spent the remainder of the afternoon listening and playing, easing his heart and its tensions in the music and its passionless, ordered passion. Too much had suddenly happened to him in too short a time, since he rode his borrowed horse home to Northumberland, not expecting to see the Earl at all, expecting no change except a longer time of quiet bitter reading and waiting. He had suddenly had and been given all he had ever wanted, and more, and the part he cared most for had only begun, and yet he was not happy. How strange human nature was, he reflected, as others had before him, its discontents, its desires, its restlessness, its inability to understand at times itself or anyone or anything else.

No, it is not so complicated, he thought, it is very simple. I have found my father again, and he has found me, I love him, I want to be with him. But we have our other work and affairs now to do. And we must each do them, separately.

It was to be a clear night, as well as a cold. As he walked back, the dusk had fallen, and one star he knew well shone brightly before him, low in the Western sky. Words came into his mind that in his dislocation he could not then place:

> *"Star of the Evening, you bring the wanderer home,*
> *You bring the shepherd to his fold and the child to its mother—"*

What was that? Homer? He could not remember, but its mood suited his own, of hope and of longing he thought to be fulfilled, and a wordless peace, despite his sorrow at the parting.

He, and for once, the Earl too, had been unaware of the events of the outside war, in their inside peace. The Earl had known that Wellesley had been replaced with Sir John Moore and that Napoleon himself had gone with his troops of more than two hundred thousand men to Spain and had taken Madrid, but he had not thought it worth mentioning, to disturb the mood of that Christmas. There was time enough for war and its news. The reports had reached him at the time of their parting of the hasty retreat of the British troops out to sea and the death of their commander Moore at Corunna, cancelling out the summer's victory over the French at Baylen when the invincible eagles had been laid low. The end of February near Edward's birthday saw the surrender of Saragossa to the French, after withstanding two sieges, with fifty thousand Spaniards killed in the streets, fighting to hold their city. Edward did hear of it, but it was remote to him, except for this fierce love these deaths showed. April would see Wellesley returned, to Lisbon and then into Spain, for a long fund-pressed campaign alternating victories and defeats that would continue until 1813, when thereafter it for him would be only winning, in his war.

❀꙳❀꙳❀꙳❀꙳❀꙳❀꙳❀꙳❀꙳❀

CHAPTER V

The Making of a Gentleman: 1809

I

THE term passed, as terms do. The presence of George made for a difference, for George had been carefully instructed by the Earl in his duties. The first time George asked to see Edward's nails, Edward was chagrined and hid them, but on being told it was by the Earl's instruction and his wish, he reluctantly produced them and let George administer to them. That ritual took place several times a day, until Edward developed the habit of automatically spreading them before George whenever he saw him, half-laughing about it.

"Gentlemen is not always clean, and some be slovenly," George said, lecturing him, "and there is nothing that more disaffects good company or a lady, than a dirty neck or dirt in the nails, or an unclean stock, unless it be a bad breath, of which there is enough. There is them I could name, but the Earl is not one of them—I am to see, the Earl says, that you fall into no such habits, and I would do it if he did not say it, also. The Earl is knowing the Beau himself, Edward, and those that follow him will have nothing unneat or unclean about them."

"Am I not clean? I thought I was."

"I do not see how you could be, living as your uncle has let you at home, and only a bedmaker and a Scout here that do for others, and water to be carried in if you have it, and then out, and you always rushing about or in your books."

"My Scout is very good for water and slops," Edward said.

"Well," George said, "it may do for a cit, but I am here now, and I shall take care of you."

He let George oil his hands, and from time to time he even slept in chicken-skin gloves, and submitted to daily manicuring of his nails, and attention to his hair. Once a day he found a bath made ready for him, and George checked him for cleanliness as thoroughly as when he was a child. He submitted because he could not help himself, and after a while, he found it pleasant to be attended and cared for. The matter of his clothes was taken entirely out of his hands; whatever he wished was simply there, clean, starched, pressed.

On his birthday, his twentieth, his father sent him the miniatures he had requested, and the miniature of his mother that Edward had thought destroyed long ago. He wept to receive them, his wounds, hardly healed, fresh reopened. The Earl also sent him, despite Edward's demurral, his horse and a young groom. Edward smiled, amused and worried, but as the weather grew milder, and even before, he found his father had been right and that the exhilaration of riding was a tonic as bracing and purging as Spring greens. He wrote twice, once about the miniatures and, more dutifully, the horse and groom, a letter that both touched and amused the Earl, and a second time, to express the genuine pleasures he received from the horse, but he assured his father he was not scanting his studies.

He was also glad to see the horse again as an old friend, although, with no close friends, not wishing one, he had many acquaintances now. Alleyn had managed to penetrate many of his defences and reticences, but no one else there could or tried to, as he had. Edward had found deep friendship impossible when the things closest and most important to him he was unwilling to speak of, but he enjoyed casual companionship, rediscovering the merry vein he had uncovered at Christmas that he had thought long ago played out. Now here it was again on the surface, fresh, bubbling, shining. Perhaps his new clothes and George's care for his appearance and the Earl's visit helped, or his horse, or his seniority. Whatever it was, these things, himself, or all together, he found himself as popular as he could have wished, beyond that of his third term, and more so than he had time for. He became adept at refusing invitations, accepting only those he enjoyed. He was showered with invitations at Easter, but he turned them all away tentatively, for he did not care about any of the senders to any degree, although he kept the invitations for the Earl to advise him on.

His trunks were packed, and his books, but the fourth of April passed, and the Earl did not come, and he did not hear. He did not understand, and he tortured himself imagining accidents of all sorts. Neither he nor George knew what to do. He considered writing Wotton, but he waited one more day. The next day, Ross arrived. Knowing the way, he simply knocked at the door, admitted by Edward who had hoped it was the Earl.

"Oh, no, Ross," he cried, falling back in dismay, "not you! You have not come for that! You can't mean it. What have I done?" His thoughts at that moment, able only to draw to one impossible conclusion, defied his own description. His face was white and his eyes completely piteous.

"No, Edward," Ross said, not unmoved, "I have come for you, but not in the way you think I mean. The Earl has sent me, because he cannot come himself, to bring you home to Tyne for your vacation weeks."

"Why can he not come?" Edward whispered, alarmed. "He told me he would. Is he ill?"

"No, Edward, he is not ill, he was called suddenly abroad."

Ross's heart was kinder and more informed than he chose to give it. He knew very well that the Earl had planned to go to Oxford and had started out. He had received an urgent message the next day asking him to go to Oxford and bring Edward and George home, and the groom and the horse if they wished, because he had himself discovered urgent business that called him abroad. Ross himself doubted, in view of the war, that the Earl had gone abroad, although it was not impossible. He shrewdly guessed the truth that the Earl, though well-intentioned, did not trust his own strength and had fled from the emotional strain of the meeting he both feared and desired. Himself, Ross thought the Earl wise, and had used good judgement. Neither had imagined or foreseen the unspeakable conclusion Edward would instantly draw and suffer from, however quickly relieved of it; or next his concern for the Earl's safety. His holiday spirits completely broken, Edward climbed into the coach, leaving both the horse and the groom. George rode on top with Ross, and he had room and time to collect his unhappy thoughts in.

He had perceived in that brief moment of horror and betrayal, as he thought, the truth of Jonson's words which he had read for himself, "A man may be secure, but safe never." He had let himself briefly feel secure, without care, secure and safe in the knowledge of his father's care and love and attention, for once as great or greater than his own, forgetting the torturous difficulties of the Earl's character. Even a letter to him would have preserved his security, but he had not had it. Ross's explanation, though relieving, had no power to mend. He saw the shaky little edifice for what it was, himself and his father for what they were, and his new found trust ended, unrecoverable. He would after that always, in his greatest joys, be aware of the possibility of immediate loss, and be always half-consciously prepared for it.

He did not see or hear from the Earl again until his oral examination, the *viva voce,* after his written examinations. The Earl was there, but Edward did not know it. On the long ride North, before Easter term began after the vacation, to be followed at once by Act, he had had time to sort his thoughts out, and to understand without being told why the Earl had changed his plans. For a moment he was sorry about his other invitations, but only for a moment, for he had much to do and to think through in the short four weeks. In the end he was even glad not to have had the excitement and disturbance of seeing the Earl. In four years he had grown used to a routine and his habits for study were not easily broken. He was glad to have the room and freedom to ride and go where he pleased, his own room and easy meals and untroubled sleep, but he was also glad for comparative solitude. The memory of the moment when he saw Ross's figure loom before him, again as in the past, though based on a delusion, had power to haunt him and turn him icy, only remembering it. But with compunction for it, and relief at Edward's return to virtue, Ross ceased to be unfriendly and relations between them had an appearance of usuality. At the end of the vacation, when he had returned to Oxford, he wrote the Earl a careful letter, neither brief nor long, expressing without emotion or reproach these thoughts and giving an account of the quiet but useful passage of his vacation. He sent it care of Wotton, and the Earl, in London, received it without delay.

His mind again at terms with itself was particularly peaceful, and he found that Spring most beautiful of all the four. He walked among the flowering chestnut, the cherry and almond, apple and pear, espaliered on the Northern walls of quadrangles and free, and his heart sang continuously within him, even as all those going away sang together on Magdalen Tower on May Day at sunrise, in the centuries-old tradition and Latin hymn, and then had strawberries for breakfast. The gardeners with their scythes were already at work on the lawns, and the rhythm of their blades sweeping reminded Edward of the rhythmic sweeping of the bow of the Earl's violin. The beech put out its rolled copper tips and the elms their green lace. The squirrels, thin after the winter, grew plump. Everything except the Fellows concentrated on families. The skies were clear at night, and he spent long evenings in the Observatory, merry after-noons drinking chocolate in Tom's Coffee-House, and daily inspections of the plants appearing in the Physic garden. Of his approaching exam-inations he felt no particular fear. He had spent fourteen years in study.

He took his *viva*, as was customary, before the examining board of four, under a new ruling, and a large audience of students of all years, and all the other degree candidates who were required to attend, and any other interested Fellows and tutors and members of the community. He was to be tested in logic, ethics, rhetoric, scholarship, and classical litera-ture, and also possibly grammar, old sciences, and elements of religion. He did not imagine the Earl there, the possibility did not occur to him that the Earl might be interested or would know the date or come. It was perhaps as well he did not, with the ordeal of the public oral of several hours' duration ahead of him to be faced and overcome with aplomb, or not at all. He had not himself sent the date, or perhaps he had. He did not know that both the Head and his tutor had written separately to the Earl, conveying that the occasion was expected by many to be a good one, and certainly worth his attending, for his ward was challenging Honours for a First in Literae Humaniores and expected by themselves to take it easily. Their expectations proved correct, and it being a time when Firsts were not easily come by, in the early years of Honours, and his College having had few, they were particularly pleased with him.

The Earl, gold-tasselled, velvet-capped and gowned in silk himself for the occasion, stood aside, watching, not attempting to see Edward or draw his attention to him, enjoying Edward's moment of triumph, while the crowd crowded as crowds will to wring his hand, clap his shoulder, utter their pronouncements and their opinions. After a time it thinned, and Edward saw his father standing, a little removed from it, his eyes fixed on him with pleasure and pride, watching him. His joy com-plete, and as always at the sight of the Earl his heart a little in his throat, he made his way quickly and gracefully through the remnant of the crowd, to the Earl, and took his hand. He was twenty now, taller, and looking it in his commoner's cap and gown, six months older in time and much older in experience and thought and steadiness than when he had last seen the Earl. He took his hand without embarrassment, and held it a moment in his, smiling at the Earl with frank pleasure expressed in all his face.

"Did you hear me?" he asked. "Were you here for it all? I did not know. I am so very glad you came."

"I was here, I heard it all," the Earl said, "and I am so very proud, although," he added, "I cannot truthfully say I understood all I heard."

"Yes," Edward said smiling, "we do rather stress the antiquities here, and English for all her beauties has not much chance or opportunity to be heard, except in the Dissenting Academies, which you abhor. There is a luncheon, rather late now, being given for me. Will you come?"

"Yes," the Earl said, "I have been particularly invited already by your tutor and by the Master."

"Old foxes," Edward said, "not to tell me, or perhaps they thought I knew. Oh, Holland, I am glad to see you. And I am just as glad I did not know at all you were there. But I am so glad you were."

An awkwardness, and a certain shyness fell between them, each wishing to look at the other, suddenly unable to meet the other's eyes, wishing to touch hands, and unwilling to. It was a shyness in no way helped by Edward's perceiving the Earl's pains on no account then or later to be left alone with him. He was not flattered by it, but distressed, and no experience he had had prepared him for meeting such a situation.

"Well, shall we go now?" the Earl said, suddenly smiling naturally and directly into Edward's eyes. "We lunch, then what is planned for us? I am staying at the Master's of Christ Church, at Dr. Fell's, did I not tell you?"

The Earl was careful not to see Edward alone, and only commonplaces passed between them. It galled the Earl to know that only his own will, which he was unaccustomed to using against his own wishes, held him from what he desired and from what he believed Edward, perhaps against his judgement but compliant, would not have withheld from him. But he did come, after he had removed his own academics, to Edward's rooms, where George and Edward together were packing, after lunch.

"Well," Edward said, his long fingers, as long now as the Earl's, touching in affectionate valediction the inside of his cap, as he put it away, thinking he would not now again feel its weight pressing his temples: "I have done that for you. What am I to do now?"

"Come to London," the Earl said, "and learn to be a gentleman."

"Can you make me one?" Edward asked, handing over his books to George. "Just like that?"

"I shall enlist help," the Earl said, smiling, "but the material is good, and the native quality is there which the finished product frequently lacks."

"I suppose I still have no choice about what I would like to do?" Edward observed, rather than asked, a little wistfully.

"None at all," the Earl said cheerfully. "I am going now to have tea at Oriel, and you may sit in, if you like. We are going to reminisce about the old days, and Haydn's concerts here. I shall be proud to have you with me, and they will be honoured."

"I should love to come with you," Edward said, and dismissed his thoughts.

"You will find the climate better," the Earl said, as they drove in to London the next day, "but the dirt will shock you."

Even despite the Earl's warning, Edward was shocked. The fresh green of the trees that had delighted him about Oxford was nowhere to be seen. The trees themselves looked dark, almost black, with the grime settled on them. Once again Edward wondered why men chose to live in London, when they could live elsewhere. He knew of course the answer: the making of money, the display of wealth, the enhancement of prestige, the inertia of having been born in it, but more than any of them, finally, the desire to be with other men, in the hubbub of their doings, and more particularly, with particular men and women. Later he would learn that it is in the great cities that one can be oneself or feel oneself most completely, or in them forget oneself most completely.

He was set at once by the Earl on a routine more exacting than any he had yet experienced. His days were taken over completely by lessons, without even a week's respite for rest from his last endeavours.

"I have won one pair of spurs for you," he complained to the Earl, "and you throw them in a corner, and ask for another."

"They were good ones, and pure silver," the Earl said absently. "Now we will set them and adorn them. Did you like Angelo?"

"Does it matter?"

"No, I just wondered. He is the foremost fencing master in London, I have heard, and himself a gentleman."

"I was struck by the name, and of course, his foil."

"The name?"

"A good one for a fencing master: measure for measure."

What comments the Earl might have made he kept to himself, contenting himself only by saying, "Tomorrow I take you to Jackson's."

" 'Gentleman' Jackson?"

"The name is a little less apt. Yes. I know him well, though I box now myself mainly with Mendoza. The time will come, Edward, when you can outmill me and outthrow me—don't wince, Edward, I still could you, when not surprised—and then I shall have to look to my tyrannies. I wonder I insist on teaching you these skills. In the afternoon we will go to Manton's, and shoot wafers. He will not praise you, do not expect it. I am reputed an excellent shot myself, and I have proved it, but according to Joe Manton I shoot 'tolerably.'"

And so on Mondays, Wednesdays, and Fridays in the morning Edward fenced, and in the afternoon he danced, learning even to waltz, perfecting his style in those skills. To his surprise, he loved doing both. On Tuesdays, Thursdays, and Saturdays, in the morning he boxed, bare-fisted by custom, with Jackson himself, learning his famous motto: "Whoever is not for you is against you, *mill* away right and left," a useful ability in an age of riots and no forces legally existing to uphold the law outside of the military and the hired bruisers; and in the afternoon he practised pistol-shooting at Manton's, developing a steady eye and a steadier hand. He began to feel qualified against any challenger but Angelo and Manton both cautioned him against overconfidence. "It is one thing," they told him, "to fire at a wafer or a dummy, quite another at a man you know, even though it is wise to pretend he is another wafer. And always wear black without trimming."

Edward had not really imagined his father seriously was preparing him to duel, but when he tasked him, he discovered that was precisely his object.

"But I could not, Holland," he said, "I would not."

"If you were challenged, and even you could be, you would have to, Edward. Your honour would demand it and I would expect it."

Edward looked at his father in wonder and in horror and saw that he was completely serious and that he meant what he said, and himself said no more. He privately thought the real world he was being dropped into stranger and more incomprehensible than the strangest parts of his life in Northumbria.

In between these lessons, he was taken to Waite's to have his teeth checked and confirmed, and again to Weston's for yet more outfitting. He saw various fights between the popular boxers of the day: Dan Dogherty vs. John Gully, the Irish Champion challenging the English; Tom Belcher, Tom Cribb, Bob Gregson. He did not know which to be the more amazed at, the fighters or the audience, straining, shouting with them, all classes mixed. Drury Lane Theatre had burned down in February while he was at Oxford, ruining its owner, the playwright-parliamentarian Sheridan, contemporary of the Earl, and the two major theatres were temporarily dark now, but he went once to Haymarket for pantomime with his father, and found it dull. He might have gone to Astley's Circus inside the Amphitheatre on Westminster Bridge Road, but he did not, his father not suggesting it.

On Sundays he went piously and decorously to church with the Earl, pleasantly aware that he excited interest behind demure lids, and made his responses, and listened to the slow nasal intoning of the hymnody, so unlike the swift joyous directly beautiful hymns of Charles Wesley his first father had taught him, and was morally instructed in easy matters in the sermon: "And his Commandments are not grievous." He was told that he was a rational being, the supreme handwork of his now removed and remote Creator, and subject to the laws of morality and charity. Inwardly he questioned, but not hard, for he was afraid to listen too carefully to his inner voice which insisted on a more difficult and demanding allegiance that he was now both unwilling and unable to give at that time.

In the afternoon the Earl took him for a drive down Piccadilly and pointed out the houses to him. "There is old Lord Queensberry, one of the Douglas family, sitting in his balcony of No. 138, richer than I am and more wicked, and eighty-five. May we all live to be eighty-five and enjoy ourselves as much. I must bring you sometime when I hear of it to watch him race his applicants for the post of Running Footman. He still has one, Gore and I do not, of course, it is not necessary now, but it is very amusing to watch, for they may wear the kilt again. He will sit there on his balcony with his stop watch, and time them down Piccadilly and up again and back. Though I cannot imagine why he should, since he is really too old to take the roads. I daresay it amuses him too. Lady Devonshire's black is in one of these houses now, I believe, Pompey she called him; John Morocco is at Knole. Her husband required her to give the child up, I forget which lady has him now. There is Francis Burdett's, he is a Whig, too much so for me. He is working for Reform, but I like my world as it is, and if he thought about it, I daresay he does himself. You see, he lives in Piccadilly all the same. He will cut himself off on the limb he saws at, and all of us. I hope his saw is blunt. There is Lord Eldon's, the Conservative, he is Lord Chancellor and God keep us out of Chancery. He is an honest man, but so thorough, the cases never seem to make an end. He was a Scott, one of the brothers at University, I told you." If he saw Edward's momentary look of distress at that memory, he ignored it. "The one draped in black is Coventry House. The Earl of Coventry is just dead, who married the elder of the two beautiful Miss Gunnings before I was born, but the impoverished beauties of no name have continued ever since to hope, on precedent. I believe the knocker is off the door. There is Lord Elgin's house, where he keeps the marbles he brought from Greece in a new shed he has had built for them: much good do they do him now with his fortune and his wife and his career lost to him after six years in and out of Napoleon's prisons, and on parole still and subject to recall. I have stopped travelling since that happened. It is a new custom, to imprison civilians, in war. But I will take you to see the marbles if you like, if we can manage to step around over the artists drawing them. West and Lawrence and Fuseli have all been there and still go frequently, and Farington and Nollekins, and Flaxman, of course. Haydon is there all the time, one night he will catch a cold in that drafty place." He looked at Edward, his face unreadable, and then he smiled. "I think I shall shock you, Edward," he said, a gleam in his eye. "Last Summer, last June precisely, I contributed a guinea and was invited with various artists and gentlemen to see Gregson pose like the statues without fig leaf among them that their respective torsi and anatomies might be accurately compared and credibility maintained, all in the best interests, of course, Mine, though, were not entirely artistic. There was a later similar showing which I did not attend, and three boxing matches which I did attend. But nothing was broken, more than it already was."

"I am truly shocked," Edward said, "I think you are all mad."

"Oh, come, Edward. Even the young ladies of London have been to Park Lane to see the marbles, though the bruisers were not there." He decided to change the subject, at the boy's face. "There is Cambridge House. The King's seventh son lives there. If Canning's friend Walter Scott is in town, he stays next door—the lawyer-poet. He is lame, too. Have you read him? The Border *Minstrelsy?*" Edward shook his head. "You should, he likes stories of Armstrongs. I must get you a copy of *Marmion* and keep you *au courant*."

He drove Edward past Parliament, where he rarely took his seat, and told him stories of Fox and Sheridan and Coke, of George III in the robing room with his heavy ermines, of young peers throwing oranges at one another in the park in extempore ball as they went leaping home, of pranks in the corridors, Sheridan lining a dark hall with dishes which he passed nimbly over, while his opponent crashed through. Edward was shocked and amused and worried all at once.

"Playwrights in Parliament," he said, "and playing? You alarm me."

"Don't be," his father said, reading his mind, "they don't play on the floor, and that is what counts."

He had little time for reading or music now, and his contacts with his father were wholly those of praeceptor and pupil. He was tutored at breakfast, at dinner, at lunch, on all possible manners in all possible situations and all possible forms of address to all possible personages. For several days Edward was even made to perform the duties of a footman both at meals, in hall and in coach, for his father.

"If you know what should be done, you will know how to respond to it easily," the Earl said, silencing his amazement before it turned to protest, "and you will learn most quickly by doing, what others have learned by years of having done for them. Knights always were squires first. I myself can do anything I require any man in my household to do, and better than he can, and therefore I know when he is shirking or ill-trained."

"I do not mind serving you," Edward said mildly, although it seemed to him still a questionable child's game. He found the Earl somewhat abstracted and crosser than his wont; he did not know, because the Earl did not explain, that there was new fighting in Austria and that his humour reflected his concern.

While waiting these reports, the Earl also gave Edward lessons in drinking, and in wine-tasting and wine-buying. On snuff he put a prohibition, because privately he could not bear to see the traces of it about Edward's face or on his fingers, or watch the affectation of the gesture in this particular person.

"How *does* one take snuff?" Edward asked.

"Do you not know?" the Earl asked in real surprise.

Edward shook his head. "No. I do not. How should I? No one has ever shown me, and I do not like to stare." He flicked a brief glance at the Earl, his eyes demure.

The Earl laughed slightly, his own eyes glittering.

"I will show you then," the Earl said. "Come here."

"I would rather not," Edward said uneasily, his hands behind his back. "I wish I had not asked."

"But you did," the Earl remarked easily, a hint of steel under his light voice. "Come here," he repeated. "I have overlooked a part of your education, I see."

After a moment, as the Earl's gaze did not falter, Edward did move a step nearer to him, and stood watching, his hands braced against the edge of the table behind him.

"You may stare now, Edward, if you like," the Earl remarked. "Watch closely." He made a few quick movements with his fingers, drawing his handkerchief and passing it before his face, gestures familiar to Edward, and after a few moments smiled slightly at his ward-and-son and said, "Satisfied? What did I do? Try it now yourself."

"I would rather not," Edward said uneasily, "and besides I still do not know what you do."

"All the same, you will essay. You have watched me."

Under his eyes, slightly mocking, quite hard now, Edward took an infinitesimal pinch, and put it to his nostril.

"Breathe in now," said the Earl pleasantly.

After an uncertain look at his father, Edward reluctantly obeyed, choked, and was overcome by a fit of sneezing. When he could control himself again, and his eyes had stopped watering, he looked up to see the Earl still watching him, his expression sardonic.

"How mean, Holland," Edward accused, coughing, some of the snuff seeming caught even in his throat. "You knew what would happen!"

"Perhaps," the Earl murmured, his eyes on Edward. "Grace, Edward, and finesse. Watch me again. I take a pinch, so, between my thumb and forefinger, and then I do *not* inhale the particles up my nose or try to eat them. Heaven forbid. Have you no eyes? I place the pinch carefully, here, at the front of one nostril only, so, and pack it into the little place, the cavity, that is there. You have it too, Edward. Feel with your finger-tip and you should see. No?" he said, his eyes glittering slightly, as Edward watching him fascinated, did not move. "No matter. We will attend later. The trick, Edward, is to learn to talk, and yet breathe through your mouth, Edward, as I am doing now, until you find a moment when it is convenient for you to take the effect of the snuff. If I breathed quickly through my nose now, Edward, I should have the same effect you did yourself. But the effort of breathing makes for a certain languor in the voice, as you may have observed in me or in others and not known the cause. It is not affectation, Edward, but necessity, if the snuff has once been placed. Now I take my handkerchief so"—and flicking it from his sleeve—"dust my fingers, my nostrils, my lips, to keep all tidy. I should have spilled nothing, but it is wise." He applied the handkerchief delicately, under Edward's fascinated, slightly horrified eyes, and tucked it away again into his sleeve. "The snuff in my box, you will notice, is slightly moist. If it is allowed to dry out, it will not pack, or hold itself in place, for any length of time at all. Now, Edward, it is, supposedly, your time to speak and I will unobtrusively inhale. Watch my expression, it should not change." He was silent for a few seconds, and then, unmoved, he spoke again, his voice unchanged. "A heady pleasure, quite private. One both accustomed and expert may keep the pinch there, conversing, inhaling, in turn, perhaps thirty minutes, but I will not. I take my handkerchief, to conceal my movements, so, but I will lay it by now for you to see, extract the pinch with my same fingers again, return it to my second box or if I am a dirty man to the first or in my pocket, or on the floor, and with the point of my handkerchief, just the lace, so, inserting it so, bring out any particle remaining, then wipe carefully but very quickly, so, to brush away any trace that may remain. In the end, however, it will yellow my nostrils, my upper lips, and the tips of my fingers if I am careless or if I take it excessively, and—even if I am careful, in the end it will discolour them. Look on our acquaintance, and you will see the marks. Now, Edward, come by me, and I will this time apply it to you." He took the pinch out of his snuffbox, with studied impersonality, and beckoned to Edward with the fingers holding it.

"Please, Holland," Edward said nervously, his calm leaving him, "I would rather not."

"Come, Edward," the Earl said impatiently. "You have used my laudanum, and did not mind. It is an honour, this using of my snuffbox, and you may not refuse." His voice softened slightly. "It will not hurt you, Edward, this time, nor will I. But stand quite still."

With one hand he steadied the boy's face, ignoring the young man's distressed, accusing eyes and his whispered, "Please, Holland, don't," and with the finger and thumb of the other inserted the tiny pinch deftly and with the tip of his first finger, packed it.

At the touch of the Earl's hands, falling silent, Edward grew very still under them. He did not move, but his eyes that did not look now at the Earl were frightened and intent.

"Now, Edward," the Earl said, his breath a little heavy, but his voice unconcerned, "shut your mouth and breathe carefully through your nose, let the breath inhale slowly and lightly first, then more deeply if you find you can bear it. Then hold your breath for as long as you can and wish, but do not breathe out your nose, and do not gasp, breathe slowly out your mouth when you must. You will do just as I have said, now, please," his tone not entreating but with the steady ordering Edward was helpless not to follow. He did as the Earl had directed and felt, it seemed to him, his head lift right off—up and away, the strangest sensation he had ever experienced, not pleasant yet the sensation by no means unpleasant, a kind of private ecstasy that though he did not know it until to his astonishment he saw his father was holding before him a mirror, was making him both grimace and grin foolishly. Unconsciously he had been holding his breath, as though that would keep the top of his head from exploding off and drifting away—now he released it, and too suddenly, and again fell into a fit of sneezing.

"An anticlimax, no?" remarked the Earl, his voice intruding into the airy realms Edward had been drifting somewhere among. He returned to reality, again choking, taking helplessly the handkerchief the Earl was holding out to him with amusement and something veiled in his eyes beyond amusement. "Did you like it, Edward?"

"I don't know," Edward said frankly. "I have never experienced anything quite like it. Is that happening to people we know all the time?"

"Much of it," the Earl said, smiling faintly.

"It hardly seems decent," Edward said. "I am very surprised. I am indeed." He looked suspiciously at his father. "Even you?"

"Sometimes," his father said. "From time to time. It is not a necessity to me. I have not let it be. Few things are. Some men I know, and women too, have let the habit take them, as some let other habits take them, and they keep a pinch there, in the little cavity, all the time. It is an almost continuous sensation with them. They have let themselves require it excessively, and it has controlled them. Now watch me once again," the Earl said, a faint gleam still in his eyes, but his breathing steady again, "and I will once again show you how properly it should be taken." He made again the unhurried graceful gestures, with a quick practised ease that Edward saw now concealed, as in so many things, his actual actions, and the fact itself, was for a moment quiet, then breathed and smiled at Edward.

"I have shown this to you now, Edward, but I hope you will not use it. Practise the mannerisms, would be my advice to you, Edward," he said, "and fake. But do not do the thing itself."

"Why?" Edward asked.

"You do not need to," the Earl said. "And I do not wish it."

His concern for Edward's health and his admonitions finally provoked Edward into comment: "I declare, Holland, there can be no one like a confirmed rake, as you keep over-informing me you are, for strictness in raising up the young. I do think it. You are certainly determined I shall be moderate. You will drive me from virtue yet."

"I know too well what I speak of, Edward. No course will serve but moderation. I have learned it at last."

"I don't feel moderate, I feel full of excess and enthusiasm or I would if I were not so exhausted from Jackson and so hot."

"I could not bear you to spoil your beauty with snuff or with heavy drinking or heavy eating, Edward. I beg you will not. Take the precepts of your Wesley in this." It was the only personal remark he made, and it silenced Edward's protests wholly. "I have learned how to manage finally at these great dinners, without rudeness and without gout, and if you let me, I will tell you. But you must be prepared for fantastic arrays of food such as you have never seen, with your one meat and one vegetable and two plates at Oxford, and the plain fare I serve here. Seven courses and seven dishes each of meats and puddings and vegetables and syllabubs and I don't know what at each course, besides the fish and the fruits and the cheeses and the sweetmeats, will be ordinary and considered small and stingy. A man must have some defence against it, or he will be swallowed up even as he swallows."

For a fortnight in July the Earl sent Edward out, to his friend Sir Andrew Pelham in Grosvenor Square for several days, and for several more to the town house of the Marquis and Marchioness of Gore, to continue his education and to test Edward's manners on strangers to Edward but his own particular friends. From their houses Edward drove to his lessons, which did not stop.

Pelham he found a courteous middle-aged gentleman, older-seeming than the Earl, graver, more sedate, correcting his errors with unerring tactful courtesy, bearing with his unaccustomed embarrassment which he did feel here in what to him was still essentially an unnecessary masquerade. He discovered that he was proud. He had not known it before, but he had always been served and never himself served. It was useless to remind himself of the words, "Let all be servants to one another," when Sir Andrew was exempt from it. The reminder of his anomalous position and that except for the Earl's grace his pride had no warrant for it did not help him either, although it increased his embarrassment. He had lived in that manner and in that estate for fourteen years, and it was all he really knew. Even when fallen from it, and confined away from it he had known he was fallen and confined and from where and from what. The discovery of the fact of his pride, however, could still humiliate him inwardly, and in that humility he performed what he was expected to do. He wondered if the Earl's motives had been mixed, and if he had wished and planned for him to make just such a discovery, so

that he would care for the inheritance that he had not been promised—
and be more careful not to lose it, as he had not cared before. He rather
thought not, he rather imagined the Earl simply had not imagined the
emotions he was feeling and inwardly writhing under, as he had not
himself before, having never had them himself. But the effect was the
same. He discovered that he still nevertheless did not care, even if it
took from him his place and left him a servitor to other men with place.
He was bound to his father, but bound only with that bond. With that
discovery, on his second day, and his acceptance of it, his embarrassment left him, and he profited more.

It was Pelham's wish to put his young servant at ease, despite the
rigourous regime he held him to, in addition to Edward's own schedule
the Earl had not relaxed, and this he did by his manner, although otherwise he paid him little mind. There was no time for anything else.
Edward discovered that the life of the servants went on long after he
had assumed it finished, and began long before but it reminded him of
his childhood at Tyne, and he found the work more restful than his own
life. The house was smaller, the life simpler, than the second he went to.
He wondered how the Baronet and the Earl were friends, but since the
Baronet never spoke to him as a person, only instructing or admonishing,
or broke the artificial barrier the Earl had raised, except by his kindness,
he did not learn until he was in the coach with the Earl again, and asked.

"We were at Sion House and Eton together," the Earl said briefly.
"I was his fag, and he did not abuse me. He is older than I am, as you
may have noticed, or I may seem immeasurably old to you."

"No, Holland," Edward said. "You do not. I noticed it."

"I repaid him the services of forbearance he did for me when I was
young when we were older. Our tastes are dissimilar and we do not often
meet but we have always been friends and we call upon one another for
what we need. There is no other man I trust to do well by me entirely."
He did not ask if Edward had minded. His thoughts were elsewhere. He
had learned while Edward was gone of the final defeat at Wagram of the
Austrian troops under Archduke Charles, after their encouraging but
now brief victory the end of May at Aspern. He was disheartened, for
he saw there was now no hope left of seeing the progress of Napoleon
checked by the arms of Austria, and Vienna, in which Haydn lay dying,
was a closed city as were the Austrian frontiers to all outside the Empire.

Without taking him home, the Earl took him to No. 25 Portland
Place to the Marquis' new town house at a time when they were not
having guests. Here he served only as a uniformed footman in all the

various possibilities of the post, and he had more time of his own. The only children he had known had been George's brothers and sisters, briefly, and even more briefly, Alleyn's. He discovered again that he liked children, and he appointed himself (or found himself) assistant to the much-tried governess of the eight, and also *ex facie* tutor to the eldest son who would shortly return to Oxford and Christ Church for his third year. He was some six weeks the elder of Edward, different in nature, younger in spiritual experience, and untried there, but more assured of the world and already wholly experienced in it. He was recovering from a treatment that Summer for a Gonorrhea, and he described the injections in detail to Edward when he learned to his surprise Edward had not experienced them.

"Scorched and drenched, as Byron says," he said, wincing in memory. "I met this lovely girl in Oxford by a well. God! what a mistake."

The sum of his debts, known and unknown to the young lord's father, staggered Edward, and he counselled full accounting which the young lord shrugged off with "You don't know my father."

"What do you mean? He would surely not whip you, and he cannot cut you off."

"Lord, no. He generally gives me what I want, he is not a bad sort. 'Well, if you must, you must,' he says. But I bought a new yacht and that bill is enough, and I want the curricle and the new matched blacks this year at Oxford, to race Lord Jeffrey, as well as my hunters. I also mean to ask for the use of the country box nearest Oxford for a private shoot this November with my friends, if he can forget this business I have got into now, and not worry about his maids there. The hunt last year left three with their aprons high, and two diseased. And if my tutor does not raise the cry. It is harder now to go in politics, you know, though of course I will have my Seat. There is a new kind of man there, and there are not that many key places, which is all I want. Lord, I am tired. I wish I'd never met that girl. Far worse than last year's—who would have thought it, I didn't, I thought I had the first honour but ho-ho for that." He laughed resignedly, but Edward was inwardly more shocked than he showed.

He thought the boy with his father's looks and his graceful athlete's carriage would have been charming, had his dark eyes not been so tired and heavy, and his white face so lacking in any animation but petulance and animal spirits. He had Alleyn's black hair curling in easy short waves, that pulled at Edward's heart, but his face was entirely different, lacking entirely Alleyn's delicacy or animating fire of expression, or his father's distinction. Edward attempted to drill him on his Latin, but the young man's attention was short and flitting, and he had to be drawn back again and again, and what he looked at he did not remember.

"I was rusticated last year for two terms, you know" (Edward shook his head slightly), "for shooting through the window of a damned cit who was having too loud a party with his damned cit friends, they do have their nerve now. The worst, though, was that the pater had a shipping contract going with his father, so I had my mouth soaped out all round. You took a First, didn't you?" he asked with briefly incredulous curiosity. "It will be Pass for me, or an M.A. more likely, courtesy my title. You don't look any older than I."

"I am not," Edward said smiling. "You have the pull on me, six weeks, I think."

"Oh, God," the boy said suddenly, "I know who you are. You are one of those too. There is one more, but his father's dead, and he is in the Fleet for debt. He inherited the traits but not the title to keep him out."

"One of what, too?" Edward asked, his heart beating fast.

"Our fathers raped our mothers for a joke. Didn't you know? There was a deal of money put on the bets. Mine had to marry my mother, yours didn't." He looked at Edward's face curiously. "You *are* Tyne's bastard, aren't you? My father said you were. I heard him, to my mother. I had forgotten."

"I don't believe you," Edward said slowly, but he did.

"Believe it or not, as you please. It is all the same true. Lyle's son told me. He held me down one night, when he took me out and got me laid out in my cups, and made me hear. He is a bit of a bastard in two ways, but he can hardly help it. His mother did not survive his birth, and his father took him off the parish, though he didn't have to. Most of the children there are some lord's byblow, you know, but not usually by the quality. We were, I suppose, the luckier. My father doesn't know I know, I'd never tell him. But it does make a difference, knowing, doesn't it? I haven't cared much what I did since. Lyle's father liked to tell him, being what he was he thought it *très amusant* he had a son at all. So now I know all about it too. Everything there is to know. You look rotten."

"I am going to be sick," Edward said.

"Go behind the bush," the young lord said, "the gardener can bury it. He has buried enough of mine." He listened dispassionately to the sounds of retching and moved away a little in courtesy. When the sounds ceased, he came up and stood by Edward, with something of compassion on his usually expressionless face. "I was myself when I first heard. I

don't think about it now. You'll find you don't either, after a bit. After
all it's just the old game of stick and cup ball, isn't it? My friends at
Oxford are just like me, and they haven't my excuse, so what's the difference. And my mother and my father are happy together, and theirs
generally are not. I forgave my father entirely when I saw my mother
was happy with him. He hasn't a mistress, you know, and my friends'
fathers all do. But I don't love him any more. I can't. Awful shock. I
haven't had any feeling for anyone at all since. Look, why don't you go
upstairs and have a rest. Your room will be hot, use mine. You have an
hour before you are on call again. Lord, what a cockbrained idea of
Tyne's. I wonder you put up with it. By the by," he said to Edward's
retreating back, "I don't think Tyne took the money—of course he didn't
need it. My father did."

When he stood behind the chairs that night, his pale face schooled
and impassive, he looked at his host and his hostess carefully when he
could without notice. He understood now the amused gleam behind his
quasi-host's dark eyes, when they had chanced to fall on him, and the
quality of interest he had been unable to define, and he understood his
quasi-host's dark eyes, when they had chanced to fall on him, and the
next day the Earl came for him. He went to say goodbye to the young
Viscount, but when he knocked and was told to enter, he found the
voice had spoken unconsciously. The Viscount was lying on his bed,
drunk, his clothes disordered, and his face flushed and swollen, his
senses stupified. His right hand, outflung, hung over the uncapped
chamber pot which was stuffed full with banknotes. The Viscount had
apparently had luck the night before. Edward sighed, made his adieux
to the Marquis and Marchioness, and left.

II

He walked beside the Earl quietly, unable to look at him, and stepped
up into the carriage. He wondered a little what he was going to do, and
then he realised to his shame he was not going to do anything at all. He
loved the Earl now more than he loved the memory of his mother, and—
as he always had—more than himself.

"It was not a good idea to send me there, Holland," he said quietly.
"You should not have, you should have known not to."

"Instructing me again, Edward?" quizzed the Earl, his face a little
surprised.

"Gore's son knows about his father and his mother, and about me, and about you and my mother. He told me. His father doesn't know he knows."

The Earl's face flattened under the unexpected words, and then he said slowly, "Could you not have spared me, too?"

"No. We do not spare one another, you and I, Holland."

There was a pause, and then the Earl said painfully, "I will not try to deny it. I suppose you did not find it hard to believe, knowing me."

"I believed it." His eyes rested on the Earl with intense sadness and with some of the acceptance of the Earl's nature that was a part of his love. "I did not want to believe it of you, but I did. I knew something must have happened, out of the ordinary, for you to be my father as you are, and my mother to have been a Clare and the person that she was, but dear love of God, Holland, I never thought to have come from a public joke." He had abruptly lost his control. "How it hurts, Holland, it cuts me like a knife. But perhaps that is the greatest part of the joke. Why don't you laugh, Holland, as you laughed then?"

"Don't, Edward," the Earl said, his lips white, his eyes suddenly watchful.

"That was ill-mannered of me. Above all things, let us be mannered. Though I do not see how one can rape with manners a girl and one who is innocent."

"I have had enough of this," the Earl said roughly. "You must stop it now, Edward. You don't know what you are saying."

"Do I not?" Edward asked queerly.

"No, I think not," the Earl said. "Am I supposed to tell you about it?" he added, his voice harsh.

"What is there to tell?" Edward asked flatly. "You put your thing in my mother when she did not want you to, and left me there, and left her. Did it give you pleasure to do that? Did it amuse you? She must have cried. I cannot see how it could. But you tell me you generally do what you want to do, so I suppose you wanted to, for some reason I cannot fathom." He saw his father's eyes upon him again, with their strange flat assessing quality. "I did not mind so much when I thought you did it because you loved her," he said, his mouth quivering. "I could not understand anyone hurting someone they loved, but I know you do not mind hurting people. How foolish, how romantic of me, to have thought I was a child at least of love. How many people know? How many eyes will I have to face as I did this past week looking at me as they did, and realising as I finally did that they know I was born from a drunken bet, just one of a group of such?"

"Damn Lyle!" the Earl exploded savagely. "I wish I had shot him, long ago. I wanted to. I should have."

"Dear Holland," the boy said, smiling pitifully, "you do not change, do you? Your reactions are always the same. You have not answered my question. Are you going to? How many people know?"

"None, I think," the Earl said without expression. "I did not think for this to happen. I would have avoided it at all cost had I imagined it possible."

"You *think*," Edward said, his voice unreadable. "We are not going home, Holland. Where are you taking me? Is a repetition to be avoided 'at all cost'? Am I dangerous now? If you think so, you need not make any elaborate precautions for disposing of me, I will not resist you. Kill me if you like. I do not care much right now what you do."

"Do not be absurd, Edward," the Earl said briefly. "I am taking you to Hampton Court, that is all, where I seduced and raped your mother. You shall see your place of origin for yourself. It was more ugly and more unnecessary and more shabby, both the doing and its consequences, than you can imagine, but when you know that, you know only the half. I cannot tell you the other half, you will have to learn it someday for yourself. But let me tell you this, Edward, and you must believe me: I made no boast of what I did, and there is no one on this earth or in heaven or in hell who knows what happened or of it at all but myself and your mother, George Armstrong, and now you. Gore's son, Gore him-himself, Lyle, Lyle's son guess for themselves, not from anything I said. Do you believe me?"

"I suppose so," Edward said, his eyes downcast.

"That is not an answer. Do you believe me?"

"Yes," Edward whispered. "Yes, I do. I have to, when you speak this way."

"Good," the Earl said. "I am glad you do. It is important to me that you should. Add it all to your scores to settle with me. The list is already long, and may grow longer."

"What I meant to say," Edward said, his voice low but firm, "and then I did not, because I lost myself, was that it changes nothing now." He lifted his eyes and met his father's surprised ones. "But you had to know I knew. I owed you that. I saw what holding back had done to Lord Gore's son and his father. It might have happened to them anyway, but I could not risk it. I am not strong enough to keep the knowledge by myself. I did not want that to happen to you or to me."

He took the Earl's hand in his, and kissed it, and laid it against his cheek, briefly, before he released it.

The Earl looked at him in amazement. "I don't think you mind. I cannot believe it. And after your angers at me."

"Oh, I minded. But when I had a moment to think, I saw as I had not how narrowly I had my existence, and how easily I might have missed you and not have known you. Then I could not mind, no matter how it was. The thought of that loss so frightened me and sobered me, I could not be angry. I could not even care. Though I must care, to speak to you as I have. Do I shock you? My mother loved you, I love you. That is enough."

"Oh, God, Edward," the Earl said, "how you shame me." He had turned his face away, but now he turned it back, and looked across at his son. Edward looked back at him steadily. "So what's to do? Do we just go on?"

"Nothing," Edward said. "We go on. I wish, somehow, you had told me yourself. The worst was hearing it as I did. But I cannot imagine your telling me." He smiled faintly. "You have never pretended to me. You told me it would be hard, to be known as your son."

"And is it? This foretaste?" Edward nodded. "Too hard? You can still go back." He shook his head.

"No, Holland, never too hard."

They were near Hampton Court, and they rode in silence which Edward did not break, until they reached the Maze and left the curricle.

"I have not been here for twenty-one years," Tyne said, "but it is not much changed. It was early Summer then, the trees were green, the harebells were blooming."

"O God," Edward said, as he realised where they were, "it is a maze." He stood as if struck.

"Yes," the Earl said, "is it so extraordinary?"

"It is too fitting," Edward whispered. "To live in a maze as I do, and to have been conceived in one." He remembered suddenly a dream of a place something like this he had had when he was nine.

"Please," the Earl said, lifting his hand slightly, "don't come over literary on me. There was nothing literary about the afternoon. Or do you visualise me in the middle, like the Minotaur, alone, hooved, horned, waiting to devour the approaching virgin? It was no such thing. There was a park keeper, many other people, your mother's brothers and sisters."

"Is it open?" Edward asked. "May one go in?"

"I think so. It is still early afternoon. But there is no point. We did not stay. We walked together, just the two of us, hand in hand, into that wood, out of the maze, your mother much too trusting."

"You were thirty, thirty-one?" Edward said, looking at him.

"Old enough to know what I was about, old enough for there to have been no excuse for what I did. I offer none." He lifted the iron latch of the gate as he spoke, and they went inside, the trees in their green leaves, their dark branches showing, arching over them, all of Summer's sensuous luxuriance showering in the light falling through them.

"There is nothing ugly here," Edward said, looking about him. He sighed. "My mother must have loved you and must have trusted you to give you opportunity."

"She did," the Earl said, his voice rough. "She did, and I took it."

"Where?" Edward asked.

"I do not remember the exact place," the Earl said with asperity. "Do not press me too far, do not ask me too much. I have few memories more painful to me now."

Edward sat down on a small hillock of ground beneath a tree, his knees drawn up, his hands clasped about them loosely, and looked about him, shivering a little. The Earl came after a moment and sat down beside him. After a moment Edward lay back in the grass and shut his eyes.

"I wonder if I shall ever find the way out of my maze," he said, half to himself.

"Every maze has a key," said the Earl. "One can always get out."

"I wonder if, when and if I do," he said, his voice the same, "it will only be to a betrayal such as this, in a wood I thought so fair." Or has that already happened, he thought. He opened his eyes and looked at his father, his eyes very like his mother's, their deeper dark-rimmed blue-grey lightened in the gold-green light of the wood, the sun shining on his fair hair and gilding its edges. " 'And so by indirections,' " he quoted softly, " 'find directions out.' That could be for a maze, that advice on a young man, couldn't it? Oh, God, how I need direction out, and you cannot give it to me, Holland, or you will not, or not directly. And if your indirections and mine will bring me out, I am a fool and know nothing. I am not going to talk about it any more—or think about it again. She came here willingly, she loved you, you loved her in the end. Then it is her affair and yours. It is not mine."

"My thought entirely," the Earl said with more of his usual manner. "I would like to hold you to it."

Edward caught his father looking at him strangely, again assessingly. He read, he thought, the look and smiled a little. "There is no danger," he said. "I shall never try to use it against you, to try to force you to anything. I could not, I would not try."

"I was not thinking of danger from you to me," the Earl said, his face heavy.

"What then?" the young man asked, looking like a boy as he lay loose in the grass among the flowers, his eyes on his father's face. "Do you want to rape me, too?"

"Yes," the Earl said, "but I am not going to, and by this, you may know that I do *not* always generally do what I want to do. Come, Edward," he said, "the wood and the park will close and we will be locked in, and that would never do." He took him by the hand and pulled him up, and held his hand a moment and then released it. They drove back in the fading falling sunlight, conversation fading between them, and with it, this particular subject to which they never openly referred again.

July drew to a close, the Walcheren Island expedition set sail, directed towards Antwerp, and August held the city in its sweaty hand. Above all things, Edward longed for the mountains at Tyne, beyond the hot moors, and the coolness of the August mornings and evenings he did not find in London. In the end he became very tired, and wished to return to his own home. If social life was so public and so demanding, he would willingly have forgone it, but he was not allowed his choice, either in that, or in any matter, great or small.

"It is time for you to set up a connection, Edward," the Earl said abruptly after breakfast one August morning. His manner was so matter-of-fact, their terrible conversation of two weeks before might not have taken place, but in part it lay behind the Earl's decision.

"I don't wish to, Holland," Edward said. He did not pretend to misunderstand his father. His voice and his face expressed shock, dismay, distaste, and panic.

"Why not?" the Earl said. "Have you gone Methody on me again, or perverted?"

"Neither," Edward said between shamed, set teeth.

"Then you will do as I order you, and you will not refine upon it too much."

The humour of the situation and to him the absurdity of the order suddenly struck Edward, and although he yet blushed, he began to laugh. "Oh, Holland," he said, "please ask something else. Must you order me in this too?"

"I see I must, Edward," his father said, less amused. "And you will refrain from your levity now, about a serious matter that is serious only if it is treated too seriously. But it can be discussed, when not in process."

"I am all ears," Edward said, "and all yours." His father gave him a quick suspicious glance.

"I hope I have not waited too long," was all he said, several meanings behind his words. "You are a virgin still, Edward?"

"Technically," Edward said, his eyes dancing ironically. Trapped into a conversation so embarrassing to him, amusement seemed his only defence. He enjoyed the flush that rose in its turn in the Earl's face. The Earl left his chair, turning his back on his irreverent son, and walked to the door to insure they were not disturbed.

"I assume that means you are," the Earl answered after a moment.

"You would know, Holland. Am I?" His shaft this time produced no effect on the Earl.

"We will assume it, Edward," the Earl said formally. "You are twenty years old. I wish you to change that condition."

"God!" exclaimed Edward, staring miserably at the Earl. He walked the length of the room and back again, while the Earl quietly waited.

"It is not so difficult as you seem to think, or so unpleasant," the Earl observed.

"I have heard that," Edward said briefly. "I am not a baby, Holland. But I am content as I am. Will you not leave me be?"

"No," the Earl said simply, "I will not. I do demand it. You are too old, and you will become too set in your ways." His voice softened a little at Edward's unhappy face. "It would seem to help if you found yourself in love, but it is that that I want you to learn to protect yourself against while you are still young."

"To protect *myself!* Am I to set up a nursery," Edward asked in angry impudence, "before I have a wife?"

"I hope not," the Earl said, unperturbed. "And I would have you learn how to avoid precisely that until you are ready to."

"Like yourself, with me?" Edward asked, wishing to strike his father, and half expecting his father to strike him.

"I did not choose to then," the Earl said briefly, without explanation. "But I knew what I was about. I would like you to."

"Oh, Lord!" said Edward under his breath. He left his father and went by the window, looking out in sudden tearing bitterness of spirit, wishing he might leave the room and a discussion he was so disinclined for, but he did stay, trained by the Earl to obedience, and he did not say the bitter words his tongue might easily have formed. He heard the Earl move within speaking distance, and then he heard his quiet, formal voice.

"This, Edward, is a skill, like any other, and like any other should be learned from someone experienced and expert in it. To present yourself as you are now to a young, gently nurtured girl would be an affront to her, and an embarrassment to you both." He ignored Edward's soft disclamation of any such intentions at the time. "And you may find, once you are in society and now you are out of your self-imposed cloister of books (no cloister for most), that you are more susceptible than you think. But it is an area where the susceptible are lost, and where your head would do well to govern your reins." He again ignored Edward's soft comment. "To let you loose at random could ruin your health and your disposition. If you allow yourself to be entangled with the married women of the *ton*, you may well be lost, more easily than with the discernibly vulgar, for there are many who are a bad and wild lot, despite their birth. The professionals, well chosen, are safer, and easier to leave, for they have rules. Women such as Lady Caroline have none. I will see that you enter on this in the hands of the best, so that you may distinguish thereafter quality among such women, and know what you may expect." He paused and his voice again softened. "I would have you learn how to give pleasure as well as to receive it. I am selfish in many things but not in that. You have pleased me," he said more softly yet, "but with a woman it is not the same. I would have you learn both grace and restraint in this most graceless and unrestrained of pursuits, so that if at some time you should choose to leave either, you may do so to some effect."

He smiled suddenly and warmly into Edward's discomfiture, lessening it somewhat. "I trust you will apply yourself to this task, however distasteful it may now seem to you, and accept instruction at the hands of your teacher. I trust you will prosper in it and become as adept at this skill as you have in the skills of your books."

His eyes grew serious, and he fixed them on a point other than Edward's. "Because I have misbehaved, Edward, and chosen to go into forbidden places, and because I have made a name of myself, does not make my advice less valuable. And though both by your birth and your upbringing at my hands, such actions may seem to you particularly distasteful, or dishonourable, they need not be in your hands. I wish you to learn the art, as well as the skill, before you are hurt or give hurt. In itself it is nothing, it is only the use you put it to."

"Would my mother have agreed with you?" Edward asked sharply and angrily.

"I cannot speak for that sex, only for my own," the Earl answered, "in advice. But Edward, your mother and I gave great pleasure to one another; she did not fear me or find me distasteful. She would have preferred my character different (and I have wished it had been many times since), but not myself. I find no fault in your character, Edward, and I cannot believe it will take hurt in these lessons." He paused, and then he said softly to Edward, as if remembering or quoting, "In getting the dangerous knowledge of the apple, do not forget a child's dream is divine."

With some tact, the Earl, having made the arrangements he considered necessary, discovered business that demanded his presence on his estate in the North. When he returned to London, some weeks later, he saw without having to ask by the withdrawn look of Edward's face and the absence of his clear, forthright gaze, that his education, or his initiation, had in this respect been completed. He made no comment, and he did not speak of it to Edward, or Edward to him. He assumed time would ease Edward's self-consciousness, and in his assumption he was correct. Edward eventually settled into his new habit with the disconcern of practise and assurance. He put it into proportion and used it less frequently, and his merriness and his particular personality, temporarily submerged, returned, though the innocent look to his eyes the Earl had both loved and hated so did not completely. Adult emotions and moods began to pass over his face, and to leave their traces on it.

The Earl sighed, but he did not regret. He considered a child in an adult's body, particularly one so beautiful as Edward's, in an adult world a danger to himself and those around him: in its way as much so as a person as consciously indulgent in vice as himself, and in some ways more because one expected to take no harm there. In course of time he gave Edward the benefit of his experience in length and leaving and exchange, and also in comparative payment, and with that, he considered his duty there finished, and turned to other parts of it.

Edward's own sensations were more complicated. The initial horror and shame of exposing himself to a person he did not know, and particularly a woman, for he had known few women since his mother, to touch and to be touched by her, unnerved him. It affected him worse than a challenge, he faced it more as he would being hanged, with an attempt at courage that left him after his father left him at the courtesan's house. Had he not been actually taken inside, and introduced, his feet would never have taken him in, as his father perceived.

"Keep him here," the Earl said gently to the woman, "until you are certain he will return." He glanced briefly at Edward, whose face, both morose and frightened, and very young, expressed complete betrayal. He had not had to be delivered over bound, but had he not believed his father from experience capable even of that, he would not have walked in of his own accord. For the Earl, outwardly unperturbed, inwardly a little amused and more than a little saddened, a glance was more than enough. He bowed, and withdrew. He had already given Edward his orders, that he was expected for some time to spend his nights entirely there, although he might later spend his days where he chose.

Edward reminded himself of a young ungelded horse brought to mate with a particular mare at Tyne, who had liked the enterprise as little as he did. I will not perform, he thought savagely, I will not. Tyne goes too far. But the Earl had chosen well. He had taken Edward to Harriett Wilson, deservedly famous among the demimonde, wholly experienced, surprisingly well-bred, intelligent and even intellectual through the men she had known, of great warmth and charm and understanding. She had loved the Earl, and when that had passed for him, as it always did, they had remained friends, for she was capable of friendship, as well as passion. She looked now at her farouche, unhappy, unwilling guest thoughtfully, his shamed eyes hidden under his lashes, but she was too wise and too kind to laugh. She sized him up swiftly as one too gentle himself to need gentleness on her part, and then permitted all her considerable charm to shine through, and suggested he sit down.

She had ordered supper to be brought up, but Edward was unable to eat, and he would drink no wine. He looked at her miserably and stiffly, lifting his lashes briefly, unable to answer her mood: "It is no use," he said hopelessly, "why do you bother? Why do you lend yourself to this farce?"

She looked at him, awkwardly poised in her rooms, appraisingly: "I do this for love of your guardian, acushla, otherwise I would not be for such as you, but you are a sweet-looking boy, and I shall not mind. Now tell me your name."

"I don't need to, you know it already."

She kept her eyes on him, and after a moment he muttered inaudibly, "Edward."

She seated herself beside him, dressed as for Almack's, only faintly perfumed, and said sharply, "Your name is Edward? Surely that is not all?" She laughed, thinking of the endlessly long names she had known. "Surely not. I want a name no one else uses for you. Tell me all of yours."

"I am called Edward Clare Armstrong," he said unwillingly, because it seemed he had to.

"I shall call you Clare, 'mon cher Clare,' and for the time here you shall forget that you are an Edward, whoever that person is and whatever that means to you. But you must have strength, cher Clare, for me, and you must eat, and a little wine will make us all happier." She noticed with dismay that he shrank from her, and she said sharply, "Shall I call your guardian back, and have him instruct you in how you must not refuse a lady's requests?" Her eyes softened her words, but he was not looking in them.

He shook his head, believing her, and she was horrified to see the extent of the power of her words, for he did eat a little, unhappily, unwillingly, and he drank the glass of wine that she held for him, taking it from his shaking hand. She saw that until the act he dreaded was accomplished, she could do nothing with him, and so, not delaying, and using the magic phrase she had stumbled upon, she was able to have him exchange his clothes for a dressing gown, while she did the same. She met him in the room and took him in her arms, but though he trembled a little he was as cold and stiffly unyielding as a statue of stone.

"Nom d'un nom," she cried, "must I order you entirely?"

"Yes," he whispered, "I don't know you, I don't love you, I don't want you, and I don't know what to do." He was ready to cry with vexation and shame, and she saw it.

"Poor acushla," she said. "You have been too much ordered, by my friend the Earl, who is a great tyrant in all things, or by someone." She drew him by the hand to her bed, and settled him in it, and then, snuffing out the candles except for her own, she came in from her side and lay near him. "You shall do the ordering here, entirely."

"Then I would order you to leave me alone," he said faintly.

She scolded him for his discourtesy gently. "Then we will leave that part for another night. Is it that you love someone else?" she asked gently.

"Don't ask me that," he cried, anguished. She was glad to see some feeling in him, of any kind.

She kissed him with her honey lips, faintly perfumed, like her breath, but his own lay cold and unresponsive beneath hers, but she was sorry for him, and she did not lose her temper.

"Tonight I must order you then, cher Clare," she said. She skipped out of bed and brought her brandy wine, and poured him a glass, and made him drink it, and then yet another.

"Don't!" he said helplessly, as she would have poured a third. "It won't help, I shall just be sick." She laughed at him then, without any mockery, and her laugh was very charming, a little intimate, a little loving, and entirely gay. Unbelievably, he found himself laughing back, and they lay among her pillows, overcome by the absurdity, laughing until the tears came, and his embarrassment and stiffness was suddenly gone.

"You are old enough to be my mother," he said, more soberly.

"I most certainly am not. You must never tell me or any lady any such remark about our age. It is you who are so very young." They began to laugh again, her kindness warming him, yet he felt no desire to do anything at all. She sensed it, and without warning, blowing out the light, she laid her hand upon him. She heard him gasp, and his limbs stiffen, but resigned now, fearing the Earl, to what he perceived now to be inevitable, if it should prove possible, he did not withdraw from her caressing hands, which held, and then left him, gently exploring, teasing and tantalising, then holding and stroking again.

"I don't want to feel this way," he cried desperately, "I don't like to, I don't want to, please don't make me." Waves of passion and nausea both together swept over him and he shut his eyes, trying to fight the nausea and the disgust at himself and at her. She guided him to her then, and helped him enter, and brought his lips down against her own, hoping nature finally would enter too and instruct him, which it did. He felt desperately sick and he wanted now only to finish what she had forced him to begin, but he could not.

"Be rough," she encouraged him, helping him again, "you cannot hurt me. Fight all the fights you have lost and not won here, you have the sole ordering of affairs here, my dear love, thrust hard as you would against all those you hate or all those who have hurt you."

The warm quivering softness of the place where she had set him intoxicated him, and he needed no further urging to attempt to overmaster her, suddenly herself grown passive, withdrawing back as he now pursued, and then meeting him, involuntarily answering her, falling finally on her belly, exhausted.

III

She left him then to sleep as long as he wished, perceiving what the Earl had not, that he was somehow exhausted of all his resources and whatever his complications, which she already guessed rather well, also just a very tired boy. She was dressed before he, and had had breakfast brought up, when she woke him with a kiss. His eyes flew open, and then shut again quickly, and he instinctively pressed himself away from her, but he had nowhere to go.

"You are very tiresome this morning, cher Clare, but last night in the end you were not tiresome."

His face flamed. "I am sorry to be tiresome. Why don't you just send me away?"

"For the same reason that you do not just go away, cher Clare. Open your eyes, tall little coward, and look at me: will I bite?" He opened his eyes and looked into her eyes, warm and brown and very kind, not very far from his own, wholly tolerant and wholly understanding. He found it impossible to continue to be ashamed in their warm amused gaze, and his own smiled back. "You are very sweet, cher Clare," she said, "that is another reason why I do not send you away."

His eyes swept over her quickly, and then his lashes fell, the picture of her imprinted before them, small, delicate, almost patrician, her hair in dark ringlets swept back, and demure morning frock of sprigged muslin.

She laughed. "I read your thoughts. You think I do not look like what I am. I do not have to. I am known."

"How can you?" he gasped. "You look like a lady?"

She laughed again, a silver laugh like quicksilver, and shrugged her small shoulders, French-style. "It is a living, and it has its moments. This, cher Clare, is one. To take a young man's virginity from him, almost to rape it, is an experience I rarely have now, indeed I may say for the second, that I have never had." She saw his face. "Oh, Clare, forgive me. But why not joke? Is it so serious? Your guardian warned me you might go Methody on me, but they too marry."

"This is not marrying."

She shrugged again. "In the end, it is all one, and all won. Your guardian also warned me you were a great talker."

He flushed. "He talks too much himself." He shut his eyes, as if ostrich-style he could wish her, himself, the entire room away.

"Your breakfast gets cold," she said. "Will you eat if I go away?"

"Is my guardian, is the Earl paying you to do this?" he asked again, opening his eyes again with a sudden thought and fixing them on her.

"Oh, yes, otherwise I would not do it, no matter how sweet you are, cher Clare."

"A great deal? Money?"

"You are not to ask that, Clare, you must not. But I will tell you that I do it for him himself, no amount otherwise could buy it for you at this time."

He sighed, a long deep sigh.

"Come, cher Clare, you are my prisoner today. Is it so bad to be a prisoner of love?"

"Do not call it that," he said turning his face into the pillow, "please."

"Love's guest, then? You are tired, cher Clare. Eat your breakfast and do not go to your lessons, but sleep all day and take your ease."

"I *am* tired. How did you know? I have sometimes felt I would break, I am so tired. I think you are truly kind."

"Perhaps, perhaps not. For some, perhaps yes, and for those connected with some, perhaps."

"What shall I call you? Mrs. Wilson?"

She laughed her stream of silver laughter again. "And you already thinking I am old? Indeed not. Call me anything else you choose;" she took his hand in hers, and felt its limp unresponsiveness and dropped it softly, "—or call me Harriett—or when you feel like this, just *you*."

She pulled his pillows up, and placed his dressing gown about his shoulders, and left him with the tray. He slept again, woke, wondering where he was, remembered, tried to forget, and slept again. Late in the afternoon, her man appeared, and directed a bath to be brought for him. His preceptress conferred with him through the opened door, while he was in it, and suggested if he did not wish to dress, he also have dinner quietly upstairs in the room, alone if he liked, and then appeared beside him, and seated herself, rolling up the sleeves of her dress.

"Go away," he cried, horrified. "You shouldn't be here!"

"Why not?" she said dimpling. "Don't cover yourself. You have nothing to be ashamed of. I always scrub the back of my guests, and then I rub them down. I learned the skill of massage in France. Submit, sir," she said, with mock severity. "You are in my power."

"Oh, God," he said, "and damn your lovely eyes."

She bent quickly and kissed him.

"Take back your oath, sir, or take punishment again."

He looked at her dumbly, and she sighed, and handed him his towel.

"Come out, now, sir," was all she said. To his surprise he found her ministrations pleasant. Made to lie down on the bed, partly covered by the sheet, his head resting on his arms, downwards, he relaxed under the kneading of her small firm hands, more capable and more skilled than they looked. For a moment, he felt a desire to turn and take her in his arms, but she was entirely dressed, and the desire passed, and he fell half-asleep. She covered him and left him. He felt too weary to try to rise or to dress, and there seemed little purpose in it. He was awakened again by the chambermaid, and the footman with his dinner. He ate, served in bed, the food then disappeared as miraculously as it had appeared. He began to feel almost as if he were in a fairytale like those his Uncle used to read him. The light of the falling sun fell in gold showers of diffused light in his room—like Danaë, he thought. He wondered what would appear if he clapped his hands, and wondering, fell again asleep.

It was dark when he woke again, and he discovered this time he was not alone.

"How long have you been here?" he exclaimed, dismayed.

"Some time. Not long." She waited, as if wondering what he would do, but he did nothing. She sensed, though he did not move, that he had become very tense again, and that they were no forwarder, or did not seem to be so.

She moved herself against him, and felt him withdraw.

"Please, no."

"Please, yes."

"I cannot."

"Anyone can. Even you. Especially you."

"I am awkward, and clumsy, and I cannot hold myself. Oh, God, girl, can't you see? You humiliate me, I don't know how or what I'm doing."

"Then I will show you, and I will tell you. Give me your hand." Laughing a little, beginning with their faces, and proceeding gently downwards, first with his hand on herself, and then with his hand under hers on his own body, she proceeded to give him instruction in anatomy, its functions and the nature of each part. She kissed each part gently on his body as she named it with her lips or with her fingertips, and in the end, felt him swell beneath her. He shivered, and she took pity on his distress, and helped him to her and a quick relief, repeating much the same words she had the first night.

The darkness hid them. They slept, and he woke and found her still in his arms and made love again almost angrily, this time at his own instigation, pouring out all his angers and his frustrations into her willing self, hammering away at her in increasing violence to which she responded in equal measure to restrain him somewhat, rejoicing inwardly the third time to see him somewhat direct her as he wished.

My poor cowed boy, she thought, holding him to her, held herself in his rough embrace, you are waking up to the world, and that you do not need to be.

"You lovely boy," she said aloud.

"No," he said, his face in her breasts, "don't call me that."

"My fierce Clare, then," she said laughing, pulling him to her, but laughing a little himself, he evaded her, and slipped his head and mouth down to her belly. "You are a very sensual person, Clare, after all. I began to think you were not."

"I know I am," he said, his lips pressed against her. "I have known it for a long time."

"Then why try to hide it?" she said quietly. "Do you think it a sin to feel so?"

He shook his head, not answering.

"Are you afraid you will hurt me?" He nodded, his head still against her belly. "I am very tough, and much used to this. Do not be afraid. Do as you like, whatever you like." He took her in his arms, in the dark, unable to see her, exploring her with his mouth and his hands, surprising her both by his gentleness and his roughness, until she felt as if she were a map in his hands he had gotten by heart.

"Enough," she said finally, "all or no more. One way or the other, be quiet and be easy."

"All, then," she heard him say. She was tired now and she made no move to help him, but he found her, as relaxed as a wave of water, floating with him.

"You are a lovely woman," he said, "and fit for a prince, and you let me do this, a stranger, when I do not love you."

"Yes," she said simply and drowsily, "but you are less fat, cher Clare. It is a sweet interlude. And it is easier without love. Love only confuses. I am not to teach you love, only passion's skill and entertainment. Serious boy, you need some entertainment, and some rest."

"Oh God," he said from his heart, "how I do."

"Is it not pleasant to take relief with someone one does not know after all, cher Clare?"

"Unbelievably restful," he said, "unbelievably sweet, my dear. How patient you have been with one so gauche and unrewarding."

"Gauche, yes, unrewarding, no," she murmured. "And do you think after all it is so hard a fate to have to love a woman?"

"Not hard at all," he murmured, "but then, it is yourself."

When they woke again, the sun had filled the room with light. He stirred and sat up and looked at the woman he had known in the dark, a desire to see her for the first time taking hold of him, and he pulled the cover back. She stretched and smiled, her eyes closed, and lay before him without shame, and let him explore her entirely with his eyes and then his lips and then his fingers. She opened her eyes then, and looked up at him laughing, and the world dissolved about him.

"I don't love you," he said, plunging upon her, "not at all."

"Thank God for that, cher Clare," she said, "nor do I you—it would do you no good if you did, or if I did."

He kept her there all morning, and she let him keep her, until finally she protested she would faint if she had no breakfast. She let her breakfast that once be brought to their rooms, and they ate then, and played again, and spent the afternoon in discovering, she teaching him little, letting him explore and learn for himself. When she bathed him, he pulled her in, laughing, and when she massaged him afterwards, he took her in his arms and pulled her beneath him and the sheet. But wiser than he, she made him take her down to dinner, dressed and suddenly strange, so that her abandon to him that night was the more exciting and the more sweet.

The next day, she sent him out to his lessons, and to his house to see his mail, and to have dinner away, but she was waiting for him in his bed when he returned. He came quickly to her, eager now, and impatient, taking her lips even before he took his coat, holding her against him.

"Your skin is soft," he murmured, "like silk."

"A sattinback, no more," she said contentedy. "You are not becoming serious, I hope, cher Clare. I have warned you it will not do."

"No," he murmured, "I am not. It is another girl I think I love."

"Love is a shield and a protection. Does your guardian know?"

"No. Don't tell him. I have not met her."

She laughed a trill of laughter, but she did not explain at all, and after a minute, she could not, in the passion of his lips. She pushed him away.

"You are well-advanced now, sir, in the lesson of impetuousness and hot-headedness. We must school you in restraint and consideration."

"Not yet," he said, seeking her lips again. "Not quite yet." He held her determinedly, and she relaxed in his arms, wondering what he would do, and how he would manage, but she found he managed easily.

"O, the fierce Scotch with their claymores," she murmured.

"I am not Scotch," he said.

"You have a Scotch name."

"Well," he said, "let it be." He kissed her, and then he sat up on his elbows, resting, his mind again at work. "It is an interesting name, though. A man named Fairbairn—"

"Like you," she murmured, "a fair child."

"—saw his king fall in battle, his horse wounded from under him, and he reached out his strong arm and rehorsed him, and was renamed Armstrong."

"A pretty story."

"Very pretty, and it may not be true. An Armstrong's ancestor marched to defeat Macbeth, they say. Their motto is 'Invictus maneo— I remain unconquered.'" He smiled a little at her. "That should show you I am no true Armstrong. But it is true for them, I suppose. They did not fight in the '45; besides being Lowland Scots, their strength had already been broken by James V who took their chief by treachery, meeting him like a king himself in full regalia, and hung him and thirty-four of his best men, on living trees, and left that new fruit hanging there, but the name itself survives. They were a very warlike Border clan, some three thousand strong at one time." He paused. "If they were a Border tribe, I wonder if they made acquaintance with the Earl's relations, I must ask him someday. It is a name to be proud of, and a name to conjure with. Do you know the ballad 'Johnnie Armstrong?'"

"No," she said, "but I know you speak of it as if it were not your name."

"But it is," he said, stopping her mouth in the most convenient way.

"How do you know so much?"

He flashed her his quick smile, in which affection and distress mixed, without mirth.

"Ross told me."

"Ross?"

"My—guardian's groom. He is a Highland Scot. We were caught once in a sudden storm of snow and sleet when he was returning me to Tyne one Christmas. The fell was one sheet of white, and the roads were like glass, and they were completely filled with snow. It was piercingly cold, like needles. I was frightened, but Ross was not; he is very skilful, the horses did not once slip with him, but finally we did stick fast. The axletree had snapped in the cold. He told me stories about the Armstrongs to stiffen me and make me ashamed."

"And did they?"

"I don't remember now," he said wearily. "Tyne heard himself about the storm, and sent a guide to fetch us out, and so we didn't freeze to death after all. The stiffening went for nothing. Or almost nothing."

"Lord Tyne must have been glad to see you."

"I didn't see him. I don't know." His mouth stiffened, remembering against his will how they had driven past the front of the house, its windows ablaze with lights, its doors open and welcoming, but not for him. Four years later it still had power to hurt. Boys from the village had been brought in, and with fur caps and mittens were holding branches of candelabra aloft to light the way of the Christmas guests who were arriving and descending from their coaches. He could hear music; and voices, and laughter, and he caught a glimpse of the Earl in an olive-green satin coat and cream embroidered waistcoat. Then they had past, and it was for him the scullery outside the busy kitchen preparing for the late supper that would be served. Ross saw that he had a hot tub of water for his cold feet, and a bowl of hot soup, and then he motioned to him to dry his feet and come.

"No," he had cried, "my guardian surely does not mean for it now, he sent for us. Ask him, surely he does not." He had been very young, not seventeen.

"Come, Edward," was all Ross said. "Your uncle is busy now, he is occupied, I cannot speak to him, and you know very well he does mean it, as well as I. He has no place now for you, there is no place set for you here."

"No," Edward had said desperately, and watched Ross take off his scarf, and advance upon him—and then in fear, "What are you going to do?"

"Take you down, with no fuss," Ross had said, and had bound his mouth as he spoke, and lifted him over a shoulder, his arm holding him fast in a vise, handling his weight without effort. He had unlocked the door in the passage, and taken back his scarf, and left him there on his bed in the dark, to sob in rage and humiliation and grief, the recent cold and fright and relief intensifying his present emotion and bereavement.

"Cher Clare, what is the matter?" he heard Harriett ask, her voice concerned and tender. He pulled himself back with an effort.

"Hold me, Harriett," he whispered "I was remembering something I would rather forget. Hold me, don't let me go."

"Is this my invincible Scotch conqueror?" she asked, attempting unsuccessfully to lighten his sudden changed mood.

"Never a conqueror. I do not want to be, I could not be. People who have power conquer whom they wish and then they sentimentalize over them. It happened with Culloden—look at Scott, look at the girls in their Tartan frocks, look at Mrs. Jordan singing 'Hieland Laddie' for the Duke of Clarence. They destroy a way of life, and a language, and the strong fighting men, and then I daresay if things continue as they point, the Prince of Wales will teach his daughter Charlotte the Highland Fling, and will go up in a new clan outfit to Edinburgh, and he is the nephew of the Butcher."

He smiled briefly. "I am one of the conquered. Tyne now sentimentalizes over me, he mistakes to do it."

"Must you be?" Her voice was entirely sympathetic, and honestly questioning.

"I don't know." He paused, and then he said, "There is nothing really sentimental about me. But I have grown to love my captor and my captivity. That is the worst of all. The poor 'broken' clan of Armstrong after that James in power finished with it could be not more broken than that." There was nothing she knew to say to him.

"May I take you out to dinner, or to the theatre?" he asked her the next day.

"You do not mind being seen with me? I am, as I said, well known."

"Why should I mind? It is you who might mind being seen with me. Will you come?"

"I cannot, Clare, I dare not. It is August, and my patron is at Brighton, otherwise I could not have taken you on. I should otherwise be glad to be seen with you, but now it would not be politick."

"Does it make any difference, here like this in private or in my box at the Haymarket in public?" he asked, surprised and taken aback.

"It makes all the difference in the world. You would be challenged, and he would kill you, or have you killed."

"Lord!" he exclaimed. "Does the Earl know this?"

"But of course. But if we are not seen in public places, my patron will not care. I know him well and of old."

"I am more content here. I asked only to please you. I perceive more and more my fortune."

They grew very attached, without loving one another, and in the end she had taught him all her arts, and many of her secrets, about the changing nature of women and the outward signs of their natural heat, and finally, how to arouse her, or one more innocent than she.

"Do not misuse this knowledge, cher Clare," she said, half teasing, half serious, "or you will make women afraid to get in carriages with you. I could be half in love with you myself, were I younger, and more free."

"Could you?" he asked, turning. "I am more than honoured, I am flattered. I shall remember always your kind words."

"They are not kind, cher Clare, only true." He kissed her, his lips sad.

"You have ruined my peace, Harriett. I shall never be quite the same again. My guardian insists I go to Brighton and to Bristol with him tomorrow. Will I see you again when I return?"

"I do not know when you return, Clare, that will determine it. When you return, send me a note, we will see. If it is possible, yes, my dear."

The Earl had received an invitation to a summer's entertainment given by the Prince of Wales at the Pavilion in Brighton, and he had determined to try out his candidate there, before the town filled again in Autumn. They drove down to the sea, which Edward enjoyed seeing again for the first time since he was twelve. He preferred the sea to the great Pavilion with its classical Rotunda, also by the architect Holland, or to the designs for the new one that looked like an inflated, overly ballooned Taj Mahal, but he kept his opinions both of that and of the Prince to himself. He also met the Prince's friend, George Brummell, to whom the Earl introduced him only briefly, taking him quickly on.

The Earl smiled. "I refused the fence after all."

"I thought him a simple and a sensible man," Edward said.

"Yes, but it is what he thinks of you that counts," the Earl said, "and I did not risk it, but he knows you are here."

Edward made a gesture of impatience. "And suppose I address the Prince of Wales incorrectly—he is the fat florid man with the blue ribbon and the diamond star?" ("Slightly overdressed, despite Brummell," the Earl interpolated, his voice a murmur) "—or spill a cup of tea on my nankeen breeches, or on a lady's muslin lap, what then? Do I fail? Am I sent away?"

"Hush, Edward, keep your face light. There is no more important man in England than Brummell, he has the Prince's ear entirely. His courtesy is misleading, he could be thinking anything. If he accepts you, your position is at once assured, among these people."

"And if he does not?"

"You will be accepted anyway, because I am your patron, but with his support it will be easier and more amusing. The Yellow Room is overdone, but interesting, and you should see it, particularly the inlays." The tone of the Earl's voice had not changed, but his hand pressed Edward's warningly.

"I think we have not been properly introduced," a voice said at their elbow. Edward turned and saw the man of their discussion had approached them. "We were interrupted, were we not? It is Edward Clare Armstrong?" he asked with a slight questioning, quickening inflection. He offered an arm, extricated Edward deftly, not including the Earl with equal deftness, and walked with Edward towards the long windows that opened onto the terraces behind. The Earl watched them go with a faint smile. If he was at all disturbed, or even concerned, he did not show it.

"It is all the conversation among us," Brummell's companion said, "and I daresay the Beau has gone to *find out* the mystery, who your protégé is—whose son, I mean—yours, Florizel's, York's, or Armstrong's after all. There have already been several bets placed on it in the book at White's."

"When I wish you to know," the Earl said unperturbed, lightly affixing one delicately pointed finger against his shoulder, "I will tell you. Until I do, I would not lose overmuch sleep or money over it, but you will of course do as you like."

When they returned, Edward's face was alive with good humour.

"What did he say to you, or ask you?" the Earl enquired curiously.

"He asked me if I had been also to Cambridge. I said I hadn't. He told me an amusing story about a young peer who went to Cambridge the same year I went up to Oxford, and who kept a bear in a tower near his rooms after the authorities would not let him keep his dog because he said there was no rule about bears on the books."

"Hum," said the Earl. "Did the bear receive an M.A. too?"

"No," said Edward, his schooled mouth breaking again into an unschooled grin, "it hugged his tutor on the stairs and was rusticated."

"Hum," said the Earl again. "What else did he ask you?"

"He asked me if we also kept bears in our rooms at Oxford, and I said no, only horses occasionally. It wasn't very witty, but he seemed to think so. He told me he heard I had taken a First after four years and on examination, and that this same young peer had received his M.A. after less than two years with no examination, and he wondered if I would rather have been a peer at Cambridge than a commoner at Oxford."

"And what did you reply?"

"I said I was content."

"And what did he say to that?"

"Nothing. He laughed. He asked me if the Fellows and peers at Oxford also wore gowns of coloured silk. He had attended a function at Cambridge where he said they looked like a garden of sweet-smelling peas, though the scent was less pleasant: purple, white, green, and rose colour all together. He told me then that he himself had been at Oxford for a time and in the army, and that he a little envied me a scholar's life. He looked almost a little sad. But then he said I seemed to have left that too. Holland, do your friends talk of nothing but each other? This man knew much too much about me already, I thought."

"Very little," the Earl answered, "but when everyone who matters can be with a little difficulty packed together into one room, you can see, I think, how that might come about."

"I did not altogether like it," Edward said.

"I hope you did not show it."

"No, I liked him. Who could not?"

"Even if you had not, I hope you would not have displayed your feelings. Did he approve your coat? I think you look rather well myself."

"He asked me who had taught me to dress, and said I should look at a book he was writing. I told him you."

"Hum," said the Earl.

" 'We are good friends, despite our disparate ages,' he said. 'I have taught Noel much, and learned some.' "

"Hum," said the Earl. "You did indeed talk."

"I found him very unaffected and agreeable."

"Because he wished to be," the Earl interpolated.

"Not entirely. He told me the Cambridge peer had published a book of bad verse and had gone in July to the Levant on his Grand Tour, or he would have introduced me, for he said we should meet, since he had a limp like yours and seemed to wish to excel your reputation." He looked anxiously at the Earl whose face registered no expression at all. "He took me then to introduce me to our host, who he said was nearer your age, and we said very little, and then he brought me here, that's all."

"It is enough," the Earl said. "He appears to like children as a novelty. He is closer to your generation actually than to mine. Come in to the next room, now there is dancing. What did you think of the Regent-to-be?" he added, smiling.

"I could not read him. He was affable, but then he introduced whatever subject he chose, discussed it just so long as he chose, and dropped it when he chose."

"For you who like to talk, I daresay that was a frustration."

"Not really."

While Edward took his place, the Earl stood to one side, by himself but not looking alone, watching the skill with which Edward made his way across the assembly room.

One never knew, he observed rather sadly, what one had until one saw them among other persons. The strange maturity and assurance that Edward had had when he first came to him, to his house, and which for a time he seemed almost to have lost, had flowered in the young man into a startling and winning combination of aloofness that his face with its expressive eyes and mouth contradicted, and of true courtesy. It made for an appearance of both ease and mystery. His naivety, instead of appearing gauche in him, appeared as interested friendliness. He was both unobtrusive and conspicuous in the crowded room, and the Earl found him more charming than at Christmas, watching him bow and bend in the ceaseless flowing and interweaving of the dance beneath the framework of gold lattice and falling flowers, within the circle of the temporary fountains and the festal music. Watching him, he felt none of his usual faint envy for an entertainment he could not participate in. The faint air of hesitant withdrawal that he had not noticed before, combined with the skills the Earl had forced upon him, and his striking colouring, the Earl found arresting, as he noticed others also did. He wondered if Edward was unaware of the eyes and the quizzing glasses turned upon him, following them, or skilled enough and inwardly well enough poised to be able to ignore them so completely.

He was not startled by the voice of the gentleman who had walked up beside him. "Unaffected, quite charming. Where have you been keeping him, Noel?" Brummell remarked to the Earl.

"In my cellars," the Earl replied truthfully, "to age like a good wine."

Brummell smiled at the witticism and remarked, "Someday you must really tell me, Noel, between friends."

The Earl lifted his own glass, as if to observe a group of persons seated, and did not make occasion for answer, immediately, and when he did, he had changed the subject.

IV

The Earl returned with Edward to London the next morning, deciding to omit Bristol, Edward remarking to him, "You remind me of Hannibal in your tactics, Holland."

"How so?" answered the Earl.

"You hit and run. But in the end, Holland, although he nearly took Rome, he did not."

"Why not?"

"The fault was not with him, but with his reinforcements."

"Well, Edward," the Earl said, "in your first engagement of the Summer you have done well: for you, for me, for us both. What can I do for you?"

Edward turned his face towards the landscape jolting by. "Afford again Harriett Wilson for me," he said in a low voice, "if her patron is not returned."

"He is not," the Earl answered briefly. "You have not fallen in love with her, Edward? That would be disastrous."

"No," Edward said. "I have not. I don't know how long you have paid for the arrangement to stand."

"It may stand as long as you wish it, Edward, but I do not want you to grow too attached. There are others much lovelier, but none so humanly kind. If events do not fall so naturally, I shall have before long to insist on some variety."

"I shall not grow too attached," Edward said, not answering the rest of the Earl's remark.

"I did not expect you, not so soon," she said, when she had received his note and sent a return by the footman who brought it.

"You are my only relief," he said. "I want to forget myself," he said, "and I know no other way to do it." He held her so tightly, her sides felt bruised and breathless.

"You are not here for instruction, cher Clare?"

"No," he said, his lips on hers. "I am not. Do you mind?" She answered with her arms and her mouth, and he carried her without ceremony to her bed, and took her. Afterwards, they had dinner, and settled down more comfortably in her bed, in one another's arms.

"I am in a position that is unbearable to me, Harriett," he said, holding her to him, "and I cannot leave it or do anything about it."

"Pauvre Clare," she said, kissing him, "did you stumble in the *danse,* or drop a glass, or become too serious? Are you disgraced?"

"Do you really think so?" he asked. She shook her head. "No, I am already a little what my guardian calls a '*succès fou,*' but I do not like it, it is not how I am meant to be. I do not know where it will all lead. But I cannot leave it until February, March really, that is nearly six months before me. It has just begun."

"What do you want to do, cher Clare?" she asked. He did not answer, but buried his mouth against hers, and his hurt heart against hers. "Do you not enjoy the parties and the theatres and the dances?" she asked, when she could speak.

"I do. That is the worst of it. I do, just as I enjoy you. But I am destroying myself with it, as I am with you. I already cannot help myself with you, and soon I will not with the other."

"You are just young to the world, cher Clare, you will find after you have been with it for a while, that you can take it or leave it, equally, as you will be able to take or to leave me. It is important to learn how *not* to have things, Clare. Have you not learned it?"

"No. I have been forced not to have things, many times, but that is not what you mean."

"No. Not at all. The control comes from within, not without. You will think it amusing for me to say this."

"No." He shook his head. "Not at all. I do not see how I am to learn it. I don't even wish to, at all, tonight."

"Please do not," she murmured. "That would be such a waste. You are so serious tonight, Clare, can we not laugh?"

"No," he said, "I am too unhappy to laugh."

"That is the time to laugh," she said. "But never mind. Is it that you want to play roughly with me?"

"Yes," he said, "I do. I cannot anywhere else. Even boxing is a mannered game. I am weary of manners, Harriett."

"Be rough, then, fierce Clare," she said, "I will match you in this fight, and we will have no manners at all."

She felt him finally sigh with weariness and relief, and fall asleep. In the morning, he felt better, and he was able to laugh, at the world and at himself. He returned, to find his father just up, and sitting down to breakfast. He joined him, for a roll, but the Earl would not let him have coffee.

"If you need coffee to stay awake," he said, "go up and sleep. You have been out all night?"

"Yes," Edward said, his eyes on his roll. "I have just come home. I am not tired, I do not need the coffee."

"You do not look tired," the Earl observed. "You must have also slept well."

"I did," Edward said, his eyes on his plate, pulling the roll in little pieces.

"You mustn't fidget your food, it betrays your feelings, which you do not want to do."

"Why not?" asked Edward. "If I have them, why must I hide them?"

"Why indeed," the Earl surprisingly agreed. "I am used to doing it myself, but in the end, why should one? My century has passed. I am in another now. But I myself and those my age do still think it tidier if one does." A silence fell between them. "What is it you are doing?" he asked irritably. "What ails you?" suddenly observing an unusual stiffness in Edward's face and demeanour.

"I am practising obedience," Edward said, his face crumbling into a smile, breaking apart like his roll.

"Well, don't any more. You unnerve me."

"Shall I go?"

"No," the Earl said, "no, don't go. Stay and talk to me."

"What shall I talk about? What would be suitable?"

"Anything at all. There is no one else here. It need not be suitable, just let it be bearable."

"I would like to ask a question, Holland, but it may not be bearable."

"Ask. You can do that. If it isn't, I will not answer."

"When were you born, Holland? Or should I not ask? I cannot tell how old you are at all."

"I was born in 1757. A midpoint. You may figure the rest yourself. The city gates still stood when I was born. I remember my nurse walking me —wheeling, I should say," with a glance at his foot, "through Moorgate before it was pulled down. When I was seven, I heard Mozart play the harpsichord and the organ and his sister Nannerl sing at Ranelagh Gardens. He was only eight, his feet hung down from the bench and did not reach the ground. And I cried, Edward, and wished with all my heart, for I had a heart still then, that he might never stop and that I might play as he did. But it was years before I had power to do as I wished. My nurse slapped me then for crying in public."

"How many people you could have known I would like to have known."

"Perhaps I did. I went around. Who did you have in mind?"

"You will be angry with me."

"Perhaps, perhaps not. I feel beneficent. Who?"

"I was thinking that if you had wished, you could have heard Wesley, and George Whitefield preach." He lowered his eyes, suddenly unable to watch disapproval, anger even, spring into his father's. How stupid, he thought, always, always to have to guard one's tongue, and never, never to be able to say what one thinks or ask what one really wants to know, or to talk about what interests one.

"Are you so afraid of me as this? Have I really deserved for you to be?" His father's voice struck on his ears surprisingly gentle in tone. "Is my disapproval of such matter to you?"

"Yes," Edward said in a low voice, "yes, it is. Too much, I know." He felt his father's hand take him beneath his chin, and tilt his head up, and for a moment he met his eyes, and then he shut them. Of all things on earth, he found he did not wish a scene, and did not wish to provoke one. He wished he had not tried to talk.

"Well," said the Earl, with a sigh. "One thinks one wants something, and then when one gets it, one finds one is no happier for it and that one wants something else after all, as my friend Fox said once." He did not explain himself. "It is no great matter. Yes, I heard him once. Whitefield, I mean."

"You did?" asked Edward, in surprise, his interest quickening. "What was he like, when you heard him?"

"A large, cross-eyed man, most enthusiastic in his language, and unrestrained. Vulgar, I thought, but all the same powerful, if one was susceptible to such things. He had left the green fields, and was very comfortably established in the Chapel of Lady Huntingdon as part of her Connexion. I was all of twelve, but well advanced, after my first term at Eton. I was pleased to learn from him that grace, if unmerited by me, and I did not feel at all elected to receive it, could not be won by me with good works. I resigned myself with no sadness to continue as I was, unless seized suddenly away, as I never have been."

"Have you not?" asked Edward, thinking of the Earl's many kindnesses to him.

"No. I have never done anything I did not myself wish to."

"Did you ever hear Wesley himself?"

"No, I never did, but I saw him once, riding towards the North on his horse, with his rein slack, reading, as I was driving by. I called to him from my curricle, I was twenty, or so, a young Blood, and said, 'Your rein is loose,' and he lifted his eyes from his book, which of all things I could see was a book by Sterne, that one called *A Sentimental Journey*, whatever that word means, and said, 'Friend, I always ride with a slack rein. I have learned that way my horse will never stumble. You should try the same.' But I never have, in anything."

"No, I think you haven't, Holland," Edward said, agreeing but without bitterness. The Earl glanced at him, and seemed about to answer, but then he continued his story.

"I did not know at that time who he was, but when I spoke of the incident at the Inn, that night, the Innkeeper enlightened me, and told me how many thousands of miles, I forget now how many—250,000?— that man had travelled with his slack rein and his open book without a stumble. Or any disaster. He must have seen and known this country as few have, before him or since, but he did not choose to use what he saw in a way understandable to me. That was after I heard Whitefield, of course. Myself, I would not compare the two men. Wesley's face and voice were those of a gentleman." He paused, considering and remembering. His eyes surveyed the effects of his words on Edward, perceiving it not excessive, and then reverted, looking back into the past. "I could have heard him preach. I saw him once again in a field, with several thousand people gathered in a crowd about him. I was in a carriage with a lady, known for her very pretty laugh and knowing of it herself. We had several of us come to the Common because Selwyn wanted to see a highwayman hanged, I forget which one—a gentleman as we called them of the High Toby—but he was expected to make an amusing end with some panache to it. Do I sicken you, Edward?"

"Yes," Edward said, his teeth set.

"I find I value your opinion, Edward, after all. I do not, and did not, find such spectacles amusing myself. I let Selwyn's crowd go to that end of the Common without me, we were early for it, anyway, to have good places, and the lady and I stayed by ourselves, although I could see the little figures moving, and the final dance. I could not help that. It does draw the eye, even as it sickens. After a time, after the lady and I had finished our personal business inside the carriage, I noticed the crowd moving away from the dangling figures, and congregating again in a different place on the Common. We drove, after a time, nearer to see what the new attraction was, and it was Wesley, who had come to give comfort to the several men who had to die, and had stayed to preach, since some members of the crowd seemed inclined to hear him. By the time we reached the place, the crowd had grown. We stopped out of curiosity, near the edge of the crowd, but we were too far away to hear clearly what he said, and I did not leave the carriage or press nearer. The lady was amused, I less so. One wag had come with a dozen rotten eggs in his satin pockets to throw at the speaker, but a friend coming up, not knowing his plans, clapped him with his hands on both pockets in a familiar friendly gesture such as wags use with one another, and liberally perfumed him and his clothes and the surrounding air. When that happened, we withdrew."

Edward made no comment on the Earl's little story, with its implications and its several aspects. He was silent, thinking.

"That was my age, when I was your age, Edward, but you can yet see a hanging in the streets by Newgate if you wish to."

"I do not," Edward said, "you know I do not. And I do not need to."

The Earl glanced at him quickly, but he did not comment, for Edward's face invited none.

"It happens. It is part of our world. One cannot ignore what one does not enjoy entirely. Sometimes a stand must be taken. I have myself, in the House, against the hanging of children, and transporting them to the mills, but to not much effect."

"You sound like Alleyn now?"

"Do I? God forbid. Let me be light again. But you see, surprisingly, even a Tory, and such as I, and Wesley may sometimes touch a common ground."

"Wesley believes, like Arminius, that election does not seize one," Edward said quietly. "One may resist it knowingly, or having had it, fall again away from it. Did you know that, Holland?"

The Earl looked at Edward sharply. "I have never paid overmuch attention to the arguments and the squabbling of churchmen. Are you presuming to lecture me?"

"No," Edward said, "God forbid I ever should."

"What then?"

Edward shook his head. "I was thinking of myself." He turned his head and stared out of the window bleakly.

"It is a fault with these enthusiasts," the Earl said sharply, "that they overtrouble and unbalance the mind, and make unnecessary sadness. I will not tolerate or be around sadness, or disturbance."

The boy seemed to shake himself, visibly, mentally, out of the despair that had seized him. "When you saw Wesley, they did not still throw things at him, did they?"

"No, not often, I think. The time of dead cats and bad eggs and rocks and mud and mob-pulling (and impressment threats) had largely past, they were then a part of the scene, very much one. The crowd I saw was wholly under the spell of his words, and would have been more likely to have thrown a cat at me, Edward. But they both—Wesley and Whitefield—had personal courage in the face of personal danger. I admired that. No one could have shown more—in the days when it was greatly needed. It is less spectacular now, and less documented. A younger son defies the disapproval of his family and loses their support and does not complain; a young boy with no friends to help him stands up to a vicious-natured older man whose character includes no mercy for saints."

"Not very well," Edward said in a low voice, more to himself than aloud. "I would not say so."

"I would," the Earl said firmly. He looked at Edward, his rare kindness visibly spread over his face, its heaviness smoothing out the roughness of his features, into an expression that never failed to melt Edward entirely when he saw it.

"I am unengaged today, Edward, I have no plans and no demands. Shall we spend it together? I have not seen you quietly for some time." For a moment he thought to ignore the frightened look that rose in Edward's eyes, but then he said directly, with the unembarrassed ease that so astonished Edward, "Do not leap to dramatic conclusions, Edward. They are not warranted. I thought we might enjoy London by ourselves. You have seen only the surface, and a limited part. As your guardian, shall I show you the Town?"

"Oh, yes, Holland," Edward said, his face relaxing and a quiet happiness dawning in it, "I should like that very much."

"Where shall we go, then? Where shall I take you? Have you any especial place you'd like to see?"

"Yes, Holland, I do, but you may not want to take me."

"And where is that? Where I seduced your mother? I thought we had had that."

"No, Holland," the boy said, the happiness draining, his eyes lowered, wondering why his father, for all his aversion to emotion, seemed to enjoy causing his own and pricking his joys.

"Where then? What worse place?"

"I would like to go to Moorfields."

The Earl began to laugh. "I should have guessed. He is not still there, Edward, he is dead, you know."

Edward's bent face flushed. "I do not find you amusing, Holland. If you read me like a book, as you say, and if you want me to go with you, why must you torment me?"

"Why, indeed," the Earl murmured. He took himself in hand, and exerted himself to be agreeable, for at that moment it happened to be and really was his desire to be so.

"You have not been, Edward, not even passing through?" Edward shook his head, his face still wary. "You will be surprised."

"Why?"

"At the variety," the Earl said smiling slightly. "We will have the horses saddled, I think, and ride out."

"Moorfields," the Earl said, riding slowly, and near Edward, "was a fen, a kind of March, or moor, that was drained, almost three hundred years ago. It has had walks for two hundred years, but the buildings have not been here so long, only since Charles II. Are you surprised? History interests me. It is much built up, since Wesley was here, but much that you will see was here then too. There used to be acres of wet sheets bleaching, one had to pick one's way carefully."

"Sheets?" asked Edward puzzled.

The Earl smiled a little and did not answer directly. "Avert your eyes, Edward," he said. "That soldier is just taking his ease by the wall and conveniently relieving himself. We are all men. The last time I saw that, a challenge and a duel followed, for a nearer gentleman passing had a lady with him." He reverted to his former subject. "Acres of sheets, literally. A very busy place. Laundresses washed, and troops mustered. Wesley, did you know, took over the old Foundry that was abandoned, for a church. The butchers fought the weavers, the weavers the butchers, here. Your men liked violent places. They also preached on Kennington Common, where please let's not go today, since it is in an opposite part of town, and I have already told you a story about it. I think we have at last removed the gallows there, but they could have seen Jemmy Dawson (he was a young student, Edward, your age) and the rebellionists hurdled out, hanged and quartered there, stripped of their hose and breeches as they hung, cut down carefully not quite half-dead and stripped entirely then, and stacked like so many naked logs by the fire for the rest of that ceremony; and they could have seen William Gibson, the highwayman, merely hanged. I could have seen Jerry Abershawe— in fact, I may have—famous rogue of the High Toby, hung, but watching men strangle has never amused me, as I told you." He looked at Edward, his eyes glinting provocatively. "If the sermons bored your Methody's audience, he did not need to practise patience, he could watch some poor devil making his way to the Hell he was hearing about, and showing a different Falling Sickness and agony of Sudden Grace and cries in earnest and shouts of a different sort. It was a double bill—I am not surprised they had large audiences. How could a church compare?"

"God, Holland," said Edward, shocked and fascinated, "you have seen more, and known more, than I hope I ever shall. Or than I want to. Why a fire?" he asked, despite himself.

"For the bowels and the heart," the Earl said briefly. "The heads went on spikes in Fleet at Temple Bar, or equally appropriate places."

Edward looked at the Earl, a question he could not ask in his eyes, that the Earl read and answered briefly: "His rank should protect him from part of that, even were he so foolish." He left the subject quickly. "I prefer Moorfields. They have bookstalls over there, under those trees. Shall we look in? One sometimes finds rare things, if one knows what to look for."

They had approached the Swan and Hoop livery-stables, near the Riding School, and the Earl dismounted.

"I am going to have Keats keep our horses while we browse the books," he said. But a man he did not recognise came to the door of the stables.

"Who are you?" the Earl asked in surprise. "Where is Jennings and where is Keats?"

"Jones, sir, I come with Rawlings. They beant here, either of them."

"Well, where are they gone?" the Earl asked impatiently. "When will they be back?"

"Won't be back, sir. Dead, sir, the both. Keats now took a fall from a horse these three years, could be going four, and Mr. Jennings died in his bed the year after, and Mr. Rawlings and the lady be both gone too. Be just me here the now."

"Do you know where the boy is now? What happened to the boy?" the Earl asked, having listened in some patience to that history.

"Happen he is in school, happen not. I am not knowing or keeping up with a feisty scrapping fister."

"I think we will walk our horses with us after all, Edward," the Earl said to Edward, dropping a small tip in the man's hand. "This man's memory is not good."

"Happen I have an address for the little boy," the man said. "If the gentlemen wait, I will look." He came back after a time with a dirty scrap of paper. "It is Mrs. Jennings' address. She wuz his mother's mother. She took the wisty little scrapper with her and left. But I hear she's sick. Look you! Don't bother her if she owes you money now."

"I will not bother her," the Earl said, leaving a larger bill in his out-stretched hand. "For your trouble." The man grinned and touched his forehead with it.

"Rogue," said the Earl. "Thomas Keats was another sort. Some Welsh there, I think, somewhere. It showed in the looks of the child. Thickset and stocky, dark, rather large mouth, beautiful eyes. I would have liked you to see him. I would not have described him as this man did. He used to make a rhyme to the last word I would say, impudently, with no effort, and throw back his head and laugh. I have not been here for some years, he was hardly nine then. An unusual child, John Keats," he said, walking with his stick with Edward, "some years younger than you still, Edward, not at all the kind of child one would have thought to find here. Manure is good for roses, one puts it for flowers and for fruit, but I never saw it produce a child like that." On their return, he did go briefly by to see Mrs. Jennings, without taking Edward, for he did not care for his kindnesses to be known.

They spent some time among the books, walking about the open stalls, and as they left the Earl, his eyes slightly teasing and altogether wicked, dropped a fat book in Edward's hands, with the comment, "You might try that, and give me your opinion of it."

"*Humphry Clinker?*" said Edward, his memory startled and puzzled.

"I mentioned it once to you as suitable for you. You will not re-member."

"I do remember now. I do not need it now, Uncle James."

"*Touché,*" said the Earl, "you improve, Edward, but look it over any way and tell me what you think. I just happened to see it."

They took horse again, down Windmill Road, where they happened to chance on an old man walking, whom the Earl stopped to speak to, and introduce Edward to.

"Nollekens," he said afterwards, when they had passed on, "has done the heads of Fox and Pitt and George the III—the Opposition and the Establishment, in stone where there are no fights."

"What a strange name," Edward commented.

"Dutch," the Earl answered briefly, his thoughts diverted into the past.

"Holland, what is that great palace-like building," Edward exclaimed, "with the statues?" breaking into the Earl's thoughts.

"A palace of the damned," the Earl said, "the living dead already damned. That is Bethlehem Hospital, that is Bedlam, we call it; shall we ride over? It is not the palace Tuileries it looks to be as you will see when we are closer, but I will show you Cibber's statues of Madness and Melancholy with their flaking paint. I hear rumours Parliament may order it torn down and removed."

Edward looked at the rotting stone building, from which he heard an occasional shriek, with feelings of particular horror, and he felt almost faint. He looked at his father, and his father, reading his face nodded.

"I could have had you committed there, as your friend knew. Yes, Edward—or Newgate, which I hope you never see."

"But you knew I was not mad."

"Did I?" the Earl asked. "You seemed so to me. I have heard some people have been sent here who were not mad, but if they were they would soon become mad. Peg Nicholson is here, she tried to shoot George III, as I suppose you do not know. I would take you inside, but there is a recent rule making it more difficult, one has to get a special order now."

"I wish I had not asked to come," Edward said, his face deadly white, at the noise and the air of disintegration. " I think I am going to faint, Holland."

For answer the Earl took his bridle and spurred their horses into a gallop until they were a little way away, and then directed him to get off his horse. The horses were well-trained and stood quietly, their reins down, while Edward put his head between his knees and waited for the waves of nausea and dizziness to pass.

"You have a tender kidney," the Earl commented. "Had you come to hear your preachers here, when you left them and their Easter sermons, if you were not edified, you could have come here to amuse yourself, and run rioting up and down the halls and the wards and played with the inhabitants there. A third bill to attract, and a very popular game. It was so even among some of my friends, before they closed it down."

"Did you, yourself, Holland?" Edward asked, unbelieving.

"Once, out of curiosity," said the Earl briefly. "But it goes without saying I did not run, since I could not. I did not go back. I did not see the amusement in watching poor wretches throw their straw about, that was more soiled with their filth than I would ever allow in my stables, chained to the floor, leather sellers and tailors' wives and would-be assassins and arsonists declaiming they were emperors and prophets, my lady Mayoress, the Duke of Monmouth, *ad infinitum*—while an audience of a hundred disported themselves riotously at the funny sight. It was the thing to do, the fashion then. Even Dr. Johnson went. Do you feel more the thing now, Edward? Are you recovered?"

"I think so," Edward said. He did not dare ask his father if he would really have had him committed there, for he was afraid of the answer; that he had said he had considered it was too much. He felt suddenly afraid of the Earl as he had never been before, in this open space before the madhouse with its lines of deceptive grace: perceiving the Earl's power in the brutality and suffering of the real world, his power to inflict, and his own powerlessness which could only suffer.

"I could have," the Earl said, again walking into his mind, "but I spoke of it only to divert Alleyn. I would not have, Edward, for any consideration. You forget, I had seen inside. Think much of me, but please, do not think that. Shall we leave, have you seen what you came to see?"

"I have had enough," said Edward, "more than I thought to. I would like to go away from here now, too."

"Where shall we go next? Shall I take you to see the lions in the Tower? I believe that is customary for guardians to do with the young?"

"Are there real lions there?"

"Of course. The Lions of England. We are not a symbolic people, Edward, we need the shaggy shabby beasts before our eyes. One there now is named for George III, but George has reigned so long, his lions have died several times, and he the King continues, mad, but very much alive. He has exploded the superstition that the king's lion's death foretells the king's. I think there is a tiger, too, and we can perhaps see the Mint there—not the disreputable one, the real one."

"I would rather not," said Edward, his face still pale. "I have seen enough."

"We can stop by an alehouse here, if you feel the need," the Earl said, a little worried.

"I would rather not."

"I would rather not too. Mount, then, Edward, and we will go to Mount Street to the Mount Street Coffee House, and you can forget these sights in Grosvenor Square. Thank God for these oases of civilisation we can reach."

The Coffee House, though popular, was quiet at that particular hour, and Edward sat gratefully over a cold lunch, and hot laced coffee which the Earl this once allowed him. The pallor of Edward's cheeks concerned him, for, for all his perspicacity, he could not conceive the depth of Edward's horror and fear.

"Look at the door, Edward, you will see a rare sight. Mr. Westbrook has a very beautiful imminently nubile daughter, who is also named Harriet," the Earl remarked mischievously, "who is all of thirteen or fourteen and quite innocent, I think. She rarely appears here, 'Jew' Westbrook is determined to raise her as a lady, and even his coffee shop will not do for her, but she is coming now in the door with her father. Don't stare. She is not for you."

"I don't wish to stare. She does have lovely hair," Edward said, "but he may keep his daughter for all of me. She looks to be in school still, and I like auburn colour the least."

They passed by the Watch-House, where the Prince of Wales had been carried once for disturbing the peace, and returned home.

V

The Earl had entered Edward for membership in several clubs, Brookes', White's, the ladies' Almack's, and he expected him not to be rejected. He considered them publicly to be essential to Edward's proposed position, as essential as his coats and his manners, but privately he was less than happy at the prospect, and he treated Edward to one of his paternal lectures which Edward found so embarrassing, wished he would not, and was thankful he seldom saw fit to give. It occurred as usual after breakfast, but at noon, with unheralded abruptness. He informed Edward of his prospective election and then he suddenly looked at him, straightly with more concern than Edward had ever seen visible on his face. They had been speaking of a duel that had occurred the day before between two members of White's who had gotten drunk and quarrelled and fought for an accusation at cards. The

Earl raised his heavy eyes and looked at his son consideringly, a note of urgency in his voice, hesitantly pleading below its surface.

"Edward," he said, "don't game. Yes, *I* say it. I. I know it all. Hazard, faro, the dice-box, the cards, écarté, piquet, the E.O. tables, the bets at White's. I know it is the fashion and that it is everywhere done. Everything, anything, is to be bet on—cocks, horses, mills, marriages, mistresses, heirs, divorce, it hardly matters what, just so the issue admits uncertainty, and down it goes on the book at White's. I never used those books," he added, his eyes briefly averted, "for what you may be thinking. I will enter you for membership in Brookes' and White's and Watier's," he continued, "for the standing of it, but if you show signs of the fever, and if you do, I will hear of it, I will not make you my heir. Nor will I need to hear. I know the look of the face." He paused, and then he said with finality, "I do not want Tyne lost in a few nights' amusement, or even encumbered. I have waited to decide partly to see if you were infected."

"And am I, do you think?" He was humiliated by his father's lack of trust, and yet he could see it was practical.

"No, I think not. It is early to tell for certain, but I think not. Perhaps you have an immunity, like the smallpox inoculation, through an excess of the vice in me. I know it all, you see, the little straw hats to protect the wigs from the heat of the play, though that's gone of course—how you would have laughed to see it, Edward, perched and decorated with flowers and ribbons, like a French Shepherdess at Petite Trianon—and that's gone too. And the leather gauntlets, the shields, we wore to protect our lace, when we were really seriously at play. The heavy curtains at the windows, guards against the pikestaffs, and Faro's Daughters pilloried, to try to stop us, but of course they could not. And 'sandwiches' with damned Montagu, because we did not want to stop to eat. But with me, in the end, the excitement wore off, though some claim it never does. I wished other things finally more than to sit forever in a smoky curtained room. I saw Fox lose his fortune, rather his father's, and regain it, and lose it again, and grow slovenly, and again regain it and quit. I have seen estates deforested, finally sold, to pay a son's or father's debts. I saw Lyle, richer than I and more skilful than I, lose all in the end and then his credit, though his rank protected him from the filth of debtors' prison, and rather than face exile in squalor and poverty in Belgium or in France, shoot himself, spoiling his clothes all the same at last. I perceived then that though I had both wealth and property, which I had done little to obtain, it was not endless. Actually," he said, looking at Edward now as if really seeing him, "I think you would prefer the Alfred Club—it is a small club, men of letters go—but I cannot help you with election there."

"Why do you think I will not game? Because I have nothing to game with?"

"You could find those who would think I would pay. No, because you are never bored, Edward, and you do not seem to me to require novelty, or excitement for excitement's sake. But never start, Edward, you may have the temperament and not know it. If you do, win, and you are lost. Lose, and you are doubly lost."

"Why did you stop?"

"I came into my full inheritance, and I wanted to lose none of it. And soon afterwards, I came into a second inheritance, unexpectedly, of a small child, and I had an additional reason, only possible but still nevertheless there, for wanting to maintain it intact. I am embarrassing you, I think."

"Yes."

"I was abroad the year you were born, as I told you. I had things I wanted to forget, being not entirely callous, though nearly so. I found the music of Vienna a more efficacious Lethe than play, and less lethal. I continued to play, but with a different instrument. My old reputation still pursues me even yet, and I am beleaguered by youngsters wanting to send their father to Newgate for the honour of sitting with Rockfort. If they ask me if I play yet, I say yes, I have my reputation to maintain, for I do, but not as they think—but I am always in a different hell than they are, or so it seems."

"I wonder you should trouble to pretend."

"You would, Edward," the Earl said smiling. "Wonder, I mean."

"If I do not play, will it not seem strange?"

"Well-taken. Perhaps in that one matter I shall reform publicly. I will think about it."

"I have not so much will, or so much control, or even so much virtue, as you like to tease me with, Holland. I read that book, you know, about Humphry Clinker, it is not really like at all." He sighed, a little desperately. "I seem to have less every day. I hardly know who I am any more." The Earl looked at him quizzically. "Inside myself, I mean. I am not used to this pace, and so much all the time, and so many people. I don't think I ever will be. I would not like to disappoint you. Would I not just be better to leave my name off the lists of these clubs?"

The Earl shook his head. "Not possible, Edward, unfortunately, in the world I want you in." He sighed. "I think I of all people am being idealistic and indulging in wishful thinking, to think you could just say 'no.' Well, then, Edward, I will instruct you myself. I can at least teach you something."

"I think I shall not be apt."

"We shall see."

He went to his desk, and took out a black box, and a pack of cards, and sat down again, shuffling them with a quick practised hand. He proceeded that day, and the next day, and for many days thereafter to give part of each day to play with Edward. Edward was not wholly unapt, being intelligent, and owning the Earl's hands, and he acquired a certain degree of skill, but he had, as the Earl had foreseen, an essential disinterest. Edward, for his part, found the Earl again in a position of adversary across the table from him, cool and experienced and watchful yet at ease, and he again discovered his masked formidableness. In the end, the Earl sighed, and looked at him with a fond patience, in which there was a touch of sadness as well as relief.

"I think, Edward," he said, "that I was initially right, and that I must rather teach you how gracefully to disengage yourself without offence, which I have learned to do. You might play better opposite someone than myself. I understand of course your reasons for not being at ease with me. But I hope you will, as I said first, not game at all. But it is well to know how to defend yourself if you must, and know the tricks to watch for and guard against. I don't like to threaten you, Edward, but here I do. Do you believe me?"

"Yes," Edward said, his eyes lifting briefly to meet his father's, and then lowering.

"Good. I am glad you do." Nevertheless, he continued to set aside some part of each full day to give to this particular social skill.

"I think it is too late," Edward said finally one day in September in despair. "My brain is ready to burst, and I have been mauled to pieces by Jackson and Angelo both. I am twice over dead, and a hundred times with the sword. It is eight years too late, Holland. I can never learn all you want now, or be all you expect of me." His fingers were shaking, and he could hardly eat his dinner.

The Earl looked at him with the eye of practised concern he would have used on a highstrung, jittery mare.

"You do look a little worn. Suppose I include your name out of the plans for the evening? Why do you not just finish your supper, and I will drop you off by Mrs. Wilson's this evening as I go out myself."

Edward gave a sharp bitter bark of laughter. "I wear myself out by day and your remedy is that I wear myself out by night! I shall burn out, Holland. I feel it. Before Spring there will be nothing left, except a real puppet—neatly dressed to fashion and elegant outside, and hollow inside, just an empty stick, a stock, with strings for you to pull. I don't want your world, Holland."

"You have hardly seen it yet. You think you do not like it? Wait until Christmas at least."

"I did not say I did not like it. I said I don't *want* it. I would rather go back to Northumberland, under any circumstances and any way at all."

"Any way?"

"Any way at all," Edward said defiantly, the dam of his defences breaking down.

The Earl decided sympathy, which he did feel, was out of place. He rose and walked to Edward, and gave him a little shake of his shoulders, and a light slap across the cheek, not to hurt.

"Well, Edward," he said, "you can't, as I have told you before. So make the best of what you must do, and pull yourself together." When Edward would have put his head in his hands, he pulled him to his feet. "It is not so hopeless at all as you indicate," he said, as he walked with him to his carriage and put him inside and joined him, giving the coachman Mrs. Wilson's address. "You have for some reason had a bad day, that is all. You shoot very well. Manton himself says so, and that is high praise. No one, not even Manton, is better for teaching shooting than Ross, and you have had his experience and practise for your eight years. Nor is there any better stalker or hunting master than my Highland Gilly, nor any one more able to teach you to ride. You do all these well, Edward, and with ease; you sit in those skills as forward as anyone might wish to. When you are not awkward about me, you have much grace, and you dance as a duck swims. Your wardrobe is in good hands, and your valet trained. Your manners are adequate, and your address charming. I say it impartially, with the judgement of the Beau himself to reinforce me. It is the vices of society that are throwing you, Edward, and you don't know whether you can survive them or not. Nor do I. But it is rather novel and amusing to be in a position to force on you experiences other fathers would well force their sons to forgo a little. By the by, the Prince of Wales has a room just for his bath, of marble. I think I may have one put in myself."

They had reached Mrs. Wilson's, and the coach stopped. Edward put out his hand blindly and took the Earl's that he had extended, and held it as though he were drowning.

"It is a straw," the Earl said warningly, perceiving something of the desperation of his intensity. "There is no help in it." Nevertheless, he drew Edward to him suddenly, by that grasp, and kissed his unhappy sad unresisting lips, and held him against him for a moment as though he were again a little child.

"Oh, Holland," Edward whispered, "no," but clinging to him in the dark of the coach with his own lips and his own arms, desperate and passionate.

"Most certainly no," the Earl said, "there can be no backsliding now." He held him a moment longer, his hands and his lips achingly tender for the boy who lay so lightly in his arms pressing himself so closely against him. For a moment he forgot where he was, his consciousness lost in the kiss of his son, their incongruous, ill-mated spirits mingled as closely as their breath and the beating of their blood. Even when he remembered, he could not draw away at once or break the embrace, that had been nine months denied, heedless of who might pass or what they might see, in the quiet street. It was a wordless communion wholly beyond mere passion now, of a bond and a love they were incapable of expressing or dealing with any other way than this one that they had meant to close. "Forget this," the Earl whispered, against his lips, "it has not happened, do not be afraid, it will not happen again."

"I am not afraid," Edward whispered. "Oh, Holland, I wish I could stay here, like this, forever, and die so."

"Nonsense," the Earl whispered, his lips brushing the boy's hair, and his face, before they came again to rest on his mouth, "of course you cannot, and we cannot, but I too wish we might. There is not even anywhere we could go in peace where we are not known, with this damned war. We are both known now, Edward, you as well as I. It is impossible and you know it and I know it. Do not tempt me. It is you who are Sathanas now, not I."

"I don't want to go anywhere away with you," Edward whispered, "that is you, not me, Holland. It is here and now I want to be."

"Absurd," the Earl whispered, tracing his features caressingly with the tips of his fingers. "There are people passing, and my crest is on the door."

"I do not care," Edward whispered, not moving, returning his lips into the Earl's own caress.

"I care," the Earl whispered. "I care very much, and if you cannot care for yourself, then I must care for you." He held him tightly for a last moment, until Edward lost his breath and thought his ribs would crack, but he did not care, their lips and mouths tightly enlaced, and then the Earl pushed the boy gently from him. "Go now," he said, "to your Mrs. Wilson," and opened the door. He did not linger, but had the coachman snap his whip and drive the horses away before Edward had reached the steps.

Edward walked up the steps and rang and was admitted to the house, and went to Mrs. Wilson without a word. Understanding him, and seeing his face, she did not speak, or question him, but lay down with him at once. However, she had her own blow to give.

"I cannot see you again, cher Clare, after tonight," she said to him gently, after they were lying quietly together. She took his face in her hands as she spoke, and kissed his cheek.

"Your patron has returned?" he asked quietly, without expression. It seemed then the Ninth Wave, and he bowed beneath it.

"But of course, no—you are here, my dear. But tomorrow he returns." His face took on so desolate an air that she said, "You are not jealous, cher Clare? I warned you, you remember, and you promised me you would not be. You are not going to enact me any bad tragedies, cher Clare, please do not."

"No," he said, "I am not jealous. I understand. I knew it was for a short time. But I am going to miss you, Harriett. You are the only person I have known who has ever really looked at me and seen me as I feel I am, just for myself. And I am very afraid my guardian will make me have another woman."

"That will be a good thing, dear Clare," she said, smiling just a little at his dismay. "I do think so. Why, will you mind?"

"Yes."

"Why will you mind? Because of me?"

"No. But with you I did not mind—all this."

"You did not *mind*—" She laughed and caught his ears and half shook him. "You dreadful, sweet, funny boy." She pressed her lips against his suddenly, quickly and with endearment. "I think perhaps it is I who am going to be a little jealous of you, with your unknown unwanted woman." She pressed her lips again against his, this time with an inviting passion and stretched against him as he sighed suddenly and put his arms about her, and turned again into her legs, and into her.

"I like being with you, you are so restful." She gave a little small throaty laugh deep down in her throat and put her arms loosely about him, accommodating him further, but he held a little away. "And I like your little pixy face," he said, kissing its several parts, "your big eyes that have somehow not entirely grown up, for all your wise wisdom, and your little nose that just turns up, and your sweet smiling tragic mouth."

"I am not tragic," she protested.

"To me you are."

"Coming it rather too strong, cher Clare," she said, her mouth breaking into a wide smile which he was impelled to match and close with his.

"I almost love you, Harriett," he whispered, kissing her mouth again and her throat.

"No, please, don't," she admonished, returning his kiss. "But I almost love you. I am almost twice your age, my dear. No Devonshires." She sighed and turned it into a laugh. "Let us not be ridiculous, at our two ages."

"What are Devonshires? Kisses?"

She laughed again. "My lady Devonshire is known for her excesses of emotion. And my lord for his plays. Have you not met her? Or heard the slang?"

"No," he said, his lips in the hollow of her breasts. "Shall I never see you again?"

"No. Yes. No. I don't know. Not soon. We must see. Is it your intention to eat me entirely before my patron returns?"

"Perhaps," he said. "We must see. Shall you mind?"

"No but he will challenge you." Their voices ceased, except for murmurings and the cries of love. He had finished, and lay still within her, peaceably, for a while. Then when he had slipped away, he seemed again to rouse. She laughed. "It is already twice. Go to sleep, cher Clare now, and let me sleep," she reproached him drowsily.

For answer he pulled her to him, and fitted her right against him, and pulled the sheet about them, and they went to sleep so, enlaced, her head on his bosom beneath his chin, his arms clasping her. In the night he took her again, their lips drowsily pressing, and slept again, and in the morning, early, he left. She was still asleep. He kissed her and did not waken her; there seemed no reason further to say goodbye.

When he returned to No. 12, the Earl made no comment on any passages of the night and seemed entirely himself. To Edward's wistful eyes he made no response. He was reading the latest news of Wellesley's campaigns in Spain, but he lifted an eye to Edward's exhausted face, now blank, advised him to go to bed, advice Edward declined because he had lessons, and told him of their plans for the evening.

For that night, the tenth of September, the Earl had engaged a box for the reopening of Covent Garden Theatre. He knew that prices had been raised, but the price of his box was a matter of indifference to him, and he gave it no thought. They arrived unfashionably early, well on time, for the Earl had a particular end in view.

"What do we see tonight? Is it Mrs. Siddons? I still cannot accustom myself to seeing Romeo in a bag-wig and a silk coat. I expect any moment to hear him say, 'pon my soul,'" Edward remarked, attempting to cover his low spirits, and his lack of interest.

"It is no odder a convention, Edward," the Earl said absently, "than for Shakespeare himself to have Romans played as Elizabethan gentlemen. It is all new scenery tonight for the occasion, and expected to be magnificent, if one cares for scenery." The Earl raised his glass, and raked the shining velvet boxes across from him, informing Edward of various personages he recognised, as they took their places. "There is Mr. Thomas Lawrence," he said, "whom I hope to have your portrait painted by when you come of age."

"To hang in your hall?" Edward remarked with uncalled for bitterness.

The Earl ignored his tone. "I thought to," he said mildly. He turned suddenly to Edward and remarked with an amused expression: "Cast an inconspicuous glance to the box second to your right, Edward, and you will see a rare London sight. The Ladies of Llangollen are here from Wales."

Edward looked and discovered that the box which he had thought to contain two middle-aged men in reality held two women. One, the elder, seeming by some years considerably older than the Earl, wore orders and decorations of the House of Bourbon across "his" chest, but both were dressed like men, with short powdered hair, and gentlemen's tall hats, coats, waistcoats, cravats. Seated, they could hardly be distinguished for their sex, even after one knew, Edward thought, amazed.

"Lady Eleanor Butler," whispered the Earl. "She disapproved of marriage and eloped with a young friend, the Earl of Bessborough's cousin. It was a great stir when I was twenty. They are very happy, she and her Sally, and the world comes to them, York himself, and Wellesley, when he is here, and all the literary men. They won't stay in London even for a night, and they will drive back all the way tonight to their vale in Wales. I doubt they stay to the end of the performance, certainly not through the farce. Look now to your left, the fifth box."

But Edward was not paying the Earl attention, for his glance was fixed on the box next to the Ladies where a group was entering. He did not need to be told who the lovely girl with dark hair lightly curling and still as close-cropped as his own was. Except for the shortness of her hair, framing her face like a cap, and the remembrance of her face, he would not have believed he had held her against him hard while she struggled and fought him in her rage of interruption. There was no other trace of her escapade—she sat now demurely in white satin, a single diamond winking at her throat, her gloved hands lightly clasped in her lap, and a thin silver-spangled scarf about her shoulders. Had he not already known who she was, he would have known by the gentleman beside her, who looked entirely like his first father, except for being in age much older. It must be, he thought, his first father's eldest brother, the old Lord Armstrong. There were other persons in the box, a middle-aged lady seating herself by the girl, and a youngish man, much older than himself, who did not resemble the old Earl or Edward's first father, but seemed related to the girl and the woman he supposed was her mother. He was staring rudely, unable to help himself, but they seemed unaware of him, and their looks were directed elsewhere. His attention was drawn as much by Lord Armstrong, as by the girl, to the man who had been oblivious of his existence, and had not cared to see him or to know him, as they were oblivious now.

"You are staring without a glass, Edward," the Earl said quietly, "and that is rude. That box does not concern you. Direct your attention to the left now where the three ladies sit."

With an effort Edward wrenched his eyes away, and turned his head. He did not wish himself to show an interest where none for him was felt, and he was grateful to the Earl for recalling him.

"I am looking. What am I to see?" he said, his voice shaken and not quite under control.

"I would suggest one of the three for your next connexion, tell me which appeals and I will arrange it. Close your mouth, Edward, don't look the fool."

"How did you know?" Edward whispered furiously. "Do you—must you—know everything? Did she tell you before she told me?"

"Hush," the Earl said, "of course not, young puppy, but I know very well who is returning to town. You have not answered me?"

"How long have you known? For several days? Yesterday?" The Earl nodded. "Oh, God," said Edward, "must you leave me nothing?"

They were very close to a quarrel, but their attention was diverted from themselves by several things happening all at once. The swelling unease and signs of unruliness in the filling pit and galleries had grown considerably, and the play was attempting to begin. "God Save the King" had been played and they had stood, and Kemble appeared before the curtains to dedicate the reopening, but for once and for the first time "Glorious" John was met with hisses. He cut the ceremony short in the face of the vociferous crowd, and ordered instead the green curtain raised. The crowd, however, was not quelled by the voices of the actors or even the Divine Sarah, and began to drown them out with their shouting, "Off, off!" to the actors, even Mrs. Siddons, and "No raised prices!", and then began the chanting of "Old prices, old prices!" that was taken up from all parts of the house.

"Let us leave this," the Earl said quickly, frowning. "It looks to be a riot beginning that is nothing to do with us. Let you and me go, Edward, before they have the bruisers in." He had risen as he spoke, and was making his way to the door at the back of the box, as the actors struggled to continue their parts against the storm. Out of the corner of his eye, turning with his father, Edward saw the girl rising also, and leaving with her party.

There were, however, few persons as yet desirous to leave what promised an exciting evening. The two parties passed on the divided stairs, but with no formal recognition given by either, except that as he passed, Edward lifted his downcast eyes at the same time as the girl, and their eyes met, and their glances crossed, with a thrill that jolted him such as he had felt in a student's room at Oxford who had been experimenting with a small electrifying machine. The second in which the gaze of each held the other seemed longer than the brief seconds before the two groups reached the bottom of the stairs and went their ways.

The Earl took a hackney-coach that was by the street, and had themselves driven to the Star and Garter for refreshment, and news, in Pall Mall that was lit by the new gas lamps, and sent a message to his coachman to meet them there. Leaning back, expressionless, at ease, he looked at Edward across the table.

"Well, Edward, you have not answered me. Which lady will suit you?"

"Are you serious, Holland?" Edward said, unbelieving.

"Never more. We will have a booth tomorrow at Vauxhall, and go by river, and you can meet them all, if you like, or have them all, in turn."

"Must you rush me?"

"I think so. If you throw the word *serious* at me, let me say I have warned you not to be serious in this."

"You are ruining my character and my continence," Edward said helplessly, "and I think I hate you for it, Holland."

"As you please," the Earl said with an indifferent air, "but if I have ruined your peace, you have ruined mine," he added unfairly with a sideways glance, "and I have other things to see to of more importance, and I would like to have this settled."

"Choose for yourself then," Edward said angrily, "if you are determined on this. Present me to her, and I will mount her." He averted his angry hurt eyes. "God, Holland, how little you know me."

"Perhaps," the Earl said. "Shall I reserve the Vauxhall booth then?"

"No. I could not go through such an evening. Make the arrangements you are determined to make, and tell me where you want me to go."

"You will not be so difficult?"

"I don't know. I wish you would leave me alone."

The Earl rose. "I know the person for you. I should have thought of it before. We will go there now."

Edward's fatigued face grew whiter. "I am tired, Holland, and I was out last night."

The Earl rose and paid his bill, and went out, expecting Edward to follow him, as he did. His coach had now arrived, and they rode for some little time in silence over the cobbled streets, until they came to a sedate house overlooking a quiet park.

"Wait here," the Earl said. "I may be some time." The Earl continued not to reappear, and after a while Edward's anger and his nervousness both disappeared and he fell asleep in the carriage while the coachman walked the horses up and down. The fog, increasing, hid houses, trees, even the ground. Some time later, he was awakened by the Earl's voice at the door he had opened, and he stumbled sleepily after the Earl.

"It will do," the Earl said, leading him up the stairs of a house that might have been the Earl's. "Stay here tonight and tomorrow and tomorrow night. I will send George tomorrow noon to bring your clothes and attend to you. I still think you should go out to Vauxhall and I will have a booth in your name. It is not yet too cold at night. The little lights in the gardens are very pretty, like suns and stars among the walks and the statues, and I will have a wherry engaged and supper laid on. These things are very pleasant done in wherries if you find a quiet place and send the waterman away. I believe there is also to be a concert in the Rotunda. I will expect you home the day after tomorrow, for we have a particular Assembly I want you to attend, but if you like this woman, she is unengaged, you may keep her as long as it both suits you. I think your appetites require less change than my own."

VI

Edward hardly heard the Earl. The prospect ahead of him struck him as unutterably dreary, but the event turned out differently. The Earl had told the woman Edward was in an exhausted state, and she left him in his bed completely to himself. He did not more than glance at her, noting she did not herself look entirely pleased, and removed the heaviest of his clothes, before he tumbled again into a deep sleep. He awoke the next morning, to find the room empty, and a cool gold light filtering into the room through the windows shaded by the turning Autumn trees outside. The dense fog of the evening before had not lifted entirely, but it was lightening. He stretched, and wondered where he was, and left his bed and walked about. The quiet elegance of the house and its fittings and its neighbourhood surprised him again. As if hearing him move, there was a knock at the door, and a footman opened it and offered to bring him breakfast. He accepted it, and ate it hungrily, and lying back on the pillows, reflected that the women his father knew seemed to live very well. It would not occur to him for some weeks, and those who knew had the tact not to enlighten him, that his father had turned over to him his own current mistress, who had his carte blanche and of whom he was growing a little tired. She was little more pleased than Edward at the change in arrangement, but she had agreed finally after various persuasions and considerable financial dealing. She appeared later in the morning, in a dressing gown, her silver-gilt hair down her back, tied with a ribbon, her fair face and violet eyes showing only a hint of sulkiness. She removed her dressing gown, easily and without self-consciousness, and Edward, his eyes suddenly filled with wicked delight, saw that she wore a second silk peignoir, silver-spangled like the girl's scarf of the night before, and sheer enough to have been drawn through the proverbial ring, through which her white full-formed slenderness gleamed.

He was rested, and he was suddenly immensely tired of virtue and complication and love and loss, and wished all at once to forget the problems that troubled him. He thought, Holland may know me better than I think, after all, or than I know myself. Or perhaps I have changed. I don't really care, any more.

He smiled at her, in a way that made her own lips smile a little, and the sulkiness retreat, and said, "You have me at the disadvantage, ma'am. Turn your back, my dear, if you will." He stripped himself of his clothes, and slipped back beneath the sheet.

"Now," he said, "come you here." She came forward, rustling slightly, and slipped beneath the sheet beside him. He parted the shimmering robe, and put his hands on her with gentle skill, holding off the moment, the second woman whose body was made free to him, exploring with quiet purposeful sensuality its similarities and its differences. She lay, not resisting, not responding.

"You will teach me later what you like," he whispered as he put his lips on hers, breathing in their delicate fragrance and intwining his fingers in the silver-gilt strands of her hair, and a moment later swung himself into position, to ride home.

She began to laugh, beneath him and his lips, shaking, and he stopped to ask the joke.

"Your guardian said you might be shy," she said, shaking and gasping. "Are you shy?" Her amusement convulsed her.

He began to laugh, too. "My guardian is not always infallibly right. Hush, now, love, and give me leave." He slipped his hands against her back under her thin robe and caught her to him, burying his mouth in hers, and all of him in her. He did not know who the woman was he had, he did not even remember her name, if he had been told, and he did not care. He was lost, floating, dissolved in the sensation of the moment, and his mind was gone. He cried out heedlessly and unself-consciously in the agony he had at last come to call pleasure, and not pain, and relaxed, sighing, in and against the pretty child he held.

"What's your name?" he asked lazily, after a time, his lips against her smooth satin cheek.

"Amanda," she whispered back.

"Amanda—she who ought to be loved," he murmured, moving his lips against her hair. "What a pretty name for you, and how well you suit. You live in a very expensive house, Amanda. Is your papa here or your mama?" She shook her head giggling. "All this house, all yours?" She nodded. "And your servants? You must belong to someone then. I wonder who?"

"I belong now to you," she said, slipping her arms about him, and biting his ear gently between her teeth. He felt passion again exploding dizzily within him, and he thought, conscious for only a moment, I shall be ruined. Does Holland know? Does he intend to ruin me this way, and destroy me with my own help? and then again he stopped thinking.

Later, her pique entirely gone, and perceiving her bargain not ill made, she responded herself to him, and without affection, or any intimacy of spirit, only a perception of mutual beauty, and a common latent gaiety, like two pagan children they proceeded to enjoy themselves that early winter and ease their need. His affection, however, and his conversation he reserved for Harriett Wilson who called him to her once or twice during that time.

He thought his father looked at him when he returned somewhat oddly. The amusement there he read clearly, but not the entire expression.

"You have enjoyed yourself?" his father asked. "You found Amanda satisfactory?" His eyebrows slightly raised.

"Yes, Holland," he said, "yes I did."

"I thought you might," the Earl said.

"Am I to thank you? Is that in good taste?"

"If you like."

"I do, then. But I am not a rich man, Holland, as you know. I haven't any means at all, and you are accustoming me to very expensive women. Is that wise?"

"Let us meet that problem another day. I am glad you have conquered your—difficulties, shall we say. And I am pleased to have you out of this house at night," he added without explanation.

When it occurred to Edward who had been Amanda's patron, partly by discovering her superficial incestuous, as he called it, resemblance to himself, and taxed both her and the Earl with it, neither denying, he was already drowned in the discovery of his nature and for the time, lost and past caring.

"Why did you not tell me?" he asked the Earl conversationally, rather than accusingly.

"I thought you might mind," the Earl answered mildly.

"If you thought I might mind," he suggested, but without heat, "did you never think not then to trick me?"

"I rather enjoy tricking you, Edward, to see your reactions when you find me out. Do you mind?"

"No, not now. I would have then."

"Yes, I thought so." The Earl nodded, repeating himself.

"You *are* a devil, Holland," Edward said thoughtfully, regarding him. "I do think you are."

"I have never been very susceptible to flattery," the Earl remarked.

Edward sighed, half exasperated, half touched with disturbed affection. "Holland," he said curiously, "did you know she looked like me, a little, when you picked her for yourself?"

"But of course," the Earl said, "how could it be otherwise, though your hair, Edward, is not silver, and your eyes are not violet, and really," he said smiling, "there is very little the same. Still there was an air, and at that time I found it helpful. But shortly I forgot that reason entirely. She is herself very charming, I think"—he waved his hand deprecatingly —"but I was nevertheless growing tired. I am glad you find her also to your liking."

"I think you are truly devilish, and I am your son," Edward said, his voice flat and tired, his face startled, in the recognition of what that could mean. The piercing despair of his tone penetrated to the Earl and did startle him, in his turn, but Edward ignored the questioning look of his face. "Never mind, we cannot either one of us help it now. I am glad to have Amanda."

And it was fortunate for him to have a place where he could be unself-conscious and happy and at ease, for the events of the Fall and the Winter proved more taxing on his conscious emotions and his mind than he had foreseen. One morning when the hunting season was in early start, he returned from his morning lesson to find a stag had eluded the chase and fled into the West Side of the city, plunging into the little park, and now stood, braced, against the door of a house, with the cries of the hunt ringing down another street, and the morning fog swirling about them both. In its greater fright, it ignored Edward, and he could see beneath its young tender horns of the two-year-old its terrified fixed eyes, soft and dark and shining, and the white froth at its nostrils and lips, and its heart pounding and shaking its chest and heaving flanks. He moved, and it looked at him, and saw him, and with a startled bound leaped away and was gone. Soon after, the square was filled with pink coats and horses and hounds and horns, leaping and blowing briefly about him, surrounding him in their tumult, before they vanished after it and the fog hid them all. Edward, in his own eyes at bay and trapped himself, felt a terrible kinship with the poor stag and he hoped without much hope it had made it away to a safe place. The organisation after it seemed much too compact and determined. He did not tell anyone about it, the impression it had made on him was too sharp, and when he heard by chance that evening that it had been taken, by the river, his face did not change. He was not surprised, and the sorrow he felt for its useless, needless anguish was beyond expression.

The invitations began to drift in like the Autumn leaves falling, a few at first, then thick and fast. The Earl, looking through them, gave Edward previews of the season ahead and promised him private theatricals at Richmond House, Faro at Mrs. Hobart's, masked balls at Wargrove. If Edward's face showed less than enthusiasm, the Earl did not appear to notice or disapprove. On October 25, there was to be the Jubilee celebration of George's fiftieth year of reign, and it was hoped that the King would be well, and in his mind, for the occasion, and that the Prince of Wales would conduct himself with public propriety and respect towards his father. The town was refilling earlier than usual, with this inducement, cancelling out the seasonal hunting exodus. The Earl himself had planned a rout for a later date in the season. And all this was merely prelude. Parliament, out in July, would not sit until February, and the customary Season would not begin until January.

Edward's fatigue became a settled thing he could not shake. The Earl, finally concerned, had in Knighton, who prescribed meat and vegetables and a tonic, and Crawley who prescribed abstinence and sleep and a tonic, but unable to see inside Edward's spirit, and he telling them little, they missed the root and the heart. Wesley could have told the Earl what was needed, as he had told others ("struck first with deep melancholy, and soon after with utter distraction. . . . Let physicians do all they will or can, yet it will be found in the end that 'this kind goeth not out but by prayer and fasting.'"), but he was dead and the Earl would not in any case have listened to him then. George as a countryman made Edward eat liver, and persuaded him to spend more nights at home, and to spend part of the afternoon resting.

"Flesh and blood can bear so much, and has so much to give," he said sternly, "and then it is used up, and the bank can't pay. You are too young to turn into a dry bob."

Edward winced at his language, but he acknowledged its sense. The Earl decided that what Edward did not now know he was in no condition to learn, and eased him of half of his lessons, leaving him some time free, which he spent napping or sleeping, when there were no visitors, to be ready for the evenings which began late and lasted until the small hours increased. He drank tea and ate thin stale slices of bread and butter and cake at Almack's and met and was met by the new crop of eligibles and the old crop of dowagers. They went, it seemed to Edward, to every possible form of entertainment, from huge shows of assemblies where the guests, eight hundred strong, were packed in tiers that rose on tiers, and crushed together in salons until a fan could hardly be unfolded, and where the decorations were fantastically elaborate, fountains and flowing fish and ices and entire ceilings festooned with flowers and satin canopies, to small dinners and chamber concerts, at Melbourne House and at Holland House, in Kensington, relations of Fox, not of the Earl.

Edward came home from one rout he had attended without the Earl, who had a slight *flu,* and described the decorations and the company to him in detail.

"And there I am, Holland, amongst them all like the little toy rabbit or cat you gave me once. Its tail is squeezed and its legs pop out and off it goes, like me, straight into the air of the middle of the room, and it sees its hostess and gives a little duck in her direction, and then it sees my lord, and off it goes bobbing and jiggling in that, and then it makes a jump for the first lady it sees, and off they go."

"I daresay, Edward, I daresay. I am yet to see you duck or bob, Edward, and I hope I am never like to."

It was at an Assembly Ball somewhere in size between the two extremes that Edward met Anne to speak. It was entirely through Brummell's doing, in a spirit of mischief provoked by the Earl's reticence; for though he had seen her sometimes at a distance, he had not been introduced, and had had no occasion to intrude himself.

The Beau came up to him and said, "You dance the new waltz very well, Mr. Armstrong, it pleases me to watch you. I have an introduction to make for you to a young lady who has expressed a wish to waltz, and alas, I am unable to oblige her." He had taken Edward's arm as he spoke, rapidly propelled him across the crowded floor, and brought him up before the lady who was Anne Armstrong.

"I have found an entirely suitable partner for you, Miss Armstrong," he said, his face serious, but his eyes faintly amused, faintly questioning, faintly malicious. "It will be almost like dancing with a sister, the reservation you expressed to me about the waltz, for I believe you are related, are you not? Mr. Armstrong? Miss Armstrong. You will find Mr. Armstrong well able to guide you through the new waltz. He comes on my recommendation." He bowed and left them together.

Edward bowed slightly, and offered his arm.

"Oh, sir," she said dimpling up at him, "you may be my cousin, though I cannot imagine how you come to be, but you on no account fill the bill, for I do not know you at all. I told Mr. Brummell that I thought the new waltz very graceful but that I could never bring myself to dance it with anyone but a lady or a near relative."

"I am sorry I cannot qualify," he said, gazing down on her, his eyes enchanted. "But I thought perhaps you did know me," he added hesitantly.

"Well," she said, a faint pucker in her brow, "I could not know you when you were with that odious Lord Tyne, but if you are my cousin, I suppose it is all right to speak." She spoke with a frankness he found unusual and winning, despite her words that sank his spirits. "Do you know him well?"

"I live with him. He is my guardian," he answered briefly. He was forced, whether he liked to or not, to prevaricate, by his father's wishes. He had realised from her first words that she had not connected him with his appearance that day into the scene in the study at Tyne. And why should she, he thought, a little piqued, a little relieved. He had been a year younger, dirty and mussed from his ride and not particularly well-dressed. And yet to him the moment was there, recreated, present in the very room as if it were just happening then. He rallied his attention, for she was speaking.

"I am sorry, but if we are cousins, perhaps we can yet be friends. I suppose it is not your fault that he is your guardian. But how very odd he should be." The pucker came again in her brow. He was again torn by the need to delay, to hold her and not repulse her, but he could not disown the older loyalty.

"You must not speak that way to me about Lord Tyne," he said quietly and warningly. "I have been fortunate in my guardianship," although as he said the words, he knew they were not true.

She looked so startled and somehow so hurt he was sorry he had spoken, but then she said, recovering herself, again with the frankness he would learn to associate with her, "I should not have said what I did. My quarrel is not yours, and I should not expect it to be. Has he been your guardian long?"

"Since I was six."

"And you have lived with him all these years?" He could see the words, "How terrible for you," in her face and hovering on her lips but she managed to suppress them.

"I have lived at his house. He was not often home."

"In London?"

"No, in Northumberland." She gave a small gasp and looked at him sharply, but he preserved his countenance.

"And were you there, at his home, last year?"

"I was still at Oxford," he said, diverting truth with truth, and saw she looked relieved.

"I am wondering how you can be my cousin. Lord Armstrong has no children. If you really are, you would have to be my Uncle George's son, Edward Clare, whom I have never seen."

"I am Edward Clare," he said simply.

"And I am your cousin Anne," she said smiling at him. "How very odd to meet you now and here. I suppose Mr. Brummell must have thought—I don't know what he thought. But surely we cannot continue saying 'Miss Armstrong' and 'Mr. Armstrong' to one another. It is ridiculous, don't you think?"

"I quite agree," he said smiling at her in turn. "May cousins dance the Country Dance? Are you promised? May I have the honour?"

"I should be most charmed, Cousin Edward."

He knew he should not allow her to think him who she did, but bearing the name he did, he saw nothing else to do, and in truth he was glad for the mistake. For all her friendliness, he had seen at once that she would have at once cut him, had she known his relationship to Lord Tyne, and that she would have done so for his mere presence with Tyne, without the tie of blood she thought existed. She will be told soon enough who I am, he thought, and then, like Montague and Capulet, we cannot speak. But Juliet spoke. They went through the patterns and mazes of two country dances, bound by an instant liking on the part of each, and then he took her down to supper.

The long tables were loaded with every kind of delicacy, lobster patties, little peas, early asparagus grown under glass, ices; they took their plates out on the terrace, but she ate very little.

"It is so hot inside," she said fanning herself, "and I want to dance some more." She flushed. "That is, if you are not engaged and if you do not mind, Cousin Edward?"

"I do not mind at all," he answered truthfully.

"I love to dance," she said. "When I dance, I forget who I am, and anything sad and everything except the music, but I have had to sit them all out, even after I could come, unless my brother would dance with me, and he does not care to very often. Mother is still in black gloves, but she did not want me to miss the Season for fear I should grow too old. It is a year now, and I am allowed to have white gloves.

But it is very little use to make a Season if one cannot be led to dance. After Christmas it will be different. You know about my father?" she said pausing.

"Yes, I know," he said, after a moment.

"Do I sound heartless? I am not, really."

"I know you are not," he said.

"You know then why I must hate Lord Tyne?"

"Yes," he said, "I know that too."

"But I need not hate you, nor you me, do you think?"

"I think one need not hate anyone," he said gently, "but I cannot speak for you."

She looked at him in surprise, but she did not speak right away.

"It is very odd," she said puzzled, "but I feel I have spoken with you before. Perhaps it was when we were children, but that does not quite seem to be it."

"We did not meet as children. I wish we had, but you would hardly have remembered, you would have been too young."

"I shall be seventeen."

"That is entirely what I mean, Cousin Anne," he said laughing. "You would have been hardly two."

She laughed. "It is good to grow up. Age makes less difference." Suddenly, unaccountably, she blushed a little, and her blush called forth his own. She laughed again. "I am glad we are cousins, Cousin Edward, my unruly tongue will lead me into less trouble. I have not yet learned not to say what I think."

"I am glad you haven't, Cousin Anne. I hope you never learn entirely. The courtesy of ladies who have I find a cold, killing thing."

"I would like for you to speak to Mama. You know her, of course?"

"No, Anne, I do not," he said simply. "Your family did not approve of Methodists or of Methodist ministers. I do not think she would be particularly pleased to see me or to see you with me."

She looked at him in consternation, and her mouth said "Oh."

"There," he said, "you see, I have been honest, too. Are you going to walk away and leave me now?"

She shook her head. "No," she said, "I am not. I like you and I am glad you are my cousin. My mother thinks Mr. Brummell can do no wrong, and if he has introduced us, it must be eligible."

Edward bowed slightly, but he did not answer. He had thrown enough away, he thought. The music drifted down the hall and out to them.

She looked up at him suddenly, and her eyes sparkled. "If I have been shocking already, Cousin Edward, why should I not be entirely shocking? If I am to be scolded for something that is no fault of my own, I might as well give some cause. Will you teach me to waltz?"

"With entire pleasure, ma'am," he said, bowing and taking her hand.

"We can hear the music out here, teach me here," she said, "before we go in."

He put his arm hesitantly about her waist, and took her hand, and drew her to him, their bodies touching, but she seemed unconscious of him as a person in her concentration upon the steps.

"There," she said. "Will I do?"

"You will do very well."

"Do I dare? Do you dare?"

"They can only eat us," he said, "and that, once," and led her in. The music swelled and flooded their ears, and they embarked upon the dance as upon a river. She was very light on her feet, and pliant and supple in his arms, and hardly needed to have had teaching. They were an arresting couple, even on the crowded floor, to eyes both approving and disapproving, he with his gold head, she with her dark, their feet flying and spinning, but at the center a heart of stillness for him that after a time included her too. She lifted her face and eyes, laughing, to his, and caught the expression of gravity that lay heavy on his, and the light pressure of his hands about her, and their faces so close, suddenly prodded her stumbling visual memory. She gasped and would have dropped his hand, but he held hers tightly.

"You!" she breathed, forgetting he might not have penetrated her disguise, and incapable of dissimulation.

"Yes, Anne," he said simply. "Don't leave yet," he whispered, as she pulled at his hand, "they are watching us. Please wait until the music stops."

"You knew!"

"Yes," he said again simply. "All the time."

"Oh," she exclaimed indignantly. "You should have told me. You have taken sad advantage of me."

"Yes," he said, "I have."

"Why?" Again indignantly.

"I was afraid you would be as angry as I see you are."

"I am not angry, I am humiliated," she said, fighting the angry tears filling her eyes, shaking her head. "I thought no one at all knew. It was sheer madness. I thought I could forget."

He said nothing, he only looked at her with his eyes kind and compassionate, the planes of his face smoothed away by his feeling, and waited for her to speak.

"You are hurting my hand," she said finally.

"I am sorry," he said, loosening his grasp.

"I won't run away off the floor. I see now I mustn't. I don't want to make a scandal either. I was so shocked. Did you know who I was?"

"Not then. Not your name. I knew you were not a boy."

"I do not see how you knew at all. I thought my disguise very good."

He gathered her more closely against him with his hand that held her waist and smiled a little. "The same way I do now."

She caught her breath, but she did not struggle. "You are not acting very much like a cousin, now, Cousin Edward, or as I would imagine a cousin would act, having never had one."

"I do not feel at all like a cousin."

"I do not know whether to laugh or cry," she said, "but I know you are holding me more tightly than you need to. Please release me."

The music had stopped, and he released her waist.

"You were not a gentleman, not to tell me," she said reproachfully.

He began to laugh helplessly, for she looked like a little puffed-up fighting cock.

"But what could I say? Was I to say you were no gentleman?" he asked, more than a little amused. "Come, Anne, be reasonable. It is you who had me at the disadvantage, as you have me still. And I approve of what you did. I think you did just what you should. Tyne should have been shot. But why you and not your brother?"

"I do not know," she said puzzled. "He said the matter of the quarrel did not interest him, and that he had warned my father to abstain. He said if a fool wanted to be shot in a hopeless contest for little cause, he did not want to be himself. And so there was no one left but me." She did not notice the sudden whiteness of his face, or its drawn lines. She looked at him with sudden interest. "Will you shoot him for me?"

He thought he would have to sit down in his shock, for he saw she was perfectly serious, but they were by the window, in its alcove, and there was no chair.

"No, I will not," he said promptly. "You should still be in the schoolroom with notions like that. You seem to already forget I stopped you once before myself. I thought you had outgrown such foolishness. And my God, girl, you hardly know me, we have just met, and I have known Tyne almost all my life. What do you take me for?" he added helplessly, bewildered by the fierce single-minded unchanging purpose shining in her lovely eyes.

"I take you now for my cousin," she said simply. "I want my blood revenged."

"I am not so much your cousin as that," he said firmly. He looked at her with a new surmise. "You have been uncommonly friendly, Anne. Has this cock-brained idea been at the back of your little head all this past hour?"

"Yes," she said, "it has."

"I don't know what to do with you," he said helplessly, "except to tell you that I am the last person in the world you should so approach. You had better go back to your mother now. I will take you."

"I am perfectly well able to take myself."

He shok his head. "It would not look right."

"I suppose you will tell your guardian what I have asked you to do?" she said, biting her lip. "I did not mean to ask you so soon, I meant to wait until we were better acquainted. But you startled me, when you said, as you know you did, that Tyne ought to be shot. It was so much my own thought, you see," she added naively. "Are you going to tell him, and put him on his guard?"

He looked at her again helplessly. "I wish I could make you grow up a little faster. No, I am not going to tell him. He does not need to be put on his guard, anyway. He is never off it. And he would just laugh. At least, I think he would. But I am not laughing, Anne, at least not any more. I think you are a little mad."

She lifted her hand and struck him a hard stinging blow across the cheek, that brought the tears to his eyes. They stood facing each other, the angry unwanted tears glistening in each their eyes now.

"Children, children," they heard a voice behind them say, and they turned to see Brummell had approached them with Tyne himself, "you forget yourselves. May I escort you where you would like to go, Miss Armstrong?" She would have taken his arm, in haughty indignation, but Tyne intervened, his eyes dark and glistening.

"Miss Armstrong will not accept. We will all go for a stroll in the garden together, and let Edward's cheek recover its natural colour, before he gives you back to your parent. We will quench this little scandal before it begins to burn, no, George? You have mischiefed me enough, don't you think?" he added, smiling at his old friend now of some years' standing, despite his being the older by a decade. "Miss Armstrong, give Edward your arm," he said, so sternly she did not dare disobey him.

He looked across at the quiveringly indignant young lady and his stiffly apprehensive ward.

"There is no cause for you to be so high-horsed. You have asked Edward to shoot me, and he has—quite rightly, I think—refused, and called you mad," he said pleasantly, smiling at their dismay. "Your intentions are no secret, Miss Armstrong, the world knows them. I do not need to read lips to reconstruct what must have been your conversation. I must say I am gratified, if not surprised, that Edward refused you, for he is an excellent shot, though not excellent enough, and I should have hated to shoot my ward. Try asking Brummell, perhaps he might oblige you."

Her only contact with Tyne had been the meeting in his study, when she felt bolder, her sex as she thought concealed. His enforced presence now was close to overpowering her, and her lip quivered. She held it between her teeth to steady it. Edward put his free hand over hers and pressed it, but she threw it off with a little jerk, and heard Tyne laugh.

"You are a spitfire, Miss Armstrong, a little fireworks. Be grateful to Edward. Were it not for his interest, which I shall respect, I should be tempted to take you in hand myself and school you."

She looked her disdain, and her chagrin was equalled only by Edward's, who perceived his father disapproved and intended to ruin that interest.

"Why did you fight my father?" she asked baldly, stopping on the walk and turning suddenly. "What cause could you have to kill him?"

"Men need little cause for killing, Miss Armstrong." He paused. "He challenged my guardianship of Edward," the Earl threw out briefly, "and I challenged his challenge, that is all. There, George, a morsel for you. Have you found what you sought? Come now, we bore Mr. Brummell with this talk of our obscure private affairs. Have you put your bet on 'Duke' or on 'Darling'?" he asked, turning his attention to Brummell, and Brummell's away from Edward into other subjects. "As an army man, tell me. Will Mrs. Clarke win her point and keep her right to commission?"

"It would be telling," Brummell answered, "but I shall still uphold the Duke. The news now is Canning's duel with Castlereagh on Putney Heath? Had you heard?"

"I should have thought," observed the Earl dispassionately, "that either could have done better. They did not shoot to miss, into the air, either one, but both bullets of their first shot went wild of a mark. What did they think they were at?"

"Tell more," murmured Brummell, "I had not heard this."

"Then Canning's second bullet catches the button of Castlereagh's coat, I am not informed of which one, and is turned back by it, but I should say that comes as near an end as his spill from a boat into the Irish lake in '88, he leads a charmed life. His second shot wounds Canning in the thigh, but only slightly, he walks off the ground unassisted. A discreditable affair, I would say, all round, but fortunate all the same for the country. Canning has the more winning manner, and he is capable, but I think we cannot spare the Viscount Stewart."

"I understand the Duke of Portland is taking this quarrel much to heart and will resign," Brummell observed.

"He is an old man," the Earl said, "he is seventy-one, and ill. I do not think he will survive it. He had no wish to be Prime Minister again, but he was a chance for peace at home in these troublesome and factious times, and he came at his King and his party's call."

The elder men turned their conversation onto the mismanagement of the Walcheren Marshes expedition that had caused both English lords to resign from the government, and then to the failure of the Antwerp enterprise through fever and delay.

"We lost Antwerp because Fouché was awake, when the Corsican was asleep. I hear Napoleon has rewarded him by taking away his portfolio. That man cannot bear any other brilliance near him."

"A dangerous conceit," observed Brummell.

"It is indeed, and I hope it will prove so to him. He has just met with Alexander at Erfurt to reconfirm their agreements at Tilsit."

"Did he not meet then also with Herr Goethe himself?"

"Goethe manages to maintain his admiration for Napoleon. I think like many of the literary, he wears blinders. But I know a better story. I hear Napoleon has jumped upon his hat, in a calculated frenzy, but that his temper did not impress Alexander."

"No! What happened then?"

"Very little. The Tsar smiled. I well remember that unmoved smile, and observed that passion did not impress him and that he would leave the room, and that ended the display."

"A pretty story," said Brummell.

"It is indeed. 'The Elbe is near but try and bite it.' That will not serve with Alexander, Napoleon has met a match there. They will not stay friends long, I am thinking. That bed is too small."

"The Treaty is now signed, is it not? In the palace of Schönbrunn, in Vienna?"

"A Corsican upstart of no name has stripped Austria entirely," the Earl said bleakly, "and there was no help to give. I would Staps had succeeded."

"Staps?" asked Brummell.

"Napoleon thought he was an enthusiast, an *illuminé,* or ill, but he was none of those things. He was only a young boy with a single heart and a clear eye who came to remove a tyrant." The Earl smiled, his expression unreadable, his eyes on the two figures walking just before them. "He had support, his fiancée approved. He had no political connections. Napoleon would have pardoned him, had he agreed to be grateful or even to ask for it, but he would not."

"Fantastic!" said Brummell. "I should have. The Emperor in a rare mood of mercy?"

"I do not know what has happened to him. He told Napoleon if he were released, he would try again to kill him."

"Fantastic," Brummell said again. "How old was this patriot?"

"Eighteen," said the Earl, "armed with a kitchen knife in a paper. The son of a Protestant minister from Naumbourg."

"An enthusiast, then, after all," remarked Brummell. "Do you stay in town for the Jubilee?"

"I suppose so," the Earl said absently. He was more disturbed by the little story than he cared to admit publicly, and the picture of the young boy, unrepentant, determined, unafraid, brought before the Emperor between two military guards, his hands bound behind him, to be questioned, had put Edward too strongly in his mind, as he told it. He shook the story off, and put his attention on the Prince of Wales.

The two young people, paying no attention to their elders, found their tongues tied, with nothing to say, but Edward's fingers spoke for him. "I love you," they said in their quiet pressure, "did you know?" "No," hers answered, trembling a little, "I did not know, I do not see how you can. Do cousins love?" but they did not try to draw away. "Sometimes," his replied, "I do." "I have been very foolish," hers said, attempting to withdraw, but then remaining. "I love you," his answered, "that is enough. Do you love me?" "You go too fast," hers said, trembling again, "We have just met. You must not ask me now," but they held in his still.

Nevertheless, when he took her back a few minutes later into the crowded room, their eyes and their voices spoke a different language.

"You need not disturb my mother," she said, her voice proudly indifferent and angry, her eyes flashing. "I see no use to further this acquaintance or this relationship would serve. Do you?"

He shook his head. "No, not now that I know your use for me, and you know I will not perform it for you."

He stood with the Earl, and watched her leave him.

VII

But their fingers remembered. And they nevertheless despite opposition and obstacles continued to meet. It would have been difficult not to meet, crossing and recrossing in the dance, their fingers touching, and despite themselves clinging, and and their eyes clinging too, although they did not waltz again. But their eyes met, over their other partners' shoulders, his demanding, pleading, hers troubled, and drawn despite herself. At first, she disengaged her glance as quickly as it chanced to fall across his, but as Advent approached, it remained longer in his before it fell.

Part of the opposition came from his father. The Earl, despite his surface control, had been entirely angry at the occasioning of the first meeting, and he had let Edward know his anger in no veiled terms, in the small hours when they reached home, in the privacy of his study. He had called Edward to him and had left the Assembly as soon as he thought the hour permitted it without stirring gossip, and they had ridden home inside the dark coach in almost unbroken silence, Edward's nerves tense, the Earl not trusting himself to use control in speaking in the coach of the subject, or for his words to have his effect with the cobbled jolting. If Edward had begun to hope, from the Earl's brief polite conversing in the coach, that the incident was to pass unnoticed, he quickly found out it was not.

The Earl invited Edward crisply into his study, and lit into him without preamble: "If you embarrass me again with that girl, I will have you whipped." His expression was uncompromising, and lacking all affection, his voice bleak with anger, and though Edward perceived it only minutes later, with hurt. At the time, Edward perceived only the anger lashing out uncontrolled at him, and from some depth, his own rose to meet it.

"Do it now, then," Edward said, his own small control snapping, his eyes flashing. He faced his father and what he felt to be his injustice unwaveringly, his hands braced against the desk behind him, yet wondering what the Earl would really do.

For a moment they stood, stiffly poised, waiting, like two fighters, their gaze hard fixed. The Earl saw his mistake, and quickly retreated and came round from another direction.

"I am angry with the wrong person," he said in an approach to apology. He sat down, to break the tension, and indicated a chair to Edward with his hand. "How foolish of me. Take in sail, Edward, the blow is past, and let you and me ride calm."

Edward sat down reluctantly, stiffly, not saying anything, while the Earl regarded him thoughtfully.

"Is it because she is an Armstrong or for herself?" he asked.

"I don't know what you mean," Edward said hopelessly.

"I am referring to this unfortunate sentiment you seem to have conceived."

"Don't, Holland," he whispered, in pain at the exposure.

"Well," the Earl said. And then he said again, "Well." There was a silence, and then the Earl looked at Edward directly and said, "I am sorry, Edward. There can be no meeting between our families. This one should never have occurred. Brummell intended to bait me, and learn how your relationship is received there. He dislikes mysteries, and not to know anything, and he smells one here." He sighed. "I do forbid it, Edward. I do not wish this acquaintance furthered."

"I cannot promise that," Edward said. "What are you going to do about it?"

"I do not know whether I am going to laugh or cry, Edward," the Earl said surprisingly, leaning back in his chair. "You have drawn my fangs. I am not going to do anything at all, I find, at least, not now, not tonight, except to ask you, rather to urge you, not to embarrass me, and not to let this madcap hoyden undermine all my work to have you received." He smiled a little. "Must you really pick for your light o' love a little girl who wants to shoot me and with whose family I am not on speaking terms, and you should not be? I cannot seem to rid myself of these Armstrongs."

"I am too tired for this, you may not be but I am; I cannot think," Edward said wearily. "Please, may I go?"

"You should never be too tired to think, or admit to it; I think you do not want to think."

"No, I don't. You take me too fast. I think you are all mad, you, Anne, Brummell, and all too cruel for me. Is it a crime to be introduced, is it a crime to have been curious, and is it a crime to have interest in a family whose name still ends my own? Is it, Holland? Is it?"

"It is an indiscretion, Edward, and at this time that may be worse.

You have asked me what I am going to do about it, and I have told you, appeal failing, I do not know. Now I ask you what you are going to do about it."

It was then that Edward saw the hurt in his father's eyes, and behind it their pleading look, that his measured words with their surface coolness hardly indicated, and he found he could not bear to be the cause. "I am going to try to do what you wish," he said, his voice unsteady, "I am going to try to please you. I hope I may. I cannot promise, but I will try."

He rose unsteadily, and made his way to the Earl and took his hand to bid him goodnight, bowing his head over it, but in his dizziness, he swayed. The Earl rising, caught him, and all their resolutions and their work were undone. There was no laughter and no joy, only hurt and anguish and impossible longing and bitter exploitation and guilt for both, meeting in an assuagement that shamed them both and neither could forgo. The Earl picked him up, fainting, in his arms, his mouth hard pressed against his, Edward's eyes closed, his head thrown back relaxed, but his arms tight as death about the Earl's neck. Without breaking the embrace, the Earl, in his strength, his foot dragging a little, carried him slowly up the stairs, heedless of eyes but there were none, and into his room.

"You are like a woman still, Edward," he said in soft amazement, "for all my work and all my care."

"I know," Edward said, "I am both, God help me, I cannot help myself." He clung to the Earl in a most desperate, unhappy, wordless abandon. Later in the night, he left the Earl's bed and crept back to his own room, ashamed, had he not been too weary to feel shame, blotting what he had again submitted to, and this time desired, from his mind, unable to face himself, or what had again been let loose upon them.

He seemed himself the next morning, only very pale, and his eyes abstracted and a little vague. He stayed as the Earl's mistress for a week, and yet another, in which he felt himself losing further and further his grip on reality. He continued his lessons and his evenings in the world, but he could feel the world visibly sliding from him, and though he clutched at it and cried out, his hands found nothing and his voice made no sound. Like the supper table, he thought, at Nevin House, when the glass and the covers and all the little dishes went sliding over and we could not catch it, and for a long time, it seemed, there was no noise. Or like the little cliff that crumbled in on me when I tried to climb up from swimming, and pushed me back, and buried me, except the Earl was there, and uncovered me, still clutching the little grasses that broke.

The Earl recovered first, aware among other things that his rout was scheduled for the next week. He took Edward by carriage to Amanda's, and told him to stay there: out of the fire into another fire, Edward thought desperately. She was not entirely pleased to see him.

"I have the flowers," she said petulantly. He began to laugh at the absurdity of it all, wildly, hardly able to stop. He seemed then to recover himself, and she was kinder then, but in the night Edward had a fit and frightened her so, she sent for the Earl, who found him raving, having cut himself with a knife. With the help of her footman, and George, whom he had brought, he had him subdued, and bound, and brought home. The Earl was at his wits' end, full of conscience, and pity, and at last good intentions but not knowing what to do. It was Edward himself who told him. The Earl had come to see him, for George had said he seemed lucid, having been stringently bled by the surgeon, despite the Earl's visual aversion to the practise, and not responding, then electrified with the surgeon's machine. The Earl was standing by his bed watching him, when Edward opened his eyes.

"I am sorry, Holland," he said, his voice weak and tired from the double loss of blood in the night. "Did I go mad at last?"

"At last?"

"I have thought I would, for some time now. Is this necessary? I am so uncomfortable." He shut his eyes. He could not move, being wrapped about with strips of torn sheeting.

"I am afraid so. You tried to hurt yourself."

"I wish you had not stopped me." The slow tears began to seep from his closed eyelids.

"You did not try to kill yourself." His eyes opened wide.

"I thought I did. Who then? That girl? You?" The Earl found he could not tell him.

"Is anyone hurt? Is she? Were you? Am I?"

"No," the Earl said, "no one really. You only tried." There was a silence.

Edward sighed. "I am so uncomfortable. Am I sick? Have you had a doctor?"

"Yes, Edward. He came in the night." The reality of his surroundings suddenly penetrated Edward's consciousness, and his face was convulsed with horror, and he struggled convulsively against his bonds, unable to move at all.

"I cannot bear it, Holland," he gasped. "It is like a nightmare, not to be able to move, and I cannot wake up. I *shall* go mad." He looked at the Earl piteously. "Am I mad? Has it already happened? Are you going to have me put away in Bedlam? Oh, Holland, are you? Oh God, oh God, no, Holland, please!"

The Earl again did not know what to say. He put his hand on Edward's forehead, but Edward twisted away with a look of horror.

"Be still, Edward," he said sternly, "or I shall call George in, and the doctor, and have you bled again, and though I should hate it, electrified again. No one is taking you away anywhere. I will not myself, and I will not let anyone else. Be still now." His words seemed to reach through to Edward and to have some effect. He stopped struggling, and his eyes grew less wild. He lay looking up at the Earl piteously. "Do you believe me, Edward?"

"Yes,—no—I don't know. If you are not going to send me away, what are you going to do with me?"

"I don't know," the Earl said truthfully. "I do not know. I wish I did." He looked at Edward with a sudden thought. "Do *you* know? What would *you* like me to do?"

"I would like to go home," the boy said faintly, "and I want Harriett."

"Harriett?" the Earl said, struck. "I had not thought of that. I think perhaps I can do something there. Do you want to see her now, like this?"

"Yes, Holland, I do not care. We do not pretend."

"I will bring her. And you want to go home? To Northumberland?"

"Oh, yes, Holland, please."

"Is that what you want?"

"Yes. I want to go home I want the clear air and the clear snow and the quiet, and to be almost by myself, and not to go to any more parties at all, please, or have them."

"Then that is what you shall have. I wonder I did not think of it myself. You are not mad, Edward, you are just worn out of yourself. I have pushed you too far. I will not, any more"—he bent down, but not very near—"and Edward, believe me, I will not ever touch you again. This time, my word; I promise it; believe me."

He left Edward and went himself at once to Harriett Wilson's, and told her in part what had occurred. He had no difficulty making her want to come, although he had considerable difficulty making it possible. In the end, he exchanged Amanda in her place, and she fabricated herself an excuse that would take her out of London for several weeks.

"I mistrust these ill mothers," her patron said, "but if you must go, go then but bury her quickly, or you may find yourself supplanted by Amanda."

She looked at him saucily and kissed his cheek, and went at once to the Earl's house. The Earl happened to be paying her prodigally well, but she had not come because of it. She breathed money as others do air, but in that air, she did much as she chose. The Earl was waiting for her, and he took her himself directly to Edward's room and let her in, and closed the door softly.

She walked over to the bed where Edward lay, and bent down and kissed his forehead.

"Oh, my poor lamb," she said, "what have they done to you? I should never have left you."

"You will not go away?" he said piteously, his large eyes fastened on hers.

"No, lamb. I am coming to Northumbria with you."

"Oh, Harriett. Are you?" His face grew very peaceful. "I am so glad." He watched her remove her gloves carefully, and lay them down, and her reticule and her little hat, like one who has come to stay, and he was reassured and filled with sudden contentment. She put her arms about him and lifted him a little, to rest against her, smoothing his hair.

"I cannot kiss you, cher Clare," she said. "They tell me you have hurt yourself, and I do not want to hurt you now."

"Oh, God," he said, understanding at last. "Like Attis. Did I do that?" He began to laugh, almost amused. "I wondered what had happened to me. Is that all?"

"Is that all?" she said, "cher Clare, how can you say it?"

"It is not so much. Are you still going to Northumberland with me?" He began to laugh again, rather quietly.

"Cher Clare, of course I am going. Did I not say so?"

"But you will not find it very amusing."

"We shall see. Wounds do not take so very long to heal." She met his look, her own now amused. "You did not entirely succeed, cher Clare, I am very glad to tell you. You must not try again, it would be such a loss."

"Oh, Harriett, I would like to kiss you." She bent down and let his lips brush her cheek. "I am so glad you have come." He paused, and then he said, "I suppose my guardian is paying you?"

" 'But of course your father is. But I would not have come otherwise, but I did not come because of it.' You rogue. You know very well how much I love your father and yourself. You only want to hear me say it."

"Oh, Harriett, I wish you were younger, or I were older, and I would marry you." He made no comment on her changing of his words.

"Fy! A green boy, and penniless. I would not! Never think it, love. And what of your little girl?" She saw his eyes cloud. "Oh, my dear, do not be sad; it will come right if it is meant to be." She laid him back down. "Must you be like this?"

He could not even shrug. "I don't know. I wish I did not. I am so very uncomfortable."

"What is the worst?"

"My feet, my knees."

"I shall find some scissors, and cut them. Be patient, dear heart, I am not afraid of you." She left the room, and after a while she came back with some scissors in her hand, and slit the pieces of material that taped his legs. He relaxed and parted them at ease, stretching, wincing a little.

"Thank you, my dear," he said, less like a child. "I shall give you no cause to regret this act. I am glad you are not afraid. I shall never forget you were not."

"I would like to cut them all, Clare. I am not afraid of you, but I am a little of your Earl, and I must have his permission first."

"It is better," he said, "I can bear it now, it will do."

"But how silly," she said, "you are no more made than I am, less so, I should think. I am going to find the Earl at once."

"Please don't go!"

"I shall be back almost at once." She bent and kissed his cheek quickly. "Lie still now."

"That is what everyone tells me, making it so I can't do anything else. So why tell me. I want to get up."

"Lie still now," she soothed, "there is some point now to me telling you, and soon you shall."

She found the Earl still in the hall where she had left him.

"That boy is no more mad than you or I, Noel. I cannot bear to see him tied. You *will* drive him mad that way."

"He could turn dangerous quickly, Harriett. He did before. Though I agree he does not seem to be."

"I am not afraid. Are you?"

"For myself? A little. Not enough to matter now. I am more afraid he may yet hurt himself than me. He has a great disgust he may not show you of himself and me and of his life. If you free him, it is a large responsibility, Harriett. I cannot entirely let you."

"Well, give me George then, and the two of us will find a way to make him easier, and not shame him so."

She took George, and explained very gently to Edward what she had to do, and then she cut the tapes confining his arms and the upper part of his body, but she took a strip and made a loose fetter that she bound loosely to either wrist, kissing his fingers as she fastened it.

"If you are not mad," she said pleading, "you will not be angry with me for such a silly precaution."

"If?" he said sombrely.

"*Because* you are not."

"And for how long?"

"You ask too many questions, cher Clare. Not long. Show it need not be long."

"Don't you realise that I could break these if I chose?"

"No," she said, surprised. "Can you?"

"Yes, easily. Especially I could if I am mad or *enragé* and need them at all. You have left too much play. Find a stronger material, or tie my hands actually together. George will not mind doing it for you," he added bitterly, avoiding the reproachful eyes of his valet.

"Oh, love," she said, putting her arms around him. "And I have worked so hard. I do not wish to, you would be uncomfortable again. You will not, will you? Your father desires you to have some restraint to protect yourself. Will you not please him?"

"All right," he said, smiling just a little, "I will do anything at all not to be sent to Bedlam. Tell my lord the Earl that, and reassure him. Please ask him when I can go to Northumberland."

"Ask him yourself. He is not far away."

"I cannot see him," he said drearily. "Do not ask me to."

"You must not be absurd," she said, distressed. "You must not build walls."

"You are right, of course, ma'am," he answered, still drearily. "I cannot do as I please. I am not yet twenty-one." He looked so desperate that she wondered if she had after all been wise to remove his restraints. He saw her anxious face and read her thoughts and shook his head. "Come here," he said, and slipped the circle of his fettered arms about her. "There, I have you," he said, smiling an echo of his once sweet tranquil smile. "You see, I am not entirely helpless. One should not ever be made to be, I think. And yet I am not fierce. I know what you were thinking, but it is not true any more. But I do want to start. I am well enough, and

I will be much better there." He slipped his arms away and lay back. "Tell my father I will see him without making a stir any time he likes. I am sorry for causing so much trouble, to him and to everyone I did. Oh God, Harriett, I am so tired, and so tired of this black grimy Hell of London, and of my life here."

"I know," she said. "Poor lamb. I remember. You told me once, and I heard you, but I did not listen. I wish I had paid better attention then."

The Earl came in after a while and sat quietly by Edward's bed. He smiled when he saw Harriett's fetter.

"That would not do much good, would it?" he commented.

"No, Holland," Edward said, his lips not smiling.

"A token of courtesy? Let us not stand on courtesy, then. I will remove it, shall I?"

"Please, Holland."

The Earl cut it in two with his knife, not touching Edward's wrists, and placed the knife by Edward's hand so that he might slice the knots himself. Edward did, and returned the knife to his father.

"Are you testing me, sir?"

"Perhaps. I see I do not need to."

"I have heard the mad are very canny."

"Please, Edward," the Earl said, rising, "Do not test *me*. Try to go to sleep now. We will leave in the morning early." He looked at Edward with eyes full of still surprised grief and hurt incomprehension and a faint but very real shadow of concern, overlaid by a warming and unselfish love that reached through to the boy beyond the other emotions.

"I will try, sir," he said. "Please do not vex yourself on my account. I will not cause you any more trouble."

"Go to sleep now, Edward," the Earl said, settling himself in a chair a little way from the bed. "I am going to."

"Are you guarding me?" Edward cried, his young voice taken by surprise, humiliated and outraged afresh.

"You have been sick," the Earl said quietly. "When you were little, and were sick, I stayed with you. I or George will now. We will not trouble you. But if you need us, one of us will be here. Go to sleep now."

The next morning they started, breakfasting in their rooms by candlelight before it was light. They made the long journey up without mishap and without being mired, for winter had not yet set in hard upon the roads. It was November, and the light rose late and set early, and in the cold, they did not dare travel after dark. Nor did the Earl travel long any day after he saw Edward's lips tight set in a continuous line of pain against the jolting of the road. He found excuse always to stop then, to rest, although it lengthened the journey. The problem of rooms might have been a difficult one, had Edward thought to think about it at all. The Earl shared one with Harriett, George one with Edward, but at night Edward was too weary to consider it. In the day George rode above outside with the coachman. It was almost too cold, but he was from the North and hardened to inclemency and to outside places. He snapped his hands, and told jokes, and filled himself with ale, and tried to forget Edward's silent formality with him, and withdrawal from their old easy friendship. The Earl, Edward, and Mrs. Wilson rode inside, the Earl facing them. Edward had nothing at all to say, but Mrs. Wilson and the Earl found a great deal to say on any number of topical subjects, and Edward, ignored, relaxed, listened to them. They were, after all, nearer contemporaries, Mrs. Wilson lagging by a decade.

When they reached Tyne, after settling them into the house, the Earl tactfully left and returned with all possible haste to London, to attend to his rout, which he conducted in Edward's absence with aplomb, excusing his absent ward. He picked up his own horses left at the first stage and arrived an hour before the guests, but his plans had been made well ahead and nothing was lacking or unready. He parried their casual inquiries with casual skill. His manner was unruffled, his wit polished, and if his thoughts were not with them, or his heart, his guests did not notice, that night or any of the following nights.

CHAPTER VI

Northumberland, in Retreat: November–April, 1809–1810

I

I N Northumberland, at Tyne, the days slipped by without incident. Edward did not miss the Earl, and for days he did not wish to go out. He sat by the window or near the open door, when he was not lying in his bed, and watched the snow fall, or looked up into it until he became dizzy, into its infinite crystalline host, remembering the other snows he had known. Some nights midnight seemed as bright as noon in its white light. Its stillness was everywhere. Nothing stirred in it. In London, the snow clinging raggedly to the black branches of the plane trees had made him think of Villon, and of patches of flesh clinging to the bones of gibbeted men, or so he imagined, but here he found no such imaginings and no images to trouble him. He could see the tiny stars of the separate crystals shining out of the loose mass. The hills lay far away, flat, rounded, smooth and white, the golden gorse showing through in some places in grey and brown patterns, entirely calm and peaceful, and his spirit expanded in their immensity and the far-stretching flat white moor, out of its tight contraction. Under this influence he even finally made peace with George.

And so the days passed. Edward recuperated quietly with Harriett who was mistress in all emotions but the fact, mother, sister, and friend. When he wished to be alone, she left him to himself, when he wished to talk, she listened, when he wished to be amused, she spoke, or read to him, or played cards, or walked with him. If he wished to be quiet but in company, she was content to read a novel to herself, or sit beside him and pull a fringe, or simply to sit, her hands folded, her face quiet. She was gay when he was gay, restrained when he was restrained. If it rained, she was content; if it shone, she was pleased; when it snowed, they went sleighing and threw snowballs like two children. He found her in his home even more enchanting than in London.

"You are a lovely woman," he said one afternoon as he lay on the chaise longue, and she sat beside him, looking at her with quietly grateful eyes, "and the only restful woman I have ever known. Except perhaps my mother. But I cannot remember her as she really was, to other people."

"I find you restful, too, Edward," she said. "That is a change for me, and a pleasant one."

"How did you come to be?" he asked. "How did you learn? I would like to myself."

"You will be very surprised, Edward," she said, "but I was reared a Quaker."

"I *am* surprised," he said, "in one way, but not another. It fits. You have the secret of the quiet heart that listens, and I see now how you came by it."

"You have it yourself, Edward, I think."

"Have I?" he said doubtfully. "The Vicar said something like that, I forget now what, not quite the same."

"You have perhaps forgotten you have."

"Why are you what you are," he asked, "or should I not ask that? I cannot understand it."

"You do not want to hear the story of my life," she said smiling.

"I do. I would like to understand you better."

"It is not complicated. It is very simple. I fell in love with a man who would not marry me, and I left church and home to be with him, and then he left me, and I could not go back."

"Was it my father?"

"No, Edward, it *is* not. Had it been, I would not have told you. Don't you know I would not have? Would he have been capable of such an act?" She paused, considering.

"I know he would have been," Edward said simply, without bitterness or reproach towards the absent Earl.

"Perhaps. You may know what I do not. I would have died sooner than I would have returned ashamed and outcast, having defied my family and been Read out of Meeting; I had perhaps too much pride. I lived in London doorways, and I fought the rats for my food, and I had been brought up gently. My family was in no way poor. Noel, your father, found me, before I did quite die. He was not the Earl then. He said," she paused remembering, "I had a lovely face. It did not matter to me why he wanted me. He was kind to me, and he taught me how to please. It was a useful art, for something happened to me in London after I was so ill and I do not seem to have children any more, after the first little one that died. I loved him, as I do still, and I do not expect him to be other than he is. We have always been good friends."

"Why do you not marry him now?"

"*Marry?*"

"It has been done. Fox did."

She laughed a little and cocked an eye at him.

"Would you not mind?"

"I would be very pleased."

"You are a strange boy, and too much accustomed to incest." She softened her words with a kiss. At his startled flush she added, "Of course I knew. No one told me. I did not have to be told."

He made no comment. There was none he could make. Instead, he asked, "Do you think you will?"

"I know that I will not. It is much too complicated, Edward, you could not understand."

"I think I could."

"No," she said, "you are too young. We are all much too set in our ways, and you are too young to understand *that* or what it is like to be it."

"Nevertheless, I wish you would. Marry my father, I mean."

"Why, dear Edward?" she asked using his name.

"Because you make me very happy, just to be around you, and you make Holland happy. I would like him to be happy. And I would like you always near me. I need your admonishments and advice."

"Well, Edward, if you are determined, you must sell my lord upon it," she said, smiling.

"I am out of influence at court, my word will not go for much there now. It will be leap year in 1812. I suppose we must wait until then."

"You are a rascal, cher Clare, and I have not said, moi-même, I would. I am quite content as I am."

"Harriett," he said hesitantly, "while we speak of incest,—will you sleep with me?"

"Are you quite recovered?" she asked, moving to sit beside him, and putting her arms about him. "I do not want to set you off again, and I do not want you to hurt yourself."

"I would like to try."

"Oh, my dear," she said, kissing him this time with their old passion, "I would like to try, too. I have missed you, cher Clare. Only tell me when, and tell me where."

"Why not now?" he said hesitantly. "Why not here, as we are? But someone might see us. You might mind."

"They would see nothing they have not already seen and do not already know. I like sunshine, myself." She closed the door, and removed what clothing was essential, and lay down beside him and let him take her, without delay.

"Oh, Harriett," he said, his lips against her face, "I am glad I can. I am glad my father stopped me and I did not take this from myself. You do have a lovely face."

"I am glad, too, cher Clare, and your petite fille will be, too." She put her finger on his lips. "I have met her. She came to see you this morning while you were asleep."

He struggled to sit up. "And you just now tell me?"

"Are you sorry?"

"No." He held her to him, and kissed the top of her hair. "You should know not to ask that. But was Anne really here? How could she be? Tell me all about it, please Harriett, tell me as quickly as you can."

"Why, Edward, you have just made love to me, and you are in love with someone else."

"Yes," he said impatiently. "You know that, Harriett, and you knew it a few minutes ago, and you knew what I didn't. Please, don't tease me."

"She is charming, Edward, she is not pretty, but she has an air."

"I know how she looks, and I think her pretty. I want to know where she is, and why she came, and how she is here at all, and what she wants."

"What shall I answer first?"

"Anything at all. Just speak, answer something."

"You will have a fever again. I must get your medicine first."

"I shall strangle you, Harriett, with my two hands and make the words pop out."

"Oho," she said, "you are mad, and must be bound again!"

"For God's sake, Harriett!" he cried, in real anguish. She took immediate pity on him.

"She heard you were here and that you had been ill. She came to call, with her maid, very properly, and brought you a blancmanger and a calves' jelly which you shall have to your tea as a restorative. She was much put about not to see you, but I was firm and would not wake you."

He laid a pleading hand on her wrist. "Has she gone away? Is she still here? Where is she staying now?"

"Of course she has not gone away, otherwise, dear Clare, I *would* have waked you. But there is much time, all you could want. You must not rush; I think she is a skittish filly. She was very nervous about coming at all, and I was hard put to reassure her. She is staying," she added, as he opened his mouth to speak again, "she is staying at her uncle's North estate, she said, apparently he has more than one, to visit him and some of her Scotch relatives who are also here at Lord Armstrong's estate. It is a kind of gathering of the clans, or so I gather, for a shooting. Last winter she went to Scotland for something like it."

"I know. Oh, Harriett, tell me, what am I to do?"

"Do? Why, you will return her call. It would be improper not to. I shall go with you. I am, in case you should not know, an old friend of your mother's, very dear, who has come to take care of you in your illness. You will write a note, thanking her for the various jellies, after you have tried them and can properly *rave*, you know that they will restore you so that you may hope to call upon her shortly, and the day after tomorrow we will go."

"Not until then?"

"Entirely not until then. For your health both and for policy."

He sighed. "I think I cannot go at all. What would Lord Tyne, what would my father have to say if he knew."

"Foo for Lord Tyne and what he has to say," she retorted, ignoring his shocked face. "In this, Edward, if you would win her, you must play the man. If you are afraid, I myself will deal with him."

He looked doubtful, but he allowed himself to be overruled. The call was duly made, in the presence of several relatives. Both Lord Armstrong and young Armstrong were in the fields hunting, but two aunts were present. The air was polite but cool, and they did not stay long enough to warm their cold chairs. Edward's spirits were less than elated, but he discovered his ungovernable hoyden was an independent hoyden still, still used to her way and doing as she wished. She proceeded to drop into the courtyard on her horse, or with her maid in her phaeton at least once a day. Mrs. Wilson was shocked, but Edward was unable to be, however unwise he privately thought it. He alluded only once to their previous meeting.

"If you are coming to see me, with something on your mind, thinking you can persuade me to it, put it out of your mind."

"Why, may I not hope?"

"No, you may not."

"Well, I do not give up hope so easily."

He sighed, sincerely, and she was immediately repentant. "You have been sick, and I am tormenting you. I am truly sorry, cousin; and I will not any more. I have really come just to see you. I have many second cousins, but you are my only first."

He looked grave. "Anne, it is not as a cousin that I feel about you. You must not come here, so securely, thinking otherwise."

"Oh?" she said. "But you *must* be my cousin or I cannot come. And I do so want to see you. It is more amusing here than at Lord Armstrong's" —she did not observe him wince at the word— "and I like to come. It is all talk there of guns and bags and poachers and high-flyers and who has peppered who by mistake in the face, or blown his gun up. I do get so bored. And they have got a poacher today that they are going to have hanged, because he had a gun, at least they say he did, and resisted the warrant." She looked at him uncertainly. "Is that fair, do you think, just for birds? There were several but the rest got away from them. He is just a boy, though he has a stupid face, and they have him in the shed, and so I thought, you see, I would just come here."

"I am sorry about the poacher too, Anne, the two things do not seem equal to me either, but there is nothing I know to do about it, and he surely knew the law was there, unfair or not, before he did it. I do know your family will not approve your coming here as you do."

"I have my maid, and Mrs. Wilson is an excellent chaperon."

"Perhaps," Edward said. He did not argue any more. "You are such a child, Anne. I do not at all know what to do with you."

"It is too cold to go outside," she said. "I would like to play piquet and have tea."

"I thought you were gently raised," he said. "Is this how gently raised young ladies of great houses behave, demanding and asking before they are asked?"

She looked at him, stricken. "Oh," she said. "I shall someday quite ruin myself. No, I suppose it is not. Edward, I am sorry. I quite lied to you at the Assembly."

"Did you?" he asked. "How was that?"

"About my mother. I don't have a mother. Not any more. She died in childbed, with the baby too, when I was ten. I pretend sometimes one of my aunts is, but of course she is not. I don't entirely know how to behave. I was raised by my father and by my brother, and I went right with them, until I was sent to school. I am afraid I have done very much just as I wanted to do. But that, you see, is why I minded so much Lord Tyne's shooting my father, you see, for he was all I really had. I do not much like my brother, not any more, even if he is my brother. He is much too overbearing, and thinks much too much of his position now."

"And what is that?"

"He is Lord Armstrong's heir now, and head of my family, and my guardian."

"Poor Anne," Edward said, "poor child. I am so very sorry for you, and about your father—"

"And your uncle—" she interposed.

"I am," he said "—but I cannot shoot Lord Tyne for you in the back, I would do no one that way, and certainly not Lord Tyne, and if I called him out, he would not accept, and if he did, he would just shoot me, and you would be no better off. Can you not see this, and forget this wild scheme?"

"Yes," she said with a little sigh, "I see you cannot, I was foolish not to see it before. I must just contrive some other way."

"It is also vindictive," he said. "Your father is dead now, and I cannot believe he would want you to use your time in this way in these morbid fancies."

"They are not fancies, as you shall see. And you did not know my father. He was a Lowlander, but his grandfather was killed at Culloden. He never accepted George, any George. He was a man of long memory and fierce honour, and it is precisely what he would have wished me to do."

"Anne, the Scotch cannot feel this way still. Why, their regiments, and even the transported, fought for King George in the Colonies' Rebellion, when the Irish there did not, and they had equal reason not to, and perhaps more."

"It will not serve, your speaking so rationally as if you were not Scotch. We use the English but we do not love them. You know very well the Scotch simply love to fight, they will fight anyone, for anyone, and use them at the same time for themselves."

"As you would use me?"

"As I would use you, and I am not ashamed for it. I am just sorry you will not. You should want to be so used. A father and his brother even dead are more important than a guardian with no blood relationship, and their claims should be stronger."

Edward listened to her in amazement, and wished he did not love her, but he did. The more he saw her, the more he knew the first drawing he had felt towards her had been a true one. But his heart nevertheless misgave him, and he wondered if she would ever grow up, or if she was fey. As he thought it, the look in her eyes vanished, and her face was that again of any young girl. He remembered very well when he had wanted himself to shoot Tyne, loving and hating him, and he wondered if it was that bond of that desire that drew him. He hoped not, for her desire seemed single-hearted and singly motivated, unmixed.

He took her small fierce hands in his, and held them, looking down at them and their small nails, wondering if she would continue now to come to see him. He understood very well that he was not welcome to visit her at her home.

"Do you not miss the Season here?"

"No. Not if I could not dance. You were gone and I had no one for waltzes. And Mr. Brummell said I was too young for a Season, if I slapped gentlemen in public. Edward," she said, "I would like still to come and play piquet with you. I wish we could ride, but it is much too cold for you when you have risen from a sick bed."

"Hardly that," he murmured.

"Well, you have, and I think it my Christian duty to come to see you and to cheer you up in your convalescence. Don't you?"

"I devoutly do," he said.

"And it is surely *comme il faut* with Mrs. Wilson," she said again anxiously, "and you my cousin."

"Surely," he said, the "not" beneath his breath.

"I do wish you had not been ill, and then we could have gone sleighing and had a winter picnic as you did—" She stopped, her tongue having run away with her, blushing, her eyes a little scared at her tongue's betrayal.

"I saw you too," he said quickly. "You were behind a curtain, and you would not come down."

"I had been sick," she said, her colour in confusion, contradicting the coolness of her words. "Let us play piquet, and make it for shillings."

"I haven't any money, Anne. We will have to play for love."

"How odd! But we could still play for shillings, and you would have mine, after I lost, or you could borrow again from Mrs. Wilson. I don't at all want to play for love. I am not interested in love."

"Aren't you, Anne?"

"Not at all."

"Well, I am not interested in shillings. Let's walk out in the garden, and see the winter plantings, and see if anything at all survived last night's frost. Did you know that you can see already the spring buds on the trees? They were underneath the leaves that fell in the Fall, they pushed them off themselves, pressing, and now they will stay there, hard-rolled, all winter, however cold, until Spring, when they will swell again and turn into flowers and leaves. Look, you can even see their colour, faintly, and imagine how they will be."

"You are a funny boy, Cousin Edward."

"Everybody seems to say that to me, at some time or other, so I suppose it must be true." He took her gloved hand in his, and walked along swinging it slightly, but after a few minutes, she withdrew it. He looked at her quizzically.

"I don't like to hold hands," she said, almost defiantly.

"'Who would have thought,'" he said, quoting softly, his eyes on hers, "'my shrivel'd heart

> *Could have recovered greennesse? It was gone*
> *Quite underground . . .*
> *Dead to the world,' kept 'house unknown.*
>
> *These are thy wonders, Lord of power,*
> *Killing and quickning, bringing down to hell*
> *And up to heaven in an houre . . .'"*

"If you are going to quote poetry at me, Cousin Edward, I am going to go home. And you are not that much older than I am to be talking about withered hearts and killing frosts. I don't know at all what it means, but I declare I think you are a deceiver after all like all men, and my father warned me about such."

"Have I ever said I was not?" he replied, his eyes half serious. "But that poem is by a clergyman, it is quite all right, you do not need to be afraid of *it*. I will show you what it means. Come here by this bench, but don't sit on it, for the stone is very cold." He took off his glove and took out his knife, and poked about in the ground for some depth until he found what he wanted, and held out a round withered papery-skinned brown bulb which he dropped into her hand. "There. That is what Herbert was talking about. Keep it, Anne, until you know what he means." She stared at him with eyes half-amazed, half-frightened. "You had better go home now, don't you think? The sun is on its way down, and you should be on your way, or they will have the Runners up here. My guardian is coming tomorrow, for Christmas," he added soberly, remembering, "and I don't think you had better come again while he is here. I don't want you shooting at him." His mouth smiled but his eyes did not.

"It is Christmas. I could call a truce."

"Anne, it is no use pretending. Your family, what there is, does not want you to see me, and you know it, and I know it, and my guardian does not want me to see you and I know it if you do not. I hate it, too, and I would like to pretend too it is not so, but you know it is so and I know it is so. I hate meeting you clandestinely and secretly, but I do not know right now what else to do. Do you?"

She shook her head. He took her hand in his two, the one still holding the little bulb, and he held it longer than manners required. At last he released it, whispering, "Merry Christmas, Anne, I will say it now."

"Well, I won't," she said. "I think you are a spoilsport, Cousin Edward," and left him bewildered and a little sad on the garden path as she walked away with a perceptible flounce towards her pony.

The Earl came the next day. He drove up in his crested coach with Foxham and his coachman and Brummell himself and Lord Monckton. They were not staying but the one night, but Brummell wished to see how the cellar-product, as he called him, was recovering, and Lord Monckton wished to shoot grouse for a day before they went on for Christmas at Lord Carnaervon's. The Earl had also been invited, but he had declined. The coach, and also the second following with more staff and provisions, was filled with packages and with cheer, and they overflowed the house and its occupants. For two days, the foundation of the house rocked with coming and going, for the Earl's guests stayed an extra day, and more, with Haydon and Lawrence, arrived from Edward did not know where.

Edward at first suffered a withdrawal.

"You promised me no parties," he said, his eyes frightened, "and it is not but a few weeks old."

"It is not a party," the Earl said crossly, "it is just a few friends—am I to have no friends?—and they would come. Can't you take even this?"

He was instantly sorry. "You need not come down, Edward. They will be gone tomorrow."

"Mr. Brummell will think it strange," he said. "I will come. I am too demanding, Holland, I am sorry, too. Of course you must have your friends, and I am quite all right. Forgive me."

"It is you to forgive me," the Earl said simply.

It was not a party, as the Earl had said. It was, as he had said, only a convivial gathering of friends meeting and crossing on their way to their respective Christmas hosts. The Earl had not, as he said, invited anyone at all for Christmas itself. Edward enjoyed himself more than he had thought to, although he talked almost not at all, and he was almost sorry when they left, but only almost. It was very peaceful, and for him, more of Christmas, to sit quietly by Harriett and listen to the Earl play. Harriett herself played slightly, well enough to accompany the Earl simply. He listened to the notes of the violin rise and fall, crying and singing all at once like the human voice, and he was very happy, without knowing why or asking why.

The Hall had been decorated with greens, the holly and the rosemary and the apples placed in bowls of chased silver, the Yule log again hauled in. Edward had this time not helped, but he had watched and appreciated. The Mummers came, as always, and with them Anne, velveted and wigged and rouged as the Queen.

Edward recognised her at once, and he could not imagine how she had been let into a man's sport, whether she had fooled them with her slight figure and her cropped hair, or persuaded them. But he was not concerned how she had managed to appear, but why. He sat in a state of frozen horror, shocked out of the mood of the heavenly Adagio, his eyes fastened on her empty hands, wondering what her long full sleeves held, hating to call out and stop the play and embarrass them all for perhaps no reason. Her eyes met his and sparkled with mischief but he could not read them entirely. She seemed unarmed, but he could not tell. She seemed merely excited at her prank, and at defying him, but he could not tell certainly that was all. His eyes never leaving her slightest motion, thinking that would serve, it suddenly struck his mind with new horror that she might have persuaded another of the Mummers to act for her. He could not watch them all, moving and changing constantly, he could not even see all their hands, and part of the Hobby Horse was entirely hidden. He looked at the child he loved and did not trust, and he glanced at the Earl, standing by Harriett, relaxed and at ease and unguarded, half-smiling, tolerantly amused, a genuine gleam of pleasure lighting his eyes. Edward rose and made his way quickly to him, without haste, and without turning to him, trying not to seem to speak.

"Do you love me, Holland?" he said urgently, but in a low voice. "Don't turn your head."

"Yes," the Earl said. "What a strange question to ask me now."

"Then, please, go at once out the door beside you, and don't turn your back. Don't ask me to explain. Please trust me, Holland, and go, and don't come back until the Mummers go. Let Harriett or let me give the money. Please, Holland."

The urgency of Edward's voice, and a quick glance at his face, convincingly sincere, moved the Earl to do as he asked, and no other reason. He quietly, with no further sign effaced himself. Edward moved into his place to shield him from the range of possible fire, his eyes hard fixed on Anne's all the time, and to his furious horror he saw her laugh at him. He could have wrung her neck at that moment, and perhaps she perceived his blazing anger, for the laugh died, and she looked convincingly pale as she died her mock death and fell and was raised again. In the confusion that followed, he walked up to her and took her wrist in his now hard grasp, and shook her a little.

"Don't," she said, unabashed, seemingly unperturbed but a little question in her eyes. "You are hurting me. Let go!"

"I would like to hurt you, Miss Armstrong. How dare you come here like this and frighten me and make a fool of me!"

"I don't know what you mean at all," she faltered. "I may have made a fool of Digby, and if you tell him he will be terribly cross and probably tell my brother and I will be kept in my room probably for a week, but I cannot see what I have done to hurt you or how I have made a fool of you. It is Christmas. I just wanted to see you, Edward. I thought you would think it a good joke, and even clever of me to brave the stronghold of the enemy. I do not see why you are so cross with me."

He looked at her exasperated but with less anger.

"I mistook you, ma'am. I thought you had come to fulfil your intentions upon Lord Tyne."

She looked back at him in honest amazement even indignant: "You thought I would come like this into your house, or any house, by a *trick*, and shoot the owner dishonourably in a disguise? Mr. Armstrong, you do me wrong to think it, I would never stoop to so base an action."

"Well, I did, you said you would—"

"I never did. And I said I would declare a truce at Christmas."

"Anne," he said gently, "my guardian is not at war with you."

"I am with him, but I will kill him honourably when I do."

"Anne, you would be the first to cry if you really hurt him, you are a girl, and people rarely die quickly or pleasantly. Be careful, Anne. You do not know what you are about."

"If I don't like it, I shall just have to bear it. I wish to dance upon his grave and shake his bones."

"Hush," he said, "hush! You have been reading Monk Lewis. Admit it. If I dared, I would stop your mouth with my hand. Look!" he said with relief, "the refreshments are out. Do you want some cake? You mustn't drink the ale."

"I have drunk it everywhere else, and I daresay yours is better. I will have it!"

"Lord," he said, going to fetch it, "I begin like my guardian to wish I might school you. You terrify me."

When he returned, her wild mood of exuberance was a little sobered.

"Do I really terrify you, Cousin Edward?"

"Yes, you do."

"Then I see I must try to behave. Was this really a madcap stunt, as my brother would say?"

"Yes. When are you going home? How many more places? I cannot come with you, and I don't like to think of you going about in this way."

"Why don't you come with me?" she said, her excitement kindling again, her compunction forgotten.

"Because I have got somehow to explain my melodramatics to my guardian, that is why."

"Oh, dear," she said. "Will it be hard? You won't tell him about me?"

"No, I won't tell him. You have Mary-Queen-of-Scots-eyes," he said helplessly, looking down into them, very close. "I thought they were dark, but they are that clear grey. It is the dark fringe of your lashes that make them seem so dark. I do not understand you Scotch, and your wounded honours."

"You are Scots yourself, you should, but I suppose it is being raised by that man. If you like him so, though I don't see how you can when he stole you from your rightful place, why don't you turn me in to the law?"

"There is not very much law here, except on poachers, and I don't want to. I keep hoping you will come to your senses. Oh, Anne," he said, almost with a groan, "why must you look so young and so innocent, and say such terrible things? I do not know what to do about you at all."

He looked down at her, his heart so plainly in his eyes that she at last saw it, and recognised it for what it was.

Her own voice faltered, wondering, dismayed. "You love me, don't you?"

"A Latin question expecting the answer *yes, nonne amas?*" he said unsteadily. "Yes. *Maxime,* my dear. Yes, I do."

"But you cannot. We are cousins."

"I know," he said, "it is a devil of a mess."

"I know they sometimes marry, but not first cousins; I thought you were safe."

"No," he said, "I am not safe. I wish you had not asked me. I am not a good liar. Your friends are leaving, little Scots Queen, go with them now. Here, catch." He tossed a gold coin into her surprised outheld hand, which she caught, her face startled.

"That is two things you have given me," she whispered, "and I have given you nothing."

"Nothing but a deal of trouble," he said ungraciously, "but you have given me enough of that."

"Oh," she said furiously, "you are intolerable, Cousin Edward. I do not believe you love me at all."

"Good," he said more calmly than he felt. "I am not a toy, little Anne, that you can wear about your neck, when you like, and play with when you like, and then tear off or put away. Go join your ring. You wanted it, go with it now."

Her eyes sparked at him under her headdress as she took her place, and her small chin pointed high. His eyes were sombre, but he smiled in spite of himself. The last noise died away, the door closed, and he found the Earl beside him.

II

"Now, Edward, what was that all about?" enquired the Earl.

"Please don't ask me," Edward said, feeling very foolish.

"But I do."

"I would not know how to begin to explain." His eyes fell before the Earl's steady penetrating ones.

"Come now, Edward. Is it so hard? You surely cannot mean to leave me in suspense, after hustling me away and causing me to miss the play and incidentally asking me to appear rude. Or can you?" A touch of asperity had come into his voice.

"I thought you were in danger, but I was mistaken. I was a melodramatic fool, Holland. Forgive me." His voice was shaky, and he wished desperately for rescue.

"Forgive you? I appreciate your concern," the Earl said, the tone of his voice not clear. "I shall breathe easier knowing I am looked after. What was to happen to me?"

"I thought—oh, Holland, I cannot say what I thought. Don't ask me! It seems impossible now, it was a delusion."

"I wonder," the Earl said thoughtfully, "and I wonder who is to look after you while you are looking after me." He paused. "I wish you would be frank with me, Edward. Then we would know better where we stood and what to do. I was on the gallery, watching you, Edward."

"Were you?" Edard said, flushing. "Then you did not need to ask. Why did you?"

"I wanted very much to know what you would choose to tell me. But I shall find out for myself. I cannot be ordered, Edward, and I did expect an explanation from you after your extraordinary request which I honoured. I did not think even to have to ask."

Edward lifted his eyes, stricken, pleading not to be shamed. Harriett at that moment walked over, into their midst, onto the battlefield between their eyes.

"Edward's petite fille came disguised as the Queen express to see him, Noel. Do you not think it quaint?" She ignored Edward's furious hurt look and the Earl's equally angry one. "They must meet in disguise in a kitchen because their hard families will neither let them see each other."

"I do not think it quaint," the Earl snapped. "I find it disobedient in the extreme, and also both rash and foolish. Go away, please, Harriett. This matter is entirely between Edward and myself." She made a small moue with her mouth but she walked away. "Did you expect this, Edward?"

"No," he said, his voice hardly more than a whisper. "I told her it was rash and foolish myself. I did not know. But I am not disobedient. You should not call me that. I never promised you. I told you instead to whip me. Do it then, lock me up again." He looked pitiful and wild, holding his own but barely, against an adversary now much stronger and with the advantage again.

"For two months it seems hardly worth while. You are making tragedies, Edward. I may disapprove of disobedience, you can expect me to"—his mouth briefly smiled—"but impersonally, let me assure you that occasionally disobedience is required and even to be commended. Where is she? Is Lord Armstrong in residence?"

Edward nodded dumbly.

"Oh, Lord," said the Earl, "how unfortunate. I trust she will not stay long, nor he. Have you plans made for seeing her again?"

"No," Edward said.

"Well, can you please refrain while I am here?"

"It was entirely my thought," the boy whispered. "I told you, I never meant her to come here." He wished he could stand up better to his father but he was like an exposed young tree in a hurricane gale, and he felt his resolution bending and cracking.

"Well," the Earl said, suddenly laughing and diverting the wind. "It is perhaps not so bad as I thought. I think myself she is rather plucky, to beard me so. Did she bring her pistol?"

"No. I was mistaken. She said she would not try to shoot you over Christmas—" He smiled himself at the absurdity of the words.

"But when you saw her, appearing there so suddenly, you did not believe her?"

"I did not dare."

"I am touched, Edward. Don't wince. I am not mocking you. And I am sorry for you. She seems to me a very impetuous and self-willed and irresponsible young lady sadly needing a governess." He smiled to himself, and excused himself.

Harriett came up to Edward with concern. "Did he eat you?" she asked. "Was it very bad?"

"Not my idea of fun, nor Christmas Eve," he said, trying to smile. "Damn Anne. How could she? Where has Holland gone? Do we go to Mass, or to the Vicarage? I have not seen the Vicar to speak since we came. But I am so tired."

The Earl did not return for dinner, or for the Christmas Eve services. Without him, Edward decided not to go. He had been badly frightened, and then bullied, for no fault of his own. He felt out of the humour for prayer and for Christmas too. "I have had enough of children," he said fiercely, trying not to worry, and went to bed with Harriett and solaced himself there in her kindness.

Had Edward known or conceived where the Earl had gone and with what intention, he would have been far more uneasy than he was and with real cause. The Earl, with no qualm, had decided to amuse himself and to frighten a young lady he considered impudent beyond her sex and in sad need of discipline by his own. If she was not alarmed to dress as she did and go out alone as she had that evening, cavorting on the moors, after her escapade of the year before, he intended now to teach her that she should have been. He took Ross and his coachman, who were accustomed to obey and not speak, and his unmarked coach, and had his own horse saddled. He put on his white many-caped greatcoat and a tall hat that fitted closely, and took a scarf which he recklessly sacrificed for a mask, cutting two holes in it for vision. He also took his largest set of silver pistols, which he primed. He knew very well the houses the Mummers visited, and the desolate stretch of heath that lay beyond the last one, and he imagined she would even now be regretting her enterprise as she saw the Mummers, fortified with ale and all a little drunk, separating from her, and the heath before her. They would already have paid their call on Lord Armstrong's hunting-box estate, it being North of the village and even more isolated than his own, earlier, though he doubted a little their going there at all. He instructed Ross and the coachman to follow him in the coach at a little distance to a certain part of the lone road across the fell and to wait for him there until they heard him shoot and then to come up as fast as they could drive. He saw the little band ahead of him, making for Digby's house, where they would change, and he saw, as he imagined he would, a small boyish figure shortly slip away to its horse. He waited until she was well into the heath and just abreast of him, and then he fired his first pistol directly before her, causing her horse to swerve. He could see her white face, and he deliberately aimed and fired behind her, her horse rearing. He could see her fighting to hold her seat and her control of the horse, and he admired her skill, even as he rode up in an unnecessarily hard gallop, pulled up short, and seized her reins, pulling out his third pistol from his pocket as he did so.

"Oh, what do you want!" she cried, very much frightened, but to his admiration keeping much of her spirit.

"I want you!" he said dramatically, as his coach drew up. "Will it please you enter," he added with a flourish.

"I will never do it," she cried. "Whoever you are, you cannot make me. I will scream."

"Scream away," he said indifferently. "There is no one here to hear you. And I can make you, as you will see, if you do not immediately dismount and enter my coach." He held the pistol negligently but purposely on her, and to his surprise she did dismount.

"My father said never to argue with a fool with a gun," she said, as if to explain her capitulation, "and I suppose you will really use it."

He was fascinated. "Did he now?"

"You talk like a gentleman, and I suppose you are. Are you Gentleman Harry?"

"I am not," he said promptly, "I am sorry to disappoint you."

"Then who are you, and what do you want?"

He was amused and piqued, for the interview was going differently than he expected.

"There are things said to be worse than death from a fool with a gun for a young lady," he said menacingly, "and perhaps you were unwise to enter my coach so reasonably, despite your father's sage advice."

If she was dismayed, she concealed it. "That will hardly avail. As you see, I am not a girl."

"I see a girl in boy's clothes, Miss Armstrong, but all the same a girl, and very attractive to me."

Again, if she felt it, she concealed her fright. "You are mistaken, sir, and I require you to let me dismount now from this coach and go home about my business."

He laughed, his old wicked vibrant chuckle, and he did see her blanch then. "Gad, that's rich, Miss Armstrong," he said, falling into an older habit of language. "'Pon rep, that's rich. Shall I prove to you that I am right and you are wrong?" He put his hand on the fastening of her breeches, with an unmistakable intention, and was rewarded by a gasp and a frantic pushing at his hands. "We will take the point as proved." He took her two wrists in his, and held them in a grip of one hand that she could not break, and with a steely strength that she had had no experience of, while with the other hand he caressed her short hair with his finger tips, and then pressed her face relentlessly in towards his.

"Your father was mistaken," he said, exaggerating the note of husky passion in his voice, "he should have told you never, never, on any account to enter a coach alone with a gentleman, particularly on a heath and one you do not know. Now, my dear, there is no help for you at all."

He felt her fight against him, but he held her head in the vise-like grip of his fingers and applied his own lips first brutally against hers, invading and pushing back, and then with cool science as he felt her struggles die away. He pushed her back upon the cushioned seat, his own body crushing down against hers, leaving her limp bruised lips for a moment, his hands tearing her buttons and entering her back against her bare skin. Her eyes were closed, and he saw she was crying, from the tears falling, and her quivering lips, but she was entirely limp, and when he pressed his lips against hers again, probing with his tongue, her lips parted and to his utter amazement he felt her respond, both her lips and her arms. He sat up abruptly.

"My God," he said in horror, "Miss Armstrong, please resist me!"

She opened her lovely teared eyes and looked up at him. "You have told me I am entirely helpless. Have I done wrong? My father told me that if I could not avoid rape, I should try to enjoy it. He said that at some time, in one way or another, almost every woman must meet it."

"Oh, Lord," the Earl said, beginning to laugh in his natural way, "Miss Armstrong, you and your admirable father and his sage advice put me at a loss. I cannot proceed, even if I would, but I only meant to frighten you. You are entirely too obliging. What would Edward say?" He helped her up, and began to tidy the front of her clothes as best he could.

"What does Edward have to do with you, that you should care what he says?" she asked, teary but surprised.

"Everything, my dear Miss Armstrong," he said, inclining his head courteously and taking off his thin mask, "but purely everything, for I am Lord Tyne!"

"You cannot mean it," she said, in the dark coach, beginning to shake now for the first time. "Oh, no, sir, you cannot be!"

"I do entirely mean it; I am indeed that monster."

"Oh, sir," she whispered, entirely surprising him again, "please then to shoot me, as you said you would with your little pistol. I shall never live down this humiliation. To have let you of all men kiss me and put your hands—oh—I should have first died. And you will tell Edward and I cannot bear it." She began to cry in terrible earnest.

"Madame," he said austerely, but with a slight twinkle invisible to her in the dark, "as a rule I do not shoot helpless females, in or out of coaches; ask something less." He perceived, however, that her distress was wholly genuine, and as her sobs grew wilder, he drew her against the breast front of his coat, and patted her, and soothed her, trying to reason with her, calling her little names of endearment, understanding something of Edward's helplessness.

"Oh what shall I do, what shall I do," she moaned to herself, "I have done such mischief, and I have ruined myself."

"You are not ruined anything of the kind," he said, "if you did not ruin yourself with your family by running off the way you did this evening. And I think that can perhaps be fixed. Now please stop crying, I really cannot abide it." He took his handkerchief out, and wiped her face, and her sobs dwindled into little coughing hiccups.

"There now, can you sit up?" he asked.

"No," she whispered, "please let me stay here."

"Lord, why, child?" he asked, startled.

"I am so afraid of you, and I hate you so," she whispered, to his consternation, "and it is impossible to be afraid of someone, or hate them, when one is lying oneself on their manly bosom."

He began to chuckle. "You read too many novels, child. It is the root of your difficulty, I think. You miss the meat and magnify the shell." But he let her stay as she was, his hands stroking her hair. He called out to Ross to come to the window, and told him to take Miss Armstrong's horse home and to tell them there that she would attend services with Lord Tyne and the Vicar's wife whom she had met, when it was too dark for her to return, and that Lord Tyne would bring her home. And to please send her maid, he added, and a church frock to the Inn as she had only her riding clothes.

"I am not going to church with you," she protested.

"Oh, but you are, Miss Armstrong," he said, chuckling. "You cannot help yourself, remember? You are also going to the Inn now with me and have supper with me while you wait for a suitable dress."

"Why would you do this to me," she asked, "a grown man, as old as my father, playing such ramshackle rascal tricks on me?"

"I do not like the tricks you have been playing on *me,*" he said seriously. "I thought we had better meet and talk them over, and see how they could be stopped. I also do not like the tricks you play on Edward. He is not entirely well, and you particularly distress him with your cockbrained romantic notions of revenge. I do not wish you to see him any more, Miss Armstrong, there can be no future there for either of you, and only more distress."

"But he is my cousin!" She sat up and retired into a corner against the squabs.

The Earl opened his mouth to speak, and shut it. "Nevertheless," he said, "I do not want your acquaintance to continue. You are much too young and much too inexperienced for a boy so immature and highstrung as Edward is right now, nor do I like your family, nor does yours like me."

"But I like you, sir," he heard a small voice say, almost inaudibly.

He was almost non-plussed. "And I like you too, Anne. The night is full of surprises, isn't it? But liking each other will avail neither of us. But if you like me, don't you think you could stop trying to shoot me?"

"No," she said with a small sob, "I shall just do it sadly now."

"Well, then," he said, half amused, more than half exasperated, "then just do it, but please stop talking about it and enlisting my neighbours' help and now my ward's. You make us all a name and something even of a laughing-stock, and I am seriously afraid you may drive Edward mad."

"I think you do not know your Edward very well," she said again with a little sob. "His nerves seem very cool to me, and I have never seen anyone less likely to run mad."

He was struck by her opinion, recalling as it did similar words two and a half years before from Alleyn, and he was filled again with conscience at himself. He ordered supper for them to be served in a private room while they waited for her abigail to arrive with her dress.

"I suggest you be undressed, when she comes," he said, "and not let her see those disreputable clothes."

"Agnes is used to finding me all kind of ways. I am rather enjoying myself, Lord Tyne," she said, looking up at him with an engagingly naive look, "although I am not certain you intend me to."

He smiled at her, a smile with a trace in it of Edward's sweetness. "I most certainly did not, not at first. I meant to frighten you severely, and to punish you, but you are hard to frighten, and I find I don't want to any more. In fact, you have almost frightened me. I have never met a young lady quite like you. Though I daresay when I get home and am away from you I will wish I had turned you over my knee and spanked you. I wanted you, you know, to be so afraid of me that you would entirely surcease from troubling me or Edward or my house any more. And I was very angry with you, Miss Armstrong."

"You will be still angrier, Lord Tyne. I *am* afraid of you, but I am not going to promise not to see Edward again."

"Not even if I frighten you again or attempt to force you to promise, now, by means that might after all prove extremely unpleasant to you, despite the helpfulness of your father's words?"

"No matter what you do," she said, bravely, biting her lower lip a little in her anxiety, but meeting his eyes without flinching.

"Well," he said. "It is a hard lot to be a highwayman and not a very profitable one. Let me say simply then, that if you do continue to see Edward, you will do so under my displeasure, as well as your guardian's, and that in the end it may work very badly against Edward himself, and perhaps even remove him from becoming my heir. No—don't speak, Miss Armstrong. I know you are going to say that he would be well off without me and that he is your cousin, but that was a long time ago, Miss Armstrong; that story is quite finished. The breach of families cannot be healed; and he has no inheritance there to come into. There is only possibly mine, if he pleases me. You know very well you cannot marry a penniless boy without prospects."

"We are cousins, what is this talk of marrying? I have no thought of it myself."

"Do not play the too innocent with me, Miss Armstrong. If you continue as you are, in the end that is the way the thing will lead. It always does—in or out of marriage."

She flushed. "You must not talk to me this way. I am not enjoying myself after all."

"Believe me, Miss Armstrong, your enjoyment is secondary and negligible for me. Will you promise me?"

"No, Lord Tyne," she said, "I won't, but I will think carefully about it. Will that satisfy you?"

"I suppose it must," he said, "I really have no inclination to any more violence tonight. I am after all getting old. But do think carefully, and try not to hurt us all in your charming and reckless orbit."

"Why, that is almost what Edward said to me."

"Is it?" said the Earl thoughtfully, somewhat startled.

"Yes, it is. Sometimes you seem very alike to me, the way you think."

"Do we?" said the Earl more thoughtfully yet. "That is natural enough, for people living closely together."

"My brother and I do not," she said, "but we are family, perhaps that is the reason."

"Perhaps," agreed the Earl. "I thought myself Edward and I thought rather differently about things."

She shook her head. "Not so differently as one might think. It is what you do that is so different."

"I am gratified to have your opinion."

"Now you are making fun of me, Lord Tyne, I think. Edward is after all your ward, and you surely know him better than I do."

"I think perhaps I do not. Perhaps I should have commended Edward instead?"

She looked at him, very distressed. "You surely did not hurt him, not at Christmas, not when he has been sick? He was in no way to blame. It was entirely my own stunt, and he was almost as angry with me about it as you have been. I had never seen him so cross before. Had I known he would mind so, I would never have done it."

"He received the lashing he deserved, Miss Armstrong, but with tongue only. You need not concern yourself in his affairs. I have asked you, I believe, that you do not." He paused, and his look and his tone were both forbidding. "Am I to understand from your words that you and Edward have been seeing one another frequently in my absence?"

"You may understand what you like and do what you like about it, to me, but you must not blame Edward for it. He is my only first cousin, and I wanted to see him, and I would come. I saw no harm in it then." She discovered a new grievance of her own, before he could reply. "How did you know about what I did tonight? Edward promised me he would not tell you."

"So that was it," said the Earl thoughtfully. "I should have known." He became aware that she was still looking at him expectantly and attentively. "He did not tell me, Miss Armstrong. Mrs. Wilson intervened, and told me. And I have yet my eyes."

"Then I did cause Edward trouble, just as he said I had," she said sadly, "and that was all I gave him, after all. I am truly sorry about it now. Will you tell him so for me?"

"No, Miss Armstrong, I will *not* tell him."

She sighed. "You are a difficult man to deal with, Lord Tyne."

"Yes, Miss Armstrong."

"I suppose Edward finds you so, too."

"He would, if he tried. He is wise enough not to try."

"Edward is too afraid of you, Lord Tyne," she said boldly, then dropping her eyes in confusion and halting, under his disapproving look.

"You find him so?" Tyne responded coldly and discouragingly, returning his attention to the finishing of his dinner. "I appreciate your enlightening me of it."

She was startled out of her shyness and confusion. "You *know* that he is?"

"I have been told so by several persons already, well-intentioned, I dare say," he remarked even more coldly, "but all the same intrusive." He ignored her little gasp at the new and unexpected set-down she had clearly been given. "It is not news to me, and I have spent considerable time and effort instilling in him that he should be. It is not his natural bent, but it is a requirement I demand in those who live about me, and I believe he knows that finally."

"How terrible," she said. "And how sad for you and for him." She looked at him consideringly, and then she rose in her boy's clothes and walked over deliberately and sat down on the bench beside him, and after hardly any hesitation she stretched upwards and kissed his surprised lips. They smiled, despite themselves. He put his arms about her, and lifted her into his lap, but after a short moment she withdrew her lips, and hid her face against his shirt.

"That is dangerous, pussy, more dangerous than your brother in the field. What did you do it for?"

"You did that to me. Is it not allowed?"

"Come now, you know it is not the same." He looked at her as closely as he could. "I do believe, Miss Armstrong, you are teasing *me*."

"I didn't want the one you gave me in that coach, I gave it back," she said muffled against his shirt.

He chuckled slightly and tilted her buried chin up with one hand. "Then please take back the one I just took." He shut his eyes, seemingly, his lowered eyes on the table knives and her hands, and felt her quick light touch. "Now," he said, opening his eyes, "tell me really why."

"You were angry with me, because you still think Edward is not my business, and I wanted to show you that *I* am not afraid of you, even when you are angry."

"Are you trying to shame me, or Edward?" he asked half-smiling. "You are a girl, Miss Armstrong, and not a young man, and you are nothing to do with me, if you will only leave me and mine alone. You have nothing to lose with me, except your virtue, and that is really quite safe, Miss Armstrong. And you do not have to live with me, and Edward does. I am not good as a steady diet. A very little of me is generally enough. I am extremely tired of talking about Edward now, who I continue to insist should not concern you, and I have promised myself I will not seduce you." He paused. "But I am not *that* old, and if you do not take yourself off my lap now, I may forget what I have promised."

She looked at him, startled, but she slid quickly off his lap and went back to her seat.

"You are a dangerous man too, Lord Tyne," she said quietly. "For a moment I quite forgot who you are and what I have promised myself to do."

His dark eyes met her grey ones, and then glanced to the window. "I think that will be your abigail," he remarked formally, and rising himself, offered her his hand to rise.

Her maid arrived, and she was tidied and dressed, and her rents explained as the result of a fall. She went demurely to church with the Earl, her small hand on his arm, wondering if she would see Edward, listening to the Earl breathing beside her and looking up sometimes into his face, hesitant and puzzled, while he, sensing her regard, turned and smiled down at her reassuringly. The night was very cold and very clear.

The stars seemed unusually near, without a shred of protective vapour between them and the earth, and through the windows of the church they threw out their hard sparkles like red and blue spears or like fireworks.

At the door to her home, before he let her from the carriage, but sending her abigail ahead, he asked curiously, "How old are you, Anne?"

"I am sixteen; I will be seventeen in March."

"You are very young," he murmured. "I am almost fifty-two," he said, "more than twice your age," and then he said again in warning, "You do not understand at all the complications of the quarrel between your father and myself, Anne. You are so young, and so sure, and you do not, I think, sufficiently perceive how very young you are, or how unsure the world can be. Can you not postpone your vengeance at least until you are older and understand just a little more than you can now?" He saw her shake her bent head almost imperceptibly. He sighed. "Then think well about it before you do. When I am dead, you might wish I were alive. Think well about it. I know very well, you see, that if you are truly determined upon it, you will succeed in your aim. I could disable you, of course, now," he said, taking her right wrist in his hand, and twisting it back very slightly, "like this, or if I am afraid of your offering bribes or other inducements, like this," he said, sliding his hand to her throat and pressing slightly, feeling her pulse come quickly beneath his fingers, and then releasing her entirely, "but for me that course will not serve. You do not seriously consider I might, I wonder why you do not. How confident you are in your rightness." He sighed again. "Well, remember, there is always the law for me, such as it is, if you continue to threaten me, and for you, little girl, if you succeed." He bent down and kissed her lips gently, and she flung her arms about his neck and kissed him with a passion that unnerved him but to which he courteously responded.

"Oh, Lud," he said, half to himself, when he could breathe, "here is a complication I did not intend. Edward will not forgive me."

"No, Lord Tyne," she said, giving him her hand, "you mistake. I was only saying farewell to certain of my illusions that I held earlier today when I found life simpler and more sure."

"Well," he said, still holding her hand, "I wish you Merry Christmas, Miss Armstrong."

"And I you, Lord Tyne," she said, "for what you have given me." He released her hand and bowed, and she knocked and was admitted into the house.

The next day was Christmas itself, and the world threw aside its difficulties and its dismays and welcomed it in in all its promise. The last Christmas, so different from this, rose vividly before the Earl's mind, and he looked at Edward sitting at Harriett's feet on the floor, near the fire, his head resting against her knees as she sat making needle-point in the chair. His hands were clasped about his knees, and his eyes were looking far away into the flickering blue flames of the oak, watching the sparks soar up like tiny spirits, and three small sparking flames against the black log like tares of ripe wheat. Edward seemed smaller, his height concealed by his position, and frailer, the firelight flickering over his hair and colouring his face. The Earl remembered very well how not long ago Edward had sat just so with him.

They exchanged gifts, very simple ones, a new piece of music for the Earl from Edward that he had purchased with money Harriett loaned him. His financial position, its lack of a definite shape, had ceased to gall him, as an old sore is accepted. He knew it was there but he did not let it fret him.

"It is Opus Twenty-six, I hope you do not already own it, Holland," Edward said. "I sent for it because it was dedicated to Von Lichnowsky whom you said you knew. I know you have Thirteen."

"I do not own it, although I know it, and I am very happy to own it now, Edward," he said with real pleasure

"Can you play it?" asked Edward.

"I think so. I have heard it. Let me work it out by myself first. I studied, did I tell you, for several years with Schenk himself who taught the composer." He was thumbing through his gift as he spoke, and now he exclaimed, "Oh my God! There is a Dead March. I had forgotten." He saw Edward's face fall, "It is very beautiful, and for a hero, and since we are not heroes, we need not worry or take it to heart. Lichnowsky writes me in Vienna there is a new one I have not heard: *Das Lebewohl, Les Adieux.* I am glad your gift was not that."

"What a strange title for a sonata," Edward murmured.

"Not so strange really: its three movements are three moods: *Les Adieux, L'Absence* and *Le Retour, Das Lebewohl, Die Abwesenheit, Das Wiederseh'n.* I should like to take you to Vienna, Edward, one day, while Beethoven is there, and playing. I wish I might take you now, but the travel is too hazardous, I think." He was still scanning his music. "The Trio is particularly beautiful, luminously clear. Listen." He sat down and played the opening bars. "It is how I feel about the three of us, sitting here. I wish it might always be so." He paused and turned to Edward. "You have not opened your gift from me."

The Earl had had the small packet of Edward's "father"'s sermons bound in leather, and had given him that and a book of published Extracts from Wesley's Journals. He had expected him to be pleased, at the books themselves and at his gesture of peace, and he was appalled at the sudden intense rage that swept over Edward, the like of which the Earl had not seen in years. Edward dropped the books from his shaking hands, his face white, his eyes blazing almost black, the pupils so enlarged.

"How could you, Holland," he cried, his voice shaking like his hands, "how could you!"

"I thought you would be pleased," the Earl said mildly.

"Pleased!" He picked them up, and walked to the Earl who was seated now by the fire again and offered them to him. "I don't want them. You have them."

"No more do I," the Earl murmured. "Poor little books. They are of no use to me."

"Nor of any to me," Edward said, and he tossed them into the fire.

Harriett gave a cry, and the Earl reached for one, singeing his finger tips, and raked the other out with his stick.

"'A brand plucked from the burning,'" he commented with a wry smile. "That was my gift to you. I will take it back. I am sorry it has met with so little favour."

"Favour! I don't want such favours." Edward's voice shook with passion. "I am not a toy, Holland, I am not! You must not play with me. When I wanted these, I could not have it. You would not let me. And you know what you did to me to break me, I will not speak of it before Mrs. Wilson, and you did break me. I am broken now, my will, my sex, my life, all of me, as you wanted it, to your will. I cannot go back. I know it, perhaps you do not. But where I am going forward to, I don't know. I can't see my way. But don't offer me a sop, Holland. This man, these men, are nothing to me now, nothing. Do you hear?"

"I hear you, Edward," the Earl said quietly, "I hear you very well. And it will do. Please lower your voice, you need not shout. I am not deaf. I hear you, but I do not believe you, not entirely."

"Then you know me better than I know myself," Edward said most bitterly, "for I know I don't want to think these thoughts any more."

"You protest too much, Edward. You sound as if you kick against the pricks."

"It may be, but I am pricked by two riders then, and your spurs are sharper and cut deeper."

"That will do now. I am not accustomed to my gifts being refused," the Earl said suddenly, with his anger rising. "Take them now, Edward, and let me hear no more of it. Do as you like with them, but out of my sight."

"No!" Edward said, his eyes blazing defiance. "No, Holland."

His own face white now with anger, the Earl took the innocent little books and threw them back on the fire, at its edge. "I took them out once, Edward, and received no thanks for it. Do so now yourself. Do it, I say, or I send you to Ross."

"Why?" Edward flamed. "Can you not deal with me yourself? I am your son, not his, not that man's," his hand outflung towards the books. "It is nothing to do with me now. He would hate me as I am now, what I have become."

Harriett had listened and watched dismayed. She rose now, and took Edward's arm, as he stood stonily watching the edges of the little books smoulder.

"Edward Clare," she said quietly, "It is Christmas, you are the son, do as your father asks. You should be ashamed."

"You will kindly sit down, Harriett," the Earl said, also smouldering, "and let this boy make up his own mind. If you are broken, as you say, Edward, you will pick up those books. If you are not, I can break you now."

"Are you threatening me?"

"No. I am reminding you."

For a moment, their eyes met. Then Edward's fell. The proud stiffness of Edward's shoulders faded, and he bent forward, and picked up the little books, blowing the ashes off of them, and smacking out the smouldering coal at the edges against the fender.

"What am I to do with these, sir, now that I have them? Instruct me." His voice was very low.

"Anything you like, Edward," the Earl said, suddenly weary. "Anything at all you like. I am tired of the matter entirely."

Edward put them on the table beside him to cool, and after a few minutes, he put them inside his coat, a movement not unremarked by the Earl's eyes. In one of his sudden characteristic reversals of mood, in which love or common sense outweighed his personal humours, Edward suddenly rose and walked swiftly to his father and kissed his cheek.

"I am sorry, Holland. I have been silly over nothing, and boorish. I have ruined our spirits for nothing at all, and spoiled your present. Will you forgive me?"

"I have already done so," the Earl said heavily. "It was a thoughtless gift, although I meant it otherwise."

Harriett endured the loaded silence in silence herself for a few moments, and then she said rising and going between them, "It is still Christmas, and you have not had *my* gifts." Harriett gave them each her lips.

"But we have had these already, ma'am," the Earl protested, his volatile spirits rising. "Where is our gift?"

"That was a gift," she said, her dimples demure. "I will send no bill."

"On Christmas, madame, such language?" the Earl said. "Fy!" But he kissed her lingeringly, whispering in her ear.

"Before Edward?" she said, blushing a little. "For shame, sir. You will make your ward jealous."

"Edward?" the Earl asked.

"Pay me no mind," Edward said drearily at her feet, sitting in his old position, "I wish you joy." Under the log he could see the bed of fallen coals, like little blocks of fiery ice, rippling beneath the glassy surface with the contained pulsating flame, all the material that held that fire penetrated with it and transformed by it. They would chime with a tinkling like glass or like icicles, if they touched the hearth or each other. He knew, for he had knocked them on other days, and yet they were fire and they would burn him, even the tiny ones winking at him in the grey ash at the edge. He put his mind most desperately on them, on anything besides himself, besides the two other people in the room with him.

He felt his mind again being dislocated, and yet he could find no way to help himself. His memory, once and not long ago so keen and so accurate, was fragmenting, under the repeated shocks of experiences and words and emotions he could not bear to keep in it or recall, in the presence of this fire-ice man whose unpredictable demands and angers (like the reverse pattern of his own) and changes in mood tore at his nerves and whom he winced inwardly now to meet and could not bear even so to contemplate living without. He felt uncontrollable shivers running through him like the little shivers playing beneath the surface of the coals. He let his mind turn away, and it went of its own accord back to an experience the fiery coals reminded it of that had happened almost nine years before, the morning after he had run away for the third time after his twelfth birthday.

He had ridden all night, on the horse of the man he did not know then was his father, afraid to stop, because of being found by Ross and whipped again, his back and sides and all his bones still aching from the memory of that first, and because he was cold. By morning he had come into the Southwestern range of hills so that they rose on all sides of him. The white thin cold mists were rising in vapours off the half-bare, half-wooded sides of the hills. The sun, rising out of the cleft where the Eastern and the Southern hills seemed to join, had just struck the white-gold frosted edge of the due Eastern hill, like a rounded flat obelisk, or the rising side of a woman's breast, he would have thought now; and sent its long gold shafts of light, far-darting flattened planed arrows over the flat valley behind him he had left, striking whatever objects lay in their path and transforming them. Gold disk itself, up long before it showed itself over that cleft, it had struck squarely the mists rising off the Southern flat slopes, with a peculiar effect like an oval or rounded two-coloured, localised rainbow—or like the Burning Bush, he had thought: the colours floating there in their breathless blinding brightness, like a diffused two-coloured enormous shimmering diaphanous egg, half orange-red, half gold-orange, floating on the vehicle of the mist. He had stared at the extraordinary sight, wondering if a voice would speak to him, out of that reflected burning, reflected from the face of the sun itself. But nothing spoke, any more than these coals or the fitful flame above them spoke now, and he had turned his eyes and his horse and ridden on. He lifted his eyes again to the man standing near him, and saw the Earl reach into his pocket and slip a silver bracelet, set with sapphires, on either arm of the woman he knew now they had both known.

"Noel, how charming," she said, colouring with pleasure, "but it was not necessary, my dear."

"Of course it was not, my dear, I wished to," he said smiling at her. "It is a little fetter, one from Edward, one from me. You see I do not wish you to forget us, or who you really belong to. Now—you are quite fettered to us both. Do not forget it." He brought her wrists together so that the bracelets touched, and as he did so, he bent his head and kissed the crevice of the palms of her hands where they met. Her fingers touched his cheeks in a brief caress.

"I do not need reminding," she said, her eyes warm, smiling back at him. "I am not likely to forget."

"Well—," he said. He looked down and became aware of Edward's face averted from his elders.

The Earl abruptly ceased his teasing. "I want to try my new music," he said. "Edward, will you help me?"

"If I can, sir," Edward said, rising obediently. His playing, however, stumbled and was spiritless.

III

They went to church, not seeing the Armstrongs who had gone to church in another parish, taking the Vicar a present of a brace of pheasant, and the Vicar and his wife came home with them to dinner. The Vicar looked searchingly at Edward, his kind eyes troubled behind their glasses, and tasked him a little for not having come to see him.

"I have been ill, sir," Edward said, "and not quite myself." "And I have sinned and I have not repented," his eyes said, as the Vicar's weak eyes nevertheless clearly saw in them, "and I am ashamed to see you in this state." He had for many nights had a recurrent dream: There were three hills before him he had to climb, for his salvation, his soul's health. The first, the sin itself and marked on its farther side Renunciation, he had climbed and had left, though each night he climbed it and left it again. The third, marked Atonement in letters on its side he could see ahead of him, and he had not been afraid of its severity, or its height, but the second, of Repentance, blocked him and stopped him, and he could not get over it.

"I would like to talk to you," the Vicar said kindly to Edward. "Will you come to see me?"

"I will come, when I am stronger," Edward said. It was weeks before he went, reluctantly, but compelled to it. And when he did go, he went directly to this matter.

"I have sinned, sir," he said, his head bent. "I have sinned and lived in sin."

"And do you still?" the old man asked.

"Not as I did."

"And do you intend to again?"

"No. I hope, I pray I may not. I have renounced it, or it has me, but I cannot repent to have done it, and I know I must repent, or it will be with me always, and I may even go back to it, for I have no will there." He told the Vicar his dream. "How can I learn to repent when I do not?"

Then the Vicar said a surprising thing, not wholly orthodox, looking at Edward's bent head and tortured face. "Your dream could be mistaken, it need not be a vision from God. You must choose, Edward, whether to live with it and accept it as having happened and as being never wholly past; or to cut it from you and repent and lose it entirely. I think you do not yet know your own mind in what you must do. To repent of a person, so long as one still loves them, is almost impossible to do. The renunciation, if it is truly necessary, and if you can do it, myself I think enough."

"And do you say to me, 'Go and sin no more'?"

"I say nothing to you, Edward, except that I have known you since you were a little boy, and I trust you in the end to do as you must."

"My guardian said that to me, something like it—'to remember that a child's dream is divine'—but I did not know what he meant then—what dream, which dream—and I do not know now."

But it was then still Christmas and Edward learned that the Earl had attended Christmas Eve services with a hooded young lady unknown to the Vicar.

Edward looked at the Earl, his attention fixed. The Earl would only say, admitting the fact nonchalantly, ignoring their surprise and Edward's concern, that he had discovered Miss Armstrong without an escort and had appointed himself escort to her. Further than that, he would not go, or admit there was any further to go; and with that Edward was for the time perforce content, for he knew very well that when the Earl did not wish to speak, there was no making him.

After cold informal Christmas supper, he curled up in a chair by the fire, the high back and wings hiding him. The Earl, coming in, came upon him unawares. He stood, his face unusually hesitant, as if to go, but Edward gave him his old smile, despite his wary eyes.

"You need not go because of me. I am reading the books you gave me, you see. I thought you were having coffee with Harriett."

"I was. She is tired. She has retired."

"It is my fault. My ill humour tired her. I am ashamed."

The Earl waved his apology aside. "Should you not go yourself to bed?"

Edward shook his head. "I like Christmas night better than any part of Christmas, better even than Christmas Eve. The expectation is over, it has happened. Everything is changed, but for a little, it is quiet. The pain of birth and miracles is past, and too much joy. The air is still, there are no angels, everyone is gone. One can rest, and think, and be quiet too."

The Earl opened a window, looking out, and the cold clear smell of the fallen snow came through into the room. "It is beginning to snow again," he remarked, closing the window.

He came and sat in the chair opposite Edward, and crossed his legs, relaxed, not speaking, in a brief camaraderie they rarely experienced.

"Wesley was a doctor, did you know that, Holland?" Edward said after a little. He was intensely aware of his father's presence, but neither attracted or repelled, poised in a brief equilibrium.

"I had heard something of it, but not licensed, I think."

"No, he used much common sense, and he had studied Lind. I was raised on treacle water, or tar water, and the applications of hot boiled nettles, because Mr. Wesley had so advised. I did not think much of the remedies then, but I find it interesting now to read of them here, and the apples and the apple-tea he used for flux and quinsy, and the vinegar for nosebleeds. Brimstone plasters, honey and lemon." He smiled, to remember, and for a moment his families and his lives seemed to merge and reconcile. "He even bought an electrifying machine for his Society in London, for his poor and his sick." (He had no remembrance of the use of one on himself and the Earl did not remind him.) "He rode through all kinds of weather on his horse—in fog, and ice, and snow, and hail, and sleet, and took no harm, so they must have done some good, these remedies. Once he rode from four in the morning until midnight, ninety miles, changing horse only once. Do you not find it amazing, Holland?"

"Yes, I do. Amazing grace, amazing luck. I do not venture an opinion."

"I see my father, my first father, used many of his sermon texts to enlarge on for his own favourite sermons."

"What were they, Edward?"

" 'Ho, everyone that thirsteth, come ye to the waters!' "

"Vigourous," commented the Earl, interpolating, "that!" Edward lifted his head and smiled faintly, a question in his eyes. "The reverent and the irreverent? I will curb my tongue. Continue, please, Edward. I would really like to hear. Read them to me."

" 'God is a Spirit, and they that worship him, must worship him in spirit and in truth.' 'We know that we are of God.' 'What doth the Lord thy God require of thee, but to do justly, to love mercy, and to walk humbly with thy God.' 'Turn ye, turn ye from your evil ways, for why will ye die, O house of Israel?' " Edward read the sermon verses, riffling the pages of the smaller book, without expression. " 'What is a man profited if he should gain the whole world and lose his own soul?' "

"What indeed?" murmured the Earl. "Pray, read me no more, Edward. I gather the meaning. What else does the excellent Mr. Wesley impart?"

"He speaks here, it is August 14, 1747, of the massacre by Cromwell in 1641, of two hundred thousand men, women and children within a few months, 'butchered in cool blood, and in such circumstances of cruelty as make one's blood run cold!' That was in Ireland, Holland. He speaks of walking himself through ruined and deserted abbeys where the unburied, uncared for, disjointed bones and skulls lay thrown about on the floor to a depth of several feet. 'It is well,' he says, 'if God has not a controversy with the nation, on this very account, to this day.' He sounds almost like Alleyn. He has procured what he names 'a genuine account.' 'Nor is it any wonder,' he says, 'that those who are born Papists generally live and die such, when the Protestants can find no better ways to convert them than penal laws and Acts of Parliament.' "

"That could be read in Parliament now," observed the Earl, "it is still pertinent."

"It has taken a hundred years, though, for that account to reach him. And listen yet to what he says of Culloden, on Thursday, October 9, 1746: 'The day of public thanksgiving for the victory at Culloden was to us a day of solemn joy.' How long must cruelty take to make itself known? I cannot find he changes that opinion. Knowing what we know now, one can hardly credit it to him. God! The country thought the Societies of the Methodists were Jacobite and directed through France and for the Pretender, yet no one more condemned the Rebels or feared them or supported the Crown. How ironic! Not one word of that massacre, not one word of pity about those prisoners. Did you know about it, Holland, do you know what was done then?"

"Ross has seen to it that I was enlightened, as I daresay he has done you. So you like my little books now?"

"Yes, Holland," Edward said with a quick smile. "When one faces what one fears to face, sometimes it is not so formidable or so fearsome after all."

"And were you afraid of these books, Edward?" the Earl asked curiously, in genuine surprise.

"Yes, Holland. Didn't you know? Couldn't you see?"

"Afraid of what? They are just books."

Edward shrugged his shoulders, or shivered, and let the question slip by. "I was afraid of what I might read. But nothing happened to me. His journals are like a little history of his time. He travelled often to Newcastle, preached in the Castle Garth—he was there inside the walls when the Rebels almost took it—and even, finally, years later travelled into Scotland, many times, and to Bass Island and Tantallon Castle, where I want someday to go."

"Then I must take you," the Earl said, "or see that someone does," he amended.

"I would love to go with you, Holland," Edward said quickly, into the awkward little pause, "in the Spring, when it is warmer." They sat again in silence, but it was companionable again. Edward's head was bent again over his book. Outside the wind was rising, and throwing bits of sleet against the window, like fingers tapping for attention.

"What are you reading now?" the Earl asked idly, his attention divided between the slight figure in the chair and the weather outside and his own thoughts, to divert his attention, a little piqued as Alleyn had once been by Edward's ability to concentrate and exclude.

"Mrs. Wesley here is describing in a letter to her son how she raised her children," Edward said, lifting his head, "how she taught them all to read at five, and to follow a temperate and ordered life, and how she broke their wills to their parents' wills when they were very young. It was easier and kinder, she said, to do it then, before they grew older, and that it was no real kindness or indulgence to a child not to do this, although some parents seemed to think so." He paused. "Why do you smile, Holland?"

"I was remembering my friend Fox and his father Lord Holland, who was permissive and indulgent by Mrs. Wesley's standards, or by anyone's, I suppose."

"How was that, Holland?"

"I think he never denied Charles anything. He grew up brilliant, precociously brilliant, spoiled to his own way and indulgent in his vices, but unusually sweet and generous in his disposition. I could hardly credit some of Charles' stories myself, having had a much different raising."

"Tell me some, Holland."

"The milder ones, perhaps. There is one of Charles still in dresses expressing a desire, or more exactly, a whim, to sit in a bowl of cream upon the table, and having it lifted down for him to gratify it."

Edward's lips smiled, though his eyes were a little sad.

"Then there was the incident of the wall. Charles' father had promised him he might watch a garden wall demolished, but he forgot to call Charles before the powder went off. So he had the wall rebuilt, and blew it up again, to keep his promise, he said. And there was the incident of his father's watch. Charles announced his intention of breaking it, I suppose to see how it worked, and his father gave it to him, saying, 'Well, if you must, I suppose you must.'"

"These are little things," Edward observed.

"It was the same, in all things, great or little. I am amused myself, but frankly these stories do also appall me."

"I can see they would," Edward said. "Mrs. Wesley said that self-will was the greatest sin, and the greatest cause for sin, and so that will must be entirely broken. She said that was essential to the making of a religious person who could later submit his will to God's, and with her sons, with her Charles and with John, it was just such that she did make." He looked at his father, his eyes unreadable, his breath a little caught in his throat, and yet his voice expressionless. "That is what you did to me, wasn't it, Holland, breaking my will. But I do not know what you did it for, even yet, or if you really thought about what you were doing while you did it, although tonight you spoke of it just again. Mrs. Wesley had a purpose that was more than just her convenience. Do you? My first father did not even try to do it, that I can remember, I cannot remember ever feeling he thought it necessary to be done, and yet he was a minister. But you are not religious, Holland, that part means nothing to you, does it? I know you do the things expected of you, and you swear by God"—he smiled slightly—"but I think you do not really yourself personally believe in God."

"No, Edward," the Earl said, "I suppose, if I should really ask myself that question, and I have never felt the need to and I am not going to now, but if I should, I suppose I would have to answer that I do not. Without refining too much on it, it is simpler, I think, just to say that I never think about that matter or that question at all. Nor do I like speaking of the subject with another person in this way," he added, but with a novel patience, he added yet again, "but if you do, go ahead, I do not mind. It is Christmas, and perhaps appropriate you do."

"I will read you, if you like, what I have been reading," Edward said, his voice quiet.

"And thinking about?" enquired the Earl.

Edward shook his head. "No, not really, just reading, that is all. This passage interests me, Holland. Wesley says that those who assert, 'God will not answer your prayer, unless your heart be wholly resigned to his will,' are entirely mistaken. For he says one such of his was answered directly when his will was still not single and was still divided and rebellious. He also says that we may sincerely repent and yet soon afterwards do again what we repented of, and though continuing to repent, one may continue to relapse, and so one's heart though trying to repent be hardened more and more. Such a person, he says, 'can say unfeignedly, without hypocrisy, the thing which I do I approve not; the evil which I would not, that I do. To will is even then present with him; but how to perform that which is good he finds not.' But then he says that he inclines to believe that there is a state attainable in this life, easier for certain natures to find than for others, being helped to it by elected grace, 'from which a man cannot finally fall. And that he has attained this, who can say, "Old things are passed away: all things in me are become new." ' "

His still quiet reflecting voice paused, and did not continue, and after a time the Earl asked, his voice equally quiet, "And what do you make of this?"

Edward smiled, a brief smile, but he did not answer directly. "I am not myself quite certain of what it means either, but Wesley is, he explains it in five ways here, principally that the image of God has been fresh stamped on the heart. One's address, one's pleasures, one's happiness, one's powers, one's desires, one's purposes, one's actions, all then experience change."

"That is more than five. I cannot say that I know what that sentence intends to convey."

"It means this," Edward said, turning several pages over, to a place he had marked. "I found this and recognised it. My father—that was —used to read it to my mother and to me. He asked me to get it by heart, and I did, but it had slipped my mind that I knew the words. You may read it for yourself, if you like. I could not now."

The Earl took the little book from Edward, and read the words so indicated:

" 'I take religion to be, not the bare saying over of so many prayers, morning and evening, in public or in private, nor anything superadded now and then to a careless or worldly life; but a constant ruling habit of soul, a renewal of our minds in the image of God, a recovery of the divine likeness, a still-increasing conformity of heart and life to the pattern of our most holy Redeemer.'

Lord," commented the Earl simply. "This is incendiary matter; I don't want this; I had as soon now I had let you leave the words in the coals."

"Do you? It means nothing to me now. To Wesley the 'single eye' and the 'inward undivided heart' are all, and they must be directed as he points out, and backed by works. They cannot fasten upon a person here, or remain private and unused. I have come from this, and it has, I suppose in part formed me, and yet I feel so little kinship with it now: the shouting, the singing, the praising, the serious talk, the concern for Salvation, the love of the Redemptive Blood. I am like the fallen away he laments and chides. The thorns have me. I wish when it snowed the wind would not wuther so." He shivered again. "There is so much death in these pages. Mr. Wesley does not mind it, but I do." He closed the second little book abruptly and laid it down on the table and stood up. "There is only one text of his I am able to understand or follow now."

"What is that, Edward?"

"'My son, give me thy heart.'" He looked at his father quickly, his eyes very dark, and then as quickly looked away. "I am going to bed now, Holland. Thank you, and goodnight." He left the room, but the Earl stayed down for some time looking through the little books, as if he would find some key there to Edward, but he found none that he recognised to use, except the text, "We love him because he first loved us."

He went upstairs, finally, fighting the compulsion overmastering him to go to Edward, hoping the door might be locked even as he turned the handle and found it turned easily. He found Edward lying in the large bed, lost-seeming in the center of it, his eyes open, watching the Earl as he walked to him, the Earl discovered when he had come near him. He held out his arms without a word, and took the Earl in them.

"Did I wake you?" He felt the boy shake his head, though he did not speak. "I am not going to undress," the Earl whispered against his lips. "I will at least keep so much of my word. I have come only for this."

"Oh, Holland," the boy said, terrified at himself, "I wanted you to. Did you know?"

"Yes, I knew. You called me strongly, and I came. We must both be stronger than this, Edward, or it will be an impossible situation for both of us. Do you mean to tantalise? Do you know when you provoke me?"

"Yes, I know. I cannot seem to help myself."

The Earl said no more, for he knew too well his own complexities, to browbeat and tonguewhip and then to prove his power still a simpler, more direct way whenever he perceived signs of the boy eluding him or turning from him to anyone else. He had never known before an attachment of this kind to last so long with him, and he did not understand why it should. He held the boy closely against him for a long time, his lips against his hair, slipping to his forehead and his features and then coming to rest again against his lips and their sweet breath.

"I love you, Edward," he said, against them, his voice a whisper.

"I love you, too, Holland."

"I do not want to hurt you, Edward. I do not. You must help me not to. You must not fight me."

"And then what, if I do not? Then this, too?"

"I hope not," the Earl whispered. "Help me, Edward."

"I cannot help anyone. I cannot even help myself. I want you now to hurt me. I know that now."

"Oh, my God," said the Earl softly to himself, "what have I done. What have I done."

"You have done what you wanted to do, as you always have, Holland, with anyone and with everyone," the boy said softly. "You have me now. There is nothing any more left to resist you, anywhere. I wanted to go away from you before this happened, but you would not let me. I want you now too. I am not fighting you any more at all. I know now what I am. I am a man's whore, and I am yours. I came from that and I am that. Go ahead, do what you want. I want it too. I am no longer ashamed to."

"You are needling me still, Edward," the Earl said warningly.

"No," Edward said, "before your face, believe me. I am not." He sat up, his eyes darkened and no longer clear, and took off himself his gown, and lay, trembling with passion and with cold, on top of the covers before the Earl with nothing to shield him from the Earl's eyes. The Earl took him in his arms, his fingers slipping over his skin, beneath his arms and between his thighs, parting, caressing, lingering, and then he took the boy's gown and put it on him again, and covered him beneath the covers of the bed.

"You have finally then grown tired?" He tried to speak lightly, but he was unable to.

"No, Edward, I have not."

"Why not then? Must you have a fight to care?"

"No, Edward, not any more."

"Why not, then, if I want you? Does my desire repulse you? Is that how you are?"

"No, Edward, it does not," the Earl said heavily.

"Why not then?"

"I cannot bear that I should have done this to you," the Earl said softly, a real despair in his voice.

"Oh come, Holland, no melodramatics from you. What else is it you have been making me into? Why should you care now about what else might have been? I do not any more. That is all finished. It does not matter now."

"Oh, God, help me," the Earl said.

"He will not hear you or help you, Holland, I think. He has not heard or helped me."

"Then I must help myself," the Earl said quietly, "and I am going to try to help you now. I cannot believe it is too late."

"How can you do that?" the boy asked.

"I don't know," the Earl said. "I wish to God I did." He took the boy's face in his hands, and looked at it long and hard. "I am not sorry I came, Edward, but I am going to leave you now, and because I do, you must not think that it is because I do not love you or that I want you any the less, or could not have willingly stayed here with you and done what you have said I might do."

"Or let me do to you?"

The Earl's face registered shock, in the faint light, and intense desire, but after a moment he took control of himself again and shook his head slowly. "My God, Edward, you must not say these things to me, you must not tempt me."

"Why must I not?"

"I am a man too easily tempted, and you must not offer me what I most want. I am going now because I do love you, more than I thought it possible for me to be able to do for anyone. You will not be angry with me, Edward, you will go to sleep?"

Edward drew the Earl's worried face down against his own, and laid it against his own, and briefly kissed his lips. "I think you are very sweet, Holland," he said, his voice harder than usual, brittle as glass. "Perhaps you can help me, if you try. I don't know. We will see. I will have to somehow want to help myself, and that part I will somehow have to manage for myself. Don't think that you must go away at once because of this. I am not going to be difficult. As you say, it is better so. I am not angry, and I can go to sleep easily." His voice grew less hard. "Do you know, Holland, I cannot remember ever your giving me or showing me so much of yourself. That is something, even if it is too late, even if nothing more than that comes of it." He turned away, and did not watch the Earl go, or see the tears sprung into his eyes, but he did not go to sleep as he had said he would for hours, refusing to touch himself. I am ungrowing, he thought, frightened at himself. I have stopped growing. I am going the other way. Christmas night passed, and he stared into the dark, sleepless, listening to the sleet.

The Earl took an easier way. He undressed and then went down to Harriett's room, and went to bed with her, never fully waking her, and rather quickly then to sleep. The next morning, however, waking and restless, he left her before she was awake, and returned to Edward's room. He found the boy still awake, as he could tell from his drawn face in the grey-white light before dawn. He looked at his father wearily, but he did not hold out his arms, and he did not speak, the tears slipping from his eyes at his father's return. The Earl took off his dressing gown, and then without a word, his gown, his eyes on Edward, and lifted the covers and put himself into the bed beside Edward, putting in his hand beneath the covers the oil he used with Edward, lying motionless and still beside him. After a moment Edward took off his own gown, and took the Earl in his arms, and kissed him, and in time, with the Earl's help, took him entirely, his mind entirely blacked out. He was weeping, without knowing he was, and he learned afterwards his father was weeping too. He lay very still, when he had finished, and after a time, he felt his father take him, in turn. They had no words at all. What words could there be, the Earl thought, for what one had said one would not do, and then did. They lay in one another's arms, and watched the snow turn pink.

"What will become of us now," he finally whispered.

"I don't know, Edward," the Earl said, "I don't know." He looked at the boy in the morning light, whose exhausted blank face he did not recognise, and put his hands against that face. "I think we cannot either one of us bear this again. I think, whatever you may think now, you are not meant to be this way." After a time, he kissed him most tenderly, and put on his dressing gown again, and left Edward's room.

All day he stayed away, without word or explanation. He returned an hour after dark, and found Edward sitting alone by the fire. He left his hat and coat, and went at once to him. The boy lifted his eyes, dark now with pain, rimmed with black circles as if he had been struck.

"Where have you been, Holland?" he asked, his face blank yet miserable.

"Out," the Earl said. "I had affairs," he added. "I am leaving to-morrow." He looked for a reaction on the boy's face, but he found none, except the blankness and the misery seemed to deepen, and the air of passive suffering and waiting that set his temper on edge. He took the boy's hands in his, but they were as nerveless and without feeling as his own, and after a moment, he returned them to Edward.

He stood by the fire, looking down at the bent head below him, and finally he said, in a low voice, "You know I must go, Edward. You know this cannot go on."

"Yes, I know," the boy said dully. After a moment, he said, "I thought you had gone already. I thought you had left without saying anything."

"I would not do that, Edward."

"I did not know, though," the boy said. "I have had a terrible day. I wish you had not left me like this, alone, to think." He shivered and turned his head away, into the fire. "Will you excuse me from dinner?" he said in a low voice.

"I thought you were hardened," the Earl said. "Dinner is a little thing."

"I thought so," Edward said, "but I am not."

"Nevertheless, come to dinner," the Earl said. "You look as though you had not eaten much all day. We will speak of this later, if we need to."

"I haven't," Edward said. "I have not felt like it. I have felt rather sick, and I do still. I can't seem to swallow things." He paused. "I don't see what there is to say."

The Earl looked at him critically, and relented. "I will have George bring you a tray in here or upstairs," he said. "Broth and tea, that should not be hard. Will you eat it then?"

The boy nodded his head. "I will try," he said, "if you ask it." The Earl turned abruptly and left the room, to change for dinner with Harriett.

That night, towards morning, he again returned to Edward's room. He found it unlocked, as before, and the boy awake, as before. Together they repeated substantially the same scene, that only when both were exhausted, found them again penitent.

"You cannot say now, Edward, you are only my whore," was all the Earl had to say.

"To me it is much the same thing, Holland," Edward said, his voice distant.

The Earl, relaxed and contented, paid no attention to his tone until a few minutes later, turning to him, he discovered the boy's eyes were completely blank and unfocussed, and that he did not seem to hear him at all. He spoke more sharply, and getting no response, even with shaking, he struck him sharply on his cheeks.

"Don't, Ross," the boy cried, putting his hands to his cheeks, and beginning to cry, the stony rigidity of his face melting.

"Ross?" repeated the Earl sharply. "Have you been to bed with him too?" He was twisted unreasonably by a sharp ugly jealousy that tore at him with the sudden suspicion. "Did he teach you this?"

"Oh, God, Holland," Edward said, sobbing and laughing, close to open hysteria, "how can you?"

"Did he?" asked the Earl sharply. "You are mine, Edward, and no one else's, you have always been, and you always will be, so long as I or you live. If he has had you, or even touched you, or you him, I will kill you both." He struck the boy again savagely, this time across the mouth. "Answer me, Edward, by God, answer me now and directly."

"No," he said wincing under the pain of the blow, his hand to his bruised mouth. "No, Holland."

"No?" the Earl said, his low voice more menacing than a shout. "You won't answer me?" He struck the sobbing boy again, and again, past reason.

"No, Holland. Please stop. I have answered you," Edward gasped, when he could. "I have said no. No man but you. You know that. No one at all but you." He was terrified now, at what he had unleashed, that he had not expected or even guessed at, and he cowered back against the pillows, his eyes black, his mouth bleeding.

"Then why did you say, 'Don't, Ross,' as you did, when you did?"

"Because he hit me, Holland! You have always let him hit me." He did not dare tell the Earl why, but his words had their effect.

"All right," the Earl said, his fury calming. "I believe you. I want to believe you." He took the boy's bleeding lips in his, ignoring their withdrawal, and after a moment, he said, "Turn over, Edward."

"No," said Edward. "No, Holland. I have had enough."

"I have not," said the Earl, his own lips stained with the blood from Edward's. "Turn over."

"No," he cried desperately, his eyes on that terrible face and the crossed veins throbbing on the Earl's forehead, "I don't know you like this, I don't want you, I don't love you. I want you to leave me alone." He tried to leave the bed, but the Earl, half rising, naked, caught his wrist and pulled him back.

"You should not have called me then as you did," the Earl said savagely, enraged, "for I have come and you have me now, and I am going to have you." He used the sheets as a weapon, trying to tangle and hamper Edward's arms and legs in their folds. The boy was fighting him in earnest now, but he took the pillow from under the boy's head, and pressed it over his face, and held it there until his struggles stopped. He removed it then, and saw the boy looking at him, catching his breath, and turned him over and took him, unresisting now, roughly. When he had finished, he lay back, still angry, at Edward and at himself, in silence. He felt a movement beside him, and Edward took his hand in his two and held it.

"Poor Holland," he said. "I thought I was in a bad way, but you are in a worse. Is this how you help me? It is perhaps the best way. I don't want to be like this." He sat up and kissed him gently, and then like a tired child he lay down inside his father's arm and slept.

When he woke, his father was gone. He rose, and dressed himself, not calling George, hardly able to move. He found his father and Harriett amicably having breakfast. He helped himself from the sideboard and took his place. His father did not speak to him directly, and their eyes did not meet, and he could not believe the night had happened. Lines from a poem would keep going through his head, by the strange Mr. Blake:

> How sweet I roam'd from field to field
> And tasted all the summer's pride,
> Till I the Prince of Love beheld . . .
>
> He caught me in his silken net,
> And shut me in his golden cage.
>
> He loves to sit and hear me sing,
> Then, laughing, sports and plays with me;
> Then stretches out my golden wing,
> And mocks my loss of liberty.

But in two months, he thought, the door of this gilded cage would open, and he could walk out, and no one then could bring him back, except himself, and he did not think now he would come near it ever again. He roused himself, for he realised he was being spoken to by Harriett. Harriett was asking about his face, and he managed to tell her he had fallen out of bed. His father made no comment, but as he left the table, he put his hand on Edward's shoulder, which jerked with an electric shudder.

"I am taking Ross to London with me," he said, removing his hand. "I have a new groom there who needs his instruction, and Lord Mowbray wants to borrow him for a hunt."

"You do not need to do that," Edward said, lifting his eyes briefly and letting them fall. "He is a Highlander, he will die in London, or with another master. Can you not trust me?" He discovered to his curious surprise that even like a cloud lifting off the trees of the mountains, the memory of the night was lifting from his mind. He could almost watch it rising and disappearing into nothing, into thin air. If he lifted his eyes again, he thought, it would be gone, and there would be only his father standing there, as he had always been, difficult but rational, not a monster. Even as the word crossed his mind, he found he could not remember the reason for thinking it.

"I thought it would please you."

"No. Once it might. I should feel badly now, if it were done now because of me. It was a long time ago. We get along."

"Then I will leave him." He pressed Edward's slight shoulder again, and for a minute he seemed about to say something more, but he did not. His son stopped him, putting his hand over his father's for a moment, briefly. Harriett had left, and they were just the two.

"I don't want to remember," Edward said, very quietly, not to break anything or disturb the rising mists, his lips quivering slightly but his eyes blank and withdrawn, watching the mists. "Don't make me. It is slipping my mind."

"That is God's mercy," said the Earl, "and more than I deserve. Christmas Peace, then, Edward?"

"Christmas Peace," the boy said.

IV

That day, two days after Christmas, the Earl left, and the air of the house relaxed again without him. It was duller but more peaceful; the tension left the air, and much of the strain disappeared from Edward's face. What had last occurred he had cut out of his memory, words and acts, to remember some day at a later time when perhaps he could bear to remember it, as he could not now, as one does with too much pain. He knew in a distant way it had occurred, but it no longer had any power to touch him. The reason for it had gone with the Earl and he could no longer conceive his incredible part in it, or fathom why he had wished what he distantly knew he had wished, or bear to remember at all the side of the Earl he had discovered. So he did not think of it; on his blank, blacked-out mind it had left no immediate visible impression. He had other reasons enough for strain. Edward knew his father visited Mrs. Wilson, he had once seen him come from her room, but he had not needed to see to know. He had no right to mind, he could not mind, and yet, despite his words to Harriett, he did, he was not certain for who most. For this, too, he was glad when the Earl left.

Harriett had only a few words to say when his eyes, though not his voice, reproached her: "Sometimes, Edward, one wants an adult, some-one of one's own generation, or near it," she said, stroking his hair, "as you sometimes want someone of your own, and you do, don't you?" He nodded, and did not speak. "Well," she said, "am I in disfavour?"

"No, never," he said, and put his arms about her, "never you." But he did not ask to sleep with her again until after the Little Christmas, and then, as if tumbling off a load, he sighed and relaxed with her, with no laughing.

He did not see Anne for several weeks, and he wondered if he or if the Earl had frightened her off. He missed her, but he did not go to see if she had left Lord Armstrong's estate, or merely her friendship with him. The sun seldom shone. When it did, it rose almost due South, progressed only a short way up into the sky and travelled in a low arc to the Southwest where it set early. The shadows all day were long and slanting, pointing away from the South. At evening air and snow turned both a deep blue. But one day when there was a break in the frost, for it was a particularly cold Winter, and Edward underestimated the Earl's devotion in travelling the roads, she appeared at the door, in her furs and muff and a blue velvet pelisse, and asked admittance.

"Are you still angry with me, Edward, over my foolishness?" she asked rather timidly and a little wistfully, when she had been shown in, giving him her bonnet. She thought momentarily he looked a little pale, but her thoughts were more on herself.

"No," he said, happy to see her but his eyes a little shadowed and a little wary. He took her hands in his in their furry mittens, and held them, but she pulled them loose and walked over to the large glassed square-bay windows overlooking the bare snowy gardens. The sun was out that day, after the night's snow, and sparkled with blue shadows and coloured lights on the cold snow, and the hoarfrosted shrubs, as it had a year ago; it was very still, there was no wind blowing, and it looked less cold than it was.

"You haven't taken off your furs," he said, coming up and standing behind her. "Don't you want to? You look to have big funny bear's paws." He slipped his hands from behind into her mittens and held her against him, his hands resting on hers inside the mittens. The novelty charmed her, and for a moment she nestled against him, her head just beneath his chin. He laid his cheek against her soft short hair, breathing in its fragrance.

"I have had all the dirt of the wig washed out, Edward," she said, "It is quite clean now. Are you looking to see?"

"Not exactly," he murmured against her hair. "I was just letting myself be happy."

"Oh, pshaw," she said, "how silly you are. I did not know it was that." She tried to pull away, but he kept her hands.

"I am sorry," he said, not penitently. "Perhaps I should have explained."

"Let go my hands now please," she said, turning her head a little towards him, "Cousin Edward." He held her a moment longer, his head a little bent, the faces of each only inches away, so near that with no very large effort they might have touched, but they did not touch, and only their eyes met, hers falling first, and then he released her, and she pulled her hands away in their mittens and moved away.

"Will you take me sleighing in your sledge, Edward?" she asked, again a little wistfully. "I came to ask you. I have wanted to go, and I may not have the chance again. The one with the three horses?"

"Of course I will," he said. "I do not exercise enough. I will get my coat and gloves."

"Have you wondered why you did not see me?" she asked, when they were in the fields, the hooves crackling and the bells chiming. "Have you missed me?"

"Yes to both," he said. There was a change in her manner, a lessening of her exuberance, that he noticed but that eluded him to define.

"I saw your guardian on Christmas Eve. Did he tell you?"

"He told me you went to church."

"We did. He had a talk with me—"

"I am sorry," Edward said. "I know my guardian's talks very well."

"Don't be, Edward. I deserved it. He lectured me on my conduct, and he asked me to think very seriously about what I was doing. And that is what I have been doing. I have been thinking."

"And what is it that you have thought?"

"I think he is right, and that I must not see you any more. I have not done well at all."

"Let me be the judge of that, Anne," Edward interposed with suppressed emotion, a pleading in his voice she did not hear.

"He showed me what I did not realise," she said hesitantly, "that it is not entirely as a cousin I come to see you, not really, that it is only part."

There was a pause, and then he said in a strained voice, "I am very glad if you do not feel about me as you would a cousin, Anne, for I do not you myself."

"Don't," she said. "Don't say that. I did not mean that. We *are* cousins, and it does matter to me. I would be afraid."

"I thought I was hard to embarrass," he murmured, "but you always contrive to do it. You go much faster than I do. I want only to see you a little, more than I do, and I think you already have our children born, and weak-headed and weak-chinned."

"Your guardian had it in his mind, I think, among other things."

"Holland is impossible to embarrass," he murmured again, "but please spare me my blushes, for him and for me. Leave him out. This is one affair I think I can conduct on my own."

"But you can't," she said, "that is just what he told me and made me see. He told me he would disinherit you, if I encouraged you or if I let you encourage me."

"Damn Holland," Edward said bitterly. "Must he frighten you, too? I cannot be disinherited, Anne, from what I have not got, or what I have not accepted. Did he tell you we were cousins?"

"Yes, but that he might make you his heir if you pleased him."

"Oh, damn him," Edward said again in bitter grief, "oh, damn him. He has frozen this tender growth, that could stand no killing frost yet." His own lips were sealed, and he could not tell her they were not cousins, if his father would not. It would only clear one of her scruples, anyway, he thought, and not the most important. With her hatred of his father, he feared her learning that relationship most of all, until she had learned to love him for himself, as he did her—if she could, and perhaps she never could.

"And so you have come to say goodbye?"

"Yes, Edward, I have. I thought I would write you, but I could not make the words come straight, and then I thought, no, I am a coward, I will not be so cowardly, and I came to tell you myself."

"Well," he said, "if that is it, then I will take you home now."

"Edward, you must not think it is not hard for me, having just found you for my cousin, but your guardian made me see that it would be harder to break off later than now, when it had led where he made me see it must."

"Must it?" he said bitterly. "Oh Anne, you are like Mr. McAdam's process, you quite flatten me. I don't really want to argue or to talk any more now. If you will not play piquet with me or walk in the garden, and if you must think of those non-existent weak-chinned babies, then I suppose you must do as you think you have to." He was suddenly and frankly angry. "But I think you have no feelings at all. You are just enjoying yourself and trying to work up a little Cheltenham tragedy here when perhaps there doesn't need to be any at all."

"Nor do I you," she said, "for all your talk. You can say what you like, Edward, but I have thought it all out very clearly."

He laughed bitterly, although he made an attempt at lightness: "And so this is the scene in which you renounce me?"

"Put it that way if you like"—her head a little turned away.

"I thought I had not offered myself, but if I am to be renounced before I do, let me tell you, Anne, you may not find me so easy to renounce."

"I like you, Edward, but I do not think your feelings are really any more involved yet than my own."

"And how would you know?" he asked, stung.

"Lord Tyne says—"

"Damn Lord Tyne," he said, cutting her off. "If you Lord Tyne me once more I shall make you wish you had not. You should not speak as if you knew me so well when you do not. It is a dangerous tone, Miss Armstrong."

"But Lord Tyne knows—"

He pulled the horses to a sudden halt, and catching the reins about his wrist, he caught her to him, her back against him, his hands on her small breasts, holding her to him. He could feel her breath quickening, but she did not try to move. "There is a great deal about me you do not know," he said quietly, "but you are going to learn something of it now." He pulled the lap rug up deliberately around them, ignoring her startled protests.

"If you are going to renounce me, my dear," he said with some grimness, "you should have something to renounce, or at least know what you are renouncing before you do." He turned her in his arms with all the strength he had held in reserve since their first meeting, easily, ignoring her struggles now to evade him, until her face lay near his, and he found her sweet protesting mouth with his own. "Hush," he said, kissing her angrily and roughly, "hush," again stilling her protests, not leaving off, once begun, until her struggles entirely stopped, and then he released her mouth back to her, kissing more gently her eyelids and her cheeks, and then again her mouth.

"You should be careful about making men angry," he said into her hair, as she hid her face against him, "we are, after all, men, and not lap dogs. And you should be careful about going for drives by yourself with men, even if you call them cousin. I never knew a little girl so rash."

"So Lord Tyne said," she began, but the words were taken swiftly off her lips and her breath by his own.

"I only meant," she said penitently, lying against him quietly as if resigned, "that a marriage between us would not be very convenient—"

"You must *not* talk of marriage, or propose it, so freely to strange men," he said, his lips against hers, but she struggled to speak—

"And since it would not be convenient or sensible, that we should not let any other reason—for wanting it—to grow. You know it is sensible. And oh, Edward, you should not have done what you have."

"As Lord Tyne says," he said gently. "No, Anne, I don't know. I was past being sensible a long time ago. I just did not want to tell you or frighten you, for you are so young. Another time, I might have been glad to see you worrying so, another time, I might have thought that a good sign. But I am not sorry for kissing you, I am only sorry you would not kiss me back. I will take you home now. You can sit up now. Do you want to slap me? You can if it will make you feel better. I won't hurt you, if you will just not say again those three words."

"Lord Tyne says?" she asked innocently.

He looked at her hard, but he could not entirely read her expression. He bent his head tentatively, and her lips met his, and she put her furred arms behind his neck and held him to her, for one sharp sweet insistent moment, and then she drew back.

"It is too cold," she said, "and oh, dear Edward, I am still going to renounce you, because I must, though I don't want to at all now. You have been unkind to make it much harder, and no gentleman. I would like to be taken back now, to my horse, at your house, if you will be so good." She moved over and crept within the circle of his left arm and rested her head against him.

"It would not be wise," she said. "You know it would not."

"All right," he said a little sharply, "you have made your decision, or my guardian has made it for you. Don't talk about it any more, please. I am too cold to talk."

She was shivering too, and he invited her to come in and have hot tea ("not hot ale," he said, smiling a little), as cousins. They sat with Harriett and toasted themselves, and bread on forks, and ate buttered toast and honey and strong tea, and talked nonsense and local news, but when Harriett left them alone, Edward said to her with his old frank directness, this time without overtones or undertones, "I don't want to fight at all with you, Anne, and I hate to do things clandestinely myself." She raised her eyes to his across the rim of her cup. "You are perhaps right in what you say, and much the wiser. There is actually nothing I can do, until after next month when I come of age. And you are nowhere near of age yourself. We are both quite helpless still. But after I come of age, if you want me to speak directly to your brother, to your guardian, about my intentions, I will."

"It is not possible," she said, shaking her head.

"It might then be, just possibly, if you loved me. I could try. I would be willing to. It is for you to say." He put his hand on her cheek, and she went of herself into his arms, and gave him the freedom of her lips and their response. He felt her begin to tremble, and he released her.

"There is a difference," she said unsteadily, "when one is warm. I don't understand how I can feel this way about you, when I know I must not. How could Lord Tyne know I did when I did not myself?"

"He has had much experience, he knows the small signs," Edward said, a touch grimly.

"Lord Tyne says," she said softly, touching his face with her hand, and standing on tiptoe to kiss him again. "But all the same, Edward, I mean to forget you, and to forget—all this."

"Can you so easily?"

"I can try. It is perhaps easier for me than for you. But if you want me, why don't you fight for me, Edward? Do you never fight for anything?"

"I thought I was fighting now."

"It is not enough. I cannot go against everything I think right just because I find I like to be kissed by you. I may be very immoral that way. I may find I like to be kissed by many people. And taking my breath away," she said, as he did just that, "will not effect anything either. Where is Mrs. Wilson?"

"Oh, my love," he said, "I could make you forget all your scruples;

you talk so wisely with your sweet lips and you do not know at all the force of what you speak of. I could take your lovely wilful prudent will entirely away and put mine in its place, you cannot imagine how easily, but I will not. I am not going to use that weapon against you, we both know now very certainly that it is there. But I have no other weapons to fight with, and my hands are tied in a way you cannot understand." He released her, and looked at her curiously.

"If you already have a taste for roughness, we will forgo all that kind of play; I shall do some renouncing myself. I want much more from you than that." He continued to look at her in a puzzled, thoughtful way, watching the colour come and go in her face. "I wonder where Mrs. Wilson is also. She is not a very conscientious chaperon. I could have sworn, Anne, when I saw you here, before Christmas and on Christmas Eve, that you had no idea of what kisses were. And now you do. I wonder how that comes to be?" He continued to look at her, soberly, as her colour deepened. A look of disgust and horror came over his own with the unspeakable idea penetrating him.

"It takes only a few minutes to make a girl a woman. Oh, God, Anne, has that happened to you? Could he have done even that? Why would Lord Tyne talk to you about getting in coaches with strange men? And why would you speak of him now so familiarly, and with less distaste? If it is true, Anne, I think I shall die. Can he leave me nothing of my own?"

"I am not yours, Edward," she said defiantly but with real concern, timidly touching his coat (he shook her arm off), "and I am not sure what you are thinking, but we only talked in the coach, that is all."

"Lord Tyne does not only talk to women in coaches, that is not his way. I do not believe you. I think perhaps that I shall shoot him after all for you." His eyes watched her narrowly.

"Oh, no, you must not, Edward," she said falteringly.

"Why must I not? Do none of your relations care what you do? I care. I will not endure it, I will not bear him. Go home, now, Anne. I am through." He sat down at the desk in the room, and ignored her, and pulled out a piece of paper and his pen and the bottle of ink, and began carefully to write, his hand made firm with his anger:

> Edward Clare Armstrong challenges James Noel Holland, Viscount Rockfort, Earl of Tyne, on a point of honour, weapons, seconds, time, and place, at his choice.

He took sand, and threw it over the paper, and folded it, and sealed it with a wafer. He rose, not looking at her, and took his coat, and went towards the door. She ran after him, and put her hand on his arm but he shook her off roughly.

"Go home, Anne, I do not want to see you now." He called George to him and instructed him to ride directly to London and to find Lord Tyne wherever he was and to deliver the note to him, there or wherever he was to be found, and to bring the answer back to him.

"But what have you done?" she cried.

"I have challenged Lord Tyne."

"You are mad! For a kiss?"

"No, not a kiss."

"But there was nothing else." Her voice faltered and her eyes fell. Her embarrassment did not escape him.

"I do not believe you. In any case you have told me that now. Even a kiss, from him, is enough and grounds sufficient. Go home, Anne, I have been a fool to think I could be happy, with you or with anyone. I do not want to see you any more."

He turned his back on her baldly, and left the room, and after a while, there seeming no point in staying, she left too. Harriett Wilson, descending again, found the room empty and learned the lady had left. When she went to find Edward, his door was locked and he would not answer her entreaty or her knocks.

Their quarrel was not patched over; they had both caught colds from the bitter air and their heated emotions. Edward, already weakened, caught a particularly severe one which settled into his lungs. He came to Harriett in the night, a day later, in a high fever, most desperately sick. He quite frightened Harriett with his racking paroxysms of coughing, and his refusal to say any word at all to her. She sent Ross down with a letter from herself to the Earl.

V

The Earl's reply to Edward came when Edward's fever had passed, but when he was still weak and miserably depressed from his illness, as well as from his several quarrels and his suspicions. The paper was crested, and the reply formal:

> "Lord Tyne regrets that he does not accept challenges except from his peers, and never those of untitled minors. He declines the honour of meeting E. C. Armstrong."

Underneath, he had written, less legibly and without heading:

> "For God's sake, Edward, what is the matter with you? What has happened? Will I be shot if I appear for your birthday?"

For answer Edward sent only the word *Yes* by George.

Meanwhile, Harriett had received a letter that particularly disturbed her, after these many years, from her father that her mother was critically ill, perhaps dying, and wished to see her.

"I must go," she said to Edward, "you can see that, can't you? I will have the Vicar's wife look in on you, and find a woman to come as a nurse, if you want one."

"Don't trouble," Edward said morosely, breaking his silence.

"Oh my sweet love, I don't know what to do. You act as if something were troubling you, and you won't tell me anything, and now this comes. Have you quarrelled with Anne? Lovers' quarrels do not last, not for true lovers: they cannot bear to see one another hurt, not for long. The pain comes of course when one loves and one does not, but that is the world, Edward, that cannot be helped. Oh," she said, much dismayed, "one should never tell a lie for an excuse, or I should not. With me it always comes true, as this has. I must go, but I shall come back as soon as ever I can, cher Clare. Be patient and be good while I am gone."

The Earl's answer to Harriett's letter arrived the next day and lay unopened on her dresser. She had herself sent her own letter, that reached his house after he had left London to deal himself with Edward's unaccountable crisis that had blown up. Ross, acting on instructions sent by fast horse, took a footman and a groom, George having been kept by the Earl, and entered Edward's room that night as he lay asleep. Edward, guarding himself against such an act, had locked his door, but Ross had an extra set of keys, and he made his way in and with the help of the men seized Edward as he lay asleep and bound his hands and his feet tightly, and took him down into the priest-hole where his old bed, musty and damp, still stood. He had brought several dry blankets to lay him on, and to cover him with, but the air of the place was dank, and Edward began to cough as though he would choke. Ross folded a blanket into a pillow which he placed under his head to raise it, and left the smaller groom to stay and see Edward came to no harm. Edward's eyes flashed in anger, and he refused to open his mouth to say anything or to eat or to drink anything. He lay there, his eyes open and staring, until the Earl arrived in the mid-afternoon of the next day. He went at once to see Edward, and sent the little groom away.

He walked over to Edward, and stood for a moment looking down at him. Edward met his eyes with a look of hatred so furious and so intense that the Earl, prepared for something but not for the degree, was startled.

"I am sorry, Edward, for this—outrage," he said gently, "but you surely did not expect me to do nothing?"

The boy did not answer, but he was seized by an attack of coughing that shook him and that he was powerless to stop. The Earl's concern grew, minute-ly.

"We are always quarrelling over something," he said, even more gently, his voice warm and winning, "and then you are always getting sick, and then we are always making up." Edward shook his head, his cough subsiding. "We always have made up before. Are we not to now?"

"No," said Edward, speaking for the first time, "if you release me, I will kill you."

"I cannot believe you," the Earl said slowly, his voice still warm. "You would not warn me if you really meant to." But remembering Staps, he wondered. He had not expected, when he heard that story, to find something like it in his own house.

"Don't deceive yourself. I warn you for things past. That is all," Edward said, his own voice bleak and his eyes implacable. "Try me and see."

"What am I supposed to have done? Will you at least not tell me that?"

Edward pressed his lips a little and turned his head away as far as he could, and did not answer. He was seized by another attack of coughing that shook him violently and disturbed the blankets, and the Earl saw that he was much frailer-looking and thinner than at Christmas. He despaired of reaching him or reasoning with him, as he was, in that present state.

"Where is Mrs. Wilson?" he asked, but Edward would not answer, and he had to find out for himself.

He had Edward carried back upstairs into his own room and his own bed, and his restraints unfastened, for he had seen at a glance that the boy was too weakened to be able to harm him, unarmed. He had a doctor called in from the village, and one from York, and he sent his own coach to bring Knighton from London if for the fee he could be persuaded to make the journey on the bad winter roads a second time for Edward. He kept Ross or George with a second man on perpetual guard in Edward's room.

When Edward saw George, he broke silence furiously, coughing as he spoke. "You are a traitor to me, George, to my guardian," Edward said. "I never want you to valet me again."

"Well, Master Edward, it is not for your own good for you to be shooting the Earl; whether he is your father or not, he has kept you and raised you. And he pays me, and I have known him longer even than you. If you keep threatening and worriting your guardian, you won't need a valet, anyway."

The Earl himself often sat there, puzzled, thinking, when Edward was asleep. He had not tried to question him further, perceiving he was not well.

In this manner Edward came of age. He was well aware of the day himself, although he gave no sign of it and neither did anyone else in the morning of the day. His cough was better, and he sat up in bed against his pillows, and looked about him. His saving common sense was close to coming to his aid, as his health returned. The Earl put his head in the door, and seeing Edward sitting up, came in.

"Well, Edward," he said, "do you intend to spend this day in bed, and have your toasts drunk here *à la salon,* or do you feel equal to coming down?"

Edward shrugged his thin shoulders.

"Everyone is wanting to see you, in the village, but I have said you were still ill. Was that right?"

Edward shrugged again.

The Earl started to check his own retort at Edward's sulkiness, and then he decided to let it fly. "When I speak to you, you can at least answer. Are you going to come down and behave in a civilised manner, or must I become very uncivilised with you?"

"I will come down," Edward said stiffly, "but I have no strength. I will have to be helped. And I don't want to see anyone."

The Earl came back in when Edward was nearly dressed, having made his peace with George, and he was again shaken by Edward's look of fragility, as if he would break if he were touched or even spoken harshly to. His strength was so lacking, as he had said, he could not do anything at all to help George. His eyes were entirely too luminous, the Earl thought, and his skin, almost translucent, except where it was reddened with a hectic flush, stretched too tightly over the bones of his face and hands.

"Knighton is here," he said, "but he will examine you tomorrow or tonight. I have brought you a list of gifts that have been coming to the house for you all day today." The Earl would have liked to take Edward's hand in his, but he did not dare. He sent George out on a pretext and sat near Edward at his dressing table.

The actions of being dressed had exhausted Edward, and he rose unsteadily, and left the Earl and lay down dressed, on the chaise longue, feeling waves of faintness and nausea sweep over him at the sight of his father.

"Can you not bear to see me at all?" the Earl asked curiously.

"No. I think I am going to faint, or be sick," Edward said, his eyes closed and his face blanched of colour.

The Earl picked up the Hartshorn that had been always in the room since Edward's illness, and handed it to him, and spoke conversationally. "The Vicar has sent you frosted grapes grown under glass," he said, "and Mr. Brummell has sent a French Champagne, from *his* cellar, he says, but smuggled in, I think, and Miss Armstrong has sent you a plaid of her clan." He saw Edward's face stiffen.

"Let us not go down on this evening of all evenings this way," he said, his voice gentle and pleading. "Why must it be this way? Can you at least not tell me what has changed you and why you are so out with me, when we have weathered so much? Is it something to do with this girl?" He watched Edward carefully. "I do think it must be, but I cannot for the life of me imagine what, out of a blue sky like that, with no warning, and me even gone. Now if it had been earlier—" Still watching Edward's transparent face, he began to smile. "You have discovered my escapade. It must be that. But Edward, did it deserve shooting? I knew you would be angry, but this angry? Why, even Miss Armstrong did not mind so much."

"I know," Edward whispered, "that makes it so much worse."

"I have done much worse things, Edward, and you have not called me out. Why now? I thought it for her own good."

"Your notions of a person's good, Holland, are impossibly removed from mine. I don't know what else to say." He spoke more drearily than angrily.

"Are you going Methody again, now your release is in sight, or just priggish? Come, Edward, Anne surely did not tell you all the story, let me tell you now, and then tell me if I have behaved so badly."

"No, Holland, don't," he cried. "I can't bear to talk about it any more."

"I wonder what you think I did," the Earl said musing. "I begin to guess, but 'fore God, Edward, you do think *too* badly of me. I am not lost to *all* conscience. I did not rape the gel, you know. It was just a drum. I dressed up like a highwayman, me, at my age, and I waylaid the girl going home alone across the heath."

"—You did what?" Edward exclaimed.

"Just what I said. I thought her far too independent and that a little schooling in life's dangers would not hurt. I wore a mask and shot my pistols off properly but quite safely, and forced her off her horse and into my coach, being treated to some very choice apothegms of her late father. A fair revenge in itself, that. I thought she came much too easily, myself, but she did not conceive her danger. She is a novel-reader, that girl, and a gossip-sheet reader, and she thought I was Gentleman Harry. A good course in Horace would have benefited her; perhaps it is not yet too late. I can see you, Edward, under a tree with her, doing just that."

"And what then, Holland?" he asked, his voice still tense.

"Why, then, I acted in the best traditions of an evil kidnapping lord and pretended to force myself upon her, but Gad, Edward, the chit frightened me more than I did her. She has considerable spirit, as we know." He forbore to tell Edward the details or expound on his lady's amazing character. "And so after stealing several kisses, which I performed only in the interests of education but of which I knew you would all the same disapprove, and so I did not tell you of before, I owned myself wholly vanquished by a very young lady, and took her and her abigail demurely to supper and to church. And I did endeavour my utmost—with words only—to dissuade her from the acquaintance—as I suppose she did tell you."

" 'Lord Tyne says,' " Edward rejoined, breaking into a slight smile.

"And now, are you satisfied? Am I still so black? Reckless, yes, and high-handed, yes, and perhaps ill-advised, but may I not be spoken to? Surely she did not tell you all that wild story?"

"Well, no," Edward said, looking more himself, "and I do appreciate your allaying the worst of my suspicions. I did leap to conclusions, and I thought I knew not to. But when I discovered she had been awakened—please don't ask *me* how—and I knew that she had been in a closed space with you who know so well how to awaken—"

"—And knowing that I have no morals at all, you leapt disreputably. I am almost ready to call you out now myself for thinking what you did of me. I am old, I am past such acts, and I do not need them. Will you let me live?" Edward nodded, his lips despite himself twisting into a little smile. "I seem always to be asking my life at the hands of you two extremely young persons (and you your virtue at mine, I suppose you might say)." He stopped and looked hard at Edward. "But you are still angry with me. I can tell now, even though you smile a little with me."

"Yes, Holland, I am. You had no right."

"Of course not, but no more do you. And you may find that unintentionally I have been a better friend to you than I intended to be." He did not explain his meaning, but Edward followed it. "Now I shall tell you another closely held secret. Today is my birthday too. I had never any excuse for not remembering yours." He smiled at Edward, who was unable to make any response. "We will not mention it tonight. Another year, who knows, perhaps we may celebrate together. But not tonight. Fifty-three has no place at the table of twenty-one. Come, let us go down now." He did not offer his hand, but he wished to, for Edward seemed hardly able to walk down the steps.

"Well," said Knighton cheerfully, "here is a decrepit twenty-one," his shrewd eyes assessing the boy.

"I am glad to see you, Knighton," Edward said with something of his old smile. "I like you as well as anyone I know, but I never get to see you unless I am sick. You must understand I have done this on purpose solely to have you here tonight. It is a bad trick."

"A very bad trick," Knighton said, smiling. "I am much honoured."

They made a quiet dinner of it, Edward becoming refreshed for the first part, but then quickly exhausted. Knighton perceived it, and signalled to the Earl the meal must end. The Earl uncorked the champagne, they drank a single toast, and Edward was put to bed again. Knighton came in and examined him with his gentle searching fingers minutely, first on his stomach, then on his back. He paid particular attention to his chest.

"How long have you had this cough, Edward?" he asked with apparent disconcern.

"A week, two perhaps. I have lost track of time. I caught cold in January, sleighing, after Christmas." He was seized by a paroxysm even as he spoke, and it was some time before he could get his breath.

"Nearer a month, then. Have you ever had one like this before?"

"No, I don't remember any."

"When you have coughed, did anything come out? Pink or brown or like blood?"

"I don't think so. Not really."

"Not really," repeated Knighton thoughtfully. "Your guardian tells me you have been tired, despite my prescribing in the Fall."

"I have forgotten how not to be tired."

"You need to be in a warm climate. You are cold here, and that is bad for your cough, and the house is dry from the fires, and drafty, both, and that also aggravates it and makes it difficult for you to rid yourself of it. It will go away when Spring comes, or when you go South, but you are not well enough to go South. I am going to have the Earl build you a little glass house, like a greenhouse, we call them solariums, and I want you to spend at least an hour there sunbathing every day there is sun, at the hottest hour. Otherwise stay entirely in bed, until these fits of coughing leave you. I shall speak to the cook about what you must eat, and what you must not, and I am going to leave you a particularly bad-smelling bottle of fish oil that you must take every day, even though you won't like it. And also a great vat of buttermilk. All right, Edward?" he said, recovering him warmly, and giving him a reassuring smile.

He walked out in the hall with the Earl and into his study.

"I am worried about him," the Earl said privately to Knighton. "His mother was of a frail constitution and died young."

"And his father?"

"His father has an extremely strong constitution."

"Well, let us hope then he takes after his father in that. Who is his father?"

"I am." Knighton's eyebrows rose in surprise. "It is not generally known."

"Did his mother die of pulmonary consumption?"

"She died of her heart, but she may have had the wasting consumption as well. She was very thin when she died."

"You called me in, I remember, this Fall, about this boy's tiredness. I see no real signs now, but I should put this boy out entirely to pasture, if I were you, Lord Tyne, if you value him. Oppose him in what you absolutely must, but otherwise let him have a wide tether and a loose rein. You will not spoil him, and you may save him. He is all ash now. He is used up. I have never seen it in one so young. I wish he were in Italy this Spring, or Greece or Southern France, but the war and the exhaustion of the trip leads me to say no to all. One would not want either of you to meet Lord Elgin's fate. Can you take him to Bath?"

"I can suggest it."

"I would. I will leave medicine for his cough, and suggest Bath myself. The soldiers are on the Scillies, which are like Southern France, you know, and the passage across is impossibly rough, otherwise I would suggest trying them."

The Earl nodded. "We may be best apart. I domineer even when I do not intend."

"Well, you would know best about that. The less that troubles him or that disturbs him now, the better for his recovery."

So the Earl went back to London, to leave Edward to recuperate in peace, alone except for George; and Edward lived for an hour each day in the little glass house, and ate as prescribed, although he had no appetite, and eventually, after a fortnight, took short walks about the house, and played softly on the pianoforte for short periods, and regained enough measure of his strength that he began to think again about his future.

He had been irrationally hurt that he had received nothing at all from his father on his birthday, although he had said nothing; irrationally, he knew, considering why the Earl had arrived and how he had found him, not realising the Earl had omitted any gift out of tact, feeling it would then come unwelcome, and remembering the reception of his well-meaning gift at Christmas. But when he was able to walk about his room, and notice things again, he discovered that the presents he received in past years from his father, his knife, his books, even the soldiers and the games, had been replaced as he had kept them, how and when he did not know, or whether found or rebought, he could not tell, both, he thought. He took them each in turn, laughing and crying over them, realising the effort and the memory entailed in the return, even if George had helped, whatever hardness or bitterness still lingered in his heart wholly softened and washed away. And then he discovered two new volumes, one a collection of songs by the Scotch poet Robert Burns, a contemporary of the Earl's, who had died the year after Edward first came to live at the Earl's house, and the other a copy of the third edition of *Lyrical Ballads* by two authors whose names Edward had heard in passing, first published in 1798, but poorly received then and new now to Edward. When he opened them, he found them inscribed, one, the Burns, "To Edward, from Caesar, February 20, 1810," and the other only, "To my dear Romantick, from J.N.H."; and marked in pencil by the Earl himself during the long evenings while he sat in Edward's room. He sat there on the floor, reading the marked passages, an Earl he did not seem to know there in the room beside him, patient and not demanding to be remarked, speaking through what he had marked, among them the lines:

"We'll tak a cup of kindness yet, For auld lang syne," and "He prayeth well, who loveth well, Both man and bird and beast," marked in "The Rime of the Ancient Mariner." He read them all, sitting there, that afternoon. But he did not write his father to acknowledge them or to thank him. They had not been given to him, he had only found them, and they cut too deep, and he did not want, now that he was free, to be bound again. A faint warning stirred somewhere in the hidden part of his mind that it was not somehow fair of his father, and he felt the rustling of the silken net, as he had not before.

Nothing at all had been said between him and his father about the crucial legal matters that lay before them. Edward himself found he no longer cared, and he preferred not to speak of them, and was glad the Earl had not spoken of them to him, or asked him any questions. The Earl had not spoken because he remembered very well what Edward had said he would do, and he did not wish to hear the words or to involve either of them in a disturbing scene, having no reason at that time to think Edward had changed his mind and every reason to think he had not.

And so despite the passing of the crucial day, Edward continued to live quietly in the Earl's house and convalesced. He had several visitors. The Vicar came to see him frequently, to chat of ordinary matters, and the Vicar's wife occasionally, though less frequently than the Vicar. Anne learned that he had been sick, and she brought a blancmange again, and herself. Her abigail accompanied her. She was much subdued from her usual self, and she had very little to say. She looked at him wistfully, and tried not to trouble him. They played piquet, and sat together quietly without talking very much.

"Will you recover?" she asked once, looking at him doubtfully.

"I think so," he said, smiling.

"You don't absolutely look as though you will."

"Thank you very much," he said, "but I do intend to."

"I had a cold too, but mine lasted only a week, perhaps a fortnight. I wish I had not asked you to take me sleighing."

"Do you? I wish it too."

"I hoped you would come to see me on my rides, but I never saw you."

"I couldn't. I was ill, you see. I am sorry if I incommoded you."

"It was not that. I wanted to see you."

"Did you? I thought I was renounced."

"You are teasing me, I think."

"Not entirely, Miss Armstrong. You are teasing *me*, and you will make me cough, and that will make everyone here cross at you. There is an absurd conspiracy in this house that I am not to cough, even for a piece of dust or a mere frog in my throat."

"Are you often ill?" she asked seriously.

He smiled crookedly. "Are you still thinking of the weak-chinned babies? No, I am not often ill, though I must seem so. Until this year I have ordinarily been rather well. And I have a very strong chin, and yours is not weak. They should be safe on that score, at least ours should."

"Are you asking me to marry you?"

"I did not mean to, but I seem to have, don't I. Do you want me to?" He asked idly, paying rather little attention.

"Yes."

He was startled into complete attention, and a little dismayed. "You are much too young still, even if you were not under age, and I am of age now, but I have still no prospects. I have nothing to offer you."

"You have yourself."

"That is nothing, Anne. Not for you. One day you will be sister to an Earl. We are simply not able or ready to marry. But I would like to court you, openly, and perhaps my prospects will improve. I will write my guardian-that-was—"

"Why must you write him now?"

"I will tell you why, but not now. And habits are hard to shake. And he is my only prospect that your guardian would consider a prospect. When I have heard from him, no matter what he says, I will approach your guardian."

"Your blood is entirely as good as mine, Edward, Edward, it is half the same. Perhaps I can support us, I do have an income."

"That is absurd. It is not yet yours to manage, and even if it were, I would never let you. I think we should play another round of piquet, Anne. I am still too convalescent to think these thorny problems through."

He did write the Earl, but remembering his letter's fiasco when he was sixteen, he asked only to see him and did not explain why. The Earl received the letter, put aside his invitations and his involvements, and came at once. He did not wait to write, arriving sooner than a letter. He found Edward in his solarium, warm in the sun and protected from the mildly cool afternoon air of early April. He foresaw trouble in Edward's uneasy face, and sighed and asked him into his study, waiting for him to put on his coat again.

"Well, Edward," he said with an attempt at lightness. "What now? This time what's to do?"

"I did not expect you so soon," Edward said, nonsequentially, delaying the moment. "You must have travelled hard. I am sorry to have put you out."

"You cannot put me out. It is my real pleasure to come. Now tell me why I am honoured."

"I found the books," Edward said, not looking at the Earl. "I do thank you for them. I should have written. And about the other things."

"I am pleased you liked them," the Earl said. "But I did not need to come, to be thanked," he observed with a slight smile that was almost wistful, "a letter would have done. Why am I here, Edward? Tell me now, I am waiting to hear why you called me."

Edward sighed and looked at his fingers, wholly. "I wrote because I wanted to see you on a matter of some importance to me."

"Again?" murmured the Earl. "I mistrust your matters of importance. I well remember the last some five years ago."

"I am twenty-one now, Holland," he said hesitantly.

"I know that, Edward," the Earl said quietly. As Edward did not speak, he added, "You surely did not call me two hundred and fifty miles to tell me what I already know."

"No. You are not my guardian any longer," he said, still hesitantly.

"I know that, very well," the Earl said. "If you had property in your name, it would now be yours to administer."

"But I do not. I know that. I have been thinking about it"—he saw the Earl look as if he were about to speak, and he forestalled him with a little motion of his hand—"but it wasn't that I called you to speak about. I haven't any, I know it, there isn't anything there for me to discuss with you. I didn't call you to talk about that. Although since I have lived on your charity for so long, perhaps I should thank you for it."

The Earl prepared himself mentally for a disagreeable interview, and dispensing with the preliminaries, directly engaged.

"Don't thank me, please," waving Edward's words aside. "What is it you want to say? Must it be said?" he added, his voice momentarily soft. "Can it not wait? It bids to be unpleasant."

"I think it must. I am sorry, Holland. I am afraid I am going to displease you, and I do not want to, but I must."

"Out with it then, if you must. I am listening." He settled back, unwilling to help Edward or to put words in his mouth, his face giving no indication of his inward distress and foreboding.

"I do not have to ask you this, Holland," Edward said miserably, "since I am of age, but I—I thought all the same I would speak to you first—"

"And inform me? All right, go on, please. Inform me." His tone was sharper.

"I am going to speak to Anne's guardian, to Robert Armstrong, and ask his permission to address her."

The expression on the Earl's schooled face did not change. "You should not have asked me here to tell me that," the Earl said quietly. "You would better have just done it, for of course I cannot agree to it. But now that I *am* here, I must see that you do not."

"It is too late, Holland, you cannot direct me any more. I have asked you only from courtesy."

"Would you risk angering me, and so throw all this"—he indicated the house and the estate that surrounded them with his hand—"and much else beside, away from you?"

"It is a matter of more indifference to me than you could possibly imagine," Edward said simply. The Earl, observing his face, saw that it was true, and he omitted entirely that aspect of the subject from his later remarks.

"I take it, then, that you will not give me your approval, and that I must do it then, without it," Edward said, when the Earl did not answer. "I am sorry, Holland, it must end this way."

"Don't be sorry," the Earl said, "and take nothing. You are going nowhere and you are asking nothing of anyone, particularly of no Armstrong. It is not too late."

Edward's eyes widened, and he stood up. "I am sorry, Holland, but it *is* too late. May I take my leave?"

"You may not. It is not too late, as I will soon show you. You are in my house and on my land, surrounded by my servants, and I do not intend to let you go. You are mad to think I would, when you are not well. I will confine you for your own good, I will have you fettered if need be, until I can speak with Armstrong myself and have the girl removed, as I should have done long ago, or until you come out of this madness."

"You would not, Holland?" Edward said desperate but now nervous. "You have no right!"

"I would. I may have no right, but I have the present power, and I will use it."

"I am not a child, Holland," Edward cried. "I am twenty-one now, and you cannot do this to me. I can have a complaint brought."

"By all means," the Earl said pleasantly, "if you can reach anybody with whom to lodge it. I shall have you stopped long before you reach the edge of my estate. For that matter, I have grounds for complaint, too. I have kept our exchange of letters. It is my house from which you threatened me, not even long ago."

Edward looked at his unmoved face in despair. "You have stopped everything I ever wanted to do," he cried bitterly and hopelessly. "You have made me into what I am, and whenever I would leave it, you have forced me back. What *is* it you want of me now? Is it what you usually do? If it is, I will strip now, here, in this room, and do with you what you want me to, as long as you like, if afterwards you will only let me go." (He saw the Earl shake his head slightly.) "I warn you, Holland, if you lay hands upon me one more time in force, you will have to keep me in chains for the rest of my life or yours. And what good will that be to you? Do you understand me? I have had enough. I really will not abide any more." He was almost in tears, between anger and despair. "I knew nothing before but you, and I loved you, and I let you do as you wished, and I forgave you, but I will not now. Force me to stay, and I will not forgive you; you will never be able to trust me again."

"I believe you," the Earl said, "but nevertheless I am not going to let you go. It would be cruel to. You are really not well—and you do not know these Armstrongs as I do. You will encounter a horrible scene. They essentially still hate you, and all Hannoverian English, not only me, despite their living in this country and making their money here, and their wild girl cannot change it. Their memories are long, longer than mine. The land near here, Edward, used to be known as the Debateable Land, and the Armstrongs and the Tynes debated it back and forth. The Armstrongs raided the cattle and sheep of Tynedale, thousands of head, and the Tynes returned in kind. At one time, and not so very long ago, they were neither more than well-dressed glorified thieves. They made sorties and retaliatory raids, and laid waste each other's strongholds and houses and lands, and saw one another imprisoned and hung by themselves or their lairds or the various kings of England and Scotland, if they did not manage it themselves. It was over a long time ago, as my time goes, and the Armstrongs came into England and did service for the Hannoverians against the Stewarts and were rewarded in English land

—they were always willing to serve whichever side most advantaged them—and you would think it all forgotten. Prince Charles, thank God, is at last dead, and though there are widows and children from Culloden still alive, and though Lord Armstrong's father was killed there, it is mere Lowland sentimentality now, for what they never really did, and the Armstrongs at heart have never been sentimental people, nor have we. The immediate end serves us best, but in this question of personal land and personal death. Publicly yes, perhaps, but not between our immediate families. Mr. Wesley's spirit of reconciliation has never deeply touched us—Armstrongs, men of Liddesdale, nor men of Tyne. It is a quality we do not know. We were and are a people here 'most easily offended at one another,' as he said. And we had our reasons. I would not go there if I were you, Edward. Really I would not."

From this speech Edward's mind had pulled one possibility the Earl had not made explicit, and he asked it directly, past horror and for the moment past embarrassment. "Did you do—what you did to me, have you treated me as you have, and as you say you will because of this?" He looked at the Earl straightly, and his eyes and his thoughts behind them were unreadable. "Because I am a way of retaliation, because of what they think me, who they think I am?"

"I hope not," the Earl said, after a startled pause, his own eyes turning away. "I hope not, Edward." His voice was heavy. "It was always impossible, you see. For Armstrong it was impossible, me, a Tyne, to raise an Armstrong child—even had I done it well. Had he known it possible, my guardianship, he would have treated your mother less harshly—but neither he nor I conceived such a possibility. Some kind of confrontation was bound to come, unless I relinquished you, and I, being a stubborn man, once engaged, would not. Were I a praying man, Edward, I might say, God help us all.

"But I am not a Tyne, at least, I think I may not be, even as you are not an Armstrong, or so you have convinced me. We are something else, both of us, both you and I, than we are thought to be. But I for my part do not intend to enlighten the world about me, or raise the possibility. I am content to be what I seem to be, and what I may actually be. I do not seek a fight, but I will not run from one. Your so-called father left all that, and went in another direction, but they are Scotch and the rest did not. I have myself abstained from either quarrel, as best I might, like the Vicar of Bray, I detest these wars of politics and reprisal, but it does me no good with such as these, nor will it you, particularly if you tell them who you are. Publicly and financially we may meet, or might before the duel, privately never, even if you yourself and our quarrel over you did not make it twice over impossible."

"I do not believe you," Edward said, listening, despite himself. "It is too long ago now."

"Forget her," the Earl urged, pressing on Edward's hesitation. "This scion-slip of a girl has caused you and has caused me nothing but trouble. She has no modesty, no shame: *'Peste sur ces filles sans vergogne!'* I hope it is not a new breed. She has harassed you when you were physically unfit to be harassed, and provoked you to acts not like you, and she has caused me to lose my temper and behave unsuitably, and she has revived suspicions on both our parts better buried."

"We *let* ourselves be harassed and provoked, and even forced," Edward said slowly.

"No philosophy, please, Edward, just tell me your answer, now you have mine."

Edward turned and walked away a few steps, away from the door but near the window. The Earl rose in his turn and followed him, his limp pronounced.

"Well, Edward? What is it? Which way is it to be?"

"Only this," Edward said, his face convulsed with anger and grief, turning quickly, and driving his fist, his "bunch of fives," straight into the Earl's jaw, dropping the surprised, unbalanced Earl to the floor. The Earl lay there, not picking himself up, amazed and almost amused.

"I think you should have done that long ago, Edward," he said rubbing his chin, " 'grace at a graceless face,' always an impossible thing," but Edward did not hear him, having let himself out by the windows through which he had entered a year and a half before. He walked quickly down the lawn, among the trees that were in tender bud, afraid to go to the stables for his horse, afraid he would be stopped.

VI

I have left now, he thought, I have cut myself free, for good or for bad, I cannot go back. Holland will not let me now. To have asserted his independence and his rights, he was surprisingly unhappy, and ominous lines would keep going through his head of the Deputy Angelo: "When once our grace we have forgot, nothing goes right; we would, and we would not." His common sense told him that with no money and with no clothes and little reserve of strength, he might as well shoot himself and be done with. He decided that his only recourse was to ask the mercy of the help of the Vicar, and he therefore bent his steps that way, to the vicarage which lay between Tyne's estate and the village and hardly half the distance between Tyne and the Armstrongs' Northumbrian holding, which he simply did not feel he could walk. He arrived, dusty and whiter than the dust, at the door about three o'clock and was received with motherly clucking by the Vicar's wife, and brought in, and sat down, and dusted off, and plied with tea and broth but no questions. He closeted himself with the Vicar and was devastatingly and almost entirely frank.

"I have fought with my father," he said to the Vicar, "both ways. I have left him on the floor. He won't forgive me, and I don't want him to. I have been his mistress, though not for some time, not since Christmas, and I want to go away."

"I have not heard you, and I have not understood you," the Vicar said, turning his eyes away. "I have known Lord Tyne for many years —one way or another since birth. You must not tell me too much, Edward. I am an old man. What do you need? Is it money?"

"Yes. I am not allowed any, since I came back. I have not a single coin of any sort. I could perhaps draw on my account in the York bank, it may not have been closed, but I haven't enough to get there, and I do not want to. It is not really mine."

"Vicars are not allowed much either," he said, smiling faintly, "but I will give you what I have."

"If you ask Tyne, he will give it back to you. He is very proud. He will hate my coming here."

"I have no intention of telling him of your visit, ever," the Vicar said.

Edward took the coins and the note, and finished his tea, and stood up. "Goodbye, sir," he said gently.

"Goodbye, Edward," the old man said, much troubled. "I have been remembering the little boy whom I first knew, and I cannot understand how this has come about."

"I am sorry I have troubled you," Edward said again gently. "If you will think back to my mother, I think you will perhaps understand better. I have been very alone, you know, I have had almost no one. Will you wish me well?"

"You know I do, Edward. Is there anything more I can do for you, of a more practical nature?"

"Yes," Edward said frankly, "you can. I am in a hurry, and I am also very tired. Would you mind taking your gig and driving me to a place I must go?"

"I will drive you wherever you want to go, Edward, or rather you shall drive me, and then I will drive myself home, and on the way I shall attempt to persuade you at least to reconcile with your father before you go."

"It is no use, sir," Edward said, harnessing the horse, "it cannot be done. I wish the break need not have come myself." He drove slowly, tired further by the effort of bringing the horse and gig together. "You cannot know all its causes. My nature is too weak. I cannot stand up to Lord Tyne's. I have always meant to leave, when I could, to try to find out who I am still, by myself, if I could. You cannot imagine, sir, what secrets these large removed acreages may hold unheard and unseen, and I do not wish to tell you."

"Nor I to hear," the Vicar murmured, "though I know much you might not think. The Church and the estates hold an uneasy truce, Edward, and it is not my wish to disturb it. I hope you do not think me unkind, Edward?"

"I do not at all," Edward said, "it is the way of the world. There is really very little you or anyone can do for me, that you are not doing." He handed the reins to the Vicar, when they reached the wall about Lord Armstrong's estate and its entrance, which Anne had pointed out on their sleigh ride, and swung himself down. He held out his hand, and the Vicar took it in his and held it, unwilling to let it go, and said looking at Edward, in a kindly, almost absent way, "Do you remember the Roman formula, Edward, we used to read, S.T.T.L.?"

"*Sit terra tibi levis,*" Edward said slowly. "That is for the dead, sir, do you mean that I am so now for you?"

"No, my dear boy, I only mean the earth of the world seems to be resting heavily upon you now, and I would wish that it would again be light upon you. That is my valediction for you. I am an old man, Edward, I was old when we met, and I have grown older with you, though I may not seem to have outwardly changed so much. It may be I shall not see you again. I have loved you, Edward, and I have believed in you, and when we were often together, though I taught you, it was more often I who listened to you. I hope that person may reappear, if not for me, then for others. Goodbye, Edward." He looked searchingly at him with his dim, watery blue eyes. "May the world rest lightly upon you." He shook Edward's hand warmly, and watched him as Edward walked away toward the gates, wanting to turn but not turning again.

He was admitted, and walked hesitantly up the drive to the house, dreading this second interview of the day that might also prove shattering. It seemed madness to him now, and he wondered how he had suggested it or allowed Anne to persuade him to it. He saw now with a sudden clarity that on this count he had fought his father for nothing, and that alone, with no name and no property and no wealth to support him, he did not need to go any farther to know the certain answer he would receive. He took his hand from the door, and turned away, and as he did so turned into Anne's brother Armstrong who had just come from the stables, still booted and spurred, in brown buckskins, from a day's hunting in the hills. Considerably taller, and twice the heavier, dark, with a cleft chin, some ten years the older, he looked Edward up and down, recognised him, and asked him curtly, with bare civility, what he wanted.

"Nothing," Edward said, "I was just going."

"Nothing?" asked Armstrong in surprise. "You must have wanted something. Come inside anyway. I have been wanting to talk to you."

He took Edward into his gun-room, but he did not offer him a chair, though he took one himself, throwing a leg over one arm.

"Well," he said again, "I have been wanting to see you. I suppose, though, you came to see my sister."

"No, I came to see you," Edward said. "May I sit down?"

"Sit if you like," Armstrong said ungraciously. "What did you want? Or perhaps I should tell you first why I wanted to see you."

"If you like," Edward said.

"I thought I'd tell you, let you know, that if you kept on seeing my sister behind my back, I'd break your neck for you. That's all."

Edward did not attempt to correct the slight injustice of the remark, for he knew he could have sent Anne away any time, had he really chosen, and that he had begun pursuit himself. Instead, he said simply, "It was about that, sir, that I came to see you. I do not like it either. I would like openly to ask your permission to see Miss Armstrong."

"You would? God, that's rich!" he said unpromisingly. "What about?"

"When I am in a position to support my offer, I would like to ask your sister to be my wife."

"I cannot believe I hear what you are saying," Armstrong said with an expression and gesture of uncomprehension. "Do you really ask me to believe you came here to ask me that?"

"I do. Is it so hard?"

"Then why was you turning off my door? You came to see her, thinking I was out, I am thinking."

"No, sir, I did not. I have never sought your sister out."

Armstrong gave a sharp bark of laughter, and pulled out his flask and drank from it, making no offer to Edward.

"It don't signify. You can't have her. The relationship is too close, as you ought to know, even if I liked you, which I don't. And with your skulking secret lying meetings which I have heard about, and considered putting an end to myself, with the butt end of my pistol, I wish you did not have the name you do. It is only that name that has held me back: I thought it was just some romantic notion she had about her disinherited cousin, that when she saw you, she would tire of. She is a silly chit and full of notions, and much too young for anything. Do you dare come here to tell me it has been more than that? Have you been fixing some interest with her? I never thought, it being you, it could be that sort of thing."

Edward flushed, and controlled himself with difficulty.

"It was not my wish to hide either my feelings or my intentions. Until I came of age, I had no choice. I think I have not pressed myself on your sister. I have not told her, what I am going to tell you now, that there is not that particular bar to a marriage between us."

"What *do* you mean?"

"That I am not her cousin and not yours. I am not George Armstrong's son."

"And whose are you then?" he sneered, hardly interested.

"I am Lord Tyne's."

"Tyne's bastard?" his interest quickening. "Gad, that is rich! I had heard the rumour but I never credited it, for Uncle George was not the kind to wear horns, I thought. And much as I hate Tyne, I did put that beyond him."

It was the second insinuation of some sort, and Edward forced himself to meet it. "I do not understand your implication; please make yourself clear."

"Don't you?" Armstrong asked, an odd inflection in his voice. "Then I will. Let us have no doubts." He looked at him with sudden absolute viciousness. "I know very well what you are and what you do. Do you not know that? Do not bother denying it." As Edward looked blank, he added, "Must I spell it out and diagram it? I know the cause of my father's duel with yours." He was overcome with indignation at the memory, and he dropped his indolent manner. "Is it not enough your father has killed my sister's father and mine because he knew the truth about you both, and wished to help you then? He did not know Tyne was your father. Had he known or Tyne told him, he would not have interfered in something so hopeless and so not his affair. But of course Tyne did not, fearing him to live—"

"Tyne did not know," Edward said with stiff lip. "Do not blame him for what he did not know."

"More fool he. But I am no longer interested in past history. It cannot be changed. Let us speak of the future. Now you listen to me very carefully, young flower. If you ever approach me or my sister again with such an intention, I shall have you brought to law and stocked and pilloried. You and Lord Tyne both. And I can. What you do is your affair as long as you keep it there, but if you intrude yourself into my family (what Tyne has left of it), I shall make it mine. Do you understand me? You are silent now."

"There is nothing more I can say, is there?" Edward said, his lips tight set, his eyes hopeless and beyond anger. "You are kind to give me your full opinion of myself as well as my suit, and leave me in no doubts or false hopes. I will go now, with your leave."

"You do not have it," the young Armstrong said. "If you imagine any upstart reprobate of no breeding and no name of his own can address me for my only sister's hand, you have much to learn. I intend to have you whipped for it before you go, without your leave." He pulled a cord, as he spoke, and a footman entered. "I want this impertinent young buck whipped, and hard," he said. "Call my groom and see to it."

Edward listened to Anne's older brother speak his intentions unbelieving. He made no move to resist or to escape. He had learned to fight well enough that he did not wholly despair of evading this surprising issue, despite his lack of condition, if he took the particular moment, but even if Armstrong had not been older and heavier, more experienced, and in his home surrounded by his paid men, he could not imagine laying hands on the brother of the girl he had asked to address. He did not feel insulted, he had been told no more than the truth. Already overcome with shame and with grief, he had nothing to say, and no way to protest. He stood there, his shocked eyes fixed full on Armstrong's face for what seemed endless moments, not even noticing the pistol hanging loosely in Armstrong's hand or that Armstrong thought him compelled by it. The older man in his turn watched him through narrowed disgusted eyes, contemptuous of his lack of spirit. Both received the entrance of two grooms with relief. One held a leather strap in his hand, and on a nod from Armstrong, advanced on Edward and took his hands in his, preparatory to binding them.

Edward let them lie there, but he said to Armstrong, "It is not necessary to bring in these men or to strap my hands like this. I cannot fight you, of all people. Just please do it quickly, whatever you think you have to do."

"Egad," his host said with contemptuous surprise, "don't you even mind? Are you entirely without honour and without shame?"

"I would mind if it would do me any good to mind," Edward said with a brief flash. "A whipping will not break me. Only hurry and have done with it, what you are going to do. You are a sportsman, don't torment me."

"Did you think I would stoop to touch you myself?" He turned his back, dismissing the matter. The two grooms put their hands on Edward's arms and took him from the room, and hustled him, though he did not resist them, to the courtyard in the stable.

"I have been whipped before, often enough, and for as little reason," he repeated dully to himself, numb still with the pain of Armstrong's cutting words, "one more time now will not matter." Again in the hands of grooms, he remembered the whipping Ross had given him. But he wished Armstrong had seen fit to do it himself, if he wanted it done, or had it done before him, for he was suddenly afraid of these big impassive men by themselves and their deliberate slowness. They were men who did not mind setting mantraps and spring guns on the Earl's hunting grounds, as his own Earl did not permit, or collecting afterwards their tortured mangled catches. He had seen the remains of such, half-living, in the village. He wished now he had fought them while he could. He looked at their brute faces, the warm familiar scent of straw and horses and manure in his nostrils and throat, and even then he could not believe in the outcome of his errand.

They unbound his hands, and laid hands upon his coat to strip him of his clothes. Filled with shame and a piercing fear, he felt then he had been a fool to endure Armstrong's attack or to have endured so many attacks made upon his person and he wondered why he had so often submitted. He lit into them, suddenly and savagely with his freed fists, with the advantage of surprise, after his passivity in their hands. For a moment he thought he would win his freedom, despite odds on alien ground, but they were two, and one hit him a hard glancing blow that missed his face, as he ducked back, but struck below his throat. He was overcome by a fit of the coughing he thought he had shaken, and while he was helpless and choking in its throes, his shirt and coat were taken from him roughly, and his hands rebound, in front of him. His resistance had only heightened the grooms' enjoyment, he saw. One held him tightly gripped against him in a bear's hold, laughing, while the other braced himself and pulled his boots from him, though he kicked him, once in the face—he felt the contact and heard the man curse; and though he continued to struggle, his stockings and breeches were peeled from him. He twisted frantically in their hands, furious with shame, without hope, except unreasonably to delay, though weakening, wishing now for the mercies of the Earl whose punishments had limits which he did not expect from these men, and bit the hand of the man holding him. The man yelled and swore, and threw him away from him hard against the stable boards, and he felt the whistle of the heavy horsewhip in the other man's hand strike him before he heard it. It knocked him back to the strawy floor, as he tried to rise, with its second blow, where he rolled over to shield his viscera, writhing beneath the stinging edge, blinded and choked with pain he could not avoid, his spirit this time seeming to die beneath it, but determined not to scream yet, so long as he could hold the screams back. It had struck him twice more, before he heard a different voice he did not know quietly order the men to stop. The whip hit him again, but its force diminished, even as the voice spoke.

"That is enough," the voice said more sternly. "Loose the boy and let him dress and go."

He lay there, still bound, his mouth full of dust and straw, coughing, angry tears of pain and rage and humiliation smarting his eyes, unable to wipe them away. His hands were released then, but they shook so, he could not use them. He shut his eyes, feeling the world once more sliding away from him. This time he did not try to catch it, but it caught him, before he quite vanished. He felt hands, cool and kind and long-fingered this time, not hot and heavy and dirty, take his shoulders and hold them up, and a flask pressed against his lips to drink which scalded his throat and set him coughing again. He heard the voice order water and wine, curtly, and then turn to him to speak, the hands still holding him, above the welts the whip had made:

"So you are the boy who might have been George's son." There was a pause, in which he did not open his eyes. "Are you certain you are not?" He nodded his head, slightly. "Well, we have given you no cause to wish to be." A tin was put to his lips, this time of water. He drank it thirstily, fighting now against the blackness that kept pressing in upon him.

"Open your eyes now," the voice said sternly, "I am not going to hurt you. Look at me." His shoulders were released. "Open your eyes, please," the voice came again. He pulled them somehow open as from an immense distance away. He looked into a pair of very hard, very angry grey eyes, which were the eyes, except for their expression, of the man who had fathered his infancy and early childhood. He recognised them instantly, so near his own, before their owner kneeling on his feet beside him stood up. They glowered at him beneath their shaggy grey brows, whose hairs grew wildly and at random, and high wiry grey hair that framed his head, standing vigorously away from it. His coat was grey, and his trousers, and he stood there, his piercing eagle eyes and jutting chin and crag-like brow, from his great height towering over Edward, like some giant Scottish bird of prey, and yet Edward was not afraid of him. He could not be, before a rugged image of another man he had loved, and he thought the anger not altogether meant for him.

"Do you know who I am?" Edward nodded his head, unable to speak, not trusting his voice.

"My nephew mistakes to use my land like this for such a purpose without my leave. I will not tolerate it. Neither will I tolerate Tyne's bastard here. Whose name are you using now? I hope not mine?"

Edward said nothing, humiliated, disadvantaged, almost naked, before the new sudden onslaught.

"Well, answer me then."

"I have not changed the name I have always had, and you know that as well as I, Lord Armstrong," Edward said, suddenly baited, the blackness receding. "It was given to me by your brother, I did not ask for it. It is not yours to take from me, or to reproach me with owing."

For a moment he thought the eyes boring through him softened, but if they did, the change was so momentary he might have imagined it. He was unable to bear the situation or the conversation, and he picked up his breeches with shaking fingers, not looking at the Scotch Earl. He felt rather than saw him turn and go towards the door, but he did not look up or around until a glass of wine was put in his hand. The surprise started him coughing again, his throat dry and constricted, and he spilled the wine. Lord Armstrong patiently refilled the glass, but this time he held it himself until the fit had passed, and then he continued to hold the stem, lifting the glass to Edward's lips.

"Why have you let my nephew use you like this?" he asked harshly. "Have you no spirit? Could you not have stopped him?"

Edward swallowed, coughing again in his dry throat, unable to answer anything that would not in his own eyes have seemed fulsome, drawn towards this stranger who seemed like no stranger, and who wanted none of Tyne's bastard. He did not belong to this family after all, and he was not going to; they did not want him, not for the past, not in the future.

"Well, speak," Earl Armstrong said with angry curiosity, his voice tapping against the empty air impatiently. He put a hand under Edward's chin, and drew his lowered face up where he could see it, studying it.

"I don't know," Edward said dully, shutting his eyes against inspection. "I could not fight him."

"Hmph," the Scotch Earl growled. "You should have done so. He had no scruples about you. Our family does not dwell on sentiment, except for our proper blood." As if denying his words, he put a hand on Edward's shoulder, and turned him, to survey the marks of the whip, that were not deep. "You will do," he said, "they had just begun. I am not sorry I came home when I did, and happened to see my nephew when I did. But my niece is not for you. I, 'Armstrong himself,' say it. I hope you understand me. Get yourself clothed now, it is indecent."

He turned on his heel towards the door. Edward was free to pick himself up as best he could from the strawy dusty floor. Hs brushed off what dirt he could, and found his stockings and his boots, but the struggle to put them on without George left him even more exhausted. He found his shirt and put it on and began to button it with shaking fingers, but he could not control them enough to manage the little holes. He had heard nothing, and he had thought Lord Havermore had gone, but he found him now again by him, his fingers quickly mastering the buttons he had not been able to subdue. He stood back then, watching, his face impassive, while Edward tried to put on his coat, stepping forward again when he saw Edward could not manage.

"If you attempt to call my nephew out," he said, walking with Edward to the door, "you will waste your time. He will not accept your challenge. I think I need not explain why. Lord Tyne, though, is another matter. If he chooses to enter your quarrel, I or my nephew will meet him when and where he will. Tell him so, when you tell him of this."

Edward shook his head. "I am not going to tell him anything at all. He told me not to come. I should have listened to him. It would have spared us all this trouble."

"I do not understand you," Lord Armstrong said, after a moment, "but it is no matter whether I do or not. My understanding you, or my liking you, is of no significance or consequence. I do not see your hat or your gloves. Did you leave them in the house?" Edward shook his head, not bothering to explain, past caring for Lord Armstrong's briefly puzzled stare. "I will ask you now never to come near me, or my house, or my niece again. If you do, I will myself have you whipped in true earnest, and I will not then interfere." He bowed formally. "Good day, Mr. Armstrong."

Edward did not speak. There was nothing he knew to say adequate to his feelings. He walked away, his face white and set, his lips pressed hard against their sudden quivering. It would have made him no happier to know that he had left Lord Armstrong in a baffled state unusual to him. He felt all ties cut now. He walked by instinct rather than by his senses out of the grounds and the gate of Armstrong's house, past the barred crest with the clenched fist that had nothing to do with him, not knowing when he had left it.

VII

He did not see Anne in an upper window, or hear her call him, or if he did, he did not turn his head. She marked that he was going away from Tyne, not towards it, on foot, and then she attacked both her brother and her uncle each in turn, attempting, for once unsuccessfully, to discover the content of the interview and learning at first only that they stood firm in unqualified disapproval of the match. She continued to besiege her brother Robert, however, threatening and pleading and arguing, and eventually because she enraged him, he did tell her several of the reasons for their dislike. He shocked and sobered her considerably, and it was an hour after he left her that she put on her bonnet and her pelisse, and followed in her pony cart in the direction where Edward had gone. The Vicar was the person who told her finally where to look.

She found Edward sitting on the ground by his mother's grave, his knees drawn up, his hands clasped about them, the sun that was setting casting a terracotta colour on his face and on the stone, and his face looked as bleak as desert stone. He did not move or make any greeting to her, and she stood uncertainly a little way from him, and wondering if he would speak. Finally he did.

"What do you want, Anne?" he asked, his eyes away from her, his voice as harsh as his particular voice could be. "What do you want of me? Why have you come here?"

Listening to his voice, and watching his face, she realised to her horror that he had been weeping, and had worn out his voice with crying. Oh, God, she thought, let me not say the wrong thing, forgetting that it was Edward she was dealing with, and that there was no wrong thing that could be said to him. He looked up at her suddenly with his eyes, and at their clear tired gaze her heart turned within her, and smiled slightly, his lips trembling a little.

"It's all right," he said, "I will be all right in a little while. I came up here to be alone for a while, that's all."

"Do you want me to go?"

"Yes," he said, "I do." He looked up at her for a quick moment and then his eyes fell. "I don't mean to hurt you, Anne. I just don't see what there is any more to say."

He seemed for once completely withdrawn and inapproachable, but she could not go away.

"You have been hurt," she said, her perception sharpened by her need to understand, suddenly realising it and speaking with a new gentleness, realising he was not really angry or with her, and feeling her way, her awareness of him and his need like an exposed nerve. She could not see beneath his coat, and her heightened perception told her only the hurt to his spirit. He did not answer. "Who hurt you? My brother?"

"You should know. I wish you would leave me."

"Was it Rockfort?" using unconsciously the older name. He did not answer.

"My brother and my uncle said *no*. I know that. Did Rockfort, too?"

He nodded, but he did not speak.

"Why? Because he does not like me?"

"No. You know that." His voice was rough. "I wish you would go away. I don't want to talk about it."

"It was my brother who hurt you," she said suddenly. "He didn't have to do that."

"I should have known how he would feel," Edward said, "but I didn't. I didn't at all, Anne, I don't want to talk about it any more. I wish you would go away and leave me now. Or I will go, myself." But he did not move.

"You are Rockfort's son," she said, stating, not asking, "not George Armstrong's, not my cousin."

"Yes," he said, his head on his arms, "I am. I am Rockfort's son, his bastard. I have never denied it, I don't want to deny it, but it is not something I care to go about shouting out and emblazoning, just any time and any place. I thought it was generally known now, by anyone who cared about knowing. I thought you knew. After the sleigh ride, I thought the word of *cousin* was a game."

"Which did he mind your marrying most, your cousin or Rockfort's son?"

"Rockfort's son, Edward," she said. "You should know that."

"His son or his natural son?" He smiled bitterly and painfully. "He did not say much to me."

"It doesn't matter. Just Rockfort's line, which he thinks has bad blood in it, and because your father killed my father, his and mine, who you thought was your family, too. He does not forgive that."

"A long time ago, I thought it," Edward said sighing. "I do not blame him for not forgiving it, or for not wanting your blood mixed with mine."

"Would you forgive it, Edward?"

"I don't know. I think I might, I have learned to forgive so much, but I don't know, and I don't blame him for it."

"What have you learned to forgive?"

He raised his head briefly. "Anything that has to be forgiven is best then forgotten, or it is not a clean forgiving, and forgiving does no good. Nothing much. I don't remember. I was just speaking in point. Or did your brother tell you things about me, too?"

"He told me certain things."

"There is nothing he can tell but rumours. Did you believe him? What did he tell you? Let me at least fight it, in your eyes."

He saw her eyes fall.

"Are you a coward, Anne? Why bring it up, if you cannot face it? Then I will tell you. Did he tell you I was my father's lover?"

Her lowered head answered him.

"Did you believe him?" She did not answer. "Never mind. It is true.

I was, I am, I always will be. But not exactly as your brother thinks. And my father is not mine. Not now, as your brother thinks. What do you think, Anne?"

She lifted her head, and her eyes to him. "I think I love you, Edward."

"Do you, Anne?" he asked, his eyes holding hers intently.

"I think I do, though I have tried not to before, as you know, and though I tried again this afternoon, not to, for I am afraid of Rockfort, too." The older name came naturally to both their lips.

"You have cause to be," Edward said. "He is a dangerous man, and I say it, who am his son. You should perhaps be afraid of me, too."

She shook her head. "You are yourself, Edward."

"That is only a romantic thought, Anne. I am all the things that have gone into the making of me, and I am not always sure myself what they are."

"If you love Rockfort—and you do?"

"I do," Edward said.

"—in time I think I should learn to, but he won't let me, will he, nor will my guardian, my brother or my uncle."

"No," said Edward, "I do not think they will either." He poked in the dirt at his feet with a stick.

"Your mother's name has not been changed."

"No. I see your brother told you that, too. My father will, I think. He has just not done it yet, as he has not me. He is adopting me, you know. His lawyer has the papers now. It all takes a little time. If you married me, I mean, without your brother's consent, I think he would disown me, too, and stop the papers. How strange he should feel as strongly about you and your family, as your family does about me and him." He did not tell her of his break with his father. He could not believe now it had happened and his mind shied from acknowledging it, or that these things he projected into the future were his real and present state.

"I did try to shoot him."

"Would you have?"

"I don't know. You didn't let me see."

"He thought you would not have, except by accident. And he had a gun too, a pistol, in his pocket, that you didn't know about."

"Did he?" She almost smiled. "He was probably right, but I don't know. I felt I should, and I usually do what I think I should."

"And what is that now, Anne?" he asked, his eyes again intent on hers.

"I think I should love you, but I do not know if you can love me?"

"I do not know what you mean. I have asked your guardian and mine if I might marry you, and I have pursued you and wooed you since I first saw you, despite having just about no encouragement from you, and rather just the opposite."

"I know that," she said. "It is sweet now to remember, but that is just a part of loving and what my brother has said has made me wonder."

"I have had experience, Anne, considerable," Edward said briefly. "Is that what you mean? My uncle, my father, did not want me crippled that way by what he did to me as a child, and later. It is, as he said, a skill."

"I did not mean exactly that," she said, not flushing. "I am wondering if you can really love anyone else, that is all."

"I don't know," Edward said slowly. "I cannot promise that. But I think I love you. I cannot have my father to love. He would not, and I would not, now, and I have never wanted any other man to love. I have not loved any other woman, either, before you, Anne, except of course my mother, but that is not what you mean, for I loved my first father too. But what it all means, I don't really know. And we shan't find out now, anyway."

"Why not?"

He looked at her, unbelieving. She was seated a few inches from him, on the other side of his mother's small narrow stone. She hardly believed she had spoken herself, the words had found themselves on her lips, and she trembled at them, but as she spoke, she leaned a little towards him, her eyes on his. She did not speak again, and he did not either, but he leaned forward, too, and his lips just touched hers, and then withdrew, and then touched again, tentatively. Her eyes shone in the soft cool twilight that was falling about them. She leaned forward in her turn, her lips parted, and kissed his more lingeringly, and his parted with hers and returned her kiss. He stood up, and took her hand, and drew her up, beside him, and into his arms for a long embrace in which he felt her limbs and all her body go soft against his.

"Do you want me to do this, Anne?" he asked, still unbelieving, trembling in his turn, his voice little more than a whisper.

"Yes," she said, "yes, I do. I want you, and I think you must."

He sat down and took her in his arms, and held her close for a long time. The dark erased the objects around them, and the ground grew cool, and the glowworms began to wink among the stems of the Vicar's soft green grass with a soft green light. The great tables of the stones on legs rose about them, some fallen, the stone next to his mother's grave, flat and smooth and grey and long as they were, was warm still from the heat of the day. He laid her on it, and himself beside her, quietly. She came into his arms as to her natural place, and after a moment, his lips pressed on hers, not leaving them, he turned her beneath him. For a moment, his restraint gone, aware only of the ache of his body and the ache of his heart, and his need for a present comfort, his mouth pressed hungrily and insistently into her trembling one, which though it did not withdraw, was unable to respond. Then he released her lips and brought her on his breast in his arms, despite his back, and after a long time he spoke:

"It is not very wise of you or of me, Anne. It is more like what my father would have done, and will only prove your brother right."

"You don't want me, Edward?" she said, sitting up and turning about in his arms. "You can tell me, if you don't. I love you, and I won't be angry, and I won't be hurt. I just want to know."

"I do want you." He took her hand and guided it against him. "Do you know what that means?"

"I think I do," she said, her voice trembling a little in its turn. "You will enter me with yourself."

He held her tightly. "Are you afraid?"

"No," she said, "I am afraid of nothing about you."

She felt something drop on her hands, and she realised that it was not dew, but tears. She looked up in surprise, and he shook them angrily from his eyes.

"Well, I am. I am afraid *for* you, Anne." He stood up, and pulled her to her feet, too, and put his hands gently on her shoulders. "Go home, Anne," he said, and gave her a little push. "You will be missed."

She looked at him, stricken. He shook his head. "I am not going to take you like this, Anne, in discomfort and tears and disgrace here in a churchyard—when I take you, if someday I do and we do this thing together, I want to be able to laugh, and you too—and I'm not going to elope with you to Gretna Green, and live in poverty and disgrace and friendless, with you. You think it would be all right, Anne, but it wouldn't, not after a while, not for you and not for me. We are not either of us made to live like that, I not very much and you not at all. Why, it would only prove your family was right about me, that I was irresponsible and not to be trusted. I have had enough of that kind of thing, with my father and my mother, and I don't want it for myself, or you, or anyone I love." He kissed the top of her head gently. "If your guardian thinks you are too young, you can wait to grow up a little more, and if he thinks I am not the right sort of person for you, then he will find out later he is wrong and change his mind, or we will find out he's right, that's all."

If his words seemed moderate to her in the light of what she did know, she could not conceive of the depth of their gentleness after what her brother had done to him. He had almost forgotten it himself, concentrated so wholly upon herself and him and her need. He put his finger on her lips as she would have spoken, and then brushed them with his lips. "And you must learn to trust me for myself, Anne. You must not try to test me, this way. It is not necessary, and it would answer nothing, really, after all. I would still be a mystery to you, and you to me. There would have been this once, but would there be another— you would be thinking that. Nothing, you see, ever settles anything for ever, Anne, nothing does, not love, not lust, not violence, not even death." She had begun to cry, and he wiped the tears with his fingers. "Are you angry with me, Anne, or just sad?"

"A little of both, after all," she said, trying to smile.

"I shall never remember anything so beautiful as your face below me, and these stars above me. What day is it?" She told him. "I shall never forget it. I had thought for a moment it had been my birthday," he said, "but that has after all passed, and will not come again for some months. Don't be angry with me, Anne," he said, pleading. "We can say the unforgivable thing, but nothing unforgivable can be said or done to us. Tomorrow I think you will be glad."

"But it is not tomorrow now. I wish I were like the people around us," she said bitterly, "for they are dead, and need nothing."

"How strange," he said, not answering her, tracing her features with his first finger, "I feel as if you were my family, and yet you aren't, really, after all. But someday, I think, we shall make a family you and I between us, that will be both what I might have been and what we are—I hope so. If you are patient, and will grow a little older. I hope we will. I do hope we will."

"And what if I am not patient, or my brother presses me into a marriage with some other man he does approve of?"

He looked at her soberly.

"If that happens, I shall just have to bear it, Anne, and you will too. It will be worse for me, than for you, Anne."

She was suddenly angry and quite impatient. "I—could go home and tell my brother you had assaulted me, done this thing to me, even though you haven't, and then he would make you marry me."

"Would you, Anne? I don't think you would. I don't blame you for being angry, I should not have kissed you as I did. But you are so young." He almost laughed. "He would be much more likely just to shoot me dead, you know." He kissed her a last time, and gave her another push, his hands lingering a moment on her shoulders, and then he turned her away from him. "Go home now, Anne," he said. He started to walk off, and then he changed his mind. "It is too dark, I will take you home." He walked quietly beside her, not speaking, or touching her again, to her pony cart, and drove her home.

"What will you do, Edward?" she asked at her gate.

"I think I will go away for a while, just by myself, Anne," he said. "I have wanted to, many times, but I could not before."

She had recovered herself, and despite her dismay at the knowledge he was going even farther away, her skin was singing with the memory of his kisses, and her fingers tingled at the memory of having touched him, under his hand. It was hard to live on memories, she had thought, but these were larger than at the time she had thought. She became aware that he had dismounted, and was holding out his hand to her, but she did not speak, and he looked at her face, turned away from him, and then he said, very quietly, "Do not be angry with me, Anne. We cannot help our families being as they are." She said nothing, but she looked down at him now and she put her hand into his. He brought it against his face, and rested his face against it. "I love you, Anne. I wonder if you do love me. I want so much to be with someone I love who loves me. I have wanted it all my life, but we shall have to wait, at least, I shall. It will not hurt for waiting. Nothing good does. When I come back, I will come to see you, and see how you are."

He left her, and without turning his head again, walked quickly up the road. He did not go home, for he could not. He reached the main road and continued walking. His figure was shadowed, and the large enclosed coach and four, its lamps lit, that came up behind him at first did not see him, and overshot him, and had to pull up. He looked up, without any fear and not much interest, as the Earl leaned out.

"Would you leave without saying goodbye?" the Earl said quietly.

"I am sorry, Holland," Edward said. "I should not have. I was unhappy, I did not think. And I did not think you would want to see me."

"You see I do. Forget this afternoon. I have. Are you alone?" Edward nodded. "I had not thought you would be. Will you get in, Edward?"

"I don't know. Are you going to try to stop me from going?"

"No, Edward. I want to talk to you, that's all." In answer Edward put his foot on the step, and swung himself up and closed the door.

"Why did you think I might not be?" Edward asked.

"I saw you go towards the churchyard, and after a time, I saw your —friend follow you, and I did not see either of you return. Under the circumstances I made an assumption that did not seem to me unusual or unwarranted."

"And you just watched?"

"I had made my wishes clear already. I was interested in what you would do, if I did not interfere. I had no particular wish to. It seemed your affair to manage in your own way," the Earl said dispassionately to one side of the carriage.

"'O God,'" Edward said softly under his breath, "'from you that I could private be,'" both cursing and praying in his humiliation to be so discovered still in his father's all-seeing eyes.

"What have you done with her? Or may one ask?"

"I have taken her home."

"Is one to expect yet another visit from her incensed guardian to-morrow?"

"I don't know what that means."

"I have had one already this afternoon, threatening to shoot me if I do not control you. Well?"

"I wouldn't know. Not on my account. I have not hurt her. You judge me once again too much by yourself, Holland. Is this all you want to talk to me about? If it is, please stop, I would like to get down."

"No. I am sorry to have misjudged you, I am glad I was mistaken. I would like to ask you where you are going, but I will not." Edward volunteered no answer. "I want to know how you are fixed."

"Not very well," Edward admitted ruefully, "and I got what I have from the Vicar. I did not want to ask you for anything."

"I thought you might not, and so I brought you what I had in the house in blunt." He handed a roll of notes and some loose silver to the boy. "And your greatcoat and your hat, and a change of shirt, there on the seat. I will instruct both my London and my Edinburgh banks, and of course the York, to honour your requests, my Dublin too if you like."

"You are too kind, Holland. I do not deserve this."

"Who is talking about kindness or deserts? You are my son, you do not need to beg. I would rather you did not. And I do not want you encumbering my estate with any post-obits some Jew-lender might be foolish enough to let you write against it."

"Do you think I would do that? I wouldn't, Holland. I think I would sooner die. I am going to take a place, a position, somewhere. Will you mind?"

"You surprise me all the time, Edward. Will my minding stop you?"

"No."

"Then I shall not waste my energy minding. What on earth will you do?"

"I don't know. I might be a tutor. With your help, though, that you've given me, I may just walk for a while, maybe all Spring and all Summer. I would like to go to Skye, when it is warmer, and through the Lake Country, I would like to go to Cornwall where it is warmer now and to Wales."

"Would you like your horse? I brought it. It is one of the four."

"No, I don't want to have to care for anything. I'd rather just walk."

"What of your clothes, Edward?"

"I hadn't thought."

"When you settle somewhere, if you write me, I will have them sent."

"Thank you, Holland. I will do that then. Where are these horses taking me? Shouldn't you stop now?"

"I am taking you to the Inn, Edward, and you can sleep there, and start your walk tomorrow. Only please do not walk. Take the mail to Bath or Cornwall, where it is warmer, as Knighton says you should, will you, Edward, and rest tonight first? I won't see you again, you will be quite free. You must be tired, Edward."

"I am. I wish you were not so kind tonight, Holland." He was very close to tears.

"The girl's brother said something to disturb you, Edward; what was it?"

"I would rather not tell you." There was a silence.

"Then I can guess." There was another silence. "I do not see why he would say it, but so much is said about me. Shall I call him out?"

"God, no! Holland! I cannot live down the first death."

"I don't know what to say, Edward, except that I am sorry."

"Don't be," Edward said briefly, "I'm not, for anything." They looked at each other in the darkness of the carriage, faintly lit by the lamps, their eyes bright, but a glass wall lay between them, and neither dared try to shatter it, a little for fear of rebuff, and principally from a feeling it was best left intact.

"Do you mind so very much about this girl Anne, Edward?" He felt Edward's spirit stiffen and withdraw. "I said only what I thought. I would not have coerced you now in any way to my will. Did you think I would?"

"Yes, I did, Holland, but you did not stop me, I stopped myself. I think now, though I didn't at the time, that her brother is right. Tell him that for me, if you like. She *is* too young, and I am too. And he is right too, in another way: I do love you, too much, Holland. I am wishing now I were a little boy again, but I'm not, and I must learn to live my own life now."

"I have always wanted you to do that."

"Oh, Holland," Edward cried suddenly, "but if you had not left me so alone, I would have been less tied to you. We only want so desperately as I have wanted you what we do not have. What you finally gave me was not what I wanted."

The Earl held out his hand. "It is too late to mend the past. That is the nature of it. Let us try what we have now. I shall not leave you again. It is you now who will leave me. Come to me when I can help you, Edward, and I will." He looked out, as the carriage slowed. "Here is the Inn."

Edward put his hand in the Earl's where it lay briefly and warmly in his cold nerveless one, and then he climbed quickly down, feeling as though a knife were cutting a part of him from him. He paused at the chaise door. "Goodbye, Holland. Thank you for coming and not letting me go as I was."

"Goodbye, Edward," the Earl said sadly but evenly. "It might have been easier if I had. You see, I am selfish to the end." Edward took the outstretched hand the Earl had handed him his coat with, and bent his head briefly over it and kissed it, and then he released it, and turned and went quickly into the Inn.

PART THREE

The End of the Story, and a Second Beginning

(1810 – 1816)

CHAPTER VII

Absence and Return:
1810–1815

I

IT was the 4 Trees Inn, where he had stayed when he was six with his mother. He had not been in it since, though he had passed it often, and when he entered it again and saw it again much as it had been then, its whitewashed walls and black settles and pewter plates and mugs, where he had eaten his lunch with George, the past swept over him and he thought he would die with grief for it and for his many losses. He managed to mount the stairs, and put himself to bed in a bedroom not unlike the room in which he had read, unaware of anything ahead of him, while his mother had talked to the man who had absorbed his person into his own.

His back hurt him so that he could not sleep, although he was exhausted, and his mind throbbed like the welts on his back, until finally he lost his fear of gossip and paid the landlord to ease it with a homemade remedy. The landlord had seen too many bruised backs in his lifetime to be much surprised or much interested, but he had enough rough practical skill to relieve Edward enough for him to sleep. He wished for laudanum, but he had none, and eventually he fell asleep from pure weariness, and was wakened by the landlord in time only to breakfast at four and to catch the Mail, blowing its yard of tin as it rumbled in. With his father's generosity, which he accepted because of the way it had been offered, and realising that he was losing his health, he did go South, in easy stages, stopping when he was tired, sleeping a great deal, trying to forget all the people he had known.

He spent two weeks in Bath at an unfashionable hotel, consulted a doctor Knighton had recommended, and then, feeling stronger, he did go to Cornwall where he did much walking, and stayed until July. He spent July in Scotland, and in Inverness and Skye, and August in Wales, and then as the Fall came on, he returned to Bath and began looking in the papers for a position as a tutor. After a week, he did find one, and was accepted, and began the third phase of his life which would last five years.

He was, for the time, both self-centered and self-oblivious, and he did not allow his mind to turn back or to think of those he had left. His first unhappiness at the parting had been matched by the Earl's, and in some ways exceeded by it both in depth and in duration. The Earl's self, which ordinarily he gave little quarter or attention to, had been thrown off center by it, and he was abnormally and uncomfortably conscious of having a self in a different manner than his usual unconscious self-interest and instinct for self-preservation, although he did not allow his unbalance or his unhappiness to show publicly at all, or privately in any open way.

He at that time bought Harriett Wilson peremptorily for himself, storming icily into her current situation, cutting short her amusement at his blunt cutting out of her present patron to whom she had returned after a curt uninformative word from Northumberland, taking her at once to his own home, later to his establishment, talking little, finding a strange comfort in sheathing himself where Edward had been. Simultaneously he sought out Amanda, for something of the same reason, whom he took perversely on Sundays. Paying her extravagantly for it, and she therefore shrugging and submitting, he kept her in rooms, not allowing her to leave them, treated her brutally, and cutting her long hair short, used her like a boy. He found a temporary alleviation in such games, but little satisfaction, and he soon gave them up, but not before he had hurt Amanda. He did not know it, and she did not at the time, but she took an infection that beginning slowly, not alarming her, reached septic proportions the doctor she finally sent for could not control. The Earl, summoned, when she had called for him in her fever, put her in the most expert care he could buy, but she was past responding, and soon after he came, past consciousness. He sat beside her, his fingers on her short cropped hair, and caught in her fingers themselves tightly, looking at her face with the skin drawn tightly over the bones, the empty stock he had used without conscience for the real person, and now an empty stock for herself and for everyone, and helpless, watched her die, as if he were watching Edward die; and in the height of his conscience and his concern for her, knew the profound relief that it was not Edward, and that the boy had escaped from him. He had not recovered from this, before he was summoned to a second deathbed, to that of the old Vicar, reluctantly, tired of death and parting.

The old man was feeble but lucid, and he asked about Edward, if he had returned, and if he was well.

"I do not know if he is well," the Earl said, "he has not returned, I do not know where he is, I have not seen him. You will say that is just as well."

"I say nothing," the old man murmured, the Earl bending to catch the words. "In my long life, that is all I have learned—sometimes, finally, to say nothing. I know I do not know what is best for one or for another, or here or there, or when, or by what seeming rule. It is for another than myself to know and to decide. I would say, in my prudence, it is well; but when I remember other things, I wonder that God in his providence should let anything that can be turned to use go to waste." He looked at the Earl with his faint, half-blind eyes, that seemed to see him clearly. "I have never been able to do much of anything with you, Noel, have I?" The Earl shook his head slowly. "I could not with your father, either. I told him he was ruining you, but he would not listen or he did not care."

"Absurd," the Earl said softly and gently, "I take credit for doing that myself. It was not done to me. I ate it like a babe its natural pap" (or a cat its vomit, he thought to himself).

"He would not give you," the Vicar said, as if he had not been interrupted, "what your nature required. He held it back, as if intentionally, when he might as easily and with no effort have supplied it. I watched him do it, and he would not pay attention to me, when I tried to tell him what was happening, what he was doing. It was a way he had found, I sometimes thought, of crucifying your mother, who had otherwise withdrawn beyond his power to hurt, through hurting you and stunting what would have been your natural growth, apart of course from your bone's growth. You forget, Noel," he said, as the Earl might have spoken, "I have known you, when you did not know yourself. But I did have your nurse dismissed. I was a young curate then, and I had not learned to keep my mouth shut, whatever my eyes saw."

"Absurd," the Earl said again, more gently yet. "Am I supposed to ask you what commodity it was, that I required and did not get?"

"I am past being mocked," the old man said, "and past being humoured. I have nothing to tell you now, it has all been said. The sins and the mistakes of the fathers, of omission and commission, shall be visited upon the sons. It is a most unfortunate truth, a most inescapable law, and our tears and our words by themselves will not change it. I only wanted to see you, Noel, for all these years, and say goodbye." A flash of wry humour lit his face. "And I thought you might like to see how a Christian dies."

"That is what I do not want to see," the Earl said soberly, but nevertheless, the next day he did see it, and saw the expression on the old man's face of one who has received good news.

He arranged for a pension to be set up for the Vicar's widow, in addition to what the Church provided, and that she should keep her house, and left. When he returned, he was more difficult than ordinary to live with, for those unfortunate enough to have to or to try to, and even more difficult and impossible to talk to, outside of drawing room inanity. He quarrelled with Harriett, who made the mistake of trying to, and threw her out of the house he had set up for her, which was unlike him, for his partings were heretofore always amicable. It had arisen over nothing, but in the course of it, she had thrown aside her charm and her placidity and blazed out at him like a vixen, he thought, or a fish wife, words out of all proportion to the situation.

"You are not God, Noel, truly you are not, not for all your money, nor all you can do, not that yet."

He could not remember afterwards what he had done or said that had prompted the words, or what the situation had been, or why the words had so angered him—in retrospect they seemed only true. He had struck her, as he never had, and put her out on the street, and shut and locked the door against her, although that last was unnecessary. When he had recovered partly from his anger, he had sent his coachman to find her, and after he had left, to bring her back for her things, to stay until she took another place, but he turned aside all her overtures of peace, as he would also have an apology, noting she did not apologise or retract.

On an impulse, as if seeking some contact with Edward, ironically since Edward himself made no such overtures in that direction or with the past, he spent considerable time and effort tracing down the present location and schedule of the Rev. Davenby. When he had done that, he appeared frequently in his small congregation, listening attentively, quietly dressed, never speaking, entirely anonymous, exposing no marks of his identity, calling himself Mr. Henry. When he discovered that the building in which, growing old, the Rev. Mr. Davenby most often came and stayed longest in, had no organ and no music of any sort, except the voice, he ordered an organ to be made for it, and sent it anonymously. Until it came, he made the offer of supplying accompaniment with his violin, an offer quickly accepted, and after the organ itself appeared, he took the position of organist until one was more permanently found. In these hymns of Charles Wesley he found much to invoke passionate loving Edward's spirit before him, and much that through that medium reached him, the word "dear desire" meaning at first only Edward, but later suggesting, faintly but still making the imprint, another possibility to him that he was not ready for:

> *The same in mind, and heart,*
> *Nor joy, nor grief, nor time, nor place,*
> *Nor life, nor death can part.*
>
> *Thy only love do I require*
> *Nothing in earth beneath desire,*
> *Nothing in heaven above;*
> *Let earth and heaven and all things go;*
> *Give me thy only love to know;*
> *Give me thy only love.*
>
> *Father, in whom we live,*
> *In whom we are and move . . .*
>
> *When shall I find my willing heart*
> *All taken up by thee?*
> *I thirst, I faint, I die to prove . . .*
>
> *God only knows the love of God;*
> *O that it now were shed abroad*
> *In this poor stony heart!*

As a musician he was drawn to one, whose words through the music imprinted themselves on his still unreceptive brain, to be remembered:

> *Where shall my wondering soul begin?*
> *How shall I all to heaven aspire? . . .*
> *That I, a child of wrath and hell,*
> *I should be called a child of God . . .*
> *Sinners alone his grace receive . . .*
> *His open side shall take you in.*
> *He calls you now, invites you home.*

And to that same music:

> *And can it be that I should gain . . .*
> *For me, who him to death pursued? . . .*
> *Long my imprisoned spirit lay,*
> *Fast bound in sin and nature's night . . .*
> *I woke, the dungeon flamed with light;*
> *My chains fell off, my heart was free,*
> *I rose, went forth, and followed thee.*

That Christmas in that small place he played on his violin the music to "Hark! the Herald Angels Sing," and "Love Divine, All Loves Excelling, Joy of Heaven, to Earth Come Down," and "Rejoice, Give Thanks and Sing":

> *Lift up your heart, lift up your voice!*
> *Rejoice, again I say, rejoice!*

And by Isaac Watts, "Joy to the World," that he played set to music by Handel. At Easter, he played Wesley's "Christ the Lord Is Risen Today, Alleluia!" to the music of the Lyra Davidica. He discovered the other hymns of Isaac Watts, among them, "O God, Our Help in Ages Past," with its sad verse:

> *Time, like an ever rolling stream,*
> *Bears all its sons away;*
> *They fly forgotten, as a dream*
> *Dies at the opening day.*

and "Alas! and Did My Saviour Bleed":

> *But drops of grief can ne'er repay*
> *The debt of love I owe;*
> *Here, Lord, I give myself away;*
> *'Tis all that I can do.*

It was a simple answer, he thought, to Wesley's lines:

> *I want a principle within . . .*
> *And let me weep my life away*
> *For having grieved thy love . . .*
> > *remove*
> *The hardness from my heart . . .*
> *And drive me to that grace again,*
> *Which makes the wounded whole.*

He could not imagine doing it, wanting to or being able to, or any such surrender of self being a requirement or a necessity or a personal gain to anything pertaining to himself. Although he felt a necessity for Edward that drove him to sit patiently among associations with Edward, his shadowed face attentive, and although he became conversant in the language of this vein, and by association aware of the emotion, he continued to look upon those sitting around him as creatures of another breed than himself, privileged, perhaps, he admitted, looking at their faces, in ways inaccessible to him, but entirely different and separate. While noting with attention certain verses, he managed without difficulty to shake them off like water drops from his impermeability. Edward would nevertheless have been surprised and amazed, had he seen him there and seen his face, and might hardly have recognised him, had he chanced to walk in. In fact, the Earl, without acknowledging it to himself, had at one time a fleeting hope that Edward might so chance, but Edward, in fact, kept himself entirely away from the Chapels. After some months, the pressures and demands of the world increased upon the Earl. The poignancy of Edward's memory did not fade but the pain grew bearable, he accepted the fact of the boy's departure and returned to his own ways, and Mr. Henry came no more.

These years, 1810–1815, privately crucial for Edward, were crucial publicly for his world, but he was hardly aware of their events, as many people in England were not. His own life went on, absorbing his interest, as it always does, if it is allowed to. Spring of 1810 under the new Perceval Administration, formed after Portland's death in 1809, saw the arrest in his house in Piccadilly of Sir Francis Burdett, a liberal peer urging internal reform, while thousands of troops lined the streets to hold back riot. It saw the early beginnings of a new ferment in Ireland, politically astir again under the leadership of Daniel O'Connell, more temperately and more cautiously now, eschewing violence, in meetings that avoided the government bans and would culminate finally after many setbacks in the Catholic Emancipation Act of 1829, though not then or ever in a repeal of the Act of Union of 1800. Perceval, meanwhile, was continuing Portland's (and the King's) opposition to the Bill for Catholic Emancipation. 1811 saw the Prince of Wales made Regent for "an old, mad, blind, despised, and dying king" who would not yet wholly die for ten years. It saw the beginning of the Luddite riots, in part an effect of Napoleon's Economic Blockade, in the over-productive manufacturing towns, taking place in a country of 11,000,000 souls where 11,000 were franchised; and heard in Parliament Lord Byron's effective but ineffectual speech against death for the breaking of frames. 1812

saw Perceval, a weak minister, not much liked by anyone but deserving
no such fate, assassinated in the House by a man unjustly arrested in
Russia, now bankrupt like Lord Elgin, angry, mad, and abused; and the
beginning of an unwanted war with the United States, ineptly and confusedly wandered into by both parties. It was an unstable time. Since
Pitt resigned in 1801, there had been five administrations: Addington
(Lord Sidmouth); Pitt returned to protect from invasion in 1804, until
his death in 1806; the brief All the Talents administration of Grenville
and Fox and again Sidmouth; the aged Duke of Portland for two years,
and then Perceval. Now, in 1812, Lord Liverpool, whom Sidmouth had
made a peer out of Jenkinson, with Sidmouth as his Home Secretary,
took the reins, and with a ministry at that time exclusively and tightly
Tory would hold them for fifteen years.

While Edward drilled Latin verbs and in his turn inspected nails,
armies drilled and inspected across all Europe. In these years Napoleon,
in 1812, reached Moscow, his alliance with Alexander broken, and the
city burned, entirely, rather than receive him. An unprecedented coalition
was formed between Russia, England, Sweden, Prussia, and Austria
against their common enemy. October of 1813 saw the Battle of Leipzig,
called the Battle of Nations, prove Napoleon vulnerable; and in England 1813 saw, though few eyes did, the publication of the revolutionary
poem *Queen Mab* in a private edition of two hundred and fifty copies,
of which seventy sold. March of 1814 saw the Allies march through to
Paris, victoriously. April and May of 1814 saw the abdication of Napoleon, the First Treaty of Paris, the reinstalling of the Bourbons with Louis
XVIII, the Continent reopened, and Napoleon's exile to his now mi-
nuscule sovereignty of Elba Island off the coast of Italy.

September, 1814, the Congress of Vienna began, with its congregation
of Kings and Emperors, not one yet fifty years of age: Alexander I of
Russia, thirty-seven; Frederick William III of Prussia, forty; Emperor
Francis II (Francis I of Austria), forty-six, their host, nephew of Marie
Antoinette once Queen of France, and father of Marie Louise, recently
Empress of France; the city crowded with its elaborate balls and en-
tertainments and its stalemated diplomacy. Castlereagh, of Irish infamy
(a bill for severer enforcement of Irish laws then in the House at home),
was there, in quiet plain dignity, attending for England, and for a time
the now Duke of Wellington also, born in the same year, both forty-four.
Tyne was there, although Edward did not know it, an unofficial am-
bassador and liaison, under his own name now in that city, having known
the shifting worldly Talleyrand, sixty, three years his senior but his par-

ticular contemporary and also lame, and the presiding conservative genius of the Congress, Metternich, fifteen years the younger. January, 1815, saw the Triple Alliance of England, Austria, and the restored Royal France against the political strength of Russia and Prussia combined.

While the politicians mànoeuvred, Napoleon manoeuvred. March, 1815, saw him land at Cannes, shocking the Congress into action and adjournment in June. As he marched inland he gathered force, including the forces of Marshal Ney who had promised Louis to bring Napoleon to Paris in a cage and instead defected to his old commander. June saw Ney's defeat at Quatre Bras by Wellington, and saw Wellington's retreat to Brussels south of the small town Waterloo when Napoleon marched to reinforce and join with Ney. On June 22, Napoleon, like Castlereagh and Wellington also forty-four, defeated at Waterloo, signed his second abdication, ending the Hundred Days, having surrendered for English asylum to the British warship *The Bellerophon,* to be shipped off instead to the fifty miles of Saint Helena safely and remotely in the mid-Atlantic. Summer saw the army returned and on the country. The immediate years under Lord Liverpool and Castlereagh continued in England the repressive Conservative policies of the War years into the Post-War years, stringent against signs of unrest or reform or any hint of home revolution.

These events, although they happened, affected Edward in no way at all. The details of this period do not concern this particular story, except in their existence and his ability to ignore them, nor in fact does this time as Edward spent it. In it, Edward regained his inner balance and his continence. To some degree he sorted his memories and came to terms with them, and to some degree he achieved tranquillity. He made no attachments that were meaningful to him, and with the people about him he kept an essential detachment and reserve. He used only his first two names, Edward Clare, and was known in the households he stayed in as Mr. Clare. He was paid decently, being a man, although not well. He dressed simply, but his training under the Earl not leaving him, with the indefinable air of taste and breeding that such training gives. His reputation, both for his personal charm, his morality, his social effacement, and his solid accomplishment, spread privately among families with young boys at home or particularly with young men who had been rusticated or were attempting to compress four years' reading into a single term. He preferred the latter situations, as being more within his experience, and shorter. At first he had answered advertisements and put up with hard work and social slights without minding, but after the first year, he was sought after, rather than seeking, and his situation eased. His connection with Tyne was not known. As a tutor he was not looked at, even had there been anyone who might have recognised him from his former life.

He did not like to stay anywhere long, for he wanted no involvements of any kind. The daughters of the house might languish, but to their mothers' satisfaction, he ignored their existence, beyond politeness. In this time, he saw the Earl once, some three years after he had left, who had come to dinner in the country at the Duchess of Melton's. He was going up the stairs to the schoolroom when he saw the Earl in the hall. The years fell away from him and he stood, helpless, as the Earl came to him, and took his hand.

"Holland!" he said, holding it warmly in his as if he would never let it go.

"Are you well, Edward?" the Earl said, his eyes fixed on Edward's face, his voice charged with emotion at the unexpected meeting.

"I am very well," Edward said.

"I miss you, Edward," the Earl said simply. "I wish you would come home. I had thought, if I should ever see you, to ask you if perhaps we might try again, in a different manner."

"I cannot, Holland," he said, dropping the Earl's hand. "I cannot. Not yet."

"Will I see you again tonight? Will you be at dinner?" Edward shook his head. "Will you meet me after dinner?"

"No, Holland," he said, and turning quickly, went up the stairs, his eyes blinded with tears, his composure wholly shaken.

He heard the Earl's voice call him, and he stopped, and turned.

"Will you at least let me know where you are, where you go after you leave here, in case I should need you suddenly? You can write Wotton, if you like, and I will not ask him myself. Will you do that?"

"Yes, Holland. Yes, I will," he answered, his voice breaking. He started to come toward the Earl, and then, resolutely, he continued up the stairs not looking back. The Earl stayed through dinner, and left immediately after.

He saw Harriett Wilson once, sitting in an open carriage, escorted. Their eyes met, and held, and her lips moved and said his name silently, in surprise and pleasure and concern. He turned his head away, towards his little boys, and walked on, and when he looked back, he did not see her.

He saw Anne once also; it was on a crowded street in London, when he was taking two little boys of ten and twelve in to Waite's to have two teeth pulled. She was driving herself a perch-phaeton, dressed in fashion, with only her tiger with her on the box, when she saw him and pulled over and called to him.

"Edward! Edward Clare." She gave her reins to the tiger to hold and climbed nimbly down, to hold out her hand. "Is it really you?"

"Yes," he said, looking at her, a little reserved, but with his warm smile breaking the reserve. "Yes, it is I. How good it is to see you, and how well you look."

"You look well, too, Edward," she said, and then a silence fell upon them, while she waited for him to speak but he did not.

She smiled again, hesitantly, looking at the little boys, and he said with a smile, "I am a bear-leader now, as you see."

"Yes, I see." She could not find anything to say to that.

"One day you will need one for your children, too—"

"For my children?" she asked, surprised.

"You are surely married, Anne? In all these years?"

She looked a little as if he had struck her, and then she said, "No. No, I have not married. It has not been so very long. I thought I loved someone once, but he did not want me, after all. But no one else has suited me." She turned away from him quickly, and not looking back or answering him when he cried her name, and taking the reins, snapped the horses off.

He had already begun to realise that he was running away from himself and his proper life, when Wotton wrote in July of 1815 to tell him that the Earl was very ill and that he should come to London at once. He was not far from London. He closed his accounts with the family where he was staying, and left within the hour, arriving in London by post-chaise that evening. He took a hackney to the Earl's house, and entered his room. The Earl opened his sick eyes and saw him and recognised him at once.

"Well, little Methody," the Earl said weakly, but with a trace of a smile. "What brings you? Have you come to gloat?" He was propped up on pillows in his big bed, where Edward had been many times, and he looked very white and only a shadow of himself. Edward walked quickly to him, ignoring his greeting, and took his hand in his.

"Holland," he said gently, "they told me you were sick. I came as quickly as I could. Don't die of this, please, Holland. I could not bear it if you did."

"Nor could I," said the Earl, with a faint gleam. "Don't disturb yourself, Edward. I have every intention of making myself well and living to be sufficiently old to annoy you much longer with my reminiscences. You shall bring my grandchildren to see me as I sit in my garden with my cane, or potter on my horse in the park, and point me out, and say, 'There goes the Viscount Rockfort, Earl of Tyne, who is a very wicked old man, who in the days when it was a fashion to be wicked, was even more so than most, but he is your grandfather, and you must love him all the same! But you must be a little quicker about it, Edward, or with all my help, they will miss me. But not this time."

"Hush now, Holland," Edward said, bending down to kiss his lips, "you will tire yourself and the doctor will send me away." He sat down in a chair pulled by the head of the Earl's bed, still holding his hand, and looked at him with immense tenderness. "I am working on it, but it all takes a little time."

"Are you staying long?" the Earl asked, his voice only a whisper.

"I am not going at all. I am here to stay, if you want me, as long as you want me."

"And your wife?"

"I have none—not yet," he said.

"Is it the young lady who wanted to shoot me?" the Earl asked, with a faint return of his old look. "That should make life amusing."

"Perhaps—I have not asked her. I doubt she wants to shoot you now."

"Well, be quick about it. I want them to remember me, and that will be at least four years away. Do not let it take too much time. I am going to sleep now, Edward, now that I have seen you. You won't go away?"

"No, Holland. I promise. I have come home."

"'*Il dit me, il tien me,*'" the Earl said wearily, but his face very peaceful.

He stayed beside the Earl all night, dozing sometimes in his chair, his hand where the Earl could reach it. His heart reproached him for having wasted so much time on his own problems and his own emotions, which now seemed small and of very little importance: even as when he was a child, he had thought the moor immense, and all there was, and then as he grew older he had seen it as part of a landscape, surrounded by other things, and in its proportion, in relation to things distant or unseen, for what it was.

For the next two weeks he stayed almost entirely in the Earl's room with him, leaving only for brief walks and exercise. Remembering the weakn s it had caused him, he insisted the letting of blood be stopped, and won a look of gratitude from the Earl, who had been too ill to prevent it. Edward during a stay in London had met the brilliant and original young Scottish doctor, Michael Hall, who happened to be a Wesleyan, and happened then to be doing residency in a London hospital and to be called into the house where he then was. He had already published his studies on galvanic action in frogs, and would later publish his controversial discovery of the concept of reflex action, found in a salamander he was dissecting. Edward knew him to be strongly opposed to the practise of bloodletting, used then so widely not only on men but on horses and hounds even for virtually any disorder, and with the Earl's permission, enquired out his whereabouts and asked him to come into attendance. Knighton, made a baronet a few years preceding, had become the Regent's personal physician and was to become much involved in affairs of state. Honest, sober, intelligent, tactful, loyal to his trust above his own interests and in the end his health, his career as a physician was near a close, as he became the Keeper of the Purse, a very entangled purse, for the Regent. The Earl missed him greatly, but secure in these new young hands, he relaxed and began to recover.

As the Earl grew better, sometimes at night Edward stretched out quietly beside the Earl and slept, too, as if his own young body and its strength by its nearness and contact could lend strength to the Earl, as perhaps it did, for the Earl grew stronger daily.

"The beginning," he thought, lying there so, listening to the breathing of the older man beside him, remembering Aristotle, "points halfway to the end. 'The Beginning is not merely half of the whole but reaches out toward the End.' I am a part of this man, as he is not of me; I do not understand it entirely, but I understand it in part. It is much stronger than I am, and I am never entirely going to be able to free myself, and I am never going entirely to want to, and I am not going to try to again. In his will is my peace, and I do not need to resist him to be myself. I wonder I should not have known that long ago. We are all too old now to continue to play around with our lives, and wasting them fighting what is better accepted."

His father had said to him once that to be naked was to be a man, but he thought Holland was mistaken, or had seen only a part, for people required covering to live. The word *passion* itself, so integral a part of a man, meant also suffering, and to him, to be a man was to suffer: to permit, to stretch out, to bear, to endure. It was not a new idea, it had been known long ago: Love suffereth long, is kind. Beareth all things, endureth all things. Gods did not suffer, unless they became men. Animals suffered pain, but rarely if ever consciously and with their wills for love. For him, it was the crux, like the cross, of the whole matter; and not only to suffer, but to suffer willingly, and even with joy, where one could. And yet it was not what one would choose for oneself. One would escape it if one could, and still retain what one had to have. He had tried, and then he had returned. One would rather be joyous easily and naturally. He would, and he knew that, but he was not free for it. He had been bound long ago beyond his ability to break. But his yoke is easy, he thought, smiling wryly at himself at his inclination still to blaspheme when he thought about his father. If his return cost him any pain, he did not mean his father to know it.

II

The world, however, was not through with Edward or with his education in her ways. When the Earl had recovered enough to leave his bed, and was convalescent in his gardens and in his sunny downstairs rooms, for it was August now, he told Edward that he had made him his heir, in fact, that he had done so five years before.

"That was kind," Edward said, not knowing what to say.

"No. You forget. I am not kind. I wished to. I would still like to adopt you, Edward," he said, "formally and legally, I would like to give you my name now and have you wear it."

"I would like that above all things too," Edward said.

"I have had much of the preliminary legal work accomplished," the Earl said, his eyes glinting, "I have been waiting only your return and your consent."

"How like you, Holland," Edward murmured, laughing just a little.

Within the next weeks Edward became of record Edward Clare Armstrong Holland, V Viscount Rockfort. The persons Edward Armstrong and Edward Clare were designated to become shadows of the past. A part of the estate was to be made over to him directly, so that he would have an adequate and independent income, and one of the smaller properties immediately and directly deeded to his name. But before this change was entirely accomplished, his world was entirely shaken in a way he had never dreamed it could be. He had been living quietly at home, as a son of the house, receiving callers for the Earl, speaking openly of his father, accepting no invitations and wanting none. The Earl had not wholly recovered his strength, and only this, and the event that followed, prevented them from returning to their older relationship.

They both knew separately that it was impossible for them, despite all promises, all resolvings, all conscience, and all good intentions, to live very long together chastely. Edward had accepted this fact when he came back, but he intended it to be a small part of his life. The Earl had recognised the impossibility also.

"Tell me, Edward," he had said, "would you like to set up an establishment of your own? Would you like your own house in town? You are twenty-six? It is quite customary."

"No," said Edward, "I would like to live with you." He had lifted his eyes to the Earl's, they met, questioningly, and his own had consented.

"And what of Anne?"

"I have not seen her. She knows what I have been. She was told. A great many people seem to know. She will never believe I am not still, I think, and I might as well be what I am thought to be."

"And is this what your five years taught you?"

"They have taught me that I do not care. And that I do not want any woman any more, not even Harriett, except Anne. But I want to be with you, Holland, because I love you, and if you also want me in your bed, I do not care."

"What of your conscience?"

"I am in better health now, in quite good health. Conscience, I think, is in part related to health."

"Myself, I think with you it is the other way around. I am afraid to disturb the balance I see working now so well together."

"As you wish, Holland. To me it does not matter. It is not an important part of me. I made too much over it."

The Earl laughed softly, in genuine amusement at Edward's unflattering approach, and so the matter stood. They were old lovers now, of old standing now, and in no hurry, both content for the time merely to be together. But had the nearness continued undisturbed, neither doubted the outcome and Edward showed no fear of it. It was no longer a matter of emotion, for with the relaxing of tension between them, the intensity had gone. Accepting and accepted, in all their relationships, there remained only the desire to please. For Edward, this meant willingness, for the Earl, at this time, restraint. During his absence, grace had returned to Edward, and looking at the young man, on whom it sat so easily, without his knowledge, the Earl could not imagine disturbing it. It had provoked him in Edward the child, and tantalized in Edward the adolescent, and by his own lack of it it had drawn him, to a degree even consciously, to destroy it. His success in its destruction, climaxed in Edward's brief total acquiescence and commitment and loss of will in his twentieth year, had managed to appall him. Therefore, although he took quiet pleasure in the easy infrequent touch of Edward's hands, the moments when he lay beside him, the occasional light caress, and the infrequent brief sweetness of his lips bent on his own, he did not respond or make any move to touch Edward himself, or to possess what he knew he might. The slight air of spiritual aloofness and the withdrawal had returned to Edward that had in other days characterised him, made more distinct by the contrasting familiar ease and pliancy of his physical person. Because of it, the Earl could not now have touched him, and he did not wish to, although knowing himself, he did not expect his unusual reticence and restraint to last. He felt rather as he had as a young child, summoning back early forgotten natural memories of Tyne, when he lay half-hidden in the grass beside the tarn, and a butterfly lit upon his hair, or when sitting with his unused gun, on the rocky hill, a doe came up to his hand, unafraid, and lay beside him. He could have destroyed either, he had chosen not to; he did not choose to now. The weakness of his late illness helped him in that; like Wesley, he had been bled and purged, and his spirits were less, and his spirit more. And for all Edward's present seeming sureness, he had seen his sureness and his spirit destroyed; he had no faith in its permanent strength; he did not wish to be the instrument of his destruction again.

Of his five years away, what he had done, and more particularly what he had thought and felt, Edward was particularly reticent to speak. The loosening of his bound spirit had occurred gradually, the change at first imperceptible, like the increase of water in mountain streams above the high timber line, out of sight, when the ice first begins to thaw beneath the surface.

"I tried to enjoy myself," he said simply. "I have always tried to do that. At first it was hard, and I thought for once I could not, but in time it became easier and I could. My mind had run in certain grooves for so long it had worn channels like water in stone; I had to redirect it, and bank it out of the old grooves until it formed new ones, but for a time it did flood me entirely over, and I thought the force would drown me. Then I learned to ride that force, and float with it, as I did once when I was younger, and then forgot again how. That is all. Don't let's talk about me, Holland, I am not really very interesting. Let's talk of something else."

"I find you interesting," the Earl said.

"It is a delusion merely," Edward said, "I am really not interesting at all."

The Earl stared at him intently—and then forced his stare away. He had once wished Edward to talk less; now he wished him to talk more, but he found Edward unwilling only in that.

He also noticed in Edward a new characteristic, or an old one more marked now, that he asked no questions about any of the people he had known. That part of his nature, or his memory, seemed yet to be frozen, or held in a distant reserve. He did not ask where George was or if he might have him, he did not enquire after the Vicar, and when told of his death, he showed no surprise. He sighed deeply, and expressed briefly a proper sentiment, and went off by himself for a while. When the Earl suggested diffidently that he might call George down from the North, where he was married now, and assistant to the Steward, Edward did shake his head and suggested he wait. This reticence spared the Earl the embarrassment of mentioning his quarrel with Harriett, which had remained unreconciled—unable to help himself, he had cut her on the street, the few times he had met her, his face frozen and blank; or mentioning Amanda's death. Nevertheless, the Earl found it unnatural, particularly in its degree. He marked it, and he wondered about it privately, not recognising a part of himself in it.

Edward expressed himself only once at any length or depth, the first Sunday his father was able to attend Church, after the Anglican service, and a bland placid Watchmaker sermon which had irritated him. The Earl noticed he was unusually quiet, and intent, as they drove home, and he asked why.

"I was thinking," Edward said briefly.

"I know that," the Earl said. "I wondered about what."

Edward flashed him a quick smile. "Nothing much."

"A profoundly interesting nothing and a considerable much to produce such a face."

"I have gotten rather in the way of keeping my thoughts to myself," Edward said apologetically, "finally. No one was interested in them, unless they had some point or application."

"I am. Tell me."

"If you like then. I was thinking that I could have preached a better sermon than that."

"If you were ordained," the Earl commented, privately dismayed.

"Don't be," Edward said, noting his expression and his inner thought.

"I have no wish for ordination, I haven't had, I have forgotten now when I did. I was just thinking that with that time to speak and we there listening, he made so little use of it."

"Nevertheless, it sounds remarkably ministerial to me, that remark," the Earl said.

"That was only a part of what I was thinking," Edward said. Under the Earl's attentive face, after a moment, he continued.

"I have been thinking," he said, "about who I am, and what it means." He spoke rather fast, his eyes turned away. "Jesus, you know, Holland, was a bastard too; in the eyes of the world, it did come down to that, and I daresay the world was no kinder about it. I mean, he was, if Joseph was not his father, and his mother did not think so, and Jesus did not either. Perhaps it was when he found out about it, whenever it was, whether his mother told him, or one of his fathers, or he just found out for himself, that he decided to act as he did, to do his father's will. He was not god himself, you know, Holland, that is a ridiculous controversy to me, but he had his father in him, who was God himself, and he was like his father. And his father did recognise him too, publicly. I sometimes wonder if these pious churchmen, properly conceived in righteous sheets, know what that really means, how upsetting it is, and what an awful, compelling power there is in it, to know one's real father, who he really is, and what he really is, to be at one with him, and to do what he wants and as he expects, to do his will, and at the same time the human will wanting to be separate and free and itself, but unable to because of this intangible, unrecognised, all-existing bond. Then he recognises and is himself recognised, and he wants only to do that will, to fulfil that nature, and finally there is no conflict or question, for that will and that nature is both outside himself and in himself."

"I don't know what to say to this, Edward," the Earl said.

"It is just an analogy, Holland, and perhaps not in good taste. I am the son of Lord Tyne, that is all, though it is a great deal to me, and that is whose nature is in *me*, with my mother's. What I mean is, of course I don't after all want to be a minister, I have no reason to want to be, any more, as I have told you. I am not like a younger son, or an orphan, or a thrown-off child, I don't have to cast my eye about to find some thing to do, that is the very thing I need not do: I am your very heir, and what that means and what it needs and does itself require of me is clear. I am not a minister's son, I never really was, it is just a skill, like carpentering, I picked up as I passed through that house. I want to do what you want and expect now, of your acknowledged son. That is all.

I do not see, now, why I cannot *do* that, and still *be* myself, as that is."

For a few minutes the Earl could not speak. He took Edward's hand in his and held it tightly. "I count myself fortunate above all my friends," the Earl said simply, when he did speak. "I hope what you say may be so."

The day, however, did come that the Earl had foreseen, when he looked at the young man sitting beside him, and saw only his particular flesh and the boy still in him, and their conversation flagged—they had been speaking of his agent's last report, brought in the morning post, for in these weeks the Earl had been opening to Edward the articles of his estate and its operations, having Wotton instruct him in its limits, and its extents, and from there moving to the latest iniquitous folly of the Regent. The darkened look to the Earl's eyes and the heaviness to his features, as of a weight flattening them, appeared that Edward had long ago recognised.

He looked at the Earl and gave him his hand. "Shall I go to your room, Holland?"

"Yes, Edward," the Earl said heavily. He followed, despite himself, some minutes later, delayed by the footman with a message, and found Edward already lying in his bed, only the sheet covering him, resting his face on his arms, his eyes closed.

"Do you want me, Edward?" the Earl asked in a whisper, sitting on the bed beside him, suddenly wanting and needing reassurance. He could not see Edward's face.

"I am here," the boy's voice said remotely. "That is all you can ask. I am not going to help you, but I am here, if you want me, and I love you." He spread his legs a little apart, beneath the sheet, and lay quietly, breathing easily, as the Earl put his hand beneath the sheet and passed it lightly over his too-loved flesh, cool as the ice of those streams.

He seemed not so much to be lying still as alit, the Earl thought; his weight, sparse and distributed, seemed hardly to press the bed, less than the Earl's hand did his flesh; and the Earl was seized as before by a compulsion to hold and tear open into his elusiveness, to search it out, until he could compel him to show himself, his real self, entirely, or at the least to hold him like Proteus tightly. He had never understood the essential singleness of Edward's nature, and he did not yet; such simplicity, underneath the complications of his mind and his imagination, lay beyond the Earl's conceiving. But it roused him, as always, to that violence of action which in effect sent Edward only further and more elusively yet away from him, despite his wish to be with him.

He drew the sheet back from Edward's shoulders, and he saw then for the first time the tracery, still visible, of the four long stripes the horsewhip had cut, and the fifth lighter mark.

"Who did that to you, Edward?" he asked, shocked, his mood changed to anger and otherwise forgotten. "Who dared?"

"Besides yourself?" murmured Edward's distant muffled voice. "I had forgotten they were there. It was a long time ago. I have forgotten."

"I never used a horsewhip or had one used. Be just." He sat in silence, brooding, but Edward said nothing. "I shall find out who did this and I shall kill him, or them."

"Do not be absurd, Holland," Edward's distant voice came. "The wounds are healed, the scars are hardly there. Why reopen them? I bear no malice for it now myself. I am sorry you had to see, but you would of course, if I undressed. Do you want me or do you not?"

"I do not, Edward," the Earl said heavily. "Not any more, I am greatly distressed."

"Oh, Holland, do not be." He turned over, hiding his back. "It was all so long ago. So much went wrong then, this was only a little part." He held out his arms, and the Earl bent down, clothed, and let the arms clasp him briefly. Then he kissed Edward, and disengaged them.

"I had forgotten," he said, "these marks put it quite from my mind. I came to tell you that a message has come for you. It is downstairs with John. It seems of some urgency. If you wish still to humour me, I will see you this evening." He left the room, to let the boy dress in private.

When Edward came down, he found John had a note for him, the seal unbroken. He slit it, and unfolded the plain piece of good white paper, from which the heading had been cut, and read the simple note:

For Edward Armstrong:

> I must see you at once alone, on a matter of urgency and secrecy. You will find me at a writing desk at Brookes'. You will know me, I think, and I will know you. On no account to bring anyone with you. Please come.

The letter was not signed, but it was written in an educated hand, and Edward could not imagine what harm could come to him in the public writing room at Brookes', or why he should not go.

"Who brought this, John?" he asked. "Is he still here?"

"No, Master Edward; it was a footman, in a good livery, who said you must have it right away, no matter where you were, but he did not stay."

"Tell the Earl," he said, taking the letter with him, "that I have stepped out, and that I should be back shortly, but not to worry if I am some hours delayed."

He took his hat, and his cane, as a precaution as well as a fashion, and walked to Brookes'. There were two men in the writing room, but one of the two rose as he entered, and passed closely to him, looking directly at him, and left the room. After a moment's surprise, Edward followed him. He had recognised him at once, despite the lapse of years, and seeing him only distantly since, as one of the two young men who had come to his room in Oxford and precipitated him into that adventure. He could have spoken to him several times on occasion five years before, but neither had chosen to.

"Did you write this note to me?" Edward asked, coming up to him in the street, and handing it to him.

"Yes, I did," the other answered, pocketing it. He seemed extremely nervous. "Have you spoken of this to anyone at all?" Edward shook his head. "Look, I don't want to be seen with you. I am staying at Miller's while I am up in town, will you meet me there? I will give you one of the keys to my room." His eyes were haunted and cast about furtively, despite the civility of his appearance and his impeccable clothes, hat, coat, waistcoat, trousers, all of a tone.

"Why should I come?" Edward asked, curiously. "You are acting very strangely. I remember you but I don't even know your name. Are you trying to kidnap me?"

"God, no!" the other said, looking at Edward directly. "Please come. It is about Marion. I could not think of anyone to ask but you."

"I will come," Edward said quietly, startled, but asking no more questions, except one necessary one. "Where is this Miller's?"

"On Westminster, of course. Don't take a hackney, and don't look to follow me." He bowed and swung off, his almost ridiculously elegant figure swinging down the pavement. Edward forced himself not to stare, and after a moment, he made his way by a different route to Miller's. He arrived first, and let himself in to the room indicated on the key, found it empty, and took a chair by a table. He took out his pistol, from his coat pocket, and laid it on the table before him, as clear evidence of his doubts. His *assigné* appeared a few minutes later.

"God!" he said. "Put that up, Armstrong. I'm not going to play tricks on you. You can do as I propose, or you cannot. When once I tell you, it is up to you. I can't urge it. Myself I haven't the courage. You will be in a terrible fix if you are caught, and you are likely to be. That's why the *hush*—I don't want myself to be connected with you. I am a fearful coward." He laughed nervously, and Edward wondered if he had gone mad.

"You said you wanted to tell me something about Marion: what is it?"

"I don't know how to begin to tell you."

"Just tell me, that's all. Where is Marion? Is he here in London?"

"Yes," the elegant young dandy said nervously, "yes, in a way. My name is Neville, Hugh Neville, Lord Hugh, but it don't signify. Call me Hugh, call me Neville, call me anything. What do you know about Allister since he left Oxford," he asked abruptly. "Anything? Anything much?"

"No," Edward said, trying to hold his patience. "I know his father put him in the Royal Navy and I know he didn't want to go, that's all. He never wrote to me. No one would tell me anything else, they would not even tell Lord Tyne. Now you tell me he is in London. Where is he? Can he be seen? Neville, what is it you know? Are you going to tell me? Do you really know anything?" He could have shaken the dilatory young effete lounging before him, with his knowledge he could not get from him.

"Well, I know something more than that, as it happens, quite a bit more." He took out an enamelled cloisonné snuffbox and extricated a pinch and inhaled it in each nostril, and blew it out, and Edward saw his hands were shaking like birch leaves, though his face was a polite white mask, its expression always faintly surprised, faintly amused, the flesh ridged and folded about the eyes and mouth. "I make it my business to know things. I like to, and I know where to go, down on the wharves and in the taverns there, among the low characters there. I find it dangerous and exciting. I like low people, and I can find out things, because I'm thought an amusing fool, but I am not really. Don't think it. I will survive. I know things no one else knows in this town, or very few. I know, for example, or I am fairly sure I do, how Marion left the Royal Navy."

Edward was startled. "I didn't know he had. Did his father help him out?"

"No, my dear. I think he simply took a ship and left with it."

"Like that?"

"Like that."

"How like him," Edward said whitely, hardly knowing whether to laugh or cry. "Is that not mutiny? He said he never would."

"Are you listening to me or telling me?"

"Go on, I am listening. Tell me. Just please tell me."

"Well, I am trying to, I thought." He treated himself to another application from his snuffbox. "The ship Marion sailed on disappeared, with its captain and its officers and its crew. It was listed as a casualty to the French, in some places, as a mystery in others. It may have been shot down and sunk by a Frenchy (as the Navy said), but myself, I think Marion took it. I have heard stories of the late Captain and certain of his officers down on the wharves, and certain deaths on board that ship. The types there like a tough captain, but this one they did not. Had I been Admiral Alleyn I would never have signed anybody to it, certainly no one I liked or no one of my kin, but he may have thought his son wanted toughening the hard way. Some fathers do. Mine would, except I have more money than he has, and he can't."

"Neville, I cannot bear this talk. Are you trying to tell me in your way that Marion has been involved in a mutiny in the Royal Navy during wartime? If you are, please say it directly. I know what it will mean, and I think I am going to faint." The shadows were looming in the sunlit room, which grew dark around him.

"Oh, for God's sake, I didn't know I'd caught a baby. Lie down, I'll find you some spirits. I thought you had more nerve." He handed Edward a glass of brandy. "I am not trying to tell you he has been involved in a mutiny, I am suggesting that he instigated one, and by his lights executed the Captain and the officers and went off with the ship and the crew, but I can't prove it and I don't want to. It is just my little idea. I think he might have. I thought I'd tell you."

"But you are speaking of murder, Neville," Edward said in horror, "and there is no going back from that."

"There are murders and there are murders, some official, some not, some sanctioned, some not, some condoned, some not. In my way I am a small authority on the subject. It is because of my interest in the field that I know where Marion is now, so I suppose it serves some purpose, after all. But you are right in what you say, there is no going back."

"Where is he, Neville?" Edward asked desperately breaking in. "You are telling me he is in trouble. And you want me to do something. I understand you. What kind? What can I do? Can I see him?"

"That depends on you. I hope you do. Do you read the papers, Armstrong?"

"Not much. I have been rather cut off," Edward answered impatiently.

"Well, it don't matter either way, I just wondered. But you will have to be less squeamish than this, Armstrong." He looked suddenly at Edward with his small sharp eyes, five years older than Edward in age, a hundred in expression. "Marion has always been in trouble ever since I have known him, one way or another, but he is in more trouble this time than you can imagine, or I could have. It is the worst of trouble, Armstrong. He is going to die sometime tonight, and it will not be pretty when he does. And there is nothing you nor I nor anyone can do to stop it from happening."

The room again swam before Edward's eyes, and his stomach felt weak and ill. Whatever he had begun to expect, he had expected nothing like this.

"You look sick," Neville said. "I am sick too. I have lost my stomach for our age, but I expect I will regain it. Have another glass of brandy. There is nothing to do yet, the sun is still too high. I called you early, I didn't know when I would find you. And I'm glad to have company. I liked Marion, you know; I really did. I have had an awful shock. Shall I tell you about it?"

"I have been asking you to, and you tell me everything else. Where is he? Is he in prison?"

"No."

"Then why must he die? Is he ill?" Edward asked wildly.

"Be patient," Neville said, pushing him back. "I will tell you that in a little. I am going to tell you a little history first about me and my day. Nothing is happening now, there is time. Don't look at me with your little balled fists as if you wanted to hit me. Without me there is nothing for you to know, and I must tell you in my own way."

"Tell me then," Edward said, his throat stiff and tight with apprehension, fighting down the nausea of helpless fear and the panic gnawing at him and blowing up inside him, "but first tell me just this. Where is Admiral Alleyn? Is he with Marion? Does he know?"

"Too many questions. He may know. I don't know. If he knows, he is not doing anything. Be quiet now a minute. Do you read the more lurid parts of the morning sheets? The assizes, that kind of things. No, I think I've asked you that already, and you say you don't."

"Sometimes," Edward said. "I have been out of town, and since I've been back my father has been ill."

"Your father? I thought Armstrong was dead."

"My father is Lord Tyne."

"Oh, my God," Neville said, whistling out his breath. "I didn't know. Lord! Here's a new angle. I thought you were superfluous, I thought you were expendable. Begging your pardon, but I really did. He will shoot me for involving you in this."

"You have now. You will have to go on or *I* will shoot you. I do have a gun, you know. Do you? I saw nothing about Alleyn in the paper."

"Hush, child, don't threaten me. There would not be. He has not been using his name. I want to tell you, I think you will not be afraid to help, that's why I called you, but if Tyne ever finds out about it, or asks you, ever, please do tell him I did it under duress then. Now be quiet and let me tell you, I really will now, for the time is going now." His unnaturally white face flushed faintly. "I am not a nice person, Edward. I am related to Selwyn, perhaps you know"—Edward shook his head—"rather distantly, but I seem to have somewhere one of his tastes. I come up for the assizes, and I go to most of the things that happen afterwards. I haven't much to do, and I—I enjoy it, or I did."

"Please go on," Edward said, his eyes intent.

"I am going on. Otherwise, you see, except for this deplorably awkward taste of mine, I would not have known, for as I said, he appeared under another name. I had a terrible shock, when I saw him, standing there with the others. I recognised him almost at once, though he is much changed. We played at too many disguises together when we were children, one gets to know."

"Yes. I know. Please. Where was this?"

"I am telling you if you will just let me. He was being tried for piracy done at sea with the other fifteen, under the law of the mercantile marine." Edward's face lost its last vestige of colour, but its expression was incredulous, unbelieving. "I can see him, you know, I really can, being a rather bonny Irish pirate, can't you, strictly by the old romantic honour codes, one for all and all for one and all that, can't you? His black hair, and his blue eyes flashing under those brows, waving his cutlass, and sparing the ladies, or whatever they spare on their little forays. Privateering on the French ships, and the American, and unfortunately on ours too? Making little huts on the Pacific isles and marrying one of those lovely Tahitian girls who Cook says believes in love, sunning on the white sands—he has finally browned, bronzed I should say—and swimming in the blue sea off some atoll. While it lasts, that is. There is not much left of the idyll, I suppose, after a long voyage back to England to be made an exhibit of, chained for months in a stinking hole, everybody beginning to look alike. Didn't you follow the story of the *Bonnyventure?* The merchant marine the pirates took in a disguised ship, oh, it has been five years ago. They kept the crew, but they sent the Captain and the officers off in a little boat, which was a foolish thing to do, for they were picked up on an island and made it to New South Wales one way and another and back here, and they have identified their own sailors. Had I been the pirates, I should have drowned them first myself. It's been a big thing in the papers, you see. This was a famous group. They were known to be somewhere in the Pacific. The Navy has been looking for them. A Royal Society expedition after some meridian comet saw them and recognized them, and the Navy took them. The ship is in the Harbour now, at Greenwich Reach, you can go on it if you pay, take the wee wifie and the little ones to have a real look. You should go."

"Damn you, Neville, tell me about Marion. That's all I want to hear. What happened? Did you get him pardoned? What did you do?"

"What could I do? I was in a horrible state of shock. I was sitting up close, you see, and I stood up like a Jack-in-the-Box all at once, to see if I could find some friends and do anything for a pardon or what-have-you, and he saw me, and saw what I meant to do, and tried to raise his hand but he could not, being double-ironed, and so he just shook his head slightly, and I knew then he would rather die any death than have his own name known. I sympathised with him on that. It was a demned embarrassin' spot to be in, that way, or even to see."

Edward made agonized fists of his hands, but he only said, "So what did you do?"

"I sat back down." (Oh, God," said Edward softly.) "After all, that was what I had come for," Neville said defensively, "it was just a different cast than I had thought. And the more I thought about it, piecing together little bits and hints I had heard over the years, the more clearly I saw that even with his own name it could lead only one way. There was no hope for any pardon, and he knew that when he shook his head. It could only have been a different place of death, a different court, and no honour anywhere, since whatever happened before that he had not gone with the Captain in the boat. Don't you see that? He was an officer himself."

Edward sat up and rested his head in his hands in agony, and felt hands push him back.

"Lie down now, little weak-stomached Armstrong, and try, if you can, not to interrupt me. I am going to tell you something really horrible, but if you can't take this now, you will never make it tonight."

III

"The trials were short," Neville said, "there being no defence possible. They had none in law. They were all fifteen, even the cabin boy, sentenced yesterday afternoon while I was there in court. The Regent had signed the warrants in advance at breakfast yesterday morning, I was with him, and stuck them in the toast rack. Oh my God, to think I found that funny, then. They were hung this morning at East Wapping, where I went—there was an enormous crowd, a real press, to see so many go, and afterwards they were staked out at Execution Dock, at Wapping Old Stairs, you know, after low tide. There were two still there from last week, but there wasn't much left of them. Don't look at me like that, Edward Armstrong, I am just telling you the facts, what happened. I did not order it."

Edward raised himself up and looked at him in an intolerable disgust. "Are you telling me that you stood there and watched Marion hung?"

"No, I sat, on my coach roof and had a good view. It was most interesting, though I never saw anyone cry so much as the boy. I could see Allister's face, how he hated it for the child, and I saw him speak to the child, before they came to hood him (he refused the hood himself, and there were so many they let him), but the child was inconsolable, and Allister was powerless. All the same it was most interesting. He had nerve, most didn't. He took it without a sound, and hung there without moving, his eyes open until near the end. Breeding, after all, counts."

"You told me he was alive." Edward turned aside, in intolerably bitter grief, and put his head in his hands.

"He is," Neville said briefly. "That is the hell of it. He should not be, but he is. Now listen, and I will tell you." He looked at him curiously. "If you can't take hearing, what will you do when you see? I want you to go there, I am trying to prepare you."

"I will be all right," Edward said, putting himself under some control. "Just go on now."

"I went down afterwards, when the crowd had thinned, to have a closer look. He was lying in the mud of the ebb, grey-black stinking stuff, they had not chained him up yet, and he looked as gone as any of the group, but when I went closer, ruining a new pair of white stockings, mind you, and my shoes, he opened one eye and he—Edward, he winked at me. I did see it, I'm not making it up. So I knew I couldn't leave it there. But he had been choked and he couldn't speak, or perhaps he didn't want it known that he was only half-dead, though I don't think they would have cared. To hang a pirate first is just a modern mercy; before they did it could take three tides to drown a tough one, or so I've heard. So I knew I had to do something—but I can watch, Edward, but I cannot *do*. The Marshall of the Admiralty and the Deputy Marshall had already left, for it was misling rain a little, and everyone was in a hurry now. Then they came to chain him to his post, and I had to leave."

"And you left him there alive?" Edward asked in horror.

"Had to. We all had to. Show was over, and guards, you know. There are two of them there now. Have to look now at a distance, or from a boat. Nice sight for boaters down to Greenwich, I always thought."

"Is it always done, this chaining?" He found his hands were trembling uncontrollably, and he could hardly speak. He put his head down again against the bitter blackness that was of no use to anyone, and after a little, refusing the brandy Neville again offered him, he lay back, in the intolerable daylight, making himself take long deep breaths, slowly and consciously, until the faintness and the shuddering passed a little, and he could control his hands and his voice. "I never knew of it before."

"For piracy, yes, and any mutiny in the mercantile marine. We un-chain to hang—we use only loose rope then, that slips, for hands and everything—and then we put some more back on the dead. I wonder sometimes what we think the dead can do. If the court had known what I suspect, though none of the fifteen indicated it, that Marion was not rank and file, they might have gibbeted him high, as they did Kidd, but I doubt he had that much name."

"It is too horrible. I do not see how the ships can bear to pass, or people live near Wapping. Neville, does his father know?" The tears were thick behind his eyes now, and he could not hold them back from spilling out and falling.

"He don't want it, child, and it would not help. I told you that. They had him. It is death on any count, just a different place had he been tried by the Royal Navy for mutiny, and a yellow flag on the ship, and no room for error there, and his name disgraced. By tomorrow it will be finished, and tomorrow will come. It always does. It will now."

"Neville," Edward said desperately, "he is still alive. He isn't dead. You have said so. Can't he yet be pardoned? Money does so much, and rank does too, you know that, when it is not made a public thing. There is time yet left. Let me go to Admiral Alleyn myself. I know him. I know the courts are slow but he has influence."

"Edward," Neville said heavily but steadily, "forget it. I know him, too. Admiral Alleyn was there. He sat on the court."

"I know he had another name, but would his father not have recognised him?" Edward asked, still desperately, for once failing to understand what Neville was trying to say and unwilling to make plain.

"If he did, he did not show it."

A look at the man's face enlightened him, and his own face whitened in horror and understanding, as the scene as it must have been presented itself to him.

"There will be no pardon then," he said slowly.

"I do not think so, though his friends continue privately to work for it. I am not as unfeeling as you think, Edward. I am doing what I can, by what means I can bring to bear, but they are both proud men. You should know that. It is a risky thing all round, and I expect nothing from it."

"Oh, God," said Edward, "what can I do?"

"If you have the courage," Neville said, his eyes fixed on him, "take opium to him. I myself do not. That is all anyone can do now. It was for that I called you."

"I will go," Edward said, "but tell me how to do it." His eyes were immense and dark, but he spoke without hesitation.

"Go to several different druggists, and buy a small amount or what you can from each, that is all. You should be able to find it, a ship docked last week for the East India Company. Liquid or powdered, either will do. But it will come dear. And then I will tell you how to go. But if you are caught there, I will not be able or willing to help you, and it could be severe for you as well."

"I will risk that. Where will you wait for me?"

"I will be here."

"How long do I have?"

"Long enough. You cannot go until it is dark, but high tide is not until nearly twelve."

Edward's eyes darkened in horror.

"I will tell you what I think is best when you come back," Neville said gently, "but see first if you can get the laudanum. When you ask, try not to look as if you wanted it to suicide with. Have you money with you?"

"Not much."

"Nor do I, but perhaps between us it will be enough. Go now," he added, pushing Edward with his hand, "if you will go, before the shops close."

Neville had given him several names to try, and his search led him to one shop by the river. The streets were narrower, and dim in the again overcast day, full of empty gaping doors and slops. He did not think to be afraid, even when his senses grew uneasy for him, when he saw an old grizzled worn pigtailed sailor looking at him searchingly, whom he had seen near the previous druggist he had visited, who had questioned him too closely and sold him only a few grains and had looked as if he might send after him. He had made several turns out of his way, in case the man had, to avoid any further inquiry or delay. He had considered then if he must try his own house, for his father's supply, but he had no idea how much he might happen to have or where he kept it, and he was most afraid of all of being questioned or stopped there. He thought he heard steps behind him, but when he stopped, they stopped, and he heard nothing. He had decided it was his imagination, already too burdened, when passing again an open door, yawning blackly into its abandoned building, he felt himself seized from behind, against an iron-like body, a huge calloused hand fixed firmly over his nose and mouth. He was pulled back into the dark of the doorway.

Oh, God, he thought, despairing, unable to believe it was happening and just then, I am being impressed. He tried desperately first to break away and then simply to breathe, but he could not move.

"Be still and lie easy and I lets you breathe," the voice said, slipping its hand from his nose but still tightly covering his mouth, "as wass more than 'e could." The large rough hand attached to the arm gripping his body fumbled about his clothes, and found and removed his pistol. "You bees Mr. Armstrong, beant you?" Edward nodded his head slightly, despite his surprise, seeing no point in concealing the fact. "It bees a piece of luck to find you now. I wass comin' to yer house. I saws you leave, and I have followed. I wass asket to give you this." There was a sound of one-handed fumbling while the hand on his mouth remained firm, and then a hand fumbled at his own hand and managed to slip a ring over a finger. "So now I have, I have done it now."

He knew what it must be, without needing to see it in this strange terrible day, and his eyes filled with tears that fell and splashed on the hand holding his mouth. He leaned against the figure quietly and he put his own fingers gently on the hand, tapping, to show he wanted to speak.

The tears had already shown that the message had been received and understood, but the hand did not release him. The other hand felt probing at the back of his neck, found what it looked for behind his left ear, and pressed. The darkness of the doorway grew even darker and he felt himself slipping away with no pain, and then the pressure was released.

"Got that, cap'n?" the voice said in a croak by his ear. "Can you find it yerself now? Remember it." He felt the fingers again pressing and he struggled convulsively against them this time and their darkness, and they instantly released him, and his mouth entirely.

"Who gave you this ring to give to me?" he asked, his fingers on Marion's signet ring on his hand.

"A gentleman as wass on hard times in the hold of mer ship," he said. "I had the charge of him, and he never give me no trouble, so I asked, before he wass unloaded, if I could do an errand fer him, fer he wass a bonny gentleman to see, when the captain first took him, before the hold and the irons worked on him. I went down to see him turned off, and I thought they mucked it, but I wassn't sure until I followed you, and saws what you wass after. Now I've showed you what to do, that bees quicker and more surer than what you've bought. He said you wass a right one, and you are."

"I would like my pistol back now, please," Edward said, not answering directly.

"You don't want that on you, cap'n," the old sailor commented, withholding it, "it beant safe."

"I don't want to be stopped again," Edward replied, holding out his hand. "It is mine, and my business. Give it to me now. I won't use it on you, you know that."

"If I wass you, I'd throw it away. It done you no good with me." But he reluctantly handed it over. A thought struck the old sailor. "Wait here, cap'n, I've something you can have that might be more useful to you." Edward waited, impatiently, worriedly, the minutes slipping by, his hands touching the ring, ready to leave and go, when the striped shirt and greasy grey pigtail reappeared with a black wad of material. "Mer uncle's" he said proudly, "that don't need it now. Good luck to you, cap'n, and God bless. I've half a mind to go merself, but just the half."

The massive grizzle-jowled figure moved away with surprising lightness and agility, and Edward went back to Miller's with an anxious eye at the light.

He was back by five, and found Neville anxiously pacing the floor.

"You were a long time. I thought you were not coming back. Could you find it? Did you get it?"

"Just barely," Edward said, "I hope it is enough." In the face of action he was cooler now than Neville. He put down on the table a small bottle of laudanum and a paper of several additional grains of opium which he carefully tilted into the little bottle. "You do care," he said, looking at Neville's sweating face.

"Of course I care, you fool. I care damnably. What is the parcel?"

"It is a black frock."

"They are not allowed there."

"Methodists go anywhere, or try," Edward said with a fleeting unhappy smile. "It might be helpful, if I am stopped before I find him. Why do they guard the dead?"

"People are strange, like me, and stranger. They will come for the rope, or take the head for a mask, or a piece of hair, a shirt, a hand, anything. The guards won't have that. The law does its work in dignity, after its fashion. And sometimes friends have tried to take them down for burial, for relatives, and the guards will not permit it. That is not the law. They are to stay and be an object to us, that we should be good and not play such games ourselves. There was one attempt at escape some years ago: the pirate bound a piece of tin about his throat and bribed the hangman, but when his friends came, the guards held them off, and so they had to watch him drown. Marion must have a throat like leather. I could see the cords in it standing out. I could tell something was wrong at the time. The knot was not behind the right ear, and there was no metal eye, someway his neck was not broken, and then it is only strangling. That is slow. Kemble was an old man, and a mere priest, that was Sarah Siddons' grandfather, in the '45, but it took him half an hour even in a hood to strangle. John Kemble told me about it. I never remember which ear is quick myself. With so many to turn off this morning, and it raining and he one of the last to put up, they missed it, or did not care, and cut him down too soon. And they would not let the crowd up to pull their feet, or no one cared to, it being pirates."

"You have horrible interests, Neville," Edward said. "You are horribly informed." He averted his eyes from the man's tight trousers. "You do not need to come with me. I am going to swim. I think that is the only way. I am a very strong swimmer, and I am going now. Whatever happens, I am glad you sent for me. Have you paper? And pen? I am going to write a note for my house that I will be dining out. Would you have it delivered for me?" He changed into the rusty black frock coat with its greasy once white bands, looking far too noticeable with his gold hair.

"I should have bought a wig," he said, "but I did not think of that and it can't be helped."

He left Neville, and walked quietly from Westminster Bridge to George Street and Whitehall and found a hackney and had himself driven a little way below the Tower, near the London Docks where, after the hackney had gone, he went down to the water.

It was dark now. He walked along the bank as far as he dared, and then he took off his boots and slipped into the water, which was colder than he expected, and swam the remaining distance, letting the current carry him partly, although he could feel already the slight inward drive of the tide pushing him partly back. He was not afraid, he simply did not wish to be stopped again by anyone, and he swam underwater at any movement or sound.

He came finally to the sloping bank of the river where it had been cut back and dug out, and the sides and back lined with stone where rough steps had been cut leading down. The river bottom was covered now, and the posts were not conspicuous, although their burdens were. He picked his way among the dead and the dying, the rotten and the stinking and the yet moaning in half-life, until he found Marion. He was lying, higher up, half in the water which lapped about his waist, dirty and brown and greasy, filled with scum and stench and debris, unable to brush the gnats and the blowflies from his face and eyes, which were shut, his hands outstretched and shackled to the sloping post, linked to the heavy chain padlocked about his waist, but the agony of pain passing on his face showed he was both conscious and alive. He was older, and harder and browner, than when Edward had known him, but the delicacy of his profile was still pronounced and outlined against the dark stubble of beard on his face.

Edward knelt beside him, and brushed the gnats from his face.

"Marion," he said, his voice low but clear, "it is a friend. Can you hear me?"

The condemned man opened his eyes and turned them towards the fair-haired young man in the black robes of a cleric.

"By God," the familiar voice exclaimed faintly, "it is Edward Clare, and gone black! How are you here?" He spoke quickly and feverishly. "Have you come, you crow, to give me last rites? I won't have them. How did you come here? God, I am glad to see your face."

Edward shook his head. "I put them on to get here. I came as soon as I heard." Despite his attempt at control, he lost his breath in a sob. "I cannot bear this, Marion."

His friend's lips twisted in a quick grimace that was all he could manage for a smile. "I can hardly bear it either, but I must. There is no pardon, is there?"

"Not when I came. Your friends are working but I think there is no hope for one."

"Not for this, I did not think there would be, and still one hopes. It is hard to be 'absolute for death,' and such a death as this, which comes so slow. It is the waiting that is worst, knowing it will happen, that it is about to happen. When it does happen, one is too busy dying and trying not to, to think anything. I have already died twice, but I cannot stay dead. Once, when they hung me on their gallows back there —with a proper ceremony that was lost on me, silver oar and all—oh God, Edward, the human care and patience, and concern, with which they killed us—before they put me here, and once before you came, in the wake of the paddle boat. I shall not live out this first high tide. This time I will die of it. Oh, God, Edward Clare, I am here and I still wonder why I must."

"I have brought you laudanum," Edward whispered, "to kill the pain. I do not know how strong it is, I do not know if there's enough to take it all away, but it should help you bear it, if it does not."

"Kill me, you mean? I don't want you to kill me, Edward Clare, I want these bastards to do their own rotten work."

"I don't think there is enough. I wish there were." He held it to his friend's lips, lifting his head to help him drink, and then giving him water from his flask, and brandy, and water again.

"Your priest's robe won't help you down here, Edward Clare, they are not allowed here for such as me. Go now, and leave me. You are too good, you don't want to end here too."

"I am not going," Edward said, "at least not now." He settled himself down in the water, slightly beneath his friend, lifting his head and shoulders, easing the strain on his arms, and kissed his face and stroked his forehead and his hair.

"Take my hand," Marion asked, and he reached and held it tightly in his. The tide was coming in again, and he could see the line rising, slowly and inexorably, but he felt the hand he held begin to relax.

"You are religious, aren't you, Edward Clare, whether those are your own robes or not," Marion's voice said near him, but not mockingly.

"Yes," said Edward simply, "I am."

"I do not see how you can be, sitting here, where we are, it is a mismanaged world. But now I wish I were. I find myself wishing it. Tell me why you are, Edward. I am going to sleep, and I will not wake again to live, I think. I hope I may not wake again, and drown through still another tide. Comfort me, Edward, if you can. I am in need of it."

"'The Lord is my shepherd,'" Edward said quietly, stroking his hair. "'I shall not want . . .'"

"I cannot believe that here," Marion said, "and if the world has a god, it has crucified him more than once. But go on."

"'Though I walk through the valley of the shadow of death, I will fear no evil, for thou art with me . . .'" The tears were falling from his eyes, but his voice was steady. "'Thy rod and thy staff they comfort me.' 'In my father's house there are many mansions, I go even now to prepare a place for you.' 'Except a man lose his life he shall not find it.'" He saw the strong opium had worked finally, and the face by him lay relaxed, the harshness and the strain gone from it. Somewhere, he knew from Marion's friend, there was the artery near the ear that when pressed, brought quick sleep. He was wondering whether to try, when he felt a hand laid on his shoulder, and rough fingers pulled at him, to lift him up to his feet. He slid out, laying Marion's head back gently, against his taut arm, like a sleeping child's.

"He is dead," he said, though it was not true, "don't waste your time on him." He could not bear that they should touch Alleyn again or wake him. He twisted loose of their hands, and began to run, among the out-stretching figures, so they would be distracted, and not examine or try. They caught him at the steps. He began to sob in agony that he had done all he could do, fighting them with his nails until one fetched him a clout over his ear that knocked him senseless.

He awoke once briefly and did not know where he was, but he thought at first his beliefs were all betrayed and that he was in Hell. He could not move, and when he opened his eyes he could see nothing in the blackness, but the smell of death was all around him, and rotten stenches, like an opened coffin or an uncleaned cloaca, and moans and cries and weird snatches of song and rustlings in the dark, and something cold flicked across his face and touched his arm. He cried out in terror, his cry lost and unheard in the other cries, but whatever the thing was went away. He was cold, and wet, and he seemed to have no coat. His head ached miserably so that he could not think, and when he tried to move, he thought it would break apart and waves of nausea swept over him and left him fainting and yet unable to faint. He realised that he could not move because he was fettered and stapled to the floor, shackled so heavily the weight of the iron held his weakness down. A returning memory of the night began to stir in his head, and his agony was so great that he did faint then.

He awoke again, some time later, ill and feverish, but his fetters removed, and a blanket pulled over him, to hear the Earl repeatedly calling his name. He came slowly and reluctantly back to consciousness, trying to keep back from himself a memory he could not bear. He thought at first he was ten years younger, and again in the priest-hole in his uncle's house, and he murmured, "Is it you, Uncle? Have you come?" But as his eyes opened, he saw he was truly in a cell in a prison, with a small heavily barred high window letting in only a dim light through which he could just distinguish his father beside him, and he knew where he was and why.

"Is he dead?" he asked hopelessly.

The Earl nodded, unable to speak. "Yes, Edward," he said after a moment.

"Can you have him brought down?"

"No, Edward, I cannot. It is the law."

Edward turned his face away towards the wall, the dry harsh sobs racking his body helplessly that shook beneath him.

"I have been searching for you, Edward," the Earl said, "I could not find you until now, or I would have come before. I have had you moved into this private cabin." He saw Edward no longer heard him, or realised the perilousness of his own position. "Edward," he said sharply, "you must wake up. I must talk to you. You *must* wake up." He shook him a little, and Edward's eyes heavy with pain and illness opened briefly. "Have you been charged?" The eyes looked at him dully, uncomprehending. "Think, Edward, have you been before a judge? Have you been unconscious all this time? I must know. Did you resist whoever brought you here? Were you armed? Your pistol is not at home. Did you have a pistol on you? It is important," he said, pleading into the dulled eyes. "I must know."

"I don't remember," Edward said weakly, stupid with illness and grief, "I don't know what you mean," and fainted again. The Earl looked at him in despair, yet with a little hope, for it seemed impossible to him that Edward could have been charged in the state in which he had found him. He had been able to find out very little, but he hoped the Ellenborough Law of 1803 had not already been invoked, directed initially against poachers, that made armed resistance to arrest in itself a hanging felony.

Lord Tyne as the Viscount Rockfort had known both Scott brothers from Newcastle-on-Tyne at University College. One, William Scott, near his age, lecturer of Ancient History then and now Judge Scott, he had become friends with because of his action in befriending the younger brother John Scott, now Lord Chancellor, who had eloped then and lost his Fellowship because of it and in poverty during the temporary estrangement of their angry families was then trying to study law. Tyne had benefited him then, and he recalled this now privately to the minds of the two judges, now Lords Eldon and Stowell. He was himself intensely afraid of the severity of the aging and ill Lord Chief Justice Lord Ellenborough, Edward Law, a very different sort of Edward, who had himself secured passage of the Treason Laws of 1796, which bill bore his name, and had initiated ten new capitol felony offenses, among them that of 1803, who supported easily and indefinitely any opportunity for suspension of *habeas corpus*, temporarily then back in effect, who was resisting successfully all efforts of Romilly to ameliorate the harshness of the present laws. As a conservative bulwark against the tide of revolution, the Earl had hitherto found no fault in the beliefs or the practises of either Lord Ellenborough or Lord Eldon, and he still found none in these men personally, but when he found the slow and impenetrable block of these laws moving impersonally and unexpectedly to crush someone of his own, he found he of necessity regarded it in a different light.

It took all the power and the influence the Earl and his friends possessed, and knowledge of technicalities to bring to bear, and certain promises he would have given for no one else, to effect Edward's release, under the several charges that might have been brought against him. Edward himself knew nothing of the unofficial trial against him, being too ill with brain fever and grief, and then Newgate fever, to regain consciousness during any of it. The chill he took in the river, with the mistreatment that followed and the shocks given his nervous system, had rendered him entirely susceptible to a too prevalent and contagious disease at any time. The severity of his illness and the necessity for treatment elsewhere lent urgency to the mitigation of his offences, and helped in part to effect it.

IV

When he woke again he was in a strange bedroom, clean, shaded against the sun that moved coolly mixed with shadows against his shutters. The linen sheets were smooth and cool and fresh and pressed, and faintly scented with Lavender, and he felt cool and light and like another person, but who the person was he did not know. He was not even sure of his name, until he heard a movement, a slight rustling near his bed beyond the bed curtains, and saw Anne's face near his. He knew, then, everything, except where he was, and why, and he did not want to talk or be asked questions or to ask them. He tried to smile, and could not, and shut his eyes again.

When he opened them, the room was shadowed with gold lights, rather than green, but Anne was by him as before, and she did not look to have moved. She looked older, her face wan and with lines of concern in it that had he not been so preoccupied with himself, absorbed in his weakness, would have shown to him how worried she had been for him.

"Whose house is this?" he asked, forming the words slowly and hesitantly, his eyes resting on hers, with no spirit in them. "I don't know where I am."

"It is my house, Edward," a second voice said. Turning his face slowly, painfully, he saw a tall man standing at the foot of his bed. For a moment his face was blank, trying to remember the face, and then he knew it was Earl Armstrong. The Scotch Earl came to stand by Edward's bed, and took his flinching hand. "Are you afraid of me, young man? Don't be, I am not here to hurt you. You are a brave young man, I am proud, I am honoured, to have you in my house, and that you bear part of my own first name."

Edward could not imagine why he was there, with people who had not wanted him, but the face seemed only concerned and filled with good will. He did not care to try to imagine why, and then a wild idea struck him that his families had been exchanged and that for some reason he was after all to be made an Armstrong. He struggled to sit up, his face wild and dismayed, and cried desperately, "Where is Holland? Where is my father?"

"He is downstairs," the Scotch Earl said reassuringly, as Anne put her hands on Edward's shoulders to ease him back on his pillows. "I will call him and tell him you are awake."

"Oh, please," Edward said, his face white and frightened.

Anne looked at him and said falteringly, "I am sorry about your friend."

He winced in intolerable pain and turned away, throwing his arm over his eyes, and she said, horrified at herself, "I never learn, I always say the wrong thing."

"Always," he said, his face turned away, "always."

The Earl entered the room and stood looking at them for a moment, before Anne was aware of his presence. If he had thought that he had only to bring Edward and the Armstrongs together for his story to end happily, he saw at once that he was mistaken, and that it would not be so easy as he had hoped.

"Your uncle is having lunch," he said kindly to Anne. "Why don't you join him, my dear?" He sat down in the chair by the bed, but Edward reached for him desperately with a feverish hand, as he had many times in delirium, although his fever had passed, and the Earl sat instead on the bed by him and took him in his arms and kissed him. The passion of the boy startled and eluded him, until Edward spoke.

"I thought you had gone. I thought you had left me here with these people I don't know." His voice was close to sobbing, and had a tone near hysteria.

"I am never going to leave you," the Earl said, holding him as he had held him when he was a child, soothing him. "I promised you before, I promise again."

"Why am I here? Why aren't we in our house? I wish I were home," he said desperately and unhappily.

"Knighton thought you would improve faster out of London and its fogs, and in a Southern exposure. Lord Armstrong kindly offered his house. You are in Devon, Edward, where you always wanted to be."

"Not any more," Edward whispered. His maturity had left him entirely and he was only a frightened child, and more frightened than ever as a child. "He told me never to come near him again. He stopped his nephew's men when they were whipping me, but he told me he would himself if I came to his house. I don't want to be here. I want to go home."

"You shall go home, but not until you are stronger. Don't work yourself up, Edward, you will make yourself worse. I thought you would like it here. And Anne is here."

"No," Edward whispered.

The Earl made no further immediate comment. Then he said: "Lord

Armstrong came to me when he heard of your trouble, and asked to be allowed to help. I thought those stripes might have come from his house. I felt no hesitation or reluctance to accept Lord Armstrong's aid. His integrity is unquestioned, and he was very helpful, very influential. I could not have done so well without him. You could have no better friend."

"You won't leave me with him?" Edward pleaded, again frightened.

"Of course not. You are my son, not his."

"What day is it, Holland?"

"I am not sure," his father said ruefully. "Some date in October, the twentieth, I think. It may not be so late."

"I remember nothing, almost nothing, since August," Edward said, frightened. "Have I been so sick?"

"Yes, Edward, we thought you would die."

"I wish I had," Edward said, turning his face away.

"No, Edward," the Earl said, turning his face back to him and against him. "If you had, you would have. You were very sick, and people do generally die of gaol fever, but you fought with us to live."

"Yes, I do. I wish I had. I wish I could now. I loved him so. I never told you. You do not know. We fought, and then it would have been all right again, except he had to go away." He began to cry, terribly, harshly, the sobs breaking over each other in gasping waves.

"I do know, I loved him too. I thought once he might be my son, but his mother said no, though she never had a head for dates, that she was certain he was his own father's."

"Don't, Holland," Edward said, between sobs.

"Do you want to tell me about it, would it help?"

"No, I can't. You went there, didn't you? Didn't you see?"

"I saw," the Earl said, holding him tightly.

"Is he there still?"

"I don't know. I have not been back."

"Oh God, oh God," cried Edward, "I cannot bear the memory, it is worse than the thing itself, and imagining what happened then, and did he know."

"It could be," the Earl said soberly, his face worried, "don't let it be. His agony is over, don't let it become yours. He would be the first to tell you that. He was not a person to be sentimental, when he lived. I considered calling Lord Alleyn out, but in the end I did not. I thought death too easy, and that living to know and to remember and to regret could be worse. You have not that to remember, Edward, and nothing really to regret." He smoothed Edward's hair. "Face it and forget it, Edward," he said, "'It is appointed unto men once to die,' your Wesley says that, with your Bible," but he saw his words did not reach Edward.

A look of terror and other memories passed over his face, and his eyes stared as though the shapes were before them. The Earl shook him by his shoulders, and the intensity of his gaze relaxed and he returned to the reality of where he was, the present room.

"How did you know? About—about either of us? How did you find me?"

The expression of the Earl's face grew pinched. "Your brave friend Neville finally told me, and then I knew where you had to be. Even knowing, it was hard to find you."

"Where was I, Holland, before I was here?"

"You were in Newgate," the Earl said between tight lips.

"Newgate Prison?" Edward asked, startled. "I thought—I don't know what I thought. How long was I there?"

"You were there three weeks," the Earl said, his face drawn. "You were ill in the public ward for several days, before I found you. I paid to have you made more comfortable and put in the cabin side, but I could not get you out at first."

The Earl's own memories were not good. He was currently out of the Regent's favour, and he had been afraid to ask his help. It was a difficult time. Apart from the war and its aftermath, apart from prime minister succeeding prime minister rapidly in that decade, and cabinets falling and being reformed, there had been the Cumberland–Sellis affair, five years ago now in 1810, but not allowed to be forgotten. The Earl knew Cumberland well, knew him to be the most intelligent and the most strong-willed and the most courageous of George III's five sons, himself the fifth, and the actual governing force and directing mind behind the Regency, more Conservative even than the Earl in his policies. The Earl did not personally believe that the Duke had cut the throat of his valet, but the strange coincidence of the Duke found wounded in his apartment in St. James's Palace, his head cloven except for a fortunate mischance, and so soon after, his valet Sellis found dead in his bed, had stirred the public mind, and the Radical newspapers were now making hay of it, regardless of threats and the sentence of imprisonment on White in 1813 for printing the rumour. After all, Cumberland was the nephew of Cumberland "the Butcher." The ministry was on the verge of falling, through an odd circumstance, on a motion to raise the Duke of Cumberland's pension from 18,000 pounds to 24,000. The motion had been defeated by a majority of one, in the House of Commons, the deciding vote having been cast by Thomas Cochrane, eldest son of the ninth Earl of Dundonald, of Lanarkshire, a Lowland district briefly annexed by Northumbria in the seventh century.

The Cochrane affair was complicated, and the Earl had offended in expressing his opinions on it tactlessly. A ruggedly self-sufficient and inventive naval officer, Cochrane had fallen foul of the Admiralty, particularly sensitive since Dundas, Lord Melville's trial for misuse of its funds, through his criticism of its methods and his exposure of its abuses. This was the Cochrane who had said he could have circumvented the entire Peninsular War, had he been given leave, with a coast-line harrying done by a few ships under his command; and who had in private submitted what became known as the "secret war plan," that he promised to be capable of destroying any fleet or fortress. Although the Royal Dukes toyed with the idea of using it, in 1811, and again later, they rejected it as being "infallible, irresistible, but inhuman." The Earl, learning of this but unable as a state secret to speak of it generally, had pointed out with interest that war *was* inhuman, and in his opinion not a game, and that if one engaged in it at all, one might as well win. When Wellington and the Allies won over Napoleon on the field near Waterloo, with a loss of 30,000 men, he recalled Cochrane's "secret war plan," and wondered what it could have been to be more inhuman than that.

The year before an uncle to Cochrane and a prospective aide had been involved in a Funds scandal. The aide, an unscrupulous French refugee, also inventive, and a prospective good gunner, had sent supposedly authentic word that Napoleon was dead, the Allies marching on Paris, and peace imminent. Funds had risen and then fallen rapidly, and the uncle under an assumed name had made a large profit. Cochrane on learning of it, and of his aide's various masquerades, had given the aide up to arrest, but he had himself been tried with them, stripped of his honours and offices, dismissed from the Navy, and sentenced to the King's Bench for a year. He was also to pay a fine of a thousand pounds and to sit in the pillory for an hour. The pillory sentence was remitted, under fear of a riot, when his colleague Sir Francis Burdett promised to stand there with him. Expelled from the House of Commons by sentence of the court, he was enthusiastically and promptly re-elected by his Westminster constituents in protest, at their own expense, and Cochrane had determined to take his seat. After seven months in the King's Bench, not quite forty years old, he had made an ingenious and daring escape over the spiked neighbouring rooftops, injuring himself in the drop, and had nevertheless arrived in the House and taken his seat, to cheers. He had been at once re-arrested, taken back to the King's Bench, and this time imprisoned in the damp strongroom that lay largely underground, in great discomfort to serve out the remaining months, but public sentiment was strongly in his favour. He had paid his fine, writing on the back of the bank cheque that he submitted to robbery to protect himself from murder, and took his seat in time to make his vote on that decisive evening. The Earl had indifferently let his opinion be known, that regardless of their different politics, he did not believe Cochrane capable of fraud. It was not an opinion popular with the Regent, nor was his private defence of Lord Castlereagh, back again now in Vienna and in Paris for the final negotiations of the peace.

Castlereagh's public image, shortly to fall, was still high, but privately the Regent was displeased with word which had reached him but not yet the general ear that Castlereagh in his disinterested statesmanship for the general European good, believing that in the end to be of most benefit to England herself, had asked for and had secured very little spoils for his country after her efforts in making and concluding the war. The Earl, contrary to his usual political retirement, had felt compelled to describe the situation at the Congress of Vienna, and Castlereagh's extraordinary diplomacy, at once suave and obstinate, in his own clearest terms, not foreseeing any immediate need to ask favours of anyone.

But when Edward looked to be going to die, before the law would act, he did go, and helped by the repeal of the property tax he privately settled an immense amount of his private funds upon that expensive debt-ridden contemporary.

He or Anne or Lord Armstrong or George or Foxham were with Edward at all times, for he could not bear to be alone. If he was left alone at any time, he sensed it and woke up, sometimes screaming, thinking huge rats were crawling on him and that he could not move. He only rested completely easily with the Earl, who stayed with him when he could.

"I am ready at this moment to step out of character and to work for the Penal Bill in the House of Lords, even with a Whig like my younger neighbour Lord Grey," he said one day in exhaustion, when Edward's nightmares seemed to grow worse rather than to improve, "but it would do no good, it will not pass. The time is not here. But perhaps you will, Edward. You will know what to say. I think I must really speak with Mrs. Fry."

Edward looked at him blankly, without much curiosity.

"Did she come to see you while you were in Newgate? A soft-spoken lady in grey? Quaker-dressed?"

Edward shivered and turned his face away. "I don't remember."

"You should try, Edward," the Earl said gently yet sternly; "you *were* there, and you cannot forget; your dreams show that, so you should try to remember."

"No," Edward whispered. "Hold me, Holland, hold me hard. Please don't leave me."

The Earl talked sometimes to Edward to pass the time, for he did not feel like reading and he did not want to be read to. Sometimes he spoke to Edward generally, sometimes he talked of people he had known, but all their conversations seemed to lead back to one point.

"Have you ever heard the name John Wilkes, Edward?"

"No," Edward said, his eyes closed.

The Earl sighed. "That does show me times change. Well," he said, "well. Things pass. I shall enlighten you now." Edward opened his eyes briefly at the word, and stared at his father. "What is it, Edward?"

"Nothing," Edward said, and shut his eyes again. "For a moment you reminded me of—of someone." The Earl followed his thought then, but he made no comment.

"Wilkes was one of the old rakes of my day, Edward, as much older than me as I am you, he was one of the Monks, that old Hell-Fire Club, and I saw him, if you can imagine it, Edward, apotheosized here and in the Colonies as a Whig martyr, until he became lord mayor of London and put down Lord George Gordon's riot. The Whigs liked him less then, but he did what had then to be done, as we all must. I always credited him for courage. Lord, which one of them was it who dressed up an ape in a coffin and terrified the rest of the Monks when it popped out, for they thought they'd really raised the devil. Could that have been Wilkes? I do believe it was. What a name he was, and how my father hated him. The only person he hated more was 'Junius,' who he thought was the son of Fox's tutor, but Fox would not talk about that. Strange story there. Francis was ten years older than Fox, twenty than myself. He quarrelled with Fox over preferment, after Fox had done so much for him: ambitious, but I suppose he had to be. But I was speaking of Wilkes." He looked across at Edward. "Are you interested, Edward?"

"Not very much."

"Well, I shall tell you anyway. He supported the Colonies' cause, and criticized the King generally in a little publication he had that he ran on satirical lines and ran into the libel law and was arrested and imprisoned on an illegal warrant. Old Judge Pratt ordered him released, not because he liked him, but because of the illegality, he was a man of courage too, and lost the Lord Chancellorship for it. I will say that for Eton, it has always bred courage. Lord, was not the George angry! He outlawed Wilkes, sent him flying to France, and four years later got him back in gaol, this time legally. Though the Lord Chief Justice, that was Lord Mansfield then, reversed the sentence of outlawry, and made George Rex angry again (though God knows Mansfield had convicted the leaders of the '45 for him, even Lords Balmerino and Kilmarnock): 'Iustitia fiat, ruat coelum,' Mansfield said, brave words then."

"Let justice be done, though the heavens fall," Edward said slowly. "Do you believe that, Holland?"

"I have shown I do not, Edward. One year's justice is another year's tyranny. Justice on earth must be by law, there is no other way, but laws change, and therefore our justice is neither absolute nor constant." He looked at the boy compassionately. "Heaven's justice, if there be such, is surely more sure, and may take into account what the law officially may not. I uphold in principle the law's justice and its right to function as it presently exists, but in actuality I have no objection to tampering with it or tempering it. In fact, these days I have noticed judges and juries frequently tempering it themselves, through erratically, and not in the areas Alleyn touched." He looked at Edward's closed face. "When you were nine, Edward, you quoted two lines to me. Do you remember them? 'Misericordia et veritas obviaverunt sibi: Iustitia et pax osculatae sunt.' The Four Virtues, but even there mercy and justice are not paired. In life they do not meet. They obviate one another. Mercy is *not* justice— by its very nature it is and it gives what justice can and will not be or give. It is mercy and truth that meet together; it is justice and peace that kiss. Think about that, Edward."

"What did I receive?" Edward asked.

"You received mercy."

"And Alleyn?"

"He received justice."

"Oh, God," whispered Edward. "I think you do not mind."

"I mind the destruction of anything beautiful to see. I would mind if for no other reason than that, and I have many other reasons. But I can see that it is fitting. If he settled for mercy ever it was because he could not find justice. Justice was a passion with him. What he demanded, in his principles, he demanded he and those he demanded for be given because it was due, and justice required it, not out of mercy."

Edward shook his head, remembering Marion's words to him about mercy, but he had been helpless then, thirsty and in discomfort. "He believed in mercy for the helpless," he said.

"Do we not all, but it is then, when we are helpless, that sometimes instead we receive justice. If we are not helpless, we do not need mercy, and justice cannot touch us. If we are not helpless, we can supply our own needs and our own ends."

"Why should I, when he did not?"

"Oh, Edward, you surely can answer that for yourself. Surely you can? And he was not himself a particularly merciful person. It is the merciful, we are told, who are to receive mercy."

"I would have given my mercy to him, and taken his justice," Edward whispered, tears blinding him.

"I know you would, Edward, and so even did those in whose power and near jeopardy that willingness put you, and that is in part why you are here now, and not somewhere else. But remember this, Edward. He would not have for you; not for yourself, as just yourself, receiving only justice. He would have been sorry, but for you as an equal, receiving justice, he would have done nothing and risked nothing."

Edward was silent. He had known a different person, who had without reason or explanation revealed a different and vulnerable side to him, as private and still as his pulse, but he was too weak to argue over something that could no longer make any difference.

Another day the Earl said, "You have seen terrible things, Edward, and not being used to them, being sheltered from the harshness of the world by my own harshness, they affect you more. That was not wise of me, you were better inoculated a little at a time, as I had you done against the smallpox. But then, I was not thinking of your good. But you knew always, I think, that I did love you and that I did care." He looked at Edward, but Edward made no response. "Even death, which you have known, and too young, is not so shattering as cruelty. It is hard to understand, I sometimes think, when we must meet so many hard things we cannot avoid, that we should be cruel to one another, but it is the world and it is human nature.

"I have seen many things in my time, Edward. I have seen the Gordon riots in London against the Catholics, when the old Newgate was burned and the government houses sacked and rifled, and I have heard about the Irish riots for the Catholics against the Protestants, and what they did to one another in retaliation and counter-retaliation. I have seen the Pacific charted, and the Southern Continents claimed and opened. I have lived through the Spithead Mutiny when London was blockaded and the Admiralty forced to bow—although it did not help Parker, for them to do so. I could have seen, had I chosen, men and women and children hung for any conceivable crime against property or morality or merely foolish act, as I can yet but not so frequently and not thanks to Romilly any longer for picking pockets, all done through due process of law, and I have known them equally dead and equally hung, without process of law, in the French and the American and the Irish Revolutions and Counter-Revolutions." He ignored the whiteness of Edward's face. "When I could, I will tell you that I have removed myself as far as possible from the scene of the disturbances. I have seen much that was bad pass away, and worse succeed it, and I have seen much that was good pass away, and worse succeed that, and I do not believe in the perfectibility of human nature, despite our country's present reformers. There is enough of vice in me alone, I think, to infect a country, and I am only one. (I do not speak of country matters.) But in all these things I have seen the power of the common people grow, and though I deplore it, I think nothing in the end will check it, until like the mob in France they again choose a tyrant to subdue them."

"How like Alleyn you sound, although you mean a different thing," Edward said in dreary grief.

"He was himself, he was, he is a sign of the times, both. Such ugly and useless deaths, in the end, Edward, will awake a conscience far more powerfully than any life. It has always been so." He paused, and spoke again more generally, when he did speak. "The temper of the country now, of the ruling part of it, that is, is one of fear, and a desire to preserve itself at any cost. Such a fear makes for a harshness in my opinion both unnecessary and self-defeating. One sees this when one sees juries begin to become unwilling to convict, though God knows they still convict enough, and merchants themselves asking for more leniency in the laws in order to secure some conviction for theft. But the laws are there, and individual interpretation is an uncertain and quixotic support on which to lean. Myself, I was afraid of these juries and these laws, equally. One sees some change must come. These fevers and riots of the body politic are like the fevers and consumptions of the body natural," he said, looking at Edward. "They are violent medicines for an incumbent ill, but if they do not destroy the body itself, if it resists them and throws them off, and returns to itself, they purify and cleanse the flesh of it and renew it, until it is like the flesh of a little child again, and it then is like to live longer. I felt some such renewal after my own last illness. But to benefit, of course, the body must survive them. I hope the body politic will survive those ravaging it now.

"I have seen Napoleon myself, Edward," the Earl said, reverting, "and he was no demi-god, he was a petty tyrant. He came out onto a little balcony in Paris, this was some years ago, lifting his hands, and the world was expected to throw up its hat and cheer, but there were only a few people in the street, and they let out a half-hearted whoop of some nature that he found very disappointing, for he frowned, and after a brief word he retired, but the papers proclaimed it a popular triumph. Wellington and Napoleon were the same age: strange, is it not? One year saw them both born, and Castlereagh, too. A year for violent births."

He was silent, thinking, and after a while he said, with a glance at Edward, "I consider Alleyn misinformed on Castlereagh. His diplomacy as I witnessed with the wrangling kings was remarkable, and his appointment of Wellington always an act of inspiration. He had reverses, but in war they occur. The last battle alone signifies. I shall honour Castlereagh always for saving the Art Collections of Paris from destruction at the hands of Blücher who wanted to make an example of Paris. God! One must honour him for that, anyone must. And it is my understanding that he moderated the general inhumanities in Ireland, rather than acerbating them, rather the opposite, in fact. He asked for amnesties the Government here refused to give afterwards, I doubt Alleyn knew that, and he might not have believed it. Freethinkers rarely think closely. They were there before him, the inhumanities. He knew the Irish, he was born there, in Dublin, and he was only twenty-four, younger than you are now, Edward, when the French attempted to take Ireland in 1793, abetting the rebellion there for their own ends, as they helped with in America. And they nearly did, then. They might well have, with the help of our general blind stupidity, except for Castlereagh's shrewdness and promptness and his balanced eye, and the wrangling stupidity of the French. He was made Irish Secretary for it when he was only twentynine, too young for wisdom, perhaps. But 'Dabbling his sleek young hands in Irish gore!' "—the Earl snorted—"that goes too far, our poet peer is a touch dramatic and more than a touch unjust, I think. He worked for the Union in 1800, as many Irish did sincerely, and it was perhaps unwise in the event, but with Pitt, he resigned from the Ministry when George III went back on his promises, as they thought, on Catholic Emancipation. You have not met him, Edward: a reserved, difficult quiet man, very plain, his elegance distingushed but very simple, of great dignity, and I myself think, entire integrity. When you are well, I should like you to meet him."

Edward's face registered no expression. The Earl paused and flicked a glance towards him, and then he asked abruptly, in direct and blunt attack, "What happened to you, Edward, at the hands of Alleyn's Irish firebrands? What could have happened that you cannot tell?" He sighed. "That boy was born to be a leader, in law or out of law. He was charming and ruthless, like all natural leaders: under their seeming humanness, their blood is entirely cold and directed to their own ends. He could capsize a nation, and laugh. You have told me now about Armstrong. Tell me about that." He paused. "I wish you would, Edward. I think you should."

Edward shut his eyes. "I do not see why you think so. What will telling about it help? I cannot imagine why anyone should want to hear, but if you do, it does not matter now." He spoke as if he were asleep, indifferently. "I was bound and stripped and cut and burned and whipped and hung, never entirely, just enough, and made to sing before them all, and made to kiss the men who hurt me, blindfolded, their hands, their feet, their mouths, their things. Then I was left for Marion to finish with, as he liked. He did not choose, he was very kind. It happened to enlighten me about the Irish, when I kept him back from some meeting he had set up. His real friends had tied him in a chair and pulled the curtains to, trying to keep him from being expelled, which happened, anyway. They asked me to sit with him, and I did, and he was very angry about it, but he did not really want me hurt. That was an accident. I was very sick, sick really, and sick inside, but I have forgotten it now. At least, I think I have." His eyes shut, he did not see the shock and disgust that passed across the Earl's face.

The Earl made no direct comment on Edward's little story. After a moment, he said, quietly, "All sentiment aside, Edward, the day of the great Irish kingdoms some say existed (but I don't know that I believe they did) has been long over. It will not and it cannot return. Nothing of that is the same. The people there are not the same, the world is not the same. The conquered are never the same, even when they can influence their conquerors, and the Irish have been too many times conquered. They exist now as a nation to be conquered, if not by us, then the French. They are entirely too easily influenced, too easily worked upon. Even the Irish leaders now, Rowan and O'Connell, know that, and they have seen revolution and excess, at home, and in France where they had to escape, and they are sickened with easy blood. We could not have the French across a narrow channel from us on two sides, one is entirely too much. I should think anyone could see that, if they stopped to think. Had it not been for Lord Portland's easy tolerance of them as Home Secretary then, this country's dissidents would have suffered more than they complain of. He had unprecedented power—through the Alien Act, the Treason Act, the Sedition Act, against 'Traitorous Correspondence and Seditious Meetings'—and he used it less than he might have— against the Irish themselves or the talkers at home. Lord Sidmouth, that was Addington, is Home Secretary now, and he is a very different matter, entirely severe, entirely stern. God knows what we shall see under him. I remember what my friend Fox, my personal friend, not my political friend, said of Addington when he was prime minister, and his Whig friends said better an incompetent Whig Addington than Pitt back again. Fox, rest him, said he would rather have Pitt than a 'fool': 'I can't bear fools; anything but fools.' I should release him into heaven myself for that remark; but that man is who we have now, and we must bear with it. One can be sentimental if one likes oneself, Edward, but one cannot count on anyone else or any other nation being sentimental too, and they are much more likely not to be. The self-interested feed on the sentimental. The French fed on our well-meaning Liberals, or thought to. But I think few people and few nations are really sentimental: it is a luxury of an illusion the very tough and the very powerful sometimes foolishly allow their children to play with."

He looked at Edward's pale shuttered unhappy face, and his eyes fixed on the boy's turned-away ones, and he said very gently, "Harriett has told me you consider yourself one of the conquered, Edward. She was most distressed, and she rounded on me in a most fierce manner. I was quite surprised. I may have treated you badly, I have even admitted to it, but I am not unique, and not even as severe as many parents, and their children survived adequately. George II imprisoned the Prince of Wales, his son, in his room, and George III, that Prince's son, would have transported the Regent, had his power been sufficient, when his son was still Prince of Wales. Have you heard those stories, Edward? I could tell you many others." He watched Edward's face, but it did not change, or move, what he could see of it. "Shall I admit then, I have been, if not the worst, among them? Must I? Is that what you would have me do? What then? You, conquered? I have heard few ideas so absurd, I hope you are not labouring under that delusion now. You, the conqueror of Rockfort and Alleyn, two unassailable citadels heretofore until you appeared. Nations are conquered, and sometimes must be, individuals

never, if they choose not to be. You are the least conquered and con-
querable person I know, Edward, you have endless reserves I for one do
not dream of having. You fall back upon them and they reinforce you,
or you call them and they come forward to your aid. There is no ultimately defeating you at all, for there is no single object you require.
You have been uncommonly sick, and your immediate reserves are exhausted, that is all. You will find them again when you are stronger and
when you open your eyes and will face what you have seen and what you
really are and what I really am and what the world is. I wish you would
look at me, Edward, I cannot talk to a cheek. Do you want Harriett?
Would you like to see her? I imagine I could arrange something. Would
you like me to rent a house and for you or for us to go stay with her?"

"No," Edward whispered, "not even to leave this house. I want to
forget that."

"Well," said the Earl, "so entirely be it. What were we speaking of?
The inexorable march of the comman man, wasn't it? And Napoleon and
Wellington and Castlereagh, no?—that year for violent births.

"But I will tell you this, Edward, though I daresay you already know
it. I may see these things but I am not a humanitarian. I love a particular
piece of music more than I do an unknown man. I am a little sorry for
suffering, but it seems to me our lot. Extension of the franchise does not
excite me, I deplore it. It does not particularly matter to me whether the
majority serves the few, or whether the few serve the majority, as I
imagine someday they will. To me, a murder is a murder, a lie is a lie,
no matter who committed by, no matter for what end. If there is any
one thing particularly abhorrent to me, it is a detestable action committed in the name of some glorious end." He paused, aware of Edward's
startled eyes fixed upon him, unaware that in his words Edward surprisingly heard the echo of his own, spoken years ago in Alleyn's rooms.
But since Edward did not speak, he continued to pursue his own line
of thought. "I have seen many such actions, and I have not found them
confined to any one race or class or government or religion, or to the rich
or to the poor. I have found them in all ranks done equally and equally
likely, depending only upon the particular natures of the particular men,
not dependent upon the circumstances of immediate hunger or satisfaction. You may say, you particularly, and with reason, I am a strange man
to speak of morality. I have only one defence for myself. Whatever I may
myself have done, I have never done for any end other than the end I
declared, and I have deceived no one in the way of doing it. If I have
the advantage of wealth, it has come from past direct service of my

family to its king, and present husbandry. But I am glad to have it. I distrust the people and I distrust the crown alike. For myself, I wish only the personal power to protect myself and my own from the cruelty, misguided or intentional, of the majority or of the few, as I have been able to do you." He paused. "I have been frightened, Edward, for the first time in my life, that I should not be able to do what I set out to do or accomplish my end."

"I can easily tell I am related to you now," Edward said, his hand over his eyes, "for you also talk at much length, dear Holland, and my head aches, and I am so wretched. Please just hold me, please don't talk. I don't want to think about these things, or about myself, or about anything."

The Earl was silent, and did as Edward asked. It was hard, the Earl thought, to lay down one's life for a friend, and for that friend to be dead, and oneself alive, and only sick. Later, when George relieved him, he met Lord Armstrong in the downstairs hall.

"What that young man of ours needs," the Earl of Havermore said to the Earl of Tyne, "is an interest outside of himself, to make him want to get well; something to do. Too much leisure, too much time, nothing he has to do. Too cold in Scotland, take him stalking there, otherwise. Is he strong enough to ride to hounds? He can shoot now, can't he? He does own land? I could take him over to the Quorn, if he is, or Robert could arrange a shoot, beaters or over dogs, either way."

"I agree with you in general principle," the Earl said gently, "but I do not think that is quite the thing for Edward just now."

"It makes the blood stir," the Scotch Earl said, "the hounds in cry, and the horses after, a hundred or more, every kind of man from dukes to chimney sweeps in full pursuit. Boy needs his blood stirred by something. Not getting well here. Thought Anne would do it, but that doesn't seem to be working out, does it?"

"His nerves are strung differently than Robert's," the Earl said quietly, "and they have been shocked off pitch. He loves that girl of yours, and one way or another I think he will come to know it again, if she will bear with him as he is now." He looked at the Earl, his eyes dark and unpenetrable, and added casually, "A whipping would rather put a young man off, don't you think? Not a good memory to connect? Monks knew that. Better than a cold bath. Someone, I think, knew what they were about, when he ordered that."

"So you know about that," Havermore remarked. "Hoped you didn't. Bad business, that. Not my doing. Stopped it, you know, would have sooner, didn't know in time. Bad mistake. Didn't know the boy, either of us then. Too much pride, on our part, all along. Far too much. Boy tell you? Told him I would meet you, tell you that. Said he wasn't going to."

The Earl shook his head. "I knew nothing at all about it until this Summer. Come, Havermore. You would have heard from me, if I had known earlier. You surely know that."

"Thought so. Glad not to. Too damned good a shot, by more than half, but would have. Past now?"

The Earl held out his hand. "For my part, most certainly past now, and for Edward's, long ago, in the sense you mean. But he does not feel about your family now, as he was disposed to do, before your nephew had that done, or you promised to repeat it. I hardly blame him for that, do you?"

The Scotch Earl shook his head. "No. Our loss. Boy has my name. Rather have him for my heir, than Robert, but Robert counting on it now."

"And he is my son, and my heir," the Earl said, somewhat absently. "You will have to be content now with something else. We may all have to be," he added, getting up, tired of the conversation. "I am seriously worried. Good God, man, a *hunt?* He cannot even walk."

❂❂❂❂❂❂❂❂❂❂❂❂❂❂❂

CHAPTER VIII

Vienna: Winter and Spring: 1815–1816

I

"You have been too long in this bed," the Earl said consideringly. "Let's see if you can get up." He pulled back the covers from Edward's fever-wasted form, and put an arm around his shoulders, and forced him to move his legs and feet to the floor, and to stand, but his weakened legs would not support him. The Earl slipped an arm under his thin legs and picked him up and carried him to the window, and sat down with him in the late Autumn sunlight.

"You are a mere featherweight," he said, lightly but very concerned, "I do not know where the rest of you has flown to. Anne says you will not eat. Are you bent on making all my efforts of no use? I am going to attend your supper tonight myself, and see that you do."

The boy—for he seemed one, his manhood seemed vanished—pressed himself against the Earl as if he would melt into him or become the Earl's mere shadow, and the Earl put his arms about him and held him closely.

"You aren't improving," he said with mock severity, "Edward, why don't you improve?"

"I can't eat, when Anne is there, or her family," he whispered.

"Well, I can't stay with you *all* the time. Robert is reconciled, I am ceding him a piece of land his family always tried to claim, and he is in the field with his hounds all day."

"I know. I hear them. I hate the sound. Robert is reconciled—reconciled to *what?*"

"To your marriage, silly Edward, with his sister. What else? Isn't that what you wanted?"

"Once," Edward whispered. "I don't want it now."

The Earl was considerably surprised, despite the signs he had observed. "You surprise me," he said slowly. "What do you want? Do you know?"

For answer Edward put his thin wasted arms about the Earl's neck and drew his mouth to his, and clung to it as though its breath were his own, and his very life. The Earl said nothing, and he made no move to disengage Edward, until the boy himself fell back, exhausted.

"It is not possible here," he said slowly, wondering how to use this revelation.

"I want to go away from here, and from these people. Oh, Holland, please take me away, please take me home."

"Northumberland is too cold, and too bleak, and too lonely, Edward. I should go mad myself there, to stay there all winter. Knighton tells me you will not survive a Winter in London with its soot and fog, in this condition. What's to do?" he said helplessly, as he had once before. "I thought we were well here."

The boy pressed his face into the Earl's chest, and did not answer. The Earl stroked his hair with his hand. "And I cannot believe you would mean it," he said gently, "if you were yourself, and stronger. It is death to you, and you know it, and I know it now. I thought us well interrupted." He picked the boy up again in his arms. "But if you do, I want you to work for me. You must try to eat, and you must try to walk. Will you do that, Edward?" The boy nodded. The Earl laid him back in his bed, and covered him again. "I will take all your meals with you, and if you will make yourself strong, I will take you for Christmas and the winter to Vienna. The Treaty will be signed then. I might even take you for the Grand Tour you have never had. Will you like that?"

Edward did not answer directly. "Would you call Dr. Lind?" he asked.

"Dr. Lind? Cook's adviser? Is he still alive?"

"I don't know. It is his son. He knows me. He is at Windsor, I think."

"I am sorry, Edward, I did not know you knew him. He died three years ago, while you were gone."

"Oh," Edward said drearily. "He might have known what to do, he knew once before, when I felt like this, just a little."

"Try to tell me then," the Earl whispered. "I will help you, Edward, but you must also help yourself, and help me to help you."

Edward shut his eyes, and his voice was barely audible. "I will try," he said, but he did not turn his head away. He opened his eyes briefly, and looked at the Earl, into his dark distressed ones, and then he shut his own again.

The Earl attended, as he had said he would, at Edward's meals, and he sent George with the Scotch Earl and Robert's assistance out for all manner of delicacies: wheatears, and fat ruffs and reaves, Devonshire cream, Severn salmon, now that the Thames salmon had stopped running, as it had about the turn of the century, Dunstable larks, Whitstable oysters. With the Earl's careful forcing, Edward did grow stronger, and he was able to take short walks on the terrace in the air that even in mid-November was still mild, but his disposition was embittered and hardhusked around his spirit which had removed itself from a world it had found too cruel. He did not want to talk to Anne at all—when he saw her hurt and bewildered, he did not care. If he realised her unstinting labour for him for weeks, it brought him no pleasure to know it.

"I am what I am," he said to her one day savagely on the terrace. "I cannot promise you anything. Do not look at me as you do."

"And what is that, that you so are?" she asked, her small pointed chin resolutely lifted against the hurt he inflicted, but her voice not firm.

"You know, and I know you know. We should lead a hellish life. There has been too much said, and too much done. We can never forget. I cannot forget. I thought I could but I cannot. Not any of it. I was whipped by your brother, by his grooms, for being what I am, did you know that, Anne? If we were in bed together, you would see the scars. He did not even know me yet he did it, he had it done. I cannot bear to be here, remembering, and seeing him, and seeing Lord Armstrong. We talk and we smile, but it is more real now than it was. I cannot forget." He saw her face, and was overcome with brief penitence. "God forgive me, I never meant to tell you, Anne. But you see, we shall always only hurt each other. That is all we do."

"It did not use to be."

"Always, I just did not care then. We mustn't talk, Anne. I am only an exposed nerve now, there's nothing else left to me. I shall only hurt you, anything I say." His voice was anguished now and rough. "You want too much from me, I don't have it now to give you. I have nothing left now to give anyone."

"Let me give to you," she offered quietly.

"I don't want what you have," he answered brutally. "And it is not leap year yet, not until next year, not for two months."

"And it was all just words, before?"

He looked at her strangely, and turned away. "I don't remember. I don't know what you mean." He turned away, a look of misery on his face. She was too sorry for him to be angry or even hurt.

"All right," she said, "but come with me, Edward. I have something I want to show you. You can at the least do that." He followed her down the wide stone steps, across the lawn, his steps slow and still dragging, to a corner of the garden beneath her room. She had stopped to take a trowel from the gardener, and now she stooped, careless of her muslin dress and her thin slippers on the ground, and began to dig beneath some yellowed withered strips that lay mattered on the surface of the ground, almost hidden by the late Michaelmas daisies and the chrysanthemums. She pulled up finally a hard-soft papery brown thing, and shook the dirt from it and from its roots.

"Here," she said, holding it out. "Take it. You gave it to me and told me to keep it and I did. I watched it bloom for five years. It had a lovely flower. Take it back now."

"What am I to do with that," he said, not offering to take it, his face showing no emotion, unless distaste.

"Cut it up, throw it away, whatever you like," she said, almost crying, offering the shrivelled thing. "You gave it to me for a lesson. I am giving it to you."

He reached out his hand, and took the bulb, and the trowel as well, and stooped down himself. "I am going to plant it again. Something may come of it yet. I don't think so, but one does not know. Anyway, that is what one does with bulbs. Because I am dead inside, it does not need to die, or be disturbed." He pushed it back into the ground, and covered it with earth, and stood up, shaking the dirt from his fingers.

"I do not want you to hope, Anne. I am not like this flower. There is nothing to hope for and nothing to expect. Please believe me." She turned her face away, loving yet humiliated, unable to leave, despite the cruel thrusts of his words. "I have bad blood in me, Anne," he said gently, suddenly speaking really to her, "bad for you, that is. I do not think the Clare in me can outweigh it, I do not think it is strong enough.

And I have been abominably and heartlessly raised, ever since I can remember now. I did not use to think it mattered; I see it does now. You do not want such blood in your children, or if you think you do, you should not."

"Edward," she said rather desperately, her face still averted, "you do not understand. I like Tyne, I like him very much. We have grown to become friends. I do not mind at all he is your father, I am glad he is."

He took her face briefly in his hands and turned it to him. "It is you who do not understand, my dear. You do not understand at all. I have consented. You do not even know what that means but it does not matter. It is too late now. I do not want you any more." She could not escape either his voice or his eyes raw with his grief he would not share, stabbing her with his unforgettable, unforgivable words that he meant to be. "I was not really raped. I consented. I did love you once. It is true, and you know I did, but I am asking you now to just forget me. I came back only for my father. Only for that. And I want nothing but him now. I want no children. I do not want to love anyone else again. I don't want to go any farther, or any part of me to. I want to end." He looked at her for a moment, his face pale with weakness, but not with emotion, his eyes remote and without feeling. Then he turned and walked away, despite his height, a slight lonely figure, and did not turn his head or look back.

The next day, his father took him away. The Second Treaty of Paris had been signed, and the acts of the Congress of Vienna were again in effect. They crossed to the coast in his travelling chaise, using post horses, on the new fast macadamized roads, and had the coach taken on board the ship itself, and disembarked in France. Edward remembered very little of the trip. He slept for most of it, his head in his father's lap. They crossed the country east of Paris, still devastated by Napoleon's last hard-pressed march across it, the crop-poor people hungry and suspicious and unfriendly, and into Switzerland, and across the passes of the Alps. When they were briefly blocked by snow and were attacked by wolves, Edward showed no fear, but sat watching the hungry slavering fire-eyed great beasts dispassionately.

"I am glad we are not in a sleigh," the Earl remarked. "I was pursued by the ugly brutes in an open troika in a forest there, when I was in Russia. Not very enjoyable." He took a pistol from its holster in the coach, and opened fire carefully, and was rewarded by a yelp. "They want the horses," the Earl said, "but I don't intend for them to have them. The Russians carried a small serf or two with them on trips just to throw out in emergencies like this, but we won't throw you or the horses to them. We shall keep you both, but we shall have to get out and clear the road, all of us, before night falls, for there is no way to kindle a fire. I wish our other coach would come up."

Edward dismounted without fear, and worked with the Earl and the coachman and the footmen. He fired off an occasional shot, and threw snowballs he rolled up, at the wolves, and worked with his hands at the debris on the road. When one seized the coachman's wrist, he walked up to the red-fanged slavering beast, and knocked it away with a hard piece of ice, and shoved snow in its face and jaws. They were all relieved when the second coach lumbered up, and George and Foxham and the grooms appeared to assist.

"Well," said the Earl, when they were finally on their way again. "You didn't seem afraid. It might have ended badly."

"I wasn't," said Edward. "I did not care."

The Earl looked at him oddly, but he did not comment. Edward did not seem the worse for the adventure. His cheeks were flushed from the exertion, and though he was shivering, the colour made him look better, except for his burnt-out eyes.

They reached Vienna, at the height of the Christmas season, where Edward for the first time saw little trees everywhere, lit with tapers. "It is a custom here," the Earl said, "each child has his own little tree. How shall we keep Christmas this year, Edward?"

"No way at all."

"Edward, your mother died, and you yourself taught me how to grieve, and you recovered. That was worse. At most you knew this young man a few weeks, eight, ten, no more."

"I was not there, I did not see it happen."

"But I was."

"He did not want to die."

"No more did she. No one does. I thought that was what your religion was about, how to die, how to let go, how not to regret the surrender, of oneself or of one's friends."

"She did not die in chains," the young man gasped.

"In a way she did that, too," the Earl said, shaken even now by the memory, "in chains of flesh." He was sorry when he had said it, and glad Edward showed no understanding.

"This was a real chain, a three-inch chain, he was chained with it, chained down. I could not get it off. He was alive, and I could not get it off." He began to shiver, like a leaf in the wind. "I cannot forget it, it is always before my eyes."

"You are sentimentalizing, Edward. He looked delicate, but he was a tough boy and a tough man. He went directly through to whatever he wanted and took it. Very little stopped him until death itself did. He was well able to take whatever the world dealt him, and to deal it back well in his turn before it took him. You know that, or you knew it once. He was not like you, and at this moment, I could wish you more like him. The world requires some toughness. I thought you had more than you show now. You always seemed to, you told me once you did. Do you remember? You see, I remember everything you have ever said to me. I do not know what has happened to you."

"I see only the water, and his face," Edward whispered.

The Earl looked at Edward thoughtfully. "Edward, you surely aren't afraid of Hell? I know some enthusiasts are. For you, or for your friend? Is that it, is that what is troubling you so? Your feeling is excessive, I do not understand it. Does this lie behind it?"

"I don't know," Edward said, his face shuttered. "I don't think about that much. I don't care. I would rather go to Hell, if there is such a dreadful place, and be there with those I love, if they are there, than go to Heaven without them. But I don't believe in Hell as a horrid place of physical pain, I think like Wesley it is Hell because it is isolation, and we carry it about with us when we are in it, now as well as later, and it is Hell because it cuts us off from the face of God, and after that from the face of everyone, even those we love, and for no other reason. We cannot help others out of it, nor ourselves. That is where Grace must come, and help us, when we cannot help ourselves any longer. I do not care about this, Holland. I am past caring. If I am in Hell now, or if I must go there, I do not care. But oh Holland, he wanted to love me, and I would not let him. Why do we not let those love us who wish to while we can."

"Why not indeed," the Earl murmured. "Why not Anne?"

"It is too late," he said wildly, "I am as dead for Anne."

"And me?"

"You do not want me any more, and I haven't the strength. And it is not the same."

It was true. Despite their closeness, it was innocent. The Earl could no more have touched him in a mature way than he could have violated him when he was actually the small child he now seemed to be, and Edward was unable to force the issue through himself. His energies were unequal to anything requiring emotional action. On Christmas Eve, he left the Earl's side, when he was sleeping, and found his laudanum, and took it all. Whether he wished to kill himself or not he did not clearly think, he wished only to obliterate Christmas from his thoughts and to evade it with its pressing certainties of pain and loss after joy. He lay down quietly by the Earl, when he had taken it, and put his arms around him, and lay still, so, until he felt the world he feared now so began to slip away from him.

When the Earl woke in the morning, he could not wake Edward. He recognised the signs, and checked his supply and found it completely gone. He sent for a doctor, and for coffee, and while the choir boys sang in the gold-crossed Cathedral of St. Stephen's across from the hotel, he and the doctor walked Edward up and down the room and gave him ipecac and made him vomit and gag, hardly conscious, and to drink endless coffee that they poured down him like a variant of the water torture. It all did no good, the opium had been absorbed into his system. There had not been enough grains in solution to kill him, only to throw his nervous system farther off. When the deep sleep wore off, he was assailed by tremors that shook him and visions that made him scream and sweat.

He was in a drawing room again, but the eyes and mouths of all the men and women, as they looked at him, were full of death worms, writhing in the hollows of the empty pupils, and their teeth were blackened and rotted and fallen away, and their luxuriously dressed hair turned grey and in wisps and hanks before his eyes, and fell away. The clinging muslin dresses that they wore over their dampened slips clung wholly transparently now to collapsed wombs and fallen breasts with eyes in place of nipples, and they carried dead embryos in their hands like fans. The members of their male partners swelled and grew and enlarged beneath their tight stretched court breeches and burst through with a life of their own eclipsing the faces of the men behind them, spraying like the fountains of the Regent's party he had attended. In the little rooms to the side, guests were playing with cards of transparent fire, and the footless glasses they held perpetually, unable to set them down, were filled with blue fire and made of fire. The clawed legs of the chairs and tables, in the new fashion of crocodiles and lions, gleamed green and gold, and undulated and swayed, leaving their places and weaving themselves in a dance about the floor, while the musicians, unperturbed, continued to play, but music that grew louder and louder and swirled and pounded against his eardrums and would not stop, even when he screamed for it to cease. It had an odd surging, retreating, and resurging rhythm, like the decaying dancers' breath, swelling and falling in discordant sounds that he had never heard before. He left the dance, and stumbled down the steps that unfolded before him and rolled up behind him as he went, the sconces in the walls made of human hands, living and fleshed, springing curled from the brackets in the wall, their fingertips burning with blue flames that dropped wax like hot rain on his face. The ground fell away beneath him, and he held to the pavement's edge to save himself, and the lights in all the beautiful buildings around him flashed on and off like lightning illuminating through the windows that had lost their glass the insides that were like the empty ruins of the fallen Abbeys. The stones themselves grew immaterial like stones of clouds, but he could see through them to the foul black gaols on which each were built instead of basements, in which ragged creatures that seemed inhuman, half-naked, but their flesh whole and human, swayed in their three-inch chains and tried to bail with rusted bottomless begging cans the river that was flowing through the cellars, inundating them and rising to drown them. He could see a moon three-quarters gone, above him, in a bloody haze. And the river did rise then, and swept them all away, himself, clinging to the pavement still, horses and carriages, patient and unconcerned, dancers and danced upon, all like leaves and straws and sticks and scum whirled away into the sea that waited to meet them and took them all. They were choking and drowning in the dirty brown flood, and then suddenly the dirt and the mud vanished and they were in the sea itself. He floated there then, not sinking, turning slowly in the dark waters, alone, he thought, until he saw beside him a small child, not an infant, not a real child, with fair hair and eyes that looked back at him that were his own.

"You are the Christmas child," he cried, his voice shaking with instant love. The child seemed to answer, "Yes." He reached out his hands, longingly, whether to save the child or merely to hold and embrace it he did not know, but the still, sucking waves carried the child away from him. He seemed to hear again the words, "remember that a child's dream is divine," and he wanted to cry to the child to wait and to explain, but it sank from him. He could see it, its face shining out of the depths, not moving or trying to save itself, through the water that had suddenly become clear and crystalline. "I would come too, wait for me, I would come too," he cried again and again, but the water held him away like a pliant pane of glass and he could neither reach the child to raise it or join it himself. He began to sob desperately, and then more quietly on and on and on, until his voice was only a whisper and he sobbed without a voice. He could still hear a voice, however, beating about him, and calling him, asking him something, wanting something of him.

He was out of the water now, and lying on a beach, or was it a table or a bed. He was a turtle now, heavily armoured, but someone was turning him over to his vulnerable side, and swollen and grotesque, jamming himself into him and inside him. He was bursting with the pain, his inner body dissolving into sand and water, unable to move beneath the force crushing and annihilating him, cracking his shell apart and forcing him out, helpless. But as fast as the shell broke, a new one appeared that hardened quickly and encased him. Then abruptly his drugged senses briefly cleared but the sensations continued, and he realised that he was actually in someone's grasp and had been taken and that the person was on him and in him. His ears were full and deafened with the shock of the physical motion, as with the waves. Even the sound of the voice faded from his closed ears. He lay quiet, on the sand or on the bed, his eyes shut against the tumultuous chaos about him. He opened his eyes briefly but the furniture swayed like trees and put out feathery fronds, and he shut them quickly. He reached for the hand he felt near him, that was his father's hand, and brought it to lie beneath his face and his lips, and relaxed. The child is father of the man, he thought to himself confusedly, the words forming and entering into his mind, we are one and the same. He became aware then of nothing but the tree within him, its shaft like a great shattering Roman spear penetrating him. When it reaches my heart, I shall die, he thought calmly, suddenly remembering his childhood imagining of the giant in the mountains, and he waited for the moment, even longing for it, to welcome the sharp piercing that would end finally his pain, but it did not come. He fell asleep, instead, the tree beneath him, above him, in him, all around him, infinitely immense, infinitely comforting. He was on the sea now again, but not drowning, safe with the tree which held him up from the spiralling depths in which others were drowning. So he spent his Christmas Day.

II

He awoke the next morning, drenched with sweat, as wet as though he had actually been in the sea itself, and still in his father's encircling arms. The Earl seemed asleep, but when Edward stirred, he opened his tired eyes and smiled a little at him.

"Well, Edward," he said, "you want whipping." That was all he said.

"Yes, sir," Edward said, "but please forgive me, Holland. I have had terrible dreams."

"I daresay," said the Earl. "You are sweating like a horse that has been run. What possessed you, Edward?" He disengaged himself and rose to find Edward a dry nightgown, which he tossed to him.

"I could not bear it to be Christmas," was all Edward said. His fingers would not obey him, and his limbs were made of soft rubber, and the Earl had to change his nightgown completely for him. "It was terrible. The world was all dissolving. I would have drowned, but you held me up."

"I thought I must do something. I merely wished to distract. Pay no attention to opium dreams, Edward, and for God's sake, take no more like that. I will go in another room if you do, and leave you to it alone. Myself, I cannot survive another such twenty-four hours." He was silent, staring at the boy, unable to take his eyes away.

"I feel so strange, and you look so strange, Holland," Edward whispered. "Your face and your forehead are all changed. I have never seen you look this way. What is the matter, Holland?" His memory only faintly stirred. Two veins, making a V-shaped mark, like a hasty check mark, in the center of the Earl's forehead just above the meeting of his arched brows, had filled beneath the skin and were throbbing and pulsing, lending together a particularly satanic countenance to his shadowed face in the half-light of the early morning.

"Haven't you?" said the Earl, breathing heavily. "Many people have. I thought you had. I am glad if you think you haven't. I suppose you mean the veins on my forehead. Are they visible now? They must be. I call it Cain's Mark. It has been there a long time. It is the only mark of God I have." He caught his breath. "I feel strange, too, Edward—I am too tired." He slipped his hands under the boy's nightgown, against the soft skin of his back and his stomach, and raised the nightgown up to his arms.

"Holland, I think I am going to faint," Edward whispered, shutting his eyes against the look directed on him, dizzy and unable to move, "please don't now. I feel so sick."

"I am unleashed now, I cannot control myself," the Earl said harshly, angrily with himself. "Oh, God, Edward, brace yourself, resist me. I am going to misuse you terribly. Do not let me," he cried, locking the boy against him with all his strength. He felt him pant and gasp, incapable of evading him, or struggling, with his useless limp limbs against which the Earl tightened his own. He pressed his mouth hard on the boy's shaking, crying, quailing lips, stifling his cries, drinking them like a food until he realised the figure he held had fainted, and then he used him as he wished, and fell asleep himself.

Edward woke again, bruised and hurt, still pressed beneath the heavier weight, feeling as if he would suffocate. I am going to die, he thought, like this, but his body struggled, and in its faint struggles woke the Earl who released him. He looked down at Edward's face, his own inscrutable, into his darkened eyes that despite their terror met him without fear.

"You were not loving me," he whispered, "you were angry, you were punishing me. As you did once before. I remember it now."

"Yes," the Earl said.

"How horrible," Edward whispered. "Are you often like this?"

"Often. You have just never quite seen me so. You did not really know me. Even after all these years."

"No," Edward whispered, still shocked, his brain and his senses preternaturally clear. "No, I did not. But it has not been long—not a year altogether, all the years told."

"I have always kept a restraint, except that other once, but my control slipped, and let the devil in me out. It was always there. I saw your flesh glistening with sweat, and your mind removed from me, and I did not care."

"Why did you tell me to resist you? I did once, and you only hurt me worse, until I stopped and did not. I would not any more, even if I could have been able to. You used to warn me not to, and then I learned why you did. Why not now? Is it more amusing for you to hit me and to choke me first?"

"Don't, Edward," the Earl said, "I don't want to. It comes over me, and I cannot help myself. I am not safe then. I am not safe now."

"I know," Edward said, his eyes on the Earl's face, on his wide, mobile, beautifully shaped lips, avoiding the veins still pulsing in his forehead with the pounding of the blood behind them.

"I have loved you, in my way, and I have tried not to let you know this. Have I hurt you?"

"Yes," Edward whispered. "It has been too long, I am not used to you now, or like this, but I do not care. Hurt me again. I think I am going to die of this, but I do not care." He felt completely helpless, ill and weak, across the water and beyond the mountains, in a city he did not know, a language he did not know, with a man grown suddenly strange to him, prey again to emotions too familiar to him.

His mind remained clear, although he was unable to move, except to move his legs a little apart. He shut his eyes, removing the last restraint of their tired clear gaze from the Earl's vision, and waited. He felt his gown stripped from him, and the Earl take entire charge of his body giving his members a life of their own that his own will could not govern. As passive a tool as ever moved upon wire, he thought to himself bitterly of himself, using a phrase of Mr. Wesley's that had struck him particularly. His senses exploded about him, but his mind remained removed, seeing all his life as in transparent pictures of glass moving before him. He did not care whether he lived or died, or whether he remained sane or lost his self, but he felt instinctively that the way he was now going would bring for him his own death, in some way, and he welcomed it.

He saw the pictures of his mother and his Armstrong father, back into years he thought he had forgotten, when his life was simple and loving and loved. He seemed to live each moment of those years again, timelessly, effortlessly, in the transparent pictures before his eyes. Nothing was forgotten. He realised again that he had only known love then, in those brief years, but he also realised that it had been enough, for he had known what it was, free and limitless and uninvolved, expecting but not demanding, guiding, not forcing. His spirit cried out for it again, but he made no cry with his lips, which were no longer his own. He was imprisoned now in fetters of flesh, and he shivered and was unable to move or to break them and to stop the destruction wreaked and converging upon him, but the child who had known love continued to struggle to be reborn, and to cry out that what was happening to him now and had taken him from himself since his sixth year, had nothing at all to do with love. And yet he felt no hate for the man who could not love him without hating him and wanting to destroy him, but his spirit struggled to be free, seeing so clearly the cruelty of the emotion.

"I have always loved you, but you do not love me, Holland," he whispered, into the lips ravaging his, "you do not know how."

"No," the Earl admitted. He turned the boy roughly over, ignoring his clear voice, aware only of his passive limbs.

"You hate me rather. You love only an accident of flesh."

"Perhaps I do."

"I know you do. I do not mind dying, but you should mind killing me."

"You will not die of this. Bite on the sheet if you cannot be quiet."

Edward was silent. He knew what he meant. Through the duality of the present moment, he perceived clearly the duality of his life since he had been brought to the North. His mind was briefly as it had been, though his body was entirely as it had been made to be. His mind urged on him the necessity of escape, but his body was incapable, and his will was nowhere. The moments of clarity clouded and merged again into a kind of delirium, the remnants of the opium dream refashioning themselves like a scattered army into semblance of a stand.

If I am a woman, he thought suddenly, and not a man, I will give birth to this child. He shut his eyes and felt his tormented body swept by waves of sensation, and he laboured to expel the weight, but when he had given birth, he imagined the Earl took the child and strangled it and threw it aside. He wrenched himself aside from the hands that would have held him, recovering a slight movement. He gave birth again and again, his body straining and expelling, and each time the Earl took the child and strangled it and threw it aside. Panic seized him that none would be left, that Cronos would swallow all, and he began to scream. He felt something bear down on his mouth, cavernous and moist, smothering his cries and his breath, and his hands without his volition, obeying his maternal panic, groped and fastened about the neck of the Earl with the strength of frenzy. The clarity that had been his had wholly vanished, and there was left only the need to fulfil an ancient expectation, he had forgotten what, and justify the hate that seemed determined to destroy him, and somehow save the child that he could hear gasping and crying. His hold was broken with a savage wrenching of arms that shocked back against the bones of his face, and the crumpled sheet was dragged against him. With exhaustion and the sudden pain he fell suddenly asleep, his face relaxed and peaceful as a child's.

When he awoke again, the bed and his night clothes were clean and quiet and cool. He did not open his eyes, but stretched out his hand, and felt the Earl's cool, strangely passionless fingertips take it.

"I have had such terrible dreams," he said slowly.

"They were not all dreams. If you wanted whipping, I do now myself. Forgive me, Edward?"

His hand tightened on the Earl's that he held clasped. "I dreamed I was reborn, I thought it was true, but now I am just the same."

"The drug is wearing off. I should put you in another's care. I am not fit, to have taken advantage of a sick boy."

"It did not matter. For a moment you made me forget—what I cannot forget—I thought only of myself. And I remembered things I had forgotten or thought I had. For that time those pictures replaced the— the others. For a while they seemed the only reality, but now they do not." He sighed. "Why did you hurt me so, Holland?" He opened his eyes, and followed the Earl's hand and arm to where he found the Earl sitting in the chair, chastened, his eyes ashamed but meeting Edward's.

"I hoped you would not remember. I behaved very ugly. My promises are worth nothing, they are straw. I think I should leave you."

"No, Holland," he pled, faintly. The clarity in which he had seen that was what he must again do had left him. "Do not tease me, you promised you would not. I cannot bear it if you go." He held out his arms, and the Earl, no more able to resist them than Edward not to offer, came into them and held the boy close.

"Did I try to kill you again, Holland," he asked after a moment, "or did I only think it?"

"After a fashion, you did. It was not much threat, and the circumstances warranted it."

"Oh, God," said Edward, "I do not want to at all. What does it mean?"

"It means you want to be free to live your life," the Earl said, looking at him compassionately.

"No," Edward said, turning his face away.

"Yes," the Earl said relentlessly, "you do, but you do not know you do yet. You are tired of grief, Edward, why hang on to it? You must read the story in Mr. Wesley's Journal about the man who dived into water to save a friend, who put his arm about his neck and held them both under until both were like to die; but the man first to need help died first and released his rescuer, who floated to the surface, recovered his breath, and struck out for shore. Strike out, Edward, you need not die too. You are afraid, I think, I am going to die too, like Alleyn, and leave you, and someday I will. But not now. You can leave me, Edward, and still see me, still be with me, still love me if you like." He realised he might as well be addressing the wall of an empty room, for all the impression his words made, and he stopped talking.

They spent the Winter quietly. The Earl took Edward to concerts several nights a week in private salons and in some public halls. He introduced him to musicians, and artists, but he did not press social evenings upon him. He introduced Edward briefly to Beethoven at the palace of Archduke Rudolph, where they heard the Trio dedicated to the Archduke, the No. 6 in B-Flat Major in which the composer did not himself take part, and the piano sonata also dedicated to the Archduke some years before, *"Das Lebewohl, Les Adieux,"* which that night he played himself. The Earl told Edward, smiling slightly, that the composer had just been given the guardianship of a nine-year-old boy.

"That man," the Earl whispered, his eyes on the man at the piano, "says that he is in direct contact with divinity, and when I hear what he has composed, I believe he may be. The *Andante Cantabile* of the Trio we heard makes open heaven as nearly for me as I think it will ever be. I would some of it might reach you. I must be quiet now. I have waited years to hear this sonata."

Edward made no comment, then or later, but his eyes continued to turn towards the musician, drawn to his harsh face, whose music through the Earl he had learned to worship, and then back to the harsh absorbed face beside him. During the third movement their eyes met, in a wordless brief communion of remembered emotion and understanding, remembering their own return.

That Winter the Earl put him to a master to continue to study pianoforte, and to a master for the violin, and they lived quietly. The Earl had hoped the music would unlock Edward's emotions, and the gaiety of the beautiful city his own gaiety, with its concerts of small Nightmusic serenades beneath the hotel windows, gypsy music on street corners and in street cafés with *maulfreundlich* wine, and the rousing morning bands of the military, the great trees of the Vienna woods, stripped and bare now, their black branches arching like choir arches, their easy distinguishing characteristics fallen from them, and the slow flowing shining Danube in its center, but neither change appeared, whatever working might be happening underneath his frozen face and his bleak blank eyes. The crisp air, however, and the Viennese cooks and the walks the Earl sent him out on changed him from a skeleton barely fleshed again into a more ordinary-weighted young man of twenty-six with some slight colour in his cheeks. He had still no appetite and no hunger, but he ate the beautiful food at his father's persistence, choking on it as if it were scraps of cardboard. As his twenty-seventh birthday approached he began to look less like an emaciated fifteen, and more like what he was, but the return was only in looks.

Sometimes to the Earl watching him listening to music, this time Mozart's G Minor, seemingly absorbed in it, his eyes seemed to soften, but more often he only seemed farther away still, locked somewhere inside himself. When the music ended, he showed no change that was visible. He was quiet, and if anything sadder. For once Edward was unaware of the Earl's eyes upon him, after that earlier brief meeting of eyes, and the Earl was free to watch him without restraint, when he chose, as he had never before felt the desire to. The Earl's eyes stayed now more upon Edward than the performers, thoughtfully observing him, in profile beside him. He oftenest sat with his hands in his lap, his face without expression, but sometimes he rested his chin upon the knuckle of his first finger, the delicate fingers of his hand falling curled, relaxed, his weight on the arm of the chair, his coat sleeve falling back from his young wrist in a way that struck the Earl most poignantly, his deepset eyes with their darker delicate tracery of brow pensive, withdrawn. The Earl looked at the face so strange in its emotions to him now whose contours his own fingers knew better than his own: the small shell-like ear set back against the hair, at the generous heart-shaped line of the jaw and the full cheek with its high wide bone and delicate hollow sloping to the ear, smooth and fair, delicately coloured, like a girl's; the delicate flush of colour staining his sweet-molded lips, once so quick to smile. The Earl studied his face with his eyes now as if by that means the emotions behind it would become clear to him. Despite its sadness and its too-old look, and despite his experiences, his face still had kept its air of young innocence. His beauty, incredible to the Earl that it should exist in a single person and that person inconceivably come from himself, had increased with his suffering, not decreased. It pierced the Earl and eluded him, although at night he held it in his arms. He did not take it again, he did not dare.

As the snows began to diminish, Edward felt for the first time a conscious emotion, afraid to be bereft of their soft shielding, covering shelter. It was the transience of snow, he thought, unaware that he was thinking again, that made one welcome and love it so. Its gaiety and insouciance, filling the air where it did not belong, in its special dance, invading a world whose natural state was not snow. He wanted its cold softening, erasing colours, erasing form, erasing sharpness and dirt and ugliness, erasing odour except its own clear clean scent, even erasing or muffling sound, covering houses, churches, trees, bushes, horses, small animals, living people, churchyards, all alike. He wanted its light, weightless, slowing, numbing hood, he did not want Spring, or a return to diffusion, distinction, burgeoning tumult, colour, scent, individual differentiated movements and forms. He welcomed each snow that continued to fall.

One particularly last cold night he slipped out of the hotel and after walking about until he was tired, he sat down on a stone bench in a small park not far from the hotel and took off his coat and hat and gloves, bent his head and shut his eyes and let the falling flakes cover him. The Earl, waking, finding him gone, without stopping to dress, enlisted help, took his coach, and searched the dark city. As dawn broke, and the sweepers with their birch brooms appeared, he found him, unconscious or deeply asleep, picked him up, shaking off the snow, and brought him back. From that with the Earl's instant care he caught only a cold, but after that, the Earl locked the doors and windows to their room at night, reluctantly cautioned the hotel personnel and all his own staff, and sent George out with him on all his walks.

Edward understood very well the reason and the Earl's intention, though he made no comment. He did not care enough to attempt to elude George or to run from him. He paid him no attention at all, as if he were not there, not speaking to him, looking through him, giving no thought or gratitude to George's old devotion that had moved him to leave his own wife and children to be of service now if he could in an unloved unloving city foreign and strange to him whose language and customs he did not understand. Edward would have been surprised had he known that in this behaviour George, though saddened and distressed, saw only that of his father the Earl, and so accepted it as unaccountable in the gentry. Or he might not have cared.

Edward's music master for the pianoforte was a young man, not so old as Edward, whom Salieri had recommended, short, stocky, powerful, his hair springing off his forehead in luxuriant wiry wild brown curls, his brows bushy over his weak near-sighted eyes and small round glasses, his lips full and well-developed but always pressed close together, his brow furrowed. He was unhappy himself, irritable and impatient with a fate that kept him poor and teaching when he had other things to do. He had no patience with Edward who could have done anything at all he wished, and he told him so, in his language that Edward understood only haltingly or in French, which he spoke haltingly. Their only real communication lay through the terms of music common to both.

"These harmonies are not for us alone, we cannot begin to understand them now, but as you butcher them, we do not hear them at all. He can do everything but we cannot understand everything. You are not trying, even, yet when you do, your right hand can sing, in the melody of the *cantabile*. Sing then, little Englishman, do you hear me, sing!"

"My hands are cold," Edward muttered, for he came to his teacher's rooms where the pianoforte stood.

"But you at least eat, no, Englishman?"

Finally, in irritation, he told Edward to go home, that he could do nothing for him.

"But first," he said, "Englishman who wants nothing, I, I who want everything, will show you something." He pushed Edward impatiently from the instrument, and sat down himself in his place. He began to play, and after a few minutes he seemed to forget Edward, and he began to sing, to a different piece of music that he began. Edward listened, fascinated yet hating its emotional pull.

"What is that?" he asked, when his teacher stopped. "What was it about? What do those words *Erl-könig* mean?"

"Earl-king," the young man said tersely, "a poem by your Ossian and our Goethe. I have set it to music myself, see, and Vogl shall sing it for me. Listen," and he played again the bass notes with their threatening triplet roll, "the father rides with his child in his arms." He began again to sing:

"Wer reitet so spät durch Nacht und Wind?"

He paused to translate, turning to Edward, after this and after each phrase that he sang, with emphatic looks and dramatic pauses:

"(Who rideth so late through night and wind?)

'Es ist der Vater mit seinem Kind'
(It is the father with his child);

'er hat den Knaben wohl in dem Arm,
er fasst ihn sicher, er hält ihn warm.'

(He has the boy so safe in his arm,
He holds him tightly, he folds him warm.)

And now the Earl-King comes, but only the child can hear what he says. The father asks:

'Mein Sohn, was birgst du so bang dein Gesicht?'
(My son, in terror why hidest thy face?)

and the little boy answers, his voice very high, so:

'Siehst, Vater, du den Erl-König nicht?'
(Oh, father, see the Earl-King is nigh!),
'den Erlen-könig mit Kron' und Schweif?'
(The Earl-King dreaded, with crown, and robe!).

But the father sees and hears nothing, and he does not believe the little

boy and he does not believe in his danger. He tells him it is only his imagination playing tricks, a streak of mist, a stirring of dead leaves, an
old grey tree. The Earl-King speaks. He calls the child to come away, so,
and entices him with pictures of what he will see and what he will do,
beautiful things, and he presses the child, so, harder and harder to come,
but hear how quiet his voice is, how dulcet, it is for a moment a little
waltz dance song, only two notes here to the bar, to persuade, as if
mesmerizing his will and taking it away; and the key itself changes, so:

> *'Du liebes Kind, komm, geh' mit mir!*
> *gar schöne Spiele spiel' ich mit dir;'*
> (My dearest child, come, go with me!
> Such merry plays I'll play with thee!)

He describes his beautiful garden, so, and the flowers, and the lovely
maidens, that are his daughters there, but the little boy will not listen.
He begs his father to tell him if he does not hear the Earl-King's soft
whispering in his ear too, but the father again tells him to be quiet. Then
the Earl-King sings, less sweetly now, the old key is gone, and you hear
the new sharps, now, no? Listen, so:

> *'Willst, feiner Knabe, du mit mir gehn?* . . .
> *Ich liebe dich, mich reizt deine schöne Gestalt*
> *und bist du nicht willig, so brauch' ich Gewalt.'*
>
> (Come, lovely boy, wilt thou go with me? . . .
> I love thee so, thy beauty has ravished my sense;
> And willing or not, I will carry thee hence.)

The child cries out, frantically, to his father to protect him, so:

> *'Mein Vater, mein Vater, jetzt fasst er mich an!*
> *Erl-könig hat mir ein Leid's getan!'*
>
> (My father, my father, now grasps he my arm,
> The Earl-King has seized me, has done me harm!)

Now the father believes him, but is it too late?

> *'Dem Vater grauset's, er reitet geschwind,*
> *er hält in Armen das ächzende Kind,'*
>
> (The father shudders, he rides like the wind,
> He clasps to his bosom the pale, sobbing child.)"

and the triplets roll again as they ride, hear, Englishman?

The young man's voice, already emotional, as if on stage singing and speaking from his swivelling piano stool in character the different roles, increased its fervour, lowering its register dramatically:

> "'erreicht den Hof mit Müh' un Not;
> in seinem Armen' . . .
>
> (He reaches home with fear and dread;
> Clasped in his arms . . .)"

The room was for a moment entirely still. Then the singer's voice pitched itself to a low awed tone, almost a whisper: "'das Kind' . . ."

He paused as if overcome by shock and grief's emotion, and then he sang the last two low notes in pitiful and final surprise: ". . . 'war tot.'"

"The child was dead," he said slowly and distinctly, playing slowly two last soft chords. He stopped singing, took his hands from the keys, and turned around entirely to Edward, his mood changed and exuberant, his speaking voice returned to its normal explosiveness. "That is a good song, no, you think not! Nothing there is like it quite before. It is for me, me only, to do, and I make my name, so! Go home, now, little boy, go home and learn to sing. You do no good here. You waste my time only. I have too much to do before the *Erl-könig* comes for me!"

Edward put his shaking hands in his pocket, the wild haunting music with its terrible and too-apt name beating in his head, and brought out all the coins he had, and left them on the table, and walked home. George did not see him, for he had left early. He passed the Earl, going out as he was coming in, without a word, as if he did not see him, his face white and set, his eyes staring and darkened. He shut himself up in his room, and would not answer any of the Earl's knocks or entreaties. The Earl could hear him, gasping, as though he were sobbing or choking, and he grew frightened, and had the door taken down.

"I want to know what is going on," he said to Edward sharply, who lay on his bed looking through him at things invisible to him, and did not answer, still catching his breath in the shuddering gasps that had so alarmed the Earl. "You will please stop this hysterical and unreasonable behaviour and explain to me what has brought it on." He took the flat of his hand and gave Edward several sharp slaps across the cheeks, systematically and dispassionately. The boy's eyes focussed on him, and he visibly took himself in hand.

"All right, Holland," he said, "all right, you can stop now!" He laughed shakily, and unhappily. "I have been dismissed. Herr Franz said I played badly, and he told me not to come back."

"Impudent puppy!" exclaimed the Earl angrily. "I will take *all* his pupils away! I will speak to Salieri about it."

"Oh no, Holland, please don't. He was quite right. I do play badly, and I don't try. I shouldn't waste anyone's time. That didn't upset me, that was just true. But he sang me a terrible frightening song he had made up, I have never heard anything like it. I didn't want to listen to it, and yet I couldn't stop myself from listening. It was about me, and you, I thought, about death and a child and a father, and it upset me as badly as he said I played. And yet I can't see now why it did. What is the matter with me? Oh Holland, oh Holland, I cannot bear to be like this, what shall I do, what shall I do?"

"I detest enthusiasts, they think to obtain the end without the means," the Earl said with compressed lips, ironically using Wesley's words, "and they are everywhere. Plague take them. But I heard this one sing as a child in the Imperial Court Chapel choir, and I will spare him. I will tell you what you will do. You will forget romantic songs and come with me to dinner and to a classical concert Beethoven will give privately at the Rasoumovsky Palace. That man is going deaf, they tell me privately. If he can bear that, can you not bear whatever it is you have to bear?"

After that Edward took lessons only on the violin, and gradually, he dropped even those. The weeks passed. The Earl could interest Edward in nothing really—not work, not play, not friends, not his future in England. The Earl was privately very concerned about the crash of the market in England, after the War. Wheat that had been 110s. a quarter in 1813 had dropped to 66s. in 1815, and was going lower. The country, victorious in war, was crippled now in peace by the unspeakably vast National Debt, excessive general taxation that promised to go higher, and a correspondingly enormous poor rate.

The North had felt the sudden post-war depression less than the South of England. The Earl, always a careful manager even in his outwardly reckless youth, under his seeming unconcern quietly observant and thoughtful of new methods, managed to remain secure, able even by his vast resources to buy when others were forced to sell for a song. He had even reduced his rents, as the cost of living rose, on a scale with the sliding price of wheat, and he made it his practise to never refuse work to any unemployed who asked it; but he was able without loss to himself to do these quiet humanitarian acts, when others, even more well-intentioned, were not. He was more concerned than he let Edward know, and with reason: it was the year the twenty-year depression began, although it would be 1830 before the government would recognise it publicly as having happened or the fortunate of the upper classes fully feel it: a few months yet before the Spring "bread or blood" riots would begin in the Southern shires.

The Earl knew Edward was interested in the land, or had been, for he had told the Earl so, when they had talked, after his return. The Earl had himself imagined Edward wishing something more public or more intellectually based, but he had only smiled and said, "There is nothing, Holland, that would more please me or interest me more than to be your heir and to learn to do with what is yours what is needful to maintain it as you have done. I can think of few things more useful or helpful, than to live as best one can in one's particular sphere, and this is now mine."

"But could you be content so, Edward?" the Earl had asked.

"Have you not been? I am a quiet sort of person, as you know, more than yourself. I do not want to be a public name. I do not see it means I would have to put away any of the things that I love, do you? You did not. It is just a third education, and I know already something of it. You forget. I grew up there, at Tyne, I lived on the land, until I was sixteen. It was not then the confining I minded so much, as the taking away, the being off the land."

But when the Earl attempted now, quietly, to bring Edward into part of his confidence, he was unable to reach through to him at all. That interest too seemed dead. Edward was dutiful and passive and without interest in anything the world had to offer, and to all outward effects, his personality dead. The Earl, willing to try any stimulus, thought again of the girl Anne, who had been the only thing Edward had ever fought at all for, and wrote the Earl of Havermore, suggesting her brother happen to bring her to Vienna, for what promised in other respects to be a brilliant Spring. Meanwhile, the Earl continued his efforts to reach his son's mind, to find some solid center of being on which he could help him help himself to build again.

"Edward," he said once in desperation. "Is there nothing you would like? I will even send you to be ordained, if you like, as any minister you choose, and I will try to like it."

"I am not fit," Edward said. He did not trouble to mention the fact, since they both knew it, that dutiful in all else, he had refused even to walk the few steps across the street into the Cathedral, not even to hear the organ or the voices of the Choir, or into any church of any kind, and when he could, on Sundays he managed to find himself somewhere else in the city and out of sight and hearing of its services and its congregation.

"Nonsense. Talleyrand was ordained."

"No," said Edward with finality. "I have changed. I don't want to. I told you that before. I still mean it."

"Is there nothing you want to do? Nothing at all?"

"I want to die," Edward said beneath his breath.

The Earl looked up sharply. "I did not hear you," he said. "Will you say it again?"

"Nothing," Edward said. "I want nothing—nothing except you. Just to have you, or to be left alone."

"Then shall I call a minister to you?" He remembered Wesley's words he had read, in the book he gave Edward: "Why then do not all physicians consider, how far bodily disorders are caused or influenced by the mind? And in those cases, which are utterly out of their sphere, call in the assistance of a Minister."

"No, I will not have one," Edward said wearily, without passion, "I will not speak if you do, or listen. I know all they can say myself."

III

Endlessly patient now, and his patience not exhausted, the lack of result made the Earl begin to wonder if he had been too patient and too kind too long. As Spring came, he began to think, and to watch Edward sharply, and what he saw did not reassure him. Edward's first contact with absolute brutality seemed to have bruised him fatally. The injury was internal now, the external signs were less visible, but in its malignancy its nature was none the less sure. The new injury, meeting and combining with the older submerged ones, looked fair to be destroying if not Edward entirely, nevertheless all the Earl found now he really cared for in him, or ever really had, he thought furiously at himself, had he had the sense to know it then.

He was daydreaming all the time now, hardly conscious of them, living in them more than in the world about him. Images, pictures, seized hold of his helpless mind. He was sitting actually beside the Earl at one of the endless musical evenings the Earl insisted on taking him to, but he had no feeling of his actual seat or any physical object or presence about him. Now, as he listened, he saw a young man in a dark room, cold, shabby, writing notes on a roll of paper, his pen flying, and then slowing, and finally stopped. He saw him roll the sheets up, and put them in a cabinet, and lock the door, and then take the key and walk slowly, his feet dragging, out into a courtyard and drop the key into a well and pull the cover over it, the key sinking slowly through the dark water like notes of music falling one by one. "Unfinished," he thought. "I am unfinished too, and I don't know how to go on."

He slept by the Earl every night, and clung to him, welcoming any contact that reassured him of the Earl's physical nearness, pressing himself against him, with an unsensual desperateness that began to frighten the Earl for him.

"This won't do, Edward, you know," he said finally, with great gentleness. "I shall die one day myself, not soon, I hope, but all the same, the time will come that I do, and you will be alone."

"Are you leaving me?" Edward said, his eyes stark. "You are tired of me? Is that what you are trying to say?"

"I will not ever leave you, I am never going to, unless I am forced to leave you, but it is time for you to leave me. It is Anne, or if not this Anne, some other Anne, you should have beside you now and find your comfort in. You have grieved enough, Edward, you have grieved sufficiently. To continue to grieve so is senseless, and indulgent. Alleyn himself would not have wished it. He would have laughed at you, and you know it."

"I know it. But I cannot find my footing."

"You are not trying to. You are drowning in shallow water, and unfettered, for no reason but because you will not put your feet down. You must try, Edward, really you must. You cannot relive always a bad time that is over. Discard it!—as a woman does the unused lining in her every month. It is worth no more thought, it is over." He did not really change the subject. "Anne is here, you know, in Vienna. Her brother has brought her."

"I don't want to see her. I wish she had not come. She is too young. And I am too old, and too young both. I cannot be any more for her what she wants. I do not even want to try."

"Harriett, then? She is older. Or another."

"I don't want a woman at all. I want only you."

"I am easy, and I take no effort. You are growing selfish, Edward, and I cannot let you."

"Oh, Holland, do not leave me, not yet."

The Earl, moved unbearably with pity, unable to be cruel then, took him in his arms and held him. But the next day he resolved upon a dreadful course his own words had suggested.

"Get up, Edward," he said, "I am going to give you only one chance this morning. I have been too kind and you have grown a bore."

"Are you leaving me?" Edward asked, hardly awake.

"No. That would not serve. You are either going to live, or I am going to drown you myself like the weak kitten you have become. I will not abide a moper. It is not so terrible to drown," the Earl said to that suddenly startled, frightened, questioning face, "not so terrible to die."

"You must be joking with me, Holland, you are making a game," Edward said uncertainly, "I cannot believe you will. Why should you want to do such a thing to me, and right now, this moment, after you did what you wanted not long ago. You don't look as if you are, but you must be. Why should you want to kill me, and right now? I cannot believe you will." He looked at his father's face for reassurance, and found none.

"You had better believe me. You would do well to. That last was for farewell." He looked at the white-faced boy, his face not softening. "I did not say I wanted to, I said I was going to. Two different things, sometimes, Edward. You were not paying attention. You should pay attention now. You tried to end yourself once in the sea when you were twelve, do you remember, and I would not let you. This time I will help you. I do not see why you should look frightened now. What was it you thought you were about then twice this Winter? I was mistaken to stop you. There are worse things than dying, even when one wants to live. It is worse to die daily, and to refuse to live, and yet you do not seem to mind that or to find it horrible. We will find out who you are and what you really want, now. I am tired of these half-measures."

"Oh, Holland," Edward said pitifully, "I do not want you to kill me."

"It is just that I am going to do, unless you wake up and prevent me. You are not chained. We will find out what you really want. Come here —come here, I say, or I will fetch you." He poured the water in the big ewer into the bowl brought for shaving.

To his horror the boy, that was all the young man seemed, did climb out of bed and come to stand in his nightgown beside the marble basin of water, his face anguished yet passive. "It lacks dignity this way, and I had not expected to die today," he whispered, his voice like a child's, his eyes wide and fixed on the basin.

"It is not deep," the Earl said, "but it will suffice. It can take you out of a place you have ceased to love. You need no dignity, no one will watch you." With no other word, he put his hand behind the boy's head, and held it in the water, below the level, his hand firmly holding him down. To his more horror, Edward did not struggle or seem to try to breathe, and the Earl felt himself in the grip of nightmare, but he continued to hold the fair head, and to his surprise, he found himself praying.

"Oh, God," he prayed, again and again, "do not take this boy," all the time his own hands were helping him on.

"Wilt thou not give him back to me, whom I have fitted for myself?" The words fell into his mind.

"No," he cried inwardly against the words, desperately pleading against them, his will fighting against them, but his hands in their action acquiescing. "Don't ask it. I cannot. I will not. Don't ask it of me, don't ask it of this child, mine, yours, whose ever he is. You must not ask it. I beg you not to ask it now, not to require it of him or of me now."

"What can you give me instead that I could want?" The words were clear and unbidden to his mind. He did not question their reality.

"I will give you myself," he answered inwardly, "when I have time, if you want me. I promise it." He felt the water in the bowl stir and he knew the boy had had to breathe, but he continued to hold him under as Edward began to choke and gasp, and his hands to flail and fight, but at the air, not at the Earl. After a minute of that, the Earl released his hands and let the boy up.

He gasped and choked and looked at the Earl murderously, but all he said was, "Why did you bring me up? It is not so bad as I thought. Another minute and I would have been gone. Tie my hands and do not let me up."

"I will not tie your hands," the Earl said, "you are a free agent, but I will hasten it. Think of Anne quickly, you have not long. Have you any word?" Edward shook his head, shivering. The Earl took his fist, and hit Edward lightly in the chest, knocking the breath out of him, and as he gasped in air, trying to regain it, he put his head again into the basin, praying wordlessly, holding him there despite his struggles until the boy himself suddenly broke his hold and brought his head out dripping.

"Back you go," the Earl said, seizing him again, "you want to die, you don't really want up, it is just an animal habit, a galvanic action." He plunged the face again, gasping and choking, into the basin, half empty now, and was sharply kicked, as Edward immediately forced his way out.

"Your reflexes are too strong, little frog," the Earl said to the furious, choking, now outraged boy, "but I know your will and it is this morning and you shall have it, though I have to knock you out to help you." He attacked the boy with his fists, and Edward was forced to defend himself, despite himself.

"Be patient," the Earl said, gasping himself now, too busy to pray, "it is a little harder than I thought, but it will soon be over. A good right to the jaw, hold still, and you will be asleep and hardly feel a thing. The injustice of the world will no longer bother you. Hold still. I can't reach you."

Edward, however, did not hold still. He had begun to fight in earnest for his life, believing now the Earl incomprehensibly was really going to take it, trying to talk to the Earl, as he dodged his blows.

"Please, Holland, stop," he panted. "I give in, I will live, I will marry the girl, I will do what you say."

"Not good enough," the Earl replied panting in his turn, "resignation not enough, we'll just go ahead now and finish."

"You are mad!"

"No, just bored, like you, but not with living. World too full of fools, will make one less now." Penetrating his guard, the Earl hit Edward a blow on the chin that knocked him flat, and he was on him, pulling him up dizzily, dragging him to the water and pressing him down. The inch of water left revived the boy, and he jerked himself backwards and rounded on his attacker, catching him back with his two hands against the wall.

"Will you leave me alone now!" he shouted.

"No," the Earl shouted back, in what voice he had.

"I did not mean it, you've made your point!"

"Of course you meant it. Mood will come back. Same thing to do tomorrow. Finish now, less work," the Earl gasped. He broke from Edward's hold, and hit him unfairly in the groin, and watched him double up, but as he approached, Edward straightened out and drew his hand back clenched, and knocked the Earl on the chin, and sent him sprawling, several feet by the force of the blow, until a corner of the room stopped his slide. He lay there, nursing his jaw, trying to keep the amusement out of his eyes, and to look properly hurt. He believed he had won, and he was able now after his fright to appreciate the humour of the repetition of their earlier fight, like the Fifth Symphony of 1809 which one thought had finished several times before it did. But life does not finish, he thought, thank God. It repeats and goes on.

"Will you leave me alone now!" Edward shouted, wholly unaware of his father's thoughts. He picked up the heavy marble basin, almost empty, shaped like a shell beneath, and hurled it against the stone floor of the fireplace where it cracked.

"Stop," cried the Earl, "the Management will hear," laughing inwardly.

"I don't care," said Edward viciously. He picked it up again and threw it harder, and it split in two halves. "Don't you ever try to do that again, Holland, or I will kill you. Do you hear me?" He glared at his prostrate father. "I'm going out now. I don't trust you; you stay there, right as you are, and don't move, until I can dress, or I will hit you again. Do you hear?"

Suddenly he thought he heard a familiar laugh, and a voice near him say, "Well done, little Edward Clare. A neat bunch of fives. Just what I'd have liked to do myself had I had a hand free."

He looked up, startled, unbelieving, and he heard nothing, and yet the room seemed somehow filled, as it had not been, and he felt the words form themselves, without his consciousness in his head, falling like still drops of water: "It is well with me now. It is over now. It happened, but it is past. Do not grieve. Do not be troubled on my account."

Edward stood listening intently, unaware of the room or his father or where he was, as the words continued like distinct drops of a healing oil to slip into his mind.

"You must make your mind wide enough to hold the earth, Edward Clare. What seemed to me of all importance then seems of less importance now. Be of good cheer. What are men's inventions but a passing day? Do not despair if around thee a web of meanness is wrought, nor if the pen is rebel to the soul and if the mind is wrung dry of thoughts; look thou upon earth again and see the playground of the gods, and the taste of beauty will be upon thy lips. When you are in trouble, think of the waters of the river that were beauteous still, and that may help you. I found them so, even then."

Then, as suddenly as it had come, the feeling was gone, the words stopped, the room was empty as before. He stood there in the room, his anger gone, his despair gone, but his face startled.

The most remarkable moments in life, Edward thought in a moment of sudden rare understanding, are those that leave no trace and have no proof and that one cannot speak of.

"What is it, Edward?" he heard his father ask twice before he could find words to answer.

"I thought—" he said, "I thought—I cannot tell you what I thought. You did not need to hear, somehow you already knew." He walked over to his father who was watching him warily, and held out his hand to him to take, to pull him up.

"Thank you, Holland," he said. "I will be all right. I have come to my senses again now. You don't need to wory about me any more."

The Earl laughed a little. "Well," he said complacently, "it was a bonny fight. I always did enjoy a scrap. Lud," he added more ruefully, "we are out of condition, we will both be stiff."

Edward dressed quickly, not waiting to call his valet, leaving the Earl to bathe and to dress at leisure. He walked without waiting for breakfast, and called a hackney, trying to remember where Anne was, at which Hotel. As he started back to ask his father, it came to his mind, and he caught his hackney, and caught Anne, as she was descending the front steps of the hotel with her brother, between the stone lions.

She looked at him, startled, and then she began to laugh. "Oh, Edward," she cried, "what have you been doing? Who did you find to fight so early?" She put her hand to his face and touched lightly the darkening bruise and his swelling eye.

He grinned, suddenly, a natural, boyish grin, free from strain or self-consciousness. "I will tell you, but not now. I have something else to tell you. When did you arrive? Have you breakfasted?"

"Hours ago," she said.

"Well, I haven't. Come with me and have some more. I am taking you to the concert tonight, it is all Beethoven, the Concerto Holland likes to play, and the Sixth Symphony. Holland is coming, and I hope Robert is. It is the Pastorale, and just how I feel." He flicked a casual glance at Robert, neither hostile nor friendly.

"I would be happy to attend with you and your father," Robert said, a trace stiffly.

"Good," said Edward, with no stiffness. "I want your sister now." He took Anne's hand beneath his arm, but the dignity was too much, and he changed it to take it in his, without dignity, and walked with her, swinging her hand lightly, towards the little tables in the nearby park. The trees were just budding, chestnut, beeches, oaks, and certain small ones and the lilacs were in flower, and the tall lindens. The scent was everywhere, delicate and pervading. He stopped with her beneath a white cherry, and pulled two tufts of blossoms and slipped them through her hair behind her ears. They were sheltered by the greenery, and he tilted her chin up, to look at her face, which answered him without a word. He kissed her ears beneath the flowers, and her lips, and then as her eyes closed, and her arms slipped around him, her eyelids, and her lips again which responded eagerly. His knees turned suddenly to water, and he sat down on the ground, regardless of their clothes, and held her in his lap, their lips saying everything they had to say, without words.

"Can you really want me, even me?" his lips asked, a certain hesitancy in them despite his returned assurance.

"I do, I do," hers answered, "just you, just as you are, however that may be, whatever you are."

"Will you ever trust me?" his asked. "I do not see how you can."

"Try me and see," hers promised without reserve.

"Oh, you lovely child," his whispered, his voice echoing their touch.

"No child now," her lips replied, proving it.

He was flooded with sudden happiness like the Spring freshets in the rivers at his home. Is this how it is, he thought, when all old things become new? I did not know, I never knew. Can it have happened to me, even to me? The joy he felt brought back into his mind long forgotten words. "How fresh, O Lord, how sweet and clean are thy returns!" he thought to himself, his spirit clear and still. He remembered the two long descending falls of piano notes, circling, wandering, yet moving steadily and purposely to their point of rest, like water falling in slow separate even drops, like grace itself, in the opening of the Adagio of another Concerto, the Fifth. Aloud, he said, looking at her, very softly,

> " 'Grief melts away
> Like snow in May,
> As if there were no such cold thing.' "

"No poetry, dear Edward," she said, stopping his lips with her fingers, then her own. "Not just now."

It was easy after all. She was real, and no part of himself, or anything connected with himself.

"We must be married at once, Anne," he said, his hands in her soft hair that was no longer so short. "We have waited too long."

"Yes," she said. "When, Edward? Today?"

He laughed in overflowing joy, his eyes once again like stars beneath his lashes. "If we can. Or tomorrow. We will go see Holland and ask him how, and how long. Do you mind if there's no ceremony?"

"I want no ceremony but yours," she said, and her voice was cut off by his kiss that took her breath with it.

"How sweet," he murmured softly, "but we must have a small one read, first, don't you think?"

"Here now," a voice said, and the park attendant was by them. "We don't allow this in the park, and you a respectable lady and gentleman. Ashamed you ought to be."

They did not look ashamed, but very pleased with one another, although Edward's face when he turned it looked less the gentleman's than his clothes. They smiled at the attendant, understanding his meaning though not his words, and Edward helped Anne to her feet.

"He will say now we are just the mad English. It doesn't matter. I'm hungry anyway," he said happily to Anne, leading her towards one of the little tables with his hand. "Let's breakfast first."

Finis non est.

Acknowledgements

I would like here to thank particularly F. W. Marsh (for A. Cameron), librarian for the Port of London Authority, for his help in locating again for me the exact place of Execution Dock (after which I could find out more about it), for telling me of the discovery in dredging of the chain supposed to have been used at some time there, and for describing and dating the last use of it for the purpose described in the novel, in December, 1830 (that was the last year of the reign of George IV, formerly the Prince Regent).

The words in the final section, "Wilt thou not give him back to me, whom I have fitted for myself?" are not mine; they come from a woman's experience reported directly to John Wesley and repeated by him in the account he gives of it in his journal for Sunday, March 19, 1769.

I would also like to thank A. D. M. Cox, History Fellow at University College, Oxford, for verifying De Quincey's term names for me and for checking the register for the year 1805–1806 for me, to confirm the term dates.

Permission has been granted from the Oliver Ditson Co. to use Arthur Westbrook's translation of *Der Erlkönig*, Goethe's poem set to music by Franz Schubert. (*Typical Piano Pieces and Songs*, selected by Clarence G. Hamilton, 1921.)

The Reverend Mr. Davenby's account of his conversion comes largely from a nineteenth-century unpublished autobiographical sketch in my family's possession.